Praise for the works of Peter Straub

Koko

"VASTLY ENTERTAINING AND BRILLIANTLY WRITTEN . . . EVOKES BIZARRE FEVERS AND BRIMSTONE TERROR. . . . Peter Straub flexes all his muscles. . . . His style is at its peak. . . . Judged as a thriller it deserves to be compared to the best."
—*The Washington Post Book World*

"A DIZZYING SPIN THROUGH EERIE PSYCHIC BADLANDS WHERE NIGHTMARE AND INSANITY SEEM TO FUSE WITH REALITY."
—*Publishers Weekly*

"GRUESOME, DOUBLE-EDGED THROBS WITH VITALITY . . . an enormously entertaining and scary story . . . rich, complex, dark, and tough to put down."
—*New York Daily News*

"A MASTERPIECE OF TERROR . . . A crime novel, a suspense novel, a horror novel and a study of human relationships . . . a fascinating and complex novel . . . lures the reader into caring about all its characters."
—*Los Angeles Times*

continued . . .

"THE CHARACTERS ARE OUTSTANDING. They're not just around to further the story—they *are* the story, appealing yet enigmatic, enshrouded by a nightmare that never lifts. The ending is unguessable and will not ease your mind. . . . Peter Straub takes bold risks, and he succeeds."

—*San Jose Mercury News*

"A RUMBLING, BIG-FIRING TANK OF A THRILLER . . . with real emotional power."

—*Kirkus Reviews*

Mystery

"THE NEAR PERFECT MYSTERY . . . HAS EVERYTHING A CLASSIC WHODUNIT SHOULD. . . . full of intricate, engrossing, flesh-and-blood suspects and heroes . . . unexpected curves and potholes. . . . The title says it all." —*Milwaukee Journal Sentinel*

"MURDER, MAYHEM, MYSTERY . . . a complex and satisfying tale . . . compelling characters . . . a pulse-pounding climax."

—*The Cleveland Plain Dealer*

"A work that will stand as a milestone for years to come . . . STRAUB IS A MASTER."

—*Los Angeles Daily News*

The Throat

"TERRIFYING PSYCHOLOGICAL HORROR . . . ONE OF THIS YEAR'S BEST CONTEMPORARY HORROR NOVELS. . . . Straub, a master storyteller, weaves a tale that's rich in detail and character."
—*The Cleveland Plain Dealer*

"AN EXCELLENT PSYCHOLOGICAL NOVEL. . . . Straub well understands the dark recesses of the psyche where the personal demons dwell. . . . We may want to turn away . . . but we cannot because the horror mesmerizes us." —*Pittsburgh Post-Gazette*

"A BLOODSTAINED TAPESTRY OF STUNNING EMOTIONAL POWER." —*San Francisco Chronicle*

Houses Without Doors

"STRAUB IS BACK IN DELICIOUSLY DARK FORM. . . . Relying more on psychological terror than real physical monsters, his stories make us think while they thrill us, and make us work a little at what they mean while we wait for the next macabre twist of the tale." —*Boston Herald*

"This is an author who can plop seemingly conventional characters down in the middle of a seemingly familiar setting and within three pages ALL HELL HAS BROKEN LOOSE."
—*Los Angeles Times Book Review*

"MASTERFUL, COMPELLING . . . the best of Peter Straub's writing." —*Houston Chronicle*

Also by Peter Straub
from Signet

Mystery
The Throat
Houses Without Doors

KOKO

PETER STRAUB

A SIGNET BOOK

SIGNET
Published by New American Library, a division of
Penguin Putnam Inc., 375 Hudson Street,
New York, New York 10014, U.S.A.
Penguin Books Ltd, 80 Strand,
London WC2R 0RL, England
Penguin Books Australia Ltd, Ringwood,
Victoria, Australia
Penguin Books Canada Ltd, 10 Alcorn Avenue,
Toronto, Ontario, Canada M4V 3B2
Penguin Books (N.Z.) Ltd, 182–190 Wairau Road,
Auckland 10, New Zealand

Penguin Books Ltd, Registered Offices:
Harmondsworth, Middlesex, England

Published by Signet, an imprint of New American Library,
a division of Penguin Putnam Inc.

First Signet Printing, November 1989
25 24 23 22 21 20 19 18

Printed in the United States of America

PUBLISHER'S NOTE
This is a work of fiction. Names, characters, places, and incidents either are the product of the author's imagination or are used fictitiously, and any resemblance to actual persons, living or dead, business establishments, events, or locales is entirely coincidental.

CONTENTS

PART FOUR: IN THE UNDERGROUND GARAGE

PART FIVE: THE SEA OF FORGETFULNESS

PART SIX: THE REAL RAW TASTE

PART SEVEN: THE KILLING BOX

PART EIGHT: TIM UNDERHILL

For Susan Straub
and
For Lila J. Kalinich, M.D.

I believe it is possible and even recommended to play the blues on everything.

—FRANK MORGAN,
alto saxophonist

PART ONE
THE DEDICATION

1

WASHINGTON, D.C.

1

At three o'clock in the afternoon of a grey, blowing mid-November day, a baby doctor named Michael Poole looked down through the windows of his second-floor room into the parking lot of the Sheraton Hotel. A VW van, spray-painted with fuzzy peace symbols and driven by either a drunk or a lunatic, was going for a ninety-eight-point turn in the space between the first parking row and the entrance, trapping a honking line of cars in the single entry lane. As Michael watched, the van completed its turn by grinding its front bumper into the grille and headlights of a dusty little Camaro. The whole front end of the Camaro buckled in. Horns blew. The van now faced a stalled, frustrated line of enemy vehicles. The driver backed up, and Michael thought he was going to escape by reversing down the first row of cars to the exit onto Woodley Road. Instead, the driver nipped the van into an empty space two cars down. "Well, damn," Michael said to himself—the van's driver had sacrificed the Camaro for a parking place.

Michael had called down twice for messages, but none of the other three men had checked in yet. Unless Conor Linklater was going to ride a motorcycle all the way from Norwalk, they would almost certainly take the shuttle from New York, but Michael enjoyed the fantasy that while he stood at the window he would see them all step out of the van—Harry "Beans" Beevers, the Lost Boss, the world's worst lieutenant; Tina Pumo, Pumo the Puma, whom Underhill had called "Lady" Pumo; and wild little Conor Linklater, the only other survivors of their platoon. Of course they would arrive separately, in taxis, at the front of the hotel. But he wished they would get out of the van. He hadn't known how strongly he wanted them to join him—he wanted to see the Memorial first by himself, but he wanted even more to see it later with them.

Michael Poole watched the doors of the van slide open. There appeared first a hand clamped around the neck of a bottle which Michael immediately recognized as Jack Daniel's sour mash whiskey.

The Jack Daniel's was slowly followed by a thick arm, then a head concealed by a floppy jungle hat. The whole man, now slamming the driver's door, was well over six feet tall and weighed at least two hundred and thirty pounds. He wore tiger-stripe fatigues. Two smaller men similarly dressed left through the sliding door in the side of the van, and a big bearded man in a worn flak jacket closed the van's passenger door and went around the front to take the bottle. He laughed, shook his head, and upended it into his mouth before passing it to one of the others. Individually and collectively they looked just enough like dozens of soldiers Poole had known for him to lean forward, staring, his forehead pressed against the glass.

Of course he knew none of these men. The resemblance was generic. The big man was not Underhill, and the others were none of the others.

He *wanted* to see people he had known over there, that was the large simple truth. He wanted a great grand reunion with everyone he had ever seen in Vietnam, living or dead. And he wanted to see the Memorial—in fact Poole wanted to love the Memorial. He was almost afraid to see it. From the pictures he had seen, the Memorial was beautiful, strong and stark, and brooding. That would be a Memorial worth loving. The only memorial he'd ever expected to have was a memorial to separateness, but it belonged to him and to the cowboys out in the parking lot, because they were forever distinct, as the dead were finally distinct. Together they were all so distinct that to Poole they almost felt like a secret country of their own.

There were names he wanted to find on the Memorial, names that stood in place of his own.

The big cowboy had taken a slip of paper from his shirt pocket and was writing, bent halfway over the hood of the van. The others unloaded duffel bags from the back of the van. The Jack Daniel's bottle circulated until the driver took a last slug and eased it into one of the bags.

Now Michael wanted to be outside, to be moving. According to the schedule he had picked up at the registration desk downstairs, the parade up Constitution Avenue had already begun. By the time he had his first look at the Memorial and came back, the others would have checked in.

Unless, that is, Harry Beevers had managed to get drunk at the bar of Tina Pumo's restaurant and was still asking for one more vodka martini, one more little teeny martooni, we'll catch the five o'clock shuttle instead of the four o'clock, or the six o'clock, or the seven. Tina Pumo, the only one of the old group Poole saw with anything like regularity, had told him that Beevers sometimes spent all afternoon in his place. Poole's only contact with Harry Beevers in four or five years had come three months before, when Beevers had called him up to read aloud a *Stars and Stripes* article, sent to Beevers by his brother, about a series of random murders committed in the Far East by someone who identified himself as Koko.

Poole stepped back from the window. It was not time for Koko, now. The giant in tiger stripes and jungle hat finished putting his note under one of the Camaro's windshield wipers. What could it say? *Sorry I beat up your car, man, come around for a shot of Jack—*

Poole sat down on the edge of the bed, picked up the receiver, and after a second of hesitation dialed Judy's number at school.

When she answered he said, "Well, I'm here, but the other guys haven't checked in yet."

"Do you want me to say, 'Poor Michael'?" asked Judy.

"No, I thought you'd like to know what's going on."

"Look, Michael, is something special on your mind? This conversation has no point. You're going to spend a couple of days going all drunk and sentimental with your old army buddies. Do I have any place in that? I'd just make you feel guilty."

"I still wish you'd have come along."

"I think the past is in the past because that's where it belongs. Does that tell you anything?"

"I guess it does," Michael said. There was a moment of silence that went on too long. She would not speak until he did. "Okay," Michael finally said. "I'll probably see Beevers and Tina Pumo and Conor tonight, and there are some ceremonies I'd like to take part in tomorrow. I'll get home Sunday about five or six, I suppose."

"Your patients are extremely understanding."

"Diaper rash is rarely fatal," Michael said, and Judy uttered a smoky exhalation that might have been laughter.

"Should I call you tomorrow?"

"Don't bother. It's nice, but don't bother, really."

"Really," Michael said, and hung up.

2

Michael moved slowly through the Sheraton's lobby looking at the men lined up at the registration desk, among them the big cowboy in tiger-stripe fatigues and his three buddies, and the groups of people sitting on padded dark green chairs and banquettes. The Sheraton was one of those hotels with no true bar. Women in clinging, filmy dresses brought drinks to the twenty or thirty tables in the sunken lobby. The waitresses all seemed to have descended from the same tall, languid, handsome family. Where these princesses might normally have served gin-and-tonics and Perriers-and-lime to men with dark suits and power haircuts—to men like Michael Poole's neighbors in Westchester County—now they set down shots of tequila and bottles of beer before wildmen in battle jackets and bush hats, in funky fatigues and funkier khaki ballcaps.

The sulphurous conversation with his wife made Michael want to sit down among the wildmen and order a drink. But if he sat down, he would be drawn into things. Someone would begin to talk to him. He would buy a drink for a man who had been in some of the same places he had been, or had been near the places he had been, or who had a friend who had been near those places. Then the man would buy him a drink. This would lead to stories, memories, theories, introductions, vows of brotherhood. Eventually he would join the parade as part of a gang of strangers and see the Memorial through the thick insulating comfort of alcohol. Michael kept moving.

"Cavalry all the way!" shouted a whiskey voice behind his back.

Michael went through a side door out into the parking lot. It was just a little too cold for his tweed jacket and sweater, but he decided not to go back upstairs for his coat. The heavy billowing sky threatened rain, but Michael decided that he didn't much care if it rained.

Cars streamed up the ramp from the street. Florida license plates, Texas plates, Iowa and Kansas and Alabama, every kind and make of vehicle, from hardcore GM pickups to tinny Japanese imports. The van cowboy and his friends had driven to Washington from New Jersey, the Garden State. Tucked beneath the Camaro's windshield wiper was the note: *You were in my way so FUCK YA!!!*

Down on the street, Michael flagged a cab and asked the driver to take him to Constitution Avenue.

"You gonna walk in the parade?" the driver immediately asked.

"That's right."

"You're a vet, you were over there?"

"That's right." Michael looked up. From the back, the cabdriver could have been one of the earnest, desperate, slightly crazed students doomed to flunk out of medical school: colorless plastic glasses, dishwater hair, pale youthful skin. His ID plate said that his name was Thomas Strack. Blood from an enormous pimple had dried on the collar of his shirt.

"You ever in combat? Like in a firefight or something?"

"Now and then."

"There's somethin' I always wanted to ask—I hope you don't take no offense or nothing."

Michael knew what the cabdriver was going to ask. "If you don't want me to take offense, don't ask an offensive question."

"Okay." The driver turned his head to glance at Michael, then looked straight ahead again. "Okay, no need to get heavy."

"I can't tell you how it feels to kill someone," Michael said.

"You mean you never did it."

"No, I mean I can't tell you."

The cabbie drove the rest of the way in boiling silence. You coulda told me something. Gimme a little gore, why don't you? Lemme see that good old guilt, lemme see that fine old rapture. The past is in the past because that's where it belongs. Don't bother, really. You were in my way, so fuck ya.

I'll take a triple Finlandia martini on the rocks, please, hold the olives, hold the vermouth, please, hold the rocks, please, and get the same thing for my four hundred buddies in here, please. They might look a little funny, but they're my tribe.

"This okay?" the cabbie asked. Beside the car was a wall of people. Michael could see flags and men carrying banners suspended between poles. He paid the driver and left the cab.

Michael could see over the heads of most of the people lining the sidewalk. Here the tribe had gathered, all right. Men who had once been soldiers, most of them dressed as though they were still soldiers, filled the width of Constitution Avenue. In platoon-sized groups interspersed with high school bands, they marched raggedly down the street. Other people stood on the sidewalk and watched them go by because they approved of what they were, what they meant because of what they had done. By standing there the bystanders applauded. Until now, Michael realized, he had resisted fully believing in the reality of this parade.

It was not ticker tape and limousines on Fifth Avenue—the Iranian hostages had been given that one—but in most ways this was better, being more inclusive, less euphoric but more emotional. Michael edged through the people on the sidewalk. He stepped off the curb and fell in behind the nearest large and irregular group. Surprised tears instantly filled his eyes.

The men before him were three-fourths jungle fighters with everything but Claymores and M-16s, and one-fourth pudgy WWII vets who looked like ex-boxers. Michael realized that the sun had come out only when he saw their long shadows stretching out to him on the street.

He could see Tim Underhill, another long shadow,

striding along with his belly before him and cigar smoke drifting in his wake. In his mind, Underhill was muttering obscene hilarious remarks about everyone in sight and wearing his summer uniform of a bandanna and blousy fatigue pants. A streak of mosquito blood was smeared across his left shoulder.

In spite of everything, Michael wished that Underhill were beside him now. Michael realized that he had been considering Underhill—not brooding or thinking about him, *considering* him—since Harry Beevers had called him up at the end of October to tell him about the newspaper articles his brother had sent him from Okinawa.

In two separate incidents, three people, an English tourist in his early forties and an older American couple, had been murdered in Singapore just about the time the Iranian hostages had returned to America. The murders were thought to have been committed at least a week to ten days apart. The Englishman's body was found on the grounds of the Goodwood Park Hotel, those of the American couple in a vacant bungalow in the Orchard Road section of the city. All three bodies had been mutilated, and on two of them had been found playing cards scrawled with an unusual and enigmatic name: Koko. Six months later, in the summer of 1981, two French journalists were found similarly mutilated in their Bangkok hotel room. Playing cards with the same name had been placed on the bodies. The only difference between these killings and those that had happened after Ia Thuc, a decade and a half earlier, was that the cards were not regimental, but ordinary commercial playing cards.

Michael thought Underhill lived in Singapore. At least Underhill had always claimed that he was going to move there after he got out of the army. But Poole could not make the mental leap required to convict Tim Underhill of murder.

Poole had known two extraordinary human beings during his time in Vietnam, two men who had stood out as exceptionally worthy of respect and affection in the half-circus, half-laboratory of human behavior that a longstanding combat unit becomes. Tim Underhill was one, and a boy from Milwaukee named M.O. Dengler was the other. The bravest people he had ever known, Underhill and little Dengler had seemed perfectly at home in Vietnam.

Tim Underhill had gotten himself back to the Far East

as soon as possible after the war and had become a moderately successful crime novelist. M.O. Dengler was killed in a freakish street accident while on R&R in Bangkok with another soldier, named Victor Spitalny, and never returned from Asia at all.

Oh, Michael Poole missed Underhill. He missed them both, Underhill and Dengler.

The group of vets behind Michael, as scattered and varied as those before him, gradually caught up with him. He became aware that he was no longer marching alone, but was moving along between the crowds lining both sides of the street with a couple Dengler-sized boonie-rats, fiercely moustached, and an assortment of polyester-suited VFW types.

As if he had been reading his thoughts, one of the Dengler-sized boonie-rats walking beside Michael sidled up to him and whispered something. Michael bent down, cupping his ear.

"I was a hell of a fighter, man," the little ex-soldier whispered a shade louder. Tears gleamed in his eyes.

"To tell you the truth," Michael said, "you remind me of one of the best soldiers I ever knew."

"No shit." The man nodded briskly. "What outfit was you in?"

Poole named his division and his battalion.

"What year?" The man cocked his head to check out Poole's face.

" 'Sixty-eight, 'sixty-nine."

"Ia Thuc," the boonie-rat said immediately. "I remember that. That was you guys, right? *Time* magazine and all that shit?"

Poole nodded.

"Fuckin'-A. They shoulda give that Lieutenant Beevers a fuckin' Medal of Honor for what he done, and then took it away again for shootin' off his mouth in front of fuckin' journalists," the boonie-rat said, sidling away with an easy fluid motion that would have been noiseless if they had been walking over brittle twigs.

Two fat women with short fluffy hair, pastel pantsuits, and placid church-picnic faces were rhythmically waving between them a red banner with the stark black letters POW-MIA. A few paces behind marched two youngish ex-soldiers bearing another banner: COMPENSATE FOR AGENT ORANGE. Agent Orange—

Victor Spitalny had tilted his head and stuck out his tongue, claiming that the stuff tasted good. *You motherfuckers, drink it down! This shit's boo-koo good for your insides!* Washington and Spanky Burrage and Trotman, the black soldiers on the detail, cracked up, falling into the thick jungly growth beside the trail, slapping each other on the back and sides, repeating "boo-koo good for your insides" and enraging Spitalny, whom they knew had only been trying, in his stupid way, to be funny. The smell of Agent Orange, halfway between gasoline and industrial solvent, stuck to all of them until sweat and insect repellent and trail grime either covered it up or washed it off.

Poole caught himself wiping the palms of his hands together, but it was too late to wash away the Agent Orange.

How does it feel to kill somebody? I can't tell you because I can't tell you. I think maybe I got killed myself, but not before I killed my son. You shit in your pants, man, you laugh so hard.

3

By the time Michael Poole reached the park, the parade had melted down into a wandering crowd, marchers and onlookers moving together across the grass. Loose, ragged groups streamed over the entire landscape, walking through the sparse trees, filling the whole scene. Though he could not see the Memorial, Michael knew where it was. About a hundred yards before him, the crowds were moving down a grade into a natural bowl from which came the psychic flare of too many people. The Memorial stood at the bottom of all those people. Michael's scalp tingled.

A phalanx of men in wheelchairs were pushing themselves across the long stretch of grass before the bowl. One of the chairs tilted over sideways and a gaunt, black-haired, legless man with a shockingly familiar face spilled out. Michael's heart froze—the man was Harry Beevers. Michael started to run forward to help. Then he checked himself. The fallen man was surrounded by friends, and in any case he could not be Poole's old lieutenant. Two others righted the chair. They held it steady as the man braced himself on his stumps. Then he pushed himself up onto the metal footrests. The man reached up, grasped the armrests, and with neat gymnastic skill deposited himself in his own seat.

The men in wheelchairs were gradually overtaken by the crowd. Michael looked around him. All about were familiar faces which at second glance resolved into the faces of strangers. Various large bearded versions of Tim Underhill were moving toward the grassy bowl, also several wiry Denglers and Spitalnys. A beaming, round-faced Spanky Burrage slapped the palm of a black man in a Special Forces hat. Poole wondered what had happened to the dap, the complicated series of handgrips that blacks in Vietnam used to greet one another. There had been a wonderful mixture of seriousness and poker-faced hilarity about daps.

People streamed down into the bowl. Old women and babies clutched tiny flags. To Michael's right, two young men on crutches were followed by an old gaffer, his bald head factory-white, with a row of medals pinned above the left pocket of his plaid shirt. Beside him a florid septuagenarian in a VFW garrison cap struggled with a shiny four-sided walker. Poole looked into the face of every man roughly his own age, and found most of them looking back at him—a crossfire of frustrated recognitions. He took a step forward across the trampled grass and looked straight ahead.

The Memorial was a long, intermittently visible line of sheer black tying together the heads and bodies of the people before it. Men ranged all along its top, walking along over its crew cut of grass as if pacing it off. Others lay down and leaned over to trace names engraved in the polished stone. Poole moved several steps forward, the crowded bowl in front of him widened and fell away, and the entire scene stood before him.

The huge broken black wing of the Memorial was surrounded by people without being engulfed by them. Poole imagined that it would take a lot to engulf this Memorial. Pictures had not quite conveyed its scale. Its strength came from its mass. Only inches high at the tapered ends, it rose to more than twice the height of a man at its folded center. Separated from it by a foot or so of earth already sprouting little flags, letters pinned to sticks, wreaths, and photographs of the dead, a sloping path of granite blocks ran its length.

The people before this emphatic scar in the earth passed slowly before the increasingly tall panels. Now and then they paused to lean forward and touch a name. Michael saw a lot of embraces. A skinnier version of an unloved basic training sergeant was inserting a handful of small red poppies one by one into the cracks between the panels. From immediately in front of the Memorial, a large wedge-shaped crowd fanned upward into the grassy bowl. A dense impacted wave of emotion came from all of these people.

Here was what was left of the war. The Vietnam War consisted of the names etched into the Memorial and the crowd either passing back and forth before those names or standing looking at them. For Poole, the actual country of Vietnam was now just another place—Vietnam was many thousands of miles distant, with an embattled history and an idiosyncratic and inaccessible culture. Its history and culture had briefiy, disastrously intersected ours. But the actual country of Vietnam was not *Vietnam*; that was here, in these American names and faces.

The ghost-Underhill had appeared beside Michael again, kneading one beefy shoulder with bloody fingers—bright smears of insect blood across his tanned skin. *Ah, Lady Michael, they're all good folks, they just let themselves get messed up by the war, that's all.* A dry chuckle. *We didn't do that, did we, Lady Michael? We tend to be above it all, don't we? Tell me we do.*

I thought I saw you smash in a car to get to a parking space, Poole said to this imaginary Tim Underhill.

I only smash up cars on paper.

Underhill, did you kill those people in Singapore and Bangkok? Did you put the Koko cards on their bodies?

I don't think you'd better pin that one on me, Lady Michael.

"Airborne!" someone shouted.

"Airborne all the way!" someone else shouted back.

Poole worked his way closer to the Memorial through the mostly stationary crowd. The sergeant who looked like his old sergeant from Fort Sill was now slipping the tiny red poppies into the crack between the last two tall panels. Protruding from between the panels, the little poppies reflected twice, so that two black shadows lay behind each red dart. A big wild-haired man held up a Texas-sized flag with a waving golden fringe. Poole stepped up beside a Mexican family posted directly beside the granite walk and for the first time saw the reflection in the tall black panel. Mirrored people streamed before him. The reflections of the Mexican family, a man and a woman, a pair of teenage girls, and a small boy holding a flag, all stared at the same spot on the wall. Between them, the reflected parents held a framed photograph of a young Marine. Poole's own uptilted head seemed, like the others, to be searching for a specific name. Then, as in an optical illusion, the real Poole saw names leap out from the black wall. Donald Z. Pavel, Melvin O. Elvan, Dwight T. Pouncefoot. He looked at the next panel. Art A. McCartney, Cyril P. Downtain, Masters J. Robinson, Billy Lee Barnhart, Paul P.J. Bedrock. Howard X. Hoppe. Bruce G. Hyssop. All the names seemed strange and familiar, in equal measure.

Someone behind him said "Alpha Papa Charlie," and Michael turned his head, his ears tingling. Now people completely filled the shallow bowl. They covered the rise behind it. Alpha Papa Charlie. Without asking, there was no way of telling which of the men, white-haired, bald, pony-tailed, with faces clear and pockmarked, seamed and scarred, electric with feeling, had spoken. From a huddle of four or five men in jungle hats and green jackets came another, rougher voice saying " . . . lost him outside Da Nang."

Da Nang. That was in I Corps, *his* Vietnam. For a moment or two there Poole could not move his arms or legs. Into him streamed place names he had not remembered for fourteen years—Chu Lai, Tam Ky. Poole saw a narrow dirt alleyway behind a row of huts; he smelled the clumps of drying marijuana hanging from the ceiling of a lean-to where a mama-san with the irresistible name of Si Van Vo lived and prospered. The Dragon Valley, oh God. Phu Bai, LZ Sue, Hue, Quang Tri. Alpha Papa Charlie. On the other side of a collection of thatched huts a line of water buffalos moved across a mud plain toward a mountain trail. Millions of bugs darkened the humid air. Marble Mountain. All those charming little places between the Annamese Cordillera and the South China Sea, where the dead SP4 Cotton, killed by a sniper named Elvis, had lazily spun in frothing pink water. The A Shau Valley: yea, though I walk . . .

Yea, though I walk through the A Shau Valley, I shall fear no evil. Michael could see M.O. Dengler bouncing along a high narrow trail, grinning over his shoulder at him, blivets and ammunition strung across his back. On the other side of Dengler's joyous face was a green, unfolding landscape of unbelievable depth and delicacy, plunging thousands of feet into mists, shading into dozens of different shades of green and rolling on all the way to a green, heavenly infinity. *You been bad?* Dengler had just asked him. *If you haven't, you ain't got nothin' to worry about. Yea, though I walk through the A Shau Valley . . .*

Poole finally realized he was weeping.

"Polish on both sides, yeah," said an old woman's voice quite near him. Poole wiped his eyes, but they filled again, so quickly he saw nothing but colorful blurs. "Whole neighborhood was Polish, both sides, up and down. Tom's father was in the Big One, but the emphysema kept him home today." Poole took his handkerchief out of his pocket and pressed it to his eyes and tried to bring his crying under control. "I said, old man, you can do what you like but nothin' is gonna keep me away from DC, come Veteran's Day. Don't you worry, son, nobody here minds if you cry your eyes out."

Poole slowly realized that this last comment had been directed at him. He lowered his handkerchief. An obese white-haired woman in her sixties was looking at him with grandmotherly concern. Next to her stood a black man in a faded Special Forces jacket, an Anzac hat astride an unruly Afro.

"Thanks," Poole said. "This thing"—he gestured behind him at the Memorial—"finally got to me."

The black ex-soldier nodded.

"Actually, I heard somebody say something, can't even remember what it was now . . ."

"Yeah, me too," said the black man "I heard somebody say 'about twenty klicks from An Khe,' and I . . . my damn *stomach* just disappeared."

"II Corps," Michael said. "You were a little south of me. Name's Michael Poole, nice to meet you."

"Bill Pierce." The two men shook hands. "This lady here is Florence Majeski. Her son was in my unit."

Poole had a strong, sudden desire to put his arms around the old woman, but he knew that he would break down again if he did that. He asked the first question that came to mind: "You get that hat off an ARVN?"

Pierce grinned. "Snatched it right off, riding by in a jeep. Poor little bastard."

Then he knew what he really wanted to ask Pierce. "How can you find the names you're looking for, in all this crowd?"

"There's Marines at both ends of the Memorial," Pierce said, "and they have books with all the names and the panels they're on. Or you could ask one of the yellow caps. They're just here today, on account of all the extra people." Pierce glanced at Mrs. Majeski.

"They had Tom right there in the book," the old lady said.

"I see one over thataway," Pierce said, pointing off to Michael's right. "He'll find it for you." In the midst of a little knot of people, a tall, bearded, young white man in a yellow duckbill cap was consulting sheets in a looseleaf binder and then gesturing toward specific panels.

"God bless you, son," said Mrs. Majeski. "If you're ever in Ironton, Pennsylvania, I want you to stop in and pay us a visit."

"Good luck," Pierce said.

"Same to both of you." He smiled and turned away.

"I mean it now!" Mrs. Majeski yelled. "You stop in and see us!"

Michael waved, and moved toward the man in the yellow cap. At least two dozen people had him circled, and all seemed to be leaning toward him. "I can only handle one at a time," the man with the cap said in a flat Midwestern voice. "Please, okay?"

Poole thought, The others ought to be at the hotel by now. This is a ridiculous gesture.

The young man in the yellow cap consulted his pages, indicated panels, wiped moisture from his forehead. Michael soon stood before him. The volunteer was wearing blue jeans and a denim shirt unsnapped halfway down over a damp grey T-shirt. His beard glistened with sweat. "Name," he said.

"M.O. Dengler," Poole said.

The man riffled through his pages, located the D's, and ran his finger down a column. "Here we go. The only

Dengler is Dengler, Manuel Orosco, of Wisconsin. Which happens to be my home state. Panel fourteen west, line fifty-two. Right over there." He pointed to the right. Small poppies like red pinpoints dotted the edges of the panel, before which stood a large unmoving crowd. NO MORE VIETNAMS, announced a bright blue banner.

Manuel Orosco Dengler? The Spanish names were a surprise. A sudden thought stopped Michael as he made his way toward the blue banner through the crowd: the guide had given him the wrong Dengler. Then he remembered that the guide had said that his was the only Dengler. And the initials were right. Manuel Orosco had to be his Dengler.

Poole was directly in front of the Memorial once again. His shoulder touched the shoulder of a shaggy-haired, weeping vet with a handlebar moustache. Beside him a woman with white blonde hair to the waist of her blue jeans held the hand of a little girl, also blonde. A child without a father, as he was now forever a father without a child. On the other side of the broken strip of sod, planted with flags and wreaths and photographs of young soldiers stapled to wooden sticks, the fourteenth panel, west, loomed before him. Poole counted down until he reached the fifty-second line. The name of M.O. Dengler, MANUEL OROSCO DENGLER, etched in black polished granite, jumped out at him. Poole admired the surgical dignity of the engraving, the unadorned clarity of the letters. He knew that he had never had any choice about standing in front of Dengler's name.

Dengler had even liked the C-rations scorned by the others. He claimed the dogfood taste of army turkey loaf, canned in 1945, was better than anything his mother had ever made. Dengler had liked being on patrol. *(Hey, I was on patrol the whole time I was a kid.)* Heat, cold, and dampness had affected him very little. According to Dengler, rainbows froze to the ground during Milwaukee ice storms and kids ran out of their houses, chipped off pieces of their favorite colors, and licked them until they were white. As for violence and the fear of death, Dengler said that you saw at least as much violence outside the normal Milwaukee tavern as in the average firefight; inside, he claimed, you saw a bit more.

In Dragon Valley, Dengler had fearlessly moved about under fire, dragging the wounded Trotman to Peters, the medic, keeping up a steady, calm, humorous stream of talk. Dengler had known that nothing there would kill him.

Poole stepped forward, careful not to trample on a photograph or a wreath, and ran his fingers over the sharp edges of Dengler's name, carved into the chill stone.

He had a quick, unhappy, familiar vision of Spitalny and Dengler running together through billowing smoke toward the mouth of the cave at Ia Thuc.

Poole turned away from the wall. His face felt too tight. The blonde woman gave him a sympathetic, wary half-smile and pulled her little girl backwards out of his way.

Poole wanted to see *his* ex-warriors. Feelings of loneliness and isolation wrapped themselves tightly around him.

2

MESSAGE

1

Michael was so certain that a message from his friends would be waiting for him at the hotel that once he got there he marched straight from the revolving door to the desk. Harry Beevers had assured him that he and the others would arrive "sometime in the afternoon." It was now just before ten minutes to five.

Poole started to scan the wall behind the desk for his messages as soon as he could read the room numbers beneath the pigeonholes. When he was three-fourths of the way across the lobby, he saw one of the white hotel message forms inserted diagonally into his own rectangular box. He immediately felt much less tired. Beevers and the other two had arrived.

Michael stepped up to the desk and caught the clerk's eye. "There's a message for me," he said. "Poole, room 204." He took the oversize key from his jacket pocket and showed it to the clerk, who began to inspect the wall behind him with an almost maddening lack of haste. At last the clerk found the correct slot and withdrew the message. He glanced at the form as he handed it to Poole, then smiled.

"Sir."

Michael took the form, looked first at the name, and turned his back on the clerk to read the message. *Tried to call back. Did you really hang up on me? Judy.* The time 3:55 was stamped on the form in purple ink—she had called just after Michael had left his room.

He turned around and found the clerk looking at him blankly. "I'd like to know if some people who were supposed to be here by now have checked in yet."

Poole spelled the names.

The clerk slowly pecked at buttons on a computer terminal, frowned, tilted his head, frowned again, and without changing his posture in any way looked sideways at Michael and said, "Mr. Beevers and Mr. Pumo have not arrived as yet. We have no booking for a Mr. Linklater."

Conor was probably saving money by sleeping in Pumo's room.

Poole turned away, folded Judy's message into his jacket pocket, and for the first time since his return saw what had happened to the lobby.

Men in dark suits and striped neckties now occupied the banquettes and tables. Most of them had no facial hair and wore white name tags crowded with print. They were talking quietly, consulting legal pads, punching numbers into pocket computers. During his first surreal eighteen months back from Vietnam, Michael Poole had been able to tell if a man had been in Vietnam just by the way he held his body. His instinct for distinguishing vets from civilians had faded since then, but he knew he could not be mistaken about this group.

"Hello, sir," said a clarion voice at his elbow.

Poole looked down at a beaming young woman with a fanatical face surrounded by a bubble of blonde hair. She held a tray of glasses filled with black liquid.

"Might I inquire, sir, if you are a veteran of the Vietnam conflict?"

"I was in Vietnam," Poole said.

"The Coca-Cola Company joins the rest of America in thanking you personally for your efforts during the Vietnam conflict. We wish to take this opportunity to express our gratitude to you, and to introduce you to our newest product, Diet Coke, in the hope that you will enjoy it and will share your pleasure with your friends and fellow veterans."

Poole looked upward and saw that a long, brilliantly red banner of some material like parachute silk had been suspended far above the lobby. White lettering said: THE COCA-COLA CORPORATION AND DIET COKE SALUTE THE VETERANS OF VIETNAM! He looked back down at the girl.

"I guess I'll pass."

The girl increased the wattage of her smile and looked amazingly like every one of the stewardesses on Poole's flight into Vietnam from San Francisco. Her eyes shifted away from him, and she was gone.

The desk clerk said, "You'll find your meeting areas downstairs, sir. Perhaps your friends are waiting for you there."

2

The executives in their blue suits sipped their drinks, pretending not to monitor the girls walking around the lobby with their inhuman smiles and trays of Diet Coke. Michael touched Judy's note in his jacket pocket. Either it or the tips of his fingers felt hot. If he sat down in the lobby bar to watch the arrivals coming through the door, within minutes he would be asked if he were a veteran of the Vietnam conflict.

Poole went to the bank of elevators and waited while an odd mixture of veterans and Coca-Cola executives, each group pretending the other group did not exist, left the car. Only one other man, a drunken mountainous being in tiger-striped fatigues, entered the elevator with him. The man studied the buttons and pushed SIXTEEN four or five times, then stumbled against the railing at the back of the car. He emitted a foggy bourbon-flavored burp. Poole finally recognized him as the van driver who had smashed into the Camaro.

"You know this, don't you?" the giant asked him. He straightened up and began to bellow out a song Poole and every other veteran knew by heart. *"Homeward bound, I wish I were homeward bound"* . . .

Poole joined him on the second line, singing softly and tunelessly, and then the car stopped and the door opened. The giant, who had closed his eyes, continued to sing as Poole stepped from brown elevator carpet to green hall carpet. The doors slid shut. The elevator ascended and Poole heard the man's voice echoing down the shaft.

3

REUNION

1

A North Vietnamese soldier who looked like a twelve-year-old boy stood over Poole, prodding his neck with the barrel of a contraband Swedish machine gun he must have killed someone to get. Poole was pretending he was dead so that the NVA would not shoot him; his eyes were closed, but he had a vivid picture of the soldier's face. Coarse black hair fell over a broad, unlined forehead. The black eyes and abrupt, almost lipless mouth seemed nearly serene in their lack of expression. When the rifle barrel pushed painfully into his neck, Poole let his head slide fractionally across the greasy earth in what he hoped was a realistic imitation of death. He could not die: he was a father and he had to live. Huge iridescent bugs whirred in the air above his face, their wings clacking like shears.

The tip of the barrel stopped jabbing his neck. An outsized drop of sweat squeezed itself out of Poole's right eyebrow and trickled into the little depression between the bridge of his nose and the corner of his eye; one of the rusty-sounding insects blundered into his lips. When the NVA did not move on to any of the real corpses near him, Poole knew that he was going to die. His life was over, and he would never know his son, whose name was Robert. Like his love for this unknown son, the knowledge that the soldier was going to blow his head apart here on the narrow field full of dead men was total.

The shot did not come. Another of the rusty insects fell onto his sweat-slick cheek like a spent bullet and took a maddening length of time scrabbling to its legs before it lumbered off.

Then Poole heard a faint click and rustle, as of some object being pulled from a casing. The soldier's feet moved as he shifted his weight. Poole realized that the man was kneeling beside him. An entirely uncurious hand, the size of a girl's, pushed his head flat into the smeary earth, then yanked his right ear. His impersonation of a dead man had been too successful—the NVA wanted his ear as a trophy. Poole's eyes snapped open by themselves, and before them, on the other side of a long grey knife where the sky should have been, hung the motionless black eyes of the other soldier. The North Vietnamese gasped. For a brimming half second the air filled with the stench of fish sauce.

Poole jackknifed up off his bed and the NVA melted away. The telephone was ringing. The first thing he was fully conscious of was that his son was gone again.

Gone too were the corpses and the lumbering insects. Poole groped for the phone. "Mike?" came tinnily from the receiver. He looked over his shoulder and saw bland pale wallpaper, a painting of a misty Chinese landscape over the bed. He found that he could breathe.

"This is Michael Poole," he said into the receiver.

"Mikey! How are you? You sound a little weirded-out, man." Poole finally recognized the voice of Conor Linklater, who had turned his head away from the telephone and was saying, "Hey, I got him! He's in his room! I told you, man, Mike's just gonna be in his room, remember?" Then Conor was speaking to him again. "Hey, didn't you get our message, man?"

Conversations with Conor Linklater, Michael was reminded, tended to be more scattered than conversations with most other people. "I guess not. What time did you get in?" He looked at his watch and saw that he had been asleep for half an hour.

"We got here about *four-thirty,* man, and we called you right away, and at first they said you weren't here and Tina made'em look twice and then they said you *were* here, but nobody answered your phone. Okay. How come you didn't answer our message?"

"I went out to the Memorial," Poole said. "I got back a little before five. I was in the middle of a nightmare when you woke me up."

Conor did not say good-bye and he did not hang up. Speaking more softly than before, he said, "Man, you sound like that nightmare really weirded you out."

A rough hand tugging his ear away from his head; the ground greasy with blood. Poole's memory gave him the picture of a field where exhausted men carried corpses toward impatient helicopters in the hazy blue light of early morning. Some of the corpses had blood-black holes where they should have had ears. "I guess I went back to Dragon Valley," Poole said, having just understood this.

"Be cool," Conor Linklater said. "We're already out the door." He hung up.

Poole splashed water on his face in the bathroom, roughly used a towel, and examined himself in the mirror. In spite of his nap he looked pale and tired. Megavitamins encased in clear plastic lay on the counter beside his toothbrush, and he peeled one free and swallowed it.

Before he went down the hall to the ice machine, he dialed the number for messages.

The man who answered told him that he had two messages. "The first one is stamped 3:55, and reads 'Tried to call back—' "

"I picked that one up at the desk," Poole said.

"The second is stamped 4:50, and reads 'We just arrived. Where are you? Call 1315 when you return.' It's signed 'Harry.' "

They had called while he was still downstairs in the lobby.

2

Michael Poole paced back and forth between the window overlooking the parking lot and the door. Whenever he got to the door, he stopped and listened. The elevators whirred in their chutes, carts squeaked past. After a little while he heard the *ping!* of the elevator, and he cracked the door open to look down the corridor. A trim grey-haired man in a white shirt and a blue suit with a name tag on the lapel was hurrying toward him a few paces ahead of a tall blonde woman wearing a grey flannel suit and a paisley foulard tied in a fussy bow. Poole pulled back his head and closed the door. He heard the man fumbling with his key a little way down the hall. Poole wandered back to the window and looked down at the parking lot. Half a dozen men dressed in unmatched parts of uniforms and holding beer cans had settled on the hoods and trunks of various automobiles. They looked like they were singing. Poole walked back to the door and waited. As soon as he heard the elevator land once again on his floor, he opened the door and leaned out into the hall.

Tall, agitated Harry Beevers and Conor Linklater turned into the hallway together, a harried-looking Tina Pumo a second later. Conor saw him first—he raised his fist and grinned and called out "Mikey baby!" Unlike the last time Michael Poole had seen him, Conor Linklater was smooth-shaven and his pale reddish hair had been cut almost punkishly short. Conor normally wore baggy blue jeans and plaid shirts, but he had taken unaccustomed pains with his wardrobe. Somewhere he had obtained a black T-shirt with the stenciled legend AGENT ORANGE in big irregular yellow letters, and over this garment he wore a large, loose, many-pocketed black denim vest with conspicuous white stitching. There were sharp creases in his black trousers.

"Conor, you're a vision of delight," Poole said, stepping out into the corridor while holding the door open with his outstretched left hand. Half a foot shorter than Michael, Conor Linklater stepped up to him and wrapped his arms around his chest and hugged him tightly.

"Man," he said into Michael's jawline, and playfully kissed him, "what a sight for poor eyes."

Smirking at this ripe Linklaterism, Harry Beevers sidled up beside Poole and, in a wave of musky cologne, embraced him too, awkwardly. The corner of a briefcase struck Poole's hip. "Michael, a sight for 'poor eyes,' " Beevers whispered into Poole's ear. Poole gently pulled himself away and got a vivid close-up of Harry Beevers' large, overlapping discolored teeth.

Tina Pumo bobbed back and forth before them in the corridor, grinning fiercely beneath his heavy moustache.

"You were asleep?" Pumo asked. "You didn't get our message?"

"Okay, shoot me," Poole said, smiling at Pumo. Conor and Beevers broke away from him and moved separately toward the door. Pumo ducked his head like Tom Sawyer, all but digging his toes into the carpet, said, "Aw, Mikey, I want to hug you too," and did it. "Good to see you again, man."

"You too," Michael said.

"Let's get inside before we get arrested for having an orgy," Harry Beevers said, already standing in the entry to Michael's room.

"Don't get weird, *Lieutenant*," Conor Linklater said, but moved toward the doorway anyhow, glancing sideways at the other two. Pumo laughed and pounded Michael on the back, then let him go.

"So what have you guys been doing since you got here?" Michael asked. "Apart from swearing at me, that is."

Wandering around the room, Conor said, "Teeny-Tiny's been sweatin' out his restaurant." Teeny-Tiny was a reference to the origins of Pumo's nickname, which had begun as Tiny when he was an undersized child in an undersized town in upstate New York, was modulated later to Teeny, and had finally altered to Tina. After a decade of working in restaurants, Pumo now owned one in SoHo that served Vietnamese food and had been lavishly praised some months before in *New York* magazine. "He made two calls already, man. Him and the Health Department are gonna keep me awake all night."

"It's not really anything," Tina protested. "I picked an awkward time to go away, that's all. We have to do certain things in the restaurant, and I want to make sure they're done right."

"Health Department?" Michael asked.

"Really, it's nothing serious." Pumo grinned fiercely. His moustache bristled, the joyless creases at the corners of his eyes deepened and lengthened. "We're doing great. Booked solid most nights." He sat on the edge of the bed. "Harry can vouch for me. We do great business."

"What can I say?" Beevers asked. "You're a success story."

"You looked around the hotel?" Poole asked.

"We checked out the meeting areas downstairs, had a

look around," Pumo said. "It's a big party. We can do some stuff tonight, if you want."

"Some party," Beevers said. "A lot of guys standing around with their thumbs in their asses." He shrugged his jacket over the back of his chair, revealing suspenders on which cherubs romped against a red background. "No organization, *nada, rien.* The only people with their shit together are the First Air Cav. They have a booth, they help you locate other guys from your unit. We looked around, but I don't think we saw anybody from our whole damn division. Besides that, they put us into a grubby dump of a hall that looks like a high school gym. There's a Diet Coke stand, if that turns you on."

"High school gym, man," Conor muttered. He was staring intently at the bedside lamp. Poole smiled at Tina Pumo, who smiled back. Linklater picked up the lamp and examined the inside of the shade, then set it down and ran his fingers along the cord until he found the switch. He turned the lamp on, then off.

"Sit down, for God's sake, Conor," Beevers said. "You make me nervous, messing with everything like that. We've got serious business to talk about, if you don't remember."

"I remember, I remember," Conor protested, turning away from the lamp. "Hey, there's no place to sit in here on account of you and Mike got the chairs and Tina's already on the bed."

Harry Beevers stood up, yanked his jacket off the back of his chair, and made a sweeping gesture toward the empty seat. "If it'll get you to settle down, I'll gladly surrender my chair. Take it, Conor—I'm giving it to you. Sit down." He picked up his glass and sat down next to Pumo on Michael's bed. "You think you can sleep in the same room with this guy? He probably still talks to himself all night."

"Everybody in my family talks to themselves, *Lieutenant,*" said Conor. He hitched his chair closer to the table. Conor began thumping his fingers on the table, as if playing an imaginary piano. "I guess they don't act like that at Harvard—"

"I didn't go to Harvard," Beevers wearily said.

"Mikey!" Conor beamed at Poole as if seeing him for the first time. "It's *great* to see you!" He slapped Poole on the back.

"Yeah," Tina Pumo said. "How are things going, Michael? It's been a while."

These days Tina was living with a beautiful Chinese girl in her early twenties named Maggie Lah, whose brother was a bartender at Saigon, Tina's restaurant. Before Maggie there had been a series of girls, each of whom Tina had claimed to love.

"Well, I'm thinking of making some changes," Michael said. "I'm busy all day long, but at night I can hardly remember what I did."

A loud knocking came from the door, and Michael said "Room service," and stood up. The waiter wheeled in the cart and arranged the glasses and bottles on the table. The atmosphere in the room became more festive as Conor opened a Budweiser and Harry Beevers poured vodka into an empty glass. Michael never explained his half-formed plan of selling his practice in Westerholm and seeing what he might be able to do in some gritty place like the South Bronx where children really needed doctors. Judy usually walked out of the room whenever he began to talk about it.

After the waiter left, Conor stretched out on the bed, rolled on his side, and said, "So you saw Dengler's name? It was right there?"

"Sure. I got a little surprise, though. Do you know what his full name was?"

"M.O. Dengler," Conor said.

"Don't be an idiot," Beevers said. "It was Mark, I think." He looked to Tina for help, but Tina frowned and shrugged.

"Manuel Orosco Dengler," Michael said. "I was amazed that I didn't know that."

"Manuel?" Conor said. "Dengler was *Mexican*?"

"Michael, you got the wrong Dengler," Tina Pumo said, laughing.

"Nope," Michael said. "There's not only one *M.O.* Dengler, there's only one Dengler. He's ours."

"A Mexican," Conor mused.

"You ever hear of any Mexicans named Dengler? His parents just gave him Spanish names, I guess. Who knows? Who even cares? He was a hell of a soldier, that's all I know. I wish—"

Pumo raised his glass to his mouth instead of finishing

his sentence, and none of the men spoke for an almost elastically long moment.

Linklater muttered something unintelligible and walked across the room and sat on the floor.

Michael stood up to add fresh ice cubes to his glass and saw Conor Linklater backed up against the far wall like an imp in his black clothes, the brown beer bottle dangling between his knees. The orange writing on his chest was nearly the same shade as his hair. Conor was looking back at him with a small secret smile.

3

Maybe Beans Beevers didn't go to Harvard or Yale, Conor was thinking, but he had gone someplace like that—someplace where everybody in sight just took it all for granted. To Conor it seemed that about ninety-five percent of the people in the United States did nothing but fret and stew about money—not having enough money made them crazy. They zeroed out on booze, they cranked themselves up to commit robberies: oblivion, tension, oblivion. The other five percent of the population rode above this turmoil like froth on a wave. They went to the schools their fathers had gone to and they married and divorced one another, as Harry had married and divorced Pat Caldwell. They had jobs where you shuffled papers and talked on the telephone. From behind their desks they watched the money stroll in the door, coming home. They even passed out these jobs to each other—Beans Beevers, who spent as much time at the bar in Pumo's restaurant as he did at his desk, worked in the law firm run by Pat Caldwell's brother.

When Conor had been a boy in South Norwalk, a kind of wondering and resentful curiosity had made him pedal his old Schwinn up along Route 136 to Mount Avenue in Hampstead. Mount Avenue people were so rich they were nearly invisible, like their enormous houses—from the road all you could see of some of them were occasional sections of brick or stucco walls. Most of these waterfront mansions seemed empty of anybody but servants, yet now and then young Conor would spot an obvious owner-resident. Conor learned from his brief sightings that although these Mount Avenue owner-residents usually wore the same grey suits and blue jackets as everyone else in Hampstead, sometimes they blazoned forth like Harry Beevers in riotous pink and bilious green, in funny-looking bow ties and pale double-breasted suits. It was sort of like the Emperor's New Clothes—nobody had the balls to tell Protestant millionaires they looked ridiculous. (Conor was certain that none of these people could be Catholic.) Bow ties! Red suspenders with pictures of babies on them!

Conor couldn't help smiling to himself—here he was, almost flat broke, thinking he ought to pity a rich lawyer. Next week he had a job taping sheetrock in a remodeled kitchen, for which he might earn a couple hundred dollars. Harry Beevers could probably earn double that sitting on a barstool, talking to Jimmy Lah. Conor looked up, his sense of humor painfully sparkling, and saw Michael Poole looking at him as if the same kind of thought had occurred to him.

Beevers had some typical bullshit up his sleeve, Conor thought, but Michael knew better than to fall for it, whatever it was.

Conor smiled to himself, remembering Dengler's word for people who never experienced dread and took everything for granted: "toons," as in cartoons. Now the toons were running everything—they were scrambling upward, running over everything in their way. These days it seemed that half the people in Donovan's, Conor's favorite South Norwalk bar, had MBAs, put mousse on their hair, and drank blender drinks. Conor had the sense that some enormous change had happened all at once, that all these new people had just popped out of their own television sets. He could almost feel sorry for them, their morality was so fucked up.

Thinking about the toons depressed Conor. He felt like drinking a lot more even though he knew he was getting close to his limit. But wasn't this a reunion? They were sitting around in a hotel room like a bunch of old men. He drained the last of his beer.

"Give me some of that vodka, Mikey," he said, and lobbed the empty beer bottle into the wastebasket.

"Attaboy," Pumo said, raising his glass to him.

Michael made a drink and came across the room to hand it to Conor.

"Okay, a toast," Conor said, and stood up. "*Man.* It

feels *good* to do this." He raised his glass. "To M.O. Dengler. Even if he was a Mexican, which I doubt."

Conor poured ice-cold vodka into his mouth and gulped it down. He felt better instantly, so good that he downed the rest. "Man, sometimes I can remember shit that happened over there like it was yesterday, and the stuff that really did happen yesterday, I can't hardly remember at all. I mean—sometimes I'll start to think about that guy who ran that club at Camp Crandall, who had that gigantic wall of beer cases—"

"Manly," Tina Pumo said, laughing.

"Manly. Fucking Manly. And I'll start to think about how did he manage to get all that beer there, anyway? And then I'll start to think about little things he did, the way he acted."

"Manly belonged behind a counter," Beevers said.

"That's right! I bet Manly's got his own little business right now, he's got everything lined up just right, man, he's got a good car and his own house, he's got a wife, kids, he's got one of those basketball hoops up on his garage . . ." Conor stared into space for a second, enjoying his vision of Manly's life—Manly would be great in suburbia. He thought like a criminal without actually being one, so he was probably making a fortune doing something like installing security systems. Then Conor remembered that in a way Manly had started all their troubles, back in Vietnam . . .

A day before they came into Ia Thuc, Manly had separated from the column and found himself alone in the jungle. Without even meaning to make noise, he started sounding like a six-foot bumblebee in a panic. Everyone else in the column froze. A sniper known as "Elvis" had been dogging them for two days, and Manly's commotion was all he needed to improve his luck. Conor knew what he should have done—he had discovered long ago how to make himself melt into the background. It was almost mystical. Conor could virtually become invisible (and he knew it worked, for twice VC patrols had looked right at him without seeing him). Dengler, Poole, Pumo, even Underhill, could do this almost as well as he could, but Manly could not do it at all. Conor began silently working through the jungle toward the sound—he was angry enough to kill Manly, if that was what it took to shut him up. Within a minute fraction of a second, he knew as if by telepathy—so silent—that Dengler was following him.

They found Manly bulling through the curtain of green, hacking away with his machete in one hand, his M-16 at his hip in the other. Conor started to glide up to him, half-thinking about slitting his throat, when Dengler simply materialized next to Manly and grabbed his machete arm. For a second they were motionless. Conor crept forward, afraid that Manly would shriek after the numbness wore off. Instead, he heard a single report from off to his right, somewhere up in the canopy, and saw Dengler topple over. He felt shock so deep and sudden his hands and feet went cold.

He and Manly had walked Dengler back to the rest of the column. Even though the impact had knocked him down and he was bleeding steadily, Dengler's wound was only superficial. A wad of flesh the size of a mouse had been punched out of his left arm. Peters made him lie down on the jungle floor, packed and bandaged the wound, and pronounced him fit to move.

If Dengler had not been wounded even so slightly, Conor thought, Ia Thuc might have been just another empty village. Seeing Dengler in pain had soured everybody. It pumped up their anxiety. Maybe they had all been foolish to believe in Dengler as they had, but seeing him bloodied and wounded on the forest floor had shocked Conor all over again—it was as bad as seeing him hit in the first place. After that, it had been easy to blow it, go over the edge in Ia Thuc. Afterward nothing was the same. Even Dengler changed, maybe because of the publicity and the court-martial. Conor himself had stayed so high on drugs that he still could not remember some things that had happened in the months between Ia Thuc and his DEROS—but he knew that just before the court-martials he had cut the ears off a dead North Vietnamese soldier and stuck a Koko card in his mouth.

Conor realized that he was in danger of getting depressed again. He was sorry he had ever mentioned Manly.

"Refill," he said, and went to the table and poured more vodka into his glass. The other three were still looking at him, smiling at their cheerleader—other people always counted on him to provide their good times.

"Hey, to the Ninth Battalion, 24th Infantry Regiment." Conor swallowed another ice-cold bullet of vodka, and the face of Harlan Huebsch popped into his mind. Harlan Huebsch was a kid from Oregon who had tripped a wire and blown himself in half a few days after turning up at Camp Crandall. Conor could remember Huebsch's death very clearly because an hour or so afterwards, when they had finally reached the other side of the little mined field, Conor had stretched out against a grassy dike and noticed a long tangled strand of wire snagged in the bootlaces on his right foot. The only difference between himself and Huebsch was that Huebsch's mine had worked the way it was supposed to. Now Harlan Huebsch was a name up on the Memorial—Conor promised himself he'd find it, once they all got there.

Beevers wanted to toast the Tin Man, and though everybody joined him, Linklater knew that only Beans meant it. Mike Poole toasted Si Van Vo, which Conor thought was hilarious. Then Conor made everybody drink to Elvis. And Tina Pumo wound up toasting Dawn Cucchio, who was a whore he met on R&R in Sydney, Australia. Conor laughed so hard at the idea of drinking to Dawn Cucchio that he had to lean against the wall to hold himself up.

But then murkier, darker feelings surfaced in him again. If you wanted to accept the reality of what was going on, he was an unemployed laborer sitting around with a lawyer, a doctor, and a guy who owned a restaurant so fancy there were pictures of it in magazines.

Conor realized that he had been staring at Pumo, who looked like a page out of *GQ*. Tina always looked good, especially in his restaurant. Conor went there once or twice a year, but spent most of his money at the bar. On his last visit he had seen a juicy little Chinese girl who must have been Maggie. "Hey, Tina, what's the best dish you make, down there in your restaurant?"

Conor slurred a little on *best*, but he didn't think the others could hear it.

"Duck Saigon, probably," Tina said. "At least, that's my favorite right now. Marinated roast duck, dried rice noodles. The taste is out of sight."

"You put that fish sauce on top of it?"

"Nuoc mam sauce? Sure."

"I don't know how anybody can eat that gook food," Conor said. "Remember when we were over there? We all knew you couldn't eat that shit, man."

"We were eighteen years old back then," Tina said. "Our idea of a great meal was a Whopper and fries."

Conor did not admit to Tina that a Whopper and fries was still his idea of a great meal. He gulped down another silver bullet of vodka and felt lower than ever.

4

But in a little while it was almost like the old days again. Conor learned that along with all the normal Pumo difficulties, Tina now had to deal with the exciting new complications caused by Maggie being nearly twenty years younger and not only as crazy as he was, but smarter besides. When she moved in with him, Tina began feeling "too much pressure." This much was absolutely typical. What was different about Maggie was that after a few months she disappeared. Now she was out-Pumoing Pumo. Maggie called him on the telephone, but refused to tell him where she was staying. Sometimes she placed coded messages for him on the back page of the *Village Voice.*

"Do you know what it's like to read the back page of every issue of the *Voice* when you're forty-one?" Pumo asked.

Conor had never read any page of any issue of the *Village Voice.* He shook his head.

"Every mistake you ever made with a woman is right there in cold hard print. Falling for someone's looks—'Beautiful blonde girl in Virginia Woolf T-shirt at Sedutto's, we almost talked and now I'm kicking myself. I know we could be special. Please call man with backpack. 581-4901.' Romantic idealization—'Suki. You are my shooting star. Cannot live without you. Bill.' Romantic despair—'I haven't stopped hurting since you left. Forlorn in Yorkville.' Masochism—'Bruiser—No guilt necessary, I forgive you. Puffball.' Cuteness—'Twinky-poo. Twiddles wuvs yum-yum.' Indecision—'Mesquite. Still thinking. Margarita.' Of course there's a lot of other stuff, too. Prayers to St. Jude. Numbers you can call if you want to get off coke. Baldness cures. Lots of Strip-O-Grams. And Jews For Jesus, every single week. But mainly it's all these broken hearts, this terrible early-twenties agony. Conor, I have to pore over this back page like it was the Rosetta stone.

I get the damn paper as soon as it hits the stands on Wednesday morning. I read the page over four or five times because it's easy to miss clues the first couple times. See, I have to figure out which messages are hers. Sometimes she calls herself 'Type A'—that's Taipei, where she was born—but other times she's 'Leather Lady.' Or 'Half Moon'—that was for a tattoo she got last year."

"Where?" Conor asked. He didn't feel so bad now, only a little drunk. At least he wasn't as fucked up as Pumo. "On her ass?"

"Just a little below her navel," Tina said. He looked as though he was sorry he had brought up the subject of his girlfriend's tattoo.

"Maggie has a half moon tattooed on her pussy?" Conor asked. He wished he had been in the tattoo parlor when that was going on. Even if Chinese girls weren't Conor's thing—they reminded him of the Dragon Lady in "Terry and the Pirates"—he had to admit that Maggie was more than normally good-looking. Everything about Maggie seemed *round.* She somehow managed to make it seem normal to walk around in chopped-up punk hair and clothes you bought already ripped.

"No. I told you," Pumo said, looking irritated, "just a little below her navel. The bottom of a bikini covers most of it."

"It's almost on her pussy!" Conor said. "Is any of it in her hair? Were you there when the guy did it? Did she cry or anything?"

"You bet I was there. I wanted to make sure he didn't let his attention wander." Pumo took a sip of his drink. "Maggie didn't even blink."

"How big is it?" Conor asked. "About half dollar size?"

"If you're so curious, ask her to show it to you."

"Oh, sure," Conor said. "I can really see me doing that."

Then Conor overheard part of the conversation Mike Poole was having with Beans Beevers—something about Ia Thuc and a grunt Poole had talked to during the parade.

Beevers asked, "He was an ex-combat soldier?"

"Looked like he got out of the field about a week ago," Mike said, giving his little smile.

"This vet really remembered all about me and he said I should get a Medal of Honor?"

"He said they should have given you a Medal of Honor for what you did, and then taken it away again for shooting off your mouth in front of journalists."

This was the first time Conor had ever heard Beevers confronted with the opinion, once widely held, that he had been a dope to brag about Ia Thuc to the press. Of course Beevers acted as though he were hearing this opinion for the first time.

"Ridiculous," Beevers said. "I can just about go along with him on the Congressional medal idea, but not on that. I'm proud of everything I did there, and I hope all of you are too. If it was up to me, we'd all have Congressional medals." He looked down at the front of his shirt, smoothed it, then lifted his chin—stuck it out. "But people know we did the right thing. That's as good as a medal. People agree with the decision of the court-martial, even if they forgot it ever happened."

Conor wondered how Beans could say these things. He didn't see how *people* could know they'd done the right thing at Ia Thuc when even the men who had been there didn't know exactly what had happened.

"You'd be surprised how many guys I meet, I'm talking about other lawyers, judges too, who know my name because of that action," Beevers said. "To tell you the truth, being a sort of a minor league hero has helped me out professionally more than once." Beans looked around at all of them with a sweet candor that made Conor want to puke. "I'm not ashamed of anything I did in Nam. You have to turn what happens to you into a plus."

Michael Poole laughed. "Spoken from the heart, Harry."

"This is important," Beevers insisted. For a second he looked both pained and puzzled. "I have the impression that you three guys are accusing me of something."

"I didn't accuse you of anything, Harry," Poole said.

"So didn't I," said Conor in exasperation. He pointed at Tina Pumo. "So didn't he!"

"We were with each other every step of the way," Harry said, and it took Conor a moment to figure out that he had gone back to talking about Ia Thuc. "We always helped each other out. We were a team, all of us, Spitalny included."

Conor could restrain himself no longer. "I wish that

asshole would have got killed there," he broke in. "I never met anybody as mean as him. Spitalny didn't like *anybody*, man. Right? And he claimed he got stung by wasps? In that cave? I don't think there are any wasps in Nam, man. I saw bugs the size of dogs there, man, but I never saw any wasps."

Tina interrupted him with a loud groan. "Don't talk to me about wasps. Don't talk to me about bugs—any kind of bugs!"

"Is this related to the trouble you're having?" Mike asked.

"The Department of Health has strong feelings on the subject of six-legged creatures," Pumo said. "I don't even want to discuss it."

"Let's get back to the subject, if you don't mind," Beevers said, giving Poole a mysteriously loaded glance.

What the hell is the subject? Conor wondered.

Pumo said, "How about we have another little blast up here and then go down, get something to eat, see some of the entertainment. Jimmy Stewart's supposed to be here. I always liked Jimmy Stewart."

Beevers said, "Mike, are you the only one who knows what I was leading up to? Remind them why we're here. Help me out."

"Lieutenant Beevers thinks it's time to talk about Koko," Poole said.

4

THE ANSWERING MACHINE

1

"Hand me my briefcase, Tina. It's somewhere back there against the wall." Beevers leaned forward from the side of the bed and extended his arm. Tina groped under the table for the case. "Take all day, there's no rush."

"You pushed your chair over it when you got up," Pumo said, now invisible beneath the table. He surfaced with the briefcase in both hands, and held it out.

Beevers put the case on his lap and snapped it open.

Poole leaned over and looked in at a stack of reprints of a familiar page from *Stars and Stripes*. Stapled to it were copies of other newspaper articles. Beevers took out the stack of papers and said, "There's one for each of you. Michael is familiar with some of this material already, but I thought we should all have copies of everything. That way everybody'll know exactly what we're talking about." He handed the first sheaf of stapled papers to Conor. "Settle down and pay attention to this."

"Sieg Heil," Conor said, and took the chair beside Michael Poole.

Beevers handed stapled pages to Poole and Pumo, placed the final set beside him on the bed, closed his case and set it on the floor.

Pumo said, "Take all day, there's no rush."

"Touchy, touchy." Beevers put his papers on his lap,

picked them up with both hands, squinted at them. He set them back in his lap and reached over to his suit jacket to remove his glasses case from the chest pocket. From the case he took a pair of oversized glasses with thin, oval tortoise-shell frames. Beevers put the empty case on top of his suit jacket, then put the glasses on his nose. Again he inspected the papers.

Poole wondered how often during the day Beevers went through this little charade of lawyerly behavior.

Beevers looked up from his papers. Bow tie, suspenders, big glasses. "First of all, *mes amis*, I want to say that we've all had some fun, and we'll have a lot more before we leave, but"—a weighty glance at Conor—"we're in this room together because we shared some important experiences. *And* . . . we survived these experiences because we could depend on each other."

Beevers glanced down at the papers in his lap, and Pumo said, "Get to the point, Harry."

"If you don't understand how much teamwork *is* the point, you're missing everything," Beevers said. He looked up again. "Please read the articles. There are three of them, one from *Stars and Stripes*, one from the *Straits Times* of Singapore, and the third from the *Bangkok Post*. My brother George, who is a career soldier, knew a little bit about the Koko incidents, and when the name caught his eye in the *Stars and Stripes* piece, he sent it to me. Then he asked my other, older brother, Sonny—he's a career sergeant too, over in Manila—to check out all the Asian papers he could locate. George did the same on Okinawa—together they could look at nearly all the English language papers published in the Far East."

"You have two brothers who're lifer sergeants?" Conor asked. Sonny and George, lifers in Manila and Okinawa? From a Mount Avenue family?

Beevers looked at him impatiently. "Eventually these other two pieces turned up in Singapore and Bangkok papers, and that's it. I did some research on my own, but read this stuff first. As you'll see, our boy's been busy."

Michael Poole took a sip of his drink and scanned the topmost article. On January 28, 1982, the corpse of a forty-two-year-old English tourist in Singapore, a freelance writer named Clive McKenna, had been found, his eyes and ears bloodily removed, by a gardener in an overgrown section of the grounds of the Goodwood Park

Hotel. A playing card with the word Koko written on its face had been placed in Mr. McKenna's mouth. On February 5, 1982, an appraiser had entered a supposedly empty bungalow just off Orchard Road in the same city to discover lying face-up and side by side on the living room floor the bodies of Mr. William Martinson of St. Louis, a sixty-one-year-old executive of a heavy equipment company active in Asia, and Mrs. Barbara Martinson, fifty-five, also of St. Louis, who had been accompanying her husband on a business trip. Mr. Martinson lacked his eyes and ears; in his mouth was a playing card with the word Koko scrawled across its face.

The *Straits Times* piece, dated three days later, added the information that while the bodies of the Martinsons had been discovered less than forty-eight hours after their deaths, Clive McKenna's body had gone undiscovered for perhaps as long as five days. Roughly ten days separated the two sets of murders. The Singapore police had many leads, and an arrest was considered imminent.

The clipping from the *Bangkok Post*, dated July 7, 1982, was considerably more emotional than the others. FRENCH WRITERS SLAIN, the headline read. Outrage and dismay were shared by all decent citizens. The provinces of both tourism and literature had been savaged. Unwelcome events of a violent nature were particularly threatening to the hotel industry. The shock to morality—therefore to trade—had potential consequences far beyond the hotel industry, affecting taxicabs, hire-car firms, restaurants, jewelers, massage parlors, museums and temples, tattooists, airport staff and baggage handlers, etc. That the crime was almost certainly the work of undesirable aliens, committed by as well as upon foreigners, had to be not only remembered but reiterated. Police of all districts were engaged in a commendable effort of mutual cooperation designed to root out the whereabouts of the assassins within days. Political hostility to Thailand could not be discounted.

Cocooned within this oddly formal hysteria was the information that Marc Guibert, 48, and Yves Danton, 49, both journalists living in Paris, had been found in their suite at the Sheraton Bangkok by a maid on her normal morning cleaning detail. They were tied to chairs with their throats cut and their eyes and ears removed. The two men had arrived in Thailand the previous afternoon and were not known to have received any messages or guests. Cards from an ordinary deck of Malaysian playing cards, the word, or name, Koko printed by hand on each, had been inserted into the dead men's mouths.

Tina and Conor continued to read, Tina with an expression of feigned detachment, Conor in deep concentration. Harry Beevers sat upright, tapping a pencil against his front teeth, his eyes out of focus.

Printed by hand. Michael saw exactly how: the letters carved in so deeply you could read the raised grooves on the back of the card. Poole could remember the first time he had seen one of the cards protruding from the mouth of a tiny dead man in black pajamas—point for our side, he'd thought, okay.

Pumo said, "The goddamned war still isn't over, I guess."

Conor looked up from his copy of the Bangkok clipping. "Hey, it could be anybody, man. These guys here say it's some political thing. To hell with this, anyhow."

Beevers said, "Do you seriously think it's a coincidence that this murderer writes the name Koko on a playing card which he puts into his victims' mouths?"

"Yeah," Conor said. "Sure it could be. Or it could be politics, like this guy says."

"But the fact is, it almost has to be our Koko," Pumo said slowly. He spread the three clippings out beside him on the table, as if seeing them all at once made coincidence even more unlikely. "These were the only articles your brothers could find? No follow-up?"

Beevers shook his head. He then bent over, picked his glass up from the floor, and made a silent, mocking toast to them without drinking.

"You're pretty cheerful about this," Pumo said.

"Someday, my friends, this is going to be a hell of a story. I'm serious, I can definitely see book rights in this thing. Beyond that, I can see film rights. But to tell you the truth, I'd settle for a mini-series."

Conor covered his face with his hands, and Poole said, "Now I know you're nuts."

Beevers turned to them with an unblinking gaze. "Some day I'll want you to remember who first said that we could all see a lot of money out of this. If we handle it right. *Mucho dinero.*"

"Hallelujah," Conor said. "The Lost Boss is gonna make us rich."

"Consider the facts." Beevers held up a palm like a stop sign while he sipped from his glass. "A law school student who does our data-gathering did some research on my instructions—on the firm's time, so we don't get billed for it. He went through a year's worth of half a dozen major metropolitan papers and the wire services. Net result? Apart of course from St. Louis stories about the Martinsons, there has never been any news story in this country about Koko or these murders. And the stories in St. Louis papers didn't mention the playing cards. They didn't mention Koko."

"Is there any possible connection between the victims?" Michael asked.

"*Consider the facts.* An English tourist in Singapore—our researcher looked up McKenna, and he wrote a travel book about Australia-New Zealand, a couple of thrillers, and a book called *Your Dog Can Live Longer!* With an exclamation point. Maybe he was doing research in Singapore. Who knows? The Martinsons were a straight Middle-American business couple. His firm sold a load of bulldozers and cranes throughout the Far East. Then we have two print journalists, Frenchmen who work for *L'Express.* Guibert and Danton went to Bangkok for the massage parlors. They were longtime friends who took a *vacances* together every couple of years. They weren't on an assignment in Bangkok, they were just cutting up."

"An Englishmen, two Frenchmen, and two Americans," Michael said.

"A pretty clear example of random selection," Beevers said. "I think these people were just in the wrong place at the wrong time. They were shopping or sitting at a bar, and they found themselves talking to a plausible American guy with a lot of stories who eventually took them off somewhere quiet and wasted them. The original Mr. Wrong. The All-American psychopath."

"He didn't mutilate Martinson's wife," Michael said.

"Yeah, he just killed her," Beevers said. "You want mutilations every time? Maybe he just took men's ears because he fought against men in Vietnam."

"Okay," Conor said. "Say it's our Koko. Then what?" He looked almost unwillingly toward Michael and shrugged.

"I mean, I ain't going to no cops or nothing. I got nothing to say to them."

Beevers leaned forward and fixed Conor with the stare of a man attempting to hypnotize a snake. "I agree with you absolutely."

"You agree with me?"

"We have nothing to say to the police. At this point, we don't even know with absolute certainty that Koko is Tim Underhill." He straightened up and looked at Poole with the trace of a smile tugging at his mouth. "Celebrated or not-so-celebrated thriller writer and Singapore resident."

Every man in the room but Beevers all but closed his eyes.

"Are his books really nuts?" Conor finally said. "You remember all that crazy stuff he used to talk about? That book?"

" 'The Running Grunt,' " Pumo said. "I couldn't believe it when I heard he published a couple novels—he talked about it so much I figured he'd never do it."

"He did it, though," Poole said. Without wanting to be, he was surprised, even dismayed that Tina had not read any of Underhill's novels. "It was called *A Beast in View* when it came out."

Beevers was watching Poole expectantly, his thumbs tucked behind his rosy suspenders.

"So you really do think it's Underhill?" Poole asked.

"*Consider the facts,*" Beevers said. "Obviously the same person killed McKenna, the Martinsons, and the two French journalists. So we have a serial murderer who identifies himself by writing the name Koko on a playing card inserted into the mouths of his victims. What does that name mean?"

Pumo said, "It's the name of a volcano in Hawaii. Can we go see Jimmy Stewart now?"

"Underhill told me 'Koko' was the name of a song," Conor said.

" 'Koko' is the name of lots of things, among them one of the few pandas in captivity, a Hawaiian volcano, a princess of Thailand, and jazz songs by Duke Ellington and Charlie Parker. There was even a dog named Koko in the Dr. Sam Sheppard murder case. But none of that means a thing. Koko means *us*—it doesn't mean anything else." Beevers crossed his arms over his chest and looked around at all of them. "And I wasn't in Singapore or Thailand last year. Were you, Michael? *Consider the facts.* McKenna was killed right after the Iranian hostages came back to parades and cover stories—came back as heroes. Did you see that a Vietnam vet in Indiana flipped out and killed some people around the same time? Hey, am I telling you something new? How did you feel?"

The others said nothing.

"Me too," Beevers said. "I didn't want to feel that, but I felt it. I resented what they got for just being hostages. That vet in Indiana had the same feelings, and they pushed him over the edge. What do you suppose happened to Underhill?"

"Or whoever it was," Poole said.

Beevers grinned at him.

"Look, I think this whole thing is nuts in the first place," said Pumo, "but did you ever consider the possibility that Victor Spitalny might be Koko? Nobody's seen him since he deserted Dengler in Bangkok fifteen years ago. He could still be living over there."

Conor surprised Poole by saying, "Spitalny's gotta be dead. He *drank* that shit, man."

Poole kept quiet.

"And there was one more Koko incident after Spitalny disappeared in Bangkok," Beevers said. "Even if the original Koko had a copycat, I think good old Victor is in the clear. No matter where he is."

"I just wish I could talk to Underhill," Pumo said, and Poole silently agreed. "I always liked Tim—I liked him a hell of a lot. You know, if I didn't have to work out that mess in my kitchen, I'd be halfway tempted to get on a plane and see if I could find him. Maybe we could help him out, do something for him."

"That's an amazingly interesting idea," Beevers said.

2

"Request permission to move, *sir*," Conor barked. Beevers glared at him. Conor stood up, clapped Michael on the shoulder, and said, "Do you know what time it is when darkness falls, bats fill the air, and wild dogs begin to howl?"

Poole was looking up in friendly amusement, Harry

Beevers—pencil frozen halfway to his mouth—with irritation and incredulity.

Conor leaned toward Beevers and winked. "Time for another beer." He took a dripping bottle from the ice bucket and twisted off the cap. Beevers was still glaring at him. "So the lieutenant thinks we ought to send a little search party after Underhill, check him out, see how crazy he is?"

"Well, Conor, since you ask," Beevers said very lightly and quietly, "something along those lines might be possible."

"Actually go there?" Pumo asked.

"You said it first."

Conor poured nearly half of the beer down his throat in a continuous series of swallows. He smacked his lips. Conor returned to his chair and took another slug of the beer. Things had just gone totally out of control—now he could sit back and relax and wait for everybody else to see it.

If the Lost Boss says that he still considers himself Underhill's lieutenant, Conor thought, I am gonna puke.

Beevers said, "I don't know if you want to call this a moral responsibility or not, but I think we should handle this situation ourselves. We knew the man, we were there."

Conor opened his mouth, swallowed air, and let the pressure build on his diaphragm. After a second or two he emitted a resounding burp.

"I'm not asking you to share my sense of responsibility," Beevers said, "but it would be nice if you could stop being childish."

"How can I go to Singapore, for Chrissakes?" Conor yelled. "I don't have money in the bank to go around the block! I spent all my money on the fare here, man. I'm sleeping on Tina's couch because I can't even afford a room at my own reunion, man. Get serious, okay?"

Conor felt immediately embarrassed at blowing up in front of Mike Poole. This was what happened when he went over his limit and got drunk—he got mad too fast. Without making himself sound like an even bigger fool, he wanted to explain things. "I mean—okay, I'm an asshole, I shouldn't ought to of yelled. But I'm not like the rest of you guys, I'm not a doctor or a lawyer or an Indian chief, I'm broke, man, I used to be part of the old poor and now I'm part of the new poor. I'm down at sore heels."

"Well, I'm no millionaire," Beevers said. "In fact, as of several weeks ago I resigned from Caldwell, Moran, Morrissey. There were a lot of complicated factors involved, but the fact is, I'm out of a job."

"Your wife's own brother gave you a pink slip?" Conor asked.

"I resigned," Beevers said. "Pat is my *ex*-wife. Serious differences of opinion came up between myself and Charles Caldwell. Anyhow, I'm not made of money any more than you are, Conor. But I did negotiate a pretty decent golden handshake for myself, and I'd be more than willing to loan you a couple thousand dollars interest-free, to be repaid at your convenience. That ought to take care of you."

"I'd help out too," Poole said. "I'm not agreeing to anything, Harry, but Underhill shouldn't be hard to find. He must get advances and royalties from his publisher. Maybe they even forward fan mail to him. I bet we could learn Underhill's address with one phone call."

"I can't believe this," said Pumo. "All three of you guys just lost your minds."

"You were the first to say you'd go," Conor reminded him.

"I can't run out on my life for a month. I have a restaurant to run."

Pumo hadn't noticed when everything went out of control. Okay, Conor thought, Singapore, what the hell?

"Tina, we need you."

"I need me more than you do. Count me out."

"If you stay behind, you'll be sorry the rest of your life."

"Jesus, Harry, in the morning this is going to sound like an Abbott and Costello movie. What the hell do you think you're going to do if you ever manage to find him?"

Pumo wants to stay around New York and play games with Maggie Lah, Conor thought.

"Well, we'll see," Beevers said.

Conor lobbed his empty beer bottle toward the wastebasket. The bottle fell three feet short and slanted off under the dresser. He could not remember switching from vodka to beer. Or had he started on beer, then gone to vodka, and switched back to beer again? Conor inspected the glasses on the table and tried to pick out his old one. The other three were giving him that "cheerleader" look again, and he wished he'd made his net shot into the wastebasket. Conor philosophically poured several inches of vodka into the nearest glass. He scooped a handful of cubes from the bucket and plopped them in. "Give me an S," he said, raising the glass in a final toast. He drank. "Give an I. Give me an N. Give me a . . . G. Give me an A."

Beevers told him to sit down and be quiet, which was fine with Conor. He couldn't remember what came after A anyhow. Some of the vodka slopped onto his pants as he sat down again beside Mike.

"Now can we go see Jimmy Stewart?" he heard Pumo ask.

3

A little while later someone suggested that he lie down and take a nap on Mike's bed, but Conor refused, no, no, he was fine, he was with his asshole buddies, all he had to do was get moving, anybody who could still spell Singapore wasn't too bent out of shape . . .

Without any transition he found himself out in the corridor. He was having trouble with his feet, and Mikey had a firm grip on his left arm. "What's my room number?" he asked Mikey.

"You're staying with Tina."

"Good old Tina."

They turned a corner and good old Tina and Harry Beevers were right in front of them, waiting for the elevator. Beevers was combing his hair in front of a big mirror.

The next thing Conor knew, he was sitting on the floor of the elevator, but he managed to get back on his feet before the doors opened.

"You're cute, Harry," he said to the back of Beevers' head.

The elevator door opened and for a long time they moved through long, blank hallways crowded with people. Conor kept bumping into guys who were too impatient to listen to his apologies. He heard people singing

"Homeward Bound," which was the world's most beautiful song. "Homeward Bound" made him feel like crying.

Poole was making sure he didn't fall down. Conor wondered if Mike actually knew what a great guy he was, and decided he didn't—that was what made him so great.

"I'm really okay," he said.

He sat down beside Mike in a darkened hall. A black-haired man with a narrow moustache, wearing what looked like a prizefighter's championship belt under his tuxedo, was singing "America the Beautiful" and jumping around onstage in front of a band.

"We missed Jimmy Stewart," Mike whispered to him. "This is Wayne Newton."

"Wayne Newton?" Conor asked, then heard that his voice was too loud. People were laughing at what he had said. Conor felt too embarrassed for Mikey to set him straight—Wayne Newton was a fat teenager who sang like a girl. This Las Vegas toughie wasn't Wayne Newton. Conor closed his eyes and the whole dark hall instantly began to swing him around with it in great zooming circles. Conor found that he was unable to open his eyes. Applause, whistles, shouts of approval filled his ears. He heard his own first snore, and less than a second later fell into unconsciousness.

4

"We don't have as many groupies as musicians," Harry Beevers said to Poole, "but they're out there. They're basically earth mothers with a kinky little yen for excitement. Is he getting heavy? Put him on your couch and come back down to the bar with us."

"I want to get to bed," Poole said. Conor Linklater, a hundred and sixty pounds of dead weight bequeathed to him by Tina Pumo, was draped over his shoulder.

Beevers breathed alcohol at Poole. "Nam groupies are complicated, but by now I've got them figured out. They get off on, one, the idea of our being soldiers and fighting men but more spiritual somehow than other vets—two, they've got a little slug of social worker in them and they want to demonstrate that our country loves us after all—and three, they don't know what we did over there and it turns them on." Beevers glittered at him. "This has got to be the place. They'd come thousands of miles in their sleep just to hang out at the bar."

Poole had the uneasy feeling that, without knowing it, Harry Beevers was describing Pat Caldwell, his ex-wife.

After Michael had rolled Conor onto the side of the bed the maid had not turned down, he pulled off his friend's black running shoes and undid his belt. Conor moaned; his pale, veined eyelids fluttered. With his cropped red hair and pale skin, Conor Linklater seemed to be about nineteen years old: without his scraggly beard and moustache, he looked very like his Vietnam self. Poole covered Linklater with a spare blanket from the closet; then he switched on the lamp on the other side of the bed and turned off the overhead light. If Conor was to have slept on a couch in Pumo's room, Pumo must have taken a suite—Poole's own room did not offer a couch for the comfort of sodden visitors. Undoubtedly Beevers had also taken a suite. (Harry had never considered turning over his own couch to Conor.)

It was a few minutes to twelve. Poole turned on the television and turned down the volume, then sat in the closest chair and removed his own shoes. He draped his jacket over the back of the other chair. Charles Bronson was standing on the grassy verge of a road in a dainty, empty landscape that looked like western Ireland, looking through binoculars at a grey Mercedes-Benz pulled up in the gravel forecourt of a Georgian mansion. For a moment anticipatory silence surrounded the Mercedes, and then a bulging wall of flame obliterated the car.

Michael picked up the telephone and set it on the table beside him. The maid had lined up the bottles, stacked clear plastic glasses, removed the empties, and wrapped the plate of cheese in cellophane. In the bucket, one bottle of beer stood neck-deep in water, surrounded by floating slivers of ice. Michael dipped the topmost glass into the bucket and scooped up ice and water. He took a sip.

Conor muttered "googol" and rolled his face into his pillow.

On impulse Michael picked up the phone and dialed his wife's private line at home. It was possible that Judy was lying awake in bed, reading something like *The One-*

Minute Manager while successfully ignoring the television program she had turned on to keep her company.

Judy's telephone rang once, then clicked as if someone had picked it up. Poole heard the mechanical hiss of tape, and knew that his wife had turned on her answering machine with its third-person message:

"Judy is unable to answer the telephone at this time, but if you leave your name, number, and message after the beep, she will get back to you as soon as possible."

He waited for the beep.

"Judy, this is Michael. Are you home?" Judy's machine was attached to the telephone in her study, adjacent to the bedroom. If she were awake in her bed, she would hear his voice. Judy did not respond; the tape whirred. Into the waiting machine he uttered a few mechanical sentences, ending by saying, "I'll be home late Sunday night. Bye-bye."

In bed, Michael read a few pages of the Stephen King novel he had packed. Conor Linklater complained and snuffled on the other side of the bed. Nothing in the novel seemed more than slightly odder or more threatening than events in ordinary life. Improbability and violence overflowed from ordinary life, and Stephen King seemed to know that.

Before Michael could turn off his light, he was dripping with sweat, carrying his copy of *The Dead Zone* through an army base many times larger than Camp Crandall. All around the camp, twenty or thirty kilometers beyond the barbed-wire perimeter, stood hills once thickly covered by trees, now so perfectly bombed and burned and defoliated that only charred sticks protruded upwards from powdery brown earth. He walked past a row of empty tents and at last heard the silence of the camp—he was alone. The camp had been abandoned, and he had been left behind. A flagless flagpole stood before the company headquarters. He trudged past the deserted building into a stretch of empty land and smelled burning shit. Then he knew that this was no dream, he really was in Vietnam—the *rest* of his life was the dream. Poole never smelled things in his dreams. He didn't think he even dreamed in color most of the time. Poole turned around and saw an old Vietnamese woman looking at him expressionlessly from beside an oil drum filled with burning kerosene-soaked excrement. Dense black smoke boiled up from the drum and smudged the sky. His despair was flat and unsurprising.

Wait a second, he thought, if this is reality it's no later than 1969. He opened *The Dead Zone* to the page of publishing information. Deep in his chest, his heart deflated like a punctured balloon. The copyright date was 1965. He had never left Vietnam. Everything since had been only a nineteen-year-old's wishful dream.

5

BEANS BEEVERS AT THE MEMORIAL

1

Poole awoke with a fading memory of smoke and noise, of artillery fire and uniformed men running in a cartoonish lockstep through a burning village. He pushed this vision into forgetfulness with unconscious expertise. His first real thought was that he would stop off at Walden Books in Westerholm and buy a book for a twelve-year-old patient named Stacy Talbot before visiting her in St. Bartholomew's Hospital. Then he remembered that he was in Washington. His second fully formed thought was to wonder if Tim Underhill was really still alive. He had a brief vision of himself standing in a neat graveyard in Singapore, looking down with both loss and relief at Underhill's headstone.

Or was Underhill simmering in craziness, still back in the war?

Conor Linklater seemed to have vanished and left behind a crushed pillow and a wildly wrinkled counterpane. Poole crawled across the bed and peered over the far edge. Curled up into himself like a cabbage leaf, his mouth lax and his eyelids stretched unmoving across his eyes, Conor lay asleep on the floor.

Michael pushed himself back across the bed and went quietly into the bathroom to shower.

"Jeez," Conor said when Michael came out of the bathroom. He was sitting in one of the chairs and holding his head in both hands. "What time is it, anyhow?"

"About ten-thirty." Poole took underwear and socks from his bag and began dressing.

"Blackout, man," Conor said. "Total hangover." He peeked out through his fingers at Poole. "How'd I end up here, anyhow?"

"I sort of assisted you."

"Thanks, man," Linklater groaned. His head sank again into his hands. "I gotta turn over a new lease on life. I been partying too much lately, getting old, gotta slow down. *Whoo.*" He straightened up and looked around the room as if he were lost. "Where's my clothes?"

"Pumo's room," Michael said, buttoning his shirt.

"Well, I don't know. I left all my shit up there. I sure wish he'd come along with us, man, don't you? Pumo the Puma. He oughta come along. Hey, Mikey, can I use your bathroom and your shower before I go back upstairs?"

"Oh dear," Poole said. "I just got it all cleaned up for the maid."

Conor left the couch and moved across the room in a fashion that Poole associated with recovering stroke victims in geriatric wards. When Conor got to the bathroom he leaned on the doorknob and coughed. His hair was standing up in little orange spikes. "Am I crazy, or did Beans say he'd loan me a couple thousand bucks?"

Poole nodded.

"Do you think he meant it?"

Poole nodded again.

"I'll never figure that guy out, I guess," Conor said, and slammed the bathroom door behind him.

After he pushed his feet into his loafers, Poole went to the telephone and dialed Judy's number. She did not answer, nor did her machine. Poole hung up.

A few minutes later Beevers called down to inform Michael and Conor that he was offering room-service breakfast for everybody in his suite *(en suite)*, commencing in thirty minutes at eleven hundred hours, and that Michael had better get hopping if he wanted more than one Bloody Mary.

"More than one?"

"I guess you didn't get the kind of exercise I had last night," Beevers gloated. "A lovely lady, the kind I was telling you about, left about an hour or two ago, and I'm as mellow as a month in the country. Michael—try to persuade Pumo that there are more important things in the world than his restaurant, will you?" He hung up before Poole could respond.

2

Beevers' suite had not only a long living room with sliding windows onto a substantial balcony but was equipped with a dining room where Michael, Pumo, and Beevers sat at a round table laden with plates of food, baskets of rolls, racks of toast, pitchers of Bloody Marys, chafing dishes holding sausages, bacon, and eggs Benedict.

From the couch in the living room where he sat hunched over a cup of black coffee, Conor said, "I'll eat something later."

"*Mangia, mangia.* Keep your strength up for our trip." Beevers waggled a fork dripping egg yolk and hollandaise sauce. His black hair gleamed and his eyes shone. His white shirt had been fresh from its wrapping when Beevers had rolled up his sleeves and his soberly striped bow tie was perfectly knotted. The dark blue suit jacket draped over the back of his chair had a broad chalky stripe. He looked as though he expected to be standing before the Supreme Court instead of the Vietnam Memorial.

"You're still serious about that?" Pumo asked.

"Aren't you? Tina, we need you—how could we do this without you?"

"You're going to have to try," Pumo said. "But isn't the question academic anyhow?"

"Not to me, it isn't," Beevers said. "How about you, Conor? You think I'm just kidding around?"

The three men at the table looked down the length of the living room toward Conor. Startled at being the object of everyone's attention, he straightened himself up. "Not if you're loaning me the air fare, you're not," he said. "Kidding, that is."

Beevers was now quizzing Michael with his annoyingly clear, annoyingly amused eyes. "And you? *Was sagen Sie*, Michael?"

"Do you ever exactly kid around, Harry?" Michael

asked, unwilling to be a counter in Harry Beevers' newest game.

Beevers was still gleaming at him, waiting for more because he knew he was going to get it.

"I suppose I'm tempted, Harry," he said, and caught Pumo's sidelong glance.

3

"Just out of curiosity," Harry Beevers leaned forward to say to the cabdriver, "how do the four of us strike you? What sort of impression do you have of us as a group?"

"You serious?" the cabbie asked, and turned to Poole, seated beside him on the front seat. "Is this guy serious?"

Poole nodded, and Beevers said, "Go on. Lay it on the line. I'm curious."

The driver looked at Beevers in the mirror, looked back at the road, then glanced back over his shoulder at Pumo and Linklater. The driver was an unshaven, blubbery man in his mid-fifties. Whenever he made even the smallest movement, Poole caught the mingled odors of dried sweat and burning electrical circuits.

"You guys don't fit together at all, no way," the driver said. He looked suspiciously over at Poole. "Hey, if this is 'Candid Camera' or some shit like that, you can get out now."

"What do you mean, we don't fit together?" Beevers asked. "We're a unit!"

"Here's what *I* see." The driver glanced again at his mirror. "You look like some kind of bigshot lawyer, maybe a lobbyist or some other kind of guy who starts out in life by stealing from the collection plate. The guy next to you looks like a pimp, and the guy next to him is a working stiff with a hangover. This one here next to me, he looks like he teaches high school."

"A pimp!" Pumo howled.

"So sue me," said the driver. "You asked."

"I *am* a working stiff with a hangover," Conor said. "And face it, Tina, you are a pimp."

"I got it right, huh?" the driver said. "What do I win? You guys are from 'Wheel of Fortune,' right?"

"Are you serious?" Beevers asked.

"I asked first," said the driver.

"No, I wanted to know—" Beevers began, but Conor told him to shut up.

The cabdriver smirked to himself the rest of the way to Constitution Avenue. "This is close enough," Beevers said. "Pull over."

"I thought you wanted the Memorial."

"I said, pull over."

The cabbie swerved to the side of the road and jerked to a stop. "Could you arrange for me to meet Vanna White?" he asked into the mirror.

"Get stuffed," Beevers said, and jumped out of the cab. "Pay him, Tina." He held the door until Pumo and Linklater left the car, then slammed it shut. "I hope you didn't tip that asshole," he said.

Pumo shrugged.

"Then you're an asshole too." Beevers turned away and stomped off in the direction of the Memorial.

Poole hurried to catch up with him.

"So what did I say?" Beevers asked, almost snarling. "I didn't say anything wrong. The guy was a jerk, that's all. I should have kicked his teeth in."

"Calm down, Harry."

"You heard what he said to me, didn't you?"

"He called Pumo a pimp," Michael said.

"Tina's a food pimp," Beevers said.

"Slow down, or we'll lose the others."

Beevers whirled about to await Tina and Conor, who were about thirty feet behind. Conor looked up and smiled at them.

Beevers tilted his head toward Michael and half-whispered, "Didn't you ever get tired of baby-sitting those two guys?" Then he yelled at Pumo, "Did you tip that shithead?"

Pumo kept a straight face. "A pittance."

Poole said, "The cabdriver I got yesterday wanted to ask me how it felt to kill someone."

" 'How does it feel to kill someone?' " Beevers said in a mocking, high-pitched voice. "I can't stand that question. Let them kill somebody, if they really want to find out." He felt better already. The other two came up to them. "Well, we know we're a unit anyway, don't we?"

"We're savage killers," Pumo said.

Conor asked, "Who the fuck is Vanna White?" and Pumo cracked up.

* * *

By the time the four of them got within a hundred yards of the Memorial they were part of a crowd. The men and women streaming from the sidewalk across the grass might have been the same people Poole had seen the day before—vets wearing mismatched parts of uniforms, older men in VFW garrison caps, women Poole's age gripping the hands of dazed-looking children. Harry Beevers' chalk-striped lawyer's suit made him look like a frustrated, rather superior tour guide.

"What a bunch of losers we are, when you come down to it," Beevers spoke into Poole's ear.

Poole said nothing—he was watching two men make their way across the grass. One, nearly six-five and skinny as a pipestem, leaned against a metal crutch and in wide arcs swung a rigid leg that must also have been metal; his bearded companion, imprisoned in a wooden wheelchair, had to hoist his body off the seat every time he pushed the wheels. The two men were calmly talking and laughing as they moved toward the Memorial.

"Did you find Cotton's name yesterday?" Pumo asked, breaking into his thoughts in a way that seemed to extend them.

Poole shook his head. "Let's find him today."

"Hell, let's find everybody," Conor said. "What else are we here for?"

4

Pumo listed all the names and their panel locations on the back of an American Express slip. Dengler, 14 West, line 52—Poole remembered that one. Cotton, 13 West, line 73 . . . Trotman, 13 West, line 18. Peters, 14 West, line 38. And Huebsch, Hannapin, Recht. And Burrage, Washington, Tiano. And Rowley, Thomas Chambers, the only man in their company killed at Ia Thuc. And the victims of Elvis, the swivel-hipped sniper: Lowry, Montegna, Blevins. And more after that. Pumo's tiny, neat handwriting covered the back of the green American Express slip.

They stood on the stone slabs of the path, looking up together at the names etched into polished black granite. Conor wept before Dengler's name, and both Conor and

Pumo had tears on their faces as they looked at the medic's name: PETERS, NORMAN CHARLES.

"Goddamn," Conor said. "Right now, Peters ought to be on top of a tractor, worried that he ain't going to get enough rain." Peters' family had worked the same Kansas farmland for four generations, and the medic had let everyone know that while he temporarily enjoyed being their medical corpsman, sometimes in the night he could smell his fields in Kansas. ("You be smelling Spitalny, not Kansas," SP4 Cotton said.) Now his brothers worked Peters' fields, and whatever was left of Peters, Norman Charles, after the helicopter on which he'd been giving plasma to Recht, Herbert Wilson, had crashed and burned was beneath the doubtless fertile soil of a country cemetery.

"He'd just be bitching about how the government is giving a royal screwing to him and all the other farmers," Beevers said.

Michael Poole saw a huge golden-fringed flag ruffling in the breeze off to his right, and remembered glimpsing the same flag yesterday. A tall wild-haired man held the flag anchored to his wide belt—beside him, nearly obscured by a glistening wreath, stood a round white sign lettered in red: NO GREATER LOVE. Poole thought he'd read that the wild-haired ex-Marine had been standing in the same place for two days straight.

"You see the story about that guy in the paper this morning?" Pumo said. "He's holding the flag in honor of POWs and MIAs."

"It won't bring them back any quicker," Beevers said.

"I don't think that's the point," Pumo told him.

In that instant, the long black length of the Memorial *announced* itself—to Poole it was as if it had just spoken and taken a step toward him. Michael remembered this from his first visit. He moved very slightly away from the others. The world was a blur. Once Poole had stood for hours up to his waist in water swarming with leeches, holding his M-16 and his Claymores out of the water until his arms ached, turned to lead, died. . . . Rowley, Thomas Chambers was standing beside him, also holding his arsenal out of the stinking water. Swarms of mosquitos buzzed around them, settling on their faces. Every few seconds they had to blow tickling mosquitos out of their noses. Poole could remember being so tired that if Rowley had offered to prop up his arms for him, he would have collapsed into sleep right there. He could remember feeling the leeches attach themselves to his thighs.

"Oh God," Poole said, realizing that he was trembling. He wiped his eyes and looked at the others. Conor was weeping too, and emotion suffused Pumo's handsome, normally impassive face.

Harry Beevers was watching Poole. He looked about as emotional as a weight-guesser at the state fair. "It got you, hmm?"

"Sure," Poole said. Profound irritation at Beevers' smugness flashed through him. "Are you immune?"

Beevers shook his head. "Hardly, Michael. I just keep my feelings inside. That's the way I was raised. But I was thinking that a bunch of names ought to be added to this thing. McKenna. The Martinsons. Danton and Guibert. Remember?"

Poole had no desire to try to explain what he had just experienced. He too could think of at least one name that could be added to those on the wall.

Beevers virtually twinkled at Michael. "You know that we're going to get rich out of this, don't you?" And for some Beeversish reason utterly opaque to Michael Poole, he tapped him twice on the chest with an extended index finger. The finger appeared to have been manicured. Then Beevers turned to Pumo and Linklater, evidently saying something about the Memorial. Michael could still feel Harry's index finger playfully jabbing at his sternum. . . . *Only problem is that it doesn't have enough names on it*, he heard Beevers saying.

A hundred dying mosquitos packed Poole's nostrils; dying leeches clamped onto his weary, dying legs. It was decided, Poole knew: as if in imitation of their ignorant, terrified, and variously foolhardy nineteen-year-old selves, they really were going to take off for the Far East all over again.

PART TWO
PREPARATIONS FOR TAKEOFF

6

BEEVERS AT REST

1

"Maggie never comes in here, Maggie had enough," said Jimmy Lah, answering Harry's question as he poured a silvery ribbon of vermouth over the ice and liquid already in the glass. He squeezed a paring of lemon rind around the rim of the glass, then slipped it down into the ice cubes.

"Enough of life, or enough of Tina?" Beevers asked.

Jimmy Lah placed on the bar a fresh paper napkin with the word Saigon printed in slanting red letters over the silhouette of a man pulling a rickshaw. He set Harry Beevers' drink on the napkin and with a sideways sweep of his hand gathered up the damp, torn napkin beside it. "Tina's too normal for Maggie."

The bartender winked at Harry, then stepped backwards. Harry was startled to find himself looking at the spiteful, jealous faces of demons with cat's whiskers and long faces, taped to the mirror. Until Jimmy Lah moved away, they had been hidden from view. Harry Beevers felt a surprising familiarity with these demons. He knew that he had seen spiteful faces like these somewhere in I Corps, but could not remember where.

It was four o'clock and Harry was killing time before calling his ex-wife. Jimmy Lah was pouring some soapy blender concoction for the bar's only customer besides himself, a fruitcake with a roosterish yellow Mohawk and oversized pink eyeglasses.

Harry swiveled around on his stool to face the large rectangular dining room of Pumo's restaurant. Before him were knobby bamboo chairs at glass-topped bamboo tables. Ceiling fans with blades like polished brown oars revolved slowly overhead. The white walls had been painted with murals of giant fronds and palm leaves. The place looked as if Sidney Greenstreet would walk in at any moment.

Behind a counter at the far end of the restaurant a door swung open, revealing two Vietnamese men in white aprons chopping vegetables. Behind them pots bubbled on a gas range. Harry caught a glimpse, unexpected as a mirage, of a fluttering translucent curtain behind the range. He leaned forward to get a better look and felt a familiar inward flinch as he saw Vinh, Pumo's head chef, darting toward the open door. Vinh was from An Lat, an I Corps village only a few klicks from Ia Thuc.

Then Harry saw who had opened the door.

Just beneath Harry's normal field of vision, a small, smiling Vietnamese girl was moving cautiously but swiftly into the restaurant. She had nearly reached the counter when Vinh managed to grab her shoulder. The child's mouth became an astonished O, and Vinh hauled her back into the kitchen. The doors swung shut on a burst of Vietnamese.

In an eerily perfect auditory hallucination, Harry Beevers could hear M.O. Dengler panting just behind his right shoulder, along with the sounds of distant fires and far-away screams. Pale faces shone dimly at the center of a vast darkness. He remembered where he had seen the demons' faces before—on small black-haired women, rushing up with their fists raised. *You numbah ten! You numbah ten!*

An abyss had just yawned before Harry Beevers. For a moment he felt the terror of not existing, a sickening feeling that he had never existed in the way simpler, healthier people existed.

He heard himself asking what a kid was doing in the kitchen.

Jimmy stepped nearer. "That's Vinh's little girl, Helen. Both of them temporarily staying here. Helen was probably looking for Maggie—they're old buddies."

"Tina must have a lot on his mind," Harry said, beginning to feel more in control of himself.

"You see the *Village Voice*?"

Harry shook his head. He realized that he had unconsciously pushed his hands into his pockets to hide their shaking. Jimmy searched around behind the bar until he found the paper in a stack of menus beside the cash register and slid it across the bar with the back page up. VOICE BULLETIN BOARD, read the headline above three dense columns of personals in varying type sizes. Harry saw that two of the ads had been circled.

The first message read: *Foodcat. Missing damned you. Will be Mike Todd Room 10 Wed. The Wanderer.* The second message was in caps. JUST DECIDED UNABLE TO DECIDE. MAY BE MIKE TODD, MAYBE NOT. LA-LA.

"See what I mean?" Jimmy asked. He began grabbing glasses from below the bar and vigorously swirling them around in a sink.

"Your sister placed both these ads?"

"Sure," Jimmy said. "Whole family's crazy."

"I feel sorry for Tina."

Jimmy grinned, then looked up from the sink. "How's the doctor these days? Any change?"

"You know him," Harry said. "After his son died, he stopped being fun to hang out with. *Totalemente*."

After a second, Jimmy asked, "He going on your hunting trip?"

"I wish you'd call it a mission," Harry snapped. "Listen, isn't Tina ever going to come up for air?"

"Maybe later," Jimmy said, looking away.

Pumo had two Vietnamese living in his restaurant, he was tearing his kitchen apart to kill a few bugs, and he was acting like a teenager over Maggie Lah. "La-La," for sure. Beans Beevers' old comrade had become just another . . . for a second he searched for Dengler's word, then had it: *toon*.

"Tell him he ought to show up at the Mike Todd Room with a fucking knife in his belt."

"Maggie will get a big kick out of that."

Harry looked at his watch.

"You planning to get to Taipei on this mission, Harry?" asked Jimmy, showing a trace of real interest for the first time.

Beevers felt a premonitory tingle. "Aren't you and Maggie from Taipei?" A nerve jumped in his temple.

Then he got it! Who was to say that Tim Underhill still lived in Singapore? Harry had been to Taipei on his R&R, and he could easily see Tim Underhill choosing to live in the raunchy amalgam of Chinatown and Dodge City he remembered. He saw that Divine Justice, mistakenly thought to be dozing, had of course been wide awake all along. It was all ordained, everything had been thought out beforehand. God had planned it all.

Harry settled back down on his bar stool, ordered another martini, and put off his confrontation with his ex-wife for another twenty minutes while he listened to Jimmy Lah describe the seamier aspects of night life in the capital city of Taiwan.

Jimmy set a steaming cup of coffee before him. Harry folded the napkin into the inside pocket of his suit and glanced up at the angry demons. He saw a child rushing toward him with an upraised knife, and his heart speeded up. He smiled and scalded his tongue with hot coffee.

2

A short time later Harry stood at the pay telephone next to the men's room in a narrow downstairs corridor. He first tried finding his ex-wife at the Maria Farr Gallery, which was on the ground floor of a former warehouse on Spring Street in SoHo. Pat Caldwell Beevers had gone to private school with Maria Farr, and when the gallery had seemed to be failing, took it on as one of her pet private charities. (In the early days of his wife's involvement with the art gallery, Harry had endured dinner parties with artists whose work consisted of rusting pipes strewn randomly across the floor, of a row of neat aluminum slab stood on end, of pink wart-encrusted columns that reminded Harry of giant erections. He still could not believe that the perpetrators of these adolescent japes earned real money.)

Maria Farr herself answered the telephone. This was a bad sign.

He said, "Maria, how nice to hear your voice again. It's me." In fact, the sound of her voice, all the consonants hard as pebbles, reminded Harry of how much he disliked her.

"I have nothing to say to you, Harry," Maria said.

"I'm sure that's a blessing to both of us," Harry said. "Is Pat still in the gallery?"

"I wouldn't tell you if she were." Maria hung up.

Another call, to Information, got him the number of *Rilke Street*, the literary magazine that was Pat's other ongoing charity. Its editorial offices were actually the Duane Street loft of William Tharpe, the magazine's editor. Because Harry had spent fewer evenings with Tharpe and his impoverished contributors than with Maria Farr and her artists, Tharpe had always taken Harry more or less at face value.

"*Rilke Street*, William Tharpe speaking."

"Billy, my boy, how do you do? This is Harry Beevers, your best flunky's best ex-husband. I was hoping to find her there."

"Harry!" said Tharpe. "You're in luck. Pat and I are pasting up issue thirty-five right this minute. Going to be a beautiful number. Are you coming down this way?"

"If invited," he said. "Do you think I might speak to the dear Patricia?"

In a moment Harry's ex-wife had taken the telephone. "How *nice* of you to call, Harry. I was just thinking about you. Are you getting on all right?"

So she knew that Charles had sacked him.

"Fine, fine, everything's great," he said. "I find myself in the mood for a celebration. How about a drink or dinner after you're through tickling old Billy's balls?"

Pat had a short discussion with William Tharpe, most of it inaudible to Harry, then returned the receiver to her mouth and said, "An hour, Harry."

"No wonder I'll always adore you," he said, and Pat quickly hung up.

3

When his cab passed a liquor store, Harry asked the driver to wait while he went in and bought a bottle. He jumped out, crossed the sidewalk, his coattails billowing, and entered a barnlike, harshly lighted interior with wide aisles and pastel blue neon signs announcing IMPORTED and BEER and FINE CHAMPAGNES. He started moving toward the FINE CHAMPAGNES, but slowed down when he saw three young women with eggbeater hair and antisocial clothing preceding him up the aisle. Punk girls always excited Harry. The three girls ahead of Harry in the aisle of the liquor store were consulting in whispers and giggles over a bin of inexpensive red wines, their fluffy multicolored heads bobbing like toxic orchids to some private joke.

One of them was blonde-and-pink-haired, and nearly as tall as Harry. She picked up a bottle of burgundy and slowly revolved it in her long fingers.

All three girls were dressed in torn black garments that looked as if they had been picked up off the street. The shortest of them bent over to examine the bottle being caressed by the tallest girl and pointed a round bottom toward Harry. Her skin was a sandy, almost golden shade. For an instant Harry was aware only that he knew who she was. Then Harry saw her profile printed sharply against a blue neon background. The girl was Maggie Lah.

Harry stepped forward, grinning, aware of the contrast between his suit and the girls' rags.

Maggie broke away from the others and glided to the top of the aisle. The other two hurried after. The tall one reached out and closed a white hand on Maggie's shoulder. Harry saw a sunken cheek covered with dark stubble. The tall girl was a man. Harry stopped moving and his smile froze on his face. Maggie rubbed the side of her hand against the man's stubbly cheek. The three of them continued up to the top of the aisle and turned toward FINE CHAMPAGNES without seeing Harry.

Maggie and her friends veered into the side aisle lined with refrigerated cases. The neon sign shed pale blue light over them. Harry remembered that he had entered this store to buy a bottle of champagne as a sweetener for Pat when he saw Maggie open the glass doors of a refrigerated case. On her face was an expression of sweetly concentrated attention. She plucked out a bottle of Dom Perignon and slid it instantly into her clothes, where it disappeared. The theft of the bottle had taken something like a second and a half. Harry had a sudden picture, vividly clear, of the dark, cold bottle of Dom Perignon nestled between Maggie's breasts.

Without any premeditation of any kind, Harry slammed open the glass door and yanked out another bottle of

Dom Perignon. He remembered the mystically smiling face of the Vietnamese girl moving toward him through Saigon's kitchen door. He shoved the bottle beneath his suit jacket, where it bulged. Maggie Lah and her ratty friends had begun to stroll toward the rank of cash registers at the front of the store. Harry thrust his hand inside his coat, upended the bottle, and jammed its neck into his trousers. Then he buttoned his jacket and coat. The bulge had become only slightly conspicuous. He began following Maggie toward the cash registers.

The clerks at the few working registers punched buttons and pushed wine bottles down the moving belts. Maggie and the others sailed past an empty counter and a uniformed security guard lounging against the plate-glass window. As Harry watched, they vanished through the door.

"Hey, Maggie!" he yelled. He trotted past the nearest unattended cash register. "Maggie!"

The guard looked up and frowned. Harry pointed toward the door. Now everybody at the front of the store was staring at him. "I saw an old friend," Harry said to the guard, who looked away without responding and leaned back against the window.

By the time Harry got to the sidewalk, Maggie was gone.

All the way to Duane Street, Harry searched the sidewalks for her. When the cab stopped and Harry stood on the stamped metal walkway before the warehouse that housed William Tharpe's loft, he thought—where I'm going there are a million girls like that.

4

Harry Beevers presented the chilled bottle of Dom Perignon to an astonished, gratified William Tharpe, and spent five or ten minutes in hypocritical raptures over the forthcoming number of *Rilke Street.* Then he took plain, greying Pat Caldwell Beevers, who was beginning more than ever to suggest an English sheepdog that had been mooning around him half his life, out to a TriBeCa restaurant of the sort he had learned from Tim Underhill to call piss-elegant. The walls were red lacquer. Discreet lamps with brass shades sat on each table. Portly waiters hovered. Harry thought of Maggie Lah, of her golden skin, of champagne bottles and other interesting things between her small but undoubtedly affecting breasts. All the while he elaborated various necessary fictions concerning his "mission." Now and then, although Pat frequently smiled and seemed to enjoy her wine, her soup, her fish, he thought she knew that he was lying. Like Jimmy Lah, she asked him how Michael looked, how he thought he was doing, and Harry answered fine, fine. Her smiles seemed to Harry to be full of regret—whether for him, for herself, for Michael Poole, or the world at large, he could not tell. When the moment came when he asked for money, she said only, "How much?" Around two thousand. She reached into her bag, took out her checkbook and fountain pen, and without expression of any kind on her face wrote out a check for three thousand dollars.

She passed the check across the table. Her face was now flushed in a mottled band from cheekbone to cheekbone, Harry thought unattractively so.

"Of course I consider this strictly a loan," he said. "You're doing a lot of good with this money, Pat. I mean that."

"So the government wants you to track down this man to see if he might be a murderer?"

"In a nutshell. Of course it's a semi-private operation, which is how I'll be able to do the book deals, the film deals, and so on. You can appreciate the need for strict confidentiality."

"Of course."

"Well, I know you could always read between the lines, but . . ." He let the sentence complete itself. "I'd be kidding you if I said there wasn't quite a bit of potential danger involved in this."

"Oh, yes," Pat said, nodding.

"I shouldn't even be thinking like this, but if I don't come back, I think it would be fitting for me to be buried at Arlington."

She nodded again.

Harry gave up and began looking around the room for the waiter.

Pat startled him by saying, "There are still times when I'm sorry that you ever set foot in Vietnam."

"What's the point," he asked. "I'm me, I always was me, I've never been anything *but* me."

They parted outside the restaurant.

After Harry had gone a short distance down the sidewalk, he turned around, smiling, knowing that Pat was watching him walk away. But she was moving straight ahead, her shoulders slumped, her overstuffed, lumpy bag swinging at her side.

He went to his bank and let himself into the empty vestibule with his bank card. There he used the cash machine to deposit Pat's check and one other he had obtained that day and to withdraw four hundred dollars in cash. He bought a copy of *Screw* at a corner newsstand and folded it under his arm so that no one would be able to identify it. Harry walked back through the cold to West 24th Street and the studio apartment he had found shortly after Pat told him, more forcefully than she had ever said anything in the entire course of their marriage, that she had to have a divorce.

7

CONOR AT WORK

1

It was funny, Conor thought, how ever since the reunion things from the old days kept coming back to him, as if Vietnam had been his real life and everything since was just the afterglow. It was hard for him to keep his mind on the present—*back then* kept breaking in, sometimes even physically. A few days before, an old man had innocently handed him a photograph taken by SP4 Cotton of Tim Underhill with his arm around one of his "flowers."

It was four o'clock in the afternoon, and Conor was lying in bed with his first serious hangover since the dedication of the Memorial. Everybody thought you got better at handling pressure as you got older, but in Conor's experience everybody had it backwards.

Three days earlier, Conor had been in the middle of the fifth week of a carpentry job that should have paid the rent at least until Poole and Beevers put their Singapore trip together. On Mount Avenue in Hampstead, only ten minutes from Conor's tiny, almost comically underfurnished apartment in South Norwalk, a millionaire lawyer in his sixties named Charles ("Call me Charlie!") Daisy had just remarried for the third time. For the sake of his new wife, Daisy was redoing the entire ground floor of his mansion—kitchen, sitting room, breakfast room, dining room, lounge, morning room, laundry room, and servants quarters. Daisy's contractor, a white-bearded old-timer named Ben Roehm, had hired Conor when his usual crew proved too small. Conor had worked with Ben Roehm three or four times over the years. Like a lot of master carpenters who were geniuses at manipulating wood, Roehm could be moody and unpredictable, but he made carpentry more than just something you did to pay the rent. Working with Roehm was as close to pleasure as work could get, in Conor's opinion.

And the first day Conor was on the job, Charlie Daisy came home early from the office and walked into the sitting room where Conor and Ben Roehm were laying a new oak floor. He stood watching them for a long time. Conor got a little nervous. He figured maybe the client didn't like the way he looked. To cut down the inevitable agony of kneeling on hardwood all day, Conor had tied thick rags around his knees. He'd knotted a speckled bandanna around his forehead to keep the sweat out of his eyes. (The bandanna made him think of Underhill, of flowers and flowing talk.) Conor thought he probably looked a little loose for Charlie Daisy. He was not completely surprised when Daisy took a step forward and coughed into his fist. "Ahem!" He and Roehm shot each other a quick glance. Clients, especially Mount Avenue-type clients, did nutty things right out of the blue. "You, young man," Daisy said. Conor looked up, blinking, painfully aware that he was down on all fours like a raggedy dog in front of this dapper little millionaire. "Am I right about something?" Daisy asked. "You were in Vietnam, right?"

"Yes, sir," Conor said, prepared for trouble.

"Good man," Daisy said. He reached down to shake Conor's hand. "I knew I was right."

It turned out that his only son was another name on the wall—killed in Hue during the Tet offensive.

For a couple of weeks it was probably the best job of Conor's life. Almost every day he learned something new from Ben Roehm, little things that had as much to do with concentration and respect as with technique. A few days after shaking Conor's hand, Charlie Daisy showed up at the end of the day carrying a grey suede box and a leather photo album. Conor and Roehm were framing a new partition in the kitchen, which looked like a bombsite—chopped-up floor, dangling wires, jutting pipes. Daisy picked his way toward them, saying, "Until I got married again, this was the only heart I had." The box turned out to be a case for Daisy's son's medals. Laid out on lustrous satin were a Purple Heart, a Bronze Star, and a Silver Star. The album was full of pictures from Nam.

Old Daisy chattered away, pointing at images of muddy M-48 tanks and shirtless teenagers with their arms around one another's shoulders. Time travel ain't just made up out of nothing, Conor thought. He was sorry that the perky old lawyer didn't know enough to shut up and let the pictures talk for themselves.

Because the pictures did talk. Hue was in I Corps, Conor's Vietnam, and everything Conor looked at was familiar.

Here was the A Shau Valley—the mountains folding and folding into themselves, and a line of men climbing uphill in a single winding column, planting their feet in that same old mud. (Dengler: *Yea, though I walk through the A Shau Valley, I shall fear no evil, because I'm the craziest son of a bitch in the valley.*) Boy soldiers flashing the peace sign in a jungle clearing, one with a filthy strip of gauze around his naked upper arm. Conor saw Dengler's burning, joyous face in place of the boy's own.

Conor looked at a haggard, whiskered face trying to grin over the barrel of an M-60 mounted in a big green Huey. Peters and Herb Recht had died in a chopper identical to this one, spilling plasma, ammunition belts, six other men, and themselves over a hillside twenty klicks from Camp Crandall.

Conor found himself staring at the cylindrical rounds in the M-60's belt.

"I guess you recognize that copter," Daisy said.

Conor nodded.

"Saw plenty of those in your day."

It was a question, but again he could do no more than nod.

Two young soldiers so fresh they could not have been more than a week in the field sat on a grassy dike and tilted canteens to their mouths. "Those boys were killed alongside my son," Daisy said. A wet wind ruffled their short hair. Lean oxen wandered in the blasted field behind them. Conor tasted plastic—that curdled deathlike taste of warm water in a plastic canteen.

With the entranced, innocent voice of a man speaking more to himself than his listeners, Daisy supplied a commentary on men hauling 3.5-inch rocket shells to the roof of a building, a bunch of privates lollygagging in front of a wooden shack soon to become the headquarters of PFC Wilson Manly, soldiers smoking weed, soldiers asleep in a dusty wasteland that looked like the outskirts of LZ Sue, hatless grinning soldiers posing with impassive Vietnamese girls . . .

"Here's some guy, I don't know who," Daisy said. Once Conor saw the face, he was barely able to hear the lawyer's voice. "Big so-and-so, wasn't he? I can guess what he was up to with that little girl."

It was an honest mistake. His new wife had jump-started Daisy's gonads—why else was he coming home at four-thirty in the afternoon?

Tim Underhill, bandanna around his neck, was the big soldier in the photograph. And the "girl" was one of his *flowers*—a young man so feminine he might have been an actual girl. Smiling at the photographer, they stood on a narrow street crammed with jeeps and rickshaws in what must have been Da Nang or Hue.

"Son?" Daisy was saying. "You okay, son?"

For a second Conor wondered if Daisy would give him Underhill's picture.

"You look a little white, son," Daisy said.

"Don't worry," Conor said. "I'm fine."

He merely scanned the rest of the photographs.

"The truth is in the pudding," he said. "You can't forget this kind of shit."

Then Ben Roehm decided he needed another new man to do the taping in the kitchen and hired Victor Spitalny.

Conor had been a few minutes late to work. When he came into the ruined kitchen a stranger with a long streaky-blond ponytail was slouching against the skeletal framing of the new partition. The new man wore a raveled turtleneck under a plaid shirt. A worn toolbelt hung beneath his beerbelly. There was a new scab on the bridge of his nose, old scabs the color of overdone toast on the knuckles of his left hand. Red lines threaded the whites of his eyes. Conor's memory released a bubble filled with the indelible odor of burning kerosene-soaked shit. Vietnam, a ground-pounder.

Ben Roehm and the other carpenters and painters in the crew sat or sprawled on the floor, drinking morning coffee from their thermoses. "Conor, meet Tom Woyzak, your new taping partner," Ben said. Woyzak stared at Conor's outstretched hand for a few beats before grudgingly shaking it.

Drink it down, Conor remembered, *boo-koo good for your insides.*

All morning they silently taped sheetrock on opposite sides of the kitchen.

After Mrs. Daisy had come and gone with a pot of fresh coffee at eleven, Woyzak growled, "See how she came on to me? Before this job is over I'll be up in the bitch's bedroom, nailing her to the floor."

"Sure, sure," Conor said, laughing.

Woyzak was instantly across the kitchen, leaving a steaming trail of coffee and a spinning cup on the floor. His teeth showed. He pushed his face up to Conor's. "Don't get in my way, faggot, or I'll waste you."

"Back off," Conor said. He shoved him away. Conor was set to move this lunatic off-center with a head fake, step into him and mash his adam's apple with a left, but Woyzak dusted his shoulders as though Conor's touch had dirtied him and backed away.

At the end of the day Woyzak dropped his toolbelt in a corner of the kitchen and silently watched Conor pack his tools away for the night.

"Ain't you a neat little fucker," he said.

Conor slammed his toolbox shut. "Do you have many friends, Woyzak?"

"Do you think these people are going to adopt you? These people are not going to adopt you."

"Forget it." Conor stood up.

"So you were over there too?" Woyzak asked in a voice that put as little curiosity as possible into the question.

"Yeah."

"Clerk-typist?"

In a rage, Conor shook his head and turned away.

"What outfit were you in?"

"Ninth Battalion, Twenty-Fourth Infantry."

Woyzak's laugh sounded like wind blowing over loose

gravel. Conor kept on walking until he was safely out of the house.

He sat straddling his motorcycle for a long time, looking down at the dark grey stones of the drive, deliberately not thinking. The sky and the air were as dark as the gravel. Cold wind blew against his face. He could feel sharp individual stones digging into the soles of his boots.

For a moment Conor was certain that he was going to fire up his Harley and *go*, just keep moving in a blur of speed and distance until he had flown without stopping across hundreds of miles. Speed and travel gave him a pleasant, light, kind of empty feeling. Conor saw highways rolling out before him, the neon signs in front of motels, hamburgers sizzling on the griddles of roadside diners.

Perched on his bike in the cold air, he heard doors slamming inside the house. Ben Roehm's big baritone rang out.

He wished that Mike Poole would call him up and say, *We're on the way, babyface, pack your bags and meet us at the airport.*

Ben Roehm opened the door and fixed Conor with his eyes. He stepped outside and pulled on his heavy fleece-lined denim coat. "See you tomorrow?"

"I got nowhere else to go," Conor said.

Ben Roehm nodded. Conor kicked his Harley into noisy life and rode off as the rest of the crew came through the door.

For three or four days Woyzak and Conor ignored each other. When Charlie Daisy finally scented another veteran and appeared with his box of medals and his photo album, Conor put down his tools and wandered out. He couldn't bear to hang around while Thomas Woyzak looked at Underhill's picture.

The night before what turned out to be his last day, Conor woke up at four from a nightmare about M.O. Dengler and Tim Underhill. At five he got out of bed. He made a pot of coffee and drank nearly all of it before he left for work. Pieces of the dream clung to Conor all morning.

He is cowering in a bunker with Dengler, and they are enduring a firefight. Underhill must be in a dark portion of the same bunker or in another right beside it, for his rich voice, sounding a great deal like Ben Roehm's, carries over most of the noise.

There had been no bunkers in Dragon Valley.

The lieutenant's corpse sits upright against the far side of the bunker, its legs splayed out. Blood from a neat slash in the lieutenant's throat has sheeted down over his trunk, staining his chest solidly red.

"Dengler!" Conor says in his dream. "Dengler, look at the lieutenant! That asshole got us into this mess and now he's dead!"

Another great light burst in the sky, and Conor sees a Koko card protruding from Lieutenant Beevers' mouth.

Conor touches Dengler's shoulder and Dengler's body rolls over onto his legs and Conor sees Dengler's mutilated face and the Koko card in his gaping mouth. He screams in both the dream and real life and wakes up.

Conor got to work early and waited outside for the others. A few minutes later Ben Roehm pulled up in his Blazer with the two other members of the crew who lived up in his part of the state. They were men with babies and rent to pay, but too young to have been in Vietnam. As he watched them get out of the cab, Conor realized that he felt surprisingly paternal toward these sturdy young carpenters—they didn't have enough experience to know the difference between Ben Roehm and most of the other contractors around.

"Okay this morning, Red?" Roehm asked.

"Right as the dew, man."

Woyzak pulled up a moment later in a long car that had been covered with black primer and stripped of all exterior ornaments, even door handles.

Once they went to work, Conor noticed for the first time that Woyzak, who had covered twice as much ground as he had, had done his taping as if he were working for a contractor rushing to finish a crap job on a row of egg-carton houses. Ben Roehm was exacting, and to satisfy him you had to get your seams flat and smooth. Woyzak's work looked as crude as his getaway car. In the tape were lumps and bulges and wrinkles that would stay there forever, visible even when the walls had been skimmed with plaster and covered with two coats of paint.

Woyzak saw Conor staring at his work. "Something wrong?"

"Just about all of it's wrong, man. Did you ever work for Ben before?"

Woyzak put down his tools and stepped toward Conor. "You little red-haired fuck, you telling me I can't do my work? You happen to notice I'm twice as good as you are? I think the only reason you're still on this job is you went crazy over the old guy's pictures. The Old Man wants to keep the civilians happy."

The Old Man? Conor thought. Civilians? Are we back in base camp? "Hey, his kid took those pictures, man," he said.

"A nigger named Cotton took the pictures."

"Oh, shit." Conor felt as if he had to sit down, fast.

"Cotton was in little Daisy's platoon. The kid made some arrangement to get copies of his pictures—you asshole."

"I *knew* Cotton," Conor said. "I was with him when he bought it."

"*I* don't care who took the pictures—*I* don't care if he's alive or dead or somewhere in between. And I don't care if everybody around here thinks you're some kind of hero, because you're just a fuckin' nuisance in my eyes, man." Woyzak took another step toward him, and Conor saw the overlapping fury and misery in him, laid down so deeply he could not tell them apart. "You hear me? I was in a firefight for twenty-one days, man, twenty-one days and twenty-one nights."

"We gotta do something about the cat faces in the tape, that's all—"

Woyzak wasn't hearing him any more. His eyes looked amazingly like pinwheels.

"PUSSY!" he screamed.

"I thought you liked pussy," Conor said.

"I'm a good taper!" Woyzak shouted.

Ben Roehm stopped everything by slamming his fist against a sheetrock panel. Coffeepot in her hand, Mrs. Daisy hovered behind the contractor.

Woyzak smiled weakly at her.

"That's enough," Roehm said.

"I can't work with this asshole," Woyzak said, literally throwing his hands up in the air.

"This guy was edging me on," Conor protested.

"Charlie would have a fit if he heard bad language in

the house," Mrs. Daisy said nervously. "He might not look it, but he's very old-fashioned."

"Who's the taper, anyhow?" Woyzak bent down and picked up his blade and brush. His eyes looked normal again. "I only want to do my job."

"But look how he's doing it, man!"

Ben Roehm turned a solemn face to Conor and told him they had to talk.

He led Conor down the hall to the demolished morning room. Behind his back, Conor heard Woyzak purr something insinuating to Mrs. Daisy, who giggled.

In the morning room, Ben stepped over the holes in the floor and slumped back against a bare wall. "That boy is my niece Ellen's husband. He had a lot of bad experiences overseas, and I'm trying to help him out. You don't have to tell me he tapes like a sailor on a three-day drunk—I'm doing what I can for him." He looked at Conor, but could not meet his eyes for long. "I wish I could say something else, Red, but I can't. You're a good little worker."

"I suppose I was on a picnic the whole time I was in Nam." Conor shook his head and clamped his mouth shut.

"I'll give you a couple extra days' pay. There'll be another job, come this summer."

Summer was a long time coming, but Conor said, "Don't worry about me, I got something else lined up. I'm gonna take a trip."

Roehm awkwardly waved him away. "Stay out of the bars."

2

When Conor got back to Water Street in South Norwalk, he realized that he could remember nothing that had happened since he had left Ben Roehm. It was as though he had fallen asleep when he mounted the Harley and awakened when he switched it off in front of his apartment building. He felt tired, empty, depressed. Conor didn't know how he had avoided an accident, driving all the way home in a trance. He didn't know why he was still alive.

He checked his mailbox out of habit. Among the usual

junk mail addressed to "Resident" and appeals from Connecticut politicians was a long, white, hand-addressed envelope bearing a New York postmark.

Conor took his mail upstairs, threw the junk into the wastebasket, and took a beer out of his refrigerator. When he looked into the mirror over the kitchen sink, he saw lines in his forehead and pouches under his eyes. He looked sick—middle-aged and sick. Conor turned on the television, dropped his coat on his only chair, and flopped onto the bed. He tore open the white envelope, having delayed this action as long as possible. Then he peered into the envelope. It contained a long blue rectangle of paper. Conor pulled the check from the envelope and examined it. After a moment of confusion and disbelief, he reread the writing on the face of the check. It was made out for two thousand dollars, payable to Conor Linklater, and had been signed by Harold J. Beevers. Conor picked the envelope up off his chest, looked inside it again, and found a note: *All systems go! I'll be in touch about the flight. Regards, Harry (Beans!)*

3

After Conor had gazed at the check for a long, long time, he replaced both it and the note in the envelope and tried to figure out somewhere safe to put it. If he put the envelope on the chair he might sit on it, and if he put it on the bed, he might bundle it up with the sheets when he went to the laundromat. He worried that if he put it on top of the TV he might get drunk and mistake it for garbage. Eventually Conor decided on the refrigerator. He got out of bed, bent to open the refrigerator door, and carefully placed the envelope on the empty shelf, directly beneath a sixpack of Molson's Ale.

He splashed water on his face, flattened his hair across his skull with his brush, and changed into the black denim and corduroy clothing he had worn to Washington.

Conor walked to Donovan's and drank four boilermakers before anyone else came in. He didn't know if he was happier over getting the traveling money than miserable about losing his job, or more miserable about losing his job because of that asshole Woyzak than happy about the money. He decided after a while that he was more happy than miserable, which called for another drink.

Eventually the bar filled up. Conor stared at a nice-looking woman until he began to feel like a coward and got off his stool to talk to her. She was in training to do something in computers. (At a certain point in the evening, about sixty percent of the women in Donovan's were in training to do something in computers.) They had a few drinks together. Conor asked her if she would like to see his funny little apartment. She told him he was a funny little guy and said yes.

"You're a real homebody, aren't you?" the girl asked Conor when he turned on the light in his apartment.

After they had made love, the girl finally asked him about the lumps spread across his back and over his belly. "Agent Orange," he said. "I sort of wish I could teach them to move around, spell out words, shit like that."

He woke up alone with a hangover, wishing he could see Mike Poole and talk to him about Agent Orange, wondering about Tim Underhill.

8

DR. POOLE AT WORK AND PLAY

1

"Well, here it is," Michael said. "There's a medical conference in Singapore next January, and the organizers are offering reduced fares on the flight over."

He looked up from his copy of *American Physician.* Judy's only response was to tighten her lips and stare at the "Today" show. She was eating her breakfast standing up at the central butcher-block counter while Michael sat alone at the long kitchen table, also of butcher block. Three years before, Judy had declared that their kitchen was *obsolete*, *insulting*, *useless*, and demanded a renovation. Now she ate standing up every morning, separated from him by eight feet of overpriced wood.

"What's the topic of the conference?" She continued to look at the television.

" 'The Pediatrics of Trauma.' Subtitled 'The Trauma of Pediatrics.' "

Judy gave him a half-amused, half-derisive glance before taking a crisp bite out of a piece of toast.

"Everything should work out. If we have any luck, we ought to be able to find Underhill and settle things in a week or two. And an extra week is built into the tickets."

When Judy kept staring silently at the television set, Michael asked, "Did you hear Conor's message on my machine yesterday?"

"Why should I start listening to your messages?"

"Harry Beevers sent Conor a check for two thousand to cover his expenses."

No response.

"Conor couldn't believe it."

"Do you think they were right to give Tom Brokaw's job to Bryant Gumbel? I always thought he seemed a little lightweight."

"I always liked him."

"Well, there you are." Judy turned away to place her nearly spotless plate and empty coffee cup into the dishwasher.

"Is that all you have to say?"

Judy whirled around. She was visibly controlling herself. "Oh, I'm sorry. Am I allowed to say more? I miss Tom Brokaw in the mornings. How's that? In fact, sometimes Old Tom kind of turned me on." Judy had ended the physical side of their marriage four years before, in 1978, when their son Robert—Robbie—had died of cancer. "The show doesn't seem as interesting anymore, like a lot of things. But I guess these things happen, don't they? Strange things happen to forty-one-year-old husbands." She looked at her watch, then gave Michael a flat, sizzling glance. "I have about twenty minutes to get to school. You know how to pick your moments."

"You still haven't said anything about the trip."

She sighed. "Where do you suppose Harry got the money he sent to Conor? Pat Caldwell called up last week and said Harry gave her some fairy tale about a government mission."

"Oh." Michael said nothing for a moment. "Beevers likes to think of himself as James Bond. But it doesn't really matter where he got the money."

"I wish I knew why it is so important for you to run away to Singapore with a couple of lunatics, in search of another lunatic." Judy tugged furiously at the hem of her short brocade jacket and for a second reminded Michael of Pat Caldwell. She wore no makeup, and there were ashy streaks of grey in her short blonde hair.

Then she gave him her first really honest glance of the morning. "What about your favorite patient?"

"We'll see. I'll tell her about it this afternoon."

"And your partners will cover everybody else, I suppose."

"All too gleefully."

"And in the meantime, you're happy about trotting off to Asia."

"Not for long."

Judy looked down and smiled with such bitterness that Michael's insides twisted.

"I want to see if Tim Underhill needs help. He's unfinished business."

"Here's what *I* understand. In war, you kill people. Children included. That's what war is about. And when it's over, it's over."

"I don't think anything is ever really over in that sense," Michael said.

2

Michael Poole had killed a child at Ia Thuc, that was true. The circumstances were ambiguous, but he had shot and killed a small boy standing in a shadow at the back of a hootch. Michael was not superior to Harry Beevers, he was *like* Harry Beevers. There was Harry Beevers and the naked child, and there was himself and the small boy at the back of the hootch. Everything but the conclusion was different, but the conclusion was what mattered.

Some years ago Michael had read in an otherwise forgotten novel that no story existed without its own past, and the past of a story was what enabled us to understand it. This was true of more than stories in books. He was the person he was at the moment—a forty-one-year-old pediatrician driving through a suburban town with a copy of *Jane Eyre* beside him on the car seat—in part because of the boy he had killed in Ia Thuc, but more because before he had dropped out of college, he had met and married a pretty education major named Judith Writzmann. After he was drafted, Judy had written to him two or three times a week, and Michael still knew some of those letters by heart. It was in one of those letters that she said she wanted their first child to be a son, and that she wanted to name him Robert. Michael and Judy were themselves because of what they had done. He had married Judy, he had murdered a child, he had drunk it down, drunk it down. Judy had supported him through medical school. Robert—dear tender dull beautiful Robbie—had been born in Westerholm, had lived his uneventful ordinary invaluable child's life in that suburban town his mother cherished and his father loathed. Robbie had been slow to speak, slow to walk, slow in school. Poole had realized that he did not give a damn if his son went to Harvard after all, or to any other college either. He shed sweetness over Poole's whole life.

At five, Robbie's headaches took him into his father's hospital, where they found his first cancerous tumor. Later there were others—tumors on his spleen, on his liver, on his lungs. Michael bought the boy a white rabbit, and the child named it Ernie after a character on "Sesame Street." When Robbie was in remission he would haul Ernie around the house like a teddy bear. Robbie's illness endured three years—years that seemed to have had their own time, their own rhythm, unconnected to the world's time. In retrospect, they had sped past, thirty-six months gone in at most twelve. Within them, each hour lasted a week, each week a year, and those three years had taken all Michael's youth.

But unlike Robbie he lived through them. He had cradled his son in the hospital room during the quiet struggle for the last breath: at the end, Robbie had given up his life very easily. Michael had put his dear dead boy back down on his bed, and then—again, nearly for the last time—embraced his wife.

"I don't want to see that damned rabbit when I get home," she said. She meant that she wanted him to kill it.

And kill it he nearly had, even though the command was like that of a vain evil queen in a tale. He shared enough of his wife's rage to be capable of the act. But instead he took the rabbit to a field at the northern edge of Westerholm, lifted its cage out of his car, swung open the little gate, and let the rabbit hop out. Ernie had looked about with his mild eyes (eyes not unlike Robbie's own), hopped forward, and then streaked off into the woods.

As Michael turned into the parking lot beside St. Bartholomew's Hospital, he realized he had driven from his house on Redcoat Park to Outer Belt Road and the hospital, through virtually all of Westerholm, with tears in his eyes. He had negotiated seven corners, fifteen stop signs, eight traffic lights, and the heavy New York-bound traffic on the Belt Road without properly seeing any of it. He had no memory of having driven through the town. His cheeks were wet and his eyes felt puffy. He pulled his handkerchief from his pocket and wiped his face.

"Don't be a jerk, Michael," he said to himself, picked up the copy of *Jane Eyre*, and got out of the car.

A huge irregular structure the color of leaf mold, with turrets, flying buttresses, and hundreds of tiny windows punched into its façade, stood on the other side of the parking lot.

Michael's first obligation at the hospital was to look over all the babies that had been born during the night. As he had once a week for two months, the period of time Stacy Talbot had been confined to a private room in St. Bartholomew's, he made this duty last as long as he could.

When the last baby had been examined and after a quick tour of the maternity floor to satisfy his curiosity about the mothers of the infants he had just seen, Michael got on the elevator to go up to the ninth floor, or Cancer Gulch, as he had once overheard an intern call it.

The elevator stopped at the third floor, and Sam Stein, an orthopedic surgeon of Michael's acquaintance, got into the car with him. Stein had a beautiful white beard and hulking shoulders and was five or six inches shorter than Michael. His massive vanity allowed him to convey the impression that he was peering down at Michael from a great height, though he had to tilt his beard upward to do it.

A decade ago, Stein had badly botched a leg operation on a young patient of Michael's and then irritably dismissed as hysteria the boy's increasing complaints of pain. Eventually, after disseminating blame amongst every physician who had treated the child, especially Michael Poole, the orthopedist had been forced to operate on the child again. Neither Stein nor Michael had forgotten the episode and Michael had never referred another patient to him.

Stein glanced at the book in Michael's hand, frowned, then glanced up at the lighted panel above the door to see where he was going.

"In my experience, Dr. Poole, decent medical men rarely have the leisure for fiction."

"I don't have any leisure, period," Michael said.

Michael reached Stacy Talbot's door without encountering another of Westerholm's approximately seventy doctors. (He figured that about a quarter of these were not presently talking to him. Even some of those who were would think twice about his presence on the Oncology floor. This was just normal medicine.)

Michael supposed that for someone like Sam Stein what was happening to Stacy Talbot was also just normal medicine. For him, it was very much like what had happened to Robbie.

He stepped inside her room and squinted into the darkness. Her eyes were closed. He waited a moment before moving toward her. The blinds were down and the lights were off. Flowers from the shop on the hospital's ground floor wilted in the dense dark air. Just visible beneath a welter of tubes, Stacy's chest rose and fell. On the sheet next to her hand lay a copy of *Huckleberry Finn*. The placement of the bookmark showed that she had nearly finished reading it.

Michael stepped toward her bed, and her eyes opened. It took her a moment to recognize him, and then she grinned.

"I'm glad it's you," she said.

Stacy was not really his patient at all anymore—as the disease rampaged throughout her brain and body, she had been handed off to one specialist after another.

"I brought you a new book," he said, and put it on her table. Then he sat down next to her and gently took her hand in his.

Stacy's dehydrated skin emanated heat. Michael could see each brown spike of her eyebrows propped against a pad of red flesh. All of her hair had fallen out, and she wore a brilliantly colored knit cap that made her look vaguely Middle Eastern.

"Do you think Emmaline Grangerford had cancer?" she asked him. "I suppose not, actually. I keep hoping I'll read a book some day that has someone like me in it, but I never do."

"You're not exactly an ordinary kid," Michael said.

"Sometimes I think all of this stuff couldn't really be happening to me—I think I must have just made it all up, and I'm really lying on my bed at home, doing a spectacular job of staying out of school."

He opened her folder and skimmed through the dry account of her ongoing catastrophe.

"They found a new one."

"So I see."

"I guess I'll get another dent in my head." She tried to smile sideways at him, but failed. "I sort of like going to the CAT-scan, though. It's *tremendous* travel. Past the nurses' station! All the way down the hall! A ride on the elevator!"

"Must be highly stimulating."

"I get faint all over and have to lie down for days and days."

"And women clothed in white minister to your every need."

"Unfortunately."

Then her eyes widened, and for a moment she closed her hot fingers over his. When she relaxed, she said, "This is the moment when one of my aunts always tells me that she'll pray for me."

Michael smiled and held her hand tightly.

"At times like that I think that whoever is in charge of listening to prayers must be really sick of hearing my name."

"I'll see if I can get one of the nurses to take you out of your room once in a while. You seem to enjoy elevator travel."

For a second Stacy looked almost hopeful.

"I wanted to tell you that I'm going to be doing some traveling myself," Michael said. "Toward the end of January I'll be going away for two or three weeks." Stacy's face settled back into the mask of illness. "I'm going to Singapore. Maybe Bangkok, too."

"Alone?"

"With a couple of other people."

"Very mysterious. I guess I ought to thank you for giving me plenty of warning."

"I'll send you a thousand postcards of men waving snakes in the air and elephants crossing against rickshaw traffic."

"Swell. I visit the elevator, and you visit Singapore. Don't bother."

"I'll bother if I want to."

"Don't do me any favors." She turned her head away from him. "I mean it. Don't bother."

Michael had the feeling that this had happened before, in just this same way. He leaned forward and stroked her forehead. Her face contorted. "I'm sorry you're angry with me, but I'll see you again next week and we can talk about it some more."

"How could you know what I feel? I'm so *stupid.* You don't have any idea about what goes on inside me."

"Believe it or not, I have some idea," he said.

"Ever see a CAT-scan from the inside, Dr. Poole?"

Michael stood up. When he bent over to kiss her, she turned her head away.

She was crying when he left the room. Michael stopped at the nurses' station before escaping the hospital.

3

That evening Poole called the other men about the charter flight. Conor said, "Wild, sign me up, man." Harry Beevers said, "Outstanding. I was wondering when you were going to come through for us." Tina Pumo said, "You know what my answer is, Mike. Somebody's got to mind the store."

"You just became my wife's hero," Michael said. "Well, anyhow . . . would you mind trying to find Tim Underhill's address for us? His paperback publisher is Gladstone House—somebody there ought to know it."

They agreed to have a drink together before the trip.

4

One night the following week, Michael Poole drove slowly home from New York through a snowstorm. Abandoned cars, many of them dented or wrecked, lay along the side of the parkway like corpses after a battle. A few hundred yards ahead the light bar on top of a police car flashed red-yellow-blue-yellow-red. Cars crawled in single file, dimly visible, past a high white ambulance and policemen waving lighted batons. For a second Poole imagined that he saw Tim Underhill, in the snow very like a giant white rabbit, standing beside his car in the storm, waving a lantern. To stop him? To light his way forward? Poole turned his head and saw that it was a tree heavy with snow. A yellow beam from the police car flashed through his windshield and traveled across the front seat.

9

IN SEARCH OF MAGGIE LAH

1

All at once everything seemed to be going wrong, Tina Pumo thought, all at once everything was falling apart. He hated the Palladium and the Mike Todd Room. He also hated Area, the Roxy, CBGB's, Magique, Danceteria, and the Ritz. Maggie wasn't going to show up at the Mike Todd Room, and she wasn't going to be at any of those other places either. He could stand at the bar for hours, drink until he fell down, and all that would happen was that hundreds of little night people would stomp him on the way to their next bottle of Rolling Rock.

The first time he talked his way past the doorman into the vast barnlike room that the Palladium used for publicity parties and private gatherings he had come from a marathon meeting with Saigon's accountants. He was wearing his only grey flannel suit, purchased before the Vietnam War and small enough to pinch his waist. Pumo wandered through the crowd searching for Maggie. He noticed eventually that nearly everybody looked at him sharply, just once, then stepped away. In an otherwise crowded room, he was surrounded by a sort of DMZ, a *cordon sanitaire* of empty space. Once he heard laughter behind his back, turned around to see if he could share the joke, and saw everybody turn to stone, staring at him. Finally he went up to the bar and managed to catch the eye of a skinny young bartender with mascara on his face and a tangle of blond hair piled up on top of his head.

"I was wondering if you knew a girl named Maggie Lah," Tina said. "I was supposed to meet her here tonight. She's short, she's Chinese, good-looking—"

"I know her," the bartender said. "She might be in later." He retreated to the other end of the bar.

Tina experienced a moment of pure rage at Maggie. *May be Mike Todd, Maybe not. La La.* He saw that this message was a trick followed by mocking laughter. He stormed away from the bar and found himself standing in front of a blonde girl who looked about sixteen, had stars painted on both cheeks, and wore a shiny, slinky black chemise. She was exactly his type. "I want to take you home with me," he said. The girl opened her flowerlike mouth and solved one mystery by saying, "I don't go home with narcs."

That had been a week after Halloween. For at least two weeks afterward, he kept the city at bay while he tore his kitchen apart. Every time he and the exterminators took down another section of wall, a million bugs scrambled to get out of the light—if you killed them in one place, the next day they surfaced in another. For a long time they seemed to be concentrated behind the Garland range. In order to keep the fumigant from spoiling the food, he and the kitchen staff taped thick sheets of clear plastic between the range and food preparation surfaces and wherever they were trying to exterminate the insects. They pushed all three thousand pounds of the Garland eight feet out into the middle of the kitchen. Vinh, the head chef, complained that he and his daughter couldn't sleep at night because they heard things moving inside the walls. They had recently moved into the restaurant's "office," a little room in the basement, because Vinh's sister was having another baby and needed their room in her house in Queens. Normally the office was furnished with a desk, a couch, and boxes of files. Now the couch belonged to Goodwill, the desk was jammed into a corner of Pumo's living room, and Vinh and Helen slept on a mattress on the floor.

This temporary, illegal situation looked as if it was becoming a permanent illegal situation. Helen not only couldn't sleep, but she wet the bed—the mattress—

whenever she did doze off. Vinh claimed that the bed-wetting got worse right after the child saw Harry Beevers sitting at the bar. That Harry Beevers was a devil who put curses on children was mystical Vietnamese hysteria, pure and simple, but they believed it, so for them it was true. Pumo sometimes felt like strangling Vinh, but if he did he'd not only go to jail, he'd never get another chef.

Headache upon headache. Maggie did not call or send word to him for ten days. He began having dreams about Victor Spitalny running out of the cave at Ia Thuc covered with wasps and spiders.

The Health Department issued him a Second Warning, and the inspector muttered about misuse of nonresidential space. The little office reeked of pee.

The day before Maggie put another ad in the *Village Voice*, Michael Poole called again, asking if he had time to see if anyone at a place called Gladstone House knew where Tim Underhill lived. "Oh, sure," Tina grumped, "I spend all day in bed reading poetry." But he looked up the number in the book. The woman who answered referred him to the editorial department. A woman named Corazon Fayre said she knew nothing about an author named Timothy Underwood, and referred him to a woman named Dinah Mellow, who referred him to Sarah Good, who referred him to Betsy Flagg, who claimed at least to have heard of Timothy Underwood, was it? No? Let me transfer you to publicity. In publicity, Jane Boot referred him to May Upshaw who referred him to Marjorie Fan, who disappeared into limbo for fifteen minutes and returned from it with the information that ten years ago Mr. Underhill had written requesting that his circumstances and whereabouts be kept secret on pain of serious authorial displeasure, and that all communications, fan mail included, be directed to him through his agent, Mr. Fenwick Throng.

"Fenwick Throng?" Pumo asked. "Is that a real name?"

The next day was Wednesday, and after getting Vinh off to the markets and Helen to school, Tina set out to buy a copy of the *Village Voice* at the newsstand on the corner of Eighth Street and Sixth Avenue. Many newsstands were closer, but Eighth Street and Sixth Avenue was only a few blocks from La Groceria, a café where Pumo could sit in pale sunlight streaming in through long windows, sip two cups of cappuccino while pretty waitresses with white morning faces yawned and stretched like ballerinas, and read every word of the VOICE BULLETIN BOARD.

He found a message from Maggie right above the drawing in the center of the page: *Namcat. Try again same place, same time? Bruises and tattoos. You should fly East with the others, taking Type A with.* Her brother must have heard about their trip from Harry and then told her.

He thought of what it would be like to go to Singapore with Poole, Linklater, Harry Beevers, and Maggie Lah. Instantly his stomach tightened up and the cappuccino tasted like brass. She would bring too much carry-on luggage, half of it paper bags. Out of principle, she'd insist on changing hotels at least twice. She'd flirt with Poole, pick fights with Beevers, and virtually adopt Conor. Pumo began to sweat. He signaled for the check, paid, and left.

Several times during the day he dialed Fenwick Throng's telephone number, but the agent's line was always busy.

At eleven o'clock he gave unnecessary instructions about closing the restaurant, then showered and changed clothes and hurried off to the Palladium's back entrance. For fifteen minutes he stood and froze with half a dozen other people in an area like a dog pound enclosed by a wire fence, and then someone finally recognized him and let him in.

If it hadn't been for that *New York* article, he thought, I wouldn't even be able to get in here.

This time he was dressed in a Giorgio Armani jacket that looked vaguely like chain mail, voluminously pleated black trousers, a grey silk shirt, and a narrow black tie. They might mistake him for a pimp, he thought, but not for a narc.

Clutching a beer bottle, Pumo walked twice up and down the entire length of the bar before he admitted to himself that Maggie had stood him up twice in a row. He wound his way through the mob to the tables. Extravagantly dressed young people, none of them Maggie, leaned toward one another in pools of candlelight.

All of a sudden, everything's falling apart, Pumo thought. Somewhere along the line, my life stopped making sense.

Young people swirled around him. Synthesizer rock blared from invisible speakers. For a moment Pumo wished he were back home, wearing blue jeans and listening to the Rolling Stones. Maggie was never going to show up, tonight or any other night. One of these days, some hulking new boyfriend would show up at his door to collect the plastic radio, the little yellow Pony Pro hairdryer, and the Bow Wow Wow records she had left behind.

Pumo fought his way up to the bar and ordered a double vodka martini on the rocks. *Hold the olives, hold the vermouth, hold the rocks,* he remembered Michael Poole saying in Manly's little club, where there had been no olives, vermouth, or ice, only a jug of suspicious yellow-tinged "vodka" Manly claimed to have obtained from a colonel in the First Air Cav.

"That's the happiest you've looked all night," said a low voice beside him.

Poole turned and saw a tall, ambiguously sexed apparition in camouflage fatigues beaming at him. Bare shaven skin gleamed above its ears. Aggressive, shiny black hair swept across the top of the apparition's head and hung down its back. Then Pumo noticed the apparition's breasts bulging beneath the fatigue shirt. Her hips flared beneath a wide belt. He wondered what it would be like to go to bed with somebody with white sidewalls.

Fifteen minutes later the girl was squeezing herself up against him in the back seat of a taxi. "Bite my ear," she said.

"Here?"

She tilted her head toward him. Pumo put one arm around her shoulder and took her earlobe between his teeth. Fine black stubble covered the side of her head.

"Harder."

She squirmed when he bit down on the gristly lobe.

"You didn't tell me your name," he said.

She slid her hand over his crotch. Her breasts nuzzled his upper arm. He felt pleasantly engulfed. "My friends call me Dracula," she said. "But not because I suck blood."

She wouldn't let him turn on the lights in his loft, and he groped his way to the bedroom in the dark. Giggling, she pushed him down on the bed. "Just lie there," she said, and undid his belt, got rid of his boots, and pulled down his trousers. He got out of the chain-mail jacket and wrenched off his tie. "Pretty Tina," Dracula said.

She bent over and licked his erect cock. "I always feel like I'm in church when I do this."

"Wow," Tina said. "Where have you been all my life?"

"You don't want to know where I've been." She lightly scratched his scrotum with a long fingernail. "Don't worry, I don't have any nasty diseases. I practically *live* at the doctor's office."

"Why?"

"I guess I just enjoy being a girl."

Exhausted, dulled by alcohol, Pumo let her proceed. When she sat up, straddling him, she looked like an Apache warrior with plucked eyebrows. "Do you like Dracula?"

"I think I'll marry Dracula," he said.

She unbuttoned the camouflage shirt and tore it off, exposing firm conical breasts. "Bite me," she said, pushing them into his face. *"Hard.* Until I tell you to stop."

He gently bit one of her nipples, and she ground her knuckles into the side of his head. "Harder." She dug her nails into his cock. Pumo bit down.

"Harder."

He increased the pressure.

When he tasted blood, she screamed and moaned and gripped his head in her arms. "Good good." Her hand left his head and found his cock again. "Still hard? Good Tina."

Finally she let him raise his head. A thin line of blood oozed from the bottom of her breast down her ribcage. "Now little Drac goes back to church."

Pumo laughed and fell back on the pillow. He wondered if Vinh or Helen had heard her scream and decided they probably hadn't—they were two floors below.

After a long delirious time Pumo's orgasm sent looping ribbons of semen over her cheeks, into her eyebrows, into the air. She moaned and hitched herself onto his body so that his arms were pinned beneath her legs and astonished him by rubbing his semen into her face with both hands.

"I haven't come like that since I was about twenty," he said. "But you're sort of hurting my arms."

"Poor baby." She patted his cheek.

"I'd really appreciate it if you got off my arms," he said.

She looked down at him triumphantly and hit him hard in the temple.

Pumo struggled to get up, but Dracula struck him again. He found himself unable to move for a second. She grinned down at him, her teeth and eyes flashing in the murk, and slammed her fist against the side of his head.

He yelled for help. She struck him again.

"Murder!" he yelled, but no one heard.

Just before the twentieth blow to his temples, Pumo's eyes cleared and he saw Dracula peering impersonally down at him, her mouth pursed and her lipstick smeared.

2

Pumo came to in darkness, he knew not how much later. His lips throbbed and felt the size of steaks. He tasted blood. His whole body ached, the pain radiating out from the twin centers of his head and groin. In sudden panic, he put his hand on his penis, and found it intact. His eyes opened. He held up his hands before his face—they were dark with blood.

Pumo lifted his head to look down his body, and a white-hot band of pain jumped from temple to temple. He fell back on the wet pillow and breathed heavily. Then he lifted his head more cautiously. He was very cold. He saw his naked body sprawled on dark wet sheets. Working its way from ache to ache, a thin hot wire of agony snaked through the middle of his head. Now his lips felt like rough red bricks. He touched his face with wet fingers.

He considered getting out of bed. Then he wondered what time it was. Pumo raised his right arm and looked at his wrist, which no longer wore a watch.

He turned his head sideways. The radio with its digital clock was gone from the bedside table.

He slid himself off the side of the bed, finding the floor first with one foot, then with both his knees. His chest slid across the sheets, and he swallowed a bitter mouthful of vomit. When he stood up, his head swam and his vision darkened. He propped himself up on the headboard with aching arms. A cut on the side of his head beat and beat.

Clutching his head, Pumo slowly made his way into the bathroom. Without turning on the light, he bathed his face in cold water before daring to look at himself in the mirror. A grotesque purple mask, the face of the Elephant Man, stared back at him. His stomach flipped over, and he threw up into the sink and passed out again before he hit the floor.

10

CONVERSATIONS AND DREAMS

1

"Yes, I've been lying low, and no, I haven't changed my mind about going," Pumo said. He was talking on the telephone to Michael Poole. "You should see me, or rather you shouldn't. I'm hideous. I stay inside most of the time, because when I go out I frighten children."

"Is that some new kind of joke?"

"Don't I wish. I got beat up by a psychopath. I also got robbed."

"You mean you got mugged?"

Pumo hesitated. "In a way. I'd explain the circumstances, Mike, but frankly, they're too embarrassing."

"Can't you even give me a hint?"

"Well, never pick up anybody who calls herself Dracula." After Michael had laughed dutifully, Pumo said, "I lost my watch, a clock radio, a brand new pair of lizard-skin boots from McCreedy and Shreiber, my Walkman, my *Watch*man, a Dunhill lighter that didn't work anymore, a Giorgio Armani jacket, and all my credit cards and about three hundred in cash. And when the asshole took off, he or she left the downstairs door open and some god-damned bum came in and pissed all over the hallway."

"How do you feel about that?" Michael groaned. "Jesus, what a stupid question. I mean, in general how do you feel? I wish you'd called me right away."

"In general I feel like committing murder, that's how I feel in general. This thing shook me up, Mike. The world is full of hurt. I understand that there's no real safety, not anywhere. Terrible things can happen in an instant, to anyone. That asshole just about made me afraid to go outside. But if you're smart, you *should* be afraid to go outside. Listen—I want you guys to be *careful* when you get over there. Don't take any risks."

"Okay," Michael said.

"The reason I didn't call you or anybody else is the only good thing that came out of this whole thing. Maggie showed up. I guess I just missed her at the place where I encountered Dracula. The bartender told her he saw me leaving with someone else, so the next day she came around to check up. And found me with my face about twice its normal size. So she moved back in."

"As Conor said, there's a flaw in every ointment. Or something like that."

"But I did talk to Underhill's agent. His former agent, I should say."

"Don't make me beg."

"Basically the word is that our boy did go to Singapore, all right, just like he always said he would. Throng—the agent's name is Fenwick Throng, believe it or not—didn't know if he was still there. They have a funny history. Underhill always had his checks deposited in a branch bank down in Chinatown. Throng never even knew his address. He wrote to him in care of a post office box. Every now and then Underhill called up to rant at him, and a couple of times he fired him. I guess over a period of five or six years the calls got more and more abusive, more violent. Throng thought that Tim was usually drunk or stoned or high on something, or all three at once. Then he'd call back in tears a couple of days later and beg Throng to work for him again. Eventually it just got too crazy for Throng, and he told Tim he couldn't work for him anymore. He thinks that Tim has been agenting his own books ever since."

"So he's probably still out there, but we'll have to find him for ourselves."

"And he's nuts. He sounds scary as shit to me, Michael. If I were you, I'd stay home too."

"So the agent convinced you that Tim Underhill is probably Koko."

"I wish I could say he didn't."

"I wish you could too."

"So consider this—is he really worth risking your neck for?" Tina asked.

"I'd sure as hell rather risk my neck for Underhill than for Lyndon Baines Johnson."

"Well, hang on, because here comes the good part," Tina said.

2

"I don't think adult men actually exist anymore—if they ever did," Judy said. "They really are just grown up little boys. It's demeaning. Michael is a caring, intelligent person and he works hard and all that, but what he believes in is *ridiculous*. After you reach a certain level, his values are completely childish."

"At least they're that mature," said Pat Caldwell. This conversation too was conducted over the telephone. "Sometimes I'm afraid that Harry's are just infantile."

"Michael still believes in the army. He'd deny that, but it's the truth. He takes that boy's game as the real thing. He loved being part of a group."

"Harry had the time of his life in Vietnam," Pat said.

"The point is that Michael is going *back*. He wants to be in the army again. He wants to be part of a unit."

"I think Harry just wants something to do."

"Something to do? He could get a job! He could start acting like a lawyer again!"

"Hmm, well, perhaps."

"Are you aware that Michael wants to sell his share of the practice? That he wants to move out of Westerholm and work in a slum? He thinks he isn't *doing* enough. I mean, he has a little tiny point, you have to be a doctor in a place like this to find out how really political it is, you wouldn't believe how much infighting goes on, but that's *life*, that's all it is."

"So he's using the trip to give himself time to think about it," Pat suggested.

"He's using the trip to play army," Judy said. "Let's not even mention how he's guilt-tripping himself about Ia Thuc."

"Oh, I think Harry was always proud of Ia Thuc," Pat said. "Some day, I ought to show you the letters he wrote me."

3

The night before he flew to Singapore, Michael dreamed that he was walking at night along a mountain trail toward a group of uniformed men sitting around a small fire. When he gets nearer, he sees that they are ghosts, not men—flames show dimly through the bodies in front of the fire. The ghosts turn to watch him approach. Their uniforms are ragged and stiff with dirt. In his dream Michael simply assumes that he had served with these men. Then one of the ghosts, Melvin O. Elvan, stands and steps forward. *Don't mess with Underhill,* Elvan says. *The world is full of hurt.*

On the same night, Tina Pumo dreams that he is lying on his bed while Maggie Lah paces around the bedroom. (In real life, Maggie disappeared again as soon as his face had begun to heal.) *You can't win a catastrophe,* Maggie says. *You just have to try to keep your head above water. Consider the elephant, his grace and gravity, his innate nobility. Burn down the restaurant and start over.*

11

KOKO

The shutters of the bungalow were closed against the heat. A film of condensation lay over the pink stucco walls, and the air in the room was warm, moist, and pink dark. There was a strong, dark brown smell of excrement. The man in the first of the two heavy chairs now and then grunted and stirred, or pushed his arms against the ropes. The woman did not move, because the woman was dead. Koko was invisible, but the man followed him with his eyes. When you knew you were going to die, you could see the invisible.

If you were in a village, say—

If the smoke from the cookfire wavered and rose straight into the air again. If the chicken lifted one foot and froze. If the sow cocked her head. If you saw these things. If you saw a leaf shaking, if you saw dust hovering—

Then you might see the vein jumping in Koko's neck. You might see Koko leaning against a hootch, the vein jumping in his neck.

This is one thing Koko knew: there are always empty places. In cities where people sleep on the pavement, in cities so crowded people take shifts in bed, cities so crowded no one single person is ever truly quiet. In these cities especially there are always hollow realms, eternal places, places forgotten. Rich people leave the empty places behind, or the city itself leaves them behind.

The rich people move everything out and forget, and at night eternity quietly breaks in with Koko.

His father had been sitting in one of the two heavy chairs the rich people had left behind. *We use everything,* his father said. *We waste no part of the animal.*

We do not waste the chairs.

There was one memory he had seen in the cave, and in memory no part of the animal is wasted.

This is one thing Koko knew: they thought the chairs weren't good enough for them. Wherever they went had better chairs.

The woman didn't count, Roberto Ortiz had just brought her along. There weren't even enough cards for the ones that counted, much less the ones they brought along. When they answered the letters they were supposed to come alone, but the ones like Roberto Ortiz thought where they were going was nothing, who they were going to see was nobody, and it would all be over in ten minutes. . . . They never thought about the cards, no one had leaned over them at night and said: *We waste no part of the animal.* The woman was half-Indian, half-Chinese, something like that, maybe just a Eurasian, someone Roberto Ortiz had picked up, someone Roberto Ortiz was planning to fuck the way Pumo the Puma fucked the whore Dawn Cucchio in Sydney, Australia, just someone dead in a chair, just someone who wouldn't even get a card.

In his right jacket pocket he had all five Rearing Elephant cards, all the regimental cards he had left, with the names written lightly, penciled lightly, on four of them. Beevers, Poole, Pumo, Linklater. These were for when he went to America.

In his left jacket pocket he had an ordinary pack of Orchid Boy playing cards, made in Taiwan.

When he had opened the door wearing the big Tim Underhill smile, the hey baby how's it shakin' smile, and seen the woman standing next to Roberto Ortiz wearing her own hello don't mind me! smile, he had understood why there were two chairs.

In the cave there had been no chairs, no chairs for the lords of the earth. The cave made Koko shake, his father and the devil made him shake.

"Of course it's okay," he had said. "There's not much here, but you have a chair apiece, so come in and sit you down, sit you down, don't mind that the place is so bare, we're making changes all the time, I don't actually work here. . . ."

Oh, I pray here.

But they took the chairs anyhow. Yes, Mr. Roberto Ortiz had brought all his documentation, he brought it out, smiling, just beginning to look curious, beginning to notice the dust. The emptiness.

When Koko took the documents from the man's hand, he switched on the invisibility switch.

It was the same letter for all of them.

Dear (name),
I have decided that it is no longer possible for me to remain silent about the truth of the events which occurred in the I Corps village of Ia Thuc in 1968. Justice must finally be done. You will understand that I myself cannot be the one to bring the truth of these events to the world's eyes and ears. I was a participant in them, and have besides turned my horror at these events to account in works of fiction. As a representative, past or present, of the world press, as one who visited the scene of a great unknown crime and saw it at first-hand, would you care to discuss this matter further? I myself have no interest whatever in the profits that might be made from publishing the true story of Ia Thuc. You may write to me at (address) if you are interested in coming East to pursue this matter. I ask only, for reasons of my own security, that you refrain from discussing this matter with, or even mentioning it to, anyone until we have had an initial meeting, that you make no notes or diary entries pertaining to myself or Ia Thuc until we meet, and that you come to our first meeting with the following proofs of identity: a) passport, and b) copies of all stories and articles you wrote or to which you contributed, concerning the American action in the I Corps village of Ia Thuc. In my opinion, you will find our meeting more than worthwhile.
Yours sincerely,
Timothy Underhill

Koko liked Roberto Ortiz. He liked him very much. I thought I could just show you my passports and drop off my material, he said, Miss Balandran and I had planned to see Lola, it's getting late for a meeting now, Miss Balandran particularly wanted me to see Lola, it's a form of entertainment well known in this city, could you come around to my hotel tomorrow for lunch, you'll have time to look over the material in the file. . . .

Do you know Lola?

No.

Koko liked his smooth olive skin, his glossy hair, and his confident smile. He had the whitest shirt, the glossiest tie, the bluest blazer. He had Miss Balandran, who had long golden legs and dimples and knew about the local culture. He had been going to drop something off and arrange a meeting on his own ground, as the Frenchmen had done.

But the Frenchmen only had each other, they did not have Miss Balandran smiling so prettily, urging him so quietly, so sexily, to agree.

"Of course," Koko said, "you must do as your beautiful escort says, you must see all the sights, just stop in for a second, have a drink and let me take an initial look at what you've brought . . ."

Roberto Ortiz never noticed that Miss Balandran flushed when Koko said "escort."

Two passports?

They were sitting in the chairs, smiling up at him with such confidence, such assurance, their clothes so beautiful and their manners so good, knowing that in minutes they would be on their way to the nightclub, to their dinner and their drinks, their pleasures.

"Dual citizenship," Ortiz said, glancing slyly at Miss Balandran. "I am Honduran as well as American. You'll see all the Spanish-language publications in the file, besides the ones you're familiar with."

"Very interesting," Koko said. "Very interesting, indeed. I'll just be back in a moment with your drinks, and we can toast the success of our venture as well as your night out on the town."

He went behind the chairs into the kitchen and turned the cold tap on and off, banged a cabinet closed.

"I wanted to say how much I've enjoyed your books," Roberto Ortiz called from the living room.

On the counter beside the sink were a hammer, a cleaver, an automatic pistol, a new roll of strapping tape, and a small brown paper bag. Koko picked up the hammer and the pistol.

"I think *The Divided Man* is my favorite," Roberto Ortiz called out.

Koko put the pistol in his coat pocket and hefted the hammer. "Thank you," he said.

They were just sitting in the chairs, looking forward. He came gliding out of the kitchen and he was invisible, he made no noise. They were just waiting for their drinks. He came up behind Roberto Ortiz and he raised his arm and Miss Balandran didn't even know he was there until she heard the squashy sound of the hammer hitting Roberto Ortiz's head.

"Quiet," he said. Roberto Ortiz collapsed into himself, unconscious but not dead. A snail trail of blood crawled out of his nose.

Koko dropped the hammer and quickly moved between the chairs.

Miss Balandran gripped the arms of her chair and stared at him with dinner plate eyes.

"You're pretty," Koko said, and took the pistol from his pocket and shot her in the stomach.

Pain and fear took people in different directions. Anything having to do with eternity made them show you their real selves. No part of the animal was wasted. Remembrance, the whole thing they had been, just sort of took over. Koko figured the girl would get up and come for him, move a couple of steps before she realized half her guts were still back in the chair. She looked like one hell of a fighter, like a scrapper. But she couldn't even get out of the chair—it never even *crossed her mind* to get out of the chair. It took her a long time even to move her hands off the arms of the chair, and then she didn't want to look down. She shit herself, like Lieutenant Beans Beevers, down in Dragon Valley. Her feet went out, and she started shaking her head. She looked about five years old all of a sudden.

"Jesus Christ," Koko said, and shot her in the chest. The noise hurt his ears—it really bounced off those stucco walls. The girl had sort of melted back into the chair, and Koko had the feeling that the sound killed her before the second bullet did.

"All I got is one rope," Koko said. "See?"

He got down on his knees and put his arms between Roberto Ortiz's twisted-up feet to pull the rope out from under the chair.

Roberto Ortiz didn't as much as groan the whole time Koko was tying him up. When the rope tightened over his chest and clamped his arms, he pushed out a little air that smelled like mouthwash. A red knot the size of a baseball had flowered on the side of his head, and a trickle of blood matted the hair behind the knot in a way that reminded Koko of a road on a map.

From the shelf in the kitchen he fetched the cleaver, the roll of strapping tape, and the brown paper bag. Koko tossed the cleaver on the floor and took a new washcloth out of the bag. He pinched Roberto Ortiz's nose between his forefinger and thumb, pulled up, and stuffed the washcloth into Ortiz's mouth. Then he peeled off a length of the tape and wound it three times around the bottom half of Ortiz's face, sealing in the washcloth.

Koko took both sets of cards out of his pockets and sat cross-legged on the floor. He placed the cards beside him and rested the handle of the cleaver on his thigh. He watched Ortiz's eyes, waiting for him to wake up.

If you thought there were good parts, if you were a person who thought about the good parts, this was the good part now, coming up.

Ortiz had webby little wrinkles next to his eyes, and they looked dirty, full of dirt, because his skin was that olive color. He had just washed his hair, and it was thick and shiny black, with the sort of waves in it that looked like real waves, one after the other. You thought he was handsome, until you noticed his boxer's dented little blob of a nose.

Ortiz finally opened his eyes. Give him this much, he got the whole situation right away and tried to jump forward. The ropes caught him short before he even got started, and he wrestled with them for a second before he got that too. He just gave up, sat back and looked from side to side—tried to take everything in. He stopped when he saw Miss Balandran melted into her chair and he really *looked* at her and then he looked straight at Koko and tried to get out of the chair again but kept on staring at Koko when he realized he couldn't.

"Here you are with me, Roberto Ortiz," Koko said.

He picked up the regimental cards and held the good old Rearing Elephant out toward Ortiz. "Recognize this emblem?"

Ortiz shook his head, and Koko could see pain floating in his eyes.

"You have to tell me the truth about everything," Koko said. "Don't go out on a lie, try to remember everything, don't waste pieces of your own brain. Come on, look at it"

He saw how Roberto Ortiz was concentrating. The awakening of some little cell way back in his head flared in his eyes.

"I thought you'd remember," Koko said. "You showed up with the rest of the hyenas, you must have seen it somewhere. You walked all around, you probably worried about getting your spit-shine boots all dirty—you were there, Roberto. I asked you here because I wanted to talk to you. I wanted to ask you some important questions."

Roberto Ortiz groaned through the washcloth and tape. He issued a plea with his big soft brown eyes.

"You won't have to talk. Just nod your head."

If you saw a leaf shaking.

If the chicken froze on one foot.

If you saw these things, no part of the animal was wasted.

"The Elephant stands for the 24th Infantry, right?"

Ortiz nodded.

"And would you agree that the elephant embodies these traits—nobility, grace, gravity, patience, perseverance, power and reserve in times of peace, power and wrath in times of war?"

Ortiz looked confused, but nodded.

"And in your opinion, did an atrocity take place in the I Corps village of Ia Thuc?"

Ortiz hesitated, then nodded again.

Koko was not in a darkened room in a pink stucco bungalow on the fringe of a tropical city, but on a frozen tundra under a sky of high hard blue. A constant wind skirled and rippled the thin layer of snow over a layer of ice hundreds of yards deep. Far off to the west sat a range of glaciers like broken teeth. God's hand hung hugely in the air, pointing at him.

Koko jumped up and rapped the butt of his pistol

against the knot on Ortiz's head Just like a cartoon, Ortiz's eyes floated up into his head. His whole body went loose. Koko sat down and waited for him to wake up again.

When Ortiz's eyelids fluttered, Koko slapped him hard, and Ortiz jerked his head up and stared wildly at him, all attention again.

"Wrong answer," Koko said. "Even the court-martials, unfair as they were, couldn't say there was any atrocity. It was an act of God. A literal act of God. Do you know what that means?"

Ortiz shook his head. The pupils of his eyes looked blurry.

"It doesn't matter. I want to see if you remember certain names. Do you remember the name Tina Pumo, Pumo the Puma?"

Ortiz shook his head.

"Michael Poole?"

Ortiz wearily shook his head again.

"Conor Linklater?"

Another shake of the head.

"Harry Beevers?"

Ortiz lifted his head, remembering, and nodded.

"Yes. He talked to you, didn't he? And he was pleased with himself. 'Children can kill,' he said, didn't he? 'It doesn't matter what you do to a killer.' And 'The Elephant takes care of its own.' He said that, 'The Elephant takes care of its own.' Right?"

Ortiz nodded.

"You sure you don't remember Tina Pumo?"

Ortiz shook his head.

"You're so fucking dumb, Roberto. You remember Harry Beevers, but you forget everybody else. All these people I have to find, have to track down . . . unless they come to me. Big joke! What do you think I should do after I find them?"

Ortiz cocked his head.

"I mean, do you think I should talk to them? These people were my brothers. I could step outside of all this shit, I could say, I cleaned up my share of the cesspool, now it's someone else's turn, I could say that, I could start all over, let it be someone else's responsibility. What's your best opinion on that, Roberto Ortiz?"

Roberto Ortiz communicated by means of mental telepathy that Koko should now let it be someone else's responsibility to clean up the cesspool.

"It's not that easy, Roberto. Poole was *married* when we were over there, for God's sake! Don't you think he told his wife about what happened? Pumo had Dawn Cucchio, don't you think he has another girlfriend, or a wife, or both, right now? Lieutenant Beevers used to write to a woman named Pat Caldwell! You see how it never stops? That's what eternity *means,* Roberto! It means Koko has to go on and on, cleaning up the world . . . making sure no part is wasted, that what travels from one ear to another ear is rooted out, nothing left over, nothing wasted. . . ."

For a second he actually saw red—a vast sheet of blood washing over everything, carrying everything with it, houses and cows and the engines of trains, washing everything clean.

"You know why I wanted you to bring copies of your articles?"

Ortiz shook his head.

Koko smiled. He reached out and picked the thick file of articles off the floor and opened it on his lap. "Here's a good headline, Roberto. DID THIRTY CHILDREN DIE? I mean, is that yellow journalism, or what? You can really be proud of yourself, Roberto. It's right up there with BIGFOOT DEVOURS TIBETAN BABY. What's your answer, anyhow? Did thirty children die?"

Ortiz did not move.

"It's cool if you don't want to say. Satanic beings come in many forms, Roberto, in many, many forms." As he spoke, Koko took a pack of matches from his pocket and set the file alight. He fanned it in the air to keep the fire alive.

When the flames neared his fingers, Koko dropped the burning papers and kicked them apart. The small flames left greasy black scorches on the wooden floor.

"I always liked the smell of fire," Koko said. "I always liked the smell of gunpowder. I always liked the smell of blood. They're clean smells, you know?"

I always liked the smell of gunpowder.

I always liked the smell of blood.

He smiled at the little flames guttering out on the floor. "I like how you can even smell the dust burning." He turned his smile to Ortiz. "I wish my work was done.

But at least I'll have two pretty passports to use. And maybe when I'm done in the States, I'll go to Honduras. That makes a lot of sense, I think. Maybe I'll go there after I check out all these *people* I have to check out." He closed his eyes and rocked back and forth on the floor. "Work never leaves you alone, does it?" He stopped rocking. "Would you like me to untie you now?"

Ortiz looked at him carefully, then nodded very slowly.

"You're so stupid," Koko said. He shook his head, smiling sadly, took up the automatic pistol, and pointed it at the middle of Roberto Ortiz's chest. He looked directly into Ortiz's eyes, then shook his head again, still smiling sadly, braced his wrist with his left hand, and fired.

Then he watched Roberto Ortiz die fighting and twitching and struggling to speak. Blood darkened the pretty blazer, ruined the pretty shirt and the luxurious necktie.

Eternity, jealous and alert, watched with Koko.

When it was done, Koko wrote his name on one of the Orchid Boy playing cards, grasped the cleaver, and pushed himself up off the floor to do the messy part of the job.

3 ♠

PART THREE

THE TIGER BALM GARDENS

3

12

MEN IN MOTION

1

"Just let me keep the books," Michael Poole said to the erect little woman, all black shining hair and deep dimples, beside him. Her name tag read PUN YIN. She tilted his carry-on bag toward him, and Poole took the copies of *A Beast in View* and *The Divided Man* from the open pouch on the side. The stewardess smiled and began making her way forward through the pediatricians.

The doctors had started to unwind as soon as the plane hit cruising level. On earth, visible to their patients and other laymen, Michael's colleagues liked to appear knowing, circumspect, and only as juvenile as conventional American ethics permitted; aloft, they acted like fraternity boys. Pediatricians in playclothes, in terrycloth jogging suits and college sweaters, pediatricians in red blazers and plaid trousers roamed the aisles of the big airplane, glad-handing and bawling out bad jokes. Pun Yin got no more than halfway toward the front of the plane with Michael's bag when a squat, flabby doctor with a leer like a Halloween pumpkin positioned himself before her and did an awkward bump and grind.

"Hey!" Beevers said. "We're on our way!"

"Give me an S," Conor said, and lifted his glass.

"You remember to get the pictures? Or did your brain collapse again?"

"They're in my bag," Poole said. He had made fifty copies of the author's photo on the back of *Orchid Blood,* Underhill's last book.

All three men were watching the unknown doctor twitch around Pun Yin while a group of medical men yipped encouragement. The pretty stewardess patted the man on the shoulder and squeezed past him, interposing Michael's bag between the doctor and herself.

"We're going to face the elephant," Beevers said. "Remember?"

"Could I forget?" Poole asked. During the Civil War, when their regiment had been founded, "facing the elephant" had been slang for going into battle.

In a loud, blurry voice Conor asked, "What traits are embodied in the elephant?"

"In time of peace or in time of war?" Beevers asked.

"Both. Let's hear the whole shootin' match."

Beevers glanced at Poole. "The elephant embodies nobility, grace, gravity, patience, perseverance, power, and reserve in times of peace. The elephant embodies power and wrath in times of war."

A few of the pediatricians nearest stared at him in affable confusion, trying to share the joke.

Beevers and Poole began to laugh.

"Damn straight," Conor said. "That's it, there it is."

Pun Yin glimmered for a moment far away at the head of the cabin, then swished a curtain before her and was gone.

2

The airplane slowly digested the thousands of miles between Los Angeles and Singapore, where the corpses of Miss Balandran and Roberto Ortiz sat undiscovered in a bungalow on a leafy road; the doctors settled into their seats, overcome by alcohol and the exhaustion of travel. Bland food arrived, considerably less delicious than the smile with which Pun Yin placed it before the passengers. Eventually the stewardess removed their trays, poured out brandy, plumped up pillows for the long night.

"I never told you what Underhill's old agent told Tina Pumo," Poole said to Beevers across a dozing Conor Linklater.

Shafts of light pierced the long dark cabin of the 747. Soon *Savannah Smiles* would be shown, to be followed by a second movie which starred Karl Malden and several Yugoslavians.

"You mean you didn't want to tell me," Beevers said. "It must be pretty good."

"Good enough," Poole admitted.

Beevers waited. At last he said, "I guess we do have about twenty more hours."

"I'm just trying to get it all organized." Poole cleared his throat. "At first, Underhill behaved like any other author. He bitched about the size of his printings, asked where his royalty checks were, things like that. Apparently he was nicer than most writers, or at least no worse than most. He had his odd points, but they didn't seem serious. He lived in Singapore, and the people at Gladstone House couldn't write to him directly because even his agent only had a post office box number."

"Let me guess. Then things took a turn for the worse."

"Very gradually. He wrote a couple of letters to the marketing people and the publicity department. They weren't spending enough money on him, they weren't taking him seriously. He didn't like his paperback jacket. His print run was too small. Okay. Gladstone decided to put a little more effort into his second book, *The Divided Man,* and the effort paid off. The book made the paperback best-seller list for a month or two and sold very well."

"So was our boy happy? Did he send roses to Gladstone's marketing department?"

"He went off the rails," Poole admitted. "He sent them a long crazy letter as soon as the book hit the list—it should have got on higher and sooner, the ad campaign wasn't good enough, he was sick of being stabbed in the back, on and on. The next day another ranting letter showed up. Gladstone got a letter every day for a week, *long* letters, five and six pages. The last couple threatened them with physical abuse."

Beevers grinned.

"There was a lot of stuff about them shafting him because he was a Vietnam veteran. I guess he even mentioned Ia Thuc."

"Hah!"

"Then after the book dropped off the list he began a

long fandango about a lawsuit. Weird letters started turning up at Gladstone House from a Singapore lawyer named Ong Pin. Underhill was suing them for two million dollars, that being the amount the lawyer had calculated had been lost to his client through Gladstone's incompetence. On the other hand, if Gladstone wished to avoid the expense and publicity of a trial, Ong Pin's client was willing to settle for a single one-time payment of half a million dollars."

"Which they declined to pay."

"Especially since they had observed that Ong Pin's address was the same post office box to which Underhill's agent, Fenwick Throng, sent his mail and royalty checks."

"That's our boy."

"When they wrote back, giving him the option of taking his next book elsewhere if he was not satisfied with their efforts, he seemed to come to his senses. He even wrote to apologize for losing his temper. And he explained that Ong Pin was a lawyer friend of his who had lost his office, and was temporarily living with him."

"A flower!"

"Well, anyway . . . he made the threat of a two-million-dollar lawsuit sound like a drunken prank. Things settled down. But as soon as he submitted his next book, *Orchid Blood,* he got crazy again and started threatening lawsuits. Ong Pin wrote some sort of goofy screed in the kind of English you get in Japanese instruction manuals, you know? And when the book came out, Underhill mailed a box with dried-up shit in it to the president of Gladstone, Geoffrey Penmaiden, who I guess everybody knew and revered. It was like sending a turd to Maxwell Perkins. Then the book came out and flopped. Just sank out of sight. They haven't heard a word from him since, and I don't think they're too eager to work with him again."

"He sent shit in a box to Geoffrey Penmaiden? The most famous publisher in America?" Beevers asked.

"I think it had more to do with self-hatred than craziness," Poole said.

"You think they're not the same?" Beevers reached over and patted Michael's knee. "Really."

When Beevers canted back his seat and closed his eyes, Michael switched on the reading light and picked up his copy of *A Beast in View.*

At the beginning of Underhill's first novel, a rich boy named Henry Harper is drafted and sent to basic training in the South. The sort of person who gradually but thoroughly undermines the favorable first impression he creates, Harper is superficially charming, snobbish, selfish. Other people chiefly either disgust or impress him. Of course he detests basic training, and is detested by every other recruit on the base. Eventually he meets Nat Beasley, a black soldier who seems to like him in spite of his faults and who detects a decent person beneath Henry's snobbery and self-consciousness. Nat Beasley defends Harper and gets him through basic. Much to Harper's relief, his father, a federal judge in Michigan, is able to fix it that Henry and Beasley are assigned to the same unit in Vietnam. The judge even manages to get Henry and Nat on the same flight from San Francisco to Tan Son Hut. And during the flight, Henry Harper strikes a bargain with Nat Beasley. He says that if Nat continues to protect him, Henry will guarantee him half of all the money he will ever earn or inherit. This is a sum of at least two or three million dollars, and Beasley accepts.

After about a month in the country, the two soldiers get separated from their unit while on patrol. Nat Beasley picks up his M-16 and blows a hole the size of a family Bible in Henry Harper's chest. Beasley switches dogtags and then destroys Harper's body so completely that it is utterly unrecognizable. He then takes off cross-country toward Thailand.

Michael read on, flipping pages at the bottom of a shaft of yellow light while an incomprehensible movie played itself out on the small screen before him. Snores and belches from sleeping pediatricians now and then cut across the humming silence of the cabin. Nat Beasley makes a fortune brokering hashish in Bangkok, marries a beautiful whore from Chiang Mai, and flies back to America with a passport made out to Henry Harper. Pun Yin, or one of the other stewardesses, audibly sighed in a last-row seat.

Nat Beasley rents a car at the Detroit airport and drives to Grosse Pointe with the beautiful Chiang Mai whore beside him. Michael saw him seated at the wheel of the rented car, turning toward his wife as he pointed to Judge Harper's great white house at the far end of a perfect lawn. Behind these images, accompanying them, arose others—Poole had not spent so many hours in the air since 1967 and moments from his uneasy flight into Vietnam, encased in the self-same uneasiness, twined around the adventures of Nat Beasley, the running grunt.

The strangeness of going to war on a regular commercial flight had stayed with him for the entire day they were in the air. About three-fourths of the passengers were new soldiers like himself, the rest divided between career officers and businessmen. The stewardesses had spoken to him without meeting his eyes, and their smiles had looked as temporary as winces.

Michael remembered looking at his hands and wondering if they would be limp and dead when he returned to America. Why hadn't he gone to Canada? They didn't shoot at you in Canada. Why hadn't he simply stayed in school? What stupid fatalism had ruled his life?

Conor Linklater startled Michael by snapping upright in his seat. He blinked filmy eyes at Michael, said, "Hey, you're poring over that book like it was the Rosetta stone," and leaned back, asleep again before his eyes were closed.

Nat Beasley strolls through Judge Harper's mansion. He muses on the contents of the refrigerator. He stands in the judge's closet and tries on the judge's suits. His wife lies across the judge's bed, flipping through sixty cable channels with the remote-control device.

Pun Yin stood beside Michael with her arms angelically outstretched, floating a blanket down over Conor Linklater's body. In 1967, a girl with a blonde pageboy tapped his arm to awaken him, grinned brightly over his shoulder, and told him to prepare for descent. His guts felt watery. When the stewardess opened the door, hot moist air invaded the aircraft and Michael's entire body began to sweat.

Nat Beasley lifts a heavy brown plastic bag from the trunk of a Lincoln town car and drops it into a deep trench between two fir trees. He takes a second, lighter bag from the trunk and drops it on top of the first.

The heat, Michael knew, would rot the shoes right off his feet.

Pun Yin switched off his reading light and closed his book.

3

The General, who was now a storefront preacher in Harlem, had left Tina alone with Maggie for a moment in the clutter of his ornate living room on 125th Street and Broadway. The General had been a friend of Maggie's father, apparently also a general in the Formosan army, and after General Lah and his wife had been assassinated, the General had brought her to America—and this stuffy apartment in Harlem had been where Maggie had fled! It was a puzzle, a relief, an irritation.

For one thing, his girlfriend turned out to be the daughter of a general. This explained a lot about Maggie: she came by her pride naturally; she was used to getting her own way; she liked to speak in communiqués; and she thought she knew all about soldiers.

"Didn't you think I was worried about you?"

"You don't mean worried about me, you mean jealous."

"What's wrong with that?"

"Because you don't *own* me, Tina. And because it only works when I'm gone and you don't know where I am. You're like a little boy, you know?"

He let that one pass.

"Because when I live with you, Tina, you wind up thinking that I'm this half-crazy little punk who really just gets in the way of thinking about business and hanging out with the guys."

"That just says that *you're* jealous, Maggie."

"Maybe you're not so dumb after all," Maggie said, and smiled at him. "But you have too many problems for me." She was sitting on an ornately brocaded couch with her legs folded under her, wrapped in some loose flowing dark woolen thing that was as Chinese as the couch. The smile made Tina want to put his arms around her. Her hair was different, less scrappy, more like a smooth thatch. Tina knew how Maggie's heavy silky hair felt in his hands, and he wished he could ruffle it now.

"Are you saying you don't love me?"

"You don't stop loving people, Tina," she said. "But if I moved back in with you, pretty soon you'd be secretly wondering how you could get rid of me—you're so guilty, you'll never let yourself get married to anybody. You'll never even get close."

"You want to marry me?"

"No." She watched his suspicious, surprised response. "I said, you have too many problems for me. But that's not the point. How you *behave* is the point."

"Okay, I'm not perfect. Is that what you want me to say? I'd like you to come back downtown with me, and you know it. But I could just as well walk away right now, and you know that too."

"Think about this, Tina. When I was putting all those ads in the *Voice* for you?"

He nodded.

"Didn't you like seeing them?"

He nodded again.

"You looked for them every week?"

Tina nodded yet again.

"Yet you never even considered putting one in yourself, did you?"

"Is that what this is about?"

"Not bad, Tina. I'm glad you didn't say you were too old for that sort of thing."

"Maggie, a lot of things are going wrong right now."

"Did the city close Saigon?"

"I closed it. It was getting to be impossible to cook and kill bugs at the same time. So I decided to concentrate on killing bugs."

"As long as you don't get mixed up and start cooking them."

Annoyed, he shook his head and said, "It's costing me a ton of money. I'm still paying a lot of salaries."

"And you're sorry you didn't go to Singapore with the little boys."

"Let's put it this way. I'd be having more fun than I am now."

"Right now?"

"Now in general." He looked at her with love and exasperation, and she looked calmly back. "I didn't know you wanted me to put ads in the *Voice* too—otherwise I would have. It never occurred to me."

She sighed and raised a hand, then slowly let it fall back to her folded knees. "Forget about it. But just remember that I know you a lot better than you'll ever know me." She gave him another calm look. "You're worried about them, aren't you?"

"Okay, I'm worried about them. Maybe that's why I wish I was with them."

She slowly shook her head. "I can't believe that you get half-killed and think that you should be able to go on the way you did before—like nothing happened."

"Plenty happened, I don't mind admitting it."

"You're scared, you're scared, you're scared!"

"Okay, I'm scared." He exhaled noisily. "I don't even like going out alone in the daytime. At night I hear noises. I keep thinking—well, weird shit. About Nam."

"All the time, or just at night?"

"Well, I can catch myself thinking weird shit at any time of the day or night, if that's what you mean."

Maggie swung her legs out from beneath her. "Okay, I'll come down and stay with you for a while. As long as you remember that you aren't the only one who can walk away."

"How the hell could I forget that?"

And that was all it took. He did not even have to confess to her that right before he had come uptown, he'd been standing in his kitchen holding a bottle of beer and for a second had *known* that it was Ba Muy Ba and that the bullet with his name on it, the one that had missed him all those years ago, was still circling the world, homing on him.

The General who was now a preacher stared at Tina just as if he was still a pissed-off general, and then barked a few words at Maggie in Chinese. Maggie answered with a phrase that sounded sullen and adolescent, and the General proved to Tina once and for all that he would never comprehend the Cantonese language by beaming at Maggie and taking her in his arms and kissing the top of her head. He even shook Tina's hand and beamed at him too.

"I think he's happy to get rid of you," Tina said as they waited for the slow-moving, odorous elevator.

"He's a Christian, he believes in love."

He could not tell if she were being sardonic or literal. This was often the case with Maggie. The elevator clanked up to the General's floor and opened its mouth. A sour stench of urine rolled out. He could not let Maggie see that he was afraid of the elevator. She was already inside, looking at him intently. Tina swallowed and stepped into the reeking mouth of the elevator.

The doors slammed behind him.

He managed to smile at Maggie. Getting inside was the hardest part.

"What did he say to you, just before we left?"

Maggie patted his hand. "He said you were a good old soldier, and I should take care of you and not get too mad at you." She glinted up at him. "So I told him you were an asshole and I was going back with you only because my English was getting rusty."

Downstairs, Maggie insisted on taking the subway, and demonstrated that she could still do an old trick of hers.

They had reached the top of the steps and were moving toward the token booth. The wind cut through his heavy coat and lifted the hood against the back of his head. When he looked around for Maggie and did not see her, the moment filled with a bright dazzle of panic.

A noisy knot of boys in black jackets and knit caps, one of them toting a huge radio, were punching the air and bopping along the platform in time to a Kurtis Blow song. Black women in heavy coats leaned against the railing and paid them no attention. Far ahead, a few men and women stared almost aimlessly down the tracks. Tina was suddenly, painfully aware of how high up in the air he was—suspended like a diver on a board. He wished that he was holding onto a railing—it was as if the wind could lift him off the platform and smack him down onto Broadway.

He had automatically fallen into line at the token booth. The boys had collected up at the head of the platform. Tina reached into his pocket, furious with Maggie for disappearing and furious with himself for caring.

Then he heard her giggle, and he snapped his head sideways to see her already past the turnstile and out on the platform beside the impassive women. Her hands were shoved deep in the pockets of her down coat, and she was grinning at him.

He got his token and went through the turnstile. He felt absurdly tangible. "How did you do that?"

"Since you wouldn't be able to do it anyhow, why should I tell you?"

When the train roared up before them, she took his hand and pulled him into the subway car.

"Are they in Singapore yet?" she asked him.

"They got there three or four days ago, I think."

"My brother says they're going to Taipei too."

"I guess it's possible. They'll go wherever they have to go to find Underhill."

Maggie gave him a half-scathing, half-sympathetic look. "Poor Tina." She took Tina's hand into her soft, down-padded lap.

He sat beside her in the loud train, his fear now mostly under control. No one was staring at him. His hand rested within both of Maggie's funny little hands, in her lap.

South they flew beneath Manhattan in the filthy train, Maggie Lah with her large secret feelings and Tina Pumo with his, which ran queerly parallel to those of his friends under the patient gaze of Pun Yin. I love Maggie and I am afraid of that. She's a kind of original. She leaves me in order to keep me, she's smart enough to get out before I kick her out, and she proves it by coming back as soon as I really need her. And maybe Underhill is crazy and maybe I'm crazy too, but I hope they find him and bring him back.

Here is Tim Underhill, Tina thought, here is Underhill out in a section of Camp Crandall known familiarly to the madmen of the good old Rearing Elephant as Ozone Park. Ozone Park is a bleak section of wasteland about the size of two city blocks between the rear of Manly's "club" and the wire perimeter. Its amenities consist of one piss-tube, which provides relief, and a huge pile of empty metal barrels, which offers shade and a pervasive smell of oil. Ozone Park does not officially exist, so it is safe from the incursions of the Tin Man, for whom, in true army fashion, *should* exactly equals *is*. Here is Tim Underhill, in the company of a number of comrades wasted on Si Van Vo's 100s and getting more wasted on a little white powder Underhill has produced from one of his pockets. Here is Underhill recounting to all the others, who include besides myself, M. O. Dengler, Spanky Burrage, Michael Poole, Norman Peters, and Victor Spitalny, who just lurks around the edges of the barrels, now and then tossing little stones toward the others, the tale of the running grunt. A young man of good family, Underhill says, the son of a federal judge, is drafted and sent to good old Fort Sill in beautiful Lawton, Oklahoma. . . .

"I sure get sick of the sound of your voice," sneers

Spitalny from off to the side, near the barrels. He flings a stone at Underhill and strikes him in the middle of his chest.

"You're still nothing but a fucking queer," Spitalny says.

—And you're still a shithead, Pumo remembers saying eloquently to Spitalny, who returned the favor by throwing a stone at him, too.

It took a long time to adjust to the "flowers," because it took a long time to understand that Underhill never corrupted anybody, that he could not corrupt anybody because he himself was not corrupt. Though most of the soldiers Puma knew claimed to despise Asian women, nearly all of them used whores and bar girls. The exceptions were Dengler, who clung to his virginity in the belief that it was the talisman that kept him alive, and Underhill, who picked up young men. Pumo wondered if the others knew that Underhill's flowers were in their early twenties, and that there had been only two of them. Pumo knew this because he had met them both. The first was a one-armed former ARVN with a girl's face who lived with his mother in Hue and made a living grilling meat at a food stall until Underhill began to support him. The other flower actually worked in the Hue flower market, and Pumo had eaten dinner with the young man, Underhill, the young man's mother, and his sister. He had seen such a remarkable quantity of tenderness flow among the other four people at the table that he would have been adopted by them if he could. Underhill supported this family, too. And now in an odd way Pumo supported them, for when Underhill's best-loved flower, Vinh, finally managed to locate him in New York in 1975, Pumo remembered the excellence of the meal as well as the warmth and kindness in the little house, and hired him. Vinh had undergone deep changes—he looked older, harder, less joyous. (He had also fathered a child, lost a wife, and served a long apprenticeship in the kitchen of a Vietnamese restaurant in Paris.) None of the others knew Vinh's history. Harry Beevers must have seen him once with Underhill and then forgotten the occasion, because for reasons of his own Beevers had convinced himself that Vinh was from An Lat, a village near Ia Thuc—whenever Beevers saw either Vinh or his daughter, he began to look persecuted.

"You look almost happy now," Maggie said to him.

"Underhill can't be Koko," Tina replied. "The son of a bitch was crazy, but he was crazy in the sanest possible way."

Maggie did not say or do anything, did not change her grip on his hand, did not even blink at him, so he could not tell if she had heard him. Maybe she felt insulted. The noisy subway clattered into their station and came to a jerky stop. The doors whooshed open, and Pumo froze for a second. As the noises outside the car resolved themselves, Maggie pulled him to his feet. When Pumo got out of the train he bent over and hugged Maggie as hard as he could.

"I love you too," she said. "But I don't know if I'm being crazy in a sane way, or vice versa."

She gasped when they turned into Grand Street.

"I suppose I should have prepared you," Pumo said.

Stacks of bricks, piles of boards, bags of plaster, and sawn lengths of discarded pipe covered the sidewalk outside Saigon. Workmen in green parkas and heavy gloves, heads bent against the wind, wheeled barrows of rubble out of the front door and laboriously dumped them into a skip. Two trucks stood doubleparked beside the skip, one marked with the name SCAPELLI CONSTRUCTION CO., the other bearing the stenciled legend MCLENDON EXTERMINATION. Men in hard hats wandered back and forth between the restaurant and the trucks. Maggie saw Vinh talking to a woman holding a wide set of unrolled blueprints, and the chef winked at her, then waved at Pumo. "Must talk," he called out.

"What's it like inside?" Maggie asked.

"Not as bad as it looks from here. The whole kitchen is torn apart, of course, and most of the dining room is too. Vinh's been helping me out, cracking the whip when I'm not around. We had to take down the whole back wall, and then we had to rebuild some of the basement." He was fitting his key into the white door next to Saigon's door, and Vinh shook the architect's hand and came over in a rush before he could open it.

"Nice to see you again, Maggie," Vinh said, and followed it with something in Vietnamese to Pumo. Tina answered in Vietnamese, groaned, and turned to Maggie with increased worry plain on his face.

"Floor fall down?"

"Someone broke in this morning. I haven't been in since about eight, when I went out to get breakfast and check in with some suppliers. We're expanding the kitchen, as long as we have to do all this work, and as usual I have to chase around all over the place, which I was doing until I was stopped in my tracks by the back page of the *Village Voice*."

"How could anybody break in with all this going on?"

"Oh," he said. "They didn't break into the restaurant. They broke into my loft. Vinh heard someone moving around upstairs, but he thought it was me. Later he went up to ask me about something, and realized that it must have been an intruder."

Tina looked almost fearfully up the narrow flight of steps that led to his loft.

"I don't suppose Dracula came back to pay a social call," she said.

"No, I don't suppose so either." Tina did not sound convinced of this. "The bitch might have remembered some stuff she forgot to steal, though."

"It's just a burglar," Maggie protested. "Come on, let's get out of the cold." She took a couple of steps up the stairs, then reached down, grasped Tina's elbows with both hands, and pulled him toward her. "You know when most burglaries are committed, white boy? Around ten in the morning, when the bad guys know everybody else is at work."

"I know that," Tina smiled at her. "Honest, I know that."

"And if little Dracula comes back for your body, I'll turn her into . . . hmm . . ." She rolled her eyes up and stuck a forefinger into her cheek. "Into egg drop soup."

"Into Duck Saigon. Remember where you are."

"So let's go up and get it over with."

"Like I said."

He followed her up the stairs to the door of his loft. Unlike the white door downstairs, it was locked.

"One better than Dracula," Maggie said.

"It locks when you close it. I'm still not sure it wasn't goddamned Dracula." Pumo unlocked the door and stepped inside ahead of Maggie.

His coats and outerjackets still hung on their hooks, his boots were still lined up beneath them.

"Okay so far."

"Stop being such a *coward*," Maggie said, and gave him a push. A little way along was the door to his bathroom. Nothing in the bathroom was disturbed, but Pumo had a vivid vision of Dracula standing in front of the shaving mirror, bending her knees and fluffing up her Mohawk.

The bedroom was next. Pumo took in the unmade bed and empty television stand—he had left the bed that way, and had not yet replaced the nineteen-inch Sony Dracula had stolen from this room. The closet doors hung open, and a few of his suits drooped from their hangers toward an untidy heap of other clothes.

"Goddamn, it *was* Dracula." Pumo felt a layer of sweat pop out over what seemed his entire body.

Maggie looked up at him questioningly.

"The first time she stole my favorite jacket and my favorite pair of cowboy boots. SHIT! She loves my wardrobe!" Pumo slammed his fists against the sides of his head.

He was instantly across the room, lifting articles of clothing from the closet floor, examining them and putting them back on hangers.

"Did Vinh call the police? Do you want to call them?"

Pumo looked up at Maggie from an armload of clothes. "What's the point? Even if they find her and by some miracle put her away, she'll be back outside in about a day and a half. That's how we do it in this country. In Taipei you probably have an entirely different system."

Maggie leaned against the doorframe. Her arms hung straight down, parallel to each other, at an angle to her body. She had funny knobby little hands, Pumo noticed for perhaps the thousandth time. She said, "In Taipei, we staple their tongues to their upper lips and hack three fingers off each hand with a dull knife."

"Now that's what I call justice," Pumo said.

"In Taipei, that's what we call liberalism," Maggie said. "Is anything missing?"

"Hang on, hang on." Pumo put the last suit on its hanger, the hanger on the rail. "We haven't even gotten to the living room yet. I'm not even sure I want to get to the living room."

"I'll look in there, if you like. As long as we can eventually come back in here and take our clothes off and do all those things we were originally intending to do."

He looked at her with undisguised astonishment.

"I'll make sure the enemy has retreated from the living room," Maggie said in her flat precise voice. She disappeared.

"GODDAMN IT! DAMN IT!" Pumo yelled a few seconds later. "I KNEW IT!"

Maggie leaned into the bedroom again, looking startled and a little breathless. Her heavy black hair swung, and her lips were parted. "You called?"

"I don't believe it." Pumo was gazing at the empty nightstand beside his bed, and looked palely up at Maggie. "How does the living room look?"

"Well, in the second I had before I was distracted by the screams of a madman, it appeared to be slightly rumpled but otherwise okay."

"It was Dracula, all right." Pumo did not like the sound of *slightly rumpled.* "I knew it, damn it. She came back and stole all the same stuff all over again." He pointed to the nightstand. "I had to buy a new clock radio, and that's gone. I got a new Watchman, and the asshole stole that too."

Pumo watched beautiful little Maggie come floating into his bedroom in her loose flowing Chinese garment and mentally saw a fearful vision of his living room. He saw the cushions ripped, the books tumbled from the shelves, his desk up-ended, his living room television gone, the answering machine gone, his checkbooks, the ornamental screen he brought back from Vietnam, his VCR, and most of his good liquor, all gone. Pumo did not consider himself immoderately attached to his possessions, but he braced himself for the loss of these things. He would mind most of all about the couch, which Vinh had made and upholstered for him by hand.

Maggie lifted a drooping corner of a blanket with one hovering foot, and uncovered the clock radio and the new Watchman, which had apparently fallen from the nightstand sometime in the morning.

Without a word, she led him into the living room. Pumo admitted to himself that it looked almost exactly as it had when he left it.

The smooth, plump, speckled blue fabric still lay unblemished over Vinh's long couch, the books still stood, in their customary disorder, on the shelves and, in piles, on the coffee tables; the television stood, stupid as an idol, in its place on the shelf beneath the VCR and the showy stereo. Pumo looked at the records on the shelf beneath and knew immediately that someone had flipped through them.

At the far end of the room two steps led up to a platform, also carpentered by Vinh. Here were shelves stacked with bottles—a couple of shelves crammed with cookbooks, too—a sink, a concealed icebox. An armchair, a lamp. Shoved into a corner of the platform was Pumo's desk and leather desk chair, which had been pulled out and moved to one side, as if the intruder had wished to spend time at the desk.

"It doesn't look too bad," he said to Maggie. "She came in here and looked around, but she didn't do any damage I can see."

He moved more confidently into the room and closely examined the coffee table, the books, the records, and the magazines. Dracula had lingered here—she had moved everything around a little.

"The Battalion *Newsletter,*" he finally said.

"The what?"

"She took the Ninth Battalion *Newsletter.* It comes twice a year—I hardly even look at it, to tell you the truth, but I never throw out the old one until I get the new one."

"She's queer for soldiers."

Pumo shrugged and went up the steps to the platform. His checkbook and the Saigon checkbook were still on the desk, but had been moved. And there beside them was the missing *Newsletter,* lying open to a half-page photo of Colonel Emil Ellenbogen, retiring from the second-rate post in Arkansas to which the Tin Man had been sent after his disappointing term in Vietnam.

"No, the bitch just moved it," he called down to Maggie, who was standing in the middle of the room with her arms wrapped about herself.

"Is everything on your desk?"

"I don't know. I think something's gone, but I can't tell what it is."

He surveyed his messy desktop again. Checkbooks. Telephone. Answering machine, message light flashing. Pumo pushed rewind, then playback. Silence played itself back. Had she called first to make sure he was out? The more Pumo looked at the top of his desk, the more he thought something was missing, but he could not attach this feeling to a specific object. Beside the answering machine was a book called *Nam* which he was certain had been on one of the coffeetables for months—he had given up in the middle of the book, but kept it on the table because to admit that he was never going to finish it felt like opening the door to the worst kind of luck.

Dracula had picked up the *Newsletter* and the copy of *Nam* and set them down on the desk while she mused through his checkbooks. Probably she had touched everything on the desk with her long strong fingers. For a second Pumo felt sweaty and dizzy.

In the middle of the night Tina woke up with his heart pounding, a mad terrible dream just disappearing into the darkness. He turned his head and saw Maggie fast asleep on the pillow, her face curled up into itself like the curl of her hand. He could just make out her features. Oh, he loved seeing Maggie Lah asleep. Without the animation of her character her features seemed anonymous and wholly Chinese.

He stretched out again beside her and lightly touched her hand. What were they doing now, his friends? He saw them walking down a wide sidewalk, their arms linked. Tim Underhill could not be Koko, and as soon as they found him they would know it. Then Tina realized that if Underhill was not Koko, someone else was—someone circling in on them, circling in on all of them the way the bullet with his name on it still circled the world, never falling or resting.

In the morning he told Maggie that he had to do something to help the other guys—he wanted to see if he could find out more about Koko's victims, find out more that way.

"Now you're talking," Maggie told him.

4

Why questions and answers?

Because they go in a straight line. Because they are a way out. Because they help me to think.

What is there to think about?

The usual wreckage. The running girl.

Do you imagine that she was real?

Exactly. I *imagine* she was real.

What else is there to think about?

The usual subject, my subject. Koko. More than ever now.

Why more than ever now?

Because he has come back. Because I think I saw him. I know I saw him.

You imagined you saw him?

It is the same thing.

What did he look like?

He looked like a dancing shadow. He looked like death.

Did he appear to you in a dream?

He appeared, if that is the word, on the street. Death appeared on the street, as the girl appeared on the street. Tremendous clamor accompanied the appearance of the girl, ordinary street noise, that earthly clamor, surrounded the shadow. He was covered, though not visibly, with the blood of others. The girl, who was visible only to me, was covered with her own. The Pan-feeling poured from both of them.

What feeling is that?

The feeling that we have only the shakiest hold on the central stories of our lives. Hal Esterhaz in *The Divided Man*. The girl comes to speak to me with her terror, with her extremity, she runs toward me out of chaos and night, she has chosen me. Because I chose Hal Esterhaz, and because I chose Nat Beasley. Not yet, she says, not yet. The story is not yet over.

Why did Hal Esterhaz kill himself?

Because he could no longer bear what he was only just beginning to know.

Is that where imagination takes you?

If it's good enough.

Were you terrified when you saw the girl?

I blessed her.

13

KOKO

As soon as the plane took off, Koko too would be a man in motion.

This is one thing Koko knew: all travel is travel in eternity. Thirty thousand feet above the earth, clocks run backward, darkness and light change places freely.

When it got dark, Koko thought, you could lean close to the little window and if you were ready, if your soul was half in eternity already, you could see God's tusked grey face leaning toward you in the blackness.

Koko smiled, and the pretty stewardess in first class smiled back at him. She leaned forward, bearing a tray. "Sir, would you prefer orange juice or champagne this morning?"

Koko shook his head.

The earth sucked at the feet of the plane, reached up through the body of the plane and tried to pull Koko down into itself, suck suck, the poor earth loved what was eternal and the eternal loved and pitied the earth.

"Is there a movie on this flight?"

"Never Say Never Again," the stewardess said over her shoulder. "The new James Bond movie."

"Excellent," Koko said, with real inward hilarity. "I never say never, myself."

She laughed dutifully and went on her way.

Other passengers filed down the aisles, carrying suitbags, shopping bags, wicker baskets, books. Two Chinese businessmen took the seats before Koko, who heard them snap open their briefcases as soon as they sat down.

A middle-aged blonde stewardess in a blue coat leaned down and smiled a false machine smile at him.

"What shall we call you today, hmm?" She raised a clipboard with a seating chart into his field of vision. Koko slowly lowered his newspaper. "You are . . . ?" She looked at him, waiting for a reply.

What shall we call you today, hmm? *Dachau,* let's call you *Lady Dachau.* "Why don't you call me Bobby?"

"Well then, call you Bobby is what I'll do," the woman said, and scrawled *Bobby* in the space marked 4B on the chart.

In his pockets, Roberto Ortiz had carried his passports and a pocketful of cards and ID, as well as six hundred dollars American and three hundred Singapore. Big time! In a pocket of his blazer Koko had found a room key from the Shangri-La, where else would an ambitious young American be staying?

In Miss Balandran's bag Koko had found a hot comb, a diaphragm, a tube of spermicidal jelly, a little plastic holder containing a tube of Darkie toothpaste and a toothbrush, a fresh pair of underpants and a new pair of tights, a bottle of lip gloss and a lip brush, a vial of mascara, a blush brush, a rat-tailed comb, three inches of a cut-down white plastic straw, a little leather kit ranked with amyl nitrate poppers, a tattered Barbara Cartland paperback, a compact, half a dozen loose Valium, lots of crumpled-up Kleenex, several sets of keys, and a big roll of bills that turned out to be four hundred and fifty-three Singapore dollars.

Koko put the money in his pocket and dropped the rest onto the bathroom floor.

After he had washed his hands and face he took a cab to the Shangri-La.

Roberto Ortiz lived on West End Avenue in New York City.

On West End Avenue, could you feel how the lords of the earth, how God himself, hungered for mortality? Angels flew down West End Avenue, their raincoats billowing in the wind.

When Koko walked out of the Shangri-La he was

wearing two pairs of trousers, two shirts, a cotton sweater, and a tweed jacket. In the carry-on bag in his left hand were two rolled-up suits, three more shirts, and a pair of excellent black shoes.

A cab took Koko down leafy Grove Road to Orchard Road and on through clean, orderly Singapore to an empty building on a circular street off Bahru Road, and on this journey he imagined that he stood in an open car going down Fifth Avenue. Ticker tape and confetti rained down upon him and all the other lords of the earth, cheers exploded from the crowds packing the sidewalks.

Beevers and Poole and Pumo and Underhill and Tattoo Tiano and Peters and sweet Spanky B, and everybody else, all the lords of the earth, who may abide the day of their coming? For behold, darkness shall cover the earth. And the lawyer boy, Ted Bundy, and Juan Corona who labored in fields, and he who dressed in Chicago as a clown, John Wayne Gacy, and Son of Sam, and Wayne Williams out of Atlanta, and the Zebra Killer, and they who left their victims on hillsides, and the little guy in the movie *Ten Rillington Place,* and Lucas, who was probably the greatest of them all. The warriors of heaven, having their day. Marching along with all those never to be caught, all those showing presentable faces to the world, living modestly, moving from town to town, paying their bills, all those deep embodied secrets.

The refiner's fire.

Koko crawled in through his basement window and saw his father seated impatient and stormy on a packing crate. *Goddamned idiot,* his father said. *You took too much, think they'll ever give someone like you a parade? We waste no part of the animal.*

He spread the money out on the gritty floor, and that did it, the old man smiled and said, *There is no substitute for good butter*, and Koko closed his eyes and saw a row of elephants trudging past, nodding with grave approval.

On his unrolled sleeping bag he placed Roberto Ortiz's passports and spread out the five Rearing Elephant cards so he could read the names. Then he rooted in a box of papers and found the copy of the American magazine, *New York*, which he had picked up in a hotel lobby two days after the hostage parade. Beneath the title, letters of fire spelled out: TEN HOT NEW PLACES.

Ia Thuc, Hue, Da Nang, these were hot places. And

Saigon. Here is a hot new place, here is Saigon. The magazine fell open automatically to the picture and the paragraphs about the hot new place. (The Mayor ate there.)

Koko lay sprawled on the floor in his new suit and looked as deeply as he could into the picture of the hot new place. Deep green fronds waved across the white walls. Vietnamese waiters in white shirts whipped between crowded tables, going so fast they were only blurs of light. Koko could hear loud voices, knives and forks clanking against china. Corks popped. In the picture's foreground, Tina Pumo leaned against his bar and grimaced—Pumo the Puma leaned right out of the frame of the picture and spoke to Koko in a voice that stood out against the clamor of his restaurant the way a saxophone solo stands out against the sound of a big band.

Pumo said: "Don't judge me, Koko." Pumo looked shit-scared.

This was how they talked when they knew they stood before eternity's door.

"I understand, Tina," Koko said to the little anxious man in the picture.

The article said that Saigon served some of the most varied and authentic Vietnamese food in New York. The clientele was young, hip, and noisy. The duck was "heaven-sent" and every soup was "divine."

"Just tell me this, Tina," Koko said. "What is this shit about 'divine'? You think soup can be *divine*?"

Tina blotted his brow with a crisp white handkerchief and turned back into a picture.

And there it was, the address and the telephone number, in the soft cool whisper of italics.

A man sat down beside Koko in the fourth row of the first-class compartment, glanced sideways, and then buckled himself into his seat. Koko closed his eyes and snow fell from a deep cold heaven onto a layer of ice hundreds of feet deep. Far off, dim in the snowy air, ranged the broken teeth of glaciers. God hovered invisibly over the frozen landscape, panting with impatient rage.

You know what you know. Forty, forty-one years old. Thick fluffy richboy-blond hair, and thin brown glasses, heavy face. Heavy butcher's hands holding a day-old copy of the *New York Times*. Six-hundred-dollar suit.

The plane taxied down the runway and lifted itself

smoothly into the air, the envious mouths and fingers fell away, and the jet's nose pointed west, toward San Francisco. The man beside Koko is a rich businessman with butcher's hands.

A black-naped tern flies across the face of the Singapore one-dollar note. A black band like a burglar's mask covers its eyes, and behind it hovers a spinning chaos of intertwined circles twisting together like the strands of a cyclone. So the bird agitates its wings in terror, and darkness overtakes the land.

Mr. Lucas? Mr. Bundy?

Banking, the man says. Investment banking. We do a lot of work in Singapore.

Me too.

Hell of a nice place, Singapore. And if you're in the money business, it's hot, and I mean *hot.*

One of the hot new places.

"Bobby," the stewardess asks, "what would you like to drink?"

Vodka, ice-cold.

"Mr. Dickerson?"

Mr. Dickerson will have a Miller High Life.

In Nam we used to say: Vodka martini on the rocks, hold the vermouth, hold the olive, hold the rocks.

Oh, you were never in Nam?

Sounds funny, but you missed a real experience. Not that I'd go back, Christ no. You were probably on the other side, weren't you? No offense, we're all on the same side now, God works in funny ways. But I did all my demonstrating with an M-16, hah hah.

Bobby Ortiz is the name. I'm in the travel industry.

Bill? Pleased to meet you, Bill. Yes, it's a long flight, might as well be friends.

Sure, I'll have another vodka, and give another beer to my old pal Bill here.

Ah, I was in I Corps, near the DMZ, up around Hue.

You want to see a trick I learned in Nam? Good—I'll save it, though, it'll be better later, you'll enjoy it, I'll do it later.

* * *

Bobby and Bill Dickerson ate their meals in companionable silence. Clocks spun in no-time.

"You ever gamble?" Koko asked.

Dickerson glanced at him, his fork halfway to his mouth. "Now and then. Only a little."

"Interested in a little wager?"

"Depends on the wager." Dickerson popped the forkful of chicken into his mouth.

"Oh, you won't want to do it. It's too strange. Let's forget it."

"Come on," Dickerson said. "You brought this up, don't chicken out now."

Oh, Koko liked Billy Dickerson. Nice blue linen suit, nice thin glasses, nice big Rolex. Billy Dickerson played racquetball, Billy Dickerson wore a sweatband across his forehead and had a hell of a good backhand, real aggressor.

"Well, I guess being on a plane reminded me of this. It's something we used to do in Nam."

Definite look of interest on good old Billy's part.

"When we'd come into an LZ."

"Landing Zone?"

"You got it. LZ's were all different, see? Some were popping, and some were like dropping into the middle of a church picnic in Nebraska. So we'd make the Fatality Wager."

"Like you'd bet on how many people would get killed? Buy the farm, like you guys used to say?"

Buy the farm. Oh, you sweetheart.

"More on *if* someone would get killed. How much money you carrying in your wallet?"

"More than usual," Billy said.

"Five, six hundred?"

"Less than that."

"Let's make it two hundred. If somebody dies at the San Francisco airport while we're in the terminal, you pay me two hundred. If not, I'll give you one hundred."

"You'll give me two to one on someone dying in the terminal while we're going through customs, getting our bags, stuff like that?"

"That's the deal."

"I've never seen anyone kick off in an airport," Billy said, shaking his head, smiling. He was going to take the bet.

"I have," Koko said. "Upon occasion."

"Well, you got yourself a bet," Billy said, and they shook hands.

After a time Lady Dachau pulled down the movie screen. Most of the cabin lights went out. Billy Dickerson closed *Megatrends,* tilted his seat way back, and went to sleep.

Koko asked Lady Dachau for another vodka and settled back to watch the movie.

The good James Bond saw Koko as soon as he came on the screen. (The bad James Bond was a sleepy Englishman who looked a little bit like Peters, the medic who had been killed in a helicopter crash. The good James Bond looked a little like Tina Pumo.) He walked straight up to the camera and said, "You're fine, you have nothing to worry about, everybody does what they have to do, that's what war teaches you." He gave Koko a little half-smile. "You did well with your new friend, son. I noticed that. Remember now—"

Ready on the right? Ready on the left? Lock and load.

Good afternoon, gentlemen, and welcome to the Republic of South Vietnam. It is presently fifteen-twenty, November three, 1967. You will be taken to the Long Binh Replacement Center, where you will receive your individual unit assignments.

Remember the darkness of the tents. Remember the metal lockers. Remember the mosquito netting on the T-bars. Remember the muddy floors. Remember how the tents were like dripping caves.

Gentlemen, you are part of a great killing machine.

This is your weapon. It may save your life.

Nobility, grace, gravity.

Koko saw an elephant striding down a civilized European avenue. The elephant was buttoned into an elegant green suit and tipped his hat to all the charming ladies. Koko smiled at James Bond, who jumped out of his fancy car and looked Koko straight in the eye, and in quiet clear italics said, *Time to face the elephant again, Koko.*

A long time later they stood in the aisle, holding their carry-on baggage and waiting for Lady Dachau to open the door. At eye level directly before Koko hung the jacket of Billy Dickerson's blue linen suit, all correctly webbed and criss-crossed with big easy-going, casual-looking wrinkles that made you want to be wrinkled yourself, as easy and casual as that. When Koko glanced up he saw Billy Dickerson's blond hair ruffling out over the perfect collar of the linen suit. A pleasant smell of soap and aftershave emanated from good old Bill, who had disappeared into the forward toilet for nearly half an hour that morning while no-time turned into San Francisco time.

"Hey," Dickerson said, looking over his shoulder at Koko, "if you want to call off that bet it's okay with me, Bobby. Pretty crazy."

"Indulge me," Koko said.

Lady Dachau got the signal she was waiting for and opened the door.

They walked into a corridor of cool fire. Angels with flaming swords waved them forward. Koko heard distant mortar fire, a sign that nothing truly serious was happening: the Tin Man had just sent out a few boys to use up some of this month's quota of the taxpayers' money. The cool fire, frozen into patterns like stone, wavered beneath their feet. This was America again. The angels with flaming swords gave flaming smiles.

"You remember me mentioning that trick?"

Dickerson nodded and lifted an eyebrow, and he and Koko strolled along toward the baggage area. The angels with flaming swords gradually lost their numinosity and became uniformed stewardesses pulling wheeled carts behind them. The flames curling in the stone hardened into stiff cold patterns.

The corridor went straight for perhaps twenty yards, then slanted off to the right.

They turned the corner.

"A men's room, thank God," Dickerson said, and sped on ahead and shouldered open the door.

Smiling, Koko sauntered after, imagining an empty white-tiled place.

A woman in a bright yellow dress who passed before him exuded the hot, bloody aroma of the eternal world. For a moment a bright sword flickered in her hand. He pushed open the door of the men's room and had to shift his case to one side to swing open another door almost immediately behind it.

A bald man stood at one of the sinks, washing his hands. Beside him a shirtless man leaned over a sink and scraped lather from his face with a blue plastic razor. Koko's stomach tightened. Good old Billy was far down a row of urinals, more than half of which were occupied.

Koko saw his tense, haunted-looking face in the mirror. He jumped at himself out of his own eyes.

He went to the first urinal and pretended to pee, waiting for everyone to leave him alone with Dickerson. Something had gotten loose inside him, buzzed under his ribs, made him so lightheaded that he wobbled.

For an instant he thought he was already in Honduras, his work was either completed or ready to be begun all over again. Under an immense sun little brick-colored people milled around a comically provincial airport with tumble-down shacks, lounging policeman, and dozing hounds.

Dickerson zipped up, moved swiftly to the sink, passed his hands through a stream of water and a stream of air, and was gone almost before Koko came back to the men's room.

He hurried out. The loose thing in his chest buzzed painfully against his ribs.

Dickerson was moving quickly into a huge room where carousels like black volcanos whirred and gouted suitcases down their ribbed flanks. Nearly everyone on their flight was already gathered around the second carousel. Koko watched Dickerson work his way around the edge of the people waiting for their bags. The thing in his chest slipped down into his stomach, where it flew like an angry bee into his intestines.

Sweating now, Koko crept through the people who stood between himself and Dickerson. Lightly, almost reverently, he brushed his fingers over the linen sleeve that held Dickerson's left arm.

"Hey, Bobby, I don't feel right, you know," Dickerson said, bending forward and lifting a big Vuitton suitcase off the belt.

Koko knew one thing: a woman had picked out that bag.

"About the money thing. Let's eighty-six the whole idea, okay?"

Koko nodded miserably. His own beat-up case was nowhere on the carousel. Everything had gone slightly blurry around the edges, as if a fine mist hung in the air. A tall black-haired woman who was a living sword plucked a tiny case off the belt and—Koko saw through the descending mist—smiled at Dickerson.

"Take care," Dickerson said.

A uniformed man walked unerringly up to Dickerson and passed him through customs with a few questions. Dickerson strode off to a window to have his passport stamped.

Dazed, Koko saw his own suitcase thump down the side of the carousel and glide past him before he thought to lift it off the belt. He watched Dickerson's steadily dwindling body pass through a door marked EXIT-TRANSPORTATION.

In Customs the inspector called him "Mr. Ortiz" and searched the ripped lining of his suitcase for diamonds or heroin.

At Immigration he saw flaming wings sprout from the uniformed shoulders of the man in the booth, and the man stamped his passport and welcomed him back to the country, and Koko grabbed his old case and his carry-on bag and ran to the nearest men's room. He dropped the bags just inside the door and sprinted into an open toilet. As soon as he sat down his bowels opened, then opened again. Fire dripped and spurted from him. For a moment Koko's stomach felt as though a long needle had pierced it; then he bent forward and vomited between his shoes. He sat in his own stink for a long time, his bags forgotten, thinking only of what was there before him.

Eventually he wiped himself off, moved to the sink, washed his face and his hands, put his head beneath the cold water.

Koko took his bags outside and waited for the transfer bus to take him to the terminal from which his New York flight would leave. The air smelled of chemicals and machinery: everything before him looked two-dimensional and newly washed, drained of color.

In the second terminal Koko found a bar and ordered a beer. He felt that time had stopped—that it waited for him to wake it into life again. His breathing was shallow and slightly rushed. At the front of his forehead was a light, empty sensation, as if some moderate pain had just ceased. He could remember very little of what had happened to him during the past twenty-four hours.

He could remember Lady Dachau.

Gentlemen, you are part of a great killing machine.

Ten minutes before boarding, Koko went to his gate

and stood looking out the window, an unobtrusive man seeing an elephant in a suit and hat rearing up out of a wide dark pool of blood. When the first-class passengers were called, he filed on board and took his seat. He told the stewardess to call him Bobby.

Then everything really was all right, the sweet ache and buzz came alive within him again, for a pudgy man in his thirties dropped a briefcase into the aisle seat, shrugged off a green knapsack and set it beside the briefcase, removed his suit jacket to expose a striped shirt and dark blue suspenders, and snapped his fingers for the girl to take his jacket. The man shoved the knapsack into the overhead compartment, picked up his briefcase and squeezed into his seat. He scowled at Koko, then began to root through the contents of the briefcase.

"I don't suppose you're a betting man," Koko said.

14

REMEMBERING DRAGON VALLEY

1

Michael Poole stood at the window of his hotel room, looking down with an almost alarming sense of freedom at a long stretch of Singapore. The surprisingly green, surprisingly neat scene before him fell away to what he supposed was the east. A long way off, tall office blocks rose in a clean white cluster that might have been a transplanted section of midtown New York City. Nothing else in the scene before Poole even faintly resembled Manhattan. Trees with broad crowns that looked as edible as vegetables filled most of the space between himself and the tall white buildings, and because Michael was far above the tops of these trees, they seemed almost carpetlike. Between the broad areas filled in by the treetops swept wide roadways with smooth unblemished surfaces. Expensive cars coursed along these perfect roads, as many Jaguars and Mercedes as on Rodeo Drive. Here and there, through gaps in the trees, tiny people drifted along broad malls. Nearer the hotel, bungalows of pink or creamy stucco with wide porches, columns, and tiled roofs occupied green hillsides. Some of these had open courtyards, and in one of them a stocky woman in a bright yellow robe hung out her wash. In the immediate foreground, not at all obscured by the ubiquitous trees, the swimming pools of his own and other hotels sparkled like tiny woodland lakes glimpsed from an airplane. A canopy of red and blue stripes bordered the most distant pool, where a woman swam dogged laps; at the intermediate pool a bartender in a black jacket set up his bar. Beside the pool nearest Michael a Chinese boy dragged a stack of thick pads toward a row of empty redwood frames.

This luxurious city both surprised him, reassured him, and excited him more than he was willing to admit. Michael leaned forward against the window as if he wanted to take flight through the glass. Everything down there would be warm to the touch. The Singapore of his imagination had been a combination of Hue and Chinatown with a generalized smear of sidewalk food vendors and trishaws. He had pictured a version of Saigon, a city he had seen only briefly and disliked. (Most of the combat soldiers Michael knew who had visited Saigon had disliked it.) Just looking at those smooth quadrants of treetops, those neat serrated roofs, the tropical bungalows and the shining pools, made Poole feel better.

He was elsewhere, without doubt he was somewhere new: he had managed to step out of his life, and until this moment he had been unaware of how much he had wanted or needed to do that. He wanted to stroll beneath those healthy trees. He wanted to walk along the wide malls and smell the perfumed air he remembered from their arrival at Changi airport.

Just then his telephone rang. Michael picked it up, knowing that Judy was on the other end of the line.

"Good morning, gentlemen, and welcome to the Republic of Singapore," came the voice of Harry Beevers. "It is presently nine-thirteen on the trusty Rolex. You will report to the coffee shop where you will receive your individual assignments. . . . Guess what?"

Michael said nothing.

"A glance through the Singapore telephone directory uncovers no listing for a T. Underhill."

A little more than an hour later they were walking down Orchard Road. Poole carried the envelope full of Underhill's jacket photos, Beevers carried a Kodak Instamatic in his jacket pocket and was awkwardly examining a map folded into the back of *Papineau's Guide to Singapore,* and Conor Linklater slouched along with his hands in his pockets, carrying nothing. During breakfast they had agreed to spend the morning like tourists, walking through as much of the town as they could cover—"getting the feel of the place," as Beevers said.

This section of Singapore was as bland and inoffensive as their coffee shop breakfast. What Dr. Poole had not seen from the window of his hotel room was that the city had a lot in common with the duty-free area of a large airport. Every structure that was not a hotel was either an office building, a bank, or a shopping mall. The majority were the latter, most of them three or four levels high. A giant poster across the topmost level of a tall building still under construction depicted an American businessman speaking to a Singaporean Chinese banker. In a balloon above the American's head were the words *I am glad I learned of the fantastic return on my money I can earn by investing in Singapore!* To which the Chinese banker replies *With our beneficial investment program for our overseas friends, it is never too late to take part in the economic miracle of Singapore!*

Right now, you could step into a glass-fronted shop and buy cameras and stereo equipment; across the six-lane street, you could climb a flight of marble steps and choose from seven shops selling cameras, stereo equipment, electric razors, and electronic calculators. Here was the Orchard Towers Shopping Center, and here, across the street, shaped vaguely like a ziggurat, was the Far East Shopping Center, which had a long red banner reading GONG HI FA CHOY, for it was just past the Chinese New Year. Next to the Orchard Towers Shopping Center stood the Hilton, where middle-aged Americans breakfasted on a terrace. Further back there had been the Singapura Forum, where a stocky Malay with the face of William Bendix had played a hose over the flagstones. Far up on a hill they had seen a gardener toiling at keeping the grounds of the Shangri-La as immaculate as the center court at Wimbledon. Ahead down Orchard Road were the Lucky Plaza Shopping Center, the Irana Hotel, and the Mandarin Hotel.

"I think Walt Disney went crazy one day," said Conor Linklater, "and said 'Fuck the kids, let's invent Singapore and just make money.' "

When they passed the Prosperity Tailor Shop a grinning little man came out and followed them, trying to talk them into a purchase.

"You tough customers!" he said after the first half block. "You get ten percent off sale price. Best offer in whole city." After they had actually crossed over the big intersection at Claymore Hill, he became more insistent. "Okay, you get one-quarter off discount price! I can go no lower!"

"We don't want suits," Conor said. "We're not *looking* for suits. Give up."

"Don't you want to look good?" the tailor asked. "What's the matter with you guys? You *enjoy* looking like tourists? Come to my shop, I make you look like sophisticated gentlemen, one-quarter off discount price."

"I already look like a sophisticated gentleman."

"Could do better," said the tailor. "What you're wearing cost you three-four hundred dollars at Barneys, I give you three times the suit for same price."

Beevers ceased his impatient jigging on the sidewalk. The expression of unguarded astonishment on his face was as good as a Christmas present to Michael Poole and, he supposed, to Conor.

"I make you look like Savile Row," said the tailor, who was a round-faced Chinese man in his fifties wearing a white shirt and black trousers. "Six hundred-fifty-dollar suit, three hundred seventy-five dollars. Discounted price five hundred, I give you one-quarter off. Three hundred seventy-five dollars, price of couple good dinners at Four Seasons. You lawyuh? Stand in front of Supreme Court, you not only win case, everybody say 'Where you get that suit? Must be from Prosperity Tailor Shop, Wing Chong, proprietor'!"

"I don't want to buy a suit," Beevers said, looking shifty now.

"You need suit."

Beevers yanked the camera from his pocket and snapped the man's picture as if he were shooting him. The tailor grinned and posed. "Why don't you attack one of these guys instead of me? Why don't you go back to your shop?"

"Lowest prices," the man said, trembling with suppressed hilarity. "Three hundred fifty dollars. I go any lower, can't pay rent. Go any lower, children starve."

Beevers shoved the camera back into his pocket and

turned to Michael with the air of an animal caught in a trap.

"This guy knows everything else, maybe he knows Underhill," Michael said.

"Show him the picture!"

Michael took the envelope of photographs from under his arm and opened it.

"We are police officers from the City of New York," Beevers said.

"You lawyuh," said the tailor.

"We are interested in knowing if you have ever seen this man. Show him the picture, Mike!"

Michael took out one of the photographs of Tim Underhill and held it up before the tailor.

"Do you know this person?" Beevers asked. "Can you recall ever having seen him prior to now?"

"I never see this person prior to now," said the tailor. "It would be honor to meet this person, but he could not pay even rock-bottom price."

"Why not?" Michael asked.

"Too artistic," the tailor said.

Michael smiled and began to slide the picture back into the envelope when the tailor bent forward and grasped the print.

"You give me picture? Have plenty more?"

"He's lying," Beevers said. "You're lying. Where is this man? Can you lead us to him?"

"Celebrity picture," the tailor said.

"He just wants the picture," Michael said to Beevers.

Conor slapped the tailor on the back and laughed out loud.

"What do you mean, he just wants the picture?"

"Hang on wall," the tailor said.

Michael handed him the photograph.

The tailor tucked it under his arm and bowed, giggling. "Thank you very much." He turned around to walk back up the broad mall. Well-dressed Chinese men and women strolled toward them beneath the overhanging trees. The men wore blue suits, neat ties, and sunglasses and looked like the banker on the banner. The women were slim and good-looking and wore dresses. Poole realized that he, Beevers, and Conor were a racial minority of three. A long way down the mall, beside a poster that surrounded Chuck Norris's scowl with leaping flames and a lot of

Chinese characters, a teenage Chinese girl idled along, looking absently into shop windows. She wore what must have been a school uniform of flat white skimmer, white middy blouse with a black tie, and loose black skirt. Then an entire pack of such girls, neat as a row of ducks, swung into view behind her. Across the street next to a poster advertising McDonald's hamburgers a square white sign advised SPEAK MANDARIN—ASSIST YOUR GOVERNMENT. Suddenly Poole could smell the perfume in the air, as if some invisible, exotic flower bloomed all around him. He felt unreasonably happy.

"If we're looking for the Boogey Street Underhill used to talk about, why don't we just take a cab?" Poole said. "This is a civilized country."

2

Stung by a recognition, Tina Pumo woke up in what at first seemed utter darkness. His heart was beating very loudly. He imagined that he must have cried out, made at least some sound, before he awakened, but Maggie slept on undisturbed beside him. He raised his arm and looked at the luminous hands on the face of his watch. It was three twenty-five.

Tina knew what had been stolen from his desk. If Dracula had not moved everything around, he would have noticed its loss immediately, and if the two days since the break-in had been normal working days, he would have noticed its absence as soon as he sat down. But these two days had been anything but normal—he had spent at least half of each working day downstairs with the builders, contractors, carpenters, and exterminators. They finally seemed to have rid Saigon's kitchen of all its insects, but the exterminator was still in a state closely resembling euphoria at the number, variety, and hardiness of the bugs he had had to kill. At least a few hours a day had to be spent convincing Molly Witt, his architect, that she was designing a kitchen and an enlarged dining room, not a high-tech operating room. The rest of the time he had spent with Maggie, talking as he had never talked in his life about himself.

Tina felt almost as if Maggie had unlocked him. In two

days she had gone a long way toward drawing him out of a shell he had barely known he was in.

In a way he was still only beginning to understand, that shell had been formed in Vietnam. Pumo felt humbled by this new knowledge—Dracula had terrorized him by awakening feelings that Pumo had fondly, even proudly, imagined he had put away with his uniform. Pumo had imagined that it was only other people who had allowed themselves to be scarred by Vietnam. He used to feel at a safe emotional distance from all that had happened to him there. He had left the Army and got on with his life. Like virtually every other veteran, he'd gone through a period of aimlessness and dislocation when he coasted just alongside life, but that time had come to an end six years earlier, when he made his move with Saigon. He had, it was true, continued to go from girl to girl, and as he grew older, the girls had gotten younger by staying the same age. He fell in love with the shape of their mouths or the shape of their forearms or the eloquence of the relationship between their calves and their thighs; he fell in love with the way their hair swung or their eyes took him in. Until Maggie Lah had stopped him dead, he thought now, he had fallen in love with everything there was about a person except the actual person.

"Do you think there is a real point where *then* stops and *now* begins?" Maggie had asked him. "Don't you know that down deep the things that happen to you never really *stop* happening to you?"

It had crossed his mind that she might think this way because she was Chinese, but he had kept silent about this theory.

"Nobody can walk away from things the way you think you walked away from Vietnam," she told him. "You saw your friends get killed, and you were just a boy. Now, after a relatively minor beating, you're afraid of elevators and you're afraid of subways and dark streets and God knows what else. Don't you think there's some connection?"

"I guess," he admitted. "How do you know about it though, Maggie?"

"*Everybody* knows about it, Tina," she said. "Except a surprising number of middle-aged American men, who really do believe that people can start fresh all over again, that the past dies and the future is a new beginning, and that these beliefs are moral."

Now Pumo carefully left his bed. Maggie did not stir, and her breathing went on quietly and steadily. He had to look at his desk to see if he was right about what had been stolen. Pumo's heart was still pounding, and his own breathing sounded very loud to him. He proceeded cautiously across the bedroom in the dark. When he put his hand on the doorknob, he was visited by the sudden image of Dracula standing just on the other side of the door. Sweat broke out on his face.

"Tina?" Maggie's crystalline voice floated on a dead-level current of breath from the bedroom.

Pumo stood in the dark empty hallway. No one was there—as if Maggie had helped dispel the threat.

"I know what's missing," he said. "I have to check it out. Sorry I woke you up."

"It's okay," Maggie said.

His head pounded, and he could still feel little tremors in his knees. If he stood in that spot any longer, Maggie would know something was wrong. She might even feel that she had to get out of bed to help him. Pumo moved down the hall into the loft's living room and pulled the cord that switched on the overhead lights. Like most rooms used almost entirely in the daytime, when seen this late at night Pumo's living room had an eerie quality, as if everything in it had been replaced by an exact replica of itself. Pumo went across the room, up the steps to the platform, and sat down at his desk.

He could not see it. He looked beneath the telephone and the answering machine. He moved the checkbooks to one side and lifted stacks of invoices and receipts. He checked behind a box of rubber bands and moved a box of tissues. Nothing. It could not have been hidden by the bottles of vitamins beside the electric pencil sharpener, nor by the two boxes of Blackwing pencils beside that. He was right: it wasn't there. It had been stolen.

To be certain, Pumo looked under his desk, leaned over the top and looked behind it, and then poked through his wastebasket. The wastebasket contained lots of balled-up tissues, an old copy of the *Village Voice*, the wrapper from a Quaker Oats Granola Bar, begging-letters from charities, grocery coupons, several unopened envelopes covered with announcements that he had already won a valuable prize, and a cotton ball and sealer from a bottle of vitamins.

Crouching beside the wastebasket, Pumo looked up and saw Maggie standing in the entrance to the living room. Her arms dangled at her sides and her face still seemed full of sleep.

"I know I look a little crazy," he said, "but I was right."

"What is missing?"

"I'll tell you after I think about it for a couple of seconds."

"That bad?"

"I don't know yet." He stood up. His body felt very tired, his mind not at all. He came down from the platform and went toward her.

"Nothing's that bad," she said.

"I was just thinking about a guy named M.O. Dengler."

"The one who died in Bangkok."

When he reached her he took one of her hands and opened it, like a leaf, on his own hand. Seen like this, her hand looked normal, not at all knobby. Lots of tiny wrinkles criss-crossed her palm. Maggie's fingers were small, slim as cigarettes, slightly curled.

"Bangkok would be a filthy place to die," she said. "I loathe Bangkok."

"I didn't know you'd ever been there." He turned her hand over. Her palm was almost pink, but the back of her hand was the same golden color as the rest of her. Maybe the joints of her hand were slightly larger than one would expect. Maybe the bones of her wrist protruded.

"You don't know much about me," Maggie said.

They both knew he was going to tell her what had been stolen from his desk, and that this conversation was only a period in which Pumo could digest the fact of its loss.

"Have you ever been to Australia?"

"Lots of times." She gave him a look of mock disgust disguised as no expression at all. "I suppose you went there on R&R and spent seven days seeking sexual release in an alcoholic blur."

"Sure," Pumo said. "I was under orders."

"Can we turn off the lights and go back to sleep?"

Pumo astonished himself by yawning. He reached up and pulled the cord, putting them in darkness.

She led him back down the narrow corridor and into

the bedroom. Pumo groped his way to his side of the bed and climbed in. He felt more than saw Maggie roll onto her side and prop herself up on one elbow. "Tell me about M.O. Dengler," she said.

He hesitated, and then a sentence appeared fully-formed in his mind, and when he spoke it, other sentences followed, as if they were appearing of their own will. "We were in a kind of swampy field. It was about six o'clock in the afternoon, and we'd been out since maybe five that morning. Everybody was pissed off, because we had wasted the whole day, and we were hungry, and we could tell the new lieutenant had no idea what he was doing. He had just come in two days before, and he was trying to impress us with how sharp he was. This was Beevers."

"Could have fooled me," said Maggie.

"What he did was take us off into the wilderness on an all-day wild goose chase. What the old lieutenant would have done, what was supposed to happen, was that we got set down in the LZ, poked around for a while to see if we could find anybody to shoot at, then we'd go back to the LZ for lift out. If you got some action, you call in an air strike or you call in artillery or you shoot it out, whatever's right. You respond. That's all we were there for—we were just there to respond. They sent us out there to get shot at so that we could shoot back and kill a lot of folks. That was it. It was pretty simple, when you come right down to it.

"But this new guy, Beans Beevers, acted like . . . You knew you were in trouble. Because in order to respond, you have to know what's out there that you are responding *to*. And this new guy who was fresh out of ROTC at some fancy college acts like he's in an old movie or something. Inside his head, he's already a hero. He's gonna capture Ho Chi Minh, he's gonna wipe out a whole enemy division, there's a Medal of Honor already minted with his name on the certificate. He's got that look."

"When do we get to M.O. Dengler?" Maggie asked softly.

Pumo laughed. "Right now, I guess. The point is, our new lieutenant took us way out of our area without knowing it. He got so excited he misread his map, and so Poole kept sending the wrong coordinates back to base. We even lost our F.D., which *nobody* does. We're supposed to be getting back to the LZ, and nothing around us looks familiar. Poole says, 'Lieutenant, I've been looking at my map, and I think we must be in Dragon Valley.' Beevers tells him he's absolutely wrong, and to keep his mouth shut if he wants to stay out of trouble. 'Watch out, you might get sent to Vietnam,' Underhill says, which really begins to piss off the lieutenant.

"So instead of confessing that he was wrong and making some kind of joke about it and getting the hell out, which would have saved everything, he makes the mistake of thinking about it. And unfortunately there's a lot to think about. An entire company had been shot to pieces in Dragon Valley the week before, and the Tin Man was supposed to be cooking up some combined action. Beevers decides that since we're supposed to provoke action and respond to it, and since we had providentially found ourselves in what might be the perfect place for action, we ought to provoke a little of it. We'll advance into the Valley a little, he says, and Poole asks if he can figure out our real coordinates and radio them in. Radio silence, Beevers says, and shuts *him* up. Poole is supposed to be chicken-hearted, get it?

"Beevers is thinking that we might spot a few Viet Cong, or maybe a small NVA detachment, which is what's supposed to be down there, and if we're lucky shoot the crap out of them and get a respectable body count, and go back with our new lieutenant blooded. Well, by the time we got back he was blooded, all right. He signals us to continue moving into the Valley, see, and everybody but him knows this is totally crazy. A creep named Spitalny asks how long we were gonna keep this up, and Beevers yells back, *'As long as it takes! This isn't boy scout camp!'* Dengler says to me, 'I love this new lieutenant,' and I see he's grinning like a boy with a big piece of pie. Dengler has never seen anything like this new lieutenant before. He and Underhill are cracking up.

"Finally we get to this thing like a swampy field. It's just getting dark. The air's full of bugs. The joke, if it is a joke, is over. Everybody's beat. On the far side of the field is a stand of trees that looks like the beginning of jungle. There are a few bare dead logs in the middle of the field, and some big shell holes full of water.

"I got a funny feeling the minute I laid eyes on the field. It looked like death. That's the best I can say. It looked like a goddamned graveyard. It had that fixin'-to-die smell—maybe you know what I mean. I bet if you go to the pound and get into that room where they kill the dogs nobody wants, you'd get that same smell. Then I saw a helmet liner lying out next to a shell crater. A little way off from it I saw the busted-off stock of an M-16.

" 'Suppose we explore this piece of real estate and see what's on the other side before we go back to camp,' Beevers said. 'Looks good, doesn't it?'

" 'Lieutenant,' Poole said, 'I think this field is probably mined.' He saw what *I* did, see?

" 'Do you?' Beevers asked. 'Then why don't you go out there first, Poole? You just volunteered to be our point man.'

"Fortunately, Poole and I weren't the only ones who had seen the helmet liner and the stock. They wouldn't let Poole go out there by himself, and they weren't about to try it for themselves either.

" 'You think this field is mined?' Beevers asked."

"You men think this field is mined?" screamed Lieutenant Beevers. "You actually think I'll fall for that one? This is a struggle for command, and like it or not, I'm in command here."

Grinning, Dengler turned to Puma and whispered, "Don't you love the way his mind works?"

"Dengler whispered something to me, and Beevers blew up. 'Okay,' he yelled at Dengler, 'if you think this area is mined, prove it to me. Throw something out there and hit a mine. If nothing blows up, we all go into the field.' 'Whatever you say,' Dengler said—"

"As the lieutenant wishes," Dengler said, and looked around him in the gloom. "Throw the lieutenant," Victor Spitalny muttered. Dengler saw a good-sized rock buried in the muck near him, pushed it free with his boot, bent down, put his arms around it, and lifted it.

"—and he picked up a rock about the size of his head. Beevers was getting madder by the second. He told Dengler to heave the goddamned thing out into the field, and Poole came up next to Dengler to take half the weight. They did a one-two-three and heaved the thing maybe twenty yards. Everybody but the lieutenant fell down and covered his face. I heard the rock land with a thud. Nothing. I think we all expected a pressure mine to send shrapnel off in all directions. When nothing happened, we picked ourselves up. Beevers was standing there smirking. 'Well, girls,' he said. 'Satisfied now? Need more proof?' And then he did an amazing thing—he took off his helmet and kissed it. 'Follow this, it has more balls than you do,' he said, and he cocked his arm back and tossed his helmet as far as he could out into the field. We all watched it sail up. By the time it started to descend, we could hardly see it anymore."

They watched the lieutenant's helmet disappear into the grey air and the swarming bugs. By the time the helmet hit the ground it was nearly invisible. The explosion surprised them all, except at that level where they could no longer be surprised by anything. Again, all except Beevers flopped into the muck. A column of red fire flashed upward and the ground bounced under their feet. Set off either by a malfunction or by the vibration, another mine detonated a beat after the first, and a chunk of metal whizzed past Beevers' face, so close he could feel its heat. He either fell down on purpose or collapsed in shock next to Poole. He was panting. Everyone in the platoon could smell the acrid stink of the two explosions. For a moment everything was still. Tina Pumo lifted his head, half-expecting another of the mines to go off, and as he did so he heard the insects begin their drilling again. For a moment Tina thought he could see Lieutenant Beevers' helmet out on the far end of the mined field, lying miraculously undamaged though somehow stuffed with leaves beside a twisted branch. Then he saw that the leaves formed a pattern of eyes and eyebrows inside the helmet. Finally he saw that they were real eyes and eyebrows. The helmet was still on a dead soldier's head. What he had taken for a branch was a severed arm in a sleeve. The explosion had unearthed a partially buried and dismembered corpse.

From the other end of the field a loud inquisitive voice called out in Vietnamese. Another voice screeched in laughter, and joyfully shouted back.

"I think we're in a situation here, Lieutenant," Dengler whispered. Poole had taken his map out of its wax case

and was running his fingers along trails, trying to figure out exactly where they were.

Looking across the field at the American head which had floated in its American helmet out of the substance of the field, Poole saw a series of abrupt, inexplicable movements of the earth—as if invisible rodents tore around, roiling the sodden earth here, tossing spears of grass there. Something trembled the log near the field's far end and pushed it backwards an inch or two. Then he finally realized that the platoon was being fired on from the rear.

"There were a couple of explosions, and a lot of yelling in Vietnamese from all around us—I think they had let us just blunder along without being really certain of where we were. Beevers' radio silence at least did that much. The ones behind us started shooting, and probably the only thing that saved our lives was that they weren't sure where we were, exactly, so they put their fire where they thought we were, the same field where they'd wiped out nearly a whole company a week before. And their fire exploded maybe eighty percent of the mines they had buried with the American bodies."

It looked as if underground fireworks were destroying the field. There came a staggered, arrhythmic series of double explosions, the booming thud of the shell answered immediately by the flat, sharp crack of the mine. Yellow-red flashes engulfed orange-red flashes, then both flashes drowned in a boil of smoke and a gout of earth, throwing up a ribcage lashed against a web belt, an entire leg still wearing a trouser leg and a boot.

"Why did they booby-trap the dead bodies?" Maggie whispered.

"Because they knew that someone would come back for them. You always come back for your dead. It's one of the only decent things about war. You bring your dead *back* with you."

"Like going after Tim Underhill?"

"No, not at all. Well, maybe. I suppose." He extended his arm. Maggie rested her head on it and snuggled closer to him.

"Two guys got blown to pieces as soon as we started moving into the field. Beevers ordered us forward, and he was right, because they were readjusting their fire to blast the shit out of us where we were. The first guy to go was a kid named Cal Hill who had just joined up with us, and the other was a guy named Tattoo Tiano. I never knew his real name, but he was a good soldier. So Tattoo got killed right away. Right next to me. There was this blast that almost tore my head off when Tattoo set off the mine, and honest to God the air turned bright red for a second. He really was right next to me. I thought *I* was dead. I couldn't see or hear anything. There was nothing but this red mist all around me. Then I heard the other one go off, and I could hear it when Hill started screaming. 'Move your tail, Pumo,' Dengler yelled. 'You still got it, move it.' Norm Peters, our medic, somehow got over to Hill and tried to do something for him. I finally noticed that I was all wet, *covered* with Tattoo's blood. We started getting a little light fire from up ahead, so we got our weapons off our backs and returned fire. Artillery rounds started landing back in the fringe of jungle we had just left. I could see Poole yelling into his radio. The fire got a little heavier. We scattered out through the field and hunkered down behind whatever we could find. Along with a few other people I flattened out behind the fallen tree. I could see Peters wrapping up Cal Hill, trying to stop his blood loss, and it looked inside out to me—it looked like Peters was torturing Hill, squeezing the blood out of him. Hill was screaming his head off. We were demons, they were demons, everybody was demons, there were no people left in the world anymore, only demons. Hill sort of didn't have any *middle*—where his stomach and guts and his cock should have been there was only this flat red puddle. Hill could see what had happened to him, and he couldn't *believe* it. He wasn't in Nam long enough to believe it! 'Stop that man screaming!' Beevers yelled. Some more light fire came at us from ahead, and then we heard someone shouting at us from up there. 'Rock'n roar,' this guy was shouting, 'Rock'n roar!' 'Elvis,' Dengler said, and a whole bunch of guys started yelling at *him,* and squeezed off a couple of shots. Because this was the sniper who had appointed himself our official assassin. He was one amazing shot, let me tell you. I raised up and got off a shot, but I knew it wasn't any good. M-16s used these little 5.56 millimeter bullets instead of 7.62 rounds, and so the cartridge clips were easier to carry, eleven ounces instead of more than twice that, but the rounds spun in the air, so they wobbled like crazy once they went a certain distance. In some ways, the old M-14 was better—not only did it have better distance, you could actually *aim* an M-14. So I squeezed off some rounds, but I was pretty sure that even if I could see old Elvis, I wouldn't be able to hit him. But at least I'd have the satisfaction of knowing what he looked like. Anyhow, so there we were, stuck in a minefield between a lot of NVA, maybe a couple of companies working their way south to link up with whatever they had in the A Shau Valley. Not to mention Elvis. And Poole couldn't tell anybody where we were, because not only had the lieutenant gotten us lost, his radio had been hit and the fucker was no good anymore. So we were locked in. We spent the next fifteen hours in a field full of dead men—with a lieutenant who was losing his mind."

"Oh God oh God," Pumo heard the lieutenant repeating over and over. Calvin Hill noisily continued to die, screaming as if Peters were poking hot needles through his tongue. Other men were screaming too. Pumo could not see who they were, and he did not want to know who they were. Part of Pumo wanted to stand up and get killed and get it over with, and part of him was as scared of this feeling as of anything else that had happened. He made the interesting discovery that there are layers of terror, each one colder and more paralyzing than the one before it. Mortar rounds landed in the field at regular intervals, and machinegunfire now and then sprayed in from the sides. Pumo and everyone else huddled in whatever troughs, shellholes, or bunkers they half-found, half-dug for themselves. Pumo had finally seen the lieutenant's ruined helmet: it rested against the kneecap of a dead soldier who had been lifted out of the ground by an exploding mine. His kneecap, attached to his calf but to nothing else and white beneath its coating of grime, lay on the ground only inches from the soldier's head and shoulders, likewise attached to nothing else. The dead soldier was looking at Pumo. His face was very dirty. His eyes were open, and he looked stupid and hungry. Every time the ground rumbled and the sky split apart with a new explosion, the head tilted a little

more toward Pumo and the shoulders swam across the ground toward him.

Pumo flattened himself against the ground. The coldest, deepest layer of terror told him that when the dead soldier finally swam up and touched him, he'd die. Then he saw Tim Underhill crawling toward the lieutenant and wondered why he bothered. The sky was full of tracers and explosion. Night had come on in an instant. The lieutenant was going to die. Underhill was going to die. Everybody was going to die. That was the great secret. He seemed to hear M.O. Dengler saying something to Poole and laughing. Laughing? Pumo was intensely aware, as the world darkened and swooned around the impossibility of that laugh, of the odor of Tattoo Tiano's blood. 'Did the lieutenant shit in his nice new pants?' Underhill said. 'Mike, get your radio to work, will you?' Dengler asked in a very reasonable voice.

A huge explosion rocked Pumo as it tore apart the sky. The air turned white, red, deep black. Womanish-sounding screams came from a soldier Pumo could immediately identify as Tony Ortega, Spacemaker Ortega, a good but brutal soldier who in civilian life had been the leader of a motorcycle gang called the Devilfuckers in upstate New York. Ortega had been Victor Spitalny's only friend in the platoon, and now Spitalny would have no friends. Pumo realized that this didn't matter, Spitalny would get killed with the rest of them. Spacemaker Ortega's screams gradually sank into the dark, as if he were being carried away. "What are we going to do, what are we going to do, oh God oh God," Beevers wailed. "Oh God oh God oh God, I don't want to die, I don't I don't, I can't die."

Peters crawled away from the dead Ortega. In a sudden loud burst of light Pumo saw him moving toward a twitching man ten or twelve yards off. Another land mine inaudibly went off for the ground shook and the dead man swam a few inches nearer Pumo.

A soldier named Teddy Wallace announced that he was going to waste that fucker Elvis, and a friend of his named Tom Blevins said he'd follow. Pumo saw the two soldiers rise into crouches and take off across the field. Before he had gone eight steps, Wallace stepped on a pressure mine and was torn apart from crotch to chest. Wallace's left leg blew sideways and seemed to run above the field for a short time before it fell. Tom Blevins got a few steps further before he pitched over as neatly as if he had tripped over piano wire. "Rock'n roar!" Elvis shouted from up in the trees.

Suddenly Pumo became aware that Dengler was beside him. Dengler was grinning. "Don't you think God does all things simultaneously?" Dengler asked him.

"What?" he asked. Life doesn't make sense, he thought, the world doesn't make sense, war doesn't make sense, everything is only a terrible joke. Death was the great secret at the bottom of the joke, and demons watched the world and capered and laughed.

"What I like about that idea is that in a funny way it means that the universe actually created itself, which means that it goes on creating itself, get me? So destruction is part of this creation that goes on all the time. And on top of that is the real kicker, Pumo—destruction is the part of creation that we think is beautiful."

"Get fucked," Pumo said. Now he understood what Dengler was doing: talking nonsense to wake him up and make him capable of acting. Dengler didn't understand that the demons had made the world, and that death was their big secret.

Pumo became aware that he had not spoken in a long time. His eyes were filled with tears. "Are you awake, Maggie?" he whispered.

Maggie breathed on easily and quietly, her perfect round head still resting on his shoulder.

"That bastard stole my address book," Pumo whispered. "Why the hell would she want my address book? So she can steal clock radios and portable televisions from everyone I know?"

In a carrying voice, Underhill said, "The demons are abroad and Dengler is trying to convince Pumo that death is the mother of beauty—"

"No, I'm not," Dengler whispered, "you got it wrong, that's not it, beauty has no mother."

'Jesus," Pumo said, and wondered how Underhill knew about the demons, he must have seen them too.

Another great light exploded in the sky, and he could see the surviving members of the platoon lying as if frozen in a snapshot, their faces turned to Underhill, who seemed as calm, peaceful, and massive as a mountain. There was another secret here, a secret as deep as the one the demons had, but what was it? Their own dead, and the booby-trapped dead of the other company, lay sprawled all over the field. No, the demons are deeper, Pumo thought, because this isn't just hell, this is worse than hell—in hell you're dead and in this hell we still have to wait for other people to kill us.

Norm Peters scurried back and forth, plugging sucking chest wounds. Then darkness enclosed them again. When another giant light illuminated the sky a few seconds later, Pumo saw that Dengler had left him and was following Peters around, helping him. Dengler was smiling. He saw Pumo staring at him, and grinned and pointed upwards. Shine on, he meant, shine on, remember everything, the universe is making itself up right now . . .

Late at night the NVA began dropping in 60-mm shells from the M-2 mortars that had been taken from the American company. Several times in the hour before morning Pumo knew that he had gone stone crazy. The demons had come back, and roamed laughing through the field. Pumo finally understood that they were laughing at him and Dengler, for even if they lived through this night they would not be saved from dying senseless deaths, and if all things were simultaneous their deaths were present now, and memory was a twisted joke. He saw Victor Spitalny sawing the ears off Spacemaker Ortega, the former ruler of the Devilfuckers, and that made the demons dance and cackle too. "What the fuck are you doing?" he hissed, and picked up a clod of earth and threw it at him. "That was your best friend!"

"I gotta have somethin' to show for this," Spitalny said, but he gave up anyhow, shoved his knife back in his belt and scuttled away like a jackal surprised at his feast of carrion.

When the helicopters finally came in the NVA company had disappeared back into the jungle, and the Cobras, the gunships, merely slammed a half-dozen rockets into the canopy and fried a few monkeys before wheeling grandly in the air and returning to Camp Crandall. The other helicopter descended over the clearing.

You never remembered how almost tranquil a UH1-B was until you were in one again.

3

"To tell you the truth, we're New York City policemen," Beevers said to the taxi driver, a gaunt, toothless Chinese in a T-shirt who had just asked why they wanted to go to Boogey Street.

"Ah," the driver said. "Policemen."

"We're here on a case."

"On a case," said the driver. "Very good. This for television?"

"We're looking for an American who liked Boogey Street," Poole hastily explained. Beevers' face had turned red and his mouth was a thin line. "We know he moved to Singapore. So we'd like to show his picture around on Boogey Street to see if anybody knows him."

"Boogey Street no good for you," the driver said.

"I'm getting out of this cab," Beevers said. "I can't stand it anymore. Stop. Pull over. We're getting out."

The driver shrugged and obediently switched on his turn signal to begin making his way across three lanes to the curbside.

"Why do you say Boogey Street is no good for us?" Poole asked.

"Nothing there anymore. Mister Lee, he clean it all up."

"Cleaned it up?"

"Mister Lee make all the girl-boys leave Singapore. No more—only pictures."

"What do you mean, only pictures?"

"You walk down Boogey Street at night," the driver patiently explained, "you go past many bars. Outside bars you see pictures. You buy pictures, take them home."

"Goddamn," Beevers said.

"Someone in one of those bars will know Underhill," Poole said. "He might not have left Singapore just because the transvestites did."

"You don't think so?" Beevers yelled. "Would you buy a jigsaw puzzle if the most important piece was missing?"

"See points of interest in Singapore," the driver said. "Tonight, Boogey Street. For now, Tiger Balm Gardens."

"I hate gardens," Beevers said.

"Not flower garden," the driver said. "Sculpture garden. Many style Chinese architecture. Depictions of Chinese folklore. Thrilling scenes."

"Thrilling scenes," Beevers said.

"Python devouring Goat. Tiger ready for attack. Ascension of White Snake Spirit. Wild Man of Borneo. So Ho Shang trapped in Spider's Den. Spider Spirit in form of Beautiful Woman."

"Sounds good to me," Conor said.

"Best part, many scenes of torture. Scenes in infernal regions depicting punishment given souls after death. Very beauiful. Very instructive. Very scary."

"What do you think?" Conor asked.

"It's the punishment given souls before death that worries me," Poole said. "But let's have a look."

The driver instantly cut across three lanes of traffic.

He dropped them off at the bottom end of a wide walk leading up to a gate with the words HAW PAR VILLA suspended between green and white columns. People streamed in both directions through this gate. Above it was a hillside of purple-grey plaster that to Poole resembled a section from a giant brain. A short distance away stood a taller, gaudier gate in the shape of a tiered pagoda. Chinese people in short sleeves and summer dresses, Chinese teenagers in wildly colored clothes, schoolgirls uniformed like boys at an English public school, old couples holding hands, crewcut boys skipping along in short pants, all these people milled up and down the broad walkway. At least half of them seemed to be eating something. The sun sparkled off the white paint of the pagoda gate and threw deep black shadows across the slabs of the walk. Poole wiped sweat off his forehead. The day grew hotter every hour, and his collar was already damp.

They passed beneath the second gate. Just past a huge allegorical figure representing Thailand was a tableau of a peasant woman sprawled on the representation of a field, her basket lost behind her, her arms outstretched in a plea for help. A child raced toward her, a peasant in shorts and a pagoda hat extended an arm to threaten or aid. (The handout booklet explained that he is offering her a bottle of Tiger Balm.) Two oxen locked horns in the background.

Sweat poured down Poole's face. He remembered a

muddy field slanting down a Vietnamese hillside and Spitalny raising his rifle to sight on a woman scampering toward a circle of hootches beyond which lean oxen grazed. Her bright blue pajamas shone vividly against the brown field. Mosquitos. The heavy pails of water suspended on a wooden yoke over the woman's shoulders hampered her movements: Poole remembered the shock of recognizing that the pails of water were as important to her as her life—she would not throw the yoke off her shoulders. Spitalny's rifle cracked, and the woman's feet lifted, and for a moment she sped along parallel to the ground without touching it. Soon she collapsed in a blue puddle beside the long curved yoke. The pails clattered downhill. Spitalny fired again. The oxen bolted away from the village, running so close together their flanks touched. The woman's body jerked forward as if it had been pushed by an invisible force, and then began to roll loosely downhill. Her forearms flipped up, out, up like spokes on a broken flywheel.

Poole turned to Harry Beevers, who had glanced at the statues on top of the brain-wall and was now staring at two pretty Chinese girls giggling together near the pagoda gate. "Do you remember Spitalny shooting that girl outside Ia Thuc? The one in blue pajamas?"

Beevers glanced at him, blinked, then looked back at the sculptures of the farmer and his wife. He nodded and smiled. "Sure. But that was in another country, and besides, the wench is dead."

"No," Conor said, "that was another *wench,* and besides, the *country's* dead."

"She was obviously VC," Beevers said. He glanced again at the Chinese girls as if they too were Viet Cong who ought to be executed. "She was there, therefore she was VC."

The two girls were now walking past Beevers as if on tiptoe. They were slender girls with shoulder-length black hair and dresses of the sort, Poole thought, that used to be called frocks. Were there still frocks? He glanced up the hill and saw another pack of schoolgirls in uniform—dark blazers and flat hats.

"This whole place is back in the fifties," Beevers said. "I don't mean the gardens, I mean Singapore. It's about 1954 over here. You get arrested for jaywalking, littering, and spitting on the street. You ever go to one of those towns out West where they reenact gunfights? Where the falls are all rehearsed and the guns have no bullets and nobody gets hurt?"

"Aw, come *on*," Conor said.

"I have a feeling that's Boogey Street," Beevers said.

"Let's find the torture chamber," Poole said, and Conor laughed out loud.

On the crown of the hill, with a view down across the terraces and ornaments of the garden, stood a giant brain of gnarled, twisted blue plaster. A white sign announced in red letters: TORTURE CHAMBER HERE. "Hey, this doesn't look so bad," Beevers said. "I ought to get pictures of this." He took his Instamatic out of his pocket and checked the number on the back. Then he went up the low concrete steps and through the entrance. Winking at Poole, Conor followed.

The cool, shady interior of the plaster grotto had been divided in half by a walkway from which one looked down through wire fences at a sequence of busy scenes. When Poole stepped inside, his friends were already well along, Beevers snapping shot after shot with his camera up to his eye. Most of the Chinese in the Torture Chamber stared at the tableaux beneath them without betraying any feeling at all. A few children chattered and pointed.

"Great, great stuff," Beevers said.

CHAMBER OF BOULDERS, read a plaque before the first scene. THE FIRST COURT. From between the halves of a giant slablike boulder protruded the heads, legs, trunks, arms of people eternally crushed to death. Claw-footed demons in robes pulled screeching children toward the boulder.

In the SECOND COURT, horned devils pierced sinners with huge pronged forks and held them over flames. Another demon ripped the stomach and intestines from an agonized man. Others hurled children into a long pool of blood.

A blue demon sliced off the tongue of a man tied to a stake.

Poole wandered along the path between the exhibits, hearing Harry Beevers' camera clicking, clicking away.

Grinning devils cut women in half, sliced men into sections, boiled screaming sinners in vats of oil, grilled them against red hot pillars. . . .

Conscious—nearly conscious—of another memory hidden beneath this one, Poole found himself remembering the emergency ward where during his internship he had spent too much time tying blood vessels and cleaning wounds, listening to screams and moans and curses, attending to people with their faces cut to pieces by knives or windshields, people who had nearly killed themselves with drugs . . .

. . . *sell me some of that fuckin' morphine, Doc?* a young Puerto Rican in a blood-soaked T-shirt asked him while he frantically sutured a long wound with baseball stitches, sweating as the addict's blood pooled around him . . .

. . . blood everywhere, blood on the concrete slab, blood on the rocks, severed arms and legs on the floor, naked men hung split open by the knives sprouting from an evil tree . . .

"Clean out of my eyesight, man," Poole heard Conor say. "Hey, Mikey, these guys really believed in survival and fitness, huh?" Survival and fitness? He realized that Conor meant survival of the fittest.

Why did Beevers want pictures of this stuff?

He heard the screaming of a long-dead soldier named Cal Hill and heard Dengler's funny, snide Midwestern voice saying *Don't you think God does all things simultaneously?*

Dengler was right, God did all things simultaneously.

Every day of those months, Poole had forced himself to go to work. He had forced himself out of bed, into the drizzle of the shower, pulled himself into his clothes, grimly started his car, struggled into his scrub suit in a depression almost too total to be seen. He had gone for days without speaking to anyone. Judy had attributed his gloom, silence, and buried rage to the stresses and miseries of the emergency room, to the presence of people dying literally under his hand, to the abuse pouring out of everyone around him. . . .

Sweating in the cool shade of the plaster cave, Poole moved a few paces along. A woman wearing the white hide of a rabbit on her back and a man covered by a pig's coarse hide knelt before an imperious judge. Poole remembered the rabbit Ernie's mild beautiful fearful eyes. Other figures busied themselves around them. A monster aimed a spear, a scribe wrote on an eternal scroll. Almost exactly a year later, during his pediatric residency at

Columbia-Presbyterian Hospital in New York, Poole had finally understood.

And here it was again, that place, in a plaster brain on top of a hill in Singapore.

The Tenth Court

> For human souls destined to be reborn as a beast and other lower forms of life, they are provided by the court with the necessary coverings such as fur, hide, feathers, or scales before entering the whirlpool of fate, in order that the eternal souls may take a definite shape.

Poole heard Beevers laughing to himself outside the grotto.

He wiped his forehead and walked outside into a blast of heat and a blinding dazzle of sunlight. Harry Beevers stood before him, grinning with all his overlapping teeth.

A little way down the hill lay a huge pit filled with plaster replicas of giant blue-green crabs. Big black toads stared fixedly out through the mesh. In another brain-grotto on the other side of the path a giant woman with a chicken's head and corpse-white arms yanked at the arm of her husband, who had the wattled head of a duck. Poole saw murder in the woman's determination, the duck-man's alarm. Marriage was murder.

Beevers snapped off another picture. "This is great," he said, and turned around to focus on the giant wrinkled brain they had just left. TORTURE CHAMBER HERE.

"There are girls in New York," Beevers said, "who will go crazy when they see these pictures. You don't think that's right? There are girls in New York who'd go down on Gabby Hayes if he showed them this stuff."

Conor Linklater strolled away laughing.

"You think I don't know what I'm talking about?" His voice was too loud. "Ask Pumo—he hangs out where I hang out, he knows."

4

After they left the Tiger Balm Gardens they walked for a long time without quite knowing where they were or where they were going. "Maybe we should go back to the Gardens," Conor said. "This is nowhere."

It was nearly a literal, though a peaceful, nowhere. They were walking uphill along a smooth grey road between a high bank covered with perfectly mown grass and a long slope dotted with bungalows set at wide intervals amongst the trees. Since leaving the Gardens the only human being they had seen had been a uniformed chauffeur in sunglasses driving an otherwise empty black Mercedes Benz 500 SEL.

"We must have walked over a mile already," Beevers said. He had torn the map out of *Papineau's Guide*, and was turning it over and over in his hands. "You can turn back by yourself if you want to. There'll be something at the top of this hill. Pretty soon Frankie Avalon and Annette Funicello will drive by in a woodie. Goddamn, I can't find where we are on the fucking map." He almost immediately stopped walking and stared at a certain point on the misleading map. "That stupid shit Underhill."

"Why?" Conor asked.

"Boogey Street isn't Boogey Street. That dodo didn't know what he was talking about. It's B-U-G-I-S Street. Boo-giss Street. That has to be it, there isn't anything else even close."

"But I thought the cabdriver . . . ?"

"It's still Boo-giss Street, it says so right here." He looked up with wild eyes. "If Underhill didn't know where he was going, how the hell does he expect us to find him?"

They trudged further uphill and came to an intersection without roadsigns. Beevers resolutely turned right and began marching off. Conor protested that the center of town and their hotel were the other way, but Beevers continued walking until they gave in and joined him.

Half an hour later an amazed-looking taxi driver stopped and picked them up.

"Marco Polo Hotel," Beevers said. He was breathing heavily, and his face had become so mottled Poole could not tell if it was pink flecked with white, or white flecked with pink. A sweat stain shaped like a torpedo darkened the back of his jacket from shoulder to shoulder and extended a damp fin down to the small of his back. "I have to have a shower and a nap."

"Why you going in opposite direction?" the driver asked.

Beevers refused to speak.

"Hey, we got a little bet going," Conor said. "Is it Boo-giss Street or Boogey Street?"

"Is same thing," the driver said.

15

MEETING LOLA IN THE PARK

1

As far as Conor was concerned, this whole Bugis Street deal stank. Fifty feet from its entrance, where the cab-driver from the restaurant had pointed to it, Bugis Street looked just right for a guy like Underhill. Lots of flashing lights, bar signs, neon, crowds of people milling around. But once you were actually there, you saw who those people were and you knew that Tim Underhill wouldn't go anywhere near them. White-haired ladies with leathery, saggy upper arms holding hands with turtle-faced old parties in baggy shorts and Supp-Hose. They had the lost, childlike air of tourists anywhere, as if what they were looking at were no more real than a television commercial. About half the people Conor could see walking up and down Bugis Street had clearly arrived in the JASMINE FAR EAST TOUR buses parked outside the entrance to the street. Way up above everybody's heads, a pale blue flag drooped from the top of a long pole held by a breezy young blonde woman in a crisp, starched-looking blazer of the same pale blue.

If this bunch of ham and eggers came traipsing through South Norwalk, Conor knew he wouldn't be able to ignore them the way the other half of the people on Bugis Street were doing. Shifty-looking little guys darted in and out of the bars and shops. Pairs of whores in wigs and tight dresses strutted up and down the street. If you were a player in Singapore, this is where you came—Conor guessed that they had developed selective vision, and no longer really saw the tourists.

Conor could hear the Stones' "Jumping Jack Flash" drilling through some slow-moving cowboy song from Porter Waggoner, both of them battling the strange caterwauling of what must have been a Chinese opera—screechy voices beating up a melody that would give a headache to a dog. This noise was piped out of different bars through little speakers set above the doors, usually right above the head of a beckoning doorman. The whole thing gave Conor a headache. Probably the brandy after their dinner at the Pine Court didn't help, even if it was XO, which Harry Beevers claimed was liquid gold. Feeling as if cymbals were being slammed together next to his ears, Conor walked along behind Beevers and Mike Poole.

"Might as well start right here," Mike said, turning toward the first bar on their side of the street, the Orient Song. The doorman straightened up as they approached and began waving them in with both arms. "Orient Song your bar," he yelled. "Come to Orient Song! Best bar on Bugis Street! Americans all come here!"

Near the door a little old man in a dirty white smock twitched into life. He grinned, showing sparse yellow teeth, and swept his arm theatrically toward the display of framed photographs next to him.

They were eight-by-twelve glossies, black and white, with names printed in the white space just above the bottom of the frame. Dawn, Rose, Hotlips, Raven, Billie Blue . . . parted lips and arched necks, sex-drenched Oriental faces framed in soft black hair, plucked eyebrows above willful eyes.

"Four dollars," the old man said.

Harry Beevers grabbed Conor's forearm and pulled him through the heavy door. Cold air-conditioned air chilled the sweat on Conor's forehead, and he yanked his arm out of Beevers' grasp. Americans, paired like Mallard ducks, turned smiling toward them from their stations near the bar.

"No luck here," Beevers said. "This is just a tour bus joint. The first bar on the street is the only one these yo-yos feel safe in."

Poole said, "Let's ask anyhow."

At least the entire front half of the bar was taken up by American couples in their sixties and seventies. Conor could dimly hear someone banging chords on a piano. Out of the general hum of voices Conor heard a female voice calling someone Son and asking where his nametag was. He eventually realized that she was addressing him.

"You gotta get the spirit, boy, you gotta wear the tag. We're a fun bunch!" Conor looked down at the sun-tanned, heavily wrinkled face of a woman beaming at him and wearing a nametag which read HI! ETHEL'S A JAUNTY JASMINE!

Conor looked over her head. Behind her a couple of old boys in rimless glasses who looked like the doctors on the flight over were checking him out less benevolently—he was wearing his Agent Orange T-shirt, and did not resemble a Jaunty Jasmine.

He saw Beevers and Poole approaching the bar, where a stocky man wearing a velvet bow tie was serving drinks, washing glasses, and talking out of the side of his mouth all at once. He reminded Conor of Jimmy Lah. The back of the bar was another world. On the far side of all the Jasmines, parties of Chinese men sat around round tables drinking brandy from magnums, shouting jokes at one another, and desultorily talking with the girls who drifted by their tables. Far at the back a black-haired man in a tuxedo who looked neither Chinese nor Caucasian sat at a baby grand, singing words Conor could not hear.

He squeezed past the woman, who went on mouthing cheerful meaningless sounds, and got to the bar just as Mikey took one of the photographs of Underhill out of the envelope. "Let's have a drink, what d'you say, gimme a vodka on the rocks."

The bartender blinked, and a brimming glass appeared on the bar before Conor. Beevers already had one, Conor saw.

"Don't know him," the bartender said. "Five dollars."

"Maybe you remember him from years back," Beevers said. "He would have started coming here around 1969, '70, around then."

"Too long ago. I was little boy. Still in school. Wif da priests."

"Take another look," Beevers said.

The bartender removed the picture from Poole's fingers and flipped it over his shoulder. "He is a priest. Named Father Ballcock. I don't know him."

As soon as they got back out onto the humid street, Harry Beevers took a step ahead of the other two and faced them with his hands in his pockets and his shoulders raised. "I don't care, I have to say it. I get the wrong vibes entirely from this place. There isn't a chance in hell that Underhill's still here. My gut tells me to go to Taipei—it's more like his kind of place. Take my word for it."

Poole laughed. "Not so fast, we just got started. There are at least twenty more bars on this street. Somewhere along the line, someone will know him."

"Yeah, someone has to know him," Conor said. He felt more confident of this after having put down his vodka.

"Ah, the peanut gallery has an opinion too," Beevers said.

"You got your rocks off in Taipei, so you want to go back there now," Conor said. "It's so fucking obvious." He stomped away to avoid hitting Beevers. Cries of "Best bar! Best bar!" erupted from various doormen. Conor felt his shirt sticking to his back.

"So it's Swingtime next, is it?" Beevers had come up on the far side of Mike Poole, and Conor felt a little flare of satisfaction: Beevers wasn't taking any chances with him.

"Yeah, let's try out good old Swingtime," Poole said.

Beevers made an ironic little bow, pushed open the door, and let the other two precede him into the bar.

After Swingtime came the Windjammer, after the Windjammer the Ginza, the Floating Dragon, and the Bucket of Blood. The Bucket of Blood was a real bucket of blood, Conor thought—that had been his father's term for any dive with rickety stools and ripped booths, a floor too scummy to be visible, and crapped-out drunks lining the bar. Beevers groaned when one of the shambling drunks followed another into the cubicle that was the men's room and, to judge by the noise, began tearing his arms out by the sockets. The flat-faced bartender just glanced at the photograph of Underhill.

Conor understood why the Jaunty Jasmines stayed down at the end of the street.

Harry Beevers looked like he wanted to suggest giving up and going back to the hotel, but Poole kept them moving from one bar to another. Conor admired the way he kept on going without getting discouraged.

At the Bullfrog the guys sitting around the tables were so drunk they looked like statues. There were moving pictures of waterfalls on the walls. At the Cockpit Conor finally noticed that at least half the whores in the place weren't women at all. They had bony knees and big shoulders; they were men. He started laughing—men with big tits and good-looking cans!—and sprayed beer all over disgusted Harry Beevers.

"I know this guy," the bartender said. He looked again at Underhill's face, and started smiling.

"See?" Conor asked. "See now?" Beevers turned away, wiping his sleeve.

"Does he come in here?" Mike asked.

"No, other place I worked. Good-time Charlie. Buy everybody a drink!"

"You sure it's the same man?"

"Sure, that's Undahill. He was around for a couple years, back in the old days. Spend lots of money. Used to come in da Floating Dragon, before it change hands. I worked nights, see him alla time. Talk, talk, talk. Drink, drink, drink. Real writah! Show me a book, something about animal—"

"A Beast in View."

"Beast, right."

When Poole asked if he knew where Underhill was now, the man shook his head and said that everything had changed from the old days. "Might ask at Mountjoy, right across street. Real hard core over there. Probably be someone there who remembers Undahill from old days, like me."

"You liked him, didn't you?"

"For a long time," the bartender said. "Sure, I liked Undahill for a long time."

2

Conor felt uneasy almost as soon as they walked into the Lord and Lady Mountjoy, and he couldn't figure out why. It was a quiet place. Sober men in dark suits and white shirts sat in booths along the sides of the room or at little square tables set out on a slippery-looking parquet dance floor.

There were no transient whores in this place, just guys in suits and ties, and one character in a glittery blouse, sprayed piled-up hair, and about a hundred scarves hung loose around his neck, who was cooling out at a back table.

"Loosen up, for God's sake," Beevers said to Conor. "You got the runs or something?"

"Don't know him, never saw him," the bartender said. He had barely glanced at the photograph. He looked like a young Chinese version of Curly, the bald stooge in the Three Stooges.

"The bartender across the street told us that this man used to frequent this place," Beevers said, pushing himself against the bar. "We're detectives from New York City, and it's important to a lot of people that we find this man."

"Bartender where?" When Beevers had said the word "detective" a lead shield had slammed down over the bartender's face, making him look a lot less like Curly.

"The Cockpit," Mike said. He gave a fierce sidelong glance at Beevers, who shrugged and began toying with an ashtray.

The bartender shrugged.

"Is there anyone here who might remember this man? Anyone who was around Bugis Street in those days?"

"Billy," the bartender said. "He's been here since they paved the street."

Conor's heart sank. He knew who Billy was, all right, and he really didn't want to have to talk to him.

"In da back," the bartender said, and confirmed Conor's fears. "Buy him a drink, he's friendly."

"Yeah, he looks friendly," Beevers said.

At the back table Billy had straightened his shoulders and was patting his hair. When they approached his table, carrying their own drinks and a double Chivas Regal, he put his hands in his lap and beamed at them.

"Oh, you bought me a little drinkie, how dear of you," Billy said.

Billy wasn't Chinese, but he wasn't anything else either, Conor thought. His eyes might have been almond-shaped, but it was hard to see them under all the makeup.

Billy's skin was very pale and he spoke with a British accent. All of his gestures suggested that a woman had been trapped inside his body and on the whole was enjoying herself in there. He raised his drink to his lips, sipped, and set it down gently on the table.

"I hope you gentlemen are going to join me?"

Mike Poole sat down opposite Billy, and Harry Beevers drew up a chair beside him. Conor had to sit on the bench beside Billy, who turned his head and flicked his eyelashes in his direction.

"Are you gentlemen new to Bugis Street? Your first night in Singapore, perhaps? You are looking for entertainment of an exotic nature? Precious little left in our city, I fear. Never mind—anyone can find what he wants, if he knows where to look."

Another lidded glance at squirming Conor.

"We're looking for someone," Poole said.

"We're—" Beevers began, and then looked up in astonishment at Poole, who had just stamped on his foot.

Poole said, "The young man at the bar thought you might be our best chance. The person we're looking for lived or still lives in Singapore, and spent a lot of time on this street ten to fifteen years ago."

"Long time ago," Billy said. He cast his eyes down, tilted his head. "This person have a name?"

"Tim Underhill," Poole said. He placed one of the photographs beside Billy's drink. Billy blinked.

"Does he look familiar?"

"He might."

Poole pushed a Singapore ten-dollar note across the table and Billy twinkled it away. "I believe I did know the gentleman." Billy made an elaborate business of scrutinizing the photograph. "He was a bit of a *one,* wasn't he?"

"We're old friends of his," Mike said. "We think he might need our help. That's why we're here. We'd appreciate any information you could give us."

"Oh, everything's changed since those days," Billy said. "The whole street—really, you'd hardly know it." He moodily inspected the photograph for a moment. "Flowers. He was the man for flowers, wasn't he? Flowers this and flowers that. He'd been a soldier in the war."

Poole nodded. "We met him in Vietnam."

"Beautiful place, once," Billy said. "Free-wheeling."

He startled Conor by asking, "Did you ever see Saigon, lover?"

Conor nodded and gulped down a mouthful of vodka.

"Some of our best girls used to work there. Nearly all gone now. The wind shifted. Got too cold for them. Can't blame them, can you?"

Nobody said anything.

"Well, I say you can't. They lived for pleasure, for delight, for illusion. Can't blame them for not wanting to start grubbing away at some job, can you? So they scattered. Most of the best of our old friends went to Amsterdam. They were always welcome in their own very elegant clubs—the Kit Kat Club. You gentlemen ever see the Kit Kat Club?"

"What about Underhill?" Beevers asked.

"All mirrors, three stages, crystal chandeliers, best of everything. It's often been described to me. There's nothing like the Kit Kat in Paris, or so I hear."

He sipped his scotch.

Conor said, "Look, do you know where we can find Underhill, or are we just dicking around?"

Another of Billy's silken smiles. "A few of the entertainers who worked here are still in Singapore. You might try to see Lola perform. She works good clubs, not these remnants left on Bugis Street." He paused. "She's *vivacious*. You'd enjoy her act.

3

Four days earlier, Tina Pumo was interrupted by Maggie Lah's giggling over the front page of the *New York Post* while they ate breakfast together at La Groceria. (Tina was sentimentally attached to the little restaurant where he had so often read and reread the back page of the *Village Voice*.) They had each purchased newspapers at the newsstand on Sixth Avenue, and Tina was deep into the *Times*'s restaurant reviews when Maggie's laughter distracted him. "Something funny in that rag?"

"They have such great headlines," Maggie said, and turned the tabloid toward him: YUPPIE AIRPORT MURDER. "Random word order," Maggie said. "How about AIRPORT YUPPIE MURDER? Or YUPPIE MURDER AIRPORT? Anyhow, it's always nice to read about the end of a yup."

Tina eventually found the story in the *Times*'s Metropolitan section. Clement W. Irwin, 29, an investment banker whose income was in the upper six figures and was regarded as a "superstar" by his peers, had been found stabbed to death in a men's room near the Pan American baggage counters at JFK airport. Maggie's paper carried a photograph of a blubbery face with small, widely set eyes behind heavy black eyeglasses. Equal amounts of appetite and aggression seemed stamped into the features. The caption read: *Yuppie financial whiz Clement W. Irwin.* On the inside pages were photographs of a townhouse on East 63rd Street, a manor on Mount Avenue in Hampstead, Connecticut, and a low, rambling beach house on the island of St. Maarten. The story in the *Post*, but not the *Times*, contained the speculation that Irwin had been murdered by either an airport employee or a fellow passenger who had been on his flight from San Francisco.

3

The morning after his tour of the Bugis Street bars, Conor Linklater swallowed two aspirin and a third of a bottle of Pepto-Bismol, showered, dressed in jeans and a short-sleeved shirt, and then joined the other two in the Marco Polo's coffee shop.

"What kept you?" Beevers said. He and Michael were garbaging down on the weirdest-looking breakfast Conor had ever seen. They had toast and eggs and that stuff, but they also had bowls of gooey white pasty porridge full of green and yellow shit and fatty evil things that would have looked like eggs if they hadn't been green. Both Mike and Beevers seemed to have taken no more than a bite or two of this substance.

"Little rocky this morning, think I'll pass on breakfast," Conor said. "What is that stuff, anyhow?"

"Don't ask," Beevers said.

Mike asked, "Are you sick, or just hung over?"

"Both, I guess."

"Diarrhea?"

"I chugged down a ton of Pepto-Bismol." The waiter came up, and he ordered coffee. "*American* coffee."

Beevers smiled at him and pushed a folded copy of the

Straits Times across the table. "Take a look and tell me what you think."

Conor scanned headlines about new sewage treatment plants, about the increase of bank loans to nonbank customers, the expected overload of bridge traffic on the New Year's holiday, and finally saw this headline in the middle of the page: DOUBLE HOMICIDE IN EMPTY BUNGALOW.

An American journalist named Roberto Ortiz, Conor read, had been found slain in a bungalow on Plantation Road. Also found was the body of a young woman identified only as a Malaysian prostitute. Forensic pathologists stated that the corpses, found in a state of putrefaction, had been dead approximately ten days. The bungalow was the property of Professor Li Lau Feng, who had left it vacant for a year while he taught at the University of Jakarta. Mr. Ortiz's body had been mutilated after death from gunshot wounds. The unidentified woman had also died of gunshot wounds. Mr. Ortiz was a journalist and the author of two books, *Beggar Thy Neighbor: United States Policy in Honduras* and *Vietnam: A Personal Journey*. Police were said to have evidence linking this crime to several others committed in Singapore during the past year.

"What kind of evidence?" Conor asked.

"I bet they found Koko cards," Beevers said. "They're finally getting cagey. You think they'd release a detail like that if it happened in New York? Don't be crazy. *Mutilated,* it says. What do you want to bet his eyes were poked out and his ears were cut off? Underhill's at work, my friends. We came to the right place."

"Jesus," Conor said. "So what do we do? I thought we were going to, ah, look for this, ah . . ."

"We are," Poole said. "I got all the papers and guidebooks in the gift shop, and we were just about to try to find out where this Lola works, if she is working. The clerks in the shop won't admit to ever having heard of anybody named Lola, so we have to do it this way."

"But this morning," Beevers said, "we thought we ought to look at the places where they found the other bodies. The bungalow where they found the Martinsons, and this one, and the Goodwood Park Hotel."

"Should we maybe talk to the police? Find out if there were cards with these other people?"

"I don't feel like turning Underhill over to the police,"

Beevers said. "Do you? I mean, is that what we came here for?"

"We still don't know it's Underhill," Poole said. "We don't even know he's still in Singapore."

"You don't shit in your backyard. You got it now, Michael?"

Poole was going page by page through the *Straits Times.*

"Here's Underhill right now," Conor said. "He still wears that funky old bandanna. He's fat as a pig. He gets stoned out of his gourd every single night. He owns a flower shop. All these young guys work for him, and he bores the shit out of them when he talks about all the stuff he did in Nam. Everybody loves the old ratbag."

"Dream on," Beevers said.

Poole had gone on to another paper, and was flipping pages with the regularity of a metronome.

"Every now and then he goes into his study or whatever, locks the door, and sweats out a new chapter."

"Every now and then he locks himself in an abandoned building and kills the shit out of somebody."

"Are those eggs really a hundred years old?" Conor asked. He had picked up the menu while Beevers spoke. "What's the green shit?"

"Tea," Poole said.

Ten minutes later Poole found a small advertisement for "The Fabulous Lola" in *Singapore After Dark*, one of the cheap guides to Singapore's night life he had picked up in the gift shop. Lola was appearing at a nightclub called Peppermint City at an address up in the ten thousands out on a road too far from the center of the city to be on Beevers' map.

All three men stared at a tiny black and white photograph of a girlish male Chinese with plucked eyebrows and high teased hair.

"I don't feel too good already," Conor said. He had turned as green as a century egg, and Poole made him promise that he would spend the day in his room and see the hotel doctor.

4

Michael did not know what he expected to learn from the murder sites any more than he could anticipate what Lola might tell him, but seeing the places where the deaths occurred would help him to see the deaths themselves.

He and Beevers walked in less than ten minutes to the villa on Nassim Hill where the Martinsons had been found.

"Picked a nice place, at least," Beevers said.

Surrounded by trees, the villa stood on a little rise in the land. With its red roof tiles, golden plaster, and big windows, it might have been one of the pretty houses Michael had seen from the window of his hotel the previous morning. Nothing about it suggested that two people had been murdered there.

Poole and Beevers walked through the trees to shade their eyes and peered into a room like a long rectangular cave. In the middle of the wooden floor, thick with balls of dust like dirty cotton, as if someone had pitched brown paint onto the floor and then made a half-hearted attempt to clean it up, was a wide eccentric stain surrounded by dots and splashes.

Then Poole realized that a third shadowy reflection had fallen between his own and Beevers', and he jumped, feeling like a child caught stealing. "Please excuse me," a man said. "I did not mean to startle."

He was a massive Chinese in a black silk suit and gleaming black tasseled loafers. "You are interested in the house?"

"Are you the owner?" Poole asked. He seemed to have appeared from nowhere, like a well-dressed ghost.

"I am not only the owner, I am the neighbor!" He swept his arm sideways toward another villa just a short distance up the hillside but barely visible through the trees. "When I saw you walk up, I thought to protect against vandalism. Sometimes young people come here to use the empty building—young people same all over, correct?" He laughed in a series of flat hollow barks. "When I see you, I know you are not vandals."

"Of course we're not vandals," Beevers said a little testily. He looked at Poole and decided not to say that they were New York City detectives. "We were friends of the people who died here, and since we came here on a tour, we decided to take a look at the place where it happened."

"Very unfortunate," the man said. "Your loss is my loss."

"Very kind," Poole said.

"I am speaking commercially. Since the event, nobody wants to look at the house. And if they did, we could not let them in to show it because the police have sealed it!" He pointed out the rain-spattered yellow notice and the seal on the front door. "We cannot even wash away the bloodstains! Oh, excuse me, please, I did not think! I regret what happened to your friends, and I do sympathize with your grief." He straightened up, and took a few steps backward in embarrassment. "It is cold in St. Louis now? You are enjoying the Singapore weather?"

"You didn't hear anything?" Beevers asked.

"Not on that night. Otherwise, I heard things many times."

"Many times?" Poole asked.

"Heard him for weeks. A teenager. Never much noise. Just one boy who slipped in and out at night like a shadow. Never caught him."

"But you saw him?"

"Once. From the back. I came down from my house and saw him walking through the hibiscus trees. I called to him, but he did not stop. Would you? He was small—just a boy. I called the police, but they could not find him to keep him out. I locked the place, but he always found a way back in."

"He was Chinese?"

"Of course. At least I assumed he was—I only saw him from the back."

"Do you think he committed the murders?" Poole asked.

"I don't know. I doubt it, but I don't know. He seemed so harmless."

"What did you mean, you *heard* him?" Beevers asked.

"I heard him singing to himself."

"What did he sing?" Poole asked.

"A song in a foreign language," the man said. "It was not any dialect of Chinese, and it was not French or English—I have often wondered if it was Polish! It went . . . oh . . ." He burst out laughing. "It went 'rip-a-rip-a-rip-a-lo.' " He sang the words almost tunelessly and laughed again. "So melancholy. Two or three times I heard the song coming from this house while I sat in my courtyard in the evening. I came down here as quietly as I could, but he always heard me coming and hid until I left." He paused. "In the end, I accepted him."

"You accepted a housebreaker?" Beevers asked.

"I came to think of the boy as a sort of pet. After all, he lived here like a little animal. He did no damage, and he sang his lonely little song. *Rip-a-rip-a-rip-a-lo.*"

He seemed a little forlorn. Poole tried to imagine an American tycoon looking forlorn in a black silk suit and tasseled loafers, but failed.

"He must have left before the murders." The man looked at his watch. "Anything else?"

He waved good-bye as they walked back down to Nassim Hill and was still waving when they turned toward Orchard Road to find a cab.

They saw where the body of Clive McKenna had been discovered as soon as their cabdriver pointed out the Goodwood Park Hotel. The white hotel stood on a rise that looked down toward the fringes of the city's business district and the land fell away in a steep green slope. When the cab dropped them off, Poole and Beevers walked through a fringe of shrubbery and looked down the hill. Some tough, dark green plant like myrtle covered it, and low hedges grew at intervals.

"He lured him here," Beevers said. "They probably met at the bar. Let's go out for some fresh air. In goes the knife. Good-bye, Clive. I wonder—I wonder if we can find out anything interesting at the desk." Beevers sounded very cheerful, almost as if he were celebrating the murder.

Inside, Beevers asked, "Was a Mr. Underhill registered here around the time Mr. McKenna was killed?" He held a ten-dollar note folded into his palm.

The clerk bent over and pushed buttons on the computer terminal set beneath the registration desk. He dismayed Michael Poole by reporting that a Mr. Timothy Underhill had been expected six days before the discovery of Clive McKenna's body, but had not arrived to claim his room.

"Bingo," Beevers said, and the desk clerk reached for the bill. Beevers pulled his hand out of reach. "Do you have an address for Underhill?"

"Sure," the clerk said. "Fifty-six Grand Street, New York City."

"How did he make the reservation?"

"No record. It must have come in by telephone. We have no credit card number."

"No record of where he called from?"

The clerk shook his head.

"Not good enough." Beevers snatched back the note and smirked at Michael.

They went back out into the sun.

"Why would he use his real name if he was paying in cash?" Michael asked.

"Michael, he was so high he thought he could get away with anything. He's a shake 'n' bake, Michael—killing people is not logical behavior. This man is drooling at the mouth and you want to know why he uses his real name! See how I saved ten bucks?" Beevers nodded to the doorman, who whistled to the rank of waiting cabs.

"You know," Poole said, "I have the feeling I've heard that address, 56 Grand Street, before. It seems so familiar."

"Jesus, Michael."

"What is it?"

"Pumo's restaurant, dumbo. Saigon is at 56 Grand Street. In the City of New York in the State of New York in the United States of America."

Plantation Road began with a tall hotel at the corner of a busy six-lane road and almost instantly became a comfortable upper-middle-class enclave of long low bungalows behind wide lawns and locked gates. When they came to number 72, Beevers told the driver to wait and the two men left the cab.

The bungalow where Roberto Ortiz and the woman had died stood out in the sunlight like a pink cake. Flowering hibiscus trees grew on either side, their shadows floating over the dark lawn. A clean yellow notice had been wired to the gates, announcing that the Singapore Police Department had sealed the house for the purposes of a homicide investigation. Two dark blue police cars were pulled up before the gates, and Poole could see uniforms moving past the windows inside the house.

"You noticed yet how good-looking the policewomen

are in this country?" Beevers asked. "I wonder if they'd let us inside?"

"Why don't you tell them that you're a detective from New York?" Poole said.

"I'm an officer of the court, that's why," Beevers said.

Poole turned around to look at the house across the street. A middle-aged Chinese woman stood at a living room window with her arm around the waist of a younger, taller woman with her right hand on her hip. Both women looked very tense. Poole wondered if they had ever heard a young man singing a strange song that sounded like *rip-a-rip-a-rip-a-lo.*

Poole and Harry Beevers returned to the Marco Polo and found a frowsy, red-eyed Conor Linklater who reminded Michael of Dwight Frye in *Dracula*. The hotel had given him the name of a doctor in the building next door, and Poole and Beevers helped him into the elevator and out into the sunlight. "I can come with you tonight, Mikey," he said. "This is a real temporary thing."

"You are staying home tonight," Poole said.

"Yeah, count me out too," Beevers said. "I'm too beat to chase around to another fag bar. I'll stay home and tell Conor what we did all day."

They were moving unsteadily down the sidewalk, Michael and Beevers on either side of Conor, who took little shuffling steps, afraid to risk walking normally.

Beevers said, "In a couple of years, we'll be sitting in a screening room, watching ourselves do this. Half the people in the world will know that Conor Linklater had the runs. I wish Sean Connery were twenty years younger. It's really too bad that all the right actors are too old now."

"Olivier really is too old, I guess," Michael said.

"I mean guys like Greg Peck, Dick Widmark, guys like that. Paul Newman's too short, and Robert Redford's too bland. Maybe they ought to go for the intensity and get James Woods. I could live with that."

5

The taxi wound through Singapore until it struck a belt road and then it went so far that Poole began to wonder if the nightclub was in Malaysia. Before long the only lights close at hand were the arc lamps above the six-lane highway. Dark empty land lay on both sides of the road, here and there punctuated by small isolated clusters of lights. They were nearly alone on the road and the driver was going very fast. It seemed to Poole that the wheels were not actually touching the road.

"Are we still in Singapore?" he asked. The driver did not respond.

Eventually the car jerked off the highway onto an access road to a shopping mall that gleamed like a space station in the darkness—longer, taller, and more elaborate than any of the shopping centers on Orchard Road. A vast, nearly empty parking lot surrounded it. Huge vertical posters covered with Chinese letters the size of a man hung down the sides of the mall. A rank of palm trees hung frozen in the white artificial light.

"Are you sure this is where Peppermint City is?" Poole asked.

The driver braked to an abrupt halt before the undead palm trees and sat behind the wheel like a statue. When Poole hesitantly repeated his question, the man bawled out something in Chinese.

"How much?"

The man yelled the same phrase.

Poole handed over a bill whose denomination he could not see, received a surprising amount of change, and tipped with another random bill. When the cab took off he was alone.

The mall seemed to have been constructed of dull grey metal. Through huge windows on the ground floor Poole could see two or three tiny figures wandering past closed shops far down at the mall's opposite end.

Glass doors whooshed open and cold air enveloped him. The doors sealed up behind him. Goose bumps rose on his arms.

Before him a vacant corridor led to a vast high-vaulted space. Poole felt as if he had entered an empty church. Mannequins posed and stretched in the display windows of closed shops. Invisible escalators whirred. God had gone home and the cathedral was as empty as a bomb crater. As Poole passed into the great vault, he saw a few scattered people moving in a waking trance across the mezzanine, past darkened rows of shops.

Poole wandered through the ground floor of the mall,

certain that the driver had taken him to the wrong place. For a long time he could not even find the escalator, and thought he would have to drift all night past Good Fortune Toys, Merlion Furniture, and Mode O'Day, Clothes for Discriminating Women. Finally he turned a corner at a restaurant called Captain Steak and saw the wizened baseball-capped head of an elderly Chinese man floating downwards toward him above the escalator's steel flank.

On the third level his feet began to ache—the floor was flat, unyielding stone. Red and orange sweatshirts, trapped birds, hung in a black window. Poole sighed and kept on walking. Could he get a taxi back to town, way out here? He felt that nobody would speak to him and he would never be able to make himself understood. He understood why George Romero had filmed *Dawn of the Dead* in a shopping mall.

This was Singapore at its most sterile and perfect. Randomness, dirt, and vitality had been ruthlessly excluded. Michael wished he were back at the Marco Polo, getting drunk with Beevers and watching the finance programs and soap operas that made up Singapore television.

On the fifth level he walked, disheartened, down corridors even darker and emptier than those on the floors below. Up here, not a single shop or restaurant remained open. He was on the fifth floor of a suburban shopping mall, and he had been stranded miles out of town. Then, at the curve of the corridor, the dark shop windows gave way to walls covered with small white tiles that shone with the light from a row of angled spots. Through an opening in the wall, Poole saw men in suits, girls in tight cocktail dresses, everybody smoking in hazy blue light. A good-looking hostess stood at a desk and smiled at him while speaking into a telephone. Just outside the entrance a pink neon sign flashed PEPPERMINT CITY! beside a leafless tree which had been painted white and hung with tiny white bulbs.

Poole went through the entrance and the shopping mall disappeared. Fanning out before and below him was an enormous fantasy that looked like tea time on the grounds of a Mississippi plantation. On the other side of the desk, hostesses led couples down to ranks of round white tables of ornate cast iron, and seated them on white cast-iron ice-cream chairs. The floor and walls had been painted flat black. Other ice-cream chairs and tables sat on the mezzanine and risers on both sides of a busy, crowded bar. In the middle of the floor, surrounded by the tables, a boy in an illuminated fountain spouted water from his mouth.

The woman at the desk led him to a small white table on a platform beyond the bar. Poole ordered a beer. Young homosexual couples who wore suits and looked like MIT graduate students shuffled around on a small dance floor in front of the stage. Other couples like them occupied most of the seats in the club—boys in round glasses gripping cigarettes and trying not to look self-conscious. Scattered through the club were a few Englishmen and Americans earnestly making conversation with their Chinese and Eurasian escorts. Most of the couples drank champagne, most of the boys, beer.

A few minutes later the quiet music suddenly ceased. The boys dancing in front of the stage grinned and applauded as they went toward their seats. The telephone rang very loudly, and the cash register went *bing!*, and a few voices obliviously rose up before they, too, ceased.

Four chunky Filipinos, one Eurasian, and a slender Chinese boy bounced onto the stage. From the opposite side, a stagehand pushed on a bulky synthesizer and rolled it past the drums. All the musicians but the Chinese were dressed alike in blousy yellow shirts and tight red velvet vest-and-trouser outfits. They carried their instruments onstage with them—two guitars, a conga drum, an electric bass—and began playing a bland, processed version of "Billie Jean" as soon as the drummer and keyboard player had reached their instruments. The Eurasian and the keyboard player had short curly hair and sunglasses like Michael Jackson, and the others had John Lennon's droopy hair, round glasses, and sly sidelong glances. It was clear that they had been a band long before Lola hired them: Poole imagined that if he came back to Singapore in twenty years, he would see the same musicians grown older and paunchier, no less mechanical, and probably in the same clothes.

It was Michael Jackson's year, and Lola too had adopted the mass of curls and sunglasses, as well as a single white glove. He wore glittery Spandex tights, glossy high black boots, and a loose white off-the-shoulder blouse. Heavy earrings glittered in the curly hair, and a clutch of heavy bracelets slithered up and down his arm. The boys at the tables in front of the stage clapped and whistled, and Lola pranced through an energetic but lifeless version of Michael Jackson's dance moves. From "Billie Jean," they went into "Maniac," then into "MacArthur Park." Lola's costume changes drew claps and whistles.

Poole picked up the request card folded at his table, flattened it out and wrote *I like your act. Would you be willing to talk to me about an old friend from Bugis Street?* He raised his arm and the waitress took the form and went down the steps to wind through the tables to pass the slip up to Lola.

Still singing "Cross My Heart" and dressed now in a red long-sleeved blouse and a necklace of heavy purple glass beads, Lola snatched the card from the waitress and twiddled it flirtatiously through his fingers before opening it. His face was still for no more than half a second before he spun around, stamped his foot, extended his arms and rattled his bracelets and sang out "Cross my heart!"

After nearly an hour Lola left the stage bowing and blowing kisses. The MIT boys stood up and applauded. The band took an almost mockingly low bow.

Poole waited for his check after the lights went up. Some of the young Chinese boys had gathered around a door at the side of the stage, and occasionally someone opened the door and let them in and out.

When the boys had left or returned to their tables for the second performance, Poole knocked on the flimsy black door. It swung open. Crowded into a small, smoky lounge, the musicians looked up from the floor and the ancient sofa. The room smelled of tobacco, sweat, and makeup. Lola half-turned from the mirror before him and peered out from beneath the towel that covered his head. He held a flat case of black powder in one hand and an eyebrow brush in the other.

Poole stepped into the room.

"Close the door behind you," one of the musicians said.

"You want to see me?" Lola asked.

"I enjoyed your performance," Poole said. He stepped forward. The fat conga player pulled back his legs to permit Poole to move forward another step. Lola smiled and pulled the towel from his head.

He was smaller and older than he appeared onstage. Beneath the makeup, a network of knifelike little wrinkles had chipped into the girlish face. His eyes were tired and cautious. Sweat still sparkled in his springy hair. He nodded at the compliment and turned back to the mirror.

"I sent the note about Bugis Street," Poole said.

Lola's hand came away from his eyes and he very slightly turned his head to take in Poole.

"Do you have a minute?"

"I don't remember ever seeing you before." Lola's English was nearly accentless.

"This is my first time in Singapore."

"And you have something extremely *pressing* on your mind."

One of the musicians guffawed.

"I heard about you from a man named Billy," Poole said. He seemed to be missing something, some secret that the others knew.

"And what were you doing with Billy? Looking for entertainment? I hope you found some."

"I was looking for a writer named Tim Underhill," Poole said.

Lola startled him by slamming down the little case of mascara with enough force to raise a dingy cloud of powder. "You know, I thought I was ready for this, but I am not ready for this."

He thought he was ready for this? Poole thought. He said, "Billy said you might have known Underhill, or might even know where he is."

"Well, he isn't here." Lola stepped forward. "I don't want to talk about this. I have another show to do. Leave me alone."

The other musicians watched with good-natured indifference.

"I need your help," Poole said.

"What are you, a cop? Does he owe you money?"

"My name is Michael Poole. I'm a doctor. I used to be a friend of his."

Lola pressed his palms to his forehead. He looked as if he wished that Poole was a dream that would simply go away. He peeled his hands away from his head and rolled his eyes upward. "Oh. God. Well, here it is." He turned to the conga player. "Did you ever know Tim Underhill?"

The conga player shook his head.

"You weren't on Bugis Street at the start of the seventies?"

"We were still in Manila," the conga player said. "We were the Cadillacs in 1970. Played Subic Bay."

"Played all those bars," said the keyboard player. "Great days, man. You got anything you wanted."

"Danny Boy," the keyboard player said.

"Danny *Boy*. Sailors got Danny *Boy*."

"Can you tell me where to find him?" Poole asked.

Lola noticed that his fingers were dusty with black powder, and gave himself a disgusted look in the mirror before plucking a tissue from a box on his table. He deliberately, slowly, wiped his fingers while gazing at himself in the mirror. "I don't have anything to hide," he told the mirror. "Quite the reverse, in fact."

Then he glanced again at Poole. "What are you going to do when you find him?"

"Talk to him."

"I hope that isn't all you're going to do." Lola exhaled loudly, clouding the mirror's surface. "I'm *really* not ready for this yet."

"Just name a time and a place."

"A time and a place," sang the keyboard player, "give me the time and the place."

"Subic Bay," said the conga player.

"Ah, do you know Bras Basah Park?" Lola asked.

Poole said that he could find it.

"I'll meet you there tomorrow at eleven, maybe." Lola again confronted himself in the mirror. "If I'm not there, forget all about it. Don't come back. Okay?"

Poole had no intention of honoring that pledge, but he nodded.

The conga player began singing "Do you know the way to Bras Basah Park?" and Poole left the room.

6

The next morning, half an hour's walk brought Poole to within sight of a small green triangle of ground set between Orchard Road and Bras Basah Road. He was alone—Conor was too weak from whatever bug had attacked him to have walked the three miles to the park, and Beevers, who had appeared in the coffee shop with bags under his eyes and a red scratch above his right eyebrow, had claimed to think it better for Michael to "feel out" the singer by himself.

Poole understood why Lola had chosen Bras Basah Park for their meeting. It was probably the most public park he had ever seen. Nothing that happened there would be hidden from the buildings on the other sides of the two wide roads, or from the drivers of the cars that ceaselessly swept past. Bras Basah Park was about as private as a traffic island.

Three broad, curving paths of amber brick intersected it and converged at the park's narrow eastern end, where a wider walkway circled an abstract bronze sculpture and led out past a wooden sign.

Poole walked along Orchard Road until he reached the stoplight that would allow him to cross into the empty park. It was five minutes to eleven.

When he sat down on one of the benches on the path nearest Orchard Road, he looked around, wondering where Lola was now, and if he was watching him from one of the windows facing the park. He knew the singer would make him wait, and wished that he had thought of carrying a book with him.

Poole sat on the wooden bench in the warm sun. An old man tottered by on a stick, and took an amazingly long time to pass before Poole. Poole watched him take his tiny steps past all the benches, past the sculpture, past the sign, and finally out into the middle of Orchard Road. Twenty-five minutes had gone by.

Here he was, sitting alone on a bench on a glorified traffic island in Singapore. He felt, all at once, monumentally alone. He considered the possibility—no, the likelihood—that if he were never to go back to Westerholm the person who would miss him most would be a little girl for whom he could do nothing but buy books.

That was okay. That was all right. He'd miss Stacy too, just as much, if she were to die while he was gone. It was funny, Poole thought: in medical school you learned one hell of a lot about matters of life and death, but you didn't learn beans about mourning. They didn't teach you anything about grief. These days, grief seemed one of the absolutely essential human emotions to Dr. Michael Poole. Grief was right up there with love.

Poole remembered standing alone in a hotel room in Washington, watching as a gaudy van crunched in the front end of a dusty little car, remembered walking in brisk cold air alongside whiskery veterans accompanied by Dengler's double and the ghost of Tim Underhill. He remembered Thomas Strack.

He saw fat ladies waving banners and cold clouds scudding through grey air. He remembered how the names had walked right out of the black wall, and his mouth flooded with the bitter, essential taste of mortality. "Dwight T. Pouncefoot," he said, and heard the glorious absurdity of that name. His eyes blurred, and he began to giggle uncontrollably.

For some time he went on laughing and crying at once. An extraordinary mixture of feelings had come steaming up through his chest, filling every crevice, leaping every synapse. He laughed and cried, filled with the taste of mortality and grief, which was both bitter and joyous. When the emotion began to fade, he yanked his handkerchief from his pocket, wiped his eyes, and saw beside him on the bench a scrawny middle-aged man who looked like a Chinese Roddy McDowall. The man was watching him with mingled curiosity and impatience. He was one of those men who look like teenagers into their mid-forties, and then suddenly wrinkle into aged boy-men.

Michael took in the man's brown trousers and pink shirt with its collar carefully folded over the collar of the brown plaid sports jacket, the carefully flattened-down hair, and only then realized that this was Lola in his civilian clothes and out of his makeup.

"I suppose you're crazy too," Lola said in a flat accentless voice. His face twitched into a complicated pattern of chips and wrinkles as he smiled. "Makes sense, if you're a friend of Underhill's."

"I was just thinking that only a really terrible war would kill a guy named Dwight T. Pouncefoot. Don't you agree?" The name brought on another spasm of those radically contradictory feelings, and Poole closed his mouth against an onslaught of mad giggling laughter.

"Sure," Lola said. Poole let his hands fall into his lap and saw, with a little shock of relief and surprise, that

Lola was almost entirely unaffected by his outburst. He had seen worse. "You were in Vietnam with Underhill?"

Poole nodded. He supposed that was all the explanation Lola needed.

"You were close friends?"

Poole said, "He saved a lot of lives in a place called Dragon Valley, just by keeping everybody calm. I guess he was a great soldier. He liked the excitement of combat, he liked being on patrol, he liked that adrenaline rush. He was smart, too."

"You have not seen him since the war?"

Poole shook his head.

"You know what I think?" Lola asked, and answered his own question as Poole waited. "I think you can't help Tim Underhill." He glanced at Poole, then looked away.

"Where did you meet Underhill?"

Lola looked straight at Poole again, his mouth working as if to locate and expel an irritating seed. "At the Orient Song. It's completely different now—they have tour groups, and a few of the Bugis Street people are paid a few dollars to sit in the back and look dissipated."

"I was there," Poole said, remembering the Jaunty Jasmines.

"I know you were there. I know every place you went. I know everything you and your friends did. Many people called me. I even thought that I knew who you were."

Poole just kept silent.

"He used to talk about the war. He used to talk about you. Michael Poole, right?" When Poole nodded, Lola said, "I think you might be interested in what he used to say about you. He said that you were destined to become a good doctor, marry a perfect bitch, and live in the suburbs."

Poole met Lola's grin with his own.

"He said you'd eventually begin to hate the job, the wife, and the place where you lived. He said he was interested in how long it would take you to get there, and what you would do after that. He also said he admired you."

Poole must have looked startled, because Lola said, "Underhill told me you had the strength to tolerate a second-rate destiny for a long time. He admired that—because he could not, he had to find a tenth-rate destiny, or a twelfth-rate, or a hundredth-rate. After his writing stopped working for him, your friend went in search of the bottom. And people who seek the bottom always find it. Because it's always there, isn't it?"

What sent him there, Poole wanted to ask, but Lola went on talking—fast. "Let me tell you about the Americans who came here during Vietnam. These people could not adjust to life in their own country. They felt more comfortable in the East. A lot of them liked Asian women. Or Asian boys, like your friend." A bitter smile. "A lot of them wanted to be where they thought drugs were plentiful. Most of the Americans who felt that way went to Bangkok, some bought bars in Patpong or Chiang Mai, others got into the drug trade." He glanced at Poole again.

"What did Underhill do?"

Lola's face broke into a wilderness of wrinkles. "Underhill was happy with his work. He lived in a tiny room in the old Chinese section, put his typewriter up on a box. Little record player—he spent his money on records, books, Bugis Street, and drugs. But he was a sick person. He loved destruction. You said he was a good soldier. What do you think makes a good soldier? Creativity?"

"But he was a creative person—nobody could say he wasn't. He even wrote his best books here."

"He wrote his first book in his head in Vietnam," Lola said. "He only had to put it down. He sat in his little room, typed, went out to Bugis Street, picked up boys, did whatever he did, took whatever he took, the next morning typed some more. Everything was easy. You think I don't know? I know—I was there. When his book was finished, he had a big party in the Floating Dragon. That's when a man I know, a friend of mine named Ong Pin, met him. Then he was all set to start his next book. He says to me, he knew all about this crazy man, he knows him from the inside, he has to write a book about him. He has something to figure out—he's very mysterious. Mysterious in lots of ways. He needs money, but he says he has a scheme that will make him set up for life. But before he can get it, he has to borrow—he needs money to stay afloat. He borrows from everybody. Me included. A lot of money. He will pay me back, of course he will. He is a famous author, isn't he?"

"Is that how the lawsuit came about?"

Lola gave him a sharp look, then a twisted smile. "It

seemed like such a good idea to him. He was going to get hundreds of thousands of dollars. Underhill had one big problem—he couldn't write anything he thought was any good. He started two, three books after *The Divided Man*. Ripped them all up. He went crazy—so he and Ong Pin threatened the publisher with a lawsuit. Get a lot of money all at once, pay everybody back. When this *brilliant* idea didn't work, Underhill got tired of Ong Pin. He threw him out of his place, he sent everybody away. He beat a boy up—crazy stuff. Then he disappeared. Nobody could find him. After that I heard stories about him. Underhill was living in hotels and running out in the middle of the night after running up huge bills. Once I heard he was sleeping under a certain bridge, and some people and I went there to see if we could at least shake a few dollars out of him, maybe beat *him* up, but he wasn't there. I heard he was spending whole days in an opium house. Then I heard he was even crazier than before—going around telling people that the world was filthy, and that I was a demon, Billy was a demon, God was going to destroy us. Scared me, Doctor. Who could tell what this crazy man would do? He hated himself, I knew that. People who hate themselves, who cannot stand what they think they are, can do anything, you know. He was blackballed from bars in every part of town. Nobody saw him, but everybody heard stories. He found the bottom, he did that."

Poole groaned inwardly. What had happened to Underhill? Maybe the drugs he had taken had ruined him by making it impossible for him to write well.

As Lola talked, Poole found himself remembering the night in Washington he had gone with a woman lawyer to see a jazz piano player named Hank Jones. He had been in town to give testimony at a hearing on Agent Orange. Poole knew very little about jazz, and now he could remember none of the actual music Hank Jones had played. But what he did remember was a grace and joy that had seemed abstract and physical at once. He could remember how Hank Jones, who was a middle-aged black man with grizzled hair and a handsome, devilish face, had tilted his head over the keyboard, purely responsive to the flow of his inspirations. The music had gone straight into Michael Poole. Passion so *light!* Passion so *singing!* Poole had known that by a miracle of sympathy, he was hearing the music as the young lawyer heard it. And after the set, when Jones was standing next to the piano talking to his fans, Poole had seen the man's blazing delight in what he had done. This shone forth even in the grace of his movements, and Poole had felt as though he were watching an old lion filled with the essence of lionhood.

And something had struck him then, that of all the people he knew, probably only Tim Underhill would have known this blazing inner weather.

But Underhill had only had a couple of years of what Hank Jones seemed to have had for decades. He had cheated himself of the rest of it.

There was a long pause. "You have read his books?"

Poole nodded.

"Are they any good?"

"The first two were very good."

Lola sniffed. "I thought they would all be terrible books."

"Where is he now? Do you have any idea?"

"Are you going to kill him?" Lola squinted at Poole. "Well, maybe somebody should kill him and end his misery before he kills someone else."

"Is he in Bangkok? Taipei? Back in the States?"

"Someone like him cannot go back to America. He went somewhere else, I'm sure of that—like a crazy animal crawling off to a safe place. I always thought he would go to Bangkok. Bangkok would be perfect for him. But he used to talk about Taipei, so maybe he went there. He never paid me the money he owed me, I can tell you that." The squint was now a look of pure malice. "The crazy man he was going to write about—that was him. He did not even know that much, and people so ignorant about themselves are dangerous. I used to think I loved him. Loved him! Dr. Poole, if you find your friend, I hope you will be very careful."

16

THE LIBRARY

1

Michael Poole and Conor Linklater had already been in Bangkok—and Harry Beevers in Taipei—for two days when Tina Pumo made his discovery, which came in the mundane surroundings of the Microfilm Room of the main branch of the New York Public Library. He was writing a book about Vietnam, he had explained to a stocky, sixtyish, bearded man in a handsome black suit, in particular a book about the Ia Thuc court martials.

Which newspapers did he want? Copies of the daily New York, Washington, Los Angeles, and St. Louis papers and the national news magazines for the months of November 1968, and March 1969. And because he wanted to see the obituaries of Koko's victims, he requested the London *Times, Guardian,* and *Telegraph* for the week of January 28, 1982, and the St. Louis papers for the week of February 5, 1982, as well as the Paris daily papers for the week of July 7, 1982.

The bearded man told Pumo that it would usually take a great deal of time to locate and assemble that amount of material, but that he had both good news and bad news for him. The good news was that the various microfilms pertaining to the Ia Thuc incident had already been assembled—there were even a couple of sources, long articles in *Harper's,* the *Atlantic,* and *American Scholar,* which he had overlooked. The bad news was that this material was still awaiting redistribution because someone else was also researching Ia Thuc. A journalist named Roberto Ortiz had requested the same information three days earlier, consulted them again a day later, and had spent Tuesday afternoon examining them again, today being Wednesday—*Village Voice* day, Pumo reflexively thought.

Tina had never heard of Roberto Ortiz, and his private emotion at this news was principally gratitude that he would not have to wait days for the microfilm to be located. He was just double-checking, Tina told himself, making up for the feeling of having missed something important by not going along with the others to Singapore. If he discovered anything they ought to know, he could call them at the Marco Polo.

Before the articles were located and assembled, he read what the news magazines and the *New York Times* had said about Ia Thuc. He was seated in a plastic chair before a plastic desk; the chair was not comfortable and the microfilm machine took up so much of the desk that he had to rest his notebook in his lap. Within minutes, none of this mattered at all. What happened to Pumo within ten minutes of starting to read a *Newsweek* story entitled "Ia Thuc: Shame or Victory?" was very similar to what happened to Conor Linklater when Charlie Daisy put an album of SP4 Cotton's photographs before him. He had managed to forget how public it all had been.

Here spoke Lt. Harry Beevers according to *Newsweek:* "In this war we are here to kill Charlies, and Charlies come in all shapes and sizes. My own personal body count is thirty dead VC." *Children Killer?* asked *Time,* which described the lieutenant as "gaunt, hollow-eyed and -cheeked, desperate, a man on the edge." *Were They Innocent?* asked *Newsweek,* which said the lieutenant was "perhaps as much a victim of Vietnam as the children he is alleged to have killed."

Tina could remember Harry Beevers at Ia Thuc. "I have a personal body count of thirty dead gooks! You guys have any balls, pin a medal on me right now." The lieutenant was high and babbling, he couldn't shut up. When you stood next to him, you could almost feel the blood zooming around his arteries. You knew that you'd burn your fingers if you touched him. "War makes everybody the same age!" he had bawled out to the reporters. "You assholes think there are children in this war, you think children even exist in this war? You know why you think that way? Because you're ignorant civilians, that's why. There are no children!"

These were the articles that had nearly hanged Beevers, and Dengler with him. In *Time:* "I deserve a goddamned medal!" Funny, Pumo thought, how in Beevers' recollections of these events he always said the rest of the platoon deserved goddamned medals too.

Surrounded by a bubble of unearthly stillness, Pumo remembered how crazy and taut everybody had felt then, how close that boundary was between morality and murder. They had been nothing but nerves hooked up to trigger fingers. The stink of the fish sauce, and the smoke rising from the pot. Up on the sloping hillside, a girl lay in a crumpled blue heap before her wooden yoke. If the village was empty, who the fuck was doing the cooking? And who were they cooking for? Everything was as still as a tiger in the grass. The sow grunted and cocked her head, and Pumo remembered whirling around, weapon ready, and almost blasting a dirty child in half. Because you couldn't know, you never knew, and death could be a little smiling child with an outstretched hand; it zapped your brain, it *fried* it, and you either blasted away at everything in sight or you made yourself melt into whatever was behind you. Like the tiger in the grass, you could save your life by becoming invisible.

He looked at the photographs for a long time—Lieutenant Beevers, skinny as a sapling, with a haggard face and spinning eyes. M.O. Dengler, unidentified, white tired eyes flashing from beneath his helmet liner. All that green around them, that palpitating, trembling, simmering green. The mouth of a cave—"like a fist," Victor Spitalny said at the court-martial.

Then he remembered Lieutenant Harry Beevers lifting a girl of six or seven out of a ditch by her ankles, a muddy naked child, with that Vietnamese fragility, those chicken bones in her neck and arms, and swinging her around like an Indian club. Her mouth was a downturned curve, and her skin had begun to pucker where the fire had gotten her.

Pumo's entire body felt wet and his sides were cold with sweat. He had to stand up and get away from the machine. He tried to shove his chair back and moved the entire desk. He swiveled his legs and got up and moved, bolted, out into the center of the Microfilm Room.

They had crossed over, all right. Koko had been born on the other side of the boundary, where you met the elephant.

A little smiling child stepped forward from a black immensity, cupping death in its small hands.

Let the guy with the Spanish name have Ia Thuc, Tina thought, it'll just be another book. I'll give it to Maggie at Christmas, and she'll be able to tell me what happened there.

He looked up and the door opened. A boy with a sparse beard and a single dangling earring stepped in with double handfuls of microfilm spools. "You Puma?"

"Pumo," Tina said, and accepted the microfilm.

He returned to his little desk, unloaded the microfilm of *Time* magazine, and loaded in the *St. Louis Post-Dispatch* for the month of February 1982. He scrolled across the pages of print until he found the headline AREA EXECUTIVE, WIFE, SLAIN IN FAR EAST.

The article contained less information about the deaths than Pumo had already learned from Beevers. Mr. and Mrs. William Martinson of 3642 Breckinridge Drive, a respectable upper-middle-class couple, had been mysteriously slain in Singapore. Their bodies were discovered by a real-estate appraiser entering a supposedly empty bungalow in a residential section of the city. The motive was presumed to be robbery. Mr. Martinson had traveled extensively in the Far East in his business as Executive Vice President and Marketing Director of Martinson Tool & Equipment Ltd., and was frequently accompanied by his wife, an equally distinguished citizen of St. Louis.

Mr. Martinson, sixty-one, was a graduate of St. Louis Country Day School, Kenyon College, and Columbia University. His great-grandfather, Andrew Martinson, had founded Martinson Tool & Equipment in St. Louis in 1890. The deceased's father, James, had been president of the company from 1935 to 1952, and had also been president of the St. Louis Founders' Club, the Union Club, and the Athletic Club as well as serving in prominent positions on many civic, educational, and religious bodies. Mr. Martinson joined his family's business, now under the presidency of his older brother, Kirkby Martinson, in 1970, using his experience of the Far East and skill as a negotiator to increase Martinson's annual revenues by what was reputed to be several hundred million dollars.

Mrs. Martinson, the former Barbara Hartsdale, a graduate of the Academie Française and Bryn Mawr College, had long taken a prominent role in civic and cultural affairs. Her grandfather, Chester Hartsdale, a second cousin of the poet T.S. Eliot, founded the Hartsdale's department store chain, for fifty years the leading retail outlet throughout the Midwest, and served as ambassador to Belgium after the First World War. The Martinsons were survived by Mr. Martinson's brother Kirkby and sister, Emma Beech, of Los Angeles; by Mrs. Martinson's brothers, Lester and Parker, directors of the interior decoration firm La Bonne Vie in New York City; and by their children: Spenser, employed by the Central Intelligence Agency, of Arlington, Va.; Parker, of San Francisco, Ca.; and Arlette Monaghan, an artist, of Cadaques, Spain. There were no grandchildren.

Tina examined the photographs of these two exemplary citizens. William Martinson had possessed close-set eyes and a fringe of white hair around a smooth intelligent face. He had a prosperous, secretive, badgerlike air. Barbara Martinson had been caught smiling, close-mouthed, almost shyly, while looking sideways. She looked as if she had just thought of something funny and rather bawdy.

On what would have been the third page was a headline reading MARTINSONS RECALLED BY NEIGHBORS, FRIENDS. Pumo began skimming the small print on the monitor's screen, wrongly suspecting that he already knew all the substantial information about the Martinsons that he was ever going to know. The Martinsons had of course been loved and admired. Of course their deaths were a tragic loss to the community. They had been handsome and generous and witty. Less predictably, William Martinson was still known to his oldest friends by his Country Day nickname, "Fuffy." It was often remembered that Mr. Martinson had shown remarkable business ability after his decision to resign from journalism and join the family firm during a crisis at Martinson Tool & Equipment.

Journalism? Pumo thought. *Fuffy?*

Successful in Two Careers, claimed a subhead. William Martinson had majored in journalism at Kenyon College and earned a Master's degree at Columbia's School of Journalism. In 1948 he joined the staff of the *St. Louis Post-Dispatch* and was soon recognized as a reporter of exceptional talent. In 1964, after holding several other prestigious journalistic posts, he became a correspondent from Vietnam for *Newsweek* magazine. Mr. Martinson reported from Vietnam for the magazine until the fall of Saigon, by which time he had become bureau chief. He still maintained his home and friendships in St. Louis, and in 1970 was given a celebration dinner at the Athletic Club for his contributions to the American understanding of the war, especially his work in reporting what at first had seemed a massacre at the village of . . .

But Pumo had stopped reading. For a time he was not conscious of hearing or seeing anything—Ia Thuc had blindsided him again. He gradually became aware that his hands were taking the St. Louis microfilm from the machine. "That goddamned Beevers," he said to himself. "That goddamned fool."

"Simmer down, man," said a flat stoned voice from behind him. Pumo tried to whirl around in his plastic chair and banged himself on the molded back hard enough to give himself a bruise. He rubbed his thigh and looked up at the boy with the tentative beard. "Puma, right?"

Pumo sighed and nodded.

"You still want these?" He held out another stack of microfilm containers.

Pumo took them, waved the boy off, and went back to the screen. He did not know what he was looking at, what he was looking for. He felt as if he had been struck by lightning. Goddamned Harry Beevers, who had made such a big deal of his research, had not even scratched the surface of Koko's murders. Pumo felt another wave of concentrated rage go through him.

He slammed in the microfilmed London *Times* hard enough to vibrate the desk. Noises of dismay, evident at a low level for some time, came more loudly through the partition separating him from the next monitor.

Pumo scanned across the text until he found the headline and subhead he wanted, JOURNALIST-NOVELIST MCKENNA SLAIN IN SINGAPORE. *Came to Prominence During Vietnam Era.* Clive McKenna had made the front page of the *Times* of 29 January, 1982, six days after his death and one day after the discovery of his body. Mr. McKenna had worked for Reuters News Service in Australia and New Zealand for ten years and was then transferred to Reuters' Saigon Bureau, where he had quickly become known as a dashing figure akin to the legendary Sean Flynn. Mr. McKenna had distinguished himself by being the first English newsman to cover the siege at Khe Sanh, the My Lai massacre, the fighting in Hue during the Tet offensive of 1968, and was the only English journalist present immediately after the disputed events in the hamlet of Ia Thuc which resulted in the court-martials and eventual acquittals of two American soldiers. Mr. McKenna left the world of print journalism in 1971, when he returned to England to write the first of a series of international thrillers that quickly made him one of England's most prominent and best-selling authors.

"He was on the goddamned helicopter," Pumo said out loud. Clive McKenna had been on the helicopter that brought the reporters into Ia Thuc, William Martinson had been on the helicopter, and no doubt the French reporters had been on it too.

Pumo removed the microfilm and replaced it with that of the microfilm of the French newspaper. He could not read French, but in the prominent black-bordered article on the first page of *L'Express* he had no trouble finding the words *Vietnam* and *Ia Thuc,* which were the same in English and French.

A square masculine head with brown eyes behind large grey glasses appeared around the side of Pumo's carrel. "Excuse me," it said. It poked a few inches further past the divider, exposing a polka dot bow tie. "If you cannot control yourself or your vocabulary I shall have to ask you to leave."

Pumo felt like hitting the pompous ass. The bow tie reminded him of Harry Beevers.

With a self-conscious awareness that most of the people in the Microfilm Room were looking at him, he gathered up his coat and handed the film in at the desk. In a furious rush he ran down the steps and out through the library's great front doors. Snow swirled about him.

Pumo turned downtown on Fifth Avenue and marched along, his hands in his pockets and a brown tweed cap from Banana Republic on his head. It was very cold, and this helped. Random violence was much less likely when everybody was trying to get indoors as fast as possible.

He tried to remember the reporters at Ia Thuc. They had been part of a larger group that had come to Camp Crandall from further down in Quang Tri province, where the brass wanted them to see various dread object lessons. After they filed their obligatory stories, or so army theory went, they could choose less embattled areas for their follow-up stories. About half of the big contingent said fuck it and went back to Saigon, where they could get smashed, smoke opium, and make fun of Rolling Thunder and the so-called "McNamara Line" that was supposed to replace it. All the television reporters went to Camp Evans so they could get to Hue easily, stand on a pretty bridge with a mike up their chops, and say things like "I am speaking to you from the banks of the Powder River in the centuries-old city of Hue." A lot of the others had stayed in Camp Evans, where they could be flown a few klicks north and write stirring stuff about the helicopters landing at LZ Sue. A handful had decided to go out into the field and see what was happening in a village called Ia Thuc.

Pumo's enduring impression of the reporters was of a crowd of men in very deliberate almost-uniforms surrounding a ranting Harry Beevers. They had resembled a pack of dogs, alternately barking and gulping bits of food.

Of the men who had surrounded Harry Beevers on that afternoon, four were now dead. How many were left alive? Pumo put his head down, walking fast down Fifth Avenue in a dry swirl of windblown snow, and tried to focus on the number of men standing around Beevers. They were a numberless pack, remembered that way, and he tried instead to see them as they left the helicopter.

Spanky Burrage, Trotman, Dengler, and himself had been carrying bags of rice out of the cave and stacking them beneath the trees. Beevers was jubilant, among other reasons because they had discovered boxes of Russian weapons underneath the rice, and he was spinning around like a dancing toy. "Get those children out," he was shouting, "stack them next to the rice, and put the weapons right beside them." He was pointing at the helicopter, which was flattening out the grass as it settled swaying toward the earth. "Get 'em out! Get 'em out of here!" Then the men had begun leaving the Huey Iroquois.

In his mind he saw them jumping out of the Iroquois

and bending over as they ran toward the village. Like all reporters, they were trying to look like John Wayne or Errol Flynn, and there had been . . . five of them? Six?

If Poole and Beevers got to Underhill in time, maybe they could save at least one life.

Pumo looked up and saw that he had walked all the way to 30th Street. Looking at the street sign, he at last clearly saw the reporters jumping out of the Huey Iroquois and running through the grass blown down like cat's fur rubbed the wrong way. One man had been followed by a pair of men, then another single man loaded with cameras, and another who ran as if his legs hurt him, and one bald man. One of the reporters had spoken in soft, fluent, rattling Spanish to a soldier called La Luz, who had muttered something that included the word *maricón* and turned away. La Luz had been killed a month later.

Cold shadows were already spilling across the street, and within the shadows layers of dead snow lifted and spun. He got them all over to Singapore and Bangkok, the reporters, he figured out a way to pluck their strings and get them to come to him. He's a spider. He's a little smiling child with an outstretched hand. The streetlamps clicked on, and for a second the middle of Fifth Avenue, crowded with taxis and buses, looked discolored, bleached. Pumo tasted the bite of vodka on his tongue and turned off on 24th Street.

2

Until Pumo had finished two drinks, he had taken in only the row of bottles behind the bartender, the hand giving him the glass, and the beautiful glass itself, filled with ice and clear liquid. He thought he might even have closed his eyes. Now his third drink had appeared before him, and he was still coming out of it.

"Yeah, I was in AA," the man beside him was saying, evidently continuing a conversation that had been in progress for some time. "But do you know what I said? I said fuck it. That's what I said."

Pumo heard the man saying that he had chosen hell. Like everyone else who had chosen hell, he recommended it very highly. Hell wasn't as bad as it was cracked up to be. His friend's purple face sagged and his breath stank.

Demons jabbed out their little fists and forks inside his fallen cheeks and lit yellow fires in his eyes. He put a heavy dirty hand on Pumo's shoulder. He said he liked his style—he liked a man who closed his eyes when he drank. The bartender barked and retreated into a smoky cave.

"Did you ever kill anybody?" Pumo's friend asked. "Pretend you're on television and you have to tell me the truth. Ever waste anybody? My money says you did."

He pushed his hand down hard on Pumo's shoulder.

"I hope not," Pumo said, and gulped a third of his new drink.

"So so so so *soooo,*" the man breathed. Inside him, the demons went wildly to work, poking out their little forks, dancing, stoking their yellow fires. "I recognize that answer, my friend, it is the answer of a former warrior. Am I right? Or—am I right?"

Pumo pulled himself free of the man's hand and turned away.

"You think that counts?" the man asked. "It does not. Except in one way. When I ask you, did you ever kill anyone, that is to say, have you ever taken a life in the way you take a drink or in the way you take a piss, I am asking if you are a killer. And everything counts, even if you killed while in the uniform of your country. Because then technically you're a killer."

Pumo forced himself to turn again toward the man's blazing face and the stench of his body. "Get away from me. Leave me alone."

"Or what? You'll kill me like you killed 'em in Vietnam? Look at this." The demon-man held up a fist. It looked like a dented grey garbage can. "When I killed him, I killed him with this one here."

Pumo felt the walls of the cave focusing down in on him like the lens of a camera. Smoke and foulness darkened the air, streaming toward Pumo from the demon-man.

"Wherever you are, see, that's where you are," the man said. "You're not safe. I know. I'm a killer too. You think you can win, but you can't win. I know."

Pumo backed away toward the door.

"Roger," the man said. "Roger wilco. Wherever you are, get it?"

"I know," Pumo said, and yanked bills out of his pocket.

* * *

When he got out of the cab, the windows on the second floor were full of light. Maggie was home, oh thank you God. He looked at his watch and was astonished that nine o'clock was so near. Many hours had disappeared from his day. How long had he spent in the bar on 24th Street and how many drinks did he have there? Pumo remembered the demon-man and thought he must have had a lot more than three.

He propped himself against the wall as he worked his way up the narrow white staircase. Pumo unlocked his door and let himself into warmth and mellow light.

"Maggie?"

No reply.

"Maggie?"

Pumo unbuttoned his heavy coat and tossed it onto one of the pegs. When he reached for the tweed cap from Banana Republic, he touched his forehead and had a sudden vision of the cap resting bottom-side up on the seat of a taxi.

He came out of the corridor into the main room of his loft and immediately saw Maggie sitting up on the platform, behind his desk, with her hands folded over the telephone. Her eyebrows were a straight line and the ruff of her live lovely hair glowed. Her mouth was closed so tightly she looked as if she had trapped some small creature within it.

"You're drunk," she said. "I just called three hospitals, and you were in a bar."

"I know why he killed them," Pumo said. "I even saw them, over in Nam. I can remember how they looked jumping out of the helicopter. Did you know, I mean do you know, that I love you?"

"Nobody needs your kind of love," Maggie said, but even though Pumo was drunk he could see that her face had softened. The small thing was no longer trapped in her mouth. He started to explain about Martinson and McKenna and how he had met a demon in hell, but Maggie was already coming toward him. Then she was undressing him. When he was naked she grabbed his penis and towed him like a tugboat down the hall and into the bedroom.

"I have to call Singapore," he said. "They don't even know yet!"

Maggie slipped into bed beside him. "Now let's make up before I remember everything I thought could have happened to you while I was waiting for you and get angry again." She put her arms out and pulled her whole body into his. Then she jerked her head back. "Ugh! You have a funny smell. Where were you, in a burning trash can?"

"It was the demon-man," Pumo said. "His smell soaked through from when he put his hand on my shoulder. He said hell wasn't really so bad because you got used to it after a while."

"Americans don't know anything about demons," Maggie said.

After a while Tina thought that Maggie made him feel so wickedly good that she must be a demon too. That was how she knew so much about things. Dracula had been a demon, and the man in the bar was a demon, and if you knew how to spot them you could probably see demons strolling up and down the streets of New York. Harry Beevers—there was another demon. But then the demon-things that Maggie Lah was doing to him would not let him concentrate on anything but the notion that after he married Maggie life would be very interesting because then he'd be married to a demon.

Two hours later Pumo awakened with a headache, the sweet, grainy taste of Maggie in his mouth, and the knowledge that he had left an important task undone. A well-known dread about the restaurant displaced all his other thoughts and would not go away until he remembered how he had spent the afternoon. He had to call Poole in Singapore and tell him what he had learned about the victims. He checked his clock radio: it was a quarter to eleven. In Singapore it would be a quarter to eleven in the morning. There was a chance he could still catch Poole in his room.

Pumo got out of bed and put on a robe.

Maggie was sitting on the couch, holding a pencil upright in her hand like a paintbrush and examining something she had drawn on a yellow legal pad. She looked up at him and smiled. "I've been thinking about your menu," she said. "Since you're redoing so much, why not work on the menu too?"

"What's wrong with the menu?"

"Well," Maggie said, and Pumo knew that she was

really going to tell him. He skirted around her and went up the platform steps to his desk. "For one thing, dot matrix printing looks ugly. It makes it look as though your kitchen is run by a computer. And the paper is pretty, but it gets dirty too fast. You need something with more gloss. And the layout isn't clean enough, and you don't need such lengthy descriptions of the dishes."

"I often wondered what was wrong with the menu." Pumo sat at his desk and began hunting for the telephone number of the hotel in Singapore. "When the Mayor comes in, he likes to read those descriptions out loud. To savor them."

"The whole thing looks like scrambled eggs. I hope the designer didn't charge you much."

Pumo had of course designed the menu himself. "He was amazingly expensive. Oh, here it is."

He dialed the operator and explained that he wanted to call Singapore.

"Take a look at how much nicer your menu could be." Maggie held up the legal pad.

"Is there writing on that pad?"

At last he was connected to the Marco Polo Hotel. The desk clerk told him that no Dr. Michael Poole was registered there. No, there was no mistake. No, there could be no mistake. There were also no guests named Harold Beevers or Conor Linklater.

"They have to be there." Pumo began to feel desperate all over again.

"Call his wife," Maggie said.

"I can't call his wife."

"Why can't you call his wife?"

The desk clerk came back on the line before he could think how to answer Maggie's question. "Dr. Poole and the others were staying with us, but they checked out two days ago."

"Where did they go?"

The clerk hesitated. "I believe Dr. Poole made travel arrangements for his party through the concierge's office in the lobby."

The man went off to see what he could find out, and Maggie asked, "Why can't you call his wife?"

"Don't have my address book."

"Why don't you have your address book?"

"It was stolen," Pumo said.

"Don't be ridiculous. You're just being nasty because of what I said about your menu."

"For once, you're wrong. I—"

The clerk returned and told Puma that Dr. Poole and Mr. Linklater had purchased air tickets to Bangkok, and that Mr. Beevers had booked a flight to Taipei. Since the gentlemen had not used the concierge to book hotel rooms in these cities, the clerk did not know where the gentlemen were staying.

"Why would anyone steal your address book? Who would steal anyone's address book, for that matter?" She paused. Her eyes widened. "Oh. When you got up that time. When you told me that awful story."

"*That's* who stole it."

"How creepy."

"That's what I say. Anyhow, I don't have Mike's home phone number."

"Please excuse my saying the obvious, but you could almost certainly get it from Information."

Pumo snapped his fingers and called Information in Westchester County for Michael Poole's telephone number. "Judy must be at home," he said. "She has to get to school in the morning."

Maggie nodded rather grimly.

Pumo dialed Michael's number. After two rings, an answering machine cut in and Pumo heard his friend's voice saying "I cannot answer the phone at this time. Please leave a message and I will get back to you as soon as possible. If you must speak to someone here, call 555-0032."

That number must belong to one of the doctors in his group, Pumo thought, and said, "This is Tina Pumo. Judy, can you hear me?" Pause. "I'm trying to get in touch with Mike. I have some information he will want to know, and he's checked out of the hotel in Singapore. Will you get back to me as soon as you have his new number? It's important that I talk to him. Bye."

Maggie carefully put the legal pad and the pencil down on the coffee table. "Sometimes you act as if women just did not exist."

"Huh?"

"When you want to talk to Judy Poole, whose number do you request from Information? Michael Poole's. And whose number do you get? Michael Poole's. It never occurred to you to ask for Judith Poole's number."

"Oh, come on. They're a married couple."

"What do you know about married couples, Tina?"

"What I know about married couples is, she's out," he said.

Soon Tina began to think that Maggie might be right after all. Both of the Pooles had demanding jobs that involved appointments and emergencies, and it was logical that they might have separate telephone lines. He had resisted the idea because it was not his own. But the next morning as he badgered the carpenters and morbidly inspected every new hole in the walls for signs of roaches and spiders, he still could find no grounds to question his certainty that Judy Poole had not been home on the night he called. People usually had their answering machines where they could hear them—especially if they turned the machines on while they were home. That was why they turned them on. Therefore he could excuse his immediate rejection of Maggie's ideas—if they had a dozen telephone lines and he had called every one the results would have been identical.

When Maggie asked him if he intended to see if there was a separate listing for Judy, and Pumo said, "Maybe. I have a lot to do today, I guess it can wait."

Maggie smiled and flicked her eyes slyly upward. She knew she had won, and was too smart to ask him a second time.

Until seven o'clock in the evening, the day after Pumo's discovery that Koko's victims had been the journalists at Ia Thuc, time went by almost normally. He and Maggie had spent the day in cabs and subways, in other restaurants, and in an office with lithographs by David Salle and Robert Rauschenberg where Lowery Hapgood, Molly Witt's partner, flirted with Maggie while he explained a new shelving system. They did not get back to Tina's loft until just before seven. Maggie asked him if he felt like eating anything and lay down on the long couch, and Tina dropped into a chair at the table and said he supposed so.

"What are we going to do about it, then?"

Tina picked up the morning's *Times*, which he had

tossed onto the table. "I understand that many women delight in creating meals."

"Let's get a little bit stoned and go to Chinatown and get duck feet. Yum."

"That's the first time you wanted to get high since you started living here."

Maggie yawned, flinging out her arms. "I know. I'm getting so boring. I said it just now out of nostalgia for when I was interesting."

"Hold on," Pumo said, staring at a small article on the third page of the first section.

He was looking at a headline that read: ORTIZ, JOURNALIST, SLAIN IN SINGAPORE. The body of Roberto Ortiz, 47, a prominent member of the press corps, had been discovered the day before by police in an empty house located in a residential section of Singapore. Mr. Ortiz and an unidentified woman had died of gunshot wounds. Robbery was not assumed to be the motive. Roberto Ortiz, born in Tegucigalpa, Honduras, educated privately and at the University of California at Berkeley, was born into an influential Central American newspaper family and became a freelance reporter contributing to many Spanish- and English-language periodicals. Mr. Ortiz had spent the years 1964–1971 in Vietnam, Laos, and Cambodia, covering the Vietnam War for a variety of journals, and out of this experience had come his book *Vietnam: A Personal Journey*. Mr. Ortiz was well known for his wit, flamboyance, and personal courage. Singapore police had released the information that the death of Mr. Ortiz appeared to be related to several unsolved killings in the city.

"Something has stolen your attention from your teenage drug addict mistress," Maggie said.

"Read this." Pumo walked to the couch and handed her the paper. She read half of it lying down, but sat up to finish it. "You think he was another one of them?"

Pumo shrugged—suddenly he wished that Maggie were somewhere else, making her smart remarks about drugs. "I don't know. There's something about this—there's something about *him*. The man who was killed."

"Roberto Ortiz."

He nodded.

"Did you ever meet him?"

"There was a Spanish-speaking reporter who came to

Ia Thuc." Dark feelings churned within Pumo. He could not stand this, any of it—his nice loft, the mess downstairs in the restaurant, and right now he could not stand Maggie either.

"He got the last one," Pumo said with what felt like the last fragments of his restraint. From now on he was running on empty. "There were five reporters who came into Ia Thuc, and now they're all dead."

"You look awful, Tina. What do you want to do?"

"Leave me alone." Pumo stood up and leaned against the wall. Without volition, as if his hand had chosen to close itself, he made a fist. Quietly at first and then with growing force, he began hitting the wall.

"Tina?"

"I said, leave me alone."

"Why are you hitting the wall?"

"Shut up!"

Maggie was silent for a long time while Pumo continued to beat his fist against the wall. Eventually he changed to his left fist.

"They're over there, and you're over here."

"Brilliant."

"Do you think they know about this Ortiz?"

"Of course they know about it!" Pumo shouted. He turned around so that he could yell better. Both of his hands felt raw and swollen. "They were in the same city!" Pumo felt murderous. Maggie was sitting on the couch staring at him with big kitten eyes. "What do you know about anything? How old are you? You think I need you? I don't need you around me!"

"Good," Maggie said. "Then I don't have to be your nurse."

A wave of pure blackness went through Tina Pumo. He remembered the demon-man who had smelled like burning garbage putting a grey hand on his shoulder and telling him he was a killer. Hell was pretty nice, Pumo thought. He found himself going toward the kitchen cabinets Vinh had hung. Look what you can do in hell. He opened the first cabinet and was almost surprised to see dishes stacked on the shelves. The neat dishes looked absolutely foreign to him. He hated the dishes. Pumo picked up the topmost dish and hefted it in both hands for a moment before dropping it. It smashed into half a dozen sections when it struck the floor. See what you could do when you lived in hell? He took another plate and threw it down. Pieces of china flew out and skidded beneath his dining table. He worked down the stack, sometimes dropping just one dish, at other times two or three. He dropped the last plate with great deliberation, as if he were conducting a scientific experiment.

"You poor bastard," Maggie said.

"Okay, okay." Pumo pressed his hands to his eyes.

"Do you want to go to Bangkok to see if you can find them? It couldn't be that hard to do."

"I don't know," Pumo said.

"If being here makes you feel so bad, you ought to go. I could even book the tickets for you."

"I don't feel so bad anymore," Pumo said. He went across the room to an armchair and sat down. "But maybe I'll go. Docs the restaurant really need me?"

"Does it?"

He thought. "Yes. That's why I didn't go in the first place." He looked over the rubble of the plates. "Whoever made that mess ought to be executed." When he grinned his face looked ghastly. "I retract that."

"Let's go to Chinatown and get soup," Maggie said. "You are a person in great need of soup."

"Would you go to Bangkok with me if I decide to go?"

"I hate Bangkok," Maggie said. "Let's go to Chinatown instead."

They found a cab on West Broadway, and Maggie gave directions to the Bowery Arcade, between Canal and Bayard streets.

Fifteen minutes later Maggie was speaking Cantonese to a waiter in a small shabby room papered with handwritten menus like scrolls. The waiter was about sixty and wore a filthy yellow uniform that had once been white. The waiter said something that made Maggie smile.

"What was that?"

"He called you an old foreigner."

Pumo looked at the shuffling waiter's bent back and the iron-grey stubble covering his head.

"It's an expression."

"Maybe I should go to Bangkok."

"Just say the word."

"If they knew that this other journalist, this Ortiz, was killed in Singapore, why would they leave there and go to Bangkok?"

The waiter set before them bowls of a creamy porridge-like substance very similar to that Michael Poole had eaten for breakfast in Singapore. "Unless they found out that Tim Underhill had left town."

"And Harry Beevers went to Taipei?" Maggie smiled at this thought, which evidently struck her as ridiculous.

Pumo nodded. "So they must have learned that Underhill was in one of those two places, and split up to try to find him. But why didn't they call me first? If they learned that Underhill was out of Singapore after they read about Ortiz, they must know that Underhill is innocent."

"Well, you can fly from Singapore to Bangkok in about an hour," Maggie said. "Eat your soup and stop worrying."

Pumo tried his soup. Like everything really funny-looking that Maggie urged on him, it did not taste at all the way it looked. The soup was not at all creamy, but tasted of wheat, pork essence, and something that tasted like cilantro but couldn't be. He wondered if he could put a variation of this soup on the new menu. He could give it some name like Strength to Carry Two Oxen Soup, and serve it in little cups with lemon grass. The Mayor would love it.

"Last fall, around Halloween, I saw the wonderful Harry Beevers," Maggie said. "I did this stupid thing, just to get him worked up. He was following me around a liquor store, and he was so arrogant he thought I didn't see him. I was with Perry and Jules, you know, my downtown friends."

"Roberto Ortiz," Pumo said, having finally remembered the detail that had nagged him since seven o'clock. "Oh, my God."

"They're nice, they're just perpetually out of work, which is why you can't stand them. Anyhow, I saw Harry gloating around after me, and when I knew he was looking I stole a bottle of champagne. I was feeling *nasty.*"

"Roberto Ortiz," Pumo repeated. "I'm sure that was the name."

"I'm almost afraid to ask what you're talking about," Maggie said.

"When I looked up the newspapers in the Microfilm Room, the librarian told me that all those files had already been assembled for someone else who was researching a book about Ia Thuc. I think the librarian said the man's name was Roberto Ortiz." Tina looked virtually bug-eyed at Maggie. "Get it? Roberto Ortiz had already been dead for something like a week. I have to call Judy Poole and see if she knows where Michael is."

"It still doesn't exactly make sense, Tina."

"I think Koko killed the last journalist, and then I think he got on a plane and came to New York."

"Maybe it was Roberto Gomez at the library, or Umberto Ortiz, or some other name like that. Or maybe it was a reporter like Ernie Anastos. J.J. Gonzales. David Diaz. Fred Noriega." She tried to think of other Hispanic reporters on New York City television, but couldn't.

"Looking up articles on Ia Thuc?"

Pumo nervously finished his soup.

As soon as he had hung up his coat in the loft he switched on the lights and went up to his desk. Still wearing her down coat, Maggie trailed into the room after him.

This time Pumo asked Information in Westchester for Judith Poole's listing in Westerholm, and was given a number that did sound to him gloomily like the alternate number on Michael's recorded message. Pumo dialed it and Judy answered after a few rings. "This is Mrs. Poole."

"Judy? This is Tina Pumo."

Pause. "Hello, Tina." Another deliberate pause. "Please excuse my asking, but would you mind my asking why you're calling? It's getting very late, and you could leave a message on Michael's machine if it's for him."

"I already left a message on Michael's machine. I'm sorry it's late, but I have some important information for Mike."

"Oh."

"When I called him at the hotel in Singapore, I was told that they had checked out."

"Yes."

What the hell is going on here? Pumo wondered. "I was hoping that you could give a number for where they are now. Michael's been in Bangkok for two or three days now."

"I know that, Tina. I'd give you his number in Bangkok, but I don't have it. We didn't have that sort of conversation."

Tina groaned silently. "Well, what's the name of his hotel?"

"I don't think he told me. I'm sure I didn't ask."

"Well, could I give you a message for him? He has to know some things I've discovered in the past few days." When Judy said nothing, Pumo went on. "I'd like you to tell him that Koko's victims, McKenna and Ortiz and the others, were the journalists at Ia Thuc, and that I think Koko might be in New York, calling himself Roberto Ortiz."

"I don't have the faintest idea of what you're talking about. What's this about victims? What do you mean, *victims?* What's this *Koko* stuff?"

Michael looked over at Maggie, who rolled her eyes and stuck her tongue out.

"What the hell is going on here, Tina?"

"Judy, I'd like you to ask Michael to call me as soon as possible after he talks to you. Or give me a call and tell me where he is."

"You can't say something like that to me and then just hang up! I want to know a thing or two, Tina. Suppose you tell me who's been calling me up at all hours and not saying anything."

"Judy, I don't have any idea who that could be."

"I suppose Michael didn't ask you to do that now and then, just to check up on me?"

"Oh, Judy," Pumo said. "If someone is bothering you, call the police."

"I have a better idea," she said, and hung up.

Pumo and Maggie went to bed early that night, and Maggie wound her arms around him, hooked her feet around the back of his legs, and held him tight. "What can I do?" he asked. "Call all the hotels in town and ask if Roberto Ortiz is registered?"

"Stop worrying," Maggie said. "Nobody's going to hurt you as long as I'm here."

"I almost believe you," Pumo laughed. "Maybe I *was* wrong about the name. Maybe it was Umberto Diaz, or whoever you said."

"Umberto wouldn't hurt a fly."

"Tomorrow I'll talk to that guy at the library," Pumo said.

Maggie fell asleep after they made love, and for a long time Pumo tested his memory without shaking his conviction that the name spoken by the librarian had been Roberto Ortiz. He finally fell asleep.

And woke all at once, as if prodded by a sharp stick, hours later. He knew something horrible, knew it absolutely and with the total unblinking certainty with which the worst things are embraced in the dark of the night. Pumo understood that when daylight came he would begin to doubt this certainty. The worst thing would no longer seem rational or persuasive once the sun came up. He would be lulled, he would accept Maggie's comforting explanations. But Tina promised himself that he would remember how he felt at this moment. He knew that it was not Dracula or any other criminal who had broken into his apartment. Koko had come into his apartment. Koko had stolen his address book. He needed their addresses in order to hunt them down, and now he had them.

Then another section of the puzzle slotted into place for Pumo. Koko had called Michael Poole's number, been given Judy's number by the answering machine, and promptly dialed it. And kept on dialing it.

Pumo did not get to sleep for a long time. Eventually a thought even he knew was paranoid joined the others, that Koko had murdered the investment banker, Clement W. Irwin, in the airport, and this thought, for all its obvious irrationality, kept him awake even longer.

3

After breakfast, Maggie went off to Jungle Red to have her hair trimmed and Pumo went downstairs to talk to Vinh. No, Vinh had not seen anyone hanging around outside the building during the past few days. Of course with all the workmen he might have missed something. No, he could not remember any unusual telephone calls.

"Were there any calls from people who hung up as soon as you answered?"

"Of course," Vinh said, and looked at Pumo as if he had lost his mind. "We get those calls all the time. Where do you think you are? This is New York!"

After he left Vinh, Pumo took a cab up to the 42nd Street library. He went up the wide steps, through the doors, past the guards, and returned to the desk where he had begun his research. The stocky bearded man was nowhere in sight, and a blond man half a foot taller than

Pumo stood behind the desk holding a telephone up to his ear. He glanced at Pumo, then turned his back to continue his conversation. When he set down the telephone he came slowly toward the desk. "May I help you?"

"I was doing some research here two days ago, and I'd like to check on something," Pumo said. "Do you know the man who was on duty then?"

"I was here two days ago," the blond man said.

"Well, the man I spoke to was older, maybe sixty, about my height, with a beard."

"That could be a million people in here."

"Well, could you ask someone?"

The blond man raised his eyebrows. "Do you see anyone here besides me? I can't leave this desk, you know."

"Okay," Pumo said. "Then maybe you could give me the information I was looking for."

"If you want a particular microfilm and you've been here before, then you know how to fill out the forms."

"It's not that kind of information," Pumo persisted. "When I requested some articles on a certain subject, the man who was working here told me that someone else had recently requested the same information. I'd like the name of that man."

"I can't possibly give you that information." The blond man arched his back and looked down at Poole as if he were standing above him, on a ledge.

"The other man did, though. It was a Spanish name."

The blond man was already shaking his head. "Not possible. It's not like the old slip in the back of the book business."

"You don't recognize the description of the other clerk?"

"I am not a clerk." There was now a straight red line across each of the blond man's cheekbones. "If you do not wish to request microfilms, sir, you are wasting the time of several people who do."

He looked pointedly over Pumo's shoulder, and Pumo, who for some time had experienced the sensation that someone was staring at him, looked back too. Four people stood behind him, none of them looking anywhere in particular.

"Sir?" the librarian said, and tilted the tip of his chin like a baton at the man immediately behind Pumo.

Pumo wandered away toward the carrels to see if the

bearded man would appear. For twenty minutes, the blond man either attended to researchers, talked on the telephone, or preened at the desk. He did not once look at Pumo. At twenty minutes past eleven he consulted his watch, raised a flap in the desk, and strode out of the room. A young woman in a black wool sweater took his place, and Pumo returned to the desk.

"Gee, I don't really know anyone here," she said to Pumo. "This is my first day—I only passed my internship two weeks ago, and I spent most of the time since then in Incunabula." She lowered her voice. "I loved Incunabula."

"You don't know the names of any well-dressed sixty-year-old men with beards in this library?"

"Well, there's Mr. Vartanian," she said with a smile. "But I don't think you could have seen *him* at this desk. There's Mr. Harnoncourt. And Mr. Mayer-Hall. Maybe even Mr. Gardener. But I don't know if any of them ever had Microfilm, you see."

Pumo thanked her and left the room. He thought he might see the bearded man if he wandered through the library and poked his head into offices.

He set off down the corridor, looking at the people who filled the upper floors of the great library. Men in cardigan sweaters, men in sports jackets, moved from the elevators to office doors, women in sweaters and jeans or in dresses hurried down the wide corridor. A wonderful dandy in a resplendent suit, a bristling beard, and gleaming eyeglasses swept through a door, and all the other staff members nodded or said hello. He was taller than the librarian Pumo had spoken to, and his beard was glossy red-brown, not salt-and-peppery black.

The visitors to the library carried their coats like Pumo and looked less certain of their destinations. The dandy passed through them like a steamship pushing through a crowd of rowboats and strode down the corridor and turned a corner.

Just as Pumo reached the corner he had the same sensation of being watched he'd had in the Microfilm Room. He looked over his shoulder and saw the crowd of visitors dispersing, some going into the Microfilm Room, others into other rooms. Still others boarded the elevator. The library staff had all gone through office doors, except for two women on their way to the ladies room. Pumo turned the corner and thought he had lost the tall dandy before he had quite realized that he'd decided to follow him. Then he saw a glossy black shoe flicking around another corner.

Pumo jogged down the hallway, hearing the soles of his shoes click against the brown marble. When he came walking fast around the corner the dandy was nowhere in sight, but a door marked STAIRS was just closing halfway down the otherwise empty hallway before him. Then from down at the far end of this corridor came a pair of young Chinese women, each carrying two or three books bristling with marker slips. As he watched them come gliding toward him across the marble floor, one of the women glanced up at him and smiled.

Pumo opened the door to the stairs and stepped onto the landing. A large red numeral 3 was painted on the wall before him. As soon as the door closed behind him, he heard footsteps, softer than his own, coming down the corridor from the same direction he had taken. The dandy's footsteps sounded on the cement stairs above. Pumo began to go up the stairs. It seemed to him that the footsteps in the corridor paused at the staircase door, but he could be certain only that he heard them no more. Footsteps climbed the stairs toward the fifth floor.

The door below him clicked open. Pumo did not look down until he was at the landing where the stairs changed direction. He went to the railing and bent over to see the person who had just come onto the staircase. He could see only the railing and a wedge of stairs twisting around and around beneath him. Whoever was down there stopped moving. Pumo could still hear the tall dandy's steps ticking hollowly upward.

He moved a step away from the railing and looked up.

The footsteps from below began to ascend toward him.

Pumo took the step back to the railing and looked down, but at once the ascending footsteps stopped again. Whoever was coming toward him had moved back under the protection of the staircase.

Pumo's stomach went cold.

Then the third-floor door opened again, and the two Chinese women entered the staircase enclosure. He saw the tops of their heads and heard their clear emphatic voices, speaking Cantonese. Above, the door to the fifth floor slammed shut.

Pumo unfroze and left the railing.

He opened the door marked PERSONNEL ONLY on the fifth-floor landing and stepped into a vast dark space filled with books. The tall dandy had disappeared into one of the aisles between the stacks. His quiet footsteps came as if from everywhere in the enormous room. Tina could not hear any noises from the other side of the staircase door, but had a sudden, urgent image of a man creeping up the last few steps.

He stepped quickly into the stacks and found himself in a long empty aisle perhaps a yard wide between towering steel bookshelves. Far above, low-wattage bulbs beneath conical shades cast dim but distinct pools of illumination. The tall man's footsteps were no longer audible.

Pumo forced himself to move more slowly. Just as he reached a wide middle aisle, he heard the clicking of the door which opened onto the staircase. Someone slipped inside and closed the door behind him.

He could virtually *hear* the person who had just entered, wondering which aisle he had gone down. Pumo could not help feeling a prickle of fear.

Then he heard slow footsteps far off to his left. Pumo began to move toward the dandy, and heard the person who had just entered the stacks start down one of the narrow aisles. His feet hushed along in the soft, slow rhythms of the good old Jungle Walk.

Either he was going completely paranoid, Pumo thought, or Koko had followed him into the stacks. Koko had stolen his address book and discovered that the other men were out of town, and he was going to begin his excellent work all over again in America with Tina Pumo. He was all stoked up from reading about Ia Thuc, and Tina was next on his list.

But of course it would turn out that the person who had just come into the fifth-floor stacks was a librarian. The door said PERSONNEL ONLY. If Pumo turned down an aisle and ran into him, he'd turn out to be a fat little guy with Hush Puppies and a button-down shirt. Pumo went as noiselessly as possible down the wide middle aisle, doing a pretty fair Jungle Walk himself. Three aisles from the end, he stopped to listen.

From off to the left came quick faint footsteps that must have been the dandy's. If anyone else moved through the stacks, he was walking too quietly to be heard. Pumo peeked down a long aisle. Pools of light lay between columns of shelved books. He ducked into the aisle.

It seemed as long as a football field, narrowing, a tunnel seen through the wrong end of a telescope. Pumo moved quietly down the long tight aisle. In a queer hallucinatory trick of vision the spines and titles of books seemed to creep by him as they moved while he stood still. W.M. Thackeray, *Pendennis,* Vol. 1. W.M. Thackeray, *Pendennis,* Vol. 2. W.M. Thackeray, *The Newcomes. The Virginians. The Yellowplush Papers, ETC.,* bound in pink cloth board with gold lettering and published by Smith, Elder & Co. *Lovel the Widower, ETC.,* in matching pink and gold from Smith, Elder.

Pumo closed his eyes and heard a man cough softly into his fist one aisle away. Tina's eyes flew open, and the titles of the books before him melted into a single gorgeous Arabic scrawl of gold over a pink background. He supposed he nearly fainted.

The man who coughed took an almost silent step forward. Pumo stood still as a statue, afraid to breathe even though the man in the next aisle could only be the librarian in Hush Puppies. Whoever it was took three swift, gliding steps down the aisle.

When Pumo thought that the other man had gone far enough up toward the middle aisle, he began to move toward the door.

In that instant, as if Tina had given a cue, someone whistled the beginning of "Body and Soul" far away toward the left side of the room—an ornate performance full of scoops and trills and vibrato.

Pumo heard the man in the next aisle begin to move less cautiously toward the whistler. Someone off that way slid several books off a shelf—the dandy had found what he had been looking for when he came into the stacks. The man in the next aisle turned into the middle aisle. Pumo realized that if he had parted the Thackeray volumes in front of him, he would have seen the face of the man in the next aisle. His heart began to pound.

Just as the other man passed before the head of the aisle in which he had been hiding, Pumo emerged from the stacks and was only a few paces from the door to the staircase. A dim, shielded light burned above it. He took a step toward the door.

The knob began to revolve and Pumo's heart stopped

for the space of a single beat. The knob revolved and the whole door swung abruptly in on a bubble of conversation and a sudden tide of light.

Dark figures stepped toward him. Pumo stopped moving; they stopped moving too. The high-pitched conversation abruptly ceased. Then he saw that they were the Chinese women he had seen in the third-floor corridor.

"Oh!" both women uttered in a whisper.

"Excuse me," Pumo whispered back. "I guess I got lost or something."

They waved him forward, grinning now that they were over the surprise of seeing him, and Pumo went past them through the door and out onto what felt like the safety of the landing.

Back in his loft that night Pumo told Maggie only that he had not been able to confirm that the other person looking at material about Ia Thuc had used the murdered journalist's name. He did not want to describe what had happened in the stacks, because nothing really had happened. After a long dinner and a bottle of Bonnes Mares at a good restaurant across the street, he was too ashamed of his panic. It had been imagination doing a nasty trick with the materials of his memory, and Maggie was right, he was still trying to get over his experiences in Vietnam. The bearded man had given him some name like Roberto Diaz, and everything else was just fantasy. A fellow passenger or a coked-up airport employee had killed the yuppie at JFK. Maggie looked so beautiful that even the bored SoHo waiter stared at her, and the wine was full of subtle tastes. He looked at her face glowing at him across the table and knew that as long as your health and your money held out, the world was sane.

The next day neither Pumo nor Maggie looked at *The New York Times*, neither of them paused to look at the headlines of the tabloids on the newsstands they hurried past on their various errands. LIBRARY CHIEF SLAIN said the *Post*, with imperfect accuracy. The *News* settled for the Agatha Christie-like touch of MURDER IN THE LIBRARY. Both tabloids gave half of their front pages to a portrait shot of Dr. Anton Mayer-Hall, a tall bearded man in a double-breasted suit. Dr. Mayer-Hall, Director of Projects for New York Public Libraries and a staff member of the library for twenty-four years, had been found slain in a section of the fifth-floor stacks reserved for library personnel. It was speculated that he had used that section of the fifth floor as a shortcut to his office, where he had been due for an appointment with the library's publicity director, Mei-lan Hudson. Ms. Hudson and her assistant Adrien Lo, using the same shortcut, had stopped and questioned an intruder in the same section of the library where Dr. Mayer-Hall was murdered a few minutes before their discovery of the body. The intruder, whose description was now in the hands of the police, was being sought for questioning. The *Times* offered its readers a smaller photograph and a detailed map with arrows and an *X* where the body was found.

4

What do you fear?

I fear that I made him up. That I gave him all his best ideas.

You fear that he is an idea come to life?

He is his own idea come to life.

How did Victor Spitalny get to Bangkok?

It was simple. He found a soldier at the airport who was willing to switch his nametag and travel documents for the sake of going to Honolulu instead of Bangkok. So everything proved that PFC Spitalny went to Honolulu on Air Pacific Flight 206—not only the tickets, but also and including check-in lists, passenger rosters, seating charts filled out in-flight, and boarding passes. A PFC named Victor Spitalny could conclusively be shown to have stayed in a single room at the Hotel Lanai costing the equivalent of twenty dollars American per night for six nights, and to have returned on Air Pacific Flight 207, arriving back in Vietnam at 2100 hours 7 October 1969. It was indisputable that PFC Spitalny had gone to and returned from Honolulu during the time that he had disappeared in the middle of a street riot in Bangkok.

Finally, a PFC named Michael Warland who claimed to have lost all his papers admitted that on the morning of 2 October 1969 he had met and spoken with PFC Victor Spitalny who had suggested that they exchange places during their R&Rs. When he did not locate PFC

Spitalny in the airport on 8 October, he stored his belongings in a locker and returned to his unit. When the deception was revealed, PFC Spitalny was listed as AWOL.

What did all this do for Spitalny?

It bought him weeks of time.

Why did Spitalny want to go to Bangkok with Dengler?

He had already planned it all.

What happened to the girl?

The girl disappeared. She ran through an enraged crowd in Patpong, showing on her palms blood shed in a cave in Vietnam, and ran invisibly through the world for years until I saw her. Then I began to understand.

What did you understand?

She was back because he was back.

Then why did you bless her?

Because if I saw her, then I was back too.

17

KOKO

1

On West End Avenue the old lady nodded at him from a window in an apartment building across the street and he waved up at her. The doorman, in an ornate uniform of blue and grey with gold epaulettes, was also looking at him, but in a far less friendly manner. The doorman, who had known Roberto Ortiz, would not let him in, though *inside* was where he had to be. He could still see the Ia Thuc photographs he had looked at in the library, and the darkness at the center of those photographs, which had made him shake, pressed him toward the *inside*, the harbor that *inside* was.

You crazy? the doorman said. You outa your mind? You can't go in there.

I have to go in there.

The world had given him Pumo the Puma, standing in the Microfilm Room like an answered prayer, and Koko switched on the invisibility switch and followed Pumo the Puma down the corridor and up the stairs and into the vast room filled with bookcases in tall rows, and then everything had gone wrong, the world had tricked him, the Joker jumped out of the pack cackling and dancing—another man died in front of him, not Pumo the Puma, and it was Bill Dickerson again. The getting away. The escape. So Koko himself had to hide, the world was slick and savage and it turned its back on you. On Broadway mad old shapes in rags with bare swollen feet rushed at you, speaking in tongues, their lips black because they breathed fire. The ragged mad shapes knew about the Joker because they had seen him too, they knew Koko was going astray, astray, and they knew about Koko's mistake in the library. This time he had won the wager again, but it was the wrong wager because it was the wrong man. Then Puma had melted away. When the mad ragged bums spoke in tongues they said, *You're making mistakes! Bad mistakes! You don't belong here!*

I can't let you in here, the doorman said. You want me to call the cops? Get away or I'll call the cops, get your ass out of here.

Koko was standing now on the corner of West End Avenue and West 78th Street, the molten center of the universe, looking up at the building where Roberto Ortiz had lived. A vein jumped in his neck, and the cold bit his face.

The old lady could come down and lead him into the building, Koko thought, where he could ride up and down on the elevators and wear Roberto Ortiz's clothes forever. In warmth and safety. Now he was in the wrong world and nothing in the wrong world was right.

This was one thing Koko knew. He was not supposed to live in a small bare room next to the crazy man at the Christian's Association.

He had the address book all laid out on the little table. He had the names and addresses circled.

But Harry Beevers did not answer his telephone.

But Conor Linklater did not answer his telephone.

Michael Poole's answering machine spoke in Michael Poole's voice and gave another number where a woman answered. This woman had a stern, unforgiving voice.

Koko remembered, *I always liked the smell of blood.*

Koko felt the cold tears on his face and turned away from the old woman's window and began to walk down West End Avenue.

The crazy man's hair was ropes and his eyes were red. He lived in the room next to Koko and he came in and he laughed and said—what all this shit on the walls, boy? Killin' is a see-yun. The crazy man was black and wore exhausted black man's clothes.

Things were going fast and Koko was going fast down

West End Avenue. Frozen bushes burst into flame, and across the street a tall woman with red hair whispered, *Once you kill 'em, they your responsibility forever.*

The woman with the hard voice knew that.

On wide crowded 72nd Street he crossed over to Broadway. And behold darkness shall cover the earth. Yet once a little while, and I will shake the heavens and the earth.

For he is like a refiner's fire.

If he said that to the woman, would she know how he felt in the toilet after Bill Dickerson walked away? In the library, when the Joker jumped out of the pack and jigged and capered between the books?

I didn't start off in this business to accept substitutes, he said to himself. I can say that to her.

Time was a needle and at the end was the needle's eye. When you passed through the needle—when you pulled the needle through its own eye after you—

a man of sorrow and acquainted with grief were you.

A man in a golden fur coat was staring at Koko and Koko stared right back. I am not troubled by the hostile stares of strangers, I am a man rejected and despised. "I am a man rejected and despised," Koko said to the staring man, who had already turned his back and was walking away.

Koko walked tense and haunted down Eighth Avenue. Everything between West End Avenue, twenty blocks north, and Eighth Avenue had passed in a blurred moment. The world glittered as a cold thing glitters. He was outside not *inside*, and back in his terrible room the black man waited to tell him about sin.

The grinning demons loved the men and women they escorted through eternity—demons had a great secret, they too were created to love and be loved.

"Are you speaking to me?" asked an old man with a polished face and a dirty black beret. The old man was not one of the ragged shapes sent to torture him: the old man spoke in English, not in tongues. A jewel of snot hung from his nose. "My name is Hansen."

"I'm a travel agent," Koko said.

"Well, welcome to New York," said Hansen. "I guess you're a visitor here."

"I've been away a long time, but they're keeping me busy. Keeping me busy in all directions."

"That's good!" the old man chortled. He was delighted to have someone talk to him.

Koko asked if he could buy him a drink, and Hansen accepted with a grateful smile. The two of them went into a Mexican restaurant on Eighth Avenue near 55th Street and when Koko called for "Mexican drinks!" the bartender placed two fizzy-looking, frothy-looking, soupy-looking drinks before them. The bartender had frizzy black hair, olive skin, and a drooping black moustache, and Koko liked him very much. The bar was warm and dark and Koko liked the silence and the bowls of salty chips placed beside the red sauce. The old man kept blinking at Koko as if he could not believe his luck.

"I'm a veteran," Koko said.

"Oh," the old man said. "I never went."

The old man asked the bartender what he thought about the guy in the library.

"He was a mistake," Koko said. "God blinked."

"What guy?" said the bartender, and the old man wheezed and said, "Newspapers eat that shit up."

To the bartender and the old man, Koko said, "I am a man despised and rejected, a man of sorrow and acquainted with grief."

"I am the same," the bartender said.

Old Hansen raised his glass and toasted him. He even winked.

"Do you want to hear the song of the mammoths?" Koko asked.

"I always liked elephants," Hansen said.

"I am the same," the bartender said.

So Koko sang the song of the mammoths, the song so ancient even the elephants had forgotten its meaning, and old Hansen and the Mexican bartender listened in reverent silence.

PART FOUR

IN THE UNDERGROUND GARAGE

18

THE STEPS TO HEAVEN

1

Two days earlier, Michael Poole stood at the window of his hotel room, looking down at Surawong Road, so jammed with trucks, taxicabs, automobiles, and the little covered motorized carts called ruk-tuks that the traffic formed a seamless body. Across Surawong Road lay the Patpong District, where the bars and sex shows and massage parlors were only just beginning to open up. The room's air conditioner set up a rattling hum beside Poole, for while the air was so grey as to be nearly grainy, the day was even warmer and more humid than Singapore had been that morning. Out of sight behind Poole and, like both the air conditioner and the traffic in full spate, Conor Linklater was walking around the room, picking up the guest book, looking at all the furniture, inspecting the postcards in the desk drawer, and all the while talking to himself. He was still excited by what the cabdriver had said to them.

"Right away," Conor mumbled. "Can you believe that? I mean, is this place about getting your rocks off, or what?"

The driver had informed them that this hotel was very convenient, being on the fringe of the Patpong area, and then had permanently impressed Conor with both himself and the city of Bangkok by asking if the gentlemen wished to stop at a massage parlor before reaching their hotel. No ordinary massage parlor, no tank with skinny country girls who did not know how to behave, but a luxurious place, real sophistication, porcelain bathtubs, elegant rooms, full body massages, girls so beautiful they made you come two-three times before you even got going. He had promised girls so pretty they looked like princesses, movie stars, *Playboy* centerfolds, girls as voluptuous and yielding as the girls in dreams, girls with the thighs of drum majorettes, the breasts of Indian goddesses, the faces of cover girls, the silken skin of courtesans, the subtle minds of poet-diplomats, the agility of gymnasts, the muscle tone of swimmers, the playfulness of monkeys, the stamina of mountain goats, and best of all . . .

"Best of all," Conor mused. "Best of all. No women's lib. How about that? I mean, I got nothing against women's lib. Everybody's a free man in this world, girls included, and I know lots of women who are better men than most men. But how much of that stuff do you have to listen to? Especially in the bedroom? I mean, most of 'em already make twice as much money as I do, they run computers, they run offices, they run companies, Donovan's is full of 'em, they won't even let you buy 'em drinks, they make a face if you open the door for 'em, I mean, maybe we shoulda done what the guy said . . ."

"Umm," Poole said. Conor himself was hardly paying any attention to his babbling, and any response was sufficient.

". . . do it later, doesn't matter, hey, they have two restaurants in this hotel, nice bar too, I bet it's nicer here than wherever the Lost Boss is now, goin' around telling everybody he's a cop or a secret agent or the Bishop of New York."

Poole laughed out loud.

"Right! I mean, one hand feeds the other, but with that guy . . ."

If by four o'clock all of Bangkok seemed congested, the few square blocks that made up Patpong were already even more crowded than that. The usual traffic filled the street, and the sidewalks were so crowded Poole could see very little of the pavement. People milled around on the sidewalks before the bars and sex clubs, flowed up and down the stairs and fire escapes. Around them signs sparkled and flashed: MISSISSIPPI, DAISY CHAIN, HOT SEX,

WHISKEY, MONTMARTRE, SEX, SEX, and many others, all crowding together and shouting for attention.

"Dengler died out there," Conor said, looking down on Phat Pong Road.

"Yes, he did," Michael answered.

"It looks like the goddamn monkey house."

Poole laughed. That was what it looked like, all right.

"I think we're gonna find him, Mikey."

"I do, too," Poole said.

2

After he and Conor returned to the hotel that evening, Michael waited while the Thai switchboard operator put through his credit card call to Westerholm, New York. He finally had something positive to say about what Beevers called their "mission." He had seen something in a bookstore that confirmed his impression that he and Conor would find Underhill in Bangkok. If it took two days, they might be coming home two days after that—with Underhill in tow or not, however it worked out. Michael wanted to find some detox clinic where Underhill could straighten himself out and get the rest Poole was sure he needed. Anybody who had survived Bangkok for a long time would need a good rest. If Underhill had committed murder, Poole would find him a great lawyer and get him started on the insanity defense that would at least keep him out of jail. That might not be sufficiently dramatic for a mini-series, but it would be the best ending for Underhill and anyone who cared about him.

What Poole had seen in Patpong's most uncharacteristic place of business, a huge bright bookstore called Patpong Books, had given him indirect proof of Underhill's innocence and his presence in Bangkok. Poole and Conor had walked into the bookstore to get out of the heat and escape the crowds for a moment. Patpong Books was cool and uncrowded, and Michael was happily surprised to see that the fiction department took up at least a third of the store. He could get something for himself, and something to give to Stacy Talbot too. He wandered down the fiction aisles, not realizing that he was looking for Tim Underhill's name until he found an entire shelf filled with Underhill's novels. There were four and five copies of every Underhill novel, hardcovers interspersed with paperbacks, from *A Beast in View* to *Blood Orchid.*

Didn't that mean that he lived here? That he was a customer of Patpong Books? The shelf of novels reminded Poole of the "Local Authors" shelf at All Booked, Westerholm's best bookstore—it was as good as a signed statement that Underhill frequented the shop. And if he did that, would he also be going out and killing people? Poole could almost feel Underhill's presence near his well-stocked shelf. If he did not come in, would the store stock so many books by a writer so obscure?

It added up, at least to Poole, and once Poole had explained it to him, to Conor too.

When he and Conor left their hotel earlier that day, Poole's first impression was that Bangkok was Thailand's Calcutta. Whole families seemed to live and work on the streets, for often Poole saw women crouching on a broken pavement, feeding the children that roiled around them while smashing up concrete with the hammers in their free hands. Down the center of every sidewalk sat a row of women hacking a trench with hammers and picks. Smoke from cook-fires drifted from the vents inside half-constructed buildings in vacant lots. Plaster dust and hard little motes that stung the skin, smoke and grease and exhaust fumes hung in the grey air. Poole felt the permeable membrane of the air settle over his skin like a cobweb.

Here was a great red sign for the HEAVEN MASSAGE PARLOR, and here were rising stairs of concrete painted with blue stars, where a barefoot, spindly woman sat morosely beating a squalling child in the midst of a welter of bags, bottles, and parcels tied with coarse rope. Her hand struck its face, her fist struck its chest. The stairs led up to a wide canopy advertising the HONEYPOT NIGHTCLUB and RESTAURANT. The woman stared through Dr. Poole, and her eyes said: This is my child, this is my dwelling, you are invisible to me.

For a second he felt dizzy; a grey shadowland surrounded him, a world of shifting dimensions and sudden abysses, where reality was no more than just another illusion. Then he remembered seeing a woman in blue tumble down a wet green hillside, and knew that he was flinching away from his own life.

Michael knew about the flinch. Once he had persuaded Judy to come into New York with him to see *Tracers*, a play written and performed by Vietnam veterans. Michael thought it was a wonderful play. *Tracers* put you very close to Vietnam, and virtually every minute of it called up pictures and echoes of his time there. He found himself crying and laughing, undone by uncontrollable feelings, as on the bench in Bras Basah Park. (Judy had thought *Tracers* a sentimental form of therapy for the actors.) At various times in the play, a character named Dinky Dau pointed an M-16 straight at Michael's head. Dinky Dau probably could not see Michael, who was in the eighth row, and the gun was not loaded, but when the muzzle swung toward him, Michael felt dizzy and faint. Helplessly, he felt himself squeezing as far back in his seat as he could go, holding tightly onto the armrests. He hoped he did not look as frightened as he felt.

Bangkok aroused some of the same feelings in him as Dinky Dau's gun. At the dedication of the Memorial, fourteen years of his life had just dropped away. He had been a raw nerve, a boy soldier again, invisible inside nice, comfortable, humane Dr. Poole. It seemed that nice comfortable Dr. Poole was only the scaffolding around that raw nerve.

How strange it was to be so invisible, his real self so invisible to others. Michael wished that Conor and Pumo had gone to *Tracers* with him.

Michael and Conor walked past a dusty window filled with trusses and artficial legs like amputations, bent at the knee. "You know," Conor said, "I'm homesick. I want to eat a hamburger. I want a beer that doesn't taste like it was made with stuff they swept up off the street. I want to be able to go to the *can* again—that shit I got from the doctor closed my asshole so tight it's just a seam. You know the worst? I even want to pick up my toolchest again. I want to come home from work, clean up, and get down to my good old bar. Don't you miss stuff like that, Mikey?"

"Not exactly," Poole said.

"Don't you miss work?" Conor's eyebrows lifted. "Don't you miss getting on your whatsit, your stethoscope, all that? Telling kids it's only gonna hurt a little bit?"

"I don't really miss that side of it," Poole said. "In fact, I haven't been very happy with my practice lately."

"Don't you *miss* anything?"

I miss a girl in St. Bart's Hospital, Michael thought, but finally said, "Some of my patients, I guess."

Conor gave him a suspicious look and suggested they turn around and take a look at Patpat before they caught Black Lung disease. They had come nearly all the way to Charoen Krung Road, the Oriental Hotel, and the river.

"Patpong," Michael corrected. "Where Dengler was killed."

"Oh, *that* Patpong," Conor said.

If Patpong held an initial surprise, it was that it was no larger than what Poole had seen from his window. The section of Bangkok that attracted male tourists from all over America, Europe, and Asia was only three streets long and one street wide. Poole had imagined that like the St. Pauli section of Hamburg it covered at least a few more blocks. At five in the afternoon, the neon signs blazed above the heads of the crowds of men going in and out of the bars and massage parlors. 123 GIRLS WET. SMOKING. A tout positioned at the bottom of a flight of stairs whistled at Poole and slipped into his hands a brochure listing the specialties of the house.

1. Beautiful girl hostesses—continuous show!
2. 1 free drink per customer
3. All languages, international clientele
4. Ping-Pong balls
5. Smoking
6. Magic Marker
7. Coca Cola
8. Striptease
9. Woman-woman
10. Man-woman
11. Man-woman-woman
12. Room for use and observe

As he read this document, a small Thai male interposed himself between Michael and Conor. "You in good time," he said. "Late is too late. Choose now, you get best." He took a fat credit-card holder from his jacket pocket, and let it drop down in segments, flipping open as it fell to reveal photographs of perhaps sixty naked girls, "Pick now—late is too late." He grinned, wonderfully at ease with himself, his product, and his message, and showed bright gold incisors.

He held the ribbon of photographs up to Conor's face. "All available! Going fast!"

Michael saw Conor's face turn red, and pulled him down the street, shooing the massage parlor tout away with his other hand.

The tout waggled his photos in the air and made them shimmy.

"Boys, too. Pretty boys, boys all sizes. Later is too late, especially for boys." From another pocket he withdrew another wad of photographs. These too he let waterfall out of his palm. "Beautiful, hot, suck you, fuck you, smoke you—"

"Telephone," Poole said, thinking he had read the word on the menu from the sex club.

The tout frowned and shook his head. "No telephone—what you want? You on death trip?" He started to fold and gather his photographs into stacks as he backed away from them. For a moment he regarded them both very shrewdly. "You two guys on real death trip? Real kinky? Must be very, very careful."

"What's with this guy?" Conor said. "Show him the picture."

The little tout was looking nervously from side to side. He had folded his wares into his jacket pockets. Poole held out one of the photographs from the manila envelope. The tout licked his lips with a long colorless tongue. The man stepped backward, grinned emptily at Conor and Michael, and transferred his attentions to a tall white boy in a Twisted Sister T-shirt.

"I don't know about you," Conor said, "but I could use a beer."

Poole nodded, and followed him up the stairs to the Montparnasse Bar. Conor disappeared through a curtain of blue plastic streamers, and Michael followed him into a small, dimly lighted room ringed with chairs. From one wall jutted a tiny bar behind which stood a huge Samoan in a tight red muscle shirt. A small raised wooden stage took up the front of the room. Conor was handing bills to an obese woman seated at a desk just inside the door. "Admission, twenty baht," she croaked at Poole.

Poole glanced toward the stage, where a chunky Thai girl wearing a bra was doing something that required her to hunch down over her splayed knees. A dozen undressed girls inspected Poole and Conor. The only other man in the room was a drunken Australian bulging out of a sweat-stained tan suit and clutching a tall can of Foster's Lager. A girl was curled up in his lap, playing with his necktie and whispering into his ear.

"You know what I was trying to think of, out on the street?" Michael asked. "Smoking."

"I hope they don't have it," Conor said.

The girl onstage flashed a broad smile and cupped her hands just below her vagina. A Ping-Pong ball appeared in its folds, then disappeared back up inside her, then finally dropped out onto her palm. Another Ping-Pong ball popped into view.

Four girls had appeared around them, smiling and cooing. Two sat in the chairs on either side of them, and the other two kneeled.

"You very handsome," said the girl before Poole. She began to stroke his knee. "You be my husban'?"

"Hey," Conor said, "if these people can do shit like that with Ping-Pong balls . . ."

They ordered drinks for two of the girls, and the others padded across the room. Onstage, the Ping-Pong balls were rotating in and out of sight with the speed of a revolving door.

The girl beside Poole whispered, "You hard yet? I make hard."

Another strikingly pretty girl emerged through the curtain of streamers beside the stage. She was naked, and to Poole she looked no older than fifteen. The girl smiled at the men and women before her, then displayed a cigarette at the end of her fingers like a tiny baton, and lit it with a pink disposable lighter.

The girl bent backwards with a smooth acrobatic motion, thrusting her slender legs and pubis at the audience, and planted one hand on the floor. With the other she reached between her legs and inserted the cigarette into her vagina.

"This is getting deep," Conor said.

The tip of the cigarette glowed, and half an inch of ash formed at the tip. The girl reached forward and removed the cigarette. A plume of smoke blew from her vagina. She repeated this performance several times. Poole's girl began stroking the inside of his thigh and talking to him about growing up in the country.

"My momma poor," she said. "My village poor-poor. Many many days, no eat. You take me back to America? I be your wife. Be *good* wife."

"I already have a wife."

"Okay, I be number-two wife. Number two be best wife."

"I wouldn't be surprised," he said, looking at the girl's dimpled face. He drank his beer and felt very tired and comradely.

"In Thailand, many men have number-two wife," she said.

The teenager onstage blew a perfect smoke ring out of her vagina. "Pussy blow fractals!" the Australian yelled. "Record collectors are fun to go around with, cricketers swing big bats, but mathematicians are in their prime!"

"You have many television sets?" the girl asked Poole.

"Many."

"You have washer-dryer?"

"Absolutely."

"Gas or electric?"

Poole considered. "Gas."

The girl pursed her lips. "You have two cars?"

"Of course."

"You get extra car for me?"

"In America, everybody gets their own car. Even children get their own car."

"You have children?"

"No."

"*I* give children," the whore said. "You nice man. Two children, three children, all you want. Give American names. Tommy. Sally."

"Nice kids," Poole said. "I miss them already."

"We have best sex, your whole life long. Even sex with your wife get better."

"I don't have sex with my wife," Poole said, amazing himself.

"Then we have twice as much sex, make up."

"Pussy smoke cigarette, now pussy talk telephone," the Australian said. "Pussy call University of Queensland, tell them I'll be late."

The nymph onstage sprang upright and bowed. All the girls, the Australian, and Poole applauded loudly. When she walked off, a tall, naked young woman came through the streamers with a big folder of paper and a handful of Magic Markers.

Poole finished his beer and watched the girl onstage plant two Magic Markers in her vagina and hunker over a large sheet of paper to draw a very creditable horse.

"Where do gay men go in Bangkok?" Poole asked. "We're looking for a friend of ours."

"Patpong three. Two streets up. Gayboys. You are not a gayboy?"

Poole shook his head.

"Come in back with me. I *smoke* you." She threw her arms around his neck. Her skin had a delicious fragrance akin to the smell of apples, oiled leather, and cloves.

Poole and Conor left as the artist onstage was completing a landscape with mountains, a beach and palm trees, sailboats, and a sun with rays.

Just down the block from the Montparnasse were two dun-colored steps leading up to an open door and a sign reading PATPONG BOOKS. While Poole discovered the row of Underhill's novels, Conor went off to look at magazines. Poole asked both the clerk on duty and the manager if they knew or had ever seen Tim Underhill, but neither man even knew his name. Poole bought the hardcover copy of *The Divided Man* he had carried up to the register to ask about, then he and Conor went out to have a beer at the Mississippi Queen.

"Hell, I signed one of those Koko cards myself," Conor said at the bar.

"I did too," Poole said. "When was yours?" He had never imagined that only one member of the platoon had cut off ears and written Koko on a regimental card, but Conor's admission gave him a mixture of surprise and pleasure.

"The day after Ho Chi Minh's birthday. We had to go out on some damn coordinated patrol with platoon two. Just like on Ho's birthday. Except that this time the NVA mined the perimeter, and one of the tanks hit a fragmentation mine. Which slowed everything way, way down. Remember crawling out along the road, probing for the rest of the mines? Shoulder to shoulder? Anyhow, after that, Underhill surprised their point man out in the bushes, and we got the rest of 'em in a killing box."

"Right," Poole said. He could remember seeing the North Vietnamese soldiers moving like ghosts, like deer, along the road. They had not been boys. They were men in their thirties and forties, lifelong soldiers in a lifelong war. He had wanted very much to kill them.

"So when it was all over, I went back and did the point man." A tiny girl in a black leather bra and black leather microskirt had taken the stool beside Conor, and was bending over the bar grinning at him to catch his attention. "I mean, I can remember cutting that dude's ears off," Conor said. "It was hard to do, man. An ear is all like *gristle.* You wind up only cutting off the top part, and it doesn't look like an ear. It was like I wasn't thinking, like I wasn't even myself. I had to keep on sawing back and forth. And when I cut through it, his head slapped right down on the mud and I was holding this ear. Then I had to roll him over and do it all over again."

The girl, who had listened carefully to this speech, pushed herself away from the bar and went across the big room to whisper to another bar girl.

"What did you do with the ear?" Poole asked.

"Threw it into the trees. I'm no pervert."

"Right," Poole agreed. "It would be pretty sick to save the cars."

"Damn straight," Conor said.

3

The telephone had gone from making a buzzing sound to total dead silence to a high-pitched whistle. Conor looked up from the pictures of naked girls in the magazine he had bought at Patpong Books.

"When did you do yours?" Conor said.

"My what?"

"Koko card."

"About a month after the court-martials were announced. It was after a patrol in the A Shau Valley."

"End of September," Conor said. "I remember that one. I picked up the bodies."

"Yes, you did."

"In the tunnel—where the other big cache was. The rice cache."

"That's the one," Poole said.

"Old *Mikey,*" Conor said. "You're an animal, man."

"I still don't know how I did it," Poole said. "Gave me nightmares for years."

Then the operator cut through the whistling to say, "We are connecting you to your party, sir," and Michael Poole readied himself to talk to his wife while still holding up before him, fresh from its long internment within him, the memory of using his K-Bar to saw off the ears of a corpse propped up against a fifty-pound bag of rice. And the darker memory of using his knife on the dead man's eyes.

Victor Spitalny had seen the body first, and had come out of the tunnel bawling *Awww Righht!*

The silence deepened and changed texture. Two deep thudding clicks came over the line, like firm but complex linkages made in deep space.

Poole looked at his watch. Seven o'clock P.M. in Bangkok, seven in the morning in Westerholm, New York.

After all this time he heard the sound, familiar as a lullaby, of the American dial tone, which abruptly ceased. More deepspace silence, followed by the dim ringing of a telephone.

The telephone ceased ringing with a clunk that meant the answering machine was on. At seven in the morning, Judy was either still in the bedroom or down in the kitchen.

Michael waited through Judy's message. When the beep came, he said, "Judy? Are you home? This is Michael."

He waited three, four, five beats. "Judy?" He was about to hang up where he heard a loud click and his wife said, "So it's you," in a flat, uninflected voice.

"Hello. I'm glad you answered."

"I guess I'm glad too. Are the children having fun in the sun?"

"Judy—"

"Are they?"

Poole had a quick, guilty flash of the girl rubbing his crotch. "I suppose you could call it fun. We're still looking for Tim Underhill."

"How nice for you."

"We learned that he left Singapore, so Beevers is in Taipei and Conor and I are in Bangkok. I think we might find him in the next few days."

"Dandy. You're in Bangkok, reliving your venereal youth, and I'm doing my job in Westerholm, which happens to be the location of your house and your medical practice. You remember, I hope, if your faulty short-term memory has not already erased it, that I wasn't exactly overjoyed when you announced that you were taking this trip of yours?"

"I didn't exactly announce it in that sense, Judy."

"Bad short-term memory, what did I tell you?"

"I thought you'd be happy to hear from me."

"I don't precisely wish you ill, no matter what you may think."

"I never thought you did."

"In a way I'm almost glad you left, because it gives me the space for some long-overdue thinking about our relationship. I really wonder whether we're doing either one of us any good anymore."

"You want to talk about that now?"

"Just tell me one thing—did you ask one of your little friends to call me up periodically, to check on whether or not I'm home?"

"I don't know what you're talking about."

"I am talking about the little gnome who loves the sound of my voice on the answering machine so much that he calls up two or three times a day. And by the way, I don't care if you don't trust me anymore than that because I am a person who takes responsibility for herself around here, Michael, and I always have been."

"You're getting anonymous phone calls?" Michael asked, grateful to have discovered a reason for his wife's hostility.

"As if you didn't know."

"Oh, Judy," he said, and his pain and regret were very clear in his voice.

"All right," she said. "Okay."

"Call the police."

"What good will that do?"

"If he calls that often, they'll be able to nail him."

There was a long silence between them that to Michael seemed almost comfortable, marital.

"This is wasting money," Judy said.

"It's probably some student's idea of a joke. You need to relax a little, Judy."

She hesitated. "Well, Bob Bunce asked me for dinner tomorrow night. It'll be nice to get out of the house."

"The wasp expert?" Michael said. "Good."

"What are you talking about?"

Two years before, Michael had told some people at a faculty party about Victor Spitalny running out of the Ia Thuc cave screaming about being stung by millions of wasps. This was one part of Ia Thuc that he was able to speak about: it was harmless, and nobody died in this story. All that happened was that Victor Spitalny tore out of the cave, scraping his face with his fingernails and screaming until Poole rolled him up in his groundcloth. When he stopped screaming, Poole unwrapped him. Spitalny's face and hands were covered with rapidly disappearing red welts. "Ain't no wasps in Vietnam, little brother," SP4 Cotton said, snapping a picture of Spitalny half-emerged from the groundcloth. "Every other kind of bug, but ain't no wasps."

A six-three English teacher named Bob Bunce, who had floppy blond hair and a thin patrician face and wore beautiful tweed suits, told Michael that since wasps were found throughout the northern hemisphere, there must be wasps in Vietnam. Michael thought that Bunce was a smug self-important know-it-all. He was supposed to come from a wealthy Main Line family and to be teaching English because he had a priestly calling to it. Bunce was a liberal's wet dream. He had gone on to say that because Vietnam was a semitropical country, wasps would be rare, and anyhow that most wasps in all parts of the world were solitaries. "And aren't there more interesting questions about Ia Thuc than this, Michael?" he had insinuatingly asked.

"It doesn't matter," Michael said now to Judy. "Where are you going to go?"

"He didn't *tell* me, Michael. *Where* he *takes* me is not so ultra-important. I'm not asking for a four-star dinner, you know, all I want is a little *company*."

"Fine."

"It's not as though you're exactly starving for companionship, is it? But I think there are massage parlors in Westerholm, too."

"I don't think so," Michael laughed.

"I don't want to talk anymore," Judy promptly said.

"Okay."

Another lengthy silence.

"Have a nice dinner with Bunce."

"You have no right to say that," Judy told him, and hung up without saying good-bye.

Michael gently replaced the receiver.

Conor was walking around the room, looking out the window, bouncing on the balls of his feet, avoiding Michael's eyes. At length he cleared his throat. "Trouble?"

"My life is becoming ridiculous."

Conor laughed. "My life always was ridiculous. Ridiculous isn't so bad."

"Maybe not," Michael said, and he and Conor shared a smile. "I think I'm going to bed early tonight. Do you mind being alone? Tomorrow we can make a list of places to visit and really get down to work."

Conor took a couple of the photographs of Tim Underhill with him when he left.

4

Relieved to be alone, Michael ordered a simple meal from room service and stretched out on his bed with the copy of *The Divided Man* he had purchased that afternoon. He had not read Underhill's most successful book in years, and he was surprised by how quickly he was caught up in it again, how thoroughly it managed to distract him from his worries about Judy.

Hal Esterhaz, the hero of *The Divided Man*, was a homicide detective in Monroe, Illinois, a medium-sized city filled with foundries, auto-body shops, and vacant lots behind chain-link fences. Esterhaz had served as a lieutenant in Vietnam, and had returned home to marry and quickly divorce his high school girlfriend. He drank a lot, but for years had been a respected police officer with an uncomfortable secret: he was bisexual. His guilt over his sexual longings for other men accounted not only for his drinking, but also his occasional brutality with arrested criminals. Esterhaz was careful about this, and let himself beat only those criminals—rapists and child molesters—most despised by other policemen.

Michael suddenly found himself wondering if Esterhaz had been based on Harry Beevers. This thought had never occurred to him when he first read the book, but now, alhough the detective was tougher and more enigmatic than Beevers, Poole virtually saw the Lost Boss's face on his body. Beevers was not bisexual, at least as far as Michael knew, but Poole would not have been surprised to learn that Beevers had a wide streak of sadism hidden within him.

Michael also saw another likelihood that had slipped past him when he first read the book. Monroe, Illinois, the gritty city through which Hal Esterhaz pursued the mystery at the heart of *The Divided Man*, sounded very much like Milwaukee, Wisconsin, the city M.O. Dengler had described so often. Monroe had a large Polish population on its south side, a large black ghetto on its near north side, and a major league ball team. The mansions of the rich stood along three or four streets near its lakefront. A dark, polluted river ran through its seedy downtown. There were paper mills and tanneries, adult bookstores, bowling allies, miserable winters, bars and taverns everywhere, barrel-shaped women in babushkas waiting at bus stops. This was the landscape of Dengler's childhood.

Poole was soon so taken up in the novel's story that it was more than an hour before a third belated recognition stung him, that *The Divided Man* was virtually a meditation on Koko.

An unemployed piano player is found with his throat slit in his room at a shabby downtown hotel called the St. Alwyn. Beside the body has been placed a piece of paper with the words Blue Rose penciled upon it. Hal Esterhaz is assigned to the case, and recognizes the victim as a regular patron of one of Monroe's gay bars. He had once had sex with the man. Of course he suppresses the information about his fugitive relationship with the victim when he files his report.

A prostitute is the next victim, found with her throat slit in an alley behind the St. Alwyn, and again there is a note: Blue Rose. Esterhaz learns that she too had lived in the hotel and was a friend of the piano player; Esterhaz suspects that she witnessed the murder or knew something that would lead the police to the killer.

A week later, a young doctor is found slaughtered in his Jaguar, parked in the garage of the lakefront mansion where he lived alone with a housekeeper. Esterhaz reports to the scene miserably hung over, still wearing yesterday's clothes, with no real memory of the night before. He had visited a bar called the House of Correction, he can remember ordering drinks, talking, he remembers putting on his coat, having trouble with the sleeves . . . after that everything is black until the telephone call from his station, which had awakened him on the couch. What makes him feel far worse than his hangover is that the young doctor had been his lover for more than a year some five years before. No one, not even the doctor's housekeeper, had known. Esterhaz conducts a competent scene-of-the-crime investigation, discovers a piece of paper with the words Blue Rose written on it, questions the housekeeper and bags and tags all the physical evidence, and when the medical examiner has finished and the body is removed, returns to the House of Correction. Another blackout, another morning on the couch with a half-empty bottle and a blaring television.

The following week another body is discovered, that of a male hustler and drug addict who had been one of Esterhaz's informants.

The next victim is a religious fanatic, a butcher who preaches to a congregation in a downtown storefront. Esterhaz not only knows this victim, he hates him. The butcher and his wife had been the most brutal of the series of foster parents who had raised Esterhaz. They had beaten and abused him almost daily, keeping him home from school to work out of sight in the back of the butcher shop—he was a sinner, he had to work until his hands bled, he had to memorize Scripture to save his soul, he was damned no matter how much Scripture he memorized so he required more beatings. He had been taken from the butcher's house only after a social worker had made an unannounced visit and discovered him covered in bruises and locked in the freezer "to repent."

In fact Hal Esterhaz is not even his real name, but had been given to him by social workers: his identity and parentage, even his exact age, are mysterious. All he knows of his origins is that he was found at the age of three or four, covered with frozen mud, wandering the downtown streets near the river in the middle of December. He had known no language; he had been starved nearly to death.

Even now, Esterhaz could not remember long stretches of his wretched childhood, and could remember none of his life before he was found wandering naked and starved on a street beside the Monroe River. His dreams of that time were of a golden world where giants petted him, fed him, and called him by a name that was never audible.

Hal Esterhaz had twice dropped out of school, been in trouble with the law, had spent his adolescence in a steamy obliterating hatred of everything about him. He had joined the army in a fit of drunken self-loathing, and the army had saved him. All his most decent, most dependable memories virtually began with basic training. It was, he thought, as if he had been three times born: once into the golden world, then into frozen, bitter Monroe, finally into uniform. His superiors had soon recognized his innate abilities and eventually recommended him for OCS. In exchange for another four years of service he would happily have served anyhow, he received the training that sent him to his second tour in Vietnam as a lieutenant.

After the murder of the butcher, Esterhaz begins to dream of washing blood from his hands, of standing sweaty and fearful at his sink, holding his bloodied hands under the steaming water, his shirt off, his chest dappled with red . . . he dreams of opening a door onto a garden of sick roses, roses of an unnatural, bright, chemical blue. He dreams that he is driving his car into deep darkness, with a familiar corpse on the seat beside him.

A second recognition came to Michael at this point, that surely he remembered M.O. Dengler once inserting into his tales of a fabulous Milwaukee—tales of finding a sick angel in a packing case and feeding him Cracker Jacks until he could fly again, of the man who made ice burn by breathing on it, of the famous Milwaukee criminal from whose mouth rats and insects flew instead of words—something about his parents being only half his parents, whatever that had meant.

Poole fell asleep with the book on his chest, no more than a hundred yards or so from the spot on Phat Pong Road where Dengler had bled to death.

19

HOW DENGLER DIED

1

According to the Army of the United States of America, Private First Class Dengler was the victim of a homicidal attack by person or persons unknown. Said attack occurred during Private Dengler's Rest and Recreation tour in the city of Bangkok, Thailand. Private Dengler suffered multiple cranial fractures, compound fractures of right and left tibia and fibula, fracture of the sacrum, rupture of the spleen, rupture of the right kidney, and puncture wounds in the upper portions of both lungs. Eight of Private Dengler's fingers had been severed, and both arms were dislocated. The nose and jaw had been splintered by multiple fractures. The skin of the deceased had been severely abraded, and much of the face torn away by the assailants. Identification had been secured through the victim's dogtags.

The Army found it unwise or unnecessary to speculate on the reasons for the attack on Private First Class Dengler, restricting its comments in this regard to a consideration of the tensions that grew up between members of the American Armed Forces and native populations.

2

In the light of the *Sergeant Khoffi* (1967) and *Private First Class Springwater* (1968) incidents in Bangkok, the formation of a commission to recommend on the advisability of restricting Rest and Recreation tours in the city of Bangkok to officer rank personnel was advised. (Attention was also drawn to less severe incidents in Honolulu and Hong Kong, and to the military-civilian-police triangle pertaining in these cities.)

Give us data, the Army pleaded, give us a Commission. (The recommendation was noted, considered, and shelved.) We advise an on-site study. (Also shelved.) Good liaison with local police being imperative, we suggest an assignment of officers with police training to police departments in Rest and Recreation areas where incidents such as above have been proven to be likely. (This recommendation, offered as a sop to the Police Department of the City of Bangkok, was never taken any further.) It was recommended that Military Police in Bangkok liaise with the Bangkok Police Department to seek out and locate local witnesses to the attack on PFC Dengler, identify and apprehend the soldier who had been seen in PFC Dengler's company just before the incident, and seek to apprehend and prosecute all those responsible for the homicide of PFC Dengler. The unidentified soldier who had been seen with PFC Dengler was finally named three weeks later as PFC Victor Spitalny, who had been sent to Honolulu for his R&R.

3

In PFC Dengler's medical files, cause of death was given as loss of blood due to gross physical trauma.

His parents were informed that he had died bravely and would be very much missed by his fellow soldiers—Beevers wrote this letter half-resentfully, loaded on popskull vodka from Manly's private stock.

Then the Army held its breath. Victor Spitalny was not pulled out of the Heaven Massage Parlor or the Mississippi Queen by the Bangkok police, and the American MPs in Bangkok did not pull him out of a Patpong gutter. Police in Milwaukee, Wisconsin, which rather surprisingly turned out to be the birthplace of PFC Spitalny, did not locate the missing soldier, charged by now with the crime of desertion, at his parents' house, the house of his former girlfriend, or at the Sports Tavern, Sam 'N' Aggie's, or the Polka Dot Lounge, where the deserter had sought diversion and entertainment before entering military service.

No one in Bangkok, Camp Crandall, or the Pentagon mentioned a little girl who had run bleeding down Phat Pong Road, no one alluded to the shouts and cries that disappeared into the polluted air. The little girl disappeared into rumor and fiction, then disappeared altogether, like the thirty children in the cave at Ia Thuc, and eventually the army, having moved on to other cases and other problems, forgot that it was holding its breath.

4

What was it like to go on R&R?

It was like being on another planet. Like being from another planet.

Why was it like being from another planet?

Because not even time was the same. Everybody moved with great unconscious slowness, everybody talked slow and smiled slow and thought slow.

Was that the only difference?

The people were the biggest difference. What they thought was important, what made them happy.

Was that the only difference?

Everybody's making money and you're not. Everybody's spending money, and you're not. Everybody's got a girl. Everybody's got dry feet and they all eat real food.

What did you miss?

I missed the real world. I missed Nam. Where there's a whole different top ten.

Top ten?

Sounds that make you feel sick with excitement. You want the songs from your own planet.

Will you tell me about the girl?

She came out of the screams the way birds come out of clouds. She was an image—that was the first thing I thought. That she *had* to be seen, that she *had* to present herself. She was from my world. She was *loose*. The way Koko got *loose*.

Why did you think she was screaming?

I thought she was screaming because of the nearness of ultimate things.

How old was she?

She might have been ten or eleven.

What did she look like?

She was half-naked, and her upper body was covered with blood. There was blood even in her hair. Her hands were outstretched in front of her, and they were red with blood too. She might have been a Thai. She might have been Chinese.

What did you do?

I stood on the sidewalk and watched her run past me.

Did anybody else see her?

No. One old man blinked and looked troubled. Nothing else.

Why didn't you stop her?

She was an *image*. She was *uncanny*. She'd have died if you stopped her. Maybe you'd die too. I just stood there in the midst of the crowd and watched her run past me.

How did you feel when you saw her?

I loved her.

I felt I saw everything that was the truth in her face—in her eyes. Nothing is sane, that's what I saw, nothing is safe, terror and pain are beneath everything—I think God sees things that way, only most of the time He doesn't want us to see it too.

I had the Pan-feeling. I felt like she had burned my brain. I felt like my eyes had been scorched. She thrashed down the bright street in the midst of all her commotion, showing her bloody palms to the world, and she was gone. *Pan*-ic. The nearness of ultimate things.

What did you do?

I went home and wrote. I went home and wept. Then I wrote some more.

What did you write?

I wrote a story about Lieutenant Harry Beevers, which I called "Blue Rose."

20

TELEPHONE

1

Michael Poole and Conor Linklater separated on their second day in Bangkok. Conor went through a dozen gay bars in Patpong 3, asking his question about Tim Underhill to baffled but kindly Japanese tourists who usually offered to buy him a drink, to jumpy-looking Americans who usually pretended that they could not see or hear him, and to various smiling Thai men, who assumed that he was looking for his lover and offered the services of decorative young men who would soon heal his broken heart. Conor had forgotten his stack of photographs in his hotel room. He looked at small, pretty boys in dresses and thought of Tim Underhill while wishing that these frothy creatures were the girls they so much resembled. The bartender in a transvestite bar called Mama's made Conor stop breathing for a few seconds when he blinked at Underhill's name and stood looking at him, smiling and stroking his chin. But at last he giggled and said, "Never saw him in here."

Conor smiled at the man, who appeared to be melting a lump of some delicious substance, chocolate or butter, on his tongue. "You acted like you knew him."

"Can't be sure," the bartender said.

Conor sighed, took a twenty-baht note from the pocket of his jeans, and slid it across the bar.

The man pocketed the bill and stroked his chin again. "Maybe, maybe," he said. "Undahill. Timofy Undahill." Then he looked up at Conor and shook his head. "Sorry, my mistake."

"You little asshole," Conor heard himself say. "You shithead, you took my money." Without in any way planning to do so and without even recognizing that he was suddenly very angry, Conor ground his teeth and reached across the bar. The bartender giggled frantically and stepped backwards, but Conor lunged for him and closed his hands on his white shirt.

"Earn your money, goddamnit. Who did you think it was? Someone who came in here?"

"Mistake, mistake!" the bartender cried. A few men who had been drinking at the bar had come toward Conor and the bartender, and one of these men, a Thai in a light blue silk suit, patted Conor on the shoulder.

"Calm yourself," the Thai said.

"Calm myself, nothing," Conor said. "This asshole took my money and now he won't talk."

"Here is money," said the bartender, still yanked half-way across his bar. "Have free drink. Please. Then please leave." He plucked the bill from his pocket and dropped it on the bar.

Conor let go of the man. "I don't want the money," he said. "Keep the goddamn money. I just want to know about Underhill."

"You are looking for a man named Tim Underhill?" asked the dapper little Thai in the blue silk suit.

"Sure, I'm looking for him!" Conor said, too loudly. "What does it look like I'm doing? I'm his friend. I haven't seen him in fourteen years. My friend and I came here to find him." Conor violently shook his head, as if to shake off sweat. "I didn't mean to get rough, or nothing. Sorry I grabbed you like that."

"You have not seen this man in fourteen years, and now you and your friend are looking for him."

"Yeah," Conor said.

"And yet you become so emotional! You threaten this man with violence!"

"Hey, it snuck up on me. And I'm sorry, but I mean, I didn't threaten nobody around here, not yet anyhow." Conor pushed his hands into the pockets of his jeans and began backing away from the bar. "Gets frustrating after a while, looking for a guy nobody knows. Look, I'll see you sometime."

"You misunderstand!" said the Thai man. "Americans are always so quick!"

To Conor's vast discomfort, everybody had a good laugh at this.

"What I mean is, we might be able to help you."

"I *knew* this shithead heard of him." He glowered at the bartender, who raised his hands placatingly.

"He is going to be your friend, do not call him names," said the Thai. "Isn't that right?"

The bartender spoke in Thai—a rush of noise that to Conor sounded like "Kumquat crap crop crap kumquat crap crap."

"Crop kumquat telephone crap crop dee crap," said the man in the blue suit.

"Hey, give me a break," Conor said. "Is he dead or something?"

The bartender shrugged and stepped away. He lit a cigarette and watched the man in the blue suit.

"We both think we may know him," said the man in the blue suit. He picked up Conor's twenty-baht note, and held it upright, like a candle.

"Crap crop crap crop," the bartender said, turning away.

"Our friend is uneasy. He thinks it is a mistake. I think it is not." He twinkled the bill into one of his pockets.

The bartender said, "Crap crop crop."

"Underhill lives in Bangkok," said the Thai in the blue silk suit. "I am sure he still lives here."

The bartender shrugged.

"Used to come in here. Used to come into Pink Pussycat. Used to come into Bronco." The man in the blue suit showed all his teeth in a laugh. "He knew friend of mine, Cham." The man grinned even more broadly. "Cham very bad. Very bad man. You know telephone? Cham like telephone. *He* knew him." He tapped the bar with a long fingernail made lustrous with lacquer.

"I want to meet this guy Cham," Conor said.

"This is not possible."

"Everything is possible," Conor said. "There's money in it for you. Where does this guy hang out? I'll go there. Does he have a telephone number?"

"We go out couple bars," Connor's new friend told him. "I take care of you, you see. I know every place."

"He know every place," the bartender said.

"And you knew Underhill?"

The man nodded, distorting his face into a mask of comical omniscience. "Very well, I know him, very well. You want proof?"

"Okay, give me proof," Conor said, wondering what he would do.

The little Thai thrust his face up close to Conor's. He smelled powerfully of anise. There were tiny white scars at the corners of his eyes, like calcified razor nicks. "Flowers," he said, and laughed.

"You got it," Conor said. "That's it."

"We have drink first," said the man in the blue suit. "Must prepare."

2

They had several drinks while they prepared. The dapper little man extracted an envelope and a fountain pen from the inside pocket of his jacket and declared that they needed to make a list of Underhill's haunts, along with a list of the bartenders and patrons who would be most likely to know where to find him. There were bars in Patpong 3, bars in an area called Soi Cowboy off Sukhumvit Road, bars in hotels, bars in Klang Toey, Bangkok's port, Chinese "tea houses" off Yaowaroj Road, and two coffee shops—the Thermae, and the one in the Grace Hotel. Underhill had been known in all these places, and might still be known in some.

"This all cost money," said Conor's new friend, putting his envelope in a side pocket of his jacket.

"I have enough money to go around a few bars." Conor saw an expression of nervous suspicion cross the little man's face. He added, "And something for you on top."

"On top, very good," the man said. "I take my share now—come out on top!"

Conor pulled a wad of crumpled bills from his pocket, and the man plucked out a purple five-hundred-baht note.

"We go now," he said.

They dropped into every bar remaining in Patpong 3, but Conor's new friend saw nothing that pleased him.

"We get taxi," the little man said. "Go all 'round city, find the best places, the most exciting, and that is where we will find him!"

They went out onto the crowded street and stopped a cab. Conor climbed into the back seat while the little man spoke to the driver for a long time. He gestured and grinned, "Crap crop katoey crap crop crap baht mai crap." Several bills passed to the driver.

"Now all is taken care of," the man announced when he climbed in beside Conor.

"I don't even know your name," Conor said, and extended his hand.

The man smiled and pumped his hand. "My name is Cham. Thank you."

"I thought Cham was your friend. Who knew Tim."

"He is Cham, I am Cham. Probably our kind driver is also Cham. But my friend is *too* bad, *too* bad." He giggled again.

"And what's *'katoey'?*" Conor asked, quoting the one word repeated in the various Thai conversations he had overheard that did not sound like a bathroom joke.

Cham smiled. "A 'katoey' is a boy who dresses up like a girl. You see? I will not lead you astray." He clamped his hand on Connor's knee for a second.

Oh fuck, Conor thought, but merely slid another inch or two away on the car seat.

"And what's this telephone stuff?" he asked.

"What is what?" Cham's attitude had subtly changed—his smile had a forced, glittering edge.

They were speeding through a river of traffic, bumping over tram tracks, going miles away from the center of town, or so it seemed to Conor. "Telephone. You said something about it back at Mama's."

"Oh, oh." Cham had returned to his normal self. "Telephone. I thought you said another word. It is nothing to concern you. Telephone is a Bangkok word. Many many meanings." He glanced sideways at Conor. "One meaning—to suck. You see? Telephone." He clapped his little hands together, and his eyes closed as if in amusement.

Conor and Cham spent the next two hours in bars filled with hungry-looking girls and sleek, prowling boys;

Cham conducted long discussions full of exclamations and laughter with a dozen bartenders, but nothing happened except the exchange of bills. Conor drank cautiously at first, but when he noticed that the excitement of feeling so near to Underhill meant that the alcohol had little effect on him, he drank as he would at Donovan's.

"He has not been here in a long time," Cham said, turning to Conor with his happy smile. Conor again noticed the white little chips of scar tissue around his eyes and mouth. It looked as though a doctor had removed Cham's real face and replaced it with this smooth, boyish mask. He laid his neat sand-colored hand over Conor's. "Do not worry. We will find him soon. Do you care for another vodka?"

"Hell, yes," Conor said. "In the next joint."

They walked out into gathering twilight, Cham's hand resting between Conor's shoulder blades. Conor wondered if he ought to call Michael Poole back at the hotel, and then stood rooted to the sidewalk, thinking that he saw Mikey getting into a cab outside a glittery place called Zanzibar across the street. "Hey, Mike!" he yelled. The man ducked through the door of the cab. "Mikey! Over here!"

Cham put the tips of his fingers to his lips. "Shall we eat?"

"I just saw my friend. Over there."

"Is he looking for Tim Underhill too?"

Conor nodded.

"Then there is no point in our staying in Soi Cowboy."

In minutes they were driving down shining streets past flashing signs in a moving traffic jam. Gangs of boys on mopeds swept past them. People spilled in and out of nightclubs.

Once Conor turned from saying something to Cham and saw peering in through the window beside him a gaunt, stricken, sexless ghost's face, empty of everything but hunger.

"You mind if I ask you a question?" Conor heard his own voice, and it was the voice of a drunken man. He decided he didn't really care. The little guy was his friend.

Cham patted his knee.

"How'd you get all those damned little scars on your face? You run into a fish hook factory or something?"

Cham's hand froze on his knee.

"It must be a hell of a story," Conor said.

Cham bent forward and said "Crap crop crap klang toey" to the driver.

"Crap crap crap," the driver answered.

"*Katoey?*" Conor asked. "I'm sick of those guys."

"Klang Toey. Port area."

"When do we get there?"

"We are there now," Cham said.

Conor got out of the cab at the end of the world. The fishy, pungent smell of sea water filled the air. The skull face pressed to the window of this cab floated up in his mind.

"Telephone!" he yelled. "I Corps! What about it!"

Cham pulled him away from the distant sight of the river toward a bar called Venus.

They had drinks at Venus and Jimmy's and Club Hung; they had drinks in places without names. Conor found himself leaning against Cham, or Cham leaning against him as the cab whirled around a corner. He looked sideways, pulling Cham's hand off his leg, and again saw a bony, sunken face peering through the window with dead eyes. A chill went over his body, as if he were standing wet and naked in a cold breeze. He yelled, and the face flickered and disappeared.

"Nothing," Cham said.

They went up flights of stairs to dark rooms smelling of incense where ceramic pillows lay at the heads of empty divans and Chinese men stopped playing mah-jongg long enough to examine Underhill's photograph. In the first such place, they frowned and shook their heads, in the second they frowned and shook their heads, and in the third they frowned and nodded.

"They knew him here?" Conor asked.

"They throw him out of here," Cham said.

Conor found himself seated at a linen-covered table in the lobby of a hotel. A great distance away a young Thai in a blue jacket read a paperback book behind the registration desk. A cup of coffee steamed before Conor, and he picked it up and sipped. Young men and women sat at every table, and girls crossed their legs on the couches that ringed the lobby. The coffee burned Conor's mouth.

"He comes here sometimes," Cham said. "Everybody comes here sometimes."

Conor bent to sip his coffee. When he looked up the

lobby was gone and he was gripping the door handle in the back seat of the cab.

"Your friend was bad, very bad," Cham was saying. "No longer welcome anywhere. Is he bad, or just sick? Please tell me. I want to know about this man."

"He was a great fucking guy," Conor said. The subject of Underhill's greatness seemed inexpressibly immense, too immense to be conquered by mere words.

"But he is very silly."

"So are you."

"But I do not vomit the contents of my stomach in public places. I do not cause consternation and despair all about me. I do not threaten and abuse those who have any sort of authority over me."

"That sure sounds like Underhill, all right." Conor said, and fell asleep.

He had a moment's dream of the ghostly face pressing against the window, and jolted awake with the recognition that the face was Underhill's. He was alone in the back seat.

"What?" he said.

"Crap crop crop crop," said the driver, leaning over the back of the seat and holding out a folded piece of paper.

"Where is everybody?" Conor vaguely took the note and looked out of his window. The cab had stopped in a broad alley between a tall concrete structure that looked like a parking garage and a windowless one-story building, also of concrete. A sodium lamp painted the concrete and the surface of the alley with harsh yellow light.

"Where are we?"

The driver jabbed the note at Conor, using it to point down at his leg. Conor confusedly followed the man's gesture and saw his penis, white as a mackerel in the darkness of the taxi, draped over his right thigh. He bent forward to shield himself from the eyes of the driver and stuffed himself back inside his jeans. His heart was pounding, and his head ached. None of this made sense anymore.

Finally Conor took the folded paper from the driver. There were a few lines of spidery black writing. *You drank too much. Your friend may be here. Take care if you go in. The driver has been well paid.* A telephone number had been written at the bottom of the paper. Conor balled up the note and got out of the cab.

The driver circled around him, switching on his lights. Conor dropped the wad of paper and kicked it away. Half a dozen men in close-fitting Thai suits had materialized outside the smaller concrete building and were slowly drifting toward him across the alley. Conor felt like running—the unsmiling men reminded him of sleek sharks. His legs barely kept him upright. The headlights of the circling cab hurt his eyes. He wanted a drink.

"You come in?" The Thai closest to him was smiling like a corpse made up by an undertaker. "Cham talked to us. We waited for you."

"Cham's no friend of mine," Conor said. All of the men were waving him toward the door of the windowless concrete building. "I'm not goin' in there. What you got in there, anyhow?"

"Sex show," said the death's head.

"Oh, hell," Conor said, and let them urge him toward the door. "Is that all?"

Inside he paid three-hundred-baht admission to a woman who wore dark glasses and earrings shaped like Coca-Cola bottles with breasts. "Love those earrings," he said. "You know Tim Underhill?"

"Not here yet," the woman said. The Coke bottles with breasts swung like hanged men.

Conor followed one of the men down a long dark corridor into a big low-ceilinged room which had been painted black. Dim red lights burned above rows of camp chairs and red spots pointed at two stages, one directly before the chairs, the other beside a crowded bar. A naked girl danced on each stage, flipping her hair and snapping her fingers. The girls had unsteady breasts, narrow hips, and pubic hair like small black badges. In the red light their lips looked black. Most of the customers in the chairs and standing at the bar were Thai men, but scattered through the crowd were a few drunken white men like himself, and even a few white couples in American clothes. Conor half-sat, half-fell into an empty chair near the back of the room and ordered a beer that cost a hundred baht from a half-naked girl who materialized beside him.

That bastard took my cock out of my pants, he thought. Guess I'm lucky he didn't cut it off and take it home in a bottle. He drank his beer, then a succession of beers as the girls onstage changed faces and bodies, swapped short hair for long hair, baseball breasts for football breasts, pillowy hips for greyhound hips. They blew out smoke and smiled like girls on dates. Conor decided that he liked these girls. One of them could open Coca-Cola bottles with her vagina—the top came off the bottle with a loud, echoing report. This girl's face was oddly harsh and wistful, with high precision-engineered cheekbones and gleaming eyes like paper cuts. After she popped open the bottles, she tilted her backside against the wall of the stage, her pretty legs in the air, and inhaled the soda from the bottle. When she stood up, she released the liquid back into the bottle in a hissing jet. As far as Conor knew, there wasn't a single girl in Donovan's who could do this trick.

He had reached that ironbound stage of drunkenness, he realized, that could not be affected by a dozen more drinks.

When he looked at the side stage he felt his face turn red, his ears blaze. A slim young creature had shimmied out of her dress to reveal that she had small, pretty breasts and an erect cock. Another slender *katoey* knelt to take the erection in her mouth. Conor turned his eyes back to the center stage, where a girl with the self-possessed face of a dictator's mistress was about to do something with a large reddish dog.

"Gimme a whiskey," Conor told the waitress.

When the dictator's mistress and the dog left the stage, a short muscular Thai male and a girl with waist-length hair bounded up. Soon they were locked in intercourse, altering their positions, drawing up their knees and revolving as if they were suspended in the air. One of the *katoeys* to Conor's side sighed and arched his girl's back. Conor ordered another whiskey. A ghostly Tim Underhill sat applauding at his side.

Suddenly Conor was unable to tell which of the people onstage were men and which were women. They were men with breasts, women with erections. They had melted together—he saw the flash of a girl's smile, plump buttocks, a broad thigh. Then all four performers were standing up and bowing like actors, the young woman delicately flushed across the top of her breasts. To Conor, the four people onstage seemed to be encased in the memory of pleasure, as different from those cheering them as Martians, as untouchable as angels.

That's it! Conor thought. It flashed before him that a moment of total clarity and truth had just passed. Conor saw himself standing before a great wall of dazzling brightness, an impenetrable, unknowable realm where the sexes melted together and language was music and things moved so swiftly and brightly they hurt the eyes.

Then he fell back into cold reason. The performers now draped in robes and shuffling offstage in the emptying club were drug addicts and whores who lived in riverfront shacks, and he was drunk. Tim Underhill was a boozy wreck, just like him. Conor groped for that moment of clarity in order to dismiss it completely, but could find only the memory of sitting in bars and the taxi, of a hunt so fruitless it might have been for a unicorn instead of a man.

He thought that his whole life was a history of not understanding what the hell was going on—a history of not getting it.

Conor wiped his hands on his jeans and dully followed the last of the customers down the dark corridor and outside into the warm night.

A handful of men from the club had drifted toward the parking garage. They were all dressed in smooth-fitting Thai suits and resembled mercenary soldiers on home leave. One of them wore dark glasses. Conor weaved outside the door of the club, sensing that they were waiting for him to leave.

It was suddenly clear to him that what they had seen in the club was only a prelude to the real event of the night. They were not satisfied with what satisfied everyone else. Me too, Conor thought, remembering the feelings he'd had while the performers took their bows. There's more—there's one hell of a lot more. And something else made Conor move toward the waiting men. Underhill would have been with them. That was why Cham had brought him here. Whatever the men were awaiting was the real last act of the performance which already had taken Conor so far.

As Conor stepped toward the men, the Thai in dark glasses muttered something to his friends and broke away to approach him. He held up a hand like a policeman halting traffic, then made a sweeping-away gesture. "Performance ovah," he said. "You must go."

"I want to see what else you guys got on tap," Conor said.

"Nothing else. Must leave now." The man repeated the whisk-broom gesture.

Without appearing to have moved at all, the other men were now much nearer to Conor, who felt a familiar surge of excitement and anticipation at the proximity of danger. Violence hung about these men like a fog.

"Tim Underhill told me to come here," he said in a loud voice. "You know him, right?"

A buzz of soft talk broke out behind the man in sunglasses. Conor heard what sounded like "Underhill," followed by suppressed laughter. He relaxed. The man in sunglasses glanced back at him in a wordless command to stand still. The men spoke to each other again, and one of them made what was obviously a joke, and even Sunglasses smiled.

"Let's see what you guys got goin' here," he said.

"Crap crop crap!" one of the men shouted, and the others showed yellow smiles.

Sunglasses walked toward Conor with an officer's strut. "Do you know where you ah?"

"Bangkok. Jesus, I ain't that drunk. Bangkok, Thailand. The goddamn kingdom of Siam."

Big yellow smile, and a shake of the head. "What street you on? What district?"

Conor said, "I don't even give a shit."

At least a few of the men must have understood him, for they called out tauntingly to Sunglasses. Conor heard in their tone a cynical, end-of-the-world edge he had heard nowhere in the world in the past fourteen years. They could have been saying either: Kill him and let's move or Let the asshole American come along.

Sunglasses squinted up at Conor with a look that mingled doubt and amusement. "Twelve hundred baht," he finally said.

"This show better be four times as good as the other one," Conor muttered, and pulled his crumpled wad of bills from his pocket. The little group of men had already begun moving toward the towering concrete garage, and Conor stumbled along behind them, trying to keep himself moving in a straight line.

The man in sunglasses moved ahead of the rest and opened a door set beside the garage's exit ramp. The little group began filing through the door into a dimly lighted stairwell. Sunglasses flapped his hand in the air and hissed, urging Conor to come in.

"Here I am," Conor said, and hurried after the others.

3

The next day Conor told himself that he could not really be certain about what had happened after he followed the other men down into the lower depths of the garage. He'd had so much to drink that he had been unsteady on his feet. In a sex club he had seen a vision of—what? angels? splendor?—and it had mix-mastered his brain. He had not understood more than one word spoken inside the garage, and he could not even be certain about that word. He had been light-headed enough to have heard unspoken words and seen imaginary things; Conor felt that in some way he had been light-headed since he and Mikey and Beevers had boarded the Singapore Airlines jet in Los Angeles. Since then, reality had bent backwards in on itself in some extraordinary way, putting him into a world where people looked at scenes from hell, where plump little girls blew smoke rings out of their pussies, where men turned into women and women into men. They were getting close to Tim Underhill, Mikey said, and Conor felt that closeness every time he wondered about what happened in the garage. Getting close to Underhill probably meant you were getting into some territory where everything was upside down by nature, where you couldn't trust your own senses. Underhill liked those places—he had *liked* Vietnam. Underhill was like a bat, he felt comfortable upside down. And Koko did too, Conor supposed. The next day, he decided not to tell anyone about what he had or had not seen, not even Mike Poole.

Conor had followed the men down the concrete stairs in the dark, thinking that civilians were always wrong about violence. Civilians thought that violence was action, one guy hitting another, crunching bones and spattering blood—ordinary people thought you could *see* violence. They thought you could avoid it by not looking at it. But violence was not action. Above all violence was a feeling.

It was the icy envelope around all the business of blows and knives and guns. This feeling was not even really connected to the people using the weapons—they had just put their minds inside the envelope. Inside the envelope they did what was necessary.

This cold, detached feeling was all around Conor as he went down the stairs.

Conor soon lost count of the number of flights they had descended. Six levels down, or seven, or eight . . . the concrete steps ended two floors beneath the level on which they had last seen a parked car. A broad step led down to an irregular grey floor that looked like lumpy cement but proved to be packed earth. The light at the base of the stairs cast a thick slow light twenty or thirty feet out into shadowy greyness melting into a deep black that seemed to go on forever. The air was cold and stale and viscous.

One of the men called out a question.

There was a rustle of sound, and a light went on far at the back of the basement. Beneath it, just now lowering his hand from the light cord, stood a Thai male in his late fifties or early sixties wearing a very tentative smile. A long bar with tall and short glasses, buckets of ice, and a double rank of bottles had been set up on a long table in front of the man. The man slowly extended both arms to lean against the bar. The top of his head shone.

The Thais moved toward the bar. They were speaking in low voices in which Conor could still hear that battlefield tone. Sunglasses summoned him imperiously to the bar.

He ordered whiskey, having an idea that a warm substance like whiskey would support him and hold him up, instead of cutting him off at the knees in the way a cold substance would. "Put some ice in it, man," he told the bartender, whose bald head was covered with tiny beads of sweat as regular as eggs in a carton. The whiskey was some single malt with an unpronounceable Scottish name, and tasted startlingly of tar, old ropes, fog, smoke, and charred wood. Swallowing the stuff was like ingesting a little island off the Scottish coast.

Sunglasses nodded curtly at Conor, and took a drink poured from the same bottle.

Who were these guys? In their smooth taut suits, they might have been gangsters; they might just as easily have been bankers and insurance executives. They had the assurance of people who had never been forced to worry about money.

Harry Beevers, he thought. They sit back and watch the money come home through the door.

Sunglasses stepped away from the other men, raised his hand, and waved to the other side of the basement.

Quiet footsteps came forward out of the darkness. Conor gulped some of the miraculous whiskey. Two figures appeared at the edge of the light. A little Thai man in a khaki suit, bald as a bullet and with deep lines and pockmarks in his cheeks, moved unsmilingly toward the group of men around the bar. With one hand he held the elbow of a beautiful Asian woman who wore only a loose black robe several sizes too large for her. The woman seemed dazed by the light. She was not Thai, Conor thought—her face was the wrong shape. She might have been Chinese; she might have been Vietnamese. She needed the subtle pressure of the man's hand at her elbow to keep her moving. Her head lolled, and her mouth parted in a half-smile.

The man brought her a few more steps forward. Now Conor saw that he wore lightly tinted wire-rimmed glasses. Conor knew his type—he was absolutely military. The bullet-headed man was not a rich man, but he had the instinctive authority of a general.

Conor thought he heard one of the men beside him whisper "telephone."

When they were squarely in the light the little man took his hand from the woman's elbow. She swayed gently, then steadied herself by widening her stance and straightening her shoulders. She looked out through half-lidded eyes, smiling mystically.

The General stepped behind her and slid the robe off her shoulders. The woman now looked mysteriously larger, more formidable, less like a captured thing. Her shoulders were slim, and there was a slim affecting helplessness in the way her rounded forearms turned out, exposing a single blue brush-stroke inside the hollow of her elbow, but all of her body, even the way her calves narrowed into her ankles, had a polished perfect roundness, so that the naked woman seemed as sturdily made as a bronze shield. Her skin, a dark smudgy gold like wet sand on a beach, finally convinced Conor that she was Chinese, not a Thai: all the other men were sallow beside her.

His first instinct, faced with the woman's beautiful unconscious defiance, was to wrap her back up in the robe and take her home. Then four decades of training as an American male reasserted themselves. She had been paid well, or would be; that she looked far healthier than the girls in the sex club across the alley meant only that she would earn many times their price for submitting to a gang bang performed by half a dozen respectable citizens of Bangkok. Conor did not at all feel like joining in, but neither did he think that the woman needed protection. That she was exceptionally good-looking was no more than a professional asset.

He looked at the men around him. They were a club, and this was their ritual. Every week or so they gathered in some inconvenient and secret place, and one after another had sex with a drugged beauty. They'd talk about the women the way wine snobs talked about wine. The whole thing was creepy. Conor asked the bartender for another drink and promised himself that he would leave as soon as everybody else got busy.

If this was what Underhill got up to when he wanted to swing, he was tamer than he used to be.

But why would Underhill join a group whose purpose was to have sex with a *girl?*

If they start to have sex with each other, Conor thought, I'm out of here.

Then he was glad he had another drink, because the General stepped in front of the woman, cocked his right arm back, and slapped her hard enough to make her stagger back. He shouted a few words—"Crap crap!"—and she straightened up and stepped forward again. Her face was tilted like a shield and she was still smiling. A red, hand-shaped blotch covered the entire surface of her left cheek. Conor took a healthy, numbing slug of his drink. The General slapped her again, and the Chinese woman tottered back and straightened herself before she fell. Tears made neat tracks down her cheeks.

This time the General struck her with a straight blow to the side of her chin and knocked her flat on the ground. She murmured and rolled over, showing them dusty buttocks and a long scratch in her golden, dust-covered back. When she succeeded in hitching herself up on her hands and knees, the ends of her hair pooled on the dirt floor. The General kicked her very hard in one hip. The woman grunted and went down again. The General stepped smartly toward her and kicked her a little less forcefully in the side just beneath her ribcage. The woman writhed away into shadow, and quite gently the General bent down to extend his hand and help her to crawl back into the best light. Then he kicked her with great determination in the thigh, almost instantly raising a bruise the size of a salad plate. He proceeded to walk around her body, giving her a flurry of kicks.

It was just like the sex club, Conor saw—the sex club was just the map. Here the map was ripped away and you saw a tough little man beat up a woman in front of other men. That was how you had your fun. Down here in the garage, you got your ultimate sex club.

It made sense of the violence he had felt, anyhow.

The General examined the prostrate, huddled woman for a moment before accepting a drink from Sunglasses. He took a good mouthful, swished it around in his mouth, and swallowed. He stood and surveyed his work, his right arm bent at the elbow, the half-empty glass held with unconscious rigidity. He looked like a man taking time out from a difficult job with the satisfaction of knowing that so far he had given a superior performance.

Conor wanted to get out.

The General set down his glass and bent to help the woman stand. It was not easy to get her up. Her pains made it difficult for her to move out of a crouch, but she willingly took the General's hand. Her dark-gold skin had bruised purple and black, and a large swelling distorted the line of her jaw. She got to her knees and rested there, breathing softly. She was a soldier, she was a ground-pounder. The General nudged her plump backside with one of his loafers, then kicked her hard. "Crap, crop crap," he muttered, as if embarrassed that the others should hear him. The woman tilted her face to the light, and Conor saw how far she was willing to go. They could not stop her. They could not even touch her. Her face was a shield again, and the side of her mouth that was not swollen moved in an echo of her earlier smile.

The General struck her temple with the back of his hand. The woman canted over, caught herself with an outstretched arm, and brought herself erect again. She sighed. A smear of red feathered the corner of one eye. The General's lips moved in a silent command, and the woman visibly focused herself and got up on one knee. Then she levered herself upright. Conor felt like applauding. The woman's eyes shone.

With the force of some crazed bird escaping his throat, a loud burp tasting of smoke and pitch flew from Conor's mouth. Most of the men laughed. Conor was amazed that the woman laughed too.

The General lifted the shirt-jacket of his Thai suit and pulled a revolver from the waistband of his trousers. He crooked his second finger through the trigger guard and displayed the revolver on his palm. Conor didn't know much about guns, but this one had flashy grips carved from some milky substance like ivory or mother-of-pearl, and filigreed scrollwork on the side plate beneath the cylinder. Intricate scrolling covered the barrel. It was a pimp gun.

Conor stepped backwards, then stepped backwards again. Finally his brain caught up with his body. He could not stand and watch while the General shot her—he couldn't save her, and he had the terrible feeling that the woman would fight him if he tried, that she did not care to be saved. Conor moved backwards as silently as possible.

The General began to speak. He was still displaying the pimp gun on his palm. His voice was soft and urgent, persuasive, soothing, and compelling at the same time. He sounded just like a General to Conor. "Crap crop crap crap crop crop crop crap," the General intoned. Give me your poor your huddled masses. O glorious we. "Crop crop crop crop crap." Gentlemen, we are gathered here today. Conor eased himself further back into the darkness. The bartender's eyes flicked at him, but the men did not move. "Crop crap." Glory glory heaven heaven love love heaven heaven glory glory.

When Conor thought he was close enough to the bottom of the staircase, he turned around. It was less than six feet away.

"Crap crop crop." There came the unmistakable metallic click that meant the firing mechanism was cocked.

A shot echoed loudly through the basement. Conor jumped for the stairs, hit the bottom step, and scrambled up, no longer caring how much noise he made. When he reached the first landing he heard another shot. It was muffled by the ceiling of the basement, and this time he knew that the General was not shooting at him, but Conor ran up the stairs until he reached ground level, and hurried outside. He was out of breath and his legs were trembling. He staggered through the hot wet air, and came out of the alley onto a main road.

A grinning one-armed man beeped the horn of his ruk-tuk and steered the rackety little vehicle straight at him. When he stopped he bobbed his head and asked, "Patpong?"

Conor nodded and got in, knowing that he could walk to his hotel from there.

On Phat Pong Road Conor staggered through the crowd to the hotel, went to his room and collapsed on the bed. He kicked his shoes off lying down, and saw the bruised naked woman and the little General with his pimp gun. Conor finally swam out into deep sleep on the tide of the recognition that he had learned what "telephone" meant.

21

THE RIVERSIDE TERRACE

1

The elephant appeared to Michael Poole a short time after Conor had seen him getting into a taxi outside a bar in Soi Cowboy. Michael had failed twice by then, as Conor was to continue failing for the rest of the day, and the elephant's appearance so thoroughly surprised him that he immediately took it as a token of success. He needed this encouragement. In Soi Cowboy, Michael had shown Underhill's photograph to twenty bartenders and fifty patrons and a handful of bouncers; not one had even bothered to look at it carefully before shrugging and turning away. Then he'd had an inspiration, to look at Bangkok's flower market. "Bang Luk," said one of the bartenders, and a taxi took him across town to Bang Luk, a narrow strip of cobbled street near the river.

Flower wholesalers had set up their wares in a series of empty garages on the left-hand side of the little alley, and displayed them on carts and tables set out before the garages. Vans pulled in and out of the alley. On the alley's right-hand side, a row of shops lined the ground floor of three-story apartment houses with French windows and abbreviated balconies. Washing on clotheslines hung before half of the open French windows, and the third of these balconies, above a shop called Jimmy Siam, had been covered with green plants and bushes in earthenware pots.

Michael paced slowly down the cobbles, breathing in the odors of a thousand flowers. Men watched him from beside the barrows of birds of paradise and carts laden with dwarf hibiscus. This was not the tourist's Bangkok, and anyone who looked like Michael Poole—a tall white man in jeans and a short-sleeved white safari jacket from Brooks Brothers—did not belong here. Without feeling in any way threatened, Poole did feel extremely unwelcome. Some men loading flats of flowers into a mustard-colored van gave him only a brief glare and returned to their work; others watched him so intently that he could feel their eyes on him long after he had passed by. In this way Michael walked all the way to the end of the alley, and he stopped to look over a low concrete wall to the silty Chaophraya River, churning with an incoming tide. A long white double-decker boat marked ORIENTAL HOTEL moved slowly downriver.

He turned around, and a few men slowly returned to their work.

He returned to Charoen Krung Road on the pavement opposite the flower stalls, looking into every shop he passed for a glimpse of Tim Underhill. In a dingy café Thai men in dirty jeans and T-shirts drank coffee at a counter; in Gold Field, A Limited Partnership, a receptionist stared back at him from behind a screen of ferns; in Bangkok Exchange, Ltd., two men spoke into telephones at large dark desks; in Jimmy Siam, a bored girl tilted her head and stared into space at a counter full of cut roses and lilies; in Bangkok Fashions a lone customer dangled a baby on her hip and flipped through a rack of dresses. The last building in the row was a shuttered bank with chains across the doors and cardboard squares on the windows. Michael passed by a stop sign and was back out onto Charoen Krung Road without having seen Underhill or even sensed the possibility of his presence. He was a baby doctor, not a policeman, and whatever he knew about Bangkok had been read in guidebooks. Michael looked out into the maze of traffic. Then a ponderous movement in a sidestreet across the road caught his attention. He focused on it and found that he was looking at an elephant, a working elephant.

It was an old elephant, a laborer among elephants,

carrying half a dozen logs rolled in its trunk as easily as if they were cigarettes. It plodded down the middle of the street past inattentive crowds. Michael Poole was charmed, as enchanted as a child would be by a mythical beast. Outside of zoos, elephants *were* mythical beasts: in this one he saw what he would have hoped to see. An elephant wandering a city street: he remembered a picture from *Babar*, one of Robbie's sacred books, and that old deep grief waved to him again.

Michael watched the elephant until it disappeared behind jiggling crowds and a wall of shop signs in enigmatic Thai.

He turned south and drifted for a block or two. Tourist Bangkok—his hotel and Patpong—might as well have been in a different country. White men might have been seen in the flower market before, but here they were unknown. In his short-sleeve safari jacket, his White Man in the Tropics regalia, Michael was an intrusive ghost. Nearly every one of the people on his side of the street stared at him as he went by. Across the street were warehouses with low, slanting tin roofs and broken windows; on his side small dark people, mostly women, carried babies and shopping bags up and down the sidewalks and in and out of dusty shops. The women gave him sharp, anxious looks; the babies goggled at him. Poole liked the babies. He had always liked babies, and these were fat, clear-eyed, and curious. His pediatrician's arms longed to hold them.

Poole moved on past drugstores with window displays of hair and snake's eggs, past shoebox restaurants with fewer people in them than flies. When he walked past a school that resembled a public housing development, he thought of Judy again with a renewal of his old despondency. He thought, I'm not looking for Underhill, I'm just getting away from my wife for a couple of weeks. His marriage seemed a kind of prison to him. His marriage seemed a deep pit in which he and Judy endlessly circled around Robbie's unspoken death with knives in their hands.

Drink it down, drink it down.

Poole walked beneath a highway overpass and eventually came to a bridge over a little stream. On the far bank was a hodgepodge village of cardboard boxes, nests of newspaper and trash. This warren smelled much worse than the compound of gasoline, excrement, smoke, and dying air that filled the rest of the city. To Poole's nose it stank of disease—it stank like an unclean wound. He stood on the quavery little bridge and peered into the paper slum. Through an opening in a large carton he saw a man lying in a squirrel's nest of crumpled paper, staring out at nothing. A smudge of smoke curled up into the air from somewhere back in the litter of boxes, and a baby cried out. The baby squalled again—it was a cry of rage and terror—and the cry was abruptly cut off. Poole could all but see the hand covering the baby's mouth. He wanted to wade through the stream and do medicine—he wanted to go in there and be a doctor.

His pampered, luxurious practice also felt like a confining pit. In the pit he patted heads, gave shots, took throat cultures, comforted children who would never really have anything wrong with them, and calmed down those mothers who took every symptom for a major illness. It was like living entirely on Heath Bar Crunch ice cream. That was why he would not let Stacy Talbot, whom he quite loved, disappear entirely into the care of other doctors: she brought him the real raw taste of doctoring. When he held her hand he confronted the human capacity for pain, and the stony questions beyond pain. That was the cutting edge. That was as far as you could go, and for a doctor it was a deep, humbling privilege to go there. Just now this unscientific notion was full of salt and savor, the real taste of things.

Then Poole caught again that cryptic exhalation from this human sewer, and knew that someone was dying, breathing in smoke and breathing out mortality, back in the rubble of packing cases and smudgy fires and bodies wrapped in newspapers. Some Robbie. The baby gasped and screamed, and the greasy smudge of smoke unraveled itself in the heat. Poole tightened his hands on the wooden railing. He had no medicine, no supplies, and this was neither his country nor his culture. He sent a feeble nonbeliever's prayer for well-being toward the person dying in the pain and stink, knowing that any sort of well-being would be a miracle for him. This was not where he could help, and neither was Westerholm. Westerholm was an evasion of everything his poor feeble prayer was sent out against. Poole turned away from the world across the stream.

He could not stand finishing out his life in Westerholm. Judy could not stand his impatience with his practice, and he could not stand his practice.

Before Poole stepped off the bridge, he knew that his relationship to these matters had irrevocably changed. His inner compass had swung as if by itself, and he could no longer see his marriage or his medical practice as responsibilities given to him by a relentless deity. A worse treachery now than to Judy's ideas of success—which were Westerholm's—was treachery to himself.

He had decided something. The grip of his habitual life had loosened. It was to allow something like this, and to allow Judy to do what she might, that he had accepted Harry Beevers' absurd offer to spend a couple of weeks wandering around places he didn't know in search of a man he wasn't sure he wanted to find. Well, he had seen an elephant in the streets, and he had decided something.

He had decided really to be himself in relationship to his old life, to his wife and his comfortable job. If really being himself put his old life at risk, the reality of his position made the risk bearable. He would let himself look in all directions. This was the best freedom, and the decision allowed him to feel very free.

I'll go back tomorrow, he told himself. *The others can keep on looking.* Koko was history, Judy was right about that; the life he had left claimed him now.

Michael nearly turned around to recross the wobbly bridge and go back to the hotel and book the next day's flight to New York. But he decided to continue wandering south for a time on the wide street that ran parallel to the river. He wanted to let everything, the strangeness of Bangkok and the strangeness of his new freedom, soak into him.

He had come upon a tiny, busy fair tucked behind a fence in a vacant lot between two tall buildings. From the street he had first seen the crown of a Ferris wheel, and heard its music competing with hurdy-gurdy music, childish squeaks of pleasure, and what sounded like the soundtrack of a horror movie played through a very poor sound system. Poole walked on a few paces and came to the opening in the fence that admitted people to the fair.

The lot, no more than half a block square, was a jumble of noise, color, and activity. Booths and tables had been set up everywhere. Men grilled meat on skewers and passed them to children, candy makers handed out paper cups of sticky candy, other men sold comic books, toys, badges, magic tricks. At the back of the lot children and adults stood in line to get on the Ferris wheel. At the far right of the lot, other children howled with pleasure or froze in terror atop wooden horses on a carousel. On the lot's far left had been constructed the gigantic plasterboard front of a castle, painted to resemble black stone and decorated with little barred windows. They suddenly reminded Michael of those in St. Bartholomew's Hospital; the whole false front of the funhouse reminded Michael of St. Bartholomew's. Looking up, he could identify the window behind which Dr. Sam Stein sat plotting, the one to the room in which Stacy Talbot lay reading *Jane Eyre*.

The huge grey hungry face of a vampire, red-lipped mouth open to expose sharp fangs, had been painted across one side of the plasterboard façade. Bursts of cackling laughter and eerie music came from behind the plasterboard. Horror's conventions were the same everywhere. Within the funhouse, skeletons jumped out of dark corners and mad leering faces gave the young a reason to put their arms around each other. Warty-nosed witches, sadistic capering devils, and malignant ghosts parodied disease, death, insanity, and ordinary colorless human cruelty. You laughed and screamed and came out on the other end into the carnival, where all the real fears and horrors lived.

After the war, Koko had decided it was too scary out there, and had ducked back inside the funhouse with the ghosts and the demons.

Across the fairground Poole saw another towering Westerner, a blonde woman who must have been wearing high heels to reach her height of about six feet—her hair was rapidly going grey, and had been tied into a braid at the nape of her neck. Then Poole took in the breadth of the shoulders and knew that the person across the fairground was a man. Of course. From the grey in his hair, from his loose embroidered linen shirt and long braid, Poole gathered that this was a hippie who had wandered east and never returned home. He had stayed in the funhouse too.

When the man turned to inspect something on a table Poole saw that he was a little older than himself. The hippie's hair had receded from his crown, and a grey-blond beard covered the lower part of his face. Oblivious to the alarm bells ringing throughout his nervous system, Poole continued to watch the man as if aimlessly—he noticed the deep lines in the tall man's forehead, the creases dragging at his wasted cheeks. Poole thought only that the man looked oddly familiar: he thought he must have been someone he'd met briefly during the war. They had met inside the funhouse, and the man was a Vietnam veteran; Poole's old radar told him that much. Then sensations of both pain and joy jostled within him, and the tall, weathered man across the fairground raised the object he had been examining to within a foot of his face. It was a rubber mask of a demon's catlike face. The man answered its grimace with a smile. Michael Poole finally realized that he was looking at Tim Underhill.

2

Poole wanted to raise his hand and shout out Underhill's name, but he made himself keep standing quietly between the vendor of grilled meat and the line of teenagers waiting to get inside the funhouse. Poole finally felt his heart beating. He took in several deep slow breaths to calm down. Until this moment he had not really been certain that Underhill was still alive. Underhill's face was of a lifeless whiteness that made it clear the man spent very little time in the sun. Yet he looked fit. His shirt was brilliantly clean, his hair was combed, his beard had been trimmed. Like all survivors, he looked wary. He had lost a good deal of weight, and Poole guessed that he'd also lost a lot of teeth. But the doctor in Poole thought that the most visible fact about the man across the fairground was that he was recovering from a good many self-inflicted wounds.

Underhill paid for the rubber mask and rolled it up and slid it into his back pocket. Poole was not yet ready to be seen, and he moved backward into the shadow of the funhouse. Underhill began moving slowly through the crowd, now and then pausing to inspect the toys and books arrayed on the tables. After he had admired and purchased a little metal robot, he gave a last satisfied, amused look at the diversions around him, and then turned his back on Poole and began working his way through the crowds toward the sidewalk.

Was this what Koko did, wander through a street fair buying toys?

Without even glancing toward the far bank, Poole clattered over the flimsy bridge after Underhill. They were moving toward central Bangkok. It had grown darker since Poole had first come upon the fair, and dim lights now burned in the shoebox restaurants. Underhill moved at an easy pace and was soon a block ahead of Poole. His height and the brilliant whiteness of his shirt made him very easy to see in the turmoil and congestion of the sidewalk.

Poole remembered how he had missed Tim Underhill on the day of the Memorial's dedication. *That* Underhill had been lost, and here was *this* Underhill, a ravaged looking man with a braid in his whitening hair, just strolling beneath a noisy concrete traffic overpass.

3

Underhill's stride lengthened as he neared the corner that led to Bang Luk. Poole saw him round the corner at the shuttered bank like a man hurrying to get home, and jogged through the darkness and the crowd of milling Thais on the sidewalk. Underhill had simply melted through all the people, but Poole had to jump down into the street. Horns blared, lights flicked at him. The street traffic too had increased, and now it was thickening into the perpetual traffic jam of Bangkok's night.

Poole ignored the honking and began running. A taxi zipped past him, then a bus, packed to the windows with people, who grinned down and called out to him. He reached the corner in a few seconds and trotted over the cobbles into Bang Luk.

Men still loaded vans and trucks with flats of flowers; the shop windows spilled out light. Poole glimpsed a billowing shirt as white as a ghost and slowed to a walk. Underhill was opening the door between Jimmy Siam and Bangkok Exchange Ltd. One of the flower wholesalers at a depleted barrow called out to him, and Underhill laughed and twisted around to shout something back in

Thai. He waved at the vendor, went inside, and closed the door behind him.

Poole stationed himself against the first of the garages. Within minutes a light went on behind the shutters above Jimmy Siam. Now Poole knew where he lived; an hour earlier he had not thought he would ever find him.

A vendor emerged from the garage and frowned at Poole. He picked up a large jade plant in a pot and carried it inside, still scowling.

The shutters opened above Jimmy Siam's. Through the opened French windows Poole could see a flaking white ceiling dripping thin stalactites of paint. A moment later Underhill appeared carrying a large jade plant very much like the one the suspicious vendor had taken inside. He set the plant down on his balcony and went inside without closing the French windows.

The vendor darted out through his garage door and glared at Poole. The man hesitated a moment, then began walking toward Poole, speaking vehemently in Thai.

"I'm sorry, I don't speak your language," Poole said.

"You go away, scum," the man said.

"All right," Poole said. "No need to be so upset."

The man uttered a long sentence in Thai and spat on the ground.

Underhill's light snapped off. Poole looked up at the windows, and the stocky little flower vendor rushed a few steps toward him, waving his hands in the air. Poole retreated a few steps. Underhill was dimly visible through the French windows, drawing them closed.

"No bother!" the man shouted. "No make sick! Go away!"

"For God's sake," Poole said. "Who do you think I am?"

The vendor shooed him back a few more paces, but scurried back into his garage as soon as Underhill appeared at his street door. Poole shot back into the darkness by the wall. Underhill had changed into a conventional Western white dress shirt and a baggy seersucker jacket that flapped around him as he walked.

Underhill turned onto Charoen Krung Road and began marching through the crowds on the sidewalk. Poole found himself stalled behind groups of men or whole gatherings of families who had assembled on a patch of sidewalk and intended to stay there. Children jumped and yelled; here and there a boy fiddled with the controls of a radio. Underhill's head floated above the rest, moving easily and steadily toward Surawong Road.

He was going to Patpong 3. It was a long walk, but presumably Underhill wanted to save the few baht of the ruk-tuk fare.

Then Poole lost sight of him. It was as if his tall form had disappeared, like the White Rabbit, into a hole in the ground. He was visible nowhere on the long stretch of sidewalk. When Poole looked at the jammed street, he did not see Underhill there either—only a priest in a saffron robe melting imperturbably through the unstoppable traffic.

Poole jumped up, but saw no tall grey-haired white man making his way through the crowds. When his heels hit the pavement again, Poole started running.

Unless Underhill had been swallowed up by the earth, he must have either gone into a shop or turned down a sidestreet. As Poole ran past all the little businesses he had passed on his way to the wobbly bridge and the fair, he looked into each window. Most of the cafés and shops were closed now.

Poole swore to himself. He had managed to lose Underhill; the earth *had* swallowed him up; he had known he was being followed and he had slipped into a secret cave, a lair. In the lair he dressed in fur and claws and became Koko—he became what the Martinsons and Clive McKenna had seen in the last minutes of their lives.

Poole saw a dark cave shaped like a fist opening out in the middle of the impoverished little shops.

He was running along through the mass of people on the sidewalk, half-pushing people out of his way, sweating, irrationally convinced that Beevers had been right all along and that Underhill had gone down into his cave. Budlike horns nestled in his thinning hair.

A few steps later Poole saw that the buildings separated a block away, and a narrow street went down toward the river.

Poole hurtled into a narrow passageway lined with stalls and vendors of silk and leather bags and paintings of elephants marching across fields of blue velvet. The inevitable tribe of women and children squatted beside the wall to Poole's left, chipping away at their eternal trench. Poole saw Tim Underhill almost at once, far ahead of him, just crossing with a lengthening step a wide empty place where the byway turned up to the right instead of continuing on the short distance to the river. A low wall and a white building lay behind the curve in the road, and Underhill strode past these as he began to move uphill.

Poole hurried down past the vendors and without quite seeing it passed an ORIENTAL HOTEL legend stenciled on a wall. When he reached the bottom of the little road, he looked right and saw Underhill passing through the large glass doors of an immense white structure which extended all the way down to Poole and all the way up past the entrance to an only partially visible garage.

Poole hopped onto the sidewalk and ran past the older wing of the hotel toward the entrance. Large plate-glass windows gave him a view of the entire lobby, and he could see Underhill making his way past a florist's window and bookshop, apparently going toward a cocktail lounge.

He reached the revolving door and was welcomed into the lobby by big smiling Thai men in grey uniforms and realized that he had followed Underhill to a *hotel.* Three of Koko's murders had taken place in hotels. Poole slowed down.

Underhill walked past the entrance to the lounge and continued briskly on through a door marked EXIT—Poole saw a flash of darkness distantly illuminated by a lantern on a tall standard. Underhill passed through the door and went out onto the grounds behind the hotel.

Clive McKenna's body had been found on the grounds of the Goodwood Park Hotel.

Poole followed his horned monster to the exit and very slowly pushed it open. He was surprised to find himself on a pebbled walk that led down past tall lanterns and a poolside garden to a series of descending terraces with candle-lit tables. On the other side of the tables the river shimmered, reflecting the lights of a restaurant on its opposite bank and the sidelights of various small craft. Uniformed waiters and waitresses attended to people eating and drinking at the tables. The scene was so different from the sordid vista Poole had expected that it took him a moment to locate Underhill's tall figure just now making his way down to the lower terraces.

Poole finally took in the presence of a restaurant behind the glowing yellow windows to his right.

Tim Underhill was making for one of the few empty tables remaining on the long flat terrace directly before the river. He sat down and began looking around for a waiter. A trickle of people coming up a sunken walkway beside the pool emerged on the lower terraces at the far side of the hotel. A young waiter approached Underhill's table and took what must have been a drink order. Underhill smiled and talked, and for a time he put his hand on the young waiter's arm, and the young waiter smiled and made a joke.

The sacred monster shriveled away, blushing. Unless he had arranged a meeting with someone, Underhill came to this elegant place to have a drink in a nice setting and flirt with the boy waiters. As soon as the waiter left him, Underhill took a paperback book from one of the pockets of the seersucker jacket, turned his chair to face the river, propped an elbow on the table, and began to read with an air of habitual concentration.

Here the river did not have the weedy, vegetal stench Poole had caught at the end of the flower market. This stretch of the river smelled only of *river*, an odor at once brisk and nostalgic, evocative of movement itself, reminding Poole that he would soon be returning home.

He told a professional young person that he merely wanted a drink on the terrace, and the professional young person waved him down the torch-lit steps. Poole went all the way down to the final terrace, and slipped into a seat at the last table in the row.

Three tables away, his legs crossed at the ankle, Tim Underhill faced the river, occasionally looking up from his book to gaze at it. Here the river's odor carried strong overtones of silt and something almost spicy. The water rhythmically splashed against the piers. Underhill sighed contentedly, sipped his drink, and dove back into his book. Poole made out from three tables away that it was a Raymond Chandler novel.

Poole ordered a glass of white wine from the same young waiter with whom Underhill had flirted. Conversations flowed and sparkled at the tables strung out along the terrace. A small white launch periodically ferried guests from the pier below the terrace to a restaurant on the island halfway across the river. At intervals, bearing lights fore and aft, wooden boats shaped as oddly as boats in dreams slipped past on the black water: boats with dragons' necks, boats with round swollen bellies and beaks like birds, long flat houseboats hung with washing from the decks of which children stared at Poole with grave, unseeing faces. The darkness deepened, and the voices from the other tables grew louder.

When Poole saw Underhill order another drink from the young waiter, again laying his hand on the boy's sleeve and saying something that made the boy smile, he took out his pen and wrote a message on his cocktail napkin. *Aren't you the famous storyteller of Ozone Park? I'm at the last table to your right.* The boy was now drifting down the row of tables, and Michael, like Underhill, caught his sleeve.

"Will you please give this note to the man whose order you just took?"

The boy dimpled, having understood this request by his own lights, and promptly moved back along the row of tables. When he reached Underhill's table he dropped the napkin, which he had folded in half, beside Underhill's elbow.

"Oh?" Underhill said, looking up from Raymond Chandler.

Poole watched him splay the book open on the table and pick up the napkin. For a moment Underhill's face betrayed no response except to become remarkably concentrated. The whole inner man came to attention. He was even more focused than he had been on his book. Finally he frowned at the little note—a frown of intense mental effort instead of displeasure. Underhill had been able to keep himself from immediately glancing to his right until he had fully considered the note. Now he did so, and his eyes quickly found Poole's.

Underhill swiveled his chair sideways and let a slow smile spread through his beard. "Lady Michael, it's better than you know to see you again," he said. "For a second I thought I might be in trouble."

For a second I thought I might be in trouble.

When Michael Poole heard those words, the horned monster in Underhill's body shriveled away for good: Underhill was as innocent of Koko's murders as any man who feared becoming the next victim had to be. Michael was on his feet before he knew it, moving forward past the intervening tables to embrace him under a brightly glowing torch.

22

VICTOR SPITALNY

1

A little more than ten hours before the meeting of Dr. Michael Poole and Tim Underhill on the riverside terrace behind the Oriental Hotel, Tina Pumo awoke in a state of uncertainty and agitation. He had more to do in one day than anyone sane would ever attempt. There were meetings not only with Molly Witt and Lowery Hapgood, his architects, and David Dixon, his lawyer, with whom he hoped to iron out an ironclad way to get Vinh his naturalization papers, but immediately after lunch he and Dixon were to go to his bank to negotiate a loan to cover the rest of the construction costs. The inspector from the Health Department had told Pumo he intended to "reconnoiter 'round about sixteen-hundred hours" to make sure that the insect problem had finally been "squared away to base-line acceptability." The inspector was a Midwestern Vietnam veteran who spoke in a mixture of military jargon, yuppie lingo, and obsolete slang that could sound alternately absurd or menacing. After these meetings, all of them either expensive, frustrating, or intimidating, he had to get down to his equipment supplier on the fringes of Chinatown and pick up replacements for what seemed dozens of pots, pans, and utensils which had managed to go astray during the reconstruction. Sometimes it seemed that only the biggest woks had stayed where they had been put.

Saigon was scheduled to reopen in three weeks, and in more ways than one Pumo's ability to meet this deadline would count heavily with the bankers. The restaurant had to be running very close to full capacity for a specific number of days before it would begin to make money again. For Pumo, Saigon was a home, a wife, and a baby too, but for the bankers it was a questionably efficient machine for turning food into money. All of this made him feel rushed, anxious, stressed, but it was the presence of Maggie Lah, still sleeping on the other side of his bed, that was most responsible for his feeling of uncertainty.

He could not help this; he regretted it, and at some miserable future hour, he knew, he would hate it, but she irritated him, lying sprawled over half of his bed as if she owned it. Pumo could not divide his life in two and give half of it away. Just concentrating on the daily details took so much energy that his eyes started to close before eleven o'clock. When he woke up in the morning, Maggie was there; when he rushed through lunch she was there; when he looked at blueprints, scanned a profit and loss projection, or even read the newspaper, she was there. He had included Maggie in so many parts of his life that now she had the feeling she belonged in all of them. Maggie had come to feel that she had a right to be in the lawyer's office, the architect's brownstone, the supplier's warehouse. Maggie had taken a temporary condition for a lifelong change and had managed to forget that she was a separate person.

So she took it for granted that she could lie across half his bed every night. So she put in her two cents with Molly Witt, suggesting changes in the floor tiles and the hardware on the cabinets. (Molly had agreed with all her suggestions, but that was beside the point.) So she told him his old menu was no good, and made up some silly new design she expected him to adopt on the spot. People *liked* those descriptions of the food. Lots of people even needed them.

Pumo could not forget that he loved Maggie, but he no longer needed a nurse, and Maggie had lulled him into forgetting what he was like when he was normal. She was so lulled herself she had lost her timing.

He would have to take her with him today. Molly's partner would flirt with her. David Dixon, a good lawyer but otherwise a grown-up adolescent who thought only about money, sex, sports, and antique cars, would amusedly tolerate her presence and give Tina knowing looks. If the banker got a look at her, he'd think Tina was a flake and turn down the loan. At Arnold Leung's, the old Chinese supplier would cast forlorn, despairing looks at her and start sidelong conversations about how she was ruining her life with an "old foreigner."

Maggie's eyes opened. She looked at Tina's empty pillow, and then rolled her head up to weigh and parcel him in one measuring glance. Maggie couldn't even wake up like other people. Her face looked smooth and dusky, the whites of her eyes glinted. Even her round full lips looked smart.

"I see," she said on a little sigh.

"Do you?" Pumo said.

"Do you mind if I don't come with you today? I ought to go up to a Hundred-twenty-fifth Street to see the General. I have been neglecting my duty. He gets very lonely."

"Oh."

"Besides, you look grumpy today."

"I'm . . . not . . . grumpy," Pumo said.

Maggie gave him another slow, measuring look and sat up in bed. Her skin seemed very dark in the half light. "He hasn't been well lately. He's worried about losing the lease on the storefront."

She jumped out of bed and skimmed over the floor to the bathroom. For a moment the bed seemed astoundingly empty. The toilet flushed, water pounded through the overhead pipes. He could feel Maggie vigorously brushing her teeth, using up all the energy and air in the bathroom, draining the power from the shaver's socket and the light fixtures, making the towels wilt on the rack.

"You don't mind, do you?" she called out brightly. Her voice was slushy with toothpaste. "Tina?"

"I don't *mind*," he said in a voice carefully calculated to be almost too low for her to hear.

She came out of the bathroom and gave him another considering look. "Oh, Tina," she said, and moved past him to the closet and began to dress.

"I have to be alone for a while."

"You don't have to tell me. Should I come back tonight?"

"Do what you like."

"I'll do what I like, then." Maggie dressed quickly in the dark woolen garment she had worn when he had fetched her from the General's apartment.

Maggie and Pumo spoke very little between then and the time they both left the loft to walk down the staircase to Grand Street. Dressed in their heavy winter coats, they stood together in the cold. A garbage truck down at the end of the street noisily crunched up some wooden object that cracked and split like human bones.

Maggie looked so misleadingly small, standing next to him in her padded coat—she might have been a girl going off to high school. It occurred to Pumo that they would not have any problems if they never had to get out of bed. A recollection of Judy Poole's caustic voice on the telephone made him say, "When Mike Poole and the other guys get back here . . ."

Maggie tilted her head expectantly, and Tina wondered if what he was going to say was more complicated than he wished. Maggie did not flinch.

"I guess we ought to see more of him, that's all."

Maggie gave him a grim, sad smile. "I'll always be nice to your friends, Tina."

She gave a wave of her gloved hand as sad as her smile, and turned to walk to the subway station. He watched, but she did not look back.

2

In most ways, Pumo's morning and early afternoon went more easily than he had imagined. Molly Witt and Lowery Hapgood gave him two strong cups of coffee and showed him their latest innovations, which were, he saw, clever adaptations of the ideas Maggie had advanced a few days earlier. These changes could be painlessly incorporated into the small amount of work remaining to be done, the only hitch being that the cabinet hardware would have to be reordered. But since even the old hardware had not arrived yet . . . and didn't he think that everything "keyed together" this way? It did, and he did. And it wasn't their concern, but if he rethought the menu in the light of these changes and brought the whole look more up to date . . . in short, adopted most of Maggie's ideas about the menu too, not excluding "streamlining" Pumo's beloved descriptions of the food. After the meeting, David Dixon juggled a handful of legal balls in the brisk, cheery air of his offices and lamented that Pumo's "cute little squeeze" had not accompanied him. At lunch he returned to this theme.

"You're not going to screw this one up too, are you, buddy?" the lawyer asked him, his eyes twinkling in his ruddy ex-athlete's face as he looked over the menu at Smith & Wollensky's. "I'd hate to see you lose that beautiful little Chink."

"Why don't *you* marry her, David?" Pumo said sourly.

"My family would kill me if I brought home a Chink. What could I tell them, that our kids'll be great in math?" Dixon continued to twinkle at him, secure in the certainty of his charm.

"You're not smart enough for her, anyhow." Pumo only partially mollified Dixon by adding, "We have that much in common."

Downtown, the meeting at the bank was conducted with a certain cold formality that seemed to distress the banker, who appeared to expect more of Dixon's usual jocularity—they had been in the same class at Princeton and were happy boyish bachelors of forty. Dixon and the banker had not of course gone to Vietnam. They were *real* Americans. (That was how they would see it.)

"Don't worry, it's in the bag," Dixon said once they were back out on the street. "But let me give you a hint, old pal. You've gotta lighten up. The world is full of that particular brand of real estate, man, you can't be dragged down by one little Oriental pussy just 'cause it walked out the door." He guffawed, and a big white scarf of steam flew from his mouth. "Can you? Hell, you threw her out!"

"I'll let you know in a week or two," Tina said, and made himself smile and shake Dixon's hand. In the pressure of the lawyer's hand on his, he could tell that Dixon was as happy as he was to be parting.

Dixon strode away, red-faced, smiling his charming, lopsided old Princetonian smile, perfect in his gleaming shirtfront, his striped tie, his neat dark bush of hair, his neat dark topcoat, and for a moment Pumo watched him go as he had watched Maggie go earlier that day. What was wrong with him, that he was driving people away from him? Tina did not have much in common with Dixon, but the man was a rogue, and rogues were usually good company.

Like Maggie, Dixon did not look back. His arm shot up, a taxi rolled to a stop, and he slid inside. Rogues had a talent for flagging down cabs. Tina watched his lawyer's cab roll down Broad Street in a yellow tide of occupied taxis. All at once he felt that, just as he was watching Dixon's getaway, someone was watching him. The hair on the back of his neck actually rose, and he whirled around to see who was looking at him. Of course no one was. Pumo scanned the crowd of brokers and bankers hurrying down Broad Street in the cold. Some of them were the grey-haired old foxes he still associated with these professions, but many more were men of his and Dixon's age, and as many were in their twenties and early thirties. They looked both flawless and humorless, human adding machines. Rogues like Dixon would take them in hand and humor them along, and he would feed them and watch them get drunk. Pumo saw that the tribe moving along Broad Street did not even give him a curious glance. They were the focused people. Or maybe he was transparent. The day seemed even colder, and the sky above the sidewalk lamps grew darker, and Pumo moved to the curb and raised his arm.

It took him fifteen minutes to get a cab, and he arrived back at Grand Street at sixteen-hundred hours plus ten minutes. He let himself into the restaurant and found the inspector, Brian Mecklenberg, pacing around the kitchen, tapping his ballpoint against his front teeth, and making little checks on a sheet inserted in his clipboard. "You've gained a few yards since the last time I saw you, Mr. Pumo," he said.

"We have a way to go, too," Pumo said, dropping his coat on a chair. He still had to get down to Arnold Leung's that day.

"Oh?" Mecklenberg regarded him with as much interest as any health inspector ever gave any of his victims. "Would you say that our target has been reached?"

"Getting rid of the bugs?"

"Affirmative—zapping the infestation. What else would I mean?"

Mecklenberg looked a little bit like a target himself in a hideous yellow-black-and-olive plaid sports jacket and a brown knit tie firmly locked into place with a conspicuous tie pin.

"Getting the kitchen finished, opening for business, *staying* open, getting the people to come in off the street, that kind of thing," Pumo said. "Having a peaceful, orderly, satisfying life that also manages to be interesting. Getting my love life in order."

He remembered David Dixon's ruddy face and lopsided smile and a crazy light went on in his brain. "You want to talk about targets, Mecklenberg? Abolishing nuclear weapons and establishing world peace. Getting everybody to see that Vietnamese food is as good as French food. Establishing a Vietnam War memorial in every major city. Finding a safe way to get rid of all toxic waste." He paused for breath, aware the Mecklenberg was staring at him with his mouth open.

"Hey, about nuclear power, hey—" Mecklenberg began.

"Scrapping all that ridiculous Star Wars bullshit. Upgrading public schools. Putting religion back in churches, where it belongs."

"I'm with you there," Mecklenberg said.

Pumo's voice rose a notch. "Taking goddamned guns away from civilians." Mecklenberg tried to interrupt, but Pumo began to shout. The crazy light was burning very brightly now. Mecklenberg hadn't heard half the targets he was going to hear. "Trying to elect officials who actually know what they're doing instead of ones who just look good while pretending that they know what they're doing! Taking the radio away from goddamned teenagers and having decent *music* on again! Abolishing television for five years! Cutting one finger off every public official who is caught telling even one public lie, and cutting off another finger every time he's caught after that! Imagine what that would have done for us in Vietnam! Hey, Mecklenberg, can you get your head around that?"

"Are you in some kind of trouble, are you sure you're okay, I mean . . ." Mecklenberg had put his ballpoint pen in his shirt pocket, where a fuzzy blue stain was blossoming out. He bent down, popped open his briefcase, and shoved the clipboard inside it. "I think—"

"You have to widen your horizons, Mecklenberg! Let's

see about abolishing bureaucratic red tape! Reducing waste in government! Let's have fair taxation! Let's get rid of executions once and for all! Reform the prison system! Let's realize that abortions are here to stay and have a little sanity about that! And how about drugs? Let's figure out a policy that makes sense instead of pretending that Prohibition worked, shall we?" Pumo shot out his arm and leveled his index finger at poor Mecklenberg. He had thought of a wonderful new target.

"I have a great idea, Mecklenberg. Instead of executing him, let's take a guy like this Ted Bundy and put him in a glass cage in the middle of Epcot Center. You get me? Your basic ordinary American families can stop in for a little talk with Ted, one family every fifteen minutes. See? *Here's one of those,* we say, *here's what one looks like, here's what one sounds like, here's how he brushes his teeth and blows his nose. Get a good, close-up gander. You want to see evil? Here the son of a bitch is!*"

Mecklenberg had struggled into his overcoat and was backing away toward the swinging doors to the dining room, where a dozen workmen had set down their tools in order to overhear Pumo's rant. Someone out there shouted, "Yeah, baby!" and someone else laughed.

"You think *bugs* are evil, Mecklenberg?" Pumo boomed.

"For God's sake, just—" He clamped his hands to the sides of his head and looked around for a place to sit down.

Mecklenberg bolted toward the swinging doors. Pumo's neck was bent, and for that reason he saw an insect cautiously emerging from beneath the side of the Garland range. It was enormous. He had never seen an insect like it, not even at the height of his "infestation," when it seemed that creepy-crawlies of all descriptions occupied every centimeter of his walls. By the time the thing had finished coming out from beneath the range, it was nearly the size of Pumo's foot.

Mecklenberg slammed the front door, and a loud cheer came up from the workmen in the restaurant.

Pumo felt like fainting—or as if he had already fainted, and this creature had appeared in a fever-dream. It was long and sleek, with feelers of copper wire. The whole brown body resembled an artillery shell. It looked polished, almost burnished. Its feet clacked audibly on the tile floor.

Pumo told himself: this is not happening. There were no monsters, and cockroaches had no King Kong.

The monster roach suddenly saw him. It froze. Then it quickly fled back under the range. For a second or two Pumo heard its little hooves tapping away on the tiles, and then there was silence.

For a moment Pumo stood in the silence, afraid to bend down and look under the range. The creature might be waiting to attack him. What could you use against a bug that size? You couldn't step on it. You almost had to shoot it, like a wolverine. Pumo thought of the gallons and gallons of fluid the exterminator had sprayed behind the walls, soaking into the wooden joists and the cement foundations.

Pumo went down on his knees to look beneath the stove. Because the floor was still only half-finished, there was not even an accumulation of dust beneath the range, only a snipped off curl of electrical cable one of the electricians had thrown away.

The antennae? Pumo wondered. He had expected to see, if not the Kong of roaches, at least a hole the size of a man's head in the baseboard; not only was there no hole, there was no baseboard—fire regulations had demanded that a seamless sheet of steel be installed behind the range.

The world seemed full of gaps and stony chasms. Pumo went out of the kitchen and the workmen clapped and shouted.

3

For decades Arnold Leung had maintained his immense, dim warehouses at the easternmost end of Prince Street, where Little Italy, Chinatown, and SoHo melted together, and now he had the aura of a pioneer—the neighborhood had not yet been completely subsumed into Chinatown, but in the past five years several Italian bakeries had been replaced by shops with Chinese characters painted on the windows and Chinese produce wholesalers. Restaurants named Golden Fortune and Soon Luck had taken over other sites. Late on a cold dark February afternoon the only people Pumo saw making their way down the narrow street were two well-padded Chinese women with broad muffin faces partially concealed behind thick dark head scarves. Pumo turned into the narrow alley that led to Arnold Leung's warehouses.

Leung was one of Pumo's great discoveries. His prices were twenty percent lower than any of the midtown suppliers, and he delivered instantly—his son-in-law's pickup would drop at your front door, no farther, the carton you had paid for, whether or not you happened to be present to carry it inside. The price and the speed of delivery made the surliness and the son-in-law more than acceptable to Pumo.

At the end of the alley was one of the city's anomalies, an empty lot a block long and ringed with the backs of buildings. In summers the lot was fragrant with garbage, and during the winter the wind whirling around the backs of the tenements rattled bits of debris like buckshot against Leung's tin warehouses. Tina had only been inside the first warehouse, where Leung kept his office. The only window in all four sheds was above Leung's desk.

Pumo rattled open the door and slipped inside the main building. Wind or air pressure took the flimsy aluminum door out of his hands and violently slammed it shut. Pumo could hear Leung carrying on a one-way conversation in Chinese, presumably on the telephone, which ceased the moment the door noisily struck the frame. The head and body of the proprietor, clad in what looked like several layers of sweat suits, leaned out of the office door to peek at him and then retreated back inside. At the far end of the shed, four men seated on packing cases around a board looked up at Pumo and returned to their game. Except for the office enclosure, the whole interior of the vast shed was a maze of cases and boxes mounted to the ceiling, through which Leung's employees threaded motorized carts. Bare, low-wattage bulbs on cords provided the only illumination.

Pumo waved to the men, who ignored him, and turned toward the office door. Pumo rapped his knuckles against it, and Leung cracked it open, frowned out at him, uttered a few words into the phone, and opened the door just wide enough for Pumo to slip through.

When Leung finally put the receiver down, he said, "So what do you want today?"

Pumo produced his list.

"Too much," Leung said after a glance. "Can't fill it

all now. You know what's happening? Empire Szechuan, that is what's happening. New branches every week, haven't you noticed? Three new ones on Upper West Side, one in Village. I have stuff on order two-three months, just to keep in stock. I say, open one across street from me so I can at least send out for good food."

"Send what you can," Pumo said. "I need everything in two weeks."

"You dreaming," Leung said. "What you need this stuff for, anyway? You already got all this stuff!"

"I used to have it. Quote me some prices."

All of a sudden, Pumo once again had the feeling of being watched. Here it made even less sense than on Broad Street, for the only person looking at him, and that one with a certain reluctance, was Arnold Leung.

"You look nervous," Leung said. "You ought to look nervous. All these knives listed here gonna cost you hundred-fifty, hundred-sixty dollars. Maybe more, depending on what I got in stock."

Okay, Pumo said to himself. Now I get it. Leung was going to hold him up. Leung may even have been punishing him for bringing Maggie Lah to this place once, on the occasion when Tina had heard Leung refer to him as a *lo fang*. He didn't know what a *lo fang* was, but it was probably pretty close to "old foreigner."

Pumo moved to look out of Leung's grimy window. He could see all the way down the cold windy alley to the street, a slash of brightness filled with a moving blur of traffic. Leung's window was not even glass, but of some irregularly transparent film of plastic which had darkened here and there with age. One whole side of the alley was only a brownish wash, a smear of color.

"Let's talk about cast-iron pans," Pumo said, and was about to turn around to watch the expression on Leung's face as he reached for his trusty abacus when he noticed the approach of a little black-tipped blur up the smeary side of the alley. Instantly he felt two absolutely opposed feelings, a surge of relief that Maggie had learned where he was from Vinh and had come down to be with him, and a counterbalanced feeling of deep annoyance that no matter what he said or did, he could not get rid of her.

When Leung saw her, his prices would probably go up another five percent.

"No problem," Leung said. "You want to talk about

iron pans? Let's talk about iron pans." When Pumo did not respond, he said, "You want to buy my window too?"

The moving blur stopped moving, and its whole general posture and attitude told Pumo that this was not Maggie Lah after all. It was a man. The man in the alley began shifting backwards in a way that reminded Tina of the giant roach ducking back beneath the range.

"Hold on a minute, Arnold," Tina said. He shot him a placating look that met implacable Chinese indifference. So much for old customers. Business is business.

"You know about iron pans?" Leung asked. "Production everywhere is way down, no matter where you look."

Tina had turned back to the window. The man had moved out closer to the middle of the alley, and was moving backwards very slowly.

"You ever have the feeling someone is following you?" Pumo asked.

"All the time," Leung said. "You too?"

The man in the alley stepped back into the brightness of the street.

"You'll get used to it," Leung said. "No big deal."

Pumo saw a blurry face, a shock of black hair, a slim body in nondescript clothes. He was aware for a second that this was someone he knew: and then he knew. For a moment he felt lightheaded. He turned around.

"Just deliver the stuff and send me the bill," he said.

Leung shrugged.

The man in the alley was Victor Spitalny, and Pumo knew now that his feelings of having been watched and followed had not been mistaken. Spitalny had probably been following him for days. He had even loitered outside the restaurant, where Vinh had seen him.

"I might be able to get you a little deal on those iron pans," Leung said. Normally Tina would now have begun the negotiating Leung expected, but instead he buttoned his coat and muttered some apology to the astonished wholesaler and hurried out of his office. A moment later he was shutting the aluminum door behind him in the cold.

He saw a small, dark-haired man slipping around the end of the alley. Pumo made himself walk at a moderate pace down toward the street—Spitalny would not know that he had been seen, and Pumo did not want to alarm him. First of all, he had to assure himself that the man watching him really had been Victor Spitalny—he'd had only a blurry glimpse of his face. Pumo sickeningly realized that it was Victor Spitalny who had broken into his loft.

Spitalny had nearly trapped him in the library, and he would continue to track him down until he killed him. Spitalny had killed Dengler, or at best left him to die, and now he was on a worldwide hunting trip.

Pumo reached the end of the alley, and turned against the raw wind in the direction Spitalny had gone. Of course Spitalny was now nowhere in sight. Pumo's world now seemed very close and dark. Spitalny had not died, he had not succumbed to drugs or disease, he had not straightened out and become a decent guy after all. He had bided his time and ticked away.

The whole long expanse of the street and sidewalk was almost empty. A few Chinese women padded toward their apartments, a long way up the block a man in a long black coat mounted a set of stairs and entered a building. Pumo wandered down the street in the cold, fearing that his lunatic nemesis hid behind every shop door.

He reached the end of the block before he began to doubt himself. No one was following him now, and if anyone were going to jump at him out of a doorway, he'd had ample opportunity. A moment's conviction based on a glimpse through a greasy window was his only evidence that Victor Spitalny was following him. It was hard to picture an oaf like Spitalny carrying off the pretense of being a journalist in the Microfilm Room—maybe Maggie was right, and the Spanish name was just a coincidence. An hour earlier he would have sworn that he had seen a giant cockroach. He looked up and down the empty street again, and his body began to relax.

Tina decided to go home and call Judy Poole again. If she had spoken to Michael, he would already be on the way home.

Pumo returned to Grand Street just past five-thirty, when the workmen were packing up their tools and loading their trucks. The foreman told him that Vinh had left half an hour earlier—during the construction, Vinh's daughter was staying with yet another of his relatives, a cousin who lived in a Canal Street apartment. Vinh himself spent half the night there. After the workmen's vans and pickups rolled off toward West Broadway, Pumo gave a long look up and down the street.

Grand Street was never empty, and at this hour the sidewalks were still crowded with the successful, middle-aged populace of New Jersey or Long Island who liked to spend their money in SoHo. Through the tourists strolled the residents of Grand Street and West Broadway, of Spring Street and Broome Street. Some of these waved at Pumo, and he waved back. A painter he knew, making his way up the steps to La Gamal for a drink, waved and yelled across the street the question of how soon he would be opening again. "Couple of weeks," Pumo yelled back, praying that it was true.

The painter went up into La Gamal and Pumo let himself into Saigon. The bar where Harry Beevers had spent so many of the hours he should have given to Caldwell, Moran, Morrissey had been extended and topped with the most beautiful sheet of black walnut Pumo had ever seen; beyond this lay the empty, still barren dining room. Pumo picked his way across the floor in the darkness and let himself into the kitchen. Here there were lights, and Pumo threw them on. Then he went down on his hands and knees and looked under the range and refrigerator, behind the freezers and the storage shelves, and at every inch of floor in the place. He saw no insect of any kind.

Pumo went into Vinh's little room. The bed was neatly made. Vinh's books—poetry, novels, histories, and cookbooks in French, English, and Vietnamese—stood in ranks on the shelves he had made. Pumo looked under the bed and the little chest of drawers without seeing any giant bugs.

He heard no little hooves rapping against his new tiles.

Pumo locked up and went upstairs to his loft. There he finally took off his coat and walked into his bedroom and, without turning on any lights, looked down onto Grand Street. More people were going up the stairs to La Gamal, some of them people who otherwise would be coming to Saigon with their stomachs empty and their wallets out. Everybody was moving swiftly up and down the street, nobody loitered or lingered, nobody was staring up at his window. Maggie would decide whether or not she would come down tonight. Probably she would stay uptown. All of this seemed very familiar. Maggie would not call for days, he'd start to go crazy, there'd be enigmatic little ads in the *Voice*, the whole thing would start up all over again. *Foodcat misses Half Moon.* Maybe this time he would not have to get half killed to bring her back—maybe this time he would have some sense. But for tonight, Maggie would be better off uptown. Pumo knew his old need to be alone, where he could not contaminate any other human being with his troubles.

He made himself a drink at the bar behind his desk and carried it down to the couch to wait for Vinh to return.

When the downstairs buzzer rang, Pumo thought that his chef must have gone off to Canal Street without his keys, and he nearly pushed the little button to let him in without speaking into the little grille that let him interview his callers. But he thought twice, and leaned toward the grille and asked, "Who is it?"

A voice said, "Delivery."

The son-in-law, with a van full of cast-iron kitchenware and two or three boxes of knives. If Leung had sent them without waiting for Tina's instructions, he must have given him the old price. Tina said, "I'll be right there," and pushed the button to unlock the door and admit his caller.

4

"So you think I ought to go back to him tonight?" Maggie trailed after the General as if clinging close to his broad military back for warmth and strength—she was not levitating now.

"I didn't say that." The General darted into one of the aisles of his impromptu church to align a chair. Everything around them, the red vinyl of the seats, the yellow walls with the garish oils of a pigtailed Jesus confronting demons in a misty Chinese landscape, the cheap blond wood of the altar, gleamed and sparkled and shone in the harsh bright light the General and his congregation preferred to any other sort of lighting. And he and Maggie spoke in the Cantonese, similarly hard and brilliant, in which he conducted his services.

Standing by herself before the shuttered Harlem window, Maggie looked nearly bereft. "Then I apologize. I didn't understand."

The General straightened up and nodded approvingly. He went back to the aisle, stepped around her, and proceeded up the side of the church to the altar rail and the altar.

Maggie followed him as far as the rail. The General made minute adjustments to the white cloth on the altar, and at length looked at her again.

"You have always been an intelligent girl. You just have never understood yourself. But the things you do! The way you live!"

"I do not live badly," Maggie said. This looked like another replay of an old, old argument, and she suddenly wanted to leave, to go downtown and stay with Jules and Perry in one of their rickety East Village tenements, to escape into their mindless club-hopping and their mindless acceptance of her.

"I mean—living in such ignorance of yourself," the General said mildly.

"What *shall* I do, then?" she asked, unable to keep the irony out of her voice.

"You are a caretaker," the General said. "You are a person who goes where she is needed. Your friend was in great need of your help. You brought him back to health so successfully that he no longer required your assistance, your caretaking, and all his usual problems returned to him. I know men like him. It will be years before he gets to the end of what combat did to him."

"Do you think Americans are too sentimental to be good soldiers?" Maggie asked, really curious to know if he did think this.

"I am not a philosopher," the General said. He went into a storeroom behind the altar and returned carrying a stack of hymnals. Knowing what was expected of her, Maggie came forward and took the hymnals from him. "But you would perhaps be a better soldier than your friend. I have known some caretakers who were excellent officers. Your father had a great deal of the caretaker in him."

"Did he go where he was needed?"

"He often went where *I* needed him," the General said.

They were walking side by side down parallel aisles, placing hymnals face up on the chairs.

"And now I suppose you want me to go somewhere," she said at last.

"You are doing nothing now, Maggie. You help me out here in my church. You live with your old soldier. I am sure you do a great many things for his restaurant."

"I try," Maggie said.

"And if you lived with a painter, you would find the best brushes in the city, you would prepare the canvases as they were never prepared before, and you would end up getting him into famous galleries and museums."

"That's right," she said, struck by this vision.

"So either you marry some man here and live his life by proxy, being his partner if he will let you, or you have your own life by yourself."

"In Taiwan," she said, for eventually they would come to this point.

"It is as good as anywhere else, and better for you. I will forget about your brother. Jimmy would be the same anywhere, so he might as well stay here. But you could go to college in Taipei now, and then train for a career."

"What career?"

"Medicine," he said, and looked at her fully and frankly. "I can pay for your tuition."

She nearly laughed out loud in astonishment, and then tried to make a joke of it. "Well, at least you didn't say nursing!"

"I thought about that, too." He went on setting down the hymnals. "It would take less time, and cost much less money. But wouldn't you rather be a doctor?"

She thought of Pumo and said, "Maybe I ought to be a psychiatrist!"

"Maybe you ought," he said, and she saw that he knew exactly what she was thinking.

"Always the caretaker," he said. "Do you remember your mother reading *Babar* to you? The book about the elephant?"

"The books," she said, for her memory of the French children's books, which both parents had read to Maggie during her early childhood, was very clear.

"I was remembering a sentence from one of them—something King Babar says. 'Truly it is not easy to bring up a family.' "

"Oh, you did all right," Maggie said.

"I wish I had done better."

"Well, I was only the tiniest of families." Maggie smiled over the rank of intervening chairs and patted his thick old hand. "I haven't thought of those books in years. Where are they?"

"I have them."

"I'd like them someday." Now they were both smiling. "I always liked the Old Lady."

"See? Another caretaker."

Maggie laughed out loud, and if Pumo had seen her at that moment, he would have said that she had begun to levitate again.

"I would never insist you follow any design of mine," the General said. "If you decide to marry your old soldier, I would be happy for you. I would just want you to know that you were his caretaker as well as his wife."

This was too much for Maggie, and she turned them back onto safer ground. "I could sing him the song of the elephants. Do you remember *that*?"

He cocked his close-shaven authoritative head. Maggie was very grateful that he had at least met Tina Pumo, and promised herself that she would bring whatever man or men became important to her up before the General's inspection.

"All I remember is that it was supposed to be very old." He smiled and said, "From the days of the mammoths," as if he were old enough to have seen them himself.

Maggie sang the song from *Babar the King:* " *'Patali di rapato/Cromda cromda ripalo/Pata pata/Ko ko ko.'*

"That's the first verse. I can't remember the other two, but they end the same way—*'Pata pata/Ko ko ko.'* "

As soon as she had sung the words again she knew that she was going to go back down to Grand Street.

5

About the same time that Tina Pumo pressed the button to unlock his street door and Maggie Lah went up the steps to the 125th Street subway stop, wondering if Tina would still be in his infantile mood, Judy Poole called up Pat Caldwell to have a serious conversation. Judy imagined that Pat Caldwell was very likely the most satisfactory person in the world with whom to have a serious conversation. She did not judge other people in the way that most people of Judy's acquaintance, and Judy herself, judged others. Judy attributed this to the liberating effect of having been born into a great fortune and grown up to be a kind of displaced princess who went around pretending to be poor. Pat Caldwell had been born far richer than even Bob Bunce, and Judy imagined that if she had been born with such an enormous silver spoon in her mouth, she, too, might have learned to be so artless about concealing it. Really rich people made the only convincing liberals. And Pat Caldwell had known Judy Poole for more than ten years, ever since Michael and Harry Beevers had left the army—they had made a perfect foursome, Judy thought. Or would have, if Harry Beevers had not been so insecure. Harry had nearly ruined their friendship. Even Michael hadn't liked him.

"It's all because of Ia Thuc," she said to Pat, once they were talking. "You know what they remind me of? The men who dropped the bomb on Hiroshima, the ones who fell apart and turned into drunks. They let it become too much for them—almost as if they *expected* to be punished for it."

"Harry never expected to be punished for it," Pat said. "But Harry never expected to be punished for anything. Don't be too hard on Michael."

"I used to try not to be," Judy said. "I'm not sure it's worth the trouble anymore."

"Oh dear."

"Well, you got divorced."

"Well, I had reasons," Pat said. "Reasons on top of reasons. Reasons inside reasons. You don't want to know about all that."

Judy did want to know—Michael had told her that he thought Beevers was a wife beater—but felt that she could not come out and ask.

"Michael called from Bangkok," she said after a pause, "and I was terrible to him. I don't like myself when I'm like that. I even told him I was going out with someone else."

"I see," Pat said. "When the cat's away?"

"Bob is a very nice, very dedicated, very stable man,"

Judy said, somewhat defensively. "Michael and I haven't really been close since Robbie died."

"I see," Pat repeated. "Do you mean you're serious about your friend?"

"I could be. He's *healthy*. He never *shot* anybody. He *sails*. He plays *tennis*. He doesn't have *nightmares*. He isn't carrying poison and *disease* around inside him. . . ." Judy astonished herself by beginning to cry. "I'm lonely—Michael makes me lonely. All I want is to be an ordinary person and to have an ordinary middle-class life." She began to cry again, and took a moment to steady her voice. "Is that a lot to ask for?"

"Depends on who's asking," Pat said reasonably. "But clearly you don't think so."

"I *don't*," Judy fairly wailed. "I've worked hard all my life! I wasn't born in Westerholm, you know. I'm proud of my home and my accomplishments, my achievements, the whole way we live! That *counts!* I've never asked for a handout, I never took anybody's charity. I made a good place for myself in one of the most exclusive, expensive towns in the entire country. That means something."

"No one would dispute that," Pat soothed.

"You don't know Michael," Judy said. "He's perfectly willing to throw it all away. I think he *hates* Westerholm. He wants to throw everything away and go live in a slum, it's like he wants to cover himself with *ashes*, he can't stand anything *nice* . . ."

"Is he sick?" Pat asked. "You said something about poison and disease. . . ."

"The war got *inside* him, he carried *death* around inside him, he sees everything upside-down, I think the only person he really likes here is a girl who's dying of cancer, he *dotes* on her, he gives her books to read and he finds excuses to see her, it's awful, it's because she's dying, she's like Robbie, she's a smart Robbie. . . ." Now Judy was in tears again. "Ah, I loved that poor kid. But when he died I put all his things away, I was determined to put it all behind me and get on with things. . . . Oh, I suppose you'll never forgive me for getting so emotional."

"Of course I forgive you, there's nothing to forgive. You're upset. But are you implying that Michael is suffering from an Agent Orange-related illness?"

"Have you ever lived with a doctor?" Judy laughed

unpleasantly. "Do you know how hard it is to get a doctor to go to a doctor? Michael's not healthy, I know that much. He won't go for a checkup, he's like some primitive old man, he's waiting for it to go away—but I know what it is! It's Vietnam, it's Ia Thuc! He *swallowed* Ia Thuc, he ate the whole thing up, he drank it the way you'd drink some poison, and it's eating *him* up. For all I know, he blames me for all his problems." She paused, and collected herself. "Then, as if all that wasn't enough, there's my anonymous caller. You ever have one of those?"

"I've had a few obscene telephone calls," Pat said. "And Harry used to call me up, after I made him move out of my apartment. He never admitted it, but he'd stay on the phone, just sort of breathing, hoping I'd get scared or feel sorry for him or something."

"Maybe *Harry's* calling me up!" Judy uttered a muffled sound that might have been laughter.

6

Intimations that something had gone wrong followed Maggie all the way to Pumo's door. A crowd of boys at the subway's exit surrounded her as soon as she came up the steps, dancing in close to her and calling her "little Chinkie." "I show you a good time, little Chinkie." They were just aimless, bored adolescents, too frightened of women to approach them individually, but Maggie suddenly felt too scared of them to risk doing anything but shoving her hands into her pockets, averting her head, and walking straight ahead. The odor of marijuana surrounded the boys like a cloud. Where was Pumo? Why didn't he answer his phone? "Look at me, look at me, look at me," one of the boys begged, and Maggie lifted her chin and gave him a look so powerful that he fell back on the spot.

The rest of the boys continued following her for nearly a block, making half-intelligible growls and yells. The night had become very cold, and the wind burned Maggie's face. The streetlamps shed a morbid yellow light.

She needed time to absorb the General's offer. She would not reject it without fully considering it, and she might not reject it at all. It was possible that in time the General might accept her training at a medical school in

New York, if any such school would take her in. If she were a medical student with her own room up in Washington Heights or over in Brooklyn, if she were busier than any four restaurant owners, if Tina could see that she had her own life . . . then he couldn't accuse her of making a meal of his own.

The worst intimation yet that something had gone wrong interrupted the pleasant pictures this possibility gave her. From the end of the block Maggie had been seeing a sliver of yellow light beside the entrance to Saigon, and had taken for granted that it was a reflection in a pane of glass or a strip of polished metal awaiting storage inside the foyer. Now it struck Maggie that it was at least half an hour too late for the workmen to be around. In this neighborhood, they would never leave anything outside at night.

As soon as she got closer to the restaurant, Maggie saw that the door itself hung open half an inch, letting the light from the staircase spill out. This was not merely an intimation of trouble, it rang like an alarm bell. Pumo would not have left his street door gaping open in a thousand lifetimes. Maggie jogged toward the shaft of light.

When she put her hand on the door, she realized that if Pumo had not left it open, some other person had. She was already pressing the buzzer that communicated with the apartment, and snatched her hand away before it gave any more than the dot of Morse code.

She hung in the doorway a moment, fairly panting with indecision. She moved a few steps to the side and pushed the buzzer for the restaurant, thinking that Vinh might be inside. She pressed it again, and this time held it down, but nothing happened. Vinh was not home.

There was a pay telephone around the corner on West Broadway, and Maggie moved away to call the police. But maybe Pumo *had* simply left the door unlocked, and was sitting upstairs in a blue funk.

Or maybe Dracula had returned to ransack the loft. The memory of how she had found Pumo lying on sheets stiff with drying blood moved her back to the door again and lifted her hand to the buzzer. She pushed, held it down longer than she had the restaurant's buzzer, and listened to the noise ring out through the loft and down the stairs.

"Look at Maggie skulk, I bet she's spyin' on someone."

She looked over her shoulder and saw Perry, her friend from the East Village, standing just behind her with a long black portfolio under one arm. Beside him Jules grimaced at her with an expression that virtually said: Isn't this terrible, isn't this deadly? They had apparently emerged from the office building on the other side of Saigon, which housed a number of art galleries. Jules and Perry had evidently resolved to sell out.

"Let's spy with her," Jules said. "Anything'd be more fun than bein' pissed on by these gallery assholes." Perry was English, and Jules had long ago begun to sound like him.

"I believe I'd fancy a bit of spyin' about now," said Perry. "Who we havin' a decco at, then? Enemy of the state? Ernst Stavro Blofeld? Italian Post-Expressionists?"

"I'm not spying on anybody," Maggie said. "I'm just waiting for my friend."

For a moment she considered asking them to come upstairs with her, but she could see too clearly how Perry would respond to Pumo's loft. He would go around knocking things over, drink up all the liquor he could find, and relentlessly insult Pumo's taste and politics.

"Funny way you have of waitin'," Perry said. "Which friend? That old geezer followed us 'round the off-license last year? Eyes hangin' out on bloody stalks?"

"That wasn't him, that was just someone he knows," Maggie said.

"Come along with us," Jules said. It was a gesture toward their old friendship. "After we take the paintings back, we'll show you this lovely new club."

"I can't."

"You *can't*?" Perry lifted an eyebrow. "I'm sure we never killed any Asian babies in any war or nuffink. Let's get out of here, Jules." He turned away from Maggie, and Jules did not even look at Maggie as he swept past.

Maggie watched them walk down the dark street in the lamplight, their ragged clothing giving them the air of loutish royalty, and knew that they would never forgive her for not joining them. People like Jules and Perry knew that they were sane and everybody else crazy, and Maggie had just stepped over the border into the land of the crazies.

All this reflection took place in a second or two. Maggie

pulled Pumo's door all the way open and stood in the doorway. Nothing but silence came from the top of the stairs.

Maggie stepped inside and closed the door behind her. Then she gripped the handrail and began slowly, quietly to mount the stairs.

7

Koko was in glory, his yoke was easy and his burden was light.

By man came death, and by man came also the resurrection of the dead.

Thirty lives to be paid for. Pumo was ten, and if there was a woman she would be eleven.

No part of the animal was wasted. The Joker had closed his eyes, and slept on in the pack.

When Pumo the Puma had opened the door and looked into Koko's face, he had known, he had seen, he had understood. Angels walked him backwards up the stairs, angels backed him into his great glowing cave. Tears spilled from Koko's eyes, for it was true that God did all things simultaneously, and Koko's heart overflowed for Pumo, who *understood*, who *took flight*, even as his soul took flight and sailed off, sailed home.

The eyes, the ears, the Elephant Card in the mouth.

Then Koko heard a great thunderous buzzing, the noise of the impatient world hungering for immortality, and he quickly moved to the light cord and pulled it down, turning off all the overhead lights in the room. Now the cave was dark. Koko went quietly to the hallway and turned that light off too.

Then he went back into the living room to wait.

Outside, traffic roared like the passing of great beasts in a jungle. His father leaned toward him and said *Work too fast and you'll never amount to nothing*. The buzzer rang again, clamoring until it found its true voice and became a giant insect swooping in great circles between the walls. Finally it settled on Pumo's body and folded its great strong wings.

Koko picked the knife off a couch and slid into his spot just inside the entrance to the cave from the hallway. He made himself invisible, still, and silent. His father and a friendly demon waited with him, silently approving, and Koko slipped into a nightmare world he had known all his life. His footsteps turned the earth black, and thirty children went into a cave and never came out, and three soldiers went into a cave, and two came out. *Gentlemen, you are part of a great killing machine.* Finally Koko saw the elephant stride toward him, his robes ermine and silk, and the Old Lady said, *Gentlemen, it is time to face the elephant again.*

For his ears had taken in the dampened, nearly soundless click of the door and his body had felt a small slight shift in the air and now he could hear a hand closing on a handrail and her feet moving with what to a civilian would be most fearful caution from one tread of the stair to another.

8

Maggie reached the top of the steps and saw at once that the door to the loft was unlocked—it looked as though someone had banged it shut with an elbow as he carried his haul outside. Or by someone going in. She touched the knob and pushed it forward with her fingertips. Light from the staircase filled Pumo's entry, with its heaps of coats and hats on hooks.

Pumo's entry always looked as if he were having a party.

At the worst, Maggie thought, he had been robbed again, and would have to be coaxed out of another depression. Any intruder was long gone. Maggie walked through the door, switched on the light, went down the little hallway. When she reached the bedroom, she reached in and turned on that light too. Nothing had been disturbed since their unhappy morning. The bed was still unmade, a sure sign that Tina was in a downswing.

Some pervasive smell filled the loft, but Maggie filed the fact away to be dealt with as soon as she had satisfied herself either that there had been no break-in, or that the burglar who had left the doors open had not done a great deal of damage. Maggie backed out of the bedroom to check the bathroom, again saw nothing out of the ordinary, and went on into the living room.

She froze about six feet into the room. The dim illumination from the hallway showed the shadowy outline of a man on one of the little wooden-backed chairs normally arranged around Tina's dining table. Her first thought was that she had been trapped by a very cool-headed burglar, and her heart jumped up into her throat. Then as her eyes continued to adjust to the darkness, she almost subliminally recognized that the man in the chair was her lover. She moved forward, in turn ready to scold, then cajole, then to soothe him. As Maggie opened her mouth to speak his name, she finally identified the odor filling the loft as the smell of blood. She was still moving forward, and her next faltering step brought her close enough to see how Tina's chest was painted with blood, and how the legs of the chair sat in a wide red pool. Something white like a tag protruded from Tina's mouth.

Instead of screaming or whirling around, which would have led almost instantly to her death, Maggie moved off to her right, into the darkest section of the loft. This movement of pure reflex felt almost as if it had been done to her, as if some force had swept her aside to get her out of the rectangle of light which was the entrance from the hall. She wound up crouching beneath the dining table at the far right of the room, too scared by what she had seen and too startled by her own movement to do anything but look out from her vantage point at the rest of the room.

Terror must have kicked her senses open wide. In the first seconds that she found herself beneath the table, she took in every nuance from the street, the happiness in the voices calling out to each other, the squeal of a brake drum, even the tap of a cane on the sidewalk. In the midst of these sounds she heard drops of liquid landing in the pool at Pumo's feet. Accompanying these sounds was a sweet, sick, limping odor: the smell of concentrated mourning.

"Come on out, Dawn," a man whispered, and Maggie could smell only the blood again. "I want to talk to you."

A column of darkness left the door and advanced into the room. Some of the light from the hall gave the column the shape of a compact man wearing a dark topcoat slightly too large for him. The man's face was only a pale blur, and his hair must have been as black as

Maggie's, for it was entirely invisible against the darkness behind him.

Then the man startled her by giggling. "I made a mistake. You couldn't still be Dawn. Don't be mad at me."

He advanced another smooth silent yard into the room. There was an ugly black-handled knife in his hand. He drifted a few feet sideways into shadow and waited.

Maggie began to inch on her hands and knees down under the table, and at the bottom end of the table she gathered herself to make a rush for the door.

"Come out and talk to me," he said. "There's a reason for everything, and there's a reason for this. I'm not a lunatic operating in a void, you know. I have come thousands of miles to stand here right now, in the middle of the world right here. It's important for you to understand that."

He hesitated in the shadows.

"I am a person who always knows when something is going to happen, and this is a thing that is going to happen. You are going to stand up and walk toward me. You are afraid. You smell blood. That is from something that already happened a long time ago, and you are here now and you have to see that what happened then was part of a general pattern and you are in that pattern too. Worthy, worthy is the lamb that was slain. He was a warrior, and I was a warrior, and I have been called back." The man stepped closer to the center of the room. "So this has to happen. Stand up and walk out toward me."

As he spoke, Maggie shrugged her coat off her shoulders and let it silently fold onto the floor. She crept back up the length of the table, crawled around the chairs at its far end, and very slowly and quietly moved up onto the platform.

The man startled her by backing a step toward her.

"I know where you are. You are under the table. I could go over to you now and pull you out. I am not going to do that. I am going to give you the chance to show yourself. Once you show yourself to me, you can leave. You can see where I am now. I am at the back of the room. I promise you that I will not move from this spot. I would like to see your face, I would like to know you."

Maggie saw him shift the knife in his hand to hold the tip between his thumb and forefinger, the handle dangling below.

"There is the Elephant," he said. "Justice does not exist in the world system. Fairness is a human invention. The world abhors only waste, waste is forbidden, and when waste is eliminated love is permitted. Behold, I tell you a mystery—I am a man of sorrows and I loved Pumo the Puma."

Maggie had begun moving backward with greater care. She was very near the desk, and when she touched it with one backwards-reaching hand she forced herself to move even more slowly until she had found the side of the empty clay pot she knew was there. It had once held a tiny hibiscus tree, a gift from Maggie; when the tree had died from lack of light and an infestation of mites around the time of the insect problem in the kitchen, Pumo had dumped the hibiscus and kept the pot, promising Maggie that they would get another. It had sat empty beside his desk ever since.

"One minute or another, we will meet one another. In this minute, or the next, or the one after that . . ."

He stood there, about five feet away from her now, as prepared as ever to throw his knife into her back. Maggie lifted the big pot off its base, and in one motion stood up and raised the pot above her head.

The man looked back over his shoulder, already beginning to react, and Maggie stepped forward and brought the pot down with imperfect accuracy. She was sobbing with terror. His own reflexes undid him. Ducking sideways, he brought himself directly beneath the heavy pot, and it connected solidly with the side of his head. There was a dull heavy thud followed almost immediately by the smashing of the pot on the floor and the loud crash as Tina's killer pitched onto the coffee table and snapped it in two like a sheet of ice.

Maggie jumped down from the platform and skimmed across the floor before Pumo's killer had picked himself up out of the wreckage of the table. She threw open the door and went pell-mell down the stairs. As if with three-hundred-and-sixty-degree vision, she saw her huge shadow on the wall beside her and a darker shape filling the opening at the top of the stairs. Even though she was flying, she seemed to be moving with terrific slowness, as if time were muscle-bound. The man must have dropped his knife, for he did not throw it. Maggie burst through the street door as she heard the man thundering down the stairs.

Again she flew, now toward noise, lights, people. She was entirely unaware of the cold.

Maggie risked a glance over her shoulder just before she reached the corner of West Broadway. The scene behind her seemed as flat and artificial as a stage set. The door to the loft hung open, and light spilling out melted into the circular light from a streetlamp. A few people had turned around on the sidewalk to watch her run past. In the midst of all the light and activity on Grand Street was a sliding shadow, a man who melted toward her invisibly, using other people as cover. Maggie snapped her head forward, her breath freezing in her throat, and did her best to narrow down to a small black line speeding along above the pavement.

Maggie ran down the block, her arms pumping in the thin sleeves of her shirt, her knees rising and falling. "*Go*, girl," a black man urged when she flew by, for her broad smooth face reflected little of her terror. A red-hot staple fixed itself into her side, and when she began to run against the rhythm of her breathing she could hear her pursuer's footsteps smoothly, evenly hitting the ground behind her. He was gaining on her.

Finally the subway was only a block ahead of her. Her face dripped sweat and the staple burned in her side, but still her elbows pumped and her knees rose and fell. The boys, still occupying the middle of the sidewalk, saw her racing toward them and went wild.

"Chinkie!"

"Baby, you came back!"

This wide-grinning boy in a Fila sweatshirt danced in front of her, giving big come-to-me gestures. A gold chain spelling out a name in letters as large as front teeth bounced on his chest. Maggie was yelling something, and they made to close on her, but when she came within a few yards of the boy he saw her face and moved out of the way. "Murder!" she yelled. "Stop him!"

Without any transition she was flying down the steps, moving as if there were no gravity. From above she heard shouts and the sound of somebody falling. Before Maggie hit the bottom of the steps she heard a train pounding into the station, and she hit the ground running. Perhaps fifteen people were in the station, another fifteen or so on the platform. Voices still came from the top of the stairs. To her right the train came to a stop, and its doors squeaked open.

Maggie kept on winding through the people, and when she reached the turnstile she pretended to drop in her token and passed beneath the motionless bar swiftly and unobserved. Once past the turnstile she risked another glance over her shoulder and saw a wall of people advancing toward the train. Then a grey shadow melted away behind a man in a black topcoat, and she saw the suggestion of a smile as the shadow flowed on toward her. The being was quietly, gleefully capering toward her, and she sprinted across the final few yards to the waiting train.

Maggie rushed into the car and darted to the nearest window as the doors closed. The man in the black topcoat was just now nearing the turnstile, and behind him something else melted and flowed, passed between the men and women waiting to get to the platform, grinned at her and danced all but invisibly, seeing her but unseen as the train pulled away from the station.

Maggie collapsed into a seat. After a time she became aware that she was trembling. "He killed him," she said to herself. When she repeated this statement, the few people around her stood up and moved farther down the length of the car. It seemed to Maggie that what had killed her lover and pursued her into the station had not been human but a supernatural force, a grinning evil thing that could change its shape or become invisible. The only proof she had of its humanity had been the way the pot had connected to its head, and how it had sprawled onto Pumo's glass table. A wave of nausea and of disbelief went through her. Maggie was sobbing now, and she swiped at her eyes. She bent over and looked at her shoes. They were not bloodstained, not even the soles. She shuddered again and wept to herself all the rest of the long way uptown. Tears streamed down her face while she changed trains. She felt like a beaten animal returning home. Now and then she started and cried out, thinking that she had caught a glimpse of Tina's crazy shadowy killer moving behind the backs of people standing at the straps in front of her, but when the people parted and fled no one was there, he had melted away again.

At 125th Street she ran down the steps, crossing her arms over her chest for warmth. Her tears were going to freeze, she thought, and she would be trapped inside the icy seal over her face.

She parted the doors of the General's storefront church and slipped inside as quietly as she could. Warmth and the odor of burning candles immediately surrounded her, and she nearly collapsed. The General's congregation sat solidly in their chairs; Maggie stayed at the back of the church, trembling and gripping her arms, uncertain of what to do next. Now that she was here, she was uncertain even of why she had returned to the bright little church. Tears streamed down her face. The General finally caught sight of her and raised one eyebrow in a kindly, questioning look that did not fail to contain a portion of alarm. *He doesn't know,* Maggie thought, hugging herself and shaking, silently crying. *How can he not know?* Then Maggie realized that Tina Pumo still sat dead in his loft and nobody but herself and his murderer knew of it. She had to call the police.

9

As yet ignorant of these events which would soon bring him back to New York, Michael Poole emerged for the second time that day from Bang Luk, the alleyway which housed the flower market and Tim Underhill's rooms, and turned north up Charoen Krung Road. It was just past twelve-thirty at night. The streets were even more congested than they had been earlier, and under normal circumstances even a passionate walker like Dr. Poole would unquestioningly have stepped to the curb, raised his arm, and taken the first vehicle that stopped for him. It was still very hot, his hotel was two or three miles away, and Bangkok is no city for long walks. But these were not normal circumstances, and Dr. Poole never considered interring himself in a car for the length of his journey back to his bed. In any case he was in no hurry to get to bed—he knew he would be unable to sleep. He had just finished spending a little more than seven hours with Timothy Underhill, and he needed time to think as much as he needed sheer thoughtless exercise. By most ways of reckoning, very little had happened during the seven hours: the two men had talked over their drinks on the terrace; still talking, they had gone by ruk-tuk to the Golden Dragon on Sukhumvit Road and eaten excellent Chinese food while they continued their conversation; they had taken another ruk-tuk back to the little set of rooms above Jimmy Siam and talked, talked, talked. Michael Poole could still hear Tim Underhill's voice in his ears—he felt as if he were walking to the rhythms of the sentences spoken by that voice.

Underhill was a wonderful man. He was a wonderful man with a terrible life, a wonderful man with terrible habits. He was terrible and he was wonderful. (Michael had had more to drink during these seven hours than was his habit, and all the alcohol had warmed and muddled him.) Poole realized that he was moved, shaken, even in a sense awed by his old companion—awed by what he had risked and overcome. But more than that, he was persuaded by Underhill. It was shiningly certain that Underhill was not Koko. All his subsequent conversation had gone to prove what Poole had felt in Underhill's first words to him on the terrace.

In all the turmoil of his life, Tim Underhill had virtually never ceased to consider Koko, to ponder and wonder over that figure of anarchic vengeance—he not only made Harry Beevers a latecomer to the issue, he demonstrated the shallowness of Beevers' methods. Poole walked northward in the dark steaming city, hemmed all about by rushing, indifferent men, and felt how thoroughly he sided with Underhill. Eight hours earlier, Dr. Poole had crossed over a rickety bridge and felt himself coming into a new accommodation with his profession, with his marriage, above all with death. It was almost as if he had finally seen death with enough respect to understand it. He had stood before it with his spirit wide open, in a very undoctorly way. The awe, the terror were necessary—all such moments of rapturous understanding fade, leaving only the dew of their passing, but Poole could remember the sharp, salty, vivid taste of reality, and the humility he had felt before it. What had persuaded him about Tim Underhill was his sense that for years, in book after book, Underhill had actually climbed over the railing and crossed the stream. He had opened his spirit wide. He had done his best to fly, and Koko had virtually given him his wings.

Underhill had flown as far as he could, and if he had crashed, an abrupt landing might have been one of the consequences of flight. All the drinking and drugs, all his excesses, had not been undertaken to aid the flight—as Beevers and people like him would instantly have assumed—but to numb and distract the man when he had gone as far as he could and still had fallen short. Underhill had gone farther than Dr. Poole, who had used his mind and his memory and his love for Stacy Talbot, which was wrapped like a layer of bandages around his old love for Robbie: Underhill had harnessed up his whole imagination, and imagination was everything.

This, along with a great deal more, had tumbled out on the terrace, over dinner in the noisy bright enormous Chinese restaurant, in the unbelievable shambles of Underhill's apartment. Almost nothing had been explained in sequence, and the unhappy details of the author's life had often dragged Poole's attention away from Koko. The outline of Underhill's life was that of a series of avalanches. At present, however, he was living quietly and doing his best to work again. "Like learning to walk again," he told Poole. "I staggered and then I fell down. All the muscles shrank, nothing worked right. For eight months, if I wrote one paragraph after six hours' work, it was a good day."

He had written a strange novella called "Blue Rose." He had written an even stranger one called "The Juniper Tree." Now he wrote dialogues with himself, questions and answers, and he was halfway through another novel. He had twice seen a girl running up the street toward him covered in blood, making an unearthly noise—the girl was part of the answer, he said, that was why he had seen her—she announced the nearness of ultimate things. Koko was Underhill's way of getting back inside Ia Thuc, and so was the vision of a girl running in panic down a city street, and so was everything he had written.

What made everything worse, Underhill said, was that Koko was the lowlife's lowlife, Victor Spitalny.

"I worked it all out," Underhill told him at the Golden Dragon. "I did one of those Koko numbers, you did one, and I think Conor Linklater did one—"

"He did," Michael said. "And I did one too—you're right."

"No kidding," Underhill said. "You think you didn't show it? You're not exactly the atrocity type, Michael. I worked out that it could only have been Spitalny. Unless it was you, of course, or Dengler, both of which were equally unlikely.

"I came to Bangkok to learn what I could about Dengler's last days, because I thought maybe that would get me started writing again. And then, my friend, all hell broke loose. The journalists started dying. As you and Beevers noticed."

"What do you mean, journalists?" Michael asked innocently.

Underhill had stared at him with his mouth open for a moment, then had burst into laughter.

Poole reached the wide, jumbled intersection of Charoen Krung Road with Surawong Road and stood still in the dense hot night for a moment. Using the resources of a few provincial libraries and bookstores in Bangkok, Underhill had discovered what Harry Beevers, with a research assistant and a vast library system, had not. It took Poole's breath away, that Beevers would have overlooked, even denied, the connection among the victims.

Because that connection put them all in danger. Underhill was certain that Spitalny had followed him, in both Singapore and Bangkok.

He had only caught glimpses. He'd had the sensation of being watched and followed. In the Golden Dragon he told Michael, "A few weeks after the bodies were found in Singapore, I came down to the street and had this feeling that something really bad, but something that *belonged* to me, was hiding somewhere and watching me. As if I had a sick, bad brother who had come back after a long time away, and was going to make my life hell before he went away again. I looked around, but I didn't see anything but the flower sellers, and as soon as I got out onto the road, the feeling went away." And in his messy room, with the demon masks nailed up on the wall and a smeary mirror and an ivory straw before him on the table, he said: "Remember my telling you about the time I walked outside and had this *feeling*—that something bad had come back for me? I thought it was Spitalny, of course. But nothing happened. He just melted away. Well, about two days after that, a few days after the Frenchmen were killed here, I had the same feeling on Phat Pong Road. It was much stronger this time. I *knew* someone was there. I turned around, almost sure that he was right behind me, and that I'd see him. I *spun.* He wasn't behind me—he wasn't even right behind the people right behind me. I couldn't see him anywhere. But you know, I did see something strange. It's hard to put this into words, even for me, but it was like, way back down there, way way down the street, there was something like a moving shadow drifting back and forth behind these people who were much more visible, no, not drifting because it was much more animated, *dancing* back and forth behind all those people, grinning at me. I just had this little glimpse of someone moving insolently fast, someone just filled with glee—and then he vanished. I almost puked."

"And what do you want to do now?" Poole asked. "Would you come back to America? I'm almost honor-bound to tell Conor and Beevers that I've met you, but I don't know how you feel about that either."

"Do what you want," Underhill said. "But I feel like you want to drag me out of my cave by my hair, and I'm not sure I want to leave it."

"Then don't!" Michael had cried.

"But maybe we can help each other," Underhill said.

"Can I see you again tomorrow?"

"You can do anything you like," Underhill had said.

As Michael Poole walked the last two hundred yards to his hotel, he wondered what he would do if a madman danced like a moving shadow on the hot crowded street behind him. Would he see a vision, as Underhill apparently had? Would he turn and try to run him down? Victor Spitalny, the lowlife's lowlife, changed everything. A moment later Michael realized that Harry Beevers might have his mini-series after all—Spitalny put a few colorful new wrinkles in Beevers' story. But was it for that he had come so far from Westerholm?

It was one of the easiest questions Poole had ever asked himself, and by the time he was going up the stairs into his hotel, he had decided to keep quiet for a little while about having found Tim Underhill. He would give himself a day before speaking to Conor and summoning Beevers. In any case, he discovered as he passed the desk, Conor was still out. Poole hoped that he was enjoying himself.

PART FIVE

THE SEA OF FORGETFULNESS

23

ROBBIE, WITH LANTERN

1

Two days later, it was as if the world had flipped inside-out. The suddenness of events and the haste of Poole's preparations had left him so breathless that he could still not be certain, carrying two bottles of Singha beer toward the table in the airport bar where Conor sat blinking at his progress, what he made of it at all.

Underhill was supposed to come with them on their flight, and part of Conor's look at Michael as he came toward him from the crowded passengers-only bar was a gathering doubt that the writer would make it to the airport on time. Conor said nothing as Michael set down his beer and took the seat beside him. He bent forward as if to examine the floor, and his face was still white with the shock of what had happened back in New York while they had been making their separate tours of Bangkok. Conor still looked as if a loud noise had just awakened him.

Michael contented himself with a sip of the strong, cold, bitter Thai beer. Something had *befallen* Conor two nights earlier, but he would not discuss it. He too looked as if he were remembering some of the sentences Underhill had written in his dialogues with himself. Poole guessed that these questions and answers were a way of kicking a disused engine back into life: Underhill was teaching himself to work again. Along the way he had described what he called the Pan-feeling. According to Underhill, this had to do with "the nearness of ultimate things."

"What are you thinking about, Mikey?" Conor asked.

Poole just shook his head.

"Stretch my legs," Conor said, and jumped up and wandered toward the gates through which the passengers came for their own and other international flights. It was fifty minutes before the scheduled flight time, which an airline official had informed them had been delayed an hour. Conor bounced on his heels and scrutinized the people streaming through the gate until Underhill's failure to arrive made him so nervous that he had to spin off and take a quick tour of the gift shop windows. At the entrance to the racks of duty-free liquor he checked his watch, shot another glance at the new arrivals, and dodged inside.

Ten minutes later he emerged with a yellow plastic shopping bag and dropped into his old seat beside Poole. "I thought if I went in there, he'd show up."

Conor forlornly examined the Thais, Americans, Japanese, and Europeans pushing into the International departures lounge. "Hope Beevers made his plane."

Harry Beevers was supposed to have taken a flight from Taipei to Tokyo, where he was to connect with a JAL flight that would bring him to the San Francisco airport an hour after their own arrival. They were all to take the same flight to New York from San Francisco. Beevers' immediate reaction to the news of Pumo's death had been the observation that the asshole would still be alive if he had come with them instead of staying behind to run around after his girlfriend. He asked clipped impatient questions about just when they were going to be in San Francisco, and why they couldn't wait for him to come back to Bangkok. He was pissed off, he thought it was unfair that Poole and Linklater had found Tim Underhill: it was his idea, *he* should have been the one. "Make sure he gets on that plane," he said. "And don't let him lie to you."

Poole had pointed out that Underhill could not have killed Tina Pumo.

"Tina lived in So Ho," Beevers said. "Open your eyes, will you? He was in the *restaurant* business. How many coke dealers do you think live in SoHo? Not everything is the way it looks."

Conor finished off his beer, jumped up again to inspect the incoming passengers, and returned. By now all the seats in the departure lounge were occupied, and the new arrivals either sat on the floor or wandered the wide aisles before the duty-free shops. As it filled, the lounge had gradually come to resemble Bangkok itself: people sat in chairs and sprawled over empty sections of the floor, the air seemed hot and smoky, voices cried out "Crap crap crop crop!"

After a long crackling burst of Thai from the loudspeaker, in which Poole thought he heard the words San Francisco, Conor again jumped up to check the board on which departures were listed. Their flight had been rescheduled to take off in fifty-five minutes. Unless they delayed it further, they would land in San Francisco at the same time as Beevers, who would never forgive them for having been duped. Beevers would insist on going back to Bangkok on the spot. He'd stage a chase through the streets, with police sirens and dashes across rooftops, concluding with the triumphant handcuffing of the villain and an astonishing explanation of how Underhill had killed the journalists and arranged Pumo's murder. Beevers saw things in the terms rendered by car chases and lockstep summations.

Poole was very tired. He had slept little last night. He had called Judy, and she had curtly given him the news of Tina's death. "Whoever did it is supposed to be the same person who killed the man in the library. Oh, you haven't heard about that yet?" Unable to keep the satisfaction from her voice, she explained the circumstances of the death of Dr. Mayer-Hall.

"Why do they think it's the same guy?"

"There were two Chinese women who saw Tina in the stacks a few minutes before they discovered the body. They recognized his picture when they saw the papers this morning. It's all on the news. Tina was the suspect they were looking for—these women saw him coming out of the stacks. It's obvious what happened."

"What happened?"

"Tina got lost in the stacks, God only knows what he was doing in the library, and he happened to see this crazy man kill the librarian. He got away, but the man tracked him down and killed him. It's obvious." She paused. "I'm sorry to cut your fun short."

He asked if she were still getting the anonymous calls.

"Lately he has been saying that there is no substitute for butter, or something like that. I just erase the tapes as soon as he says his piece. When this guy was a kid, somebody drummed nonsense into his head from morning to night. I bet he was an abused kid."

Their conversation ended soon after.

For a moment Michael Poole saw Victor Spitalny before him, small, slope-shouldered, dark-haired, his dark eyes shifting back and forth beneath his narrow forehead with its widow's peak, his wet little mouth and his pointed chin. At eighteen years of age, there had been a self-erected psychic wall around Victor Spitalny. If he saw you coming near him, he would stop and wait until you had gotten far enough away to let him feel safe. He had probably decided to kill someone and desert very soon after hearing Tim Underhill's story of the running grunt.

Perhaps because of something his wife had said, Poole thought for the first time that it might be interesting to go to Milwaukee and see where Victor Spitalny had grown up.

And Milwaukee was Underhill's Monroe, Illinois, where Hal Esterhaz had been run down by his own destiny. If Underhill ever appeared at the airport, he might want to come along on this fantasy journey and look at the childhood of one of his own characters.

Then he heard Conor gasp, and an instant later all of this went out of his head. He was looking at Tim Underhill loping toward them, carrying a box bound with twine under one arm, a leather satchel in one hand, and a case containing an ancient portable typewriter in the other, which also gripped the handles of a plastic carrying bag. The loose seersucker jacket flapped around his frame. He looked startlingly different—in the next beat Michael saw that Underhill had cut his hair.

"You made it," he said.

"I'll be a little short of funds until I finish my book," Underhill said. "Could one of you gentlemen buy me a Coke?"

Conor jumped up to go to the bar.

2

It was like a parody of their trip out, finally—Tim Underhill in the window seat instead of Harry Beevers, Conor in the middle, Michael on the aisle on a planeful of tourists. Michael missed Pun Yin's dimples and shining hair: this was an American airline, and the stewardesses were tall women with distracted professional faces. The other passengers were not pediatricians but mainly young people who fell into two categories: the employees of multinational corporations who read *Megatrends* and *The One-Minute Manager* and married couples with or without babies, dressed in jeans and shirts. When Michael was their age, they would have been reading Herman Hesse and Carlos Castaneda, but the bulging paperbacks they dug out of their packs were by Judith Krantz and Sidney Sheldon, or were written by ladies with three names and had jacket paintings of misty castles and yearning unicorns. In 1983, bohemia, if that was what these people represented, was not very literary. That was okay, Michael thought. He read airplane books too. Conor didn't read at all. Underhill had placed on his tray a fat paperback that looked as if three people had read it before him.

Michael took from his carry-on bag a copy of *The Ambassadors,* a Henry James novel Judy had pressed on him. He had been enjoying it, back in Westerholm, but when he held it in his hands he realized that he did not feel like reading. Now that they were actually in the air, he could not imagine what he was returning to.

The sky outside the little windows was black, shot with violent, unearthly streaks of red and purple. Such a sky was suitable: it seemed to draw them into Koko's world, where no gesture could be ordinary, where angels sang and demons fled down long corridors.

Conor asked the stewardess if they got a movie.

"As soon as we clear the dinner things. It's *Never Say Never Again*—the new James Bond movie."

The stewardess looked offended when Conor grinned.

"It's because of this guy we know," Poole explained. He did not feel like calling Beevers a friend, not even to a stewardess who would never meet him.

"Hey," Conor said mockingly, "I'm a homicide detective from New York, I'm a big deal, I'm another double-oh-seven."

"Your friend is a homicide detective in New York?" the girl asked. "He must be a busy man these days. There was a guy stabbed to death at JFK a week or two ago." She noticed the sudden attention being paid to what she was saying, and added, "Some wheeler-dealer who was on one of our flights. A girlfriend of mine works in first class on the San Francisco–New York run a lot, and she said he was one of her people—a regular." She paused. "I guess he was a real jerk." Another pause. "The newspapers said he was a yuppie, but they just called him that because he was a young guy with a lot of money."

"What's a yuppie?" Underhill asked.

"A young guy with a lot of money," Poole said.

"A girl in a grey flannel suit and a pair of Reeboks," Conor said.

"What are Reeboks?" Underhill asked.

"He was killed at JFK after he arrived on a flight from San Francisco?" Poole asked.

The stewardess nodded. She was a tall blonde whose name tag said she was named Marnie, and she had an eager, playful expression in her eyes. "My friend Lisa said she saw him a couple of times a month. She and I used to go around together and do all this crazy stuff, but she moved to New York last year and now we just talk on the phone. But she told me all about it." She gave Conor a curious sidelong look.

"Can I tell you something? I want to tell you something."

Conor nodded. Marnie bent down and whispered into his ear.

Poole heard Conor nearly gasp in astonishment; then he laughed so loudly that the people in the seats before them stopped talking.

"See you guys later," Marnie said, and pushed her cart up the aisle.

"What was that about?" Michael asked. Conor's entire face had turned red. Tim Underhill flicked a little lizard smile at Poole and looked like William Burroughs, very wise and dry as a desert.

"Nothing."

"She came on to you?"

"Not exactly. Lay off."

"Good old Marnie," Underhill said.

"Change the subject. Lay off."

"Okay, listen to this," Michael said. "Somebody off a San Francisco flight was killed when he landed in New York. Spitalny could have landed in San Francisco, just as we are doing, and then connected to a New York flight, as we are also doing."

"Farfetched," Underhill said, "but very interesting. What was the name of the stewardess's friend? Who knew the dead man?"

"Lisa," Conor said, still blushing.

"I wonder if Lisa noticed anybody talking to the man who was killed?"

At the beginning of *Never Say Never Again,* James Bond was sent to a health spa. Every ten minutes someone new tried to kill him. Pretty nurses went to bed with him. A beautiful woman took a snake from around her neck and threw it into a car window.

When Marnie returned Poole asked her, "What's your friend Lisa's last name?"

"Mayo. Like in Ireland. Like in Hellman's."

It was farfetched, but so was Bangkok. So was Westerholm. Life in general was farfetched

"Did you know," Underhill was saying, "in Bangkok you can give a guy about sixty bucks and go down into a basement and see a guy kill a girl? First he beats her up. Then he kills her. You watch her die and you go home."

Conor had removed his earphones and was staring at Underhill. "I guess you know about that."

"What, did you go there?"

Conor said nothing. "Did you?" he finally asked.

Underhill shook his head.

"Come on," Conor said.

"Never. Just heard about it."

"Don't lie to me, man."

"I'm not lying."

Conor frowned.

"I have the feeling you met some interesting people," Underhill said. "I want to tell you something."

3

How Dengler Died (2):

You have to see Captain Batchittarayan, you have to see his desk, his office, his face . . .

Everything was hard, pocked, suspicious—everything smelled like death and Lysol. One light, of dull metal, shone at first down on his neat brown hands on the scarred empty metal surface of his desk; later, as if by itself, it swung upward, hurting my eyes.

Yes, it was his men who had responded to the near-riot, to call it that, the "near-riot" in the Patpong area on the day in question, it was he, at that time Sergeant Batchittarayan, who had supervised the transportation of the mutilated body to the city's morgue. It was he who had pulled the tags out of the mush on the man's chest. It was distasteful: it *had been* distasteful, and the memory of the white American's body was still unhappy. And the man before him was distasteful, with his connection to it, and with his possession of a secret.

There had been others—other Americans on R&R who had gone mad. Two years before PFC Dengler's death, a Sergeant Walter Khoffi had hacked several patrons of the Sex-Sex bar to death before going outside and killing a massage parlor tout on the street, and a quiet Bible-quoting boy from Oklahoma named Marvin Springwater had knifed three little boys to death before the traffic ran him down on Sukhumvit Road.

So the officer's distaste had some justification.

He was interested in how one knew about the child. The child existed, but had never been located or identified.

Weren't you asking about the child?

Questions about the child had attracted the Captain's attention.

Fortunately she had cried out, this unknown child. The two men and the girl had been in a narrow alley. Her screams drew attention to them. She did not cease screaming when she burst out of the alley.

Nobody knew the girl. She was a stranger. That was to be expected, Patpong being the opposite of a settled residential area. There was agreement on two points, however. She was not a bar girl or massage parlor employee—that much was clear to all those who saw her emerge from the narrow alley and run screaming down the street. And she was not a Thai. She was perhaps a Cambodian child, or Chinese, or Vietnamese.

It was not supposed that the young soldiers knew that. To the young soldiers, it was supposed, all young Asian women looked alike.

And so the crowd of men who happened to be in that particular block of Phat Pong Road that afternoon jumped the American soldier—jumped both of them—and one got away and one was torn to pieces.

Do you know who was innocent? asked the Captain. The girl was innocent. And the crowd was innocent.

So one soldier fell beneath the innocent crowd, or both did. Witnesses were vague about this. The witnesses had seen only the running girl, they had not of course participated in the assault.

A thousand years ago it would have been a great epic, this story (said the Captain). The innocent girl, her attacker torn to pieces by the righteous mob. Four hundred years ago it would have become a legend told in a song, and every child in southern Thailand would have known the song. The disappearing girl—she could have disappeared into *that*. Now there is not even a novel about her, not even a rock and roll song, not even a cartoon strip.

A month before this conversation with the Captain, Timothy Underhill had stood on Phat Pong Road and saw a girl rushing toward him down the middle of the street. He had been totally clean for something like nine weeks. He had been trying to write—a novel again at last, something still coming to life in his mind about a boy who had been raised in a shed behind his house, like an animal. He had been sober for three months. He heard the screams, which sounded as if she carried a microphone in her throat. He saw her bloody palms and blood-spattered hair. She came threshing toward him with her hands out and her mouth open. No one but he saw her.

Underhill wept on the pavement, unnoticed by the men pushing past him. He was *there* again, alive inside himself.

I went home, he told Poole, and I wrote a story called "Blue Rose." It took six weeks. After that I wrote a story of the same length called "The Juniper Tree." It took a month. I've been writing ever since.

Did you really think I'd miss this plane?

After I saw her, then I had to see everything—then I had to follow the story. It wouldn't come to me anymore. You were going to come to me, or he was, but not it. I didn't know I was waiting for either you or Koko to show up, but that's what I was doing.

4

Another movie began, but Poole had closed his eyes before the titles came up on the screen.

He was driving his car down a long dark road into an emptiness like a desert. He had been traveling many days; though the means by which he knew this were unclear, he was in a novel called *Into the Darkness,* written by Tim Underhill. The long road went straight on through the night, and as he drove Michael realized that he was Hal Esterhaz, a homicide detective, and that he had been summoned from the scene of one murder to that of another, far distant. He had been traveling for weeks, going from corpse to corpse, following the killer's footsteps without getting any nearer to him. There had been many bodies, and all of them were those of people he had known long ago in a dreamlike existence before everything had darkened.

Far ahead in the darkness he saw two dots of yellow light shining out beside the road.

In *Into the Darkness* he would drive through the dark in a gradually emptying world. There would always be another body, and he would never find the killer, for *Into the Darkness* was like a theme that repeated itself through a thousand variations, circling around and around the same cycle of chords. There would be no true ending. In *Into the Darkness* one day the killer would retire to raise orchids or turn into smoke, and then all meaning would be gone; the melody would trickle out in meaningless random sounds. For his job was to catalogue the killings, and the only truly satisfactory conclusion to that task would be to enter one of those dripping slum basements and find the killer waiting for him with a raised knife.

Now he could see that the yellow lights by the roadside were lanterns—little lanterns sending out beams of light.

Only when he had come directly abreast of the lanterns could he see who held them up. His son Robbie, whose name was Babar, stood by the roadside holding one of the lanterns aloft. Exactly his size, gigantic, the rabbit Ernie stood beside him on his hind legs, holding out the other lantern.

The boy named Babar and the rabbit turned their soft eyes on the man driving past; their lamps gleamed.

He felt a great spreading peace.

The car pulled past the tender boy and the big upright rabbit, and for a long time he could see the lights of their lanterns in his rearview mirror. The sense of peace stayed with him until the road ended at the bank of a great grey rushing river. He got out of his car and watched the great muscular river move past, rolling up a huge sinewy shoulder here, a vast thigh there.

Then he knew that he and the killer too were a part of the river's great rushing body, and a terrible mingling of pain and joy, deep deep joy and pain, spread through him and spoke in their loud joined voice, and he cried out and woke up with the river in his eyes.

The river was gone. "Hey, Mikey," Conor said, smiling almost shyly at him.

And then he only knew that he knew Koko's identity. Then the feeling of knowing went too, and he remembered only that he had dreamed of looking at a great river and driving a car past Robbie, named Babar, who held up a lantern.

Into the darkness.

"You okay, Mikey?" Conor asked.

Poole nodded.

"You made a noise."

"Noise, nothing," Underhill said. "You practically sang 'The Star-Spangled Banner.' "

Poole rubbed the stubble on his face. The screen had been folded back up into the bulkhead, and most of the cabin was dark. "I thought I understood something about Koko, but it went away as soon as I woke up."

Conor uttered a wordless exclamation full of recognition.

"Those things happen to you?" Underhill asked Conor.

"I can't really talk about it—I thought I understood something too," Conor half-mumbled. "It was real strange." He tilted his head and looked at Underhill. "You were at that place, weren't you? Where they shot the girl?"

"Sometimes I think I must have an evil twin," Underhill said. "Like the man in the iron mask."

They fell silent, and the lost understanding stirred within Michael once again. It was as if his son's lantern shone its light on the events in that village fifteen years ago: he saw a long hillside leading down to a circle of hootches, a woman carrying water downhill, oxen grazing. Smoke rose in a narrow grey column. Into the darkness, there it is.

24

IN THE CAVE

1

Dengler's arm was wrapped in gauze and tape, and his face was white and his eyes blurry. He said he didn't feel anything, and he refused to lie down and wait for them to come back for him. Ia Thuc was supposed to be where Elvis the sniper came from, it was supposed to be the village that sheltered and fed him, and Dengler wanted to be with the platoon when they got there. Lieutenant Beevers had been leading search-and-avoid missions since Dragon Valley, playing it very cool, and Ia Thuc was his chance to shine. Intelligence said that it was a stockpile for food and weapons, and the Tin Man was eager to make a good haul, boost the body count, move himself a little further up along the way to full colonel. The Tin Man was always eager to make a good body count, because only half the lieutenant colonels in Nam ever got promoted, and after making every cut along the way he did not intend to flunk this one. The Tin Man saw himself as a future division commander, two stars. He was desperate to move out of middle management before the war dried up on him.

Did Lieutenant Beevers know this? You bet your ass the lieutenant knew it.

The woman was running down the hillside as they came out of the trees. The water splashed out of the pails at the ends of her yoke each time her feet hit the ground, but she had made a computation—the pails would still be better than half full when she got to the village. Poole did not know why she was running. Running was a serious error.

"Waste her before she gets to the village," Beevers said.

"Lieutenant—" Poole said.

"Waste her," Beevers said.

Spitalny was already aiming, and Poole saw him smile against the stock of his rifle. Behind them, just coming out of the trees, a few men watched it happen: the woman racing downhill, Spitalny with his weapon to his shoulder.

"Don't lead her much, Spit," someone said. It was a joke. Spitalny was a joke.

He fired, and the girl lifted up and skimmed along for a yard or two before collapsing and rolling down the hill.

When Poole walked past the girl's body he remembered the card called "Nine Rule," which he had been given along with another called "The Enemy in Your Hands" when he had been processed into his unit. "Nine Rule" said of the VC: *You can defeat them at every turn by the strength, understanding, and generosity you display with the people.*

The third of the nine rules was: *Treat women with politeness and respect.*

And the fourth was: *Make personal friends among the soldiers and the common people.*

Oh, it got funnier and funnier. Rule five was: *Always give the Vietnamese the right of way.*

Down in that village, he thought, they were going to make some personal friends. Dengler stumbled along, making a visible effort to look as if he were not exhausted and in pain. Peters had given him a shot, "a cool one," he said, enough to keep him moving since he refused to be left behind. The sniper was still back in the jungle behind them, and the platoon was strung out, checking both directions, ready to blast at anything they saw move back in the jungle.

"Peters, are you sure that Dengler is gonna make this?" Poole asked.

"M.O. Dengler could walk from here to Hanoi," Peters said.

"But could he walk *back*?" Poole asked.

"I'm okay," Dengler said. "Let's check out this village. Let's grab those maps. Let's raid that rice. Let's orient those armaments. Let's put the whole damn place in an evidential killing box."

Beevers' platoon had successfully taken part in a killing box the week before, when one of the Tin Man's reports of North Vietnamese troop movements had turned out to be accurate. A company-sized detachment was reported to be moving down a trail called Striker Tiger, and the captain sent out platoons Alpha and Bravo to position themselves on Striker Tiger in advance of the detachment to eliminate it. They had arranged themselves above Striker Tiger, which was a trail about a yard wide through thick wooded jungle, so that all in all they had a mostly unobstructed view of maybe thirty feet of the trail. They held their weapons sighted down on the open stretch of Striker Tiger and waited.

For once, a prearranged concept worked the way it was supposed to. One lone NVR soldier, a lean, worn-looking man who appeared to be in his early thirties, strolled into the killing box. Poole nearly fell out of the tree. The NVR simply kept mooching along. Behind him, loosely bunched, followed what looked to Poole like fifty or sixty men. They too were not boy soldiers—they were real ones. They made about as much noise as a pack of grazing deer. Poole wanted very much to kill them all. For an instant, every soldier on the road was visible to Poole. A bird yammered above them in a harsh feminine voice, and the lead man looked upward with an expression for a moment almost wistful. Then everybody in the trees and up above the trail on the slope began firing at once, and the air was obliterated, rent to shreds, destroyed, and the men on Striker Tiger flopped and jittered and spun and shuddered. Then there was a total silence. The trail glistened with a bright, brilliant red.

When they had counted the bodies, they learned that they had killed thirty-two men. By counting separate arms, legs, heads, and weapons, they were able to report a total body count of one hundred and five.

Lieutenant Harry Beevers loved the killing box.

"What that boy say?" asked Spanky Burrage.

Beevers looked at Dengler as if he expected mockery. *Evidential,* he would have thought, was more his vocabulary than any grunt's. Beevers was tensed up, and Poole saw how close to the edge he was already. Poole saw only trouble in the new Beevers. Triumph had made him lose his grip—a few days ago he had said something about his days at Harvard, a college Poole was certain Beevers had never seen, much less attended.

For a second Poole looked out across the plain on the other side of the village. Two oxen that had bolted when Spitalny shot the water bearer were cropping at the grass, their noses buried deep in wet, electrified green. Nothing moved. In the village before them everything was as still as a photograph. Poole hoped that the people who lived in the scatter of hootches had heard that the round-eyes were coming and fled, leaving behind trophies of bags of rice and maybe an underground hole full of grenades and ammunition clips.

Elvis didn't have a village, Poole thought: Elvis lived in the jungle like a monkey, and he ate rats and bugs. Elvis wasn't really human anymore. He could see in the dark and he levitated in his sleep.

Underhill faded off to the right side of the village with half the men, while Poole took the other half off to the left.

The only noise was that made by their feet moving through the vibrant grass. A strap creaked, something rattled in a pot; that was all. Manly was breathing hard: Poole thought he could just about hear Manly sweat. The men began spacing themselves out. Spitalny began shadowing after Dengler and Conor as they faded toward the quiet hootches.

A chicken went *buk-buk-buk,* and a sow grunted in a pen.

A wooden stick popped in the fire, and Poole heard sparks and ash hissing down. Make them be gone, he thought. Make them all be in An Lat, two or three klicks through the forest.

Off to his right, someone's hand slapped the plastic stock of an M-16, and the sow, not yet alarmed, grunted a question.

Poole came up alongside a hootch and had a clear sightline across the center of the hamlet to Tim Underhill, who was moving silently alongside another hootch. Off to Poole's left, twenty or thirty yards beyond the perimeter of the village, the sparsely wooded forest, a hanger from the wooded slope, took over again, and for a second Poole had the ghastly fantasy that a hundred North Vietnamese soldiers crouched among the trees, aiming their weapons at them. He shot a panicky look into the woods and saw no soldiers, only a tall half-concealed mound. It caught his eye for a moment, looking almost manmade, of painted concrete and plaster, like a hill at Disneyland.

But it was too ugly for Disneyland, not picturesquely ugly like a haunted castle or a romantic crag, but naturally ugly, like a wart or a skin eruption.

Across the clearing Tim Underhill held his back against the hootch and looked at him; between them a big black pot sat on a communal fire. A column of smoke wisped up into the air. Two hootches down from Underhill, Lieutenant Beevers silently worked his mouth in a question or command. Poole nodded at Underhill, who immediately shouted *"Come out!"* in Vietnamese.

"Out!"

No one moved, but Poole heard whispers in the hootch beside him, and the other whispers of bare feet on the hootch's wooden floor.

Underhill fired a round into the air.

"Now!"

Poole trotted around to the front of the hootch, and nearly knocked down an old woman with sparse white hair and a toothless smile who was just emerging from the opening. An old man with a sunken sun-dried face hobbled after her. Poole jabbed his rifle toward the low fire in the center of the village. From the other hootches came people with their hands in the air, most of them women in their fifties and sixties. "Hello, GI," said an old man scuttling beside his old woman, and bowed with his hands still in the air.

Spitalny yelled at the man, and clouted him in the hip with the butt of his rifle.

"Stop!" Underhill yelled. Then, in Vietnamese, *"Drop to your knees!"* and all the old people went down on their knees in the trampled grass around the cooking fire.

Beevers went up to the pot, peered inside, and with his boot gave it a push that sent it rolling off the fire.

The sow began to squeal, and Beevers whirled around and shot it in its pen. An old woman yelled at him.

"Poole, get your men to check out these hootches! I want everybody out of here!"

"They say there are children, Lieutenant," Underhill said.

Beevers spotted something in the ashes where the big pot had been, and he darted forward and thrust his hand almost into the fire, jabbing at whatever he had seen, and finally pulled out a charred piece of paper that looked as if it had been torn from a notebook. "Ask them what this is!" Instead of waiting for a response, he danced up to one of the old men who had been watching him and said, "What's this? What's this writing here?"

"No bik," said the old man.

"Is this a list?" Beevers shouted. "This looks like a list!"

"No bik."

Poole also thought it looked like a list. He signaled Dengler, Blevins, Burrage, and Pumo into the hootches nearest them.

A wave of noisy protest came up from the old people kneeling near the guttering fire and the toppled pot.

Poole heard a child begin to scream in one of the other hootches, and jumped into the one the old couple had left. The interior was murky, and he gritted his teeth with tension.

"He says it's a list of names," he heard Underhill explain to the lieutenant.

Poole stepped into the center of the hootch. He tested the floor for a trap door, jabbed the mats with the barrel of his rifle, and stepped outside to go on to the next hootch.

"Ask them about the sniper!" Beevers was shouting. "Let's get it out of them." He saw Poole. "Get everything!" he shouted.

"Yes, sir," Poole said.

Pumo was hauling a screaming child of five or six toward the center of the village, and an old woman leaped up and took the little boy from him. Dengler stood slumped in the sun, listlessly watching.

A feeling of utter waste and emptiness went through Michael Poole, and he turned to enter the hootch on his left. He heard crying from the meadow side of the village and saw Beevers send Spitalny and Spanky Burrage in that direction with an impatient gesture. He stepped into the hootch, and something moved in the gloom at its far end. A furtive shape came toward him.

There was a burst of machine-gun fire from outside the village, and Poole instinctively fired on the figure advancing toward him, knowing that it was too late. He was already dead.

2

Loud terrible moans came from just outside the hootch's entrance. Miraculously not dead but knowing that the hootch was seconds from blowing up along with the grenade in the enemy's hand, Poole threw himself outside and saw Thomas Rowley on the ground, most of his stomach blown away and his purple and silver guts looped all over the grass. Rowley's face was very white and his mouth was opening and closing. No sounds came out. Poole crawled over the ground. People were firing everywhere. At first Poole thought that all the old people had been killed, but as he crawled away from the hootch he saw that they were huddling together, trying to stay under the fire.

The hootch behind him did not blow up.

Beevers ordered Dengler to check out the woods to the left of the village. Dengler began to trot toward the narrow trees. Another burst of fire came from the woods, and Dengler flopped into the grass and signaled that he was unhurt. He began firing into the woods.

"Elvis!" Beevers yelled, but Poole knew this was nonsense because Elvis did not use a machine gun. Then Beevers saw Poole and yelled, "Air support! Heavy contact!" He turned to the other soldiers and yelled, "Get them all out of the hootches! This is it! This is it!"

After a time there was no more firing. Rowley lay dead before the hootch where Poole had killed the VC. Poole wondered what Beevers had meant by "This is it," and stood up to see what was going on. He caught Pumo's eye as Pumo came out of another hootch. Pumo looked like a man who simply did not know what to do, and Poole could not tell him because he did not know either.

The Vietnamese were crying, screaming, shouting.

"Heavy contact!" Beevers was still yelling, and Poole called it in.

"Burn the village!" Beevers yelled at Underhill, and Underhill shrugged.

Spitalny shot a blast of flame into a ditch and burst out laughing when the ditch began to shriek.

Beevers yelled something and ran over to see what was in the ditch. All around Poole men were running between the hootches, setting them on fire. It was hell now, Poole thought. Beevers was reaching down into the ditch. He pulled out a naked pink girl. They hid the children, Poole thought, that's why it was so quiet, they heard us coming and sent the children into hiding. All around Poole, rising up like the screeches and yells of protest from the old people, were the fireplace smells of burning wood and the choking smells of burning grass and the flat dead odor of burned earth. Poole could hear fire snapping at the dry hootches. Beevers held up the pink squirming girl like a fisherman holding up a particularly good catch. He was screaming something, but Poole could not hear the words. Beevers began to move toward the village, now holding the girl out in front of him with both hands. Her skin was beginning to shrivel. When Beevers came to a tree with a vast fleshy head and a winding mazy trunk made of many trunks combined, he swung the girl by her heels and struck her head against the tree.

"This is it!" he screamed. "This is it, okay?"

Spitalny fired a flamethrower blast into a pen and incinerated two hens and a rooster.

Beevers swung the little girl around once more and this time split open her head against the mazy tree. He threw down her body and came raging toward the center of the village. "Now ask these people about Elvis," he yelled. "Let's get the truth out of these motherfuckers for once."

Underhill spoke to the old man, who was now trembling with mingled terror and rage, and got back a rapid tirade that made him shake his head.

"You want to see how to do this? Watch." Beevers stormed into the circle of cowering Vietnamese and pulled to his feet the little boy Pumo had taken from a hootch. The little boy was too frightened to speak, but the old woman who had been clutching him began to wail. Beevers clipped her in the forehead with the butt of his .45, and she toppled. Beevers clutched the child's throat, pointed the .45 at his head, and said, "Elvis? Elvis?"

The little boy gargled something.

"You know him. Where is he?"

Layers and curls of smoke drifted around them, carrying odors of burning straw and singed meat. Spitalny was training his flamethrower on whatever was left in the ditch. The hootches crackled around the lieutenant, the little boy, and the old people. Underhill knelt beside the child and spoke to him in soft Vietnamese. The child did not look as though he understood anything Underhill was saying. Poole saw Trotman approach the hootch where he had killed the VC, and waved him off. Trotman went on to the next hootch in the circle. A second later yellow flame grew along the roofline.

"I want his head!" Beevers yelled.

Poole began to trudge through the smoke toward the hootch where he had killed the VC. He wanted to drag him outside before the hootch was fired. Everything was all fucked up anyway. None of the hootches had been properly searched—Beevers had gone crazy when he had been fired on. Where was that list, anyhow? Poole thought that after the hootches burned down, they could still check beneath them for secret compartments—maybe it would not be a total loss. He saw Dengler, dazed and covered in dust, walking back toward the ditch to see what Spitalny was doing.

The problem was going to be to keep Beevers from killing all the old people. If he found Elvis back in that hootch, which Michael had begun to think might be very likely, Beevers would want to execute the whole village as VC. Then they'd double or triple the body count, and the Tin Man would be another little step along the way to his brigade.

For the first and only time in his military career, Michael Poole asked himself what it was that the army wanted him to do—what America wanted him to do. His radio popped and sizzled, and he ignored it. He stepped over Rowley's body and went into the hootch.

The hootch was full of smoke and the smell of gunpowder.

Poole took another step through the smoke and saw the body kneeling before the far wall of the hootch. A small black head, a brown shirt now wet with blood. The body seemed to be all trunk—"main housing unit," Beevers would have said. Poole saw no grenade. Then he finally took in the size of the body curled up before the wall and knew that he had not killed Elvis—he had killed a dwarf. He took another look around for the dud grenade, breathing hard now without knowing why. He looked at the dwarf's hands, which were small and dirty. They were not a dwarf's hands: they were not any adult's hands, being very delicate as well as crusted with dirt. Poole shook his head, sweating, and lifted the shoulder of the VC's body to get a look at his face.

The shoulder gave him almost no resistance at all, and the small body rolled over to expose the face of a small boy of nine or ten. Poole allowed the boy's body to relax back down onto the floor. "Where's that grenade?" he asked himself in a voice that sounded normal. He kicked over a little table, scattering pins and combs and a pair of round sunglasses. He tossed everything that was in the hootch upside-down—the pallets, the tin cups, straw baskets, a few old photographs. He realized that he was doing this to keep himself from fully understanding what he had done. There was no grenade. He stood very still for a moment. The radio sizzled again, and Beevers yelled his name.

Poole bent down and picked up the child's corpse. It was about as heavy as the body of a dog. He turned around and walked through the smoke to the hootch's entrance. The shrieking went up a notch when he came out.

Underhill blinked when Poole came toward him carrying the dead child, but said nothing. A woman jumped up with her arms outstretched and her face broken into craziness by grief. Poole moved up to her and gave her the dead child. She sank down into the circle of old people, crooning to the child.

Then at last the Phantom jets came wailing in over the village, their noise drowning out the sounds of fire and human voices. The old people huddled close to the earth, and the big jets screamed over the village and turned in the air. Off to the left the forest around the cave became a single huge fireball. The forest made a noise like a thousand wind machines all going at once.

I shot a little boy, Poole said to himself.

In the next instant he realized that absolutely nothing

was going to happen to him because of what he had done. Lieutenant Beevers had smashed a girl's head against a tree. Spitalny had burned children to death in a ditch. Unless the entire platoon was court-martialed nothing was going to happen. This too was terrible. There were no consequences. Actions that took place in a void were eternal actions, and that was terrible. Everything that surrounded Poole, the burning hootches, the curling smoke, the earth beneath his boots, and the huddled old men and women, for a moment seemed utterly unreal. He felt as if he could float up off the ground, if he wanted to.

He decided not to float up off the ground. That was some serious shit. If you did something like that, you'd be like Elvis, you couldn't be sure you could ever get back down.

He looked to his left and was surprised to see most of the men in the platoon standing at the fringe of the village, watching the incineration of the forest. When had they left the hootches? It seemed to him that there had been a break in time, an irrational space, an area of blockage in which everything had changed positions without his knowing or seeing it. The unreality of everything around him was much clearer now—the burning forest was a kind of movie on a screen, and the burning hootches were places where people lived in a story. It was an ugly story, and if you told it backwards by burning down the little houses it would disappear. Totally. It would never have been. Things were much better that way—the way in which the story got pulled backwards out of the world through its own asshole and disappeared. He should have levitated while he had the chance, because it no longer made any difference if he got back to earth or not. Because it was not the real earth anymore, it was a movie. What they were watching now was the unhappening of the story.

The whole village was going to unhappen.

Poole could see the ugly purple hill very clearly now. At the base of the hill, like a fold in the rock, lay the entrance to a cave.

"That's where everything is," he heard Lieutenant Beevers say.

3

Poole almost called out when M.O. Dengler began to run toward the cave after the lieutenant. Lieutenant Beevers was a human unhappening—nobody should follow him into a cave, but especially not M.O. Dengler.

Poole wanted to yell, to keep Dengler from going into that place as Harry Beevers' shield. Then he noticed Victor Spitalny sprinting after M.O. Dengler and Lieutenant Beevers. Spitalny wanted to go in there with them. Spitalny was a soldier today, Spitalny was red hot.

Pumo yelled Spitalny's name, but Spitalny only turned his head and kept on running. Running with his head turned, he looked like an image on a frieze.

The three men disappeared into the cave.

Poole turned back to the village and saw Tim Underhill trudging toward him through the smoke.

Both men heard a muffled rattle of fire come from the cave. It died with such swiftness it seemed never to have been. Behind them came the snapping and crunching of a hootch falling in on itself. The villagers continued wailing. From the cave came again the muffled sound of an M-16 firing in bursts. Poole's mind and body unfroze, and he began to run through the smoke toward the cave. He dimly saw the old man who must have been the village chief stand up in the middle of the circle. He held the charred piece of paper in his hands, and was yelling something in a squeaky high-pitched voice.

The brush still burned, sending runners of sparks along the blackened stalks. Here and there the ground itself was burning. Trees had keeled over and collapsed into themselves like cigarette ash. A cloud of smoke blocked the narrow entrance of the cave, and as Poole ran toward it, he heard enraged painful screams coming from behind the unmoving cloud.

A second later Victor Spitalny came windmilling through the smoke. His face was bright red and he was screaming as if he had been tortured. Spitalny moved in an irregular series of agitated, aimless hops and jumps, like a man being given a series of powerful electrical shocks. He must have been hit somewhere, but there was no blood on him. He was uttering a series of high-pitched syllables which at length resolved themselves into "Kill 'em! Kill 'em!" Then he lost his footing and fell into the ash near the mouth of the cave. He began to thrash around, incapable of controlling himself enough to get back on his feet. Poole pulled his groundcloth out of his pack, flipped it open, and bent over Spitalny to roll him up inside it. Raised red welts covered Spitalny's face and neck. His eyes were swollen shut.

"Wasps!" Spitalny shrieked. "All over me!"

Through the smudges where the hootches had been, Poole could see all the villagers standing up, straining to look toward them.

He yelled a question about the lieutenant and Dengler, but Spitalny kept shaking and jerking. Spanky Burrage had knelt down and was pounding the groundcloth all over Spitalny's chest, flipped him over and began beating on his back. Then he burst out laughing. "Fool, there ain't nothin' in there but you."

"Look inside here and count all the dead wasps," Spitalny said.

Poole stood up just as Dengler emerged through the cave's narrow opening. He looked whiter than ever, almost grey under the dirt. His rifle dangled from his right hand, and his eyes seemed blurry with shock or exhaustion.

"Koko," Dengler said, and half a dozen men looked at each other.

"What?" Poole asked. "What happened?"

"Nothing."

"You waste Elvis?" asked Spanky Burrage.

"Nothing happened," Dengler said. He took a few steps, stirring up sparks and ashes with his boots, and looked over the expanse of destroyed earth to the old people, all of them now standing in the center of what had been their village and looking straight back at him.

Poole heard the villagers shouting something, but it took him a moment to separate the voices enough to make out the words. What they were yelling was "Numbah ten!"

"Who was firing?"

"The good guys," Dengler said, giving a faint smile to the reeking, smoke-filled air between himself and the village.

"Is the lieutenant okay?" Poole wondered what he really hoped the answer to that question would be.

Dengler shrugged.

"You numbah ten!" came from the villagers, repeated in a ragged random chaos of high-pitched voices.

Poole realized that at some point he would no longer be able to delay going into that opening in the rock. He would go in and a child would stand before him holding out its hand in the darkness.

"You know something?" Dengler spoke in a monotone. "I was right."

"You were right about what?"

"I was right about God."

Now Spitalny stood in the sunlight with his shirt off, breathing hard. Red swellings puffed out his shoulders, arms, and back, and his face was a collection of large, red, angry-looking lumps. He looked like a plateful of yams. Norm Peters had begun to spread a greasy white ointment over Spitalny's shoulders.

Poole turned away from Burrage and walked across the smoking ground toward the medic and Spitalny. After a second Burrage came too, as unwilling as Poole to go into the cave.

Poole had taken only a few steps when he heard the approaching helicopter and looked up toward a gnat-sized black dot in the sky. Wrong, he thought, go away, go back.

4

"I can't figure this out," Peters was saying. "Will you look at this? It doesn't make sense, not to me it doesn't."

"Is Dengler out?" Spitalny asked.

Poole nodded. "What doesn't make sense?" But as soon as he had asked the question, he saw. Spitalny's narrow sharp-featured face had begun to reappear as the swellings sank down into it. His eyes were visible now, and his forehead no longer bulged out in a series of lumpy corrugations but ascended almost smoothly through eruptions like undeclared pimples to his black widow's peak.

"These aren't wasp stings," Peters said. "They're hives."

"Fuck you, they ain't wasp stings," said Spitalny. "The lieutenant ain't outa there yet. You better wrap yourself up in something and drag him out."

"Even if they were wasp stings, the stuff I'm putting on

wouldn't reduce the swelling, it'd just reduce the pain. You see how these things are going down?"

"Suck my dick," Spitalny said. He held out his skinny arms and examined them—the swellings had shrunk to the size and shape of leeches.

"You tell me," Poole said. The helicopter had grown in the distance to the size of a housefly.

"Wasps," Spitalny insisted. "Man, I'll bet the Lost Boss is in there, down and out, man. We gonna get us a new lieutenant."

He looked at Poole with the sort of expression a dog wears when you are made to realize that it too can think. "The good part of this is obvious, isn't it? You can't court-martial a dead man."

Poole watched the poisoned red lumps shrink into Spitalny's filthy sallow skin.

"There's one way out of this, and you know what it is as much as I do. We put it all on the lieutenant. Which is exactly where it oughta be."

The helicopter was huge in the sky now, descending toward them through the harsh sunlight. Beneath it the grass flattened out in sealike waves and ripples. Beyond the ruined village, beyond the ditch, lay the meadow where the oxen grazed. Far to the left, the forested hillside they had descended appeared to continue the waves and ripples caused by the helicopter far out beyond the valley.

Then he heard Harry Beevers' voice, loud and jubilant. "Poole! Underhill! Give me two men!" When he saw that they were gaping at him, he grinned. "Jackpot!"

He came striding toward them. The man was *up,* Poole saw. The nervous, jittery energy was all octane now. He was like a man who does not know that the reason he feels so good is that he's drunk. Sweat flew off his face and his eyes were liquid. "Where are my two men?"

Poole motioned to Burrage and Pumo, who began to move toward the cave.

"I want everything out of that cave, and I want it piled up right out here where everybody can see it. Troops, we're going to make the six o'clock news."

Troops? Beevers had never seemed more like an alien visitor who had learned earthling "ways" from television programs.

"You numbah ten!" an old woman shouted at them.

"Number ten on your programs, number one in your hearts," Lieutenant Beevers said to Poole, then turned away to greet the reporters running hunched over through the grass.

5

And everything else flowed from what came out of Harry Beevers' mouth. *Newsweek* and *Time* and stories in hundreds of daily newspapers, a blip passing over the screen of what is seen and read and talked about. Then only a cooling memory, stored in old photographs, of a mountain of rice and a tall pile of Russian weapons which had been carried out of a cave by Spanky Burrage and Tina Pumo and the other members of the platoon. Ia Thuc was a VC village, and everybody in it wanted to kill American soldiers. But there were no photographs of the bodies of thirty children because the only bodies found at Ia Thuc were those that had been incinerated in a ditch—three children, two males and a female, roughly thirteen years of age—and that of a single small boy of perhaps seven, also incinerated. Later the body of a young woman was found on the hillside.

After the reporters left, the old people were relocated to a refugee camp at An Lo. The Tin Man and those above him described this action as "penalizing the insurgents and depriving the VC of a recruiting base." The crops were poisoned and the people, Buddhists, taken from their family burial plots. They had seen this coming from the moment their houses were burned—maybe from the moment Beevers had killed the sow. They disappeared into An Lo, fifteen old people among thousands of refugees.

When Poole and Tim Underhill had gone deep into the cave a cloud of transparent moths had filled the air around them, buffeting against them, flattening out over their mouths and eyes, then beating off again—Poole waved his hands before his face and moved as quickly as he could, Underhill behind him, into another section of the cave, which the moths did not enter. This was the chamber where the firing had taken place. The blood was already disappearing into the bullet-pocked wall the way Spitalny's skin eruptions, his yams, leeches, eggs, and almonds had faded back into his body. The cave folded and unfolded, branching apart like a maze. Farther on they found another large store of rice, farther on a little wooden desk and chair—the desk looked as though it had been taken from one of Poole's own grade school classrooms in Greenwich, Connecticut. It began to seem hopeless, they would never find the end of it: it seemed to have no end at all, but to twist back around in on itself.

They came out again past the chamber where the empty metal casings lay like thrown coins, and Underhill inhaled deeply and shook his head. Poole smelled it too. The chamber was filled with a complex odor compounded of terror, blood, gunpowder, and some other odor Poole could identify only in negatives. It was not piss, it was not shit, it was not sweat or rot or fungus or even the reeking dew all animals exude when they are frightened unto death, but something beneath all these. The indefinable odor in the stone chamber stank of pain to him. It stank like the place where Injun Joe had made Tom Sawyer watch him rape Becky Thatcher before he killed them both.

He and Underhill finally came back out into the main part of the cave. M.O. Dengler was saying something to Spitalny as he carried a case of Russian rifles out through the opening.

"A man of sorrow and acquainted with grief," Spitalny replied, or more likely, repeated. "A man of sorrow and acquainted with grief, a man of sorrow and acquainted with dickheads, Jesus Christ."

"Calm down, Vic," Dengler said. "Whatever it was, it was a long time ago." Then he wobbled, and his rear end dropped as if a strong hand had suddenly pushed his head down into his neck. Dengler's legs folded sideways, and the case of rifles landed with a loud thud, Dengler nearly soundlessly. Spitalny heard the crash as the box of rifles landed, turned around, looked down, and continued carrying his box of rifles toward the stack.

"There are no children!" Beevers was yelling. "Not in war! No children!" Well, he was right: there were no children. For the first but not the last time, Poole wondered if the villagers from An Lac had taken more children out through another entrance.

Dengler groaned as Peters unwrapped the final length

of gauze. Everybody backed up for a second. Compact as a puff of cigarette smoke, a deep brown odor floated up from the exposed wound.

"You're out of here for a couple of days," Peters said.

"Where'd the lieutenant go?" Dengler's eyes moved almost fearfully from side to side while Peters rewrapped his arm.

"Did you see the bats flying out of his mouth?" Dengler asked.

"I gave him something a little extra," Peters said. "Tide him over."

Into the darkness, which tides us over.

25

COMING HOME

1

Groggy with cognac and too little sleep, they landed in San Francisco at some hour that seemed like four or five in the morning but was actually noon. In a vast hall hundreds of passengers milled around a luggage carousel and watched their bags thump and slide down a metal ramp onto a moving belt. His beard trimmed and his thinning hair cut short, Tim Underhill looked gaunt and tired. His shoulders were as stooped as an old scholar's, and now his questing face was also a scholar's. Poole wondered if it had been a mistake to bring him back with them.

As they moved toward Customs and Immigration with their bags, a uniformed man appeared among them, awarding instant customs clearance to a few of the passengers. The people he selected to receive this convenience were invariably middle-aged males who looked like corporate executives. Koko had been here, Poole thought while the official's eye rested upon him and moved on. Koko stood on this spot and saw everything I am seeing. He left a flight from Bangkok or Singapore and changed to a New York flight where he met a stewardess named Lisa Mayo and an unpleasant young millionaire. He talked to the unpleasant young man on the flight, and shortly after they landed at JFK airport, he killed him. I bet he did, I bet he did, I bet, I bet—

He stood right where I'm standing, Poole thought. His skin shivered.

Harry Beevers bounced up off his seat as soon as the others found their departure gate in the United terminal. He stepped over the semicircle of suitbags and carry-on luggage arranged before him and began tacking toward them through the rows of seats.

They met before the desk, and Beevers silently braced Poole at arm's length, then embraced him, enclosing him in the odors of alcohol, cologne, and airline soap. Poole supposed he was being commended for actions in the field.

Beevers melodramatically dropped his hands from Michael's arms and turned to Conor. But before Beevers could give the French Foreign Legion seal of approval to him too, Conor stuck out his hand. Beevers gave in and shook it. Finally he turned to Tim Underhill. "So this is you," he said.

Underhill almost laughed out loud. "Disappointed?"

Poole had wondered all during their flight how Beevers would handle Underhill's arrival among them as an innocent man. There was the small possibility that he would do something really nutty, such as put handcuffs on him and make a citizen's arrest. Harry Beevers' fantasies died hard, and Poole did not expect him to give up this one, which had been the foundation of many others, without being paid heavily for its loss.

But the good grace, and even the good sense of his response surprised Poole. "Not if you're going to help us, I'm not."

"I want to stop him too, Harry. Of course I'll help you, however I can."

"Are you clean?" Beevers asked.

"I'm not doing too bad," Underhill said.

"Okay. But there's one more thing. I want your agreement that you won't use any of this Koko material in a work of nonfiction. You can write all the fiction you want—I don't care about that. But I have to have the nonfiction rights to this."

"Sure," Underhill said. "I couldn't write nonfiction if I tried. And I won't sue you if you won't sue me."

"We can work together," Beevers declared. He dragged Underhill too in for a hug and said he was on the team. "Let's make some serious money, okay?"

Michael sat next to Beevers on the flight to New York. Conor was in the window seat, and Tim Underhill sat just ahead of Michael. For a long time Beevers told improbable stories about his adventures in Taipei—stories about drinking snake's blood and having incredible sex with beautiful whores, actresses, and models. Then he leaned toward Michael and whispered. "We have to be careful with this guy, Michael. We can't trust him, that's the bottom line. Why do you think I'm inviting him to stay with me? I'll be able to keep my eye on him."

Poole nodded wearily.

In a voice loud enough to be overheard, Beevers said, "I want you guys to think about something. We are going to be seeing the police at some point after we get back, and that gives us a problem. How much do we tell them?"

Underhill twisted around in his seat to look back with an interested, quizzical expression.

"I think we should consider holding to a certain confidentiality here," Beevers said. "We started off on this thing by wanting to find Koko ourselves, and that's how we want to finish up. We ought to stay a step ahead of the police all the way."

"Okay, I guess," Conor said.

"I hope I have the agreement of the rest of you on this point."

"We'll see," Poole said.

"I don't suppose we're exactly talking about obstruction of justice," Underhill said.

"I don't care what you call it," Beevers said. "All I'm saying is that we hold back on one or two details. Which is what the police do all the time as a matter of course. We hold back a little. And when we come up with a course of action, we keep it to ourselves."

"Course of action?" Conor asked. "What can we do?"

Beevers asked them to consider a few possibilities. "For instance, we have two bits of information the police do not have. We know that Koko is Victor Spitalny, and we know that a man named Tim Underhill is in New York—or soon will be—and not back in Bangkok."

"You don't want to tell the cops that we're looking for Spitalny?" Conor asked.

"We can play a little dumb. They can find out who is missing and who isn't." He gave Michael a superior little smile. "It is the other bit of information that I see being most useful to us. Spitalny used this man's name"—he pointed at Underhill—"didn't he? To get the reporters to come to him? I think he did, based on what we found out at Goodwood Park. So I say let's turn the tables on him."

"And how would you do that, Harry?" Underhill asked.

"In a way, Pumo gave me the idea when we all met in Washington back in November. He was talking about his girlfriend, remember?"

"Hey, *I* remember," Conor said. "He was talking to me. That little Chinese girl was driving him out of his gourd. She used to put ads in some paper for him. Signed them 'Half Moon.' "

"Trés bon, trés, trés bon," Beevers said.

"You want to put ads in the *Village Voice?"* asked Michael.

"This is America," Beevers said. "Let's advertise. Let's put Tim Underhill's name up all over town. If anybody asks about it, we can say that we're looking for someone who used to be in our old unit. And that way we never use Koko's real name. I think we'll shake a couple of peaches out of the tree."

2

The Star Limousine was actually a van with three rows of seats and a luggage rack on the roof. Even inside the van the air was very cold, and Poole pulled his coat tightly around himself and wished that he had packed a sweater. He felt isolated and strange, and the country outside the windows of the van seemed as foreign as it was familiar. He seemed to have been gone a long time.

Buttoned up against the cold, ugly row houses huddled on the desolate land on either side of the highway. The air had already turned dark. Nobody in the van spoke, not even the married couples.

Michael remembered seeing Robbie in a dream, holding up a lantern.

26

KOKO

1

Coming home was always the same. Coming home, there was always the fear factor. Blood and Marbles were always home. You had to make straight in the desert a highway, yet once a little while, and then you could shake the heavens and the earth, the sea and the dry land. Make straight in the desert, for who shall abide the day of his coming?

You came home to what was undone and rebuked you, to what had been badly or ill done, which spat you out of its mouth, and to that which had been done which should not have been done, which came at you with a board, a strap, a brick.

All this was in a book, even Blood and Marbles were in a book.

In this book the cave was a river where a small naked boy walked smeared with frozen mud. (But it was a woman's blood, it was.) He had read this book backwards and forwards. That was one thing they said at home—*backwards and forwards.* Koko remembered buying that book because once in another life he had known the author and soon the book revolved and grew in his hands and became a book about himself. Koko had felt as if he were in free fall—as if someone had thrown him out of a helicopter. His body had left itself, in familiar total fear his body had stood up and walked out into the book in his hands.

Fear total and familiar.

He had remembered the most terrible thing in the world. This was true—there was a most terrible thing. The most terrible thing was how his body had learned to leave itself. It was Blood opening the bedroom door at night and sidling into the little room. The hot wet smell of the eternal world on his body. His blond hair almost silver in the darkness.

Are you awake?

Anyone awake could see the police cars, anyone awake could see what was happening. Koko stood on the corner looking at the two cars pulled up before the YMCA. They expected him to just walk in there.

It was the black man, who said, *Killin' is a see-yun.* He had gone and told Mr. Partridge, who sat at a desk downstairs, about the room. Mr. Partridge had walked into Koko's room and Koko's body had walked out of his body.

—What is the meaning of this? Mr. Partridge had said. You crazies always end up here, don't you have anywhere else to go?

—This is my place, not yours, Koko said.

—We'll see about that, said Mr. Partridge, and walked out, not before taking another long look at the walls.

The children turned and cried after him.

—You ain't no travel agent, the black man said. You ain't got but a one-way ticket yourself.

Koko turned away and began walking downtown toward the subway. He carried everything essential with him in the knapsack now, and there were always empty places.

Then he remembered that he had lost the Rearing Elephant cards, and he stopped walking and put his hand over his stomach. Blood towered up before him, his hair silvery and his voice flat and cold and crazy with rage.

You lost them?

His entire life seemed as heavy as an anvil he carried in his arms. He wanted to drop the anvil. Someone else could take up the job now—after all he had done, it would be easy for someone else to finish up. He could quit. He could turn himself in, or he could flee.

Koko knew one thing—he could get on an airplane right now and go anywhere. For Honduras, you went to

New Orleans. He had looked it up. You went to New Orleans and there was your plane. Bird = Freedom.

An image from the book that had so surprised him floated up into his mind, and he saw himself as a lost child streaked with frozen mud wandering beside a cold, dirty river in the middle of a city. Dogs and wolves turned their sharpened teeth toward him, the door cracked open, through the frozen mud emerged the tips of fingers turning green with putrefaction. Feelings of loss and terror swarmed at him, and Koko staggered toward the shelter of a doorway.

The dead children held their spindly hands up before their faces.

He had no home, and he *could* quit.

Trying not to sob or at least not to show that he was sobbing, he sat down in the doorway. On the other side of the great glass door, an empty marble hallway led toward a row of elevators. He saw the cartoon policemen strutting around his room. He saw the jackets on their hangers, the shirts in the drawers. (The cards on the dresser.) Tears spilled over his cheeks. His razor, his toothbrush. Things taken away, things lost, things raped and left dazed, dying, dead. . . .

Koko saw Harry Beevers in the close darkness at the back of a cave. His father whispered his question. Harry Beevers leaned toward him with his eyes gleaming, his teeth, his whole face shining and sweating and gleaming. *Get the fuck out of here, troop,* he said, and a bat flew out of his mouth. *Or share the glory.* In the mess on the ground on the other side of the lieutenant he saw in the narrow beam one little outflung hand with fingers curling toward the palm. Koko's body had walked out of itself. Right under the stench of eternity hovered the smells of powder, piss, shit. Beevers turned and Koko saw his long erection straining out of his trousers. His history slammed together—he met himself, he was traveling *backwards and forwards.*

He looked up from his place within the shelter of the doorway and saw a blue and white police car roll past, followed closely by another. They had left his room. Maybe one would be left. Maybe he could go there and talk about the lieutenant.

Koko stood up and hugged himself tight. In his room would be one man to whom he could talk, and this thought was like an unaccustomed substance in his blood. Once he talked, everything would be different and he would be free, for after he talked the man would understand *backwards and forwards.*

For the space of several seconds Koko saw himself as if from a great distance, a man standing in a doorway with his arms wrapped around himself because he was oppressed by a great grief. Flat, even daylight, the light of ordinary reality, lay over everything before him. During these seconds Koko saw his own terror, and what he saw both astonished and frightened him deeply. He could go back and say: I made a mistake. No demons or angels surrounded him; the drama of supernatural redemption in which he had been so long enfolded had fled away down the long street crowded with taxicabs, and he was an ordinary man, out in the cold by himself.

He was trembling, but he was not crying anymore, anymore. Then he remembered the face of the girl in Tina Pumo's living room, and the face suggested to him the one neighborhood in all the city where he might feel most at home.

He would carry the anvil a little further, and see what happened.

And when he left the subway at Canal Street his whole body told him that he had been right. The subway had taken him someplace absolutely out of America. He was in an Asian world again. Even the smells were at once subtler and denser.

Koko had to force himself to walk slowly and breathe normally. With a pounding heart he passed beneath a sign in Chinese characters and turned south into Mulberry Street. It seemed to him that he was hungry as he had not been in a week. The last meal he could actually remember eating had been served by a stewardess.

Suddenly Koko was so attacked by hunger that he could have opened his mouth and let slide into him every store, every brick, every blaring yellow sign, every teapot and chopstick, every duck and eel, and every man and woman on the street along with the stop signs and traffic lights and mailboxes and telephone booths.

He paused only long enough to buy a *Times,* a *Post,* and a *Village Voice* at a newsstand before turning into the first restaurant where a row of ducks the color of buckwheat honey hung above pots of brown soup and white sticky porridge.

When the food came, the world melted, time melted, and as he ate he was back in the times when he had lived within the elephant and every time he drew breath he drew in the elephant.

In the papers today a bus driver had won nearly two million dollars in something called Lotto. A ten-year-old boy named Alton Cedarquist had been thrown off a roof in a part of town called Inwood. A block of buildings in the Bronx had burned down. In Angola, a man named Jonas Savimbi posed with an ugly Swedish machine gun and promised to fight through eternity; in Nicaragua, a priest and two nuns had been killed and beheaded in a tiny village. Backward and forward, yes indeedy. In Honduras, the government of the United States had claimed two hundred acres of land as a training site—it used to be theirs and now it was ours. We issued the usual heartfelt promises that one day soon it would be theirs again. In the meantime our mouths were open and two hundred acres had disappeared down our throats. Koko could smell the grease in which weapons were packed; he could hear the sound of crunching boots, of hands slapping the stocks of rifles.

The lords of the earth turned to him with a question on their faces.

But the real estate pages, in which he had hoped to find a good cheap room for rent, were written in code, most of which he did not understand, and showed almost no rentals at all in Chinatown. The only space available down here appeared to be a two-bedroom apartment at Confucius Plaza, at a price so high that at first he thought it must be a misprint.

Anything more? the waiter asked in Cantonese, the language in which Koko had ordered his meal.

I have finished, thank you, Koko said, and the waiter scribbled on a slip, tore it off and placed it on the table beside his plate. A grease spot instantly blossomed in the center of the green piece of paper.

Koko watched the grease spot swell out another two centimeters in diameter. He counted out money and placed it on the table. He looked up at the waiter, who was moving slowly toward the back of the restaurant.

They took my home from me, he said.

The waiter turned around and blinked.

I have no home now.

The waiter nodded.

Where is your home?

My home is in Hong Kong, the waiter said.

Do you know of some place where I might live?

The waiter shook his head. Then he said, *You should live with your own kind.* He turned his back on Koko and proceeded to the front of the restaurant, where he leaned on the cash register and in a loud complaining whine began to speak to another man.

Koko flipped over to the back page of the *Village Voice* and found himself reading the words, at first as meaningless as the code in the real estate ads, TWIDDLE: UR BEAST I EVER SCENE. PAIN IS ILL-U-SHUN. SURVE-LIVE. LUMINOUS DIAL. Beneath this one was another addressed to the universe at large and perhaps one other like himself, whirling loose within it. A STIFLED DROWSY UNIMPASSIONED GRIEF. WEYOUI MUST FIND THAT WHICH WAS LOST. Koko felt his tension breaking deep within him, just as if this ad really had been placed for him by someone who knew and understood him.

But in the meantime the other man at the front of the restaurant, more prosperous and managerial than the waiter, was looking at him with a cocked head and a light in his eye that only the promise of money could have put there. Koko folded his paper and stood up to approach him. He already knew that he had found a room for himself.

There came the customary formalities, including the customary expressions of surprise at Koko's facility with Cantonese.

I have a great love for all things Chinese, Koko said. *It is a great shame that my purse is not as large as my heart.*

The avaricious gleam in the restaurant owner's eye suffered a slight diminution.

But I will happily give a fair price for whatever you may be good enough to make available to me, and you will also earn my everlasting gratitude.

How did you come to be homeless?

My room was appropriated for other uses by my landlord.

And your possessions?

I carry all I own.

You have no job?

I am a writer, of some small reputation.

The owner extended a fat hand. *I am Chin Wu-Fu.*

"Timothy Underhill," Koko said, taking the man's hand.

Chin gestured for him to follow. They went outside, Koko shrugging on his knapsack, to bustle down the block in the cold and turn into Bayard Street. Chin Wu-Fu hustled on ahead of him, hunching his shoulders against the cold. Koko strode on behind him for two blocks, and followed him as he turned north into narrow, empty Elizabeth Street. Halfway up the block, Chin ducked through a curved archway and disappeared. He ducked back out and waved Koko in through the arch, and then ushered Koko into a small enclosed brick courtyard that smelled faintly of cooking oil. Koko saw that the court would always be sunless. Surrounded by tenement walls and fire escapes that clung like giant mantises to the dingy brown brick, the court was no more than an insulating dead space between the tenements and Elizabeth Street. It was perfect. The Chinese man in the dark suit who had admitted him to this dead still space was pulling at one of the rough doors set into the tenement's ground level.

We go downstairs, the owner said, and plunged into the cold darkness of the stairwell.

Koko followed.

At the bottom of the stairs Chin switched on a bare lightbulb and flipped through the hundreds of keys on a large ring before unlocking another door. Wordlessly, he swung it open and with a sweeping gesture motioned Koko inside.

Koko stepped into a clammy absolute blackness. He knew instantly that this was going to be just what he needed, and in the instant before Chin Wu-Fu groped for the cord and turned on the light within, he already saw the windowless rectangular chamber, the walls of a dark flaking green, the stained mattress on the floor, the population of roaches, the rickety chair, and the rusty sink and rough toilet behind a screen. He could not talk to the police, but he could find Michael Poole and Michael Poole was a man who would understand *backwards and forwards*. Harry Beevers was the road backwards, and Michael Poole was the narrow lonely path leading forward out of his cell. Another bare lightbulb came dimly to life. Down beneath the surface of Elizabeth Street, he felt on his skin the wind that blew across a frozen river. Pain was an ill-u-shun.

PART SIX

THE REAL RAW TASTE

27

PAT AND JUDY

1

"As bad as that?" Pat asked.

"You don't know the half of it." Judy Poole exhaled loudly, oddly satisfied to have at last arrived at this stage of their conversation. It was seven-thirty in the evening of Michael's third day back home, and the two women had been speaking on the telephone for perhaps twenty-five minutes.

Judy heard a sigh from Pat Caldwell's end of the line and quickly asked, "Am I keeping you from anything?"

"Not really." She paused. "Harry's only called me once, so I can't report anything. They still plan to talk to the police, do they?"

This point had already been covered within ten minutes of the beginning of this conversation, and Judy took it up again impatiently. "I told you that—they think they know something about why Tina was murdered. Do you think they're daydreaming? I *want* to think they're daydreaming."

"All this sounds so familiar," Pat said. "Harry always knew the inside of a million stories."

"Anyhow," Judy said, reverting to an earlier theme, "you don't know the worst. I don't know what to do anymore. I'm incredibly anxious. I can hardly get out of bed in the mornings, and when school's over and it's time to come home, I dawdle and dawdle, but I'm hardly even aware of what I'm doing. I go around the school looking for litter. I check to make sure the classroom doors are locked. When I get home, it's like, I don't know, some kind of bomb went off and everything got leveled and there's only this terrible *silence* left."

Judy paused, less for effect than to accommodate the thought that had just surfaced within her. "You know what this is really like? It's like what happened right after Robbie died. But at least then Michael stayed home, he went to work and he did what he was supposed to do. He was *around* at night. And I knew what was happening to him, so I knew what to do."

"And you don't know what to do now?"

"Obviously. That's why I can hardly make myself come home at night. Michael and I have scarcely had a good conversation in . . . he hasn't been working, I can tell you that. You think Harry's been working? I doubt it."

"Harry isn't my problem," Pat said promptly. "I wish him luck. I hope he sits down and starts to work. You know he lost his job, don't you? My brother couldn't put up with him any longer and let him go."

"Your brother sounds like a great man, he always has," Judy said, for a moment distracted by the old grievance that she had never met Pat Caldwell's distinguished older brother.

"Well, I think Charles gave him some money too," Pat said. "Charles has a good heart, basically. He doesn't want Harry to suffer—my brother is what I guess you have to call a Christian gentleman."

"A Christian gentleman," Judy said. Envy made her voice go dull and flat. "Are there still such creatures?"

"In the ranks of fifty-eight-year-old heads of law firms, I guess."

"Can I ask you a personal question? I promise you, it's not just out of curiosity." She paused, either for effect or out of curiosity. "I want to know about your divorce."

"What do you want to know about it?"

"More or less everything."

"Oh, poor Judy," Pat said. "I see, I guess. It's never easy—not even getting divorced from Harry Beevers was easy."

"He was unfaithful."

"Of course he was unfaithful," Pat said. "Everybody's unfaithful." She did not sound at all cynical, saying this.

"Michael wasn't."

"But you were, which I assume is one of the real topics of this conversation. But if you want to know why I left Harry, I suppose I don't mind talking about it a little bit. In a way, Ia Thuc was really the reason."

"Oh, come on," Judy said.

"What he did at Ia Thuc. I don't even know what it was. I don't think anyone else knows, either."

"You mean he killed those children after all?"

"I'm sure he killed the children, Judy, but I'm talking about something else. I don't know what, and I don't want to know, either. After we had been married ten years, I took a look at him tying his bow tie in the mirror one morning, and I knew that I couldn't live with him anymore."

"Well, *what*?"

"It's too black. I don't know. Charles told me he thought that Harry had a demon inside him."

"You got divorced because you had this mystical *feeling* about something that happened about ten years before, and for which Harry had already been put on trial and found innocent?"

"I got divorced because I couldn't stand the thought that he might touch me again." She was silent for a moment. "He wasn't like Michael. Michael feels he has to atone for whatever happened over there, but Harry never felt a second of regret."

Judy could say nothing to this.

"So I looked at him tying his bow tie and I just finally *knew* and before I even knew I was going to say it I told him that he had to move out and give me a divorce."

"What did he do?"

"Finally he saw that I really meant it, and in order to protect his job with Charles, he left without making much of a fuss." After a second she added, "Of course I felt that I should give him regular alimony payments, and I have. Harry can live at a decent level for the rest of his life without working."

What was a decent level, Judy wondered. Twenty thousand dollars? Fifty thousand? A hundred thousand?

"I take it that you're interested in the practicalities of divorce," Pat eventually said.

"Can't fool you, can I?"

"Everybody else has, why not you too," Pat said, laughing a little theatrically. "Has Michael said anything?"

"Enough." Silence. "No." Silence. "I don't know. He's in a kind of daze because of Tina."

"So you haven't talked about it with him."

"It's like—he's just sinking out of sight, and he won't let me pull him back up on land. *My* land, with *me.*"

Pat waited until Judy had stopped crying into the telephone, and then said, "Did you tell him about the man you dated when he was gone?"

"He *asked* me," Judy wailed, losing control again. "It's not that I wanted to hide it, it's not *that*—it's the way he asked me. It was like—did you ever find the car keys? He was a lot more interested in the girl, Stacy Talbot, than he was in me. I know he *hates* Bob."

"The nice, stable guy who sails and plays tennis."

"Right."

"It's not important, but I didn't know they knew each other."

"They met at a faculty Christmas party once, and Michael thought he was conceited. Maybe Bob *is* a little conceited. But he's a very dedicated man—he teaches high school English because he thinks it's important. He doesn't have to do it."

"Sounds like Michael decided he doesn't 'have to' keep his practice." Or to stay married, Pat silently added.

"Why doesn't he have to?" Judy asked in a plaintive voice. "Why did he work so hard to get it, if he doesn't have to keep it?"

That was not the question she was really asking, and Pat did not answer it.

"I feel scared," Judy said. "It's so humiliating. I hate it."

"Do you think you have a future with your friend?"

"Bob Bunce doesn't have much extra room in his life." Judy now sounded very dry-eyed. "In spite of seeming to have nothing *but* room in his life. He has his sports car. He has his sailboat and his tennis. He has his job and his students. He has Henry James. He has his mother. I don't think he'll ever make room for a wife."

"Ah," Pat said, "but you didn't start seeing him with the idea of marrying him."

"Isn't that a comfort. Wait a minute . . ." Judy apparently set down the telephone and was gone for several minutes. Pat Caldwell could hear what sounded like ice cubes cracking out of a metal tray. There came the chink of glass against glass. "Mr. Bunce fancies the whiskey that comes in a little blue bag with a drawstring. So I helped myself to some of it. Maybe I should have made him come into a little blue bag with a drawstring."

Pat heard the ice cubes chinking as Judy raised or lowered her glass.

"Don't you ever get lonely?" Judy asked.

"Give me a call if you need me," Pat said. "I'll come up and keep you company, if you like."

28

A FUNERAL

1

"What do you mean, the police will be there?" Judy asked. "I think that's completely ridiculous."

It was ten o'clock the next morning, and the Pooles were driving Harry Beevers and Conor Linklater north to the small town of Milburn, New York, for Tina Pumo's funeral. They had been driving for two hours and, thanks to Harry's directions, had managed to lose their way in search of a shortcut. Harry now sat with empty hands in the front passenger seat of Michael's Audi, fiddling with the digital dial of the radio; Judy sat in back with Conor and the unfolded map.

"You don't understand the first thing about police work," Harry said. "Are you always this aggressive about your ignorance?"

Judy opened both her eyes and her mouth, and Harry hurriedly added, "I apologize, I'm sorry, I should not have said that. Pardon, pardon. I take Tina's death very personally, and I'm also a little touchy. Honest, Judy—I'm sorry."

"Follow the signs to Binghamton," Conor said. "We're about forty-fifty miles away now, the way I figure it. Can you find something besides that noise?"

"This is a murder case," Harry said, ignoring Conor but changing the station anyhow. "It's big business. Whoever is in charge of the case will be at the funeral, looking us and everybody else over. This is his chance to meet the cast of characters. And he's thinking that whoever killed Tina might show up to see him buried. Cops always come to things like this."

"I wish Pat could have come with us," Judy said. "And I hate big bands, all that phony nostalgia."

Harry switched off the radio.

For a time they drove on in silence past a landscape of snowy empty fields and dark stands of trees straight as soldiers in formation. Slashes of grey and black stood out starkly in the snow. Now and then a farmhouse stood like a mirage between the fields and the woods. The map rattled in Conor's hands, and Judy made a series of little sniffling noises. The past had died, Michael thought, died as part of the present so that now it was really just the past.

When he had arrived back in Westerholm, a nervous Judy had welcomed him with a kiss in which he could taste resentment. Home. She had asked about Singapore, about Bangkok, about traveling with Harry Beevers; she poured out measures of an expensive whiskey that she must have bought for this moment and which, he saw, she had generously sampled in his absence. She followed him upstairs and watched him unpack. She followed him into the bathroom while he ran a tub. She was still sitting in the bathroom, listening to his edited version of the trip, when he asked her if she had enjoyed her meal with Bob Bunce.

She gave a jerky nod.

He had merely remembered to ask, but he felt as though she had shrieked at him, or thrown something at him. She raised her glass and took a swallow of the expensive whiskey.

He asked the question to which he already knew the answer, and she gave him a prompt, flat denial.

"Okay," he said, but he knew, and she knew that he did. She gulped at her drink and walked out of the bathroom.

"It's hard to believe that Tina Pumo could have come from a place like this," Judy said. "He seemed so urbane. Didn't Tina always seem urbane?"

That's right, Michael realized with a shock: Tina would have seemed urbane to Judy.

"Look good on his tombstone," Conor said. " 'This was one urbane motherfucker.' "

2

St. Michael's Cathedral, surprisingly imposing for so small a town, dwarfed the little congregation that had gathered for Anthony Francis Pumo's funeral. From where the pallbearers stood Michael could see a handful of old women, half a dozen men with weather-roughened faces who must have gone to school with Tina, a few younger couples, single old men and women beautiful in their unreflective dignity, and a gaunt Asian man holding the hand of a beautiful child. Vinh and his daughter. At the back of the church stood a tall moustached man in a handsome suit, and another, younger man in an even handsomer suit whose roguish face looked vaguely familiar. Among the other pallbearers were a stocky, brusque man with a wider, less interesting version of Tina's face, and a short powerful old man with heavy shoulders and hands like scoops: Tina's brother, who managed a muffler shop, and his father, a retired farmer.

An angular old priest with shining white hair described a shy, eager schoolboy who had served "with great honor and distinction in Vietnam" and "proved his inner strength by triumphing in the turbulent waters of the restaurant business in the city that eventually claimed his life." That was how it looked from here—one of their children had wandered into the forest of New York City and fallen prey to savage animals.

Out at the cemetery, Pleasant Hill, Michael stood alongside Judy, Beevers, and Conor while the priest read the service. Now and then he looked up at the dull grey granite clouds. He was aware of Tommy Pumo, Tina's brother, staring at Vinh with outright hostility. Tommy was evidently a difficult character.

First the father and brother, then all in turn dropped clods of earth onto the lowered coffin.

As Poole stepped back from the edge of the grave he heard a loud voice coming from further down the hill. Near the row of parked cars, Tommy Pumo was waving his arms at the well-dressed man whose face had seemed familiar in the cathedral. Pumo's brother took a furious, almost swaggering step forward. The other man smiled and spoke, and Tommy Pumo's face twisted, and he stepped forward again.

"Let's see what's going on," Beevers said. He began to

move downhill toward the little group of people frozen near the cars.

"Excuse me, sir," came a voice from just behind him, and Poole looked back to see the tall moustached man who had been in the congregation. Close up, his moustache was thick and lustrous, but the man conveyed no impression of vanity—he seemed easily authoritative, calm and commanding. He was an inch taller than Michael and very solidly built. "You are Dr. Poole? Mrs. Poole?"

Harry had stopped moving downhill, and was standing still, looking back up at the man.

"And you are Mr. Beevers?"

Beevers' face went very smooth, as if he had just been paid some tremendous compliment.

"My name is Lieutenant Murphy, and I am the detective conducting the investigation of your friend's death."

"Aha," Beevers said to Judy.

Murphy raised his thick eyebrows.

"We were wondering when we would meet you."

Murphy took it in slowly, easily. "I'd like to have a short talk with you back at the father's house. You were going there before you left to go back to the city?"

"We are at your disposal, Lieutenant," Harry said.

Smiling, Murphy turned away and walked down the hill.

Beevers raised his eyebrows and tilted his head in Judy's direction, wordlessly asking if Poole had told her about Underhill. Poole shook his head. They watched the detective reach the bottom of the hill and say a few words to Pumo's father.

"Murphy," Beevers said. "Isn't that perfect? Talk about type-casting."

"Why does he want to talk to you?" Judy asked.

"Background checks, filling in the blank spaces, getting the complete picture." Beevers shoved his hands in his coat pockets and swiveled around to look back at the gravesite. Now only a few of the older people still lingered there. "That little Maggie didn't show up, damn it. I wonder what *she* told Murphy about our little jaunt."

Beevers intended to say more, but he closed his mouth as another mourner approached them. It was the man at whom Tommy Pumo had shouted.

"Good cop, bad cop," Beevers whispered, and turned away, all but whistling.

The man turned a lopsided grin on Poole and Judy and introduced himself as David Dixon, Tina's lawyer. "You must be his old service friends. It's nice to meet you. But haven't we met before?" He and Michael worked out that they had met at Saigon several years ago.

Beevers had turned back to the group and Michael introduced everybody. "It's nice of you to come," Beevers said.

"Tina and I spent a lot of time together, working on various little things. I'd like to think we were friends, and not just lawyer and client."

"The best clients do become friends," Harry said, instantly adopting the professional pose Poole had seen in Washington. "I'm a fellow attorney, by the way."

Dixon paid no attention to these statements. "I tried to get Maggie Lah to drive up here with me, but she didn't think she could handle it. And she didn't know if Tina's family would know how to take her."

"You have Maggie's number?" Harry asked. "I'd like to get in touch with her, so if you do have it—"

"Not this second," Dixon said.

Michael filled the silence by asking about the Vietnamese chef. He wondered if the man had gone back to the house with the other mourners.

Dixon guffawed. "He wouldn't be very welcome at the house. Didn't you see Tommy Pumo going nuts down there?"

"He must be taking his brother's death very hard," Judy said.

"It's more greed than grief," Dixon said. "Tina left everything, including the restaurant and his loft, to the person he felt had done the most to help him make his place a success."

They were all attentive now.

"Who happened to be Vinh, of course. He's going to keep the restaurant going. We ought to be open again just about on schedule."

"The brother wanted the restaurant?"

"Tommy wanted the money. Years back, Tina borrowed money from his father to buy the first two floors of his building. You can imagine what happened to the value of the real estate. Tommy thought he was going to get rich, and he's hopping mad."

Down at the bottom of the hill, one of the two old

couples who had lingered at the grave shyly approached Michael and said that they would guide him to the Pumo house.

As they drove up a long unpaved drive past thick old oaks toward a neat two-story farmhouse with a wrap-around porch, the old woman, an aunt of Tina's, said, "Just pull up next to the house alongside the drive. Everybody does it. Ed and I always do it, anyhow." She turned to Conor, who held Judy on his lap. "You're not married, are you, young man?"

"Nope."

"Well, I want you to meet my daughter—she'll be inside the house helping out with the food and the coffee, I'm sure. Good-looking girl, and named after me. Grace Hallet. You be sure to have a nice talk with her."

"Grace."

"I'd be happy to help your daughter dispense the mead and sweet potato pie," Harry said. "How about me?"

"Oh, you're too famous, but this fellow here is just good folks. You work with your hands, don't you?"

"Carpenter," Conor said.

"Anybody can plainly see," said Grace.

3

Almost as soon as they got through the door, Walter Pumo, Tina's father, took Michael and Beevers aside and said he wanted to talk to them in private. In the dining room, the table had been heaped with food—a sliced ham, a turkey ready to be carved, vessels nearly the size of rowboats filled with potato salad, platters of coldcuts and pots of mustard, doughy little muffins and slabs of butter. A crowd circled the table, carrying plates and talking. The rest of the room seemed filled with women. Conor had been taken by the hand and introduced to a very pretty young blonde woman who had a bright distracted manner that was like a welded carapace.

"I know where we can find a little open space," Walter Pumo told them, "at least I hope I do. Your friend seems like he's busy with young Grace."

He was leading them down the hallway that led to the back of the farmhouse. "If they come into this room, we'll just heave 'em out." He was a head shorter than both men, and as wide as the two of them together. His shoulders nearly filled the hall.

The old man poked his head through a doorway, then said, "Come in, boys."

Michael and Beevers entered a small room crowded with an old leather sofa, a round table stacked with farming magazines, a metal filing cabinet, and an untidy desk with a kitchen chair before it. Clippings, framed photographs and certificates covered the walls. "My late wife used to call this my den. I always hated the word den. Bears have dens, badgers have dens. Call it my office, I used to say, but whenever I came in here, she'd say, 'Going off to hide in your den?' " He was talking the edge off his nervousness.

Tina's father straddled the kitchen chair backwards and waved the two younger men toward the couch. He smiled at them, and Michael found himself liking the old man very much.

"Everything changes on you, doesn't it?" he said. "Time was, I'd be certain I knew more about my boy than anyone else in the world. Both my boys. Now I don't even know where to begin. You met Tommy?"

Michael nodded. He could almost smell Harry's impatience.

"Tom's my son and I love him, but I couldn't say I like him very much. Tommy doesn't care if you like him or not. He's one of those people who mainly wants what's coming to him. But Tina—Tina went out and away, the way sons are supposed to, I guess. You two young men knew him better than I did, and that's why I wanted to see you alone for a second."

Michael felt uncomfortable now. Harry Beevers crossed and uncrossed his legs.

"I want to *see* him," the old man said. "Help me to *see* him. I won't be shocked by anything you say. I'm ready to hear anything."

"He was a good soldier," Harry said.

The old man looked down, struggling with his feelings. "Look," he said, "in the end, everything's a kind of mystery. Listen to me, Lieutenant. This land here—my grandfather plowed it and fertilized it and watched what the weather did to it all his life, and my father did the same, and I did too, nearly fifty years. Tommy didn't have the kind of love for it you have to have to do that kind of work, and Tina never even saw the farm at all—he was always looking out toward the world. The last time my name was in the Milburn paper they called me a real estate developer. I'm no real estate developer, but I'm not a farmer either. I'm the son of a farmer, is what I am. That's a goddamned good thing to be." He looked straight at Michael, and Michael felt a current of feeling go through him. "They drafted Tina. Tommy was too young to get called up, but Tina went away to that war. He was a boy—a beautiful boy. I don't think he was a good soldier. He was ready for life. When he came back he didn't know who he was anymore."

"I still say he was a good soldier," Beevers said. "He was a man. You can be proud of him."

"You know what tells me Tina was a man? He left his property to someone who deserved it. Tommy was rarin' up to sue, but I talked him out of it. And I talked to that girl on the phone. Maggie. I liked her. She knew what was going through my mind before I even said anything—a man might meet a woman like that in his life, if he's lucky. She almost got killed too, you know." He shook his head. "I'm not letting you boys talk."

"Tina was a good person," Michael said. "He was responsible and generous. He didn't like bullshit and he loved his work. The war touched everybody who was in it, but Tina came out better than most."

"Was he going to marry that Maggie?"

"He might have," Poole said.

"I hope she would have married him."

Michael said nothing, seeing that the old man was full of another question.

"What happened to him over there? Why did he have to be afraid?"

"He was just there," Michael said.

"It was like—like he knew something was coming for him. He was braced for it." He looked straight at Poole again. "My grandfather would have bribed the cop in there, taken the killer out into a field, and beaten him to death. Or at least he would have thought about it for a long while. I don't even have a field anymore."

"It's a little early to bribe Lieutenant Murphy," Beevers said.

The old man put his hands on his knees. "I thought Murphy talked to you, out at Pleasant Hill."

"Excuse me," said Beevers. "Pit stop."

Pumo's father leaned back on the seat of the chair and watched Beevers leave the room. Both men heard him turn left toward the living room. "Tina didn't like that fella much."

Michael smiled.

"He did like you, Doctor. Can I call you Michael?"

"I hope you will."

"The police picked up a man this morning—Murphy told me as soon as he got here. He hasn't been identified yet. Anyhow, they think he's the one who killed my boy."

Soon after they left the office and returned to the living room. A crowd of relatives surrounded Walter Pumo and began crosstalking at him. Judy frowned at Michael from across the room, where she was talking with a slightly older man.

Harry Beevers grabbed his elbow and pulled him sideways toward the arch of the entrance. In his attempt to conceal his distress he had become so stiff he hardly seemed able to bend. He hissed in Michael's ear. "It's terrible, Michael. They got him! He confessed!"

Over Harry's blue pin-striped shoulder Michael saw Lieutenant Murphy bearing down on them from across the room. "Spitalny?"

"Who the fuck else?"

Lieutenant Murphy had come close enough to give them both a confidential, almost conspiratorial glance that was as good as a command.

"Calm down," Michael said.

The big policeman stepped up beside them. "I wanted to tell you our good news. Unless you've already heard it from Mr. Beevers."

"I didn't say anything," Beevers said.

Murphy gave him an indulgent look. "We had what looks like a good confession this morning. I haven't seen the suspect yet, because I was on my way up here when he was apprehended on another charge. He confessed during questioning."

"What other charge? What's his name?"

"The man is not quite in this world, I gather, and he won't give his real name. I hope the two of you would be willing to have a look at him for us."

"Why do you want us to see him?" Beevers asked. "He already confessed."

"Well, we think you might have known him in Vietnam. It's possible he doesn't even remember his real name. I want to be sure about who this character is, and I'd like you to help me out."

Poole and Beevers agreed to come to a line-up at a precinct-house in Greenwich Village the following Monday.

"We arrested this guy on various charges of attempted murder and assault with a deadly weapon, and assault with intent to kill," Murphy said. "The story is a little strange. This character flipped out in a Times Square movie house during a showing of *Bloodsucking Freaks* or some such masterpiece. He whipped out a knife and started to saw the head off a guy who put his hand on his crotch. When he pretty well accomplished that, he started in on the people in front of him. Apparently they never noticed that someone was being decapitated right behind them. Anyhow, the people in front raised enough of a ruckus for the bouncer to jump the guy. The bouncer got a knife in one lung for his troubles, and by this time our hero is making a speech about how the sinners of the world have degraded him long enough, and now he's going to set things straight. Starting with Forty-second Street."

Conor Linklater and young Grace had wandered up to listen to the detective's story. Young Grace had entwined Conor's hand into her own.

"You've got one punctured bouncer, one man bleeding to death, two people with less serious stab wounds, and the whole theater is going nuts."

Murphy was an entertainer, and he enjoyed the spotlight. His eyebrows arched, his eyes gleamed.

"Anyhow, this guy finally creates so much commotion that he has to run out into the lobby. Somebody called us by then, and four patrolmen jumped him by the popcorn counter. We take him to the station and get statements from a dozen witnesses. The funny thing is, as soon as we get our guy into the station he is perfectly calm. He says he didn't want to cause so much trouble. Things have been bothering him lately, and they just got too much for him. He hopes he will not be kept too long because he has important things to do for the Lord. After we book him and tell him that he will have to stay with us for a while, he says, oh yeah, I guess you ought to know that I killed that man Pumo last week, upstairs in a loft over a restaurant in Grand Street."

Conor looked down and shook his head; Harry Beevers pursed his lips and blinked.

"The man can describe the loft perfectly, but there are a couple of points we're not satisfied on. So after the line-up there are some things I'd like to go over with the three of you."

After Murphy left them, Judy walked in from the dining room. "Have you spoken to that detective? Everybody's saying that they caught the man who killed Tina."

"It looks like they did," Michael said. He told her about being asked to appear at the line-up.

4

All Sunday the Pooles behaved toward each other with a conscious courtesy that would have suggested to an onlooker that they were comparative, slightly unfriendly, strangers in a neutral setting. It was the first full day they had spent together since Michael's return from Bangkok, and the surface of their life together felt eggshell-thin. Michael saw that Judy wished to "put the past behind them," which for the two of them meant to live exactly as they had for the four years since their son's death. If he could forgive her affair—forgive it by wrapping it in layers of silence—she would make it not have happened.

Judy brought a cup of coffee and the Sunday *Times* to the bedside. Feeling oddly more dutiful than she, Michael drank the coffee and leafed through the magazine section while Judy sat beside him and talked brightly about what had happened in her school over the last few weeks. This is an ordinary life, she was saying; this is how we live. Don't you remember this? Isn't it good?

Together they limped through the day. They ate brunch at the General Washington Inn: Bloody Marys and pickled okra and blackened red snapper, for it was "Cajun Festival." They took a long walk through the neighborhood past brown winter lawns dotted with FOR SALE signs and new houses rising like fantasies of glass and chrome on lots rutted with tire tracks. The walk ended at a long duck pond in the middle of little Thurlow Park. Mallards paddled sedately in pairs, each green-headed male insistently driving off the other males who approached his mate. Michael sat on the bench beside the pond and for a moment wished he was back in Singapore.

"What was it like, having sex again after all that time?" he asked.

"Dangerous," she said.

That was a better answer than he had expected.

After a little while, she said, "Michael, this place is where we belong."

"I don't know where I belong," he said.

She told him he was feeling sorry for himself: behind these words was the assumption that their life was fixed, unavoidable; their life *was* life.

To Michael the entire day seemed to be happening to someone else. Actors must feel this way, he thought, and only then realized that all day he had been acting the part of a husband.

He went to bed early, leaving Judy watching "Masterpiece Theatre" in apparent contentment. He undressed, put on his pajamas, and began brushing his teeth while he read Newgate Callendar's reviews in the book section of the *Times*.

Judy amazed him by easing around the bathroom door and twinkling at his reflection in the mirror. Also amazing was that she was wearing a pink satin nightie and clearly intended to go to bed before the end of "Masterpiece Theatre." "Surprise!" she said.

The person whose role he was acting said, "Hi."

"Mind if I join you?" Judy plucked her own toothbrush from the rack and nudged him an inch to the side. She ran water over the brush, squeezed on a fat curl of toothpaste, and raised the brush to her mouth. Before she inserted it, just as he was swishing water in his mouth, she asked his face in the mirror, "You're surprised, aren't you?"

Then he got it: she was acting too. That was deeply comforting. Any reality in a scene like this would have made him lose his mind with pain and fear.

When he edged around her and left the bathroom, she waved with her free hand. "Bye."

Michael walked to his side of the bed on someone else's feet, switched on the bedside lamp with someone else's fingers, and pushed his stranger's legs down into the stranger's bed. Then he picked up *The Ambassadors* and was disproportionately relieved to discover that it was really himself and not the person he was pretending to be who was reading it.

The Ambassadors was about about a man named Strether who had been sent to Paris to fetch back a young man suspected of dissipation. Strether soon found that Chad Newsome, the boy, had been enhanced instead of corrupted by the experience of Paris, and was not at all sure that he ought to go back. Strether himself put off his own return for weeks, discovering newer, subtler, better flavors and refinements of manners and feeling—he was alive and at home in himself, and he did not want to go home either.

As soon as Michael began reading, he realized that he felt he had a lot in common with Strether. They too had gone out to find a corrupt man and had found him a different, better man than they had expected. Poole wondered if Strether was ever going to bite the bullet and go home. This was a very interesting question.

Judy slid into her side of the bed and advanced nearer to him than was usual.

"This is a great book," he said. The statement was nearly not acting, but it was acting.

"You're certainly engrossed in it."

He put down the book just to make sure that Judy was still acting and he saw instantly that she was.

"I think you're mistaking me for Tom Brokaw," he said.

"I don't want to lose you, Michael." She was acting her head off, but she was serious about it. "Put down the book."

He placed the book on the bedside table and let Judy come into his arms. She kissed him. He play-acted kissing her. Judy slipped her hand past the waistband of his pajamas and fondled him.

"Are you really doing this?"

"Michael," she said. In a second she had tossed the pink nightie aside.

He kissed her back with real play-actor's fervor. For an instant his penis stirred as she rubbed and squeezed it, but his penis could not act, and it did no more.

Her arms tightened around him and she hoisted herself up onto his body. The humor in all this play-acting melted away, and all that was left was the sorrow. Judy squirmed on top of him for a time, frantically kissing his face and his neck.

Judy lapped at him with her tongue and pushed her breasts into his face. He had forgotten how Judy's nipples felt in his mouth, round and sly. For an instant filled with danger and violence he remembered how her breasts had swelled early in her pregnancy, and his cock stiffened in her hand. But she shifted, and he felt how her real emotions turned her body to steel and balsa wood, and his cock went back to sleep. Judy labored over him for a long time, and then she gave up and merely hugged him. Her arms were trembling.

"You hated doing that," he said. "Let's tell the truth. You detested it."

She uttered a low, feral sound, like a thick fold of silk being ripped in half, hoisted herself up onto her knees and struck him very hard in the middle of his chest. Her face was distorted by passion and her eyes were wild, glowing with hatred and disgust. Then she scrambled off the bed and her solid little body flashed through the room. He wondered how many times in the past four years he had, with increasing tentativeness and foreknowledge of failure, tried to have sexual intercourse with that body. Maybe a hundred times—not at all in the past year. Judy snatched up her nightgown and slipped it unceremoniously over her head. She slammed the bedroom door.

Michael heard her stamping across her dressing room. The chair creaked beneath her. She dialed a local number on her telephone. Then she slammed the receiver down so forcefully that the telephone clanged like a bell. Michael's body began to relax and became his own body again. Judy dialed a local number again, presumably the same one. He heard her inhale, and knew that her face was rigid as a mask. The receiver clanged down once more. He heard her say *"Shit."* Then she dialed a nine-digit number, probably Pat Caldwell's. After a few suspended seconds, she began to speak in a low, choked, barely recognizable whisper.

Michael picked up the James novel and found that he could not read it—the words seemed to have come alive, and to squirm around on the page. Michael wiped his eyes and the page cleared.

Strether was at a party in the city garden of a sculptor named Gloriani. Brilliant beautiful people drifted through the garden, lanterns glowed. Strether was talking to a young American named Little Bilham, whom he rather cherished. Michael wished he were there in the garden, holding a glass of champagne beside Little Bilham, listening to Strether. Had other people read this book in this way, or was it just him? "What one loses, one loses, make no mistake about that," Strether said. He could hear Judy muttering and mumbling, and her voice was that of some destructive ghost.

He realized what he was thinking just as Judy hung up the telephone and padded across the dressing room, opened the door, and flashed through again, her head turned away from him. She went out into the upstairs hall. He heard her descending the stairs. A series of taps and rattles came from the kitchen. Whatever had happened, Poole was back in his real life. His body felt like his own real body again, not an actor's. He closed his book and got out of bed.

In Judy's little dressing room, the telephone rang. Michael thought to pick it up; then he remembered that the answering machine would get it. He moved to the door of the dressing room. Then a male voice spoke.

"The world goes backward and forward at the same time, and is there any sorrow like unto my sorrow? I will wait, I am waiting now. I need your help. The narrow path vanishes beneath my feet."

This voice too, it struck Michael, was the voice of a ghost.

When he walked into the kitchen Judy backed away from the stove, where a kettle had been put on to boil, and stood with her back against the window and her arms dangling at her sides. She stared at him as if he were a savage animal who might attack her.

If she had smiled or said anything conventional, he would at once have felt again like an actor in a role, but she did not smile or speak.

Michael circled around the butcher block counter and leaned on its far side. Judy seemed smaller and older than the fierce wild-eyed woman who had hit him.

"Your crazy man called."

Judy shook her head and walked back to the stove.

"Seems he can't find his way. I know what he means."

"Stop it." She raised her fists.

The kettle began to whistle. Judy put her fists down and poured hot water over instant coffee. She stirred it with short choppy strokes.

Finally she said, "I'm not going to lose everything I have. You might have lost your mind, but I don't have to give up everything I care about. Pat says I should just calm down, but then Pat never had to worry about anything, did she?"

"Didn't she?"

"You know she didn't." She sipped her coffee and made a face. "I'm surprised you managed to put down your stupid book."

"If you thought it was stupid, why did you give it to me?"

Her eyes flew sideways, like those of a child caught in a lie. "You give books to your little girlfriend all the time. Somebody gave that one to me. I thought it might help you settle down again."

He leaned on the butcher block counter and looked at her.

"I'm not leaving this house," she said.

"You don't have to."

"I'm not going to do without anything just because you're sick." Her whole face blazed at him for a moment, then shrank back into itself. "Pat was telling me about Harry the other day. She said he repelled her—she couldn't stand the thought of his touching her. You're that way about me."

"It's the other way around. You feel that way about me."

"We've been married for fourteen years, I ought to know how I feel."

"I should too," he said. "I'd tell you how I feel, how you make me feel, but you wouldn't believe it."

"You should never have gone on that crazy trip," she said. "We should have stayed at home instead of going up to Milburn with Harry. That just made things worse."

"You never want me to go anywhere," he said. "You think I killed Robbie, and you want me to stay here and keep on paying for it."

"Forget Robbie!" she shrieked. *"Forget him! He's dead!"*

"I'll go into therapy with you," he said. "Are you listening to this? Both of us. Together."

"You know who should have therapy! *You!* You're the sick one! Not me! Our marriage was fine before you went away."

"Went away where?" Michael turned away, left the room, and went up the stairs in silence.

He lay in bed a long time, listening in the dark. Chinks and rattles and the opening and closing of cabinets came from the kitchen. Eventually Judy came up the stairs. To Michael's surprise, her footsteps came toward the bedroom door. She leaned in. "I just want to say this even though I know you won't believe it. I wanted this day to be special for you. I wanted to *make* it special for you."

"I know."

Even in the darkness he could see rage, disgust, and a kind of disbelief go through her body.

"I'm going to sleep in the guest room. I'm not sure we're married anymore, Michael."

Michael lay awake with his eyes closed another half hour, then gave up, switched on his light, and picked up the Henry James novel. The book was a perfect little garden glimpsed far down at the bottom of a landfill. Seagulls screeched over the landfill's great mountains of garbage, rats prowled through it, and right at the bottom, safe within the page, men and women clothed in an intellectual radiance moved in a beautiful, inexorable dance. Poole went cautiously down the hills of garbage toward the perfect garden, but it receded backward with every step he took.

5

He woke to the sounds of Judy showering. A few minutes later she came into the bedroom wrapped in a long pink towel. "Well," she said, "I have to go to work. Are you still going to insist on going to New York this morning?"

"I have to," he said.

She took a dress from the closet and shook her head, as if at some hopeless case. "I imagine that you won't have time to go to either your office or the hospital this morning, then."

"I might drop in at the hospital."

"You might drop in at the hospital and then drive to New York."

"That's right."

"I hope you remember what I said last night." She tore the dress off the hanger and slammed through the door to the dressing room.

Michael got out of bed. He felt tired and depressed, but he did not feel like an actor or that he had been placed in an unfamiliar body. Both the body and the unhappiness were his own. He decided to bring Stacy Talbot another book, and searched his shelves until he found an old underlined copy of *Wuthering Heights*.

Before he left home he went down into his basement to open a trunk where he had placed a few things after Robbie's death. He had not told Judy that he was doing this, because Judy had insisted that they give away or destroy everything their son had owned. The trunk was an awkward relic from the days when Michael's parents had taken cruises, and Michael and Judy had filled it with books and clothes when they had moved to Westerholm. Michael knelt down before the open trunk. Here was a baseball, a short-sleeve shirt with a pattern of horses, a worn green Dimetrodon and a whole set of smaller plastic dinosaurs. At the bottom of these things were two books, *Babar* and *Babar the King*. Poole took out the books and closed the trunk.

29

THE LINE-UP

1

An hour and a half later, driving as if on automatic pilot toward Manhattan, Michael finally noticed the worn old Riverside Edition of *Wuthering Heights* on the other seat and realized that he had held it in his hand during the whole of his visit to the hospital. Like glasses their owner searches for while wearing, the book had become transparent and weightless. Now, as if to make up for its earlier tact, the novel seemed denser than a brick, nearly heavy enough to tilt the car on its springs. At first he felt like pitching the book out the window, then like pulling up at a gas station and calling Murphy to tell him that he could not make the line-up. Beevers and Linklater could identify Victor Spitalny, Maggie would say that he was the man who had tried to kill her, and that would be that.

His next thought was that he needed something to fill up his day with reality, and driving to New York to attend a line-up was as good as anything else.

He put the car in a garage on University Place and walked to the precinct house. The weather had brightened in the past few days, and though the temperature was still under forty, warmth had begun to awaken within the air. On both sides of the narrow Greenwich Village streets, people of the generation just younger than Poole's walked coatless, smiling, looking as if they had been released from prison.

His idea of police stations had been formed by movies, and the flat modern façade surprised him when he came upon it. Lieutenant Murphy's precinct building looked like a grade school. Only the steel letters on the pale façade and the police cars drawn up before it declared the identity of the building.

The interior was another surprise. Instead of a tall desk and a bald veteran frowning down, Poole first saw an American flag beside a case of awards, then a uniformed young man, leaning toward him from the other side of an open window.

"I'm supposed to meet Lieutenant Murphy for a line-up at eleven," he said.

The young man disappeared from the window; a buzzer went off. Poole opened the door beside the window, and the young man looked up from a clipboard. "The others are on the second floor. I'll get someone to take you up." Behind him plainclothes officers glanced at Poole, then away. There was an impression of busyness, conversation, male company. It reminded Poole of the doctors' lounge at St. Bart's.

Another, even younger, policeman in uniform led Poole down a corridor hung with bulletin boards. The second policeman was breathing loudly through his mouth. He had a lazy, fleshy, unintelligent face, olive skin, and a fat neck. He would not meet Poole's eyes. "Up da stairs," he said when they arrived at a staircase. Then he labored up beside Poole and slouched off through another school corridor. Soon he stopped at a door marked B.

Poole opened the door, and Beevers said, "My man." He was leaning against the wall with his arms crossed over his chest, talking to a small round-faced Chinese woman. Poole greeted Beevers and said hello to Maggie, whom he had met two or three times at Saigon. A little ironic breeze seemed to blow about her, separating her from Harry Beevers. She shook his hand with a surprisingly firm, competent grip. One side of her face dimpled in a lopsided smile. She was extraordinarily pretty—the impression of her intelligence had momentarily filtered out her good looks.

"It's nice of you to come in all the way from Westchester

County," she said in a flat accentless voice that sounded almost English in the precision of its consonants.

"He had to join all us plebs in the dirty city," Beevers said.

Poole thanked Maggie, ignored Beevers, and sat down at a board room table beside Conor. Conor said, "Hey." The resemblance to a grade school persisted. Room B was like a classroom without a teacher's desk. Directly before Michael and Conor, on the other side of the room, was a long green blackboard. Beevers went on saying something about film rights.

"Are you okay, Mikey?" Conor asked. "You look kinda down."

Poole saw the copy of *Wuthering Heights* on the passenger seat of his car.

Beevers glared down at them. "Use the brains God gave you, man! Of course the man is down. He had to leave a beautiful town where the air is clean and they don't even have sidewalks, they have hedges, and spend hours on a stinking highway. Where he came from, Conor, they have partridges and pheasants instead of pigeons. They have Airedales and deer instead of rats. Wouldn't you be down? Give the man some understanding."

"Hey, I'm from South Norwalk," Conor said. "We don't have pigeons either. We got seagulls."

"Garbage birds," Beevers said.

"Calm down, Harry," Poole said.

"We can still come out of this okay," Beevers said. "We just don't say any more than we have to."

"So what happened?" Conor whispered to Michael.

"A patient died this morning."

"A kid?"

Michael nodded. "A little girl." He felt impelled to speak her name. "Named Stacy Talbot." The act of putting his loss into these specific words had an unexpected and nearly physical effect on him. His grief did not shrink, but became more concrete: Stacy's death took physical form as a leaden casketlike form located deep in his chest. He, Michael Poole, was intact and whole around this dense, leaden weight within him. He realized that Conor was the first person to whom he had spoken of her death.

Stacy had been feverish and exhausted when he had last seen her. The lights had hurt her eyes; her usual gallantry was at low ebb. But she had seemed interested in his little fund of stories, and had held his hand and told him that she loved the beginning of *Jane Eyre,* especially the first sentence.

Poole opened the book to read the sentence. *"There was no possibility of taking a walk that day."*

Stacy was grinning at him.

This morning one of the nurses had tried to head him off as he walked past their station, but he had barely noticed her. He had been intent on some words Sam Stein had spoken to him in the first-floor corridor. Stein, who had evaded responsibility for a surgical error with a combination of cowardice and superiority Michael found repulsive, had said that he was sorry his medical group had not made more progress with Michael's "boys"—the other doctors of his own group practice. Stein was assuming that Michael would be familiar with the background of this remark, but Michael could fill it in with informed guesswork. Stein's own "boys" were building a new medical center in Westerholm, and wanted to make it the most important in the county. To do that they needed a good pediatric practice. Michael himself was the stumbling block to the effective union of their practices, and in his grumpy, conceited way Stein had been asking him to spare him the trouble and implied insult of having to go after a second-rung pediatric group. A brand new facility like the one Stein was planning would draw about fifty percent of all the new people in Westerholm, and maybe a quarter of the houses in Westerholm changed hands every year. Michael's partners had been talking things over with Stein while he had been gone.

Michael had sailed past the gesturing nurse, the germ of a brilliant idea beginning to form in his mind, and opened the door to Stacy's room.

He strode into a room where a bald middle-aged man with a grey moustache and a double chin lay asleep with an IV in his arm and the *Wall Street Journal* open on his chest. The man did not awaken and wink at him like an actor in a farce, he slept on noiselessly, but Michael felt a change in his inner weather like the sudden hot airlessness that precedes a tornado. He ducked outside and checked the number of the room. Of course it was the right room. He ducked back again and looked at the drugged tycoon. This time he even recognized him. The man was a housing contractor named Pohlmann whose teenage children went to Judy's school and whose imitation chateau with a red tile roof and a five-car garage was located a mile and a half from Poole's own house. Michael backed out of Pohlmann's room.

For an instant only he became aware of the soft old green book in his hand, and it weighed twenty or thirty pounds. He saw the nurse watching him as she spoke into her telephone. He knew what had happened as soon as he saw her eyes. He knew it by the way she put down her telephone. But he walked up to the station and said, "Where is she?"

"I was afraid you didn't know, Doctor," the nurse had said. He had felt as if he were in an elevator falling through a long shaft, just falling and falling.

"I'm sorry, man," Conor said. "Must remind you of your own kid."

"The man is a doctor, Conor," Beevers said. "He sees things like this all the time. The man knows how to be detached."

Detached was just how Dr. Poole felt, though not at all as Beevers imagined.

"Speaking of the man," Beevers said.

Lieutenant Murphy's big aggressive-looking head appeared in the meshed window set into the door. He grinned at them through the window, his mouth set around a pipe, and opened the door.

"Glad you could all make it," he said. "Sorry I'm a little late." He looked like an athletic college professor in a tweed jacket and fawn trousers. "We're all set for the line-up and we will be going down there in a minute, but I wanted to talk to you about some things before we do that."

Beevers caught Poole's eye and coughed into his fist.

Murphy sat opposite them. He took the pipe from his mouth and held it balanced in his fingertips as if offering it for inspection. It was a big curved black sandblasted Peterson, with a tarnished silver band around the top of the neck. A plug of grey tobacco filled the bowl. "We didn't really have a chance to speak to each other up in Milburn, though there were some things I was curious about, and at the time it looked as if we had this case pretty well sewn up." He looked at each of them in turn. "I was happy about that, and I guess it showed. But this wasn't an ordinary case, not by a long shot, not even an ordinary murder case, if there is such an animal. There have been some changes since then."

Murphy looked down at the heavy pipe balanced in his fingers, and Beevers spoke into the silence. "Are you implying that the man you are holding has given a false confession?"

"Why do you sound hopeful?" Murphy asked him. "Don't you want us to nail this guy?"

"I didn't mean to sound hopeful. Of course I want the man apprehended."

Murphy regarded him steadily for a moment. "There's a lot of information pertinent to these cases that has not reached the public. And that should not reach the public, if we don't want our investigation to be compromised. Or actually interfered with, to give you the worst case. I want to go over some of this information with you people before we go to the line-up, and Miss Lah, if you know something too, I'd like you to please speak up."

Maggie nodded.

"Miss Lah has already been very helpful to us."

"Thank you," she said very softly.

"You gentlemen all met Mr. Pumo as members of the same platoon in Vietnam? And you were the lieutenant of that unit, Mr. Beevers?"

"Correct," Beevers said, smiling with his mouth but glaring at Maggie.

"How many members of that unit besides yourselves are still living, do you know?"

Beevers pursed his lips and cocked his head.

"Dr. Poole?"

"I don't know, really," Poole said. "Not many of us are left alive."

"Do you really not know?" Murphy asked in a level voice. Poole shook his head. "None of you?"

"I guess we'd be grateful for whatever you can tell us," Beevers said. "But I'm afraid I don't really follow your train of thought."

Murphy raised his expressive eyebrows. He stuck the pipe in his mouth and puffed. The dead-looking tobacco glowed red, and the detective let smoke escape his mouth.

"You are familiar with the nickname Koko, however," he said.

Beevers frowned at Maggie.

"Miss Lah passed on some background information to us. Do you think she was wrong in doing so?"

Beevers coughed. "Of course not."

"I'm glad you feel that way." Murphy's mouth twitched in a smile. "Besides the three of you, there seem to be only four survivors of the platoon that took part in the action at Ia Thuc. A PFC named Wilson Manly is living in Arizona—"

"Manly's alive?" Conor asked. "Goddamn."

Poole too was surprised. Like Conor, he had last seen Manly being carried to a stretcher—he had lost a leg and a lot of blood, and Poole had thought that he would never survive.

"Wilson Manly is disabled, but he owns a security business in Tucson."

"Security systems?" Conor asked and Murphy nodded. "Goddamn."

"Who else?" Poole asked.

"George Burrage is working as a drug counselor in Los Angeles."

"Spanky," Conor and Poole said more or less in unison. He too had been carried away after a firefight, and since nothing more had been heard of him, he too had been presumed dead.

"They both send their regards to you, and remembered Mr. Pumo very well and were sorry to hear about what happened to him."

"Of course," said Beevers. "You were in the service, weren't you, Lieutenant? Weren't you in Vietnam?"

"I was too young for Vietnam," Murphy said. "Both Mr. Manly and Mr. Burrage have an extremely good recall of various incidents involving the use of the name Koko."

"I bet they do," said Beevers.

"A PFC named Victor Spitalny might be presumed to be living," said Murphy. "There has been no record of him since he went AWOL back in Bangkok in 1969. But given the circumstances under which he disappeared, I don't think it's very likely that he would suddenly take it into his head to kill journalists and members of his old unit, do you?"

"Couldn't say," Beevers said. "What do you mean, journalists?"

"Whoever calls himself Koko has been killing the foreign and American journalists who covered the Ia Thuc atrocity story. He's been very thorough, too." He regarded Beevers with a steady detached gaze, and then looked at Poole in the same way. "This man has killed at least eight people. There is a possibility he killed one other man."

"Who's that?" Beevers asked.

"A businessman named Irwin, out at JFK a few weeks ago. We've just managed to put all the information together, using sources from all over the world. It's hard to get different police departments to cooperate when they're right next door to each other, but we're proud of ourselves on this one. We're getting ready, and we're going to take our man. But in order to do that, we need your full cooperation. And I have a feeling I'm not really getting it."

But before anybody could protest, he took an envelope out of his jacket pocket, opened the flap, and removed three playing cards encased in separate clear plastic bags. "Take a look at these, please."

He used a pencil to separate the cards on the surface of the table. Poole looked at the three cards. Every blood vessel in his body seemed to constrict. There was the Rearing Elephant, reproduced three times. "A Legacy of Honor," read a slogan beneath the emblem. Poole had not seen a regimental playing card since he had left Vietnam. The elephant looked angrier than he had remembered.

"Where'd you find these, man?" Conor asked.

Murphy flipped each of the cards face up. There it was, scrawled in the old manner. *KOKO*, three times. Before Beevers was an eight of clubs; before Conor a two of hearts; before Poole a six of spades. With a bang of his heart Poole saw the faint penciling of his name at the top of the card before him.

"Mr. Pumo had one of these, with his name on it, in his mouth," Murphy said.

LINKLATER and BEEVERS, Poole saw, had been lightly penciled on the other cards.

The line-up was a pretext to get the four of them together for questioning. They had been summoned not to identify a killer, but to be frightened into saying more than they wished.

Beevers and Conor spoke at the same time: "Where

did you get these?" "You must have gotten pretty close to him."

Murphy nodded. "We learned where he had been staying through a tip. Unfortunately, we didn't find him, so he must have learned somehow—we probably missed him by a couple of minutes. But we *never* get as close as that without getting him in the end."

Murphy used his pencil to nudge the cards back into the envelope. "There was one other survivor from your unit."

For a moment Poole could not remember who this was.

"You all remember Timothy Underhill."

"Sure,' Conor said, and the other two nodded.

"What can you tell me about him?"

There was silence for a moment or two.

"I can't figure you characters out," Murphy said.

Poole remembered Judy talking about Bob Bunce: lies of denial always transparent. "We looked for Underhill in Singapore,' he said. Then he stopped talking, because Harry Beevers' well-shod foot had come down heavily on his.

"It was what you'd call a lark," Beevers said. "We were in this interesting part of the world, on a vacation, and we thought maybe we could locate him. All we found were traces. People that used to know him, things like that. We went hither and yon in three countries. Had a ball."

"You went to a lot of trouble to find an old army buddy," Murphy said.

"That's *right*," Beevers said. He looked carefully at Maggie, then candidly back at Murphy. "We had a hell of a trip."

"No luck?"

"The man disappeared." Beevers' mouth opened. "Ah. You think this Koko is Tim Underhill?"

"It's one of the possibilities we're considering." He smiled with as much false candor as Beevers. "He certainly isn't Wilson Manly or Spanky Burrage. Or any of you."

Other questions came crowding up, but Harry asked only the most immediate. "Then who's the guy who went crazy in Times Square?"

Murphy pushed himself away from the table. "Let's go find out."

2

Murphy stayed close to Michael Poole as they walked toward the stairs. "Our friend still won't give his name. He claims to have forgotten it. In fact, he claims to have been born in New York City at the age of eighteen." He coughed. "In the back room of a bar called The Anvil." He gave Poole an almost human glance. "He drew us a map of Pumo's apartment. Then he clammed up and refused to say anything except that he had a mission to clean up the filth in the world."

Murphy led them through the big office space on the ground floor, through a door at the back, and down a wide set of stairs. Over the noise of typewriters clacking in nearby offices, Poole heard Harry Beevers speaking softly and urgently to Maggie Lah.

"Here we are," Murphy said, swinging open a broad set of doors that resembled a theater with its rows of banked seats, raised platform, and overhead lights.

Murphy took them to the second row of seats, where Maggie filed in behind Poole, followed by Beevers and Conor Linklater. Then he stepped to a podium in the central aisle one row behind them, and flipped on the stage lights. He picked up a microphone on a cord, scrutinized it for a switch, and turned it on. "We are here now," he spoke into the microphone. "Let's get the screen in place, and you can send the men out." He frowned down at the podium and flipped another switch. A long screen marked with height registrations rolled out on a track across the stage.

"Ready," Murphy said. "Each man on his mark. Once they are onstage, I will direct each man in turn to step forward, tell us a few words about himself, and then step backward."

Five men emerged from the left side of the stage and began moving uncertainly toward what Poole supposed were numbers embedded in the stage. At first glance, the three short, dark-haired men in the lineup could have been Victor Spitalny. One wore a grey business suit, one a checked sports jacket, and the third jeans and a denim jacket. The man in the checked jacket looked most like Spitalny, but his eyes were more widely spaced and his chin was broader. He looked bored and impatient. The fourth was a heavyset blond man with a lively cynical Irish face. The fifth man, who was wearing a loose khaki shirt, fatigue pants, and cowboy boots, had shaved his head some time ago and then let it grow out to a uniform dark cap still short enough to show the scalp beneath. He alone smiled at the row of people looking up at him.

Murphy called out their numbers in a toneless voice.

"My name is Bill and I work as a bartender on the Upper East Side."

"My name is George. I am the leader of the Boy Scout troop in Washington Heights."

"My name is Franco and I am from Ocean Avenue in Brooklyn.

"My name is Liam. I am in the security business."

When number five was called, the last man stepped forward. "I have no name because I have no past."

"Oh, my God," Maggie said. "I don't believe it."

Murphy ordered the fifth man to step back, and then asked all five to leave the stage. When the stage was empty he leaned on the podium and scowled down at Maggie. "Well?"

"The last man, the one in the middle of his sex change, was wearing Tina's boots. I'm sure of it. I know who he is."

"Who is he?"

"I mean—I don't know his real name, but he called himself Dracula and had a long Mohawk before he shaved it off. Tina picked him up at a club last year, or was picked up by him. He was pretending to be a girl. After they got back to the loft, he beat Tina unconscious and stole a lot of things from him. Including the boots he was wearing up there. They were Tina's favorites. I think they cost a lot of money."

"Dracula," Murphy said.

"But he isn't the man I saw in the loft."

"No," Murphy said. "I guess he wouldn't be. Gentlemen, you may leave. I want to thank you for your cooperation, and I will be speaking to each of you again. Please call me if you can think of anything I ought to know. Miss Lah, will you come back upstairs with me, please?"

Maggie stood up slightly before the other three and went out into the central aisle where Murphy stood waiting for her. She caught Michael's eye and raised her eyebrows. Michael nodded, then stood up with the other two.

3

After seeing the others into a cab and promising to join them at Harry's apartment in half an hour, Michael walked back down Tenth Street to wait outside the police station. The weather was still too cold to be really comfortable, but Michael enjoyed standing on Tenth Street in the tingling air. The sunlight lay like gilt on the pretty brownstones across the street. He felt suspended between the end of something and the beginning of something absolutely new. Stacy Talbot had been his last real tie to Westerholm—everything else that held him there could be carried away in a suitcase.

He saw how he easy it would be to keep watching the television program that his life had become. The bright dailyness of his work, the stream of snuffling children and their worried mothers, Judy and her anxieties, the lax dull partnership of the long mornings, the nice white house, the walks to the duck pond, Bloody Marys at Sunday brunch, the numbing details that rushed you forward minute by minute.

The door of the police station opened with a click as decisive as the crack of a bone, and Michael turned around and straightened up as Maggie Lah came out. Her beautiful hair caught the sun in a smooth mesh of rich deep lustrous black.

"Oh, good," she said. "I wasn't sure you'd still be here. I couldn't say anything back in there."

"I know."

"I really just wanted to see *you.* Conor is wonderful, but he isn't too sure about me. And Harry Beevers is a tremendous . . . distraction."

"Especially to Harry Beevers."

"They can spare you for a little while?"

"For as long as you like."

"Then they may never get you back," Maggie said, and put her arm through his. "I want you to help me go someplace. Will you do it?"

"I'm yours." Poole suddenly, strongly felt that he and

this girl were Tina Pumo's survivors: as much as Walter and Tommy Pumo, they were the family Tina had left behind.

"It isn't very far. It isn't even much of a place, just a little neighborhood restaurant. Tina and I used to go there—really *he* used to go there, it was *his* place and he shared it with me, and I don't want to feel like sinking into the sidewalk everytime I walk past it. Do you mind?"

"I'm very pleased," Poole said. Maggie's arm was linked with his and she matched him stride for stride. "Is there any other place I can take you to after this one?"

She glanced up. "There might be."

He let her have her own time in which to say whatever she wished to say.

"I want to know you," Maggie finally said.

"I'm glad."

"He liked you best of all—of all the men he had been over there with."

"That's very nice to know."

"He was always very pleased when you came into Saigon. Part of Tina was not very secure. It meant a lot to him that when you came all the way into town, you would pick his place to come to. That proved to him that you hadn't forgotten him."

"I haven't forgotten him, Maggie," he said, and she tightened her grip on his arm.

They were walking down Sixth Avenue, and the sunlight seemed warmer here than the cross streets. Colorful, ordinary street life flowed around them, students and housewives and businessmen and a few boys in lipstick. At the corner they walked past a hunched, bearded man in rags whose feet had blackened and swollen like footballs. Just past him a blurry-looking man of about Michael's age thrust at him a paper cup containing a few dimes and quarters. He had a bloody crusty scab on his chin, and in the slits of his eyes his pupils gleamed feverishly, tigerishly. Vietnam. Michael dropped a few quarters in the cup.

"Not far now," Maggie said, and her voice was trembling.

Poole nodded.

"It's like living with a big—emptiness." She threw out her free hand. "It's so hard. And because I'm afraid, it's even worse than that. Oh, I'll tell you about it when we get there."

A few minutes later, Maggie led him up the steps into La Groceria. A tall dark-haired woman in black tights led them to a table by the window. The sunlight drifted in the big windows and lay across the polished, rippling pattern of the caramel-colored wooden tabletops. They ordered salads and coffee. "I hate being afraid," Maggie said. "But all by itself, grief is too much. Grief gets you when you're not looking. It comes up and blindsides you." She glanced up at him in a way that mingled intelligence and sympathy. "You were talking to Conor about a patient of yours . . . ?"

Poole nodded. "Just before I drove down here I learned that she died." He tried to smile at her, and was glad that he did not have to see the result.

Her face altered, smoothed out, became more inward. "In Taipei my mother used to catch rats with traps in our garden. The traps didn't kill the rats, they just held them. My mother poured boiling water over them. The rats knew exactly what was going to happen to them. First they fought and jumped at my mother, and then finally everything left them but fear. They just became fear." A cloud somewhere east of Sixth Avenue separated, and the sunlight doubled in color and intensity. She was looking at him with a troubled but defiant gaze, and Poole experienced her concentrated attention as an undivided blessing. Right now, in the sudden drenching fall of yellow light, he became extraordinarily conscious of the smooth roundness of her arms, the beautiful golden shade of her skin, her small witty sensuous intelligent mouth. Her youth was deceptive, he understood, seeing her in the blaze of light, and if you judged her youth as being one of the central facts of her being, you made a great mistake. A moment ago he had been moved by her sheer prettiness, and now he saw so much more in the wide unblinking face before him that her prettiness became irrelevant.

"They were the worst things in the world when that happened," she said. "The most pathetic. I felt like that when—when it happened. When he almost caught me." She paused for a moment, and her face smoothed out again with the weight of what she was remembering. "I could see him, but not his face. I suppose I was a little crazy. I felt as though I must have been covered in blood, and I kept checking myself, but there wasn't a drop on me." Her eyes met his with an electric jolt.

"You want to pour boiling water over him," Poole said.

"That could be." Her mouth twisted in an odd little smile. "Could someone like that ever be afraid?"

When he said nothing, Maggie went on in a rush. "When I was in the loft—during that time—if you had seen him too—you wouldn't think so. He talked very smoothly. He was almost seductive. I don't mean he wasn't utterly crazy, because he was, but he was in control of himself. Confident. He was trying to charm me out of hiding, and if Tina's body hadn't been right in front of me, he might have done it." Her hands, of the same golden tan as the rest of her, with long elegant fingers and incongruously square, sturdy wrists, had begun to tremble. "He was like a—a demon. I thought I'd never get away."

Now she looked really stricken, and he took her hands in his. "It sounds funny, but I think he's been frightened all his life."

"You sound like you almost feel sorry for him."

Poole thought of Underhill's long labor. "It isn't that so much—I guess I feel we have to invent him in order to understand him."

Maggie slowly drew her hands out from under his. "You must be learning about that from your friend Timothy Underhill."

"What?"

Maggie propped her chin in her hand. Wholly fraudulent, wide-eyed innocent incredulity, comic right down to its core, flashed at him for a perfectly timed beat. "Your friend Harry Beevers can't act very well."

So she knew: she had seen it. "I suppose not," he said.

"This man Underhill came back with you."

Poole nodded. "You're wonderful."

"Harry Beevers is the one who is wonderful. I suppose he wants the police to waste time trying to locate Tim Underhill while he actually finds Koko himself."

"Something like that."

"You'd better be careful, Doctor." A multitude of unspoken warnings crowded in behind this one, and Poole did not know if he had been advised to beware of Koko or Harry Beevers. "Do you have time to take me to one more place? I don't want to go there alone."

"I suppose I don't have to ask where it is?"

"Hope not." She stood up.

They went outside to a Sixth Avenue that seemed to have been darkened by their conversation. Poole felt that Koko, Victor Spitalny, might be watching them from behind the big windows across the avenue, or through binoculars from some high hidden vantage point.

"Get a cab," she said. "There's one more thing I want to do."

She picked up something at the newsstand, joined Michael as a cab pulled over, and climbed into the back seat. He looked down at her lap and saw that what she had bought was a copy of the *Village Voice*.

Michael told the driver to stop first on Grand Street off West Broadway, then to take him to Twenty-fourth and Tenth.

"This is a present for buying me lunch." She moved the thick tabloid onto Michael's lap, and then took a pair of large, round, wire-rimmed sunglasses from her bag and put them on. For a moment she appeared to be reading the yellow DRIVER ALLERGIC DO NOT SMOKE and DRIVER NOT REQUIRED TO CHANGE BILLS OVER TWENTY signs applied here and there to the grimy plastic window before them.

"Are you sure you want to go to Saigon?"

"I want to see Vinh," she said. "I like Vinh. Vinh and I have long confidential talks. We agree that white Americans are an incomprehensible and exotic people."

"Have you been there since that night?"

"Don't you know the answer to that?" She removed the sunglasses and gave him an almost sullen look.

"I'm glad we could talk," he said.

At this she unself-consciously took his hand. Michael could feel the pulse beating in her warm dry hand.

At Grand Street Michael was surprised to see a brass-bound case displaying a menu and a small sign in the restaurant window.

"Doesn't it look great?" she asked him in her flat crisp voice. "We'll open as soon as the court lets us. Vinh asked me to help him out. Of course I'm grateful to have the work. It means that I don't have the feeling that I lost quite all of him."

When the cab stopped, she swung the door open, and said, "Maybe I shouldn't say this, but you seem very unsettled. There's room for you in here"—she nodded toward the building—"if you need a place to stay." She waited for him to say something.

"I'll come in and see you before long," he finally said. "Are you planning to stay here now?"

She shook her head. "Call me at the General's." Then she smiled in the face of his mystification and left the cab.

"Who is the General?"

Maggie glanced down at the paper in his lap.

He looked at the front page, where she had somehow managed to write a telephone number. When he looked back up, she was already opening the door of the restaurant.

30

A SECOND REUNION

1

"Is this really your idea of half an hour?" Beevers scowled as he let Poole into his messy dark studio apartment. Conor smiled enigmatically at him from a chair, and Tim Underhill, dressed in worn jeans and an old hooded sweatshirt, waved at him from another. Even in the dim light, Tim looked far more like his old self than he had in Bangkok—broader, healthier, less wasted. Shaking his hand and grinning, Tim was nothing like a criminal, nothing like a madman, nothing like the person Poole had thought he had been searching for.

"We ordered a pizza," Beevers said. "There's some left."

On the table, dark with grease, sat a curdled slice of pizza in a cardboard box.

Poole refused, and Beevers snapped the lid down over the remains and took the box into the kitchen.

Conor winked at Poole.

"Now that he's here," Beevers called from the kitchen, "does anybody want a drink?"

"Sure," Conor said.

"Coffee," said Underhill, and Poole said, "Me too."

They heard cabinet doors popping open, glasses slamming down on a counter, the refrigerator opening, ice cubes cracking from the tray. "So what the hell took you so long?" Beevers shouted. "You think we're playing a game here? I got news for you—you'd better begin to take this seriously."

Underhill grinned at Poole from his seat by the main window in Beevers' apartment. Beside him on the little table that held a telephone was a thick stack of papers.

"Writing something?" Michael asked.

Underhill nodded, and Beevers yelled again, "Sometimes I think I'm the only person here who really takes this whole project seriously."

He appeared with two short squat glasses filled with ice and a clear liquid, one of which he set down before Conor. Then he walked brusquely around Poole to get to the other side of the table, where he had evidently been sitting before Michael's arrival. "You can make your own coffee, you live here too," he said to Underhill.

Underhill immediately stood up and went into the kitchen.

"I suppose I had better fill in Dr. Poole on what we have been discussing in his absence," Harry said. He sounded grumpy and pleased with himself at the same time. "But I want to settle something first." Beevers raised his glass and squinted unpleasantly over the rim. "I don't suppose that you waited for the rest of us to leave so that you could go running back to Murphy and tell him everything you know. I don't really suppose that, Michael. Or do I?"

"Why would you?" Michael had to suppress both his surprise and the desire to laugh. Beevers had become very taut.

"You might want to destroy the work we've been doing. To get in good with Murphy. You might just think you have to become a sort of double agent in order to cover your ass."

"Double agent," Conor said.

"Keep quiet," Harry snapped. "I want to know about this, Michael."

Poole suddenly understood from the way they were looking at him that both Conor and Underhill knew that he had spent the past hour with Maggie Lah. "Of course I didn't go back to Murphy. He was busy with Maggie, anyhow."

"So what did you do?"

"I had to pick up some things for Judy."

Underhill smiled.

"I don't know why all you guys are against me," Beevers said. "I am working, night and day, on something that ought to make you all rich." Another suspicious look at Poole. "And if Judy wanted some things, I don't know why she didn't just ask Pat to bring them up to her."

"Pat's going to Westerholm?"

"This afternoon. She told me this morning. You didn't know?"

"I left in kind of a rush." Poole folded the newspaper on his lap.

Underhill brought him his cup of coffee, and Michael sipped, grateful for the interruption. He had never been in Beevers' apartment, and his curiosity at last made him take a good look at his surroundings.

His second impression, like his first, was of a mess so pervasive it could nearly be called squalor. On the table between Beevers and Conor stood a small stack of plates topped with dirty silverware. Underhill's cases and bags sat behind his chair beside a disorderly heap of newspapers and magazines. Beevers still read *Playboy* and *Penthouse*, Poole saw. What most gave the room its air of utter disorder were the videotapes that lay heaped and scattered on the floor. There were hundreds of them, in and out of their boxes, tossed on the carpet as though a small child had been playing with them. Dirty shirts, underwear, and khaki trousers lay on the far side of the grey convertible couch where Tim must have slept. To one blank space of wall had been taped a long photograph of the actress Nastassia Kinski entwined with a snake. Beside this hung two framed covers of national news magazines, each showing Lieutenant Harry Beevers' haggard face. In a little L-shaped alcove was a small bed like a child's with a pillow in a black pillowcase and black sheets visible beneath a rumpled duvet. The entire apartment smelled of pizza and unwashed laundry.

In his immaculate suits, his braces and his bow ties, Harry came back every night to this depressing sty. The one purposeful, orderly corner of the apartment, Poole saw, was the little island Underhill had made of his chair and the table with its stack of typed pages.

"I know the place is a little messy," Harry said. "What do you think happens when you put a couple of bachelors together? I'm really going to clean it up pretty soon." He looked around energetically, as if ready to begin now, but his eye stopped on Conor Linklater, who stirred uneasily.

"I'm not going to clean your apartment for you," Conor said.

"Tell him what we were talking about," Beevers said.

2

"Harry wants us to do a few things for him," Conor said, resenting the way Beevers got his kicks by ordering everybody around.

"For *me? Me*?"

"Okay, you can explain it yourself if you don't like the way I do it, Harry."

"I have my reasons."

With Beevers you never reached the end of these little games.

"Well," Conor began, "when we were just sort of shooting the breeze in here we found something out."

And there Mikey was—he heard it and he was tuned in, all of him.

"It was something I didn't tell you about, back in Bangkok. I figured I wanted to think about it myself, and then, you know, Tina got killed and we came back, and all that."

Poole nodded.

"Remember when we were talking about that place where you go—where a bunch of rich guys watch somebody kill a girl?"

"I remember."

"Well, I figured Tim was lying when he said he never went there. Because I got in by using his name. That's the reason I got in. Tim's name was like a kind of code, like a password or something."

"Exactly," Underhill said.

"So when he dodged around it on the plane, I figured he didn't want to admit he went in for this sick little death trip, you know?"

"But I had never been there," Underhill said.

"And a lot of other things. He didn't know anybody named Cham, and the Cham I met knew all about him. And he was never blackballed from all the bars and places I went to, but the guy who took me around heard that Tim Underhill had been kicked out of at least half of them."

"I thought you had a picture," Poole said.

"Well, I forgot it that day. But everybody knew his name, so I thought it must be Tim. But—"

Mikey got it right away.

"It was another man," Mike said.

"Bingo."

"Truth is," said Tim, "in Bangkok I pretty much laid low. I was busy getting myself together. Mainly I was trying to get back to work. In the two years I lived in Bangkok, I don't think I set foot in Patpong more than twice."

"So," Beevers said, unable to be silent any longer, "remember the time we went to Goodwood Park?"

"He used Tim's name."

"He always used Tim's name. Everywhere he went. Even when they were in the same city."

"Which explains why my reputation was even worse than my own efforts should have made it," Tim said. "The amazing Victor Spitalny was going around telling people he was me."

"So it's perfect that Murphy is looking for Underhill," Beevers said. "And what I have been suggesting to our friends while we were waiting for you is the next logical step. It's what we were talking about on the plane. We look for him too."

"Just the way we did in Singapore and everywhere else."

Very pleased with himself, he took a big swallow of his drink. "We do exactly what we did before. With this difference. Now we know who we're really looking for. I think we have a better chance of finding him than the police do. Where do you think he would be most at home?"

Nobody spoke.

"Where in New York City?"

Conor could not stand this anymore, and said, "Go on, tell us."

Beevers smirked. "Chinatown. I think he'd roll down to Mott Street the way a stone rolls downhill. The man has not been in this country in fifteen years! How does it look to him? Like a foreign country! It is a foreign country to him."

"You want us to go around Chinatown looking for him, like instant replay?" Conor asked. "I don't know."

"We're five yards from the end zone, Conor. Do you want to quit now?"

Poole asked if Beevers really wanted Tim Underhill to go around Chinatown looking for himself.

"I have a couple of other ideas for you and Tim. What I'm talking about isn't just walking around Chinatown talking to waiters and bartenders. That part of it I'm willing to take on myself. But do you remember my mentioning advertising? I want to put Tim's name where Koko will see it every time he goes outside. Let's surround him with it. And when he's feeling totally hemmed in, let's give him an out. And run him straight into a trap."

"A killing box," Mikey said.

"A trap. We capture him. We hear whatever he has to say. And then we turn him over to the police."

He looked around as if he expected disagreement and was prepared to face it down. "We've spent too much time and money to settle for anything less. Spitalny killed Tina Pumo. He is out there right now, trying to figure out how to kill *us*. Three of us, anyhow—he doesn't know Tim is here any more than the police do." He sipped from his drink. "Michael, I'm in the telephone book. I'm sure that by now he knows where I live. I have every reason to want this lunatic put out of the way. I don't want to spend the rest of my life wondering if a madman is going to come up behind me and cut my throat."

Sometimes Conor could almost admire Harry Beevers.

"So I'm talking about putting up flyers on windows, on lampposts, bus shelters, anywhere he might notice them. And I worked out a couple of ads for the *Village Voice*. It's an outside chance, but one worth taking. And there's another idea Tim was interested in—I'd like you to consider this seriously, Michael. You two could go out to Milwaukee to see Spitalny's parents and his old girlfriends or his what have you. You might be able to learn something crucial out there. It's not impossible that he has written, called them, something. Anything!"

Beevers' eyes shone with his satisfaction in this scheme.

For one thing, it got Tim Underhill out of his hair for a couple of days. Beevers had already asked Conor if he wanted to go to Milwaukee too, but he had refused. Ben Roehm needed a second carpenter for a small renovation job, and he had told Conor that Tom Woyzak "wasn't a problem anymore." His niece Ellen had filed for divorce in December. Woyzak had beaten her up once too often, and was now in a drug and alcohol treatment center.

Mikey surprised Conor by saying, "I've been thinking along those lines myself. Do you want to give it a try, Tim?"

"It could be interesting," Underhill said.

"Tell me what you think of the newspaper ads first." Beevers handed Poole the sheet of paper on which he had printed the messages for the back page of the *Voice*:

TIM UNDERHILL—END THE WAR AND COME HOME. CALL HARRY BEEVERS 555-0033.

UNDERHILL—THE GRUNT CAN STOP RUNNING. 555-0033.

"And here's one of the flyers I had run off." Beevers stood up and removed the top sheet from a stack of papers on a bookshelf above his head. "I had three hundred of these made up at a print shop around the corner. I can put one on every lamppost—he'll see it, don't worry about that."

On the flyer's yellow paper was a message in large black letters:

TIM UNDERHILL
YOU WHO WERE AT IA THUC
AND LAST SEEN IN BANGKOK
COME HOME
WE WHO KNOW YOUR REAL NAME
NEED YOUR NOBILITY
AND PATIENCE NOW
CALL THE LIEUTENANT
555-0033

3

Mike Poole nodded at the flyer, said something agreeable, and put it down.

"Think it'll work?" Conor asked him.

"It might," Poole said. He looked only half awake.

Conor wondered what had happened between Mike and Judy since Tina's funeral, but he didn't really have to know the particulars to know that it was coming apart. Back in Washington those few months ago, he would never have seen these signs or put them together in this way. Back in Washington, the only loser in a club of successful men, self-pity had made him drink himself into a stupor. He looked at the glass in his hand and carefully set it down on the table. There was no need for it now. He hoped Mikey would come out of it all right, would *do* something. Doing something was pretty much the only way out of a situation like Mike's. It almost didn't matter what you did.

For a moment Conor considered the idea of inviting Mike to stay with him in South Norwalk and trying to get a job as a kind of unpaid assistant to Ben Roehm—banging on nails and carrying sheetrock would be great therapy. But that was as impossible as it would be for him to go on hospital rounds alongside Mike. Anyhow, Conor hoped that Mike would go along with Beevers' plan and spend a day or two out in the Midwest looking for Spitalny's tracks. Anything he did would help him.

"As of now," Beevers was saying, "this is my full-time job. Once the ads run and the flyers are up, I'm staying here to man the phone. Tim can go to Milwaukee—I think that's an essential part of our strategy. The three of you should get going on that as soon as possible, and I'm the logical man to stay here."

"You're planning to tell us when anything happens, aren't you, Boss?" Conor asked.

"Absolutely." Beevers put one hand over his face and shook his head. Then he pointed at Mike with his glass. "What did *he* do? Ask yourself that. Did he call me right after he found Tim?" He turned to Underhill. "Did he even give me a chance to talk to you? When you guys ask questions, make sure you're asking the right person."

"I arranged things so that we could all arrive back in America as quickly as possible," Mike said. "I'm sorry that you feel cheated of something."

"Sometimes I wonder what would have happened if you had seen me first, instead of Michael," Tim said.

"The same thing would have happened," Harry said. His face had turned a hot, unpleasant shade of red. "I'm just making a point, that's all. Don't get paranoid."

When Mikey decided that he'd had enough and stood up to go, Conor got up too.

"We'll do some of the flyers this afternoon," Beevers said. His voice was tight and unhappy. "You guys get to go back to fresh air and clean streets, but there's work to do here. I'll let you know if anything happens, but I think he'll chew on it for a week or so before he makes his move."

"And I'll arrange tickets to Milwaukee," Poole said. "We'll go as soon as I can get away."

Conor hated to leave Tim Underhill in that apartment.

They went outside into air that seemed surprisingly springlike, and the warmth of the day as well as what he had been thinking prompted Conor to risk making a fool of himself. "Look, I don't know why I should say this, Mikey, but if you need a place to stay or anything, just give me a call, you know? You can always stay with me if you need a place."

Mike didn't laugh at him—he stuck out his hand and gave him a good handshake. "Why don't you come along on this trip to Milwaukee?"

"Bread, you know," Conor said. "Gotta get that bread. I wish I could, though. But really . . . this whole thing . . . don't you think it's time to hang it up and tell everything to that cop? We're just following Beevers around, and that's no good, man."

"It'll only be a couple more days, Conor. I'm in a funny period anyhow, and this gives me something to do."

Conor nodded, wishing he knew what to say or the way to say it, and they parted. After a few steps toward the subway, Conor turned around and watched Mikey walking in the sunlight toward Ninth Avenue. He wondered if he knew where he was going, or if he was really going anywhere at all, and for a second felt like rushing after him.

4

Poole realized that he could walk to the garage on University Place. It would be an enjoyable way to delay his arrival back in Westerholm, a free zone given him by the unseasonal weather. Right now a free zone seemed welcome.

He crossed Ninth Avenue and turned right toward 23rd Street. It occurred to him that he could walk down through the Village, cross Houston Street, and go to SoHo. Maggie Lah was probably still at Saigon. It would be interesting to see what she and Vinh were doing with the restaurant. Poole decided against doing this, but wondered if Maggie would be interested in going to Milwaukee with Underhill and himself. She might be able to identify Spitalny from photographs at his parents' house. A positive identification from Maggie would be helpful when they made their case to the police. His thoughts drifted along pleasantly as he walked down Ninth Avenue toward Greenwich Village.

5

Maggie, in the meantime, had decided in the middle of a conversation to tell Vinh that the writer Timothy Underhill, Tina's friend in Vietnam, had secretly come back to America and was now staying in Harry Beevers' apartment. As far as Maggie was concerned, this information was another proof of Beevers' instability. She knew that Vinh detested Beevers, and assumed that he would feel as she did about his attempting to continue his private efforts to find the man who had murdered Tina. She also knew that Vinh could be trusted with any secret told him. But his response startled her—he stared at her for a long time, then asked her to repeat what she had just said. All the rest of the afternoon he worked in silence, and around five o'clock, just before Maggie left, said, "I must call him," and put down his blueprints and went to the telephone in the kitchen.

6

Michael rolled up his windows, put into the tape deck a cassette of Murray Perahia playing Mozart piano concertos, and rolled out onto University Place. Music of great delicacy and melancholy began to come through the speakers. It was the wrong music. Michael ejected the tape, put it back in its case, opened another, and fed it to the machine. The first bars of *Don Giovanni* filled the car. The opera would get him home.

On the expressway into Westchester County he remembered the *Babar* books in his trunk—why had he put them there?

Because he wanted to have them with him if he did not go back to Westerholm. He had not wanted to lose them, and if Judy found them she would throw them out.

But an hour later here he was, home again, the good Dr. Poole, turning off at the Westerholm exit, winding in his little car through streets without signs or lights and lined with hedges, beneath branches that would soon begin to bud, across Westerholm's Main Street with its branches of Laura Ashley and Baskin Robbins, the garage where the proprietor "dialogued" with you about scientology while he filled your tank, then past the General Washington Inn and the duck pond, "O misery misery, *Lascia le donne? Pazzo!*" Don Giovanni bawled, "Leave women alone? You're mad—why I need them more than the bread I eat, than the air I breathe." On impulse Michael did not turn into his street but kept on going until he had come to the site of Sam Stein's new medical center.

A large sign announcing WESTERHOLM MEDICAL CENTER in tasteful, almost unreadable green on brown stood before a large lot. Behind the lot was a nature preserve. As soon as spring came, this lot would be filled with bulldozers and excavators. This was the future kingdom of Dr. Sam Stein.

Michael got back into his car and drove home. He had lost track of what was going on in *Don Giovanni*, and the big voices boomed and cajoled, fighting for air and space. He turned into his driveway, and the gravel crunched beneath his tires. This was home, he was safe. Zerlina sang, "In happiness and joy let's pass our days and nights." Like a magic light that could pass through stone, brick, lead, wood, and skin, music streamed through the world, on its way to somewhere else. Michael drew up before his garage and switched off the engine. The tape cut off and leaped noisily up into the slot. Michael picked up the novel beside him and got out of the car. For a moment he saw his wife and Pat Caldwell looking at him from the living room window. They broke apart as he began to walk toward the front door.

31

ENCOUNTERS

1

"The thing is, I like her," Conor said. "I can hardly believe I'm saying this, but I not only like her, I think about her a lot. You know what she told me? She said she likes the way I talk."

"No kids?" Poole asked.

"Thank God, no. This Woyzak guy never wanted 'em. Kids drove him crazy. But this Woyzak guy, everything drove him crazy. Didn't I ever tell you about him?"

Poole shook his head, and Conor ordered another round of drinks and began describing how he had been reminded of Victor Spitalny as soon as he had met Tom Woyzak. They were in Donovan's on the Friday night following Michael's return from New York on Monday. On Tuesday night Michael had brought a jumble of clothes in a suitcase to Conor's apartment. Every day he drove to his office, where he saw patients and tried to settle his affairs before returning to South Norwalk.

"What I mean is, nothing really ever disappears. We should have known it'd turn out to be Spitalny. He was *there*. He was there in everything." Conor's eyes were shining with uncharacteristic inspiration. "We even talked about him in Washington, remember?"

"I remember. But Beevers was so positive. And I guess I thought Spitalny was dead. I certainly couldn't see him calling himself Koko and going out and murdering a bunch of people."

Conor nodded. "Well, at least now we're that far ahead. Beevers says he didn't get any responses to his ads yet."

Poole too had spoken to Beevers, who had spent ten minutes complaining about the way Tim Underhill had deserted him.

"He's all pissed off at us, man."

"He's pissed off at everybody."

"I didn't know about Vinh, though."

"I guess *we* didn't know *Vinh*."

Beevers was still furious that Poole had told Maggie Lah about Underhill, for Maggie had told Vinh.

"So what are they doing?" Conor asked. "Are Underhill and Vinh and Vinh's kid all living in the restaurant?"

"I don't think so. I think Vinh and his daughter live with relatives. I guess Underhill used to help Vinh's family, back in the old days, and Vinh is repaying the favor."

"I hope your thing works out all right, man," Conor said.

As soon as Michael had seen Pat Caldwell standing beside Judy in his window, he had known that his marriage had reached its final stages. Judy had hardly been able to speak to him, and had soon retreated to her bedroom. Pat, grimacing with the difficulty of her position and managing by her very sympathy to suggest that she would speak privately with him later, had said that Judy felt hurt and betrayed by something that had happened between them. She no longer wanted to stay alone in the house with him. Pat was there to supply moral courage and womanly support—and to be witness to what Judy perceived as her humiliation.

"Of course you can tell me to get out, and if you do I'll go," Pat said. "I have only the most general idea of what this is all about, Michael. I like both of you. Judy asked me to come here, and so I did."

Michael had spent the night on the couch in his little office downstairs, Pat in the guestroom; when Judy had told him that she would never be able to forgive him for the way he had treated her—a statement she appeared to believe—Michael had moved out to the George Washington, which had a few rooms it let out to boyfriends and grandparents. The following night he had gone to Conor's. Now he spent hours each day talking to Max Atlas, his lawyer, who had visible difficulty keeping himself from showing that he thought his client had lost his mind. Max Atlas never smiled anyhow, his big fleshy face naturally expressed gloom and doubt, but during the hours Michael spent with him his dewlaps sagged and even his ears seemed to droop. It was not Michael's marital difficulties that depressed him, but that a client of his should voluntarily leave a business just before it began to mint money.

"She came to the job one day," Conor was saying. "In a Blazer. The Blazer was beautiful, man. I saw her get out, and she looked good. The woman looked real good, let's face it. In spite of the fact you could see that she was down on account of her old man being put away. Ben Roehm hauls me out from where I'm working and says, 'Well, Conor, I guess you ought to meet my niece Ellen.' Right away I think I don't have a chance with this woman. But it turns out that her father was a carpenter, her grandfather was a capenter, Ben Roehm is her uncle, and even her husband, who was bughouse ever since he came back from the war, was a sort of a half-assed carpenter. Guess what she likes?"

"I think I got it," Michael said.

"No—guess what she likes to do?"

"The same things you do," Poole said.

An expression of blissful amazement spread across Conor's face. "She likes sitting around the apartment and talking. She likes coming in here to the bar and having a drink. We have great times. She claims she gets a big kick out of me. She wants to have a little house up in Vermont. She wants to have a man to hang out with. She wants kids. That asshole wouldn't let her have kids, which was really okay seeing what a rat in the grass he turned out to be. I'd like to have kids, Mikey, I really would. You get tired of living by yourself."

"How many times have you gone out with Ellen?"

"Fourteen and a half times. Once we just had time for a couple of beers before her parents took her out. They're concerned about her." He revolved his beer glass on the bar. "Ellen gets a little money from Ben Roehm, but she's about as strapped as I am."

"I ought to get out of your way," Poole said. "You

don't want me sleeping in your place, Conor. You should have told me when I called you. I can go somewhere else."

"No, her mother's down with something, and Ellen's taking care of her. So we wouldn't be together anyhow, for a couple days. And besides, I wanted to tell you about her." Conor looked away for a moment. "But I was wondering when you were planning to make that trip to Milwaukee. Her mother is getting up and around a little more these days."

"I could do it the day after tomorrow," Poole said, laughing. "I have to go to another funeral. That patient of mine I told you about."

"Mikey, would you mind if I, if I, you know . . ."

"Of course not."

"You'll like her," Conor said, and slid off the stool to go to the pay phones.

Ten minutes later he returned with a big grin on his face. "She'll be here in fifteen minutes." He kept on grinning. "It's a funny thing. I feel like I'm joining up with the world again—like I was floating around in space, and I finally came back to earth. It took a long time, man."

"Yes," Poole said.

"That whole time we were on that trip, when I look back, it was like I wasn't really *there.* Everything was like swimming underwater with your eyes open. It was like I was in a dream and nothing was real. I was a human blur. And now I'm not anymore."

Conor gulped down his beer and set the glass on the bar. "Did I say that right?"

"I'm like Ellen," Poole said. "I like listening to you talk."

2

A little while later Poole too went to the telephone, thinking that it was not so very different for him. During their time in Singapore and Bangkok, everything had seemed very sharp and clear—he had been reminded of what it had been like in Vietnam. But in a short time everything had switched around. Singapore and Bangkok felt like peacetime, and what was around him now felt like Victnam. Another version of Elvis was following them. Like Conor, Poole had not thought that he was asleep and dreaming when he had walked through the Tiger Balm Gardens and Bugis Street; but maybe his first moment of real awakening had come on the rickety bridge beside the cardboard shacks. That was where he had started to give things up.

He dropped in coins and dialed his wife's number. He expected to hear her message, but someone lifted the receiver after the first ring.

Silence.

"Hello, who is this?" he asked.

"Who is *this*?" asked a strange female voice.

Then he knew who it was. "Hello, Pat. This is Michael. I'd like to speak to Judy."

"I'll do what I can."

"Please." Poole waited for long minutes while he watched Conor look at the door whenever someone walked in. He would have to leave Conor's apartment and check into a hotel that night—it was not fair to keep him from his girlfriend.

Pat's mild voice came back on the line. "She won't, Michael. I'm sorry. She just won't talk to you."

"Try again. Please."

"One more try," she said.

This time Judy came to the telephone almost immediately.

"Don't you think we ought to get together and talk about things?"

"I'm not under the impression we have anything to talk about," Judy said.

"We have a lot to talk about. Do you really want the lawyers to take over?"

"Just stay away from here," Judy said. "I don't want to see you, I don't want you sleeping on the couch, and I don't want to talk to you now."

It was all a game—sooner or later Judy would want everything back the way it used to be. For now she wanted him to suffer. He had kept her from doing something she had been pretending with all her heart to want to do.

"Have it your way," he said, but she had already hung up.

Poole wandered back to the bar. Conor took one look at him and said, "Hey man, Ellen and me can always stay at her place, you know. The only reason we use mine is that she lives over in Bethel and it'd take me a little longer to get to work, but the real main reason is that Woyzak's got all his stuff all over the walls, pictures of himself in uniform and a bunch of medals all framed, everywhere you look there's Tom Woyzak sighting down on you. It gets to you after a while."

Poole excused himself and went back to the telephone. By now the bar was full of people, and he could barely hear the mechanical voice instructing him in the use of his credit card.

A man answered, asked for his name, and said that he would bring Maggie to the telephone. He sounded very paternal.

In a moment Maggie was on the line. "Well, well, Dr. Poole. How did you know I wanted to talk to you?"

"I have an idea that might be interesting to you."

"Sounds interesting already," she said.

"Has Tim Underhill mentioned our trip to Milwaukee to you?"

He had not.

"It hasn't been too definite yet. We're going to look up Victor Spitalny's parents and spend a little time seeing if we can pick up some new information on him. He might have sent a postcard, there might be someone who's heard something—it's a long shot, but it's worth trying."

"And?"

"And I thought that maybe you should come along. You might be able to identify Spitalny from a photograph. And you're a part of what's going on. You're already involved."

"When will you be going?"

Michael said that he would book tickets that night for Sunday, and that he expected to be gone only a couple of days.

"We're opening the restaurant in a week."

"It might only take a day or two. We might find out that it's just a cold trail."

"So why should I come along?"

"I'd like you to," Michael said.

"Then I will. Call me back with the flight times, and I'll meet you at the airport. I'll give you a check for my ticket."

Michael hung up smiling.

He turned to face the bar and saw Conor standing face to face with a woman who was perhaps an inch taller than he. She had long, unruly brown hair and wore a plaid shirt, a tan sleeveless down jacket, and tight faded jeans. Conor nodded in his direction, and the woman turned to watch him approach them. She had a high, deeply lined forehead, firm eyebrows, and a strong intelligent face. She was not at all what Michael had expected.

"This is the guy I was telling you about," Conor said. "Dr. Michael Poole, known as Mike. This is Ellen."

"Hello, Dr. Poole." She gripped his hand in hers.

"I hope you'll call me Michael," he said. "I've been hearing about you too, and I'm glad to meet you."

"I had to get away for a little while so I could check up on my sweetie," Ellen said.

"If you guys ever have babies, you'd better ask me to be their doctor," Poole said, and for a time they all stood in the noisy bar grinning at each other.

3

When Michael slid into the last pew at St. Robert's on the village square the service had already begun. Two pews near the front had been filled with children who must have been Stacy's classmates. All of them looked taller, older, and at once more worldly and more innocent than she. Stacy's parents, William and Mary, "like the college," they said to those who met them for the first time, sat with a small group of relatives on the other side of the church. William turned around and gave Michael a grateful glance as he sat down. Light streamed in through the stained glass windows on both sides of the church. Michael felt like a ghost—he felt as if bit by bit he were becoming invisible, sitting in the bright optimistic church as an Episcopalian priest uttered heartfelt commonplaces about death.

He and the Talbots met at the church door at the end of the service. William Talbot was a beefy good-hearted man who had made a fortune with various investment banking firms. "I'm happy you came, Michael."

"We heard you're leaving your practice." There was a question in Mary Talbot's statement, and Michael thought he heard a criticism too. In the world of Westerholm, doctors were not supposed to leave their posts until they retired or dropped dead.

"I'm thinking about it."

"Are you coming out to Memorial Park?"

Mary Talbot had begun to look oddly worried and doubtful.

"Of course," Michael said.

There were two cemeteries in Westerholm, located at opposite ends of the town. The older of the two, Burr Grove, had filled up shortly before World War II, and was a leafy, hilly, shady place with rows of pitted old eighteenth-century tombstones. Burr Grove was known locally as "the graveyard." Memorial Park, a straightforward modern cemetery, occupied a long level field bordered by woods near the expressway on the north end of town. It was neat, very well tended, and without charm or character of any kind. In Memorial Park there were no tilting tombstones, no statuary of angels of dogs or wailing women with dripping hair, no stone bungalows testifying to the fortunes of merchant families—only straight rows of small white headstones and long, level stretches of unbroken ground.

Stacy Talbot's grave lay at the far end of the occupied section. The mounds of excavated earth had been covered with strips of imitation grass of an unearthly, chemical green. The young priest from St. Robert's stood beneath a canopy and performed with what looked to Poole like fussy satisfaction in his own elegance. The schoolchildren, presumably considered too young for an actual burial, were not present. William and Mary Talbot stood with bowed heads among their relatives and neighbors. Poole knew better than half of the crowd of neighbors, who appeared more numerous outside in the cemetery than inside St. Robert's. They were parents of his patients, some of them his own neighbors. Poole stood a little distance away from these people. He had really only been a doctor here: none of these people were his friends. Judy had been too busy and too anxious to invite people to their house; she had been secretly scornful of their lives and their ambitions. During the service Poole saw a few of them notice him—a little outburst of whispers, a few glances and smiles.

Because this was a child's burial, Poole found himself

remembering Robbie's. He felt drained by too much recent grief: an era, in many ways the calmest and most productive of his life, seemed to be sliding into the ground with Stacy Talbot's coffin. His heart ached for William and Mary Talbot, who had no other children and whose daughter had been so bright and brave. For an instant this grief pierced him like an arrow, and Stacy Talbot's death was an abyss—a monster had taken her, whittled at her body, killed her inch by inch. Poole wished he had someone to hold, someone with whom he could cry, but he stood at the edge of the mourners and cried by himself.

It was over soon, and the people who had known Stacy turned away toward their cars. William Talbot came up to Michael and put his arms around him and then backed away, too moved to speak. Mary Talbot put her patrician face beside his and embraced him. "Oh, I miss her," Michael said. "Thank you," Mary Talbot whispered.

Into the darkness, Poole thought, for the moment forgetting where he had seen or heard the phrase.

Poole said good-bye to the Talbots and turned away to walk deeper into the cemetery on one of the narrow paths that ran between the neat rows of stones.

In other years he had come here every week. Judy had come with him twice, then ceased to come—she said the visits were morbid. Maybe it was morbid: Poole did not care, because they were necessary. Eventually they had ceased to be so necessary. His last visit had been the day before he had gone to Washington to meet Beevers, Conor, and Tina.

Behind him he heard the slamming of car doors as Stacy Talbot's mourners began to leave.

Poole wished that Tim Underhill was beside him—his was the company he most wanted now. Underhill could make sense of what was happening, he could do justice to sorrow. Poole felt that he had gone through the funeral in an unfeeling daze from which he had awakened at only the last possible minute. Poole left the path and began to walk a narrow invisible line between individual graves in the direction of the woods that bordered the cemetery.

Into the darkness, Poole thought again, and then remembered the dream of the boy, the rabbit, and the cold grey rushing river.

A wave of dizziness went through him, and the air

went very dark, then very light before the dizziness left him.

The scent of strong sunlight and massed flowers had suddenly filled the cooling air, a scent so powerful and beautiful that it nearly lifted Poole off the ground, and in another quick white dazzle of light Poole saw a man who must have been six and a half feet tall standing between himself and Robbie's grave. The man was smiling at him. He had curly light brown hair and was a slim muscular man who looked as though he could move very quickly. Poole felt an instantaneous love for this man, and then realized that this was not a man at all. Time had stopped. Poole and the being were encased in a bubble of silence, and the being moved gracefully to one side to allow Poole the sight of Robbie's headstone . . .

. . . and a car door slammed, and a few quiet voices murmured back at Stacy's gravesite, and a tribe of sparrows wheeled over his head and settled onto the ground for an instant only before shooting off again toward the woods. Poole still felt light-headed, and his eyes hurt. He stepped forward again and found himself wrapped in the last traces of a strong clear scent of sunshine and flowers. The being was gone.

There was Robbie's white stone before him: Robbie's full name, which now seemed so formal, Robbie's dates.

The unearthly odor was gone, but it seemed to Poole that as if in compensation all the natural earthly odors around him had doubled or tripled in intensity. He was inundated with the odors of the grass, the life and freshness of the soil, the fragrance of roses in one of the cemetery's vases beside the next headstone, ALICE ALISON LEAF 1952–1978, even the clean strong slightly dusty smell of the gravel on the cemetery paths, the colors of all things about him boomed and snapped and sizzled. For a moment the world had split open like a peach to reveal an overpowering sweetness and goodness.

Who had appeared before him? What? A god?

The charged radiance was slipping away. Poole felt the priest's eyes on him, and he turned around and found himself looking at an indifferent landscape. The last cars had nearly reached the cemetery gates, and only his Audi and the hearse were still drawn up on the narrow drive. The funeral director and one of his assistants busily dismantled the electronic scaffold that had lowered Stacy's coffin. Two men in green pants and donkey jackets, cemetery employees, lifted the grassy carpet off the mounds of raw earth and made ready to fill the grave. A yellow earth-moving machine had appeared from behind a screen of bushes. Poole felt as if he had just passed through some kind of extraordinary psychic bubble that still had the power to invest these homely activities with its ebbing power, as if what Poole saw before him were only the visible traces of a great glory.

Certain that he was still being watched, Poole turned around again and sensed more than saw a quick, surprised movement at the edge of the woods. He looked up toward it just in time to see a shadowy figure melting back between the trees. Poole's whole body felt a jolt. He was about thirty yards from the edge of the woods. The extraordinary feeling of well-being that had surrounded him until a few seconds ago completely vanished into its own afterglow. Whatever had withdrawn into the trees seemed to vanish back even further, flickering between the trunks of trees. Poole stepped forward between his son's grave and Alice Alison Leaf's.

This time Michael knew that he had seen Koko. Koko had somehow followed him to the cemetery, which meant that he had followed him to Conor's apartment.

Poole walked between the graves until he reached the empty part of the graveyard and then walked over brown winter grass toward the trees. Far back in the darkness of the woods he thought he could see a still pale figure watching him from beside a tree. "Come on out!" Poole yelled. The figure far back in the woods did not move.

"Come on out and talk to me!" Poole shouted.

He heard the funeral director and the cemetery workmen stop whatever they were doing to look at him.

The figure in the woods wavered like a match flame. Poole moved closer to the first bare trees, and the figure disappeared backward to flicker out behind a massive trunk deep in the woods. "Come out here!" Poole yelled.

"You okay?" a voice called out, and Poole turned around to see a man as heavy as a professional wrestler standing on the bulldozer, his hands cupped around his mouth.

Poole waved him off and began to trot toward the woods. The figure had disappeared. The woods, of heavily overgrown birch, oak, and maple, home to several families of foxes and raccoons, ran for another fifty yards down into a ravine and up over a crest, and down to the expressway.

A dim shape, dark now instead of pale, moved like a deer between two oaks.

Poole yelled for him to stop and passed between the first of the trees. Ahead of him was a low bristling tangle of brush, the grey diagonal line of a dead toppled ash tree, the rough accidental suggestion of a path that led around the tangle of brush, beneath the toppled ash, and on between the trees until it split apart into a hundred narrow byways of fallen leaves and spangles of light. The little shadow was inching almost provocatively backward toward the ravine, coaxing him forward.

Poole glanced again over his shoulder and saw all four men around Stacy's grave, including the beefy gravedigger on the bulldozer, staring at him.

He ran around the dry tangle of brush, thinking that a god standing by his son's grave had beckoned him forward, ducked to pass beneath the slanting line of the fallen ash, and saw a silver wire thin as a strand from a spiderweb gleaming up at him above the pulpy leaves and twigs on the floor of the forest. If he had been running normally he would never have seen it. Instincts he did not know he still had almost literally kicked into place, and as his right ankle moved forward to trip the wire, Poole sprang forward, lifting both feet off the ground, and sailed over the wire without touching it. For a moment that lasted long enough for him to feel proud of himself his whole body stretched out in the air parallel to the ground; then he thudded into the ground with a jolt that rattled all his bones. He pulled up his knees and kneaded his shoulder, greasy with leaf mold.

Poole got up, rubbing his shoulder, and trotted a few steps deeper into the woods. Spitalny appeared briefly in a vertical mesh of birch trunks, then vanished again. Michael knew he could not catch him. By the time he got halfway down into the ravine, Spitalny could be in a car and a couple of miles south.

Michael took another step forward, scanning the ground for indications of work. Tripwire usually meant mines or homemade explosives. Even a madman like Victor Spitalny could probably buy explosives in New York, once he had learned where to look. He wouldn't be able to find any bouncing bettys or cluster bombs any more than he could find a LAW anti-tank rocket, but probably all sorts of automatic and semi-automatic weapons, plastic explosives, and grenades were for sale in underground weapons markets. Maybe crates of old M-14 plastic mines went up on the block.

Poole moved cautiously through the leaf mold, placing feet carefully, examining every inch of the ground before him. He moved forward another step, then another, feeling the earth yield beneath the soles of his shoes.

The flat, cynical laughter of a raven jeered at him from overhead. Poole looked up into the thick dark weave of branches. Sunlight penetrated about halfway down, then split and fractured to pick out a squirrel's nest and a huge hairy black bole like a tumor. He continued to walk slowly toward the ravine. Wherever they were, Koko would rig his booby traps well, and they would stay in place, still armed, until they were tripped. Spitalny had been soldier enough for that. Poole wanted to find what he had set up and disarm it before some child went running through the woods.

Some little boy.

Poole shook his head, then made himself move forward, one step at a time, mapping every inch of territory in his head. Ahead of him something gleamed on the trunk of a slender maple: it caught his eye, and he heard voices calling out. He turned to see five men—the gravediggers, the undertaker and his assistant, and one other man in a grey coat and dark tie—standing in the sunlight at the edge of the woods on the dead grass of the unused section of the cemetery.

"Keep out!" he yelled, and motioned them back.

The man in the grey coat raised his hands to his mouth, and Poole heard him shout something that included the word trespassing.

". . . police!" the man yelled.

Poole waved, and looked ahead of him again. He had nearly reached the ravine. If Spitalny had planted more booby traps, he thought he would have seen them.

"I'm coming," he shouted back to the men, who huddled closer to one another, having probably heard him no better than he had heard them. The man in the grey coat was pointing at Poole, yelling again.

". . . out now . . . police . . ."

"Don't move!" Poole shouted. "I'll be out in a second. *Stay there!*" He waved and tried to find what he had seen a moment before. It had been something incongruous: a flash of color? He scanned a rank of trees and saw nothing but a squirrel circling around the trunk of an oak. Beyond the squirrel's head, grey brush reared up in the ravine. Spitalny had cut through that impenetrable-looking stuff in something like forty seconds—he was a better jungle fighter now than he had been in Vietnam. Michael shifted his eyes and saw it at last, a white rectangle on a maple's thin dark trunk.

For a moment it looked like a scrap of white fur pinned to the bark; then he saw that what was pinned to the tree was a playing card.

He gave a flapping wave of his hand to the men at the edge of the woods and yelled, "Don't come in! Danger!"

He hoped they heard him. "Danger!" he yelled one more time, waving his arms over his head in and out of an X, and walked backwards, still semaphoring, until he sensed he was near the maple tree with the playing card attached to its trunk.

The tree stood perhaps a yard behind him, slightly off to his right.

Warning signals went off all through his body. If Koko had rigged another booby trap, this was where it would be. He gave the men another semaphore and carefully inspected the ground around his feet. This close to the ravine, the earth seemed softer and damper.

"Come out . . . out . . ." came to him.

"Wait!" Poole bawled, inspecting the earth that lay between his feet and the maple tree. No silver wires glinted in the grey-green leaf mulch, no indentations or depressions cut through the patchwork surface of the ground. Grey leaves lay on top of green leaves on top of red leaves on top of silver leaves. Each leaf fitted smoothly into its part of the jigsaw puzzle, all the colors exposed to the sun and rain were uniformly weathered, there were no sharp lines of demarcation where a busy hand slid some long-hidden maple leaf out from under the others as it worked away, concealing the marks of its passage the way a broom would sweep away footprints in sand . . . the way, it occurred to him, some unseen hand had concealed the work done by Harry Beevers in that stone egg underneath the earth.

Some little boy.

Poole stepped onto the multi-colored patchwork of moldering leaves. His foot came down onto the smooth mulch of leaves he had so carefully inspected, and—

—kept on going, breaking through the constructed surface and kept going down, past the ankle past the knee in a flash, and then his whole body had become unbalanced and he was helplessly falling forward into the deep hole uncovered by the shredding leaves, he threw his arms out too late and saw before him the long spears pointing up at his chest, his neck, his groin—

—and the ground held his weight, yielding only that springy half-inch.

". . . AN ORDER!" a man yelled.

Poole saw nothing on the card at first. It was an Ace of Hearts. Then he saw faint slanting pencil lines on the white of the card between the heart in its center and the top left center.

He moved a step forward and put his face right up before the card. The faint markings resolved into words. Poole read the words, then breathed in and read them again. He exhaled. Very delicately he raised his hand to the card and touched its smooth surface. It had been affixed to the tree with a tiny pin like those that come in a new shirt. Michael tugged the pin out of the tree as he held the edges of the card. He looked at the words on the card again, then dropped the pin in his pocket. He turned the card over. On its back was the image in black and white of a plump bare-chested little boy with round eyes and curly hair holding out a basket overflowing with lavish orchids.

4

This was the message left for him on an Orchid Boy playing card:

I HAVE NO NAME I AM ESTERHAZ
DYING IS BEFORE LIFE ETERNAL
BACKWARDS AND FORWARDS

5

Holding the card by its edges, Michael slipped it into his coat pocket and began walking out of the woods. He yelled to the men that he was coming out, but the man in the grey coat had become very excited. As Poole moved toward him, still checking the ground for tripwires and signs of disturbance, the cemetery official gripped the sleeve of the taller of his two employees and beat the air with his other arm. Poole could hear only muffled waves of sound. He waved to show that he was coming out, there was nothing to worry about, he was unarmed and a good citizen, nothing to get excited about. The man in the grey suit was paying no attention to him now. A younger man in a dark coat with square padded shoulders whom Poole recognized as the undertaker's assistant moved up beside his boss, who appeared uneasy and even slightly embarrassed by the other man's agitation. Michael took another step forward, realizing that he had to give the playing card in his pocket to the police, and was suddenly stopped cold.

He had caught the smell of the god again, that wonderful clean fragrance of sunshine and massed flowers. Here it was even stronger than it had been beside Robbie's grave. But the air did not darken and there were no trembling flashes of light. The god smell was natural, not supernatural. A slight meandering breeze took it away, then brought it to him again. Then Poole saw a rank of lolling blue and white wildflowers off to his left and knew that they were the source of the magical scent. They had bloomed in the sudden good weather and had somehow survived the fall in temperature. He could not identify the flowers, which were as tall as tulips, with wide blue blossoms striped white toward the center. They grew before a group of oak trees, and their sturdy green stalks protruded like spears up out of the leaf mold. The powerful scent came to him again.

When he looked forward, the man in the grey topcoat was leveling his index finger at him.

". . . want that man out of there right now, Watkins," Poole heard.

Watkins took a slow step forward, and the cemetery official shoved him in the small of his back.

"Get a move on!"

Watkins began to half-stumble, half-trot toward Poole. He was shading his eyes to see into the woods, and Poole knew that his form must have been flickering in and out of sight, like Koko's a few minutes earlier. Watkins' arms pumped, and his big belly heaved. The pale blob of his face looked set and unhappy.

"Nothing's wrong!" Poole yelled, holding out his hand.

Watkins moved to run in on the same wandering path Poole had taken. He ducked to pass beneath the dark slanting line of the dead ash tree.

"Stop!" Poole yelled.

The man in the grey coat stepped forward as if he were going to chase after Poole himself, and Watkins took another heavy, lumbering step into the shade, and toppled over out of sight.

Poole heard him thud into the ground. He began to run toward him. Watkins' big fuzzy head showed above a tangle of crisp vines, and his face turned toward Poole and showed a round O of mouth. Then the O began to emit ragged screams.

"Shut up," said his boss.

"He cut me!"

"What the hell are you talking about?"

Watkins held up a hand streaming with blood. "Look, Mr. Del Barca!"

Del Barca squared off in front of Poole and pointed his index finger at him again. "Stop right there," he said. "I'm having you arrested. You were trespassing on private cemetery grounds, and you injured my employee here."

"Calm down," Poole said.

"I demand to know what you were doing back there."

"I was trying to find the man who strung up this booby trap." Poole moved over the last bit of ground between himself and the fallen man. Watkins lay on his side with his left leg out before him. He was red in the face, and his fuzzy hair was matted with sweat. A widening blurry line of blood had already soaked through his left trouser leg.

"What booby trap?" Del Barca asked.

"Just relax," Poole said. "I'm a doctor, and this man needs my help. He ran into a wire, and it did some damage to his leg."

"What goddamned *wire*?" Del Barca yelled. "What the hell are you talking about?"

Poole bent down and ran his hand over the ground four or five inches behind Watkins. There was the wire, shiny and taut. It looked very much like razor wire. He lightly touched it. "You're lucky it didn't cut his leg off. Did you hear me telling him to stop?"

"You telling him?" Del Barca shouted. "Whose fault is this?"

"Yours, for one. Suppose you see what this line is connected to at either end. If it's anything but a rock or a tree trunk, leave it alone."

"Check it out," Del Barca told his other employee, a younger man with the face of a moustached gerbil.

"Don't touch anything."

Poole knelt beside the man and gently urged him to lie flat on the ground. "You're going to need stitches," he said, "but we'll see how bad the damage is."

"You better be a real doctor, buddy," Del Barca said.

"John. John," the undertaker said in a soft, urgent voice. "I know him."

Poole hooked his fingers into the cut in the fabric and ripped. A big bloody flap of cloth came away in his hand. "That line might still be hooked up to explosives," he said to the young man with the gerbil's face. The young man jerked his hand away from the wire as if he had been scalded. There was a deep gash in Watkins' leg from which blood pulsed out at a slow steady rate. "You need St. Bart's emergency ward," he said, and looked up at Del Barca. "Give me your necktie."

"My what?"

"Your tie. Do you want this man to bleed to death?"

La Barca resentfully untied his necktie and handed it to Poole. He turned to the undertaker. "All right, who is he?"

"I don't remember his name, but he's a doctor, all right."

"My name is Dr. Michael Poole." He wound Del Barca's Countess Mara necktie three times around Watkins' leg to stop the flow of blood and twisted it tight before knotting it. "You'll be okay as soon as you get to St. Bart's," he told Watkins, and stood up. "I'd get him there as soon as you can. You could drive right up here and put him in your car."

An almost aesthetic expression of distaste passed over Del Barca's features. "Wait a second. Did you set up this . . . this booby trap?"

"I just recognized it," Poole said. "From Vietnam."

Del Barca blinked.

"That wire's just tied to trees on both ends," called the rabbit-faced boy. "Cut right through the bark."

Watkins whimpered.

"Go on, Traddles," Del Barca said. "Use your hearse. It's closer."

Traddles nodded gloomily and padded away downhill toward his hearse. His assistant followed him. "I was here for the Talbot funeral," Poole said to Del Barca. "I walked over here to look at my son's grave, and I saw a man disappearing into these woods. He looked so odd that I followed him, and when I saw that tripwire I got interested enough to follow him deeper into the woods. Then you started yelling at me. I guess the man just got away."

"Musta been parked alongside the expressway," said the younger man.

They watched Traddles drive toward them along the narrow lane. When he had come as close as he could, he got out of the cab and waited by the door. The assistant ran around and opened the back.

"Go on, get him up," Del Barca said. "You can stand, Watkins. It wasn't exactly an amputation." He turned a sour, suspicious face to Michael. "I'm going to the police about this."

"Good idea," Michael said. "Have them check out that whole area back there, but tell them to be careful."

The two men watched the big man limp off toward Traddles' hearse, leaning on his small companion and hissing with every step. "Do you know the name of those flowers growing just inside the woods?" Michael asked Del Barca.

"We don't plant flowers." Del Barca gave a grim little smile. "We *sell* flowers."

"Big blue and white ones," Poole persisted. "With a strong, carrying scent."

"Weeds," Del Barca said. "If it grows back there, we pretty much let it go to hell by itself."

6

When Michael returned to Conor's empty apartment he looked out of the window down onto Water Street. He did not expect to see Victor Spitalny looking back up at him, for Spitalny would have had no trouble melting into his particular form of invisibility among the crowds of tourists that filled the renovated Water Street all during the weekends, but he gave the crowd a long look anyhow. He had to assume that Spitalny knew about the apartment, and that he was staying in it.

Poole had been shaken that afternoon, in more than one way. The appearance of Victor Spitalny had forced him to delay thinking about it, but something had shown itself to him—had revealed itself—before Robbie's grave. Of course it had been a hallucination. Stress, anxiety, and guilt had pushed him over the edge of rationality. The wonderful odor that had seemed to accompany the appearance of a supernatural being had been the scent of early wildflowers. Still it had been a wonderful experience. In the midst of his pains and troubles he had momentarily seen everything as if for the first time. The internal weight of every particle of being had *seized* him with its own seriousness and power. He wished that he could describe this experience to someone who might understand it or have shared it.

He wanted to talk about it with Tim Underhill.

Poole gave a last look down at busy Water Street, and went back into the empty room. Conor's jacket was not on the hook inside the front door. Michael went to the dining table and finally saw what he should have seen as soon as he entered. It was a small rectangle of paper torn from the pad beneath the phone in Conor's little galley kitchen and on it was printed MIKEY.

Poole smiled and turned it over to read Conor's message: *Going up to Ellen's place to be with her a couple days. You understand. Good luck in Milwaukee. Love, Conor. PS. She liked you. PPS. Here's the number in case you have to call.* A 203 number had been scrawled at the bottom of the note.

He took the playing card from his pocket and set it down next to the note on Conor's table. *I have no home.* Koko had seen Beevers' flyers. *I am Esterhaz*. This revealed that Spitalny had read Tim Underhill's best book, and it also answered the phrase "We who know your real name." And maybe it was a declaration that Spitalny intended to kill himself, as Esterhaz had done. If he felt like Esterhaz, Spitalny was in torment: like Esterhaz, he had killed too often and was becoming conscious of what he had done. Poole wanted to believe that Koko's appearance in the cemetery had been a kind of farewell gesture, a last look at someone from his old life before he slit his wrists or put a bullet in his brain and found *life eternal.*

Backwards and forwards was still the locked door of a madman's private code.

On another of the white message sheets from beneath Conor's telephone Michael copied out the three lines of the message. Then he took a plastic baggie from a drawer, inserted the original with a tweezers, and folded down the flap. The paper fit neatly into the baggie. He dropped the little pin into the baggie.

He wrote a message to Lieutenant Murphy on another sheet of paper: *I wanted to get this to you as soon as possible. It was pinned to a tree in the woods behind Memorial Park Cemetery in Westerholm. Koko must have followed me there when I went to a patient's funeral. I am going out of town tomorrow, will call when I return. This note has been handled only by its edges. Dr. Michael Poole.* He would buy a manila envelope before going to the airport, and mail everything to Murphy's precinct.

Next he dialed Saigon's telephone number to talk to Tim Underhill.

7

"So you escaped from Harry."

"It just kind of made sense to move over here," Underhill said. "There isn't much room, but I can get out of Harry's way, and I can get on with what I'm writing." He paused. "And I can see my old friend Vinh, which is pure amazement. I couldn't even be sure he was alive anymore. But he got out of Vietnam, made it to Paris, got married, and came here after a bunch of his relatives who were already living here made it possible. His wife died giving birth to his daughter, Helen, and he's been raising her ever since. She's a charming kid, and she took to me right away, too. I'm a sort of uncle, or maybe I should say auntie. She really is a dear little thing. Vinh brings her over here nearly every day."

"Vinh isn't living there with you?"

"Well, I'm just in a little room off the kitchen—the

police still haven't unsealed Tina's loft. Vinh moved into the apartment where Helen had been staying. He had been staying there most nights anyhow, which is why he wasn't around the night Tina was killed. One of his sister's boys got married and moved to Astoria, so there's an extra bedroom. Anyhow, I started writing again, and I'm about a hundred pages into a book."

"You're still planning to come to Milwaukee?"

"More than ever," Underhill said. "I gather we will have Maggie's company."

"I hope so," Poole said. "There's something you ought to know about, which is the real reason I called." He told him about seeing Koko and finding the card, and read its three lines aloud.

"He's pretty confused. Something got to him. Maybe he regained enough sanity to want to quit what he's doing. Being back in America would give him a whole series of shocks, if I can go by my own example. Anyhow, that mention of Hal Esterhaz makes me all the more interested in going to Milwaukee."

Poole arranged to meet Tim at the airport at ten-thirty the next morning.

Then he called Conor, told him about seeing Koko, and advised him to stay at Ellen Woyzak's house until their party returned from Milwaukee. Before he hung up he gave Conor the telephone number of the hotel where he had booked rooms for the next three nights.

"The Pforzheimer?" Conor asked. "Sounds like a brand of beer."

He called Westerholm, but Judy was still refusing to speak to him. Michael told Pat Caldwell to switch on the elaborate yard lights he had installed the year after Robbie's death and to be sure to call the police if she saw anyone near the house or heard any noises. He did not think that Koko would go after the women, but he wanted them to be prepared. He also told Pat about a shotgun he had taken down into his basement about the time he had stopped switching on the arc lights around his house every night, and gave her the number of the Pforzheimer Hotel. Pat asked him if all this was related to the man they had tried to find in Singapore, and Michael told her that it was not as simple as that, but that she was more right than wrong. Yes, he was going to Milwaukee to try to search for the man, and yes, he thought everything would be over soon.

When he hung up he walked to the window, looked again at the parade of people passing between the ice cream stores and the restaurants, then left the window and packed a couple of days' clothing into a suitcase. Then he called his house again. Pat answered immediately.

"Are you sitting next to the phone?"

"Well, you didn't exactly reassure me the last time you called."

"I probably over-reacted," Poole said. "This guy isn't going to come out to my house. He has never attacked women alone. It's people like Harry and me that he wants. Did you turn on those yard lights?"

"It looks like we're opening a gas station."

"When I put them in, I wanted to make everything as bright as possible. No hiding places."

"I see what you mean. Haven't the neighbors ever complained?"

"I kept them on for a few months a couple of years ago, and they never said anything about it. I think the trees screen everything pretty well. How's Judy?"

"She's okay—I told her I was humoring you."

Judy still would not speak to him, so he and Pat said goodbye.

Finally he telephoned Harry Beevers.

"I'm here," Beevers answered.

"It's Michael, Harry."

"Oh. You. Something on your mind? You're still going, aren't you?"

"Tomorrow morning."

"Okay. Just checking. You hear about Underhill? What he did to me? The man moved out. It wasn't enough for him that I gave him room and board and totally respected his privacy—it wasn't enough that while he was here that crazy junkie was able to write whenever he wanted—I'm telling you, be careful around that guy. You can't trust him. What I think—"

"Hold on, Harry. I know about that, but—"

"You know about that, huh?" Beevers' voice had gone small and cold.

"Yes, Harry."

"You *should* know about it, Michael. Who opened his mouth to a little girl, and told her that a certain person was in New York? I don't think I did that, Michael. I'm pretty sure Conor didn't do it. Somebody compromised our mission, Michael, and I'm afraid it's you."

"I'm sorry you feel that way about it."

"I'm sorry you did what you did." Beevers drew in another long breath. "I don't suppose you even remember all the things I've done for you and this mission. I've done nothing but give, give, give all the way through this thing, Michael. I was court-martialed for you, Michael, I sat in a Quonset hut and waited for a verdict, I hope you never have to go through that—"

"I have something to tell you," Poole broke in.

"I guess I better brace myself."

Michael told him about the incident in the cemetery.

"You had an unconfirmed sighting? I suppose you'd better tell me everything."

"I just did."

"Okay, we're into endgame. That's all that means. He saw my stuff. Everything is working. I hope you did not call Murphy with this information."

"I didn't," Poole said, not telling Beevers that he intended to mail the card to the policeman.

"I suppose I ought to be grateful for small favors," Beevers said. "Give me the name and number of your hotel. If he's at the stage of following us around and leaving notes, things are going to pop pretty soon. I might have to get in touch with you."

Poole read in the little apartment for an hour or two, but felt so unsettled that he kept losing himself in the long sentences. At seven he realized that he had grown very hungry, and went out to eat. On the street he saw his car parked before the ice cream shop and remembered that Robbie's *Babar* books were still in the trunk. He promised himself that he would remember to bring them up into the apartment after he had eaten.

8

He ate dinner in a little Italian restaurant and again immersed himself in *The Ambassadors*. The next day, he told himself, he would fly off into Koko's childhood. He felt poised on the brink of some great change, but ready for it. The Health and Hospitals Corporation of New

York gave fifty-thousand-dollar grants to doctors to set up storefront offices in places where people needed medical care, and after that loaned you money at the prime rate which you did not have to start repaying for two years. Two, three, four more days at the most, Poole thought; then he could finally get off the bridge and go into the places where he was needed. His whole body warmed.

9

When Poole got back to Conor's apartment he turned on all the lights and sat down on a kitchen chair to read until he could go to bed. A feeling of unfinished business nagged at him until he remembered the *Babar* books and nearly decided to put on his coat and fetch them from the car. He stood up, walked past the telephone, and remembered something else.

He had never called the stewardess who had known Clement W. Irwin, Koko's first American victim. Poole was surprised that he had remembered the man's name.

But what was the name of the stewardess? He tried to remember the name of their own stewardess. Her name had been something like his. Mikey. Marsha. Michaela, Minnie, Mona. No—it had reminded him of an Alfred Hitchcock movie. Grace Kelly. A blonde . . . Tippi Hedren, the actress who had been in *The Birds*. Then he remembered the name as easily as if the name tag was still in front of him: Marnie. And Marnie's friend had been named . . . Lisa. He groped for her last name. How could he have been stupid enough not to write it down. What's your friend's last name, he had asked her. "——," She had said. Something about Ireland. Lisa Dublin. Lisa Galway, That was close. Lisa Ulster. Like in Hellman's, Marnie had said. Lisa *Mayo*.

Poole rushed to the phone and dialed information in New York City. She would not have a listed number, of course, nothing was that easy, and he would have to work out a way to get a stewardess's telephone number from the airline that employed her. He asked for the listing, and the line went silent with an electronic clunk. That's it, Poole thought, no listing, but a robot's voice immediately came on the line, saying *"The number you have requested is*" and gave him seven digits, then repeated them.

Poole dialed, hoping it was the same Lisa Mayo. If it was, she was probably thirty thousand feet in the air, on her way back to San Francisco.

The telephone rang four, five times, and was picked up a second before Poole hung up.

A young woman said, "Yes."

"My name is Dr. Michael Poole, and I am looking for the Lisa Mayo who is a friend of Marnie's."

"Marnie *Richardson*? Where did you meet her?"

"In an airplane coming back from Bangkok."

"Marnie's pretty wild. Uh, I gave up doing a lot of stuff when I moved out of San Francisco. It's nice of you to call, but—"

"Excuse me," Poole said. "I think you have the wrong idea. I'm calling about the man who was killed at JFK about three weeks ago, and Miss Richardson said that you knew him."

"You're calling about Mr. Irwin?"

"In part," Poole said. "You did see him on the flight just before he was killed?"

"You bet I did. I saw him maybe a dozen times a year. He went back and forth to San Francisco almost as often as I do." She hesitated. "I was shocked when I read about what happened to him, but I can't say I was real sorry. He wasn't a very nice man. Oh, I shouldn't have said that. Mr. Irwin wasn't popular with any of the crews, that's all, he was a very demanding man. But what business is it of yours, anyway? Did you know Mr. Irwin?"

"I am primarily interested in the man who sat beside Mr. Irwin on the flight to New York. I wondered if you could remember anything about him."

"Him? This is very mysterious. Besides, it's getting late and I have an early call tomorrow. Are you a cop?"

The implications of that "him?" put goose bumps on Poole's arms. "No, I'm a doctor, but I do have some connection with the police investigation of Mr. Irwin's murder."

" 'Some' connection?"

"I'm sorry it's so vague."

"Well, if you think that guy who sat next to Mr. Irwin had anything to do with it, you're really barking up the wrong tree."

"Why?"

"Because he couldn't have had anything to do with it. He couldn't. I see a lot of people in the work I do, and that guy was one of the nicest, shyest . . . I felt sorry for him, having to sit next to the Beast. That's what we called Mr. Irwin. Well, come to think of it, he even sort of charmed the Beast—he got Mr. Irwin to talk to him, and he got him to make a bet on something or other."

"Do you remember his name?"

"It was some kind of Spanish name—Gomez, maybe? Cortez?"

There you are, Poole thought, and drew in a sharp breath.

"What?"

"Does Ortiz sound right? Roberto Ortiz?"

She laughed. "How did you know that? That's right—and he said to call him Bobby. Bobby seemed just right, you know, he was just like a Bobby."

"Is there anything specific you can remember about him? Anything he said, or talked about, or anything in particular?"

"It's funny—when I look back on him, all I get is this blur with a smile in the middle of it. The whole crew liked him, I remember. But as for anything he said . . . wait . . . wait."

"Yes?" Poole asked.

"I can remember something funny he did. He kind of sang. I mean, he didn't sing a song, you know, a song with words, but he sang this kind of weird little *thing*."

"What was it like?"

"Well, it was kinda strange. Like nonsense words—like a foreign language. But you could tell it wasn't any real language. It was like . . . 'pompo-po, pompo-po, polo, polo, pompo-po,' something like that."

The goosebumps were back on Poole's arms. "Yes," he said. "Thank you."

"Is that all you wanted?"

" 'Pompo-po, pompo-po . . .' or like 'rip-a-rip-a-rip-a-lo'?"

"Pretty close," the girl said.

PART SEVEN

THE KILLING BOX

32

FIRST NIGHT AT THE PFORZHEIMER

1

"I don't know if there's any name for those experiences," Underhill said. He sat near the window, Poole on the aisle, Maggie between them. They were somewhere in the air over Pennsylvania, or Ohio, or Michigan. "You could call them peak experiences, but that's a term that covers a lot of ground. Or you might call it ecstasy, since that's what it sounds like. You might even call it an Emersonian moment. You know Emerson's essay, 'Nature'? He talks about becoming a transparent eyeball—'I am nothing; I see all; the currents of Universal Being circulate through me.' "

"Sounds like just another way to face the elephant," Maggie said in her precise unsentimental voice. Both Poole and Underhill laughed. "You should not make so much of it. When you saw your son, you should have expected something like this . . . *experience* to follow."

"I didn't see my son," Poole began, and then his objections dried to powder in his mouth. He had not been certain that he was going to tell Underhill and Maggie about the "god," and his uncertainty had continued even while he described what he had seen, but Maggie's short sentence rang within him.

"But you did," Maggie said. "You saw what he would

be like as a man. You saw the real Robbie." She looked at him very quizzically. "That's why you loved the figure you saw."

"Are you for hire?" Underhill asked.

"How much money you got?" Maggie asked in the same disinterested voice. "Going to cost you plenty, if you want me to keep saying the obvious."

"I liked the theory that it was an angel."

"I did too," Maggie said. "Very possible."

They rode on for a time in silence. Michael knew that Robbie could not have grown into the man he had seen: but he thought that he had been given a vision of a perfect Robbie, one in whom all his best instincts had flowered. It would have been some quality beyond happiness, something like rapture, to have fathered the man he had seen beside his son's grave. In a sense he had fathered that man, exactly. No one else had. He had not hallucinated or imagined the man so much as he had *authored* him.

Poole felt as though with a few simple words Maggie Lah had restored his son to him. For as long as he lived, that boy was his, that man was his boy. His mourning was really over.

When at last he could speak again, Poole asked Tim if he had done any research for *The Divided Man*. "I mean, did you consult any guidebooks, anything like that?"

"I don't think there are any guidebooks to Milwaukee," Underhill said.

Maggie permitted herself an amused little noise that sounded very like a snicker.

"Most American cities don't have guidebooks," Underhill said. "I mainly remembered what M.O. Dengler used to say about it. After that I turned my imagination loose on it, and I guess it did a reasonable job."

"In other words," Michael said, "you could say that you authored the city."

"I authored it," Underhill agreed, looking faintly puzzled.

Maggie Lah turned a gleaming eye upon Poole. She astounded him by lightly patting his knee, as if in congratulation or commendation.

"Am I missing something?" Underhill asked.

"You're doing pretty well so far," Maggie said.

"Well, I have a thought about Victor Spitalny and his

parents," Tim said, trying to cross his legs and learning that he did not have enough room. "Imagine how most parents would feel if their child disappeared. Don't you think that they would keep telling themselves that the child was still alive, no matter how long the disappearance lasted? I suppose that Spitalny's parents are a little different from most. Remember—they made their kid feel like an adopted orphan, if my imagination is any good. They turned their kid into the Victor Spitalny we knew, and he later turned himself into Koko. So I'll bet that his mother says she knows he's dead. She already knows he killed Dengler. But I bet she knows that he's done other killings."

"So what will she think about us and what we're doing?"

"She might just think we're fools and humor us along with cups of tea. Or she might lose her temper and throw us out."

"Then why are we on this airplane?"

"Because she might be an honest lady who had a cuckoo for a son. There are lots of different kinds of misfortune, and her son might have been one of the worst. In which case she'll share any information she has."

Underhill saw the expression on Michael's face and added that the only thing he really knew about Milwaukee was that it was going to be about thirty degrees colder than New York.

"I think I can see why they don't have many tourists," Maggie said.

2

At one o'clock in the afternoon, Michael Poole stood at the window of his room in the Pforzheimer Hotel, looking down at what would have been a four-lane street if parallel drifts of snow nearly the height of the parking meters had not claimed half of the first lane on either side. Here and there cars had been submerged beneath the parallel ranges of old snow, and channels like mountain passes had been cut between the cars to provide passage to the sidewalk. On the cleared portion of the road, intermittent cars, most of them crusted with frozen khaki-colored slush, streamed past in single file. The green of the traffic light on Wisconsin Avenue, at the front of the hotel and at the very edge of Michael's vision, gleamed out in the oddly dusky air as if through twilight. The temperature was zero degrees Fahrenheit. It was like being in the middle of Moscow. A few men and women bundled in thick coats moved quickly down the sidewalk toward the light. The light changed from a gleaming green nimbus to a gleaming red nimbus, and even though no cars appeared in the intersection, the pedestrians stopped to obey the DON'T WALK command.

It really was the city Dengler had described. Poole felt like a Muscovite looking at Moscow with eyes washed clean. He had finished the long, long process of mourning his son. What was left of Robbie was within him. He did not even feel that he needed the *Babar* books, which were still in the trunk of the Audi. The world would never be whole again, that was that, but when had the world been whole? His grief had flared up, then subsided again, and his eyes had been *washed clean*.

Behind him Tim Underhill and Maggie Lah were laughing at something Tim had drawled.

The lights at the end of the block changed to green, and the command switched to WALK. The pedestrians began to move across the street.

Maggie had been put into a single room next to this one, where Poole and Underhill had placed their bags on the two double beds. It was a high-vaulted room with faded flocked wallpaper, a threadbare carpet with a floral pattern, and a rococo mirror in a gilt frame. On the walls hung large nineteenth-century paintings of dogs panting over mounds of bloody dead pheasants and portraits of smug, big-bellied burghers in frock coats and striped satin waistcoats. The furniture was nondescript, worn, and sturdy, and the size of the room made it look small. In the bathroom the taps and fittings were brass, and the tub stood like a lion on four heavy porcelain paws. The windows, through which the three of them now looked down onto the street, extended nearly from floor to ceiling and were hung with dark brown swag curtains drawn back with worn, heavy velvet ropes. Poole had never been in a hotel room like it. He thought it was like being in some splendid old hotel in Prague or Budapest—through twenty-foot windows like these with such a vast, elegant, decaying room at his back, he should have heard the sounds of sleigh bells and horses's hooves.

In the Pforzheimer's lobby, uniformed midgets the size of the numerous ferns had stood before the polished mahogany of the registration desk; the clerk had worn half-glasses and a narrow bow tie, and looked out upon a rich landscape of shining brass, yards of tartan carpet, glowing lamps, and immense paintings so dark that big shapes loomed out of a general blur. There was of course no computer behind the desk. A wide staircase curved up toward what a plaque identified as the Balmoral Room, and down at the far end of the lobby, a corridor led past trees in pots and glass cases filled with the stuffed heads of animals toward a dimly glowing bar.

"I sort of feel that the Neva is only a pace or two away," Poole said, looking out at the snow.

"And police in bearskin hats and leather boots to the knees strut up and down on the Prospekt," Underhill said.

"Waiting to apprehend the naked men who have been forced out of the forest by the extreme cold," Maggie said.

Yes, that was it. There would be a great forest only a mile or two distant, and at night if you opened the windows of ballrooms you would hear the cries of wolves.

"Let's take a look at the telephone book," Poole said, turning from the window.

"Let's find the telephone book," Underhill said.

The telephone itself, an old-fashioned black Bakelite model with a rotary dial but without the usual instructions for dialing the laundry, room service, the concierge, and the desk—without even a message light—stood on a military table beside Poole's bed.

The two men began opening drawers in the various chests and cabinets against the walls. In a tall highboy Underhill found a television set that swiveled out on a shelf. Poole found a Gideon Bible and a booklet entitled "The Pforzheimer Story" in a long drawer lined with crinkly paper imprinted with Christmas trees. Underhill opened a cabinet between the tall windows and discovered rows of books. "My God," he said, "a library. And what books! *Kitty's Pretty Muff, Mr. Ticker's Toenail, Parched Kisses, Historic Residences of the Malay Peninsula* . . . Oh!" He pulled out a battered copy of *The*

Divided Man. "Does this mean I'm immortal, or does it mean I'm ridiculously obscure?"

"Depends on how you feel about *Kitty's Pretty Muff,*" Maggie said, taking the book from the shelf. "Isn't the telephone book in here somewhere?" She began to root in the lower half of the cabinet.

"Faeries, Tales, and Confusions at Birth," Underhill said, removing another book from the shelves.

Maggie pulled a hidden lever, and another shelf moved into view from the back of the cabinet, carrying a silver cocktail shaker containing a musty collapsed web and a shriveled spider, a tarnished ice bucket, a nearly empty bottle of gin, a nearly full bottle of vermouth, and a bottle of rusty-looking olives. "This stuff must have been here since Prohibition," Maggie said. "No telephone book, though." She stood up, shrugged, and took her book to the couch.

"This isn't much like traveling with Harry Beevers and Conor Linklater," Poole said. "When I asked Conor if he wanted to change his mind about coming along with us, he said, 'I got better ways to idolize my time.' " He looked out the window and saw big flakes of snow spinning through the close dark air.

"What's your book about?" Underhill asked behind him.

"Torture," Maggie said.

Poole heard car horns blasting, and stepped closer to the window. The heads of horses appeared at the far right of his vision, gradually pulling into view an empty hansom cab driven by a man with a fat purple face. The driver steered his cab imperiously down the center of the street, forcing oncoming cars out of its way.

"So is mine," Underhill said. "Just kidding, Maggie. Keep your hands off."

"No pictures in yours. Mine is nothing but pictures."

"We got the right books."

Poole turned from the window as Maggie left Underhill grinning on the couch behind her and marched with a look of mock determination to a low wooden chest beneath the mirror. Poole walked over and picked up Maggie's book. On every page was a photograph of kittens dressed in jackets and hats of the 1920s. The kittens seemed to be held in place with metal straps and braces concealed beneath their outfits, and had been posed reading novels, dealing cards, playing tennis, smoking pipes, getting married. . . . The kittens' eyes were glassy with terror, and all of them looked dead.

"Aha!" Maggie said. "The secret of the Pforzheimer!" She was brandishing a green telephone directory so thick she had to hold it with both hands.

"By George, I think she's got it," Underhill said.

Maggie sat on the end of the couch beside Poole and flipped open the book. "I didn't think it would have so many *names* in it. What are we looking for? Oh yes, S, that's right, Sandberg, Samuels, Sbarro . . ." She turned a wad of pages, then one other. "Here we are. Sperber. And Spitalny. And Spitalny and Spitalny and Spitalny, you wouldn't think there'd be so many."

Michael looked at the place where Maggie's slim finger rested on the page. The finger moved down a column that began with Spitalnik, changed to Spitalny and stayed that way for something like twenty entries until it became Spitalsky.

He took the book across the expanse of the room to the bed, propped himself up on the pillows, held the book open on his lap, and moved the phone beside him. Maggie and Tim watched him from the couch, looking like the kittens in Maggie's book. "Talk among yourselves," Poole said. " 'Idolize your time.' "

"Did it ever occur to you that Conor Linklater is a genius?" Underhill asked Maggie.

"Mr. Spitalny?" Poole asked. "My name is Michael Poole, and I'm looking for the family of a man named Victor Spitalny who was in Vietnam with me. I wondered if you were related to him, or if you knew how I could get in touch with his family . . . Victor, that's right . . . So nobody in your family was named Victor . . . Yes, he was from Milwaukee . . . Thanks anyhow."

He depressed the button, dialed the next number, and when there was no answer, the one beneath that. A man who had been celebrating the snowfall answered and informed Michael in a slow, slurry voice that no such person as Victor Spitalny had ever existed, and hung up.

On the seventh listing, for E. Spitalny on South Mogrom Street, Poole had better luck. "You were in Vietnam with Victor?" a young woman asked him. "My goodness. All that seems a long time ago."

Poole signaled to the two on the couch for writing

paper. Underhill found a pad of hotel stationery and tossed it to Michael.

"He is in your family?"

"Oh, my goodness," the girl said. "Vic was my cousin. You mean he's still alive? You don't know what this does to me."

"There is a chance he's still alive. Can you give me his parents' telephone number? Are they both still living?"

"If you call it living. I don't have their number right here, but you can find it in the book. George and Margaret, Uncle George and Aunt Margaret. Look, didn't something funny happen to Vic? I thought he was in a hospital overseas, I guess I thought he must have died there."

Poole scanned down the listings until he found *Spitalny, George, 6835 S. Winnebago St.*, and circled it with his pen.

"It's your impression he was hospitalized?"

"Well, I thought Uncle George . . . it was a long time ago."

"You haven't heard anything from him since the war?"

"Well, *no*. Even if he was alive, he'd hardly write to me, would he? We weren't exactly buddies. Who did you say you were again?"

Michael repeated his name and that he and Victor were in the same unit in Vietnam. The girl said that her name was Evvie.

"I'm here with some friends from New York, Evvie, and we wanted to learn if anyone in his family had heard from Victor recently."

"Not that *I* know about."

"Can you tell me the names of any of your cousin's friends? Names of girls he went out with? Or any of the places he used to go?"

"Gee, I don't know," said Evvie. "Vic was the sort of a guy who was kind of a loner. He did go to Rufus King, I know that. And for a while he went out with a girl named Debbie. I met her once, when I was a little kid. Debbie Maczik. She was so cute, I thought. And I think he used to go to a place called The Polka Dot. But mainly he used to work on his car, stuff like that, you know?"

"Can you remember the names of his friends?"

"One guy was named Bill, one guy was named Mack—that's all I ever knew. I was only ten when Vic got drafted. My aunt and uncle will know all that stuff."

"Would your uncle be home now?"

"You wanna call him? Probably not, he's probably at work. *I* ought to be at work, I'm a secretary at the gas company, but I just couldn't face it today, so I decided to stay home and watch the soap operas. Aunt Margaret ought to be home, though. She never goes anywhere." Evvie Spitalny paused. "I guess I don't have to tell you, this feels real strange. Talking about my cousin Vic. It's funny. It's like—you think you forgot all about a certain person, you know, and then bang, you get reminded all over again. My cousin wasn't a real nice guy, you know."

"No," Poole said. "I guess he wasn't."

After Evvie had hung up, he dialed the number on Winnebago Street. An older woman with a flat nasal voice answered.

"Is this Mrs. Spitalny? Margaret Spitalny?"

"Yes, it is."

"Mrs. Spitalny, you don't know me, but I was in Vietnam with your son. We served together in the same unit for a year. My name is Michael Poole—Dr. Poole, now."

"Oh, my goodness. Say what?"

He repeated most of what he had said.

"What did you say your name was?"

He repeated his name. "I'm in Milwaukee with Tim Underhill, another member of our unit, and a friend of ours. We'd very much like to see you and your husband, if that is at all possible."

"See us?" Mrs. Spitalny seemed to speak only in questions.

"We'd like to come over and meet you, if we could. We arrived this morning from New York, and I found your name in the telephone book."

"You came all the way from New York to see me and George?"

"We very much wanted to talk to you about Victor. I hope this isn't too much of a nuisance, and I apologize for the suddenness of it, but do you think we could come out either this afternoon or tonight? We'd be interested in hearing anything you have to say about Victor, looking at photographs, that kind of thing."

"You want to come to our *house*? Tonight?"

"If we can. Please don't feel you have to feed us. We are just very interested in learning whatever we could about Victor."

"Well, there isn't that much to learn. I can tell you that right away. . . . You aren't from the police, are you?"

Poole's blood began to move a little faster. "No. I am a doctor, and Mr. Underhill is a writer."

"The other one is a writer? This isn't anything about the police? You promise?"

"Of course."

" 'Cause otherwise it would just kill my husband."

"We are just old friends of Victor's. There's no need to worry."

"I'd better call George at the Glax plant, that's where he works. I'd better check with George. He has to know about this, or I'm in Dutch. It sounds so *funny*. Tell me where you are and I'll call you back after I talk to George."

Poole gave her the number and then, on impulse, asked, "Have you heard anything from Victor lately? We were very interested in knowing where we might be able to find him."

"Heard from him lately? Nobody's heard from Vic for more than ten years, Dr. Poole. I'll call you back."

Poole hung up. "Looks like you're going to be right about his parents," he said to Underhill.

"She'll call back?" Maggie asked.

"After she talks to George."

"What if George says no?"

"Then they probably have something to hide, and we'll work on them until we talk them into letting us in the door."

"And we'll know everything they know in an hour," Underhill said. "If they play it like that, they'll be dying to get it off their chests."

"So you're hoping she will call back and say no?"

Underhill smiled and went back to reading his book.

After half an hour of reading and pacing the room, Poole looked out the windows again. Outside in Moscow, a small black car, turned the color of dead skin by winter filth, had burrowed head first into one of the mountain ranges of snow. The traffic had narrowed down to a single line in order to squeeze past it.

"Cards were invented for times like this," he said.

"Mah-jongg was invented for times like this," Maggie said. "Not to mention drugs and television."

The telephone rang, and Poole snatched it up. "Hello?"

"This is George Spitalny," said an aggressive male voice. "My wife said you called her up with some kind of cockamamy story."

"I'm glad you called, Mr. Spitalny. My name is Dr. Michael Poole, and I was in your son's unit in Vietnam—"

"Look, I only got a fifteen-minute break. Suppose you tell me what's on your mind."

"I was hoping that I could come over with another old friend of Victor's tonight, to talk to you."

"I don't get it. What's the point?"

"We'd like to know more about him. Victor was an important member of our unit, and we have a lot of memories of him."

"I don't like it. I don't have to let you and your friend walk into my house."

"No, you don't, Mr. Spitalny. And I apologize for doing all this on such short notice, but my friends and I came from New York this morning, we don't know anybody in Milwaukee, and we were just interested in hearing anything you had to say about Victor."

"Damn. Who are these friends?"

"The man I mentioned, Tim Underhill, and a friend of ours named Maggie Lah."

"She over there too?"

"No, she wasn't. She came along to help us."

"You say Victor was an important member of your unit? How so?"

"He was a good combat soldier. Victor was very reliable under fire."

"Jeez, what horseshit," Spitalny said. "I knew Vic better than you did, mister."

"Well, that's exactly why we wanted to talk to you. We do want to know more about him."

Spitalny hummed to himself for a second. "You told my wife you wasn't cops."

"That's right."

"You just come out here to see us? In the middle of winter?"

"Last year we had a kind of reunion in Washington. There aren't many of us left. We were interested in seeing what we could learn about Victor and another guy in our unit from Milwaukee. This is the time we had free."

"Okay, you just wanta talk about Vic, I guess you could come out. Around five. I gotta get back to work."

He gave directions to his house, and hung up.

Poole said, "He doesn't want us there, but he gave in anyhow. He was nervous, and he doesn't sound like the kind of man who gets rattled easily."

"Now I think *I'm* nervous," Maggie said.

Poole wandered back to the window. The black car was still stuck in the drift, and its rear wheels spun so hard that smoke lifted up from the road.

"Let's look for Dengler's parents," Underhill said behind him.

Poole heard Underhill stand up and walk across the room to the telephone book. A yellow city bus was making its way up the street. Tired-looking people wrapped in coats and scarves sat like museum exhibits in the lighted windows. For a time the bus waited for the black car to get out of the snowbank. The driver cracked open his window and shouted something. The driver of the black car opened his door, stood on the ledge, and yelled to the bus driver. He was wearing a small tweed cap. *Go around*, he motioned. The driver shouted again, then disappeared into his car. The bus moved forward until it touched the right rear bumper of the black car. The car shuddered.

"Only one Dengler," Underhill said. "On something called Muffin Street."

The driver hopped out of the black car. The bus ground forward, and the car shuddered another few feet into the snow. The man in the cap was screaming at the bus—he made a rush at it and pounded at its side. His car slid another slanting inch or two into the bank. One of the parking meters began to tilt backwards in the snow. The man in the cap ran to his car, opened the trunk, and took out a tire iron. He whanged the front of the bus, then closed his trunk with the other hand. He went around to the side of the bus and began to slam the tire iron against the silver metal as the bus methodically pushed his car deeper into the snowbank. The head of the parking meter gradually sank out of sight. Then the bus swerved out into the center of the street. Car horns blasted. The man in the tweed cap ran after the bus as it toiled up the icy street, slamming the tire iron against the bus's rear bumper. Each time he swung he took a little jump to clear the

L'eggs advertisement on its back end. He looked like a furious little wind-up toy as he chased after the bus. The passengers in the back seat had turned around and were staring down with round rubbery faces that reminded Poole of the faces of newborn babies.

3

As they turned onto a wide long bridge Poole looked out of the window of their cab, expecting to see a river beneath them. Far beneath in a wide valley, smokestacks pushed out grey clouds like wings that froze and hung in the black air. Small red fires burned and danced at the tops of columns, and red lights shone far down at the heads of trains that clanked slowly forward, showering sparks.

"What's that called?" Poole asked the cabdriver.

"Nothing." The driver was an ageless being who smelled like curdled milk and must have weighed three hundred pounds. Tattoos covered the backs of both his hands.

"It doesn't have a name?"

"We call it the Valley."

"What's down there?"

"Local companies. Glax. Dux. Muffinberg. Firms like that. Fluegelhorn Brothers."

"Instrument makers?" Underhill asked.

"Ditching equipment, garbage bags, stuff like that."

The Valley's resemblance to a surrealist hell increased as they progressed over the bridge. The frozen grey wings mutated to slabs of stone, the flames became more numerous. Sudden spasmodic illuminations revealed, as if by lightning bolt, crooked streets, stalled trains, long factories with broken and boarded windows. What seemed like half a mile down a tiny red sign winked MARGE 'N' AL'S . . . MARGE 'N' AL'S.

"There are bars down there?"

"There's everything down there."

"Do people live in the Valley? Are there houses down there too?"

"Look," the driver said. "You're an asshole, that's okay with me. If you don't like it, you can get outa this cab. All right? I don't need your shit."

"I didn't mean—"

"Just shut up and I'll take you where you wanna go. Okay with you?"

"Okay with me," Poole said. "Sure. You bet."

Maggie put her hands over her mouth. Her shoulders were shaking.

"Driver, is there a bar called The House of Correction in this town?" Underhill asked.

"I hearda that one," the driver said.

The cab hit a patch of ice at the end of the bridge, skidded nearly halfway around, then straightened out again. The smell of chocolate momentarily filled the cab.

"What's that from?" Underhill asked. "The smell."

"Chocolate factory."

Now they drove endlessly on streets both broad and narrow bordered by two-story houses with tiny porches. Every block had its own bar named something like Pete 'N' Bill's and covered with the same peeling brickface or asphalt siding as the little houses. Some blocks had two bars, one on each corner. Tall chain fences blocked off vacant lots heaped with snow that looked blue and cancerous beneath the streetlamps. Every now and then a beer sign burned in the window of what otherwise looked like a private house. On the brightly lighted corner before SAM 'N' ANNIE'S GOOD TIMES LOUNGE, a fat man in a wolfskin parka was braced before a big black dog. The cab stopped at the traffic light. The man struck the dog with his left hand, slapping it hard enough to rock it to its side. Then he struck it with his right hand. Poole could see the man grinning, showing his teeth inside the parka. He hit the dog again, and the animal backed up, crinkling its lip away from its long teeth. Again the man smashed his hand against the dog's head. This time the dog slipped, and skittered on the ice pavement before it got its footing again. The dog lowered its shoulders and inched backward. Poole was staring at the man and the dog—the man owned the dog, this was how he played with it. The light changed, and the cab moved ahead through the empty intersection just as the dog charged. Both Poole and Underhill craned their necks to look through the rear window. All they could see was the man's pale furry back, broad as a tractor, jerking from side to side as he and the dog engaged.

Ten minutes later the cab pulled up before one of the two-story frame houses. The numbers 6 8 3 5 had been nailed to the top of the porch. Poole opened the door and began paying the driver. The air instantly burned his cheeks, his forehead, his nose. His fingers had turned clumsy in the cold. "Were you in Vietnam?" he asked. "I saw the Airborne insignia on your hands."

The driver shook his head. "I'm only twenty years old, pop."

They hurried up the icy concrete walk. The steps sagged, and the porch tilted to the right. Over the original surface of the house, green pebbly asphalt paper had been applied, and flaps had begun to peel away from the door and windows. Poole pushed the bell. The smell of chocolate surprised him again.

"Just a sweet and sour kind of town," Underhill said.

"Sweet *'n'* sour," Maggie said.

The door opened, and a short stocky man with thinning black hair plastered straight back against his skull frowned through the storm door. He was wearing khaki trousers and a clean, starched khaki work shirt with double front pockets. His hard little eyes scanned the two men and stopped moving when they reached Maggie. He had not expected anything like her, and he did not really recover until she smiled at him. He gave Poole a dark look, then broke down and cracked the storm door open a few inches.

"You the people who called?"

"Mr. Spitalny?" Poole asked. "May we come in?"

George Spitalny pushed open the storm door and stood there propping it open and scowling until the three visitors had edged around him into the entry. Poole smelled sausage and boiled cabbage. "Go on," Spitalny's father said, "I gotta close the door." Everybody jostled together to allow it to swing closed. "In there."

Poole followed Maggie and Underhill through a doorway into a living room where an anxious-looking woman in a flowered housedress stood clutching her hands before a sofa covered in plastic. Her face froze when she saw Maggie, and her eyes darted toward her husband. George Spitalny stayed in the entrance, unwilling to help. It was clear that both of them had been sitting on the sofa, staring out the window, waiting for a car to pull up, and now that the company had come neither one of them knew what to do.

Maggie stepped forward and held out her hand to Mrs.

Spitalny. She introduced the two men, who also stepped forward.

Mr. Spitalny hurriedly shook the hands of the men, and said, "Well, I guess you better take a pew." He moved to a large green recliner and hitched up his trouser legs before he sat down. Maggie still smiling for all she was worth, sat down next to Mrs. Spitalny.

"Well," George Spitalny said.

"You have a beautiful home, Mrs. Spitalny," said Maggie.

"It suits us. What did you say your name was?"

"Maggie Lah."

Margaret Spitalny tentatively held out her hand toward Maggie, then realized that she had already shaken her hand, and snatched her hand back.

"Still snowing, is it?" she asked.

Her husband looked out the window. "Stopped."

"Oh. My."

"Couple hours back."

Poole realized that he was looking at a photograph of Governor George Wallace, beaming from his wheelchair in the midst of a crowd. Porcelain deer, gnomes, and dairy maids stood on a round table beside him. The floor had been covered with green linoleum. Everything was very clean.

George Spitalny took another shuttered look at Maggie, then frowned down at his shoes on the bright linoleum.

These people had no idea of how to act when other people were in their house, Poole realized. If it had not been for Maggie, they would all still be standing inside the door.

"So you people knew Victor," George Spitalny said. He looked at Poole, then gave another doubtful glance at Maggie.

"Dr. Poole and I served with him," Underhill said.

"Doctor, are you?"

"Pediatrician."

"Umm." George pursed his lips. "Well. I still don't know what you people expect to find. I think all this is a big waste of your time. We got nothing to say on the subject of Victor."

"Oh, George."

"Maybe you got something to say. I don't know what."

"Maybe these men would like a beer, George?"

"Got some Hamm's," George said.

"Please," they said, and George walked through the door, relieved to have something to do.

"I hope you don't think we're wasting our time, Mrs. Spitalny," Underhill said, leaning forward and smiling at her. In his bulky sweater and blue jeans, Underhill looked utterly at ease, and for as long as she could focus on him, Mrs. Spitalny relaxed.

"*I* don't know why George said that. He's still upset about Vic, I guess. He's proud, you know—very proud."

She closed her mouth and threw her eyes out of focus again as her husband returned to the room carrying three bottles of beer with water glasses upended on their necks. He held them out toward Michael, who gingerly took the first from his fingers. The second beer went to Underhill, and he kept the third for himself. Maggie gave Mrs. Spitalny another bright smile.

George Spitalny sat down and poured his beer. "Bet you don't get this where you come from, huh? Most people around here won't drink nothing but the local brews. It's all Pforzheimer's with most of your people here. They don't know what they're missing. And I've tried your New York beer. Swill, I thought. Plain swill."

"George."

"Wait till they try this. It's the water that makes the difference. I always say that, it's the water."

"Sure it's the water," Underhill said. "You bet it's the water."

"What else could it be?"

"Did Vic have friends?" Margaret Spitalny broke in, speaking directly to Tim Underhill. "Did you people like him?"

"Well, sure he had friends," Underhill said. "He was very close to Tony Ortega. And a lot of other people. Isn't that true, Mike?"

"Sure," said Poole, trying not to see Victor Spitalny attempting to saw the ear off Anthony Ortega's corpse with his K-bar. "We were his friends. We went out on a lot of missions with Victor."

"Victor saved their lives," Maggie said with a smile so forced that Poole could feel its strain. "Why don't you tell the Spitalnys about that?" Poole and Underhill looked at each other for a moment, and Maggie chimed in, "In Dragon Valley. Well, maybe he didn't save your lives exactly, but he kept everybody calm and he followed the medic around. . . ."

"Oh," Poole said. Both George and Margaret Spitalny were staring at Poole, and with a silent apology to Dengler's ghost, he began, "Well, on Lieutenant Beevers' first day in the field, he got lost and led us into an ambush . . ."

When he had finished, Margaret Spitalny said, "Vic never told us anything like that."

"Vic never bragged about himself," Underhill said.

"Anything else like that ever happen?" George asked.

"Did he ever tell you about the time he carried a wounded soldier named Hannapin on his back about three or four miles?"

Both Spitalnys shook their heads, absolutey riveted, and Poole told another Dengler story.

"Well, maybe the service made a man of him after all," his father said, looking sideways at George Wallace in his wheelchair. "I believe I'll have another beer." He stood up and left the room again.

"God bless you, boys," said Margaret Spitalny. "And you too, miss. Do you all work for the army?"

"No, we don't," said Poole. "Mrs. Spitalny, do you have any letters or postcards, or anything at all from Victor? Any photographs of him?"

"After—you know, after we *heard*, George took everything of Vic's from the service and burned it. Every little scrap." She closed her eyes for a moment. "I have all the pictures from when he was little and some from high school."

"Has he been in touch with you at all since he left the army?"

"Of course not," she said. "Vic's dead."

Mr. Spitalny came through the door with more beer bottles, this time with one for Maggie. "I forgot a glass," he told her. "Can you drink it out of the bottle?"

"No, George, she's a lady, she needs a glass," his wife said, and, after distributing the other bottles of Hamm's, he left the room again. "George won't admit it, but I know. Vic's been dead a long time."

"It seemed to us that he might be alive," Michael said. "We—"

George Spitalny returned with a glass and gave it to

Maggie with a long look. "Where'd a girl like you pick up such good English?"

"New York City."

Blink.

"I came here when I was six."

"Born over there in Vietnam, were you?"

"I was born in Formosa."

Blink.

"I am Chinese." Maggie was smiling so broadly Poole thought her cheek muscles must hurt.

"But you knew Victor."

"I only heard about him."

"Oh." He was deterred for only a moment. "Think you're ready for one of our good old Milwaukee suppers?"

"Not yet, George," said his wife.

"You ever hear of the Glax Corporation, honey? One of the biggest outfits in the States. You ever hear about it over in China?"

Maggie's expression of rapt interest did not waver.

"Circuit breakers. Big plant in the Valley. You probably saw it on the way over here. If you're in town long enough, you oughta pay a visit, I'll show you around, introduce you to everybody. How about that?"

"Very exciting," Maggie said.

"Lots of good places around there, too—lots of surprises in this little old town."

Poole watched George Spitalny leaning forward in his reclining chair, eating up Maggie Lah with his eyes. He had forgotten his wife and the two men. He felt great—he had heard unexpectedly good news about his son, he had a beer in one hand, and a girl who looked like Sex Incarnate was sitting on his living room couch. He was an awful man. He had burned Victor's effects because of wounded narcissism. Poole felt an unexpected stab of pity for Victor Spitalny, growing up under the thumb of this vain, arrogant, inadequate man.

"What was Victor like as a boy?" he asked.

George Spitalny turned his face heavily, almost warningly toward Poole. *Don't mess with my action, sonny.* Before he answered, he chugged down his beer and nearly winked at Maggie. "He didn't amount to much, that's the sad truth. Vic was kind of an unhappy kid. Cried a lot, didn't he?"

A look of pure cold indifference for his wife.

"Oh, Vic cried. All babies cry."

"He was a big disappointment. Never had friends until he got to high school. Never made his grades. He wasn't even any good at sports, like I thought he was gonna be. Here, I got something to show you." He gave Maggie a tight, almost shy smile and stood up again and left the room. They could hear him rapidly climbing the stairs.

"You said that Vic might be alive?" Margaret Spitalny asked Poole.

"We think it might be a possibility."

"There's no record of his death," Underhill said in a gentle voice. "He just disappeared. And he was in Thailand, so he could have just stayed there—or gone any of a dozen different places. He could have bought a new identity. You really haven't had even a postcard from him since his disappearance?"

Heavy footsteps came thumping back down the stairs, and Margaret Spitalny shook her head and glanced at the door. Her hands had begun to tremble. "I don't think—" She stopped speaking when her husband burst into the room, this time carrying a photograph in an old silver frame.

"Take a look at that, Maggie." He thrust it at her. Margaret looked sidelong at Poole, then looked down into her lap.

"Better see to the supper." She stood up and without looking at him moved around her husband, who was still grinning down at Maggie and breathing a little hard from his exertions on the stairs.

Poole moved closer to Maggie to look at the photograph. It was an old studio picture of a young man in a baseball uniform, posing with a bat in his hands. At eighteen or nineteen, George Spitalny had looked much like the son he would father—the same narrow head and widow's peak. He was more muscular than Victor had been, however, sturdier, more forceful: the face was that of a young man as unpleasant as Victor, but in a completely different way.

"Not bad, huh? That was me, 1938. What do you think of that?"

Maggie made no comment, and Spitalny took her silence as an inability to find adequate words. "I don't think I look too different now, even though it's about fifty years later. Next year I hit my retirement, and I'm still in damn good shape." He angled the photograph toward Michael for a moment, then toward Underhill before turning it back to Maggie. "That's the way a young man ought to look. Right? Well, when I looked at my kid—I mean the day Vic was born, when they brought him out to me so I could see him, I looked down at this little baby, and I got this tremendous shock. Here I was thinking I would just love this kid, love him to death. Isn't that supposed to be automatic? I thought that was supposed to be automatic. But I couldn't feel anything, really. I couldn't get over how goddamned ugly the kid was. Right away, I saw he was never gonna measure up to me. And you might call that psychic, or whatever, but I was right—he never did. Never. Not once. When he had that girlfriend in high school, that Debbie Maczik, I couldn't figure out how he could hold onto a girl cute like that. Tell you the truth, I used to think she used to come around here to see me, more than she liked to see him."

"Ready," Margaret called from somewhere in the rear of the house.

George Spitalny let Maggie feast a while longer on the photograph, then set it down on top of the television. "You guys go on back to the kitchen and sit down. I gotta go to the little boy's room."

4

"And what happened when we finally saw the pictures?" Tim asked, smiling at Maggie in the backseat of the cab during their ride back to the hotel.

Michael too had been waiting to ask this question.

After their dinner—"Put some of the ketchup on your kielbasa, Maggie, it's what we have here instead of soy sauce"—Mrs. Spitalny had finally gone upstairs and brought back from wherever they had been cached her pictures of Victor. Both Spitalnys had resisted showing these photographs, but when they had arrived George had taken charge, declaring some of them useless, others ridiculous, a few too ugly to be shown. In the end, they had been shown three photographs: one of a confused-looking boy of eight or nine on a bicycle, one of a teenage Victor leaning against the hood of an old black Dodge, and the third the standard end-of-basic-training yearbook photograph.

None of these precisely had resembled the Victor Spitalny remembered by Poole and Underhill. It was something of a shock that Victor Spitalny had ever looked as innocent as the boy in the warrior photograph. Leaning against the car with his arms crossed over his T-shirt, he looked surly but proud, for once in control of himself. In his pose was a long history of Elvis-worship. Oddly, it was the picture of the little boy that had most evoked the Victor Spitalny of Vietnam.

"Could you recognize him?" Michael asked.

Maggie nodded, but very slowly. "It had to be him. It was very dark in the loft, and the face in my memory has been getting vaguer and vaguer—but I'm pretty sure it was him. Also, the man I saw was crazy, and the boy in the pictures didn't look crazy. But if I were a boy and had that man for a father, I'd be crazy too. He thought the worst thing about his son's being a deserter was the injury it gave to his own ego."

"You have those telephone numbers?" Underhill asked.

She nodded again. George and Margaret Spitalny had looked up the numbers of Bill Hopper and Mack Simroe, both of them now married, living in their old neighborhood and working in the Valley, and of Deborah Maczik Tusa. Tomorrow they would rent a car to go back to the South Side. Poole remembered the unfocused, inward-gazing expression of the unattractive little boy on his bicycle. *Desperate*, someone had said (probably Maggie): that was why the photo of the eight-year-old Victor Spitalny looked more like the man they had known than the more adult photographs they had been shown. Only in the face of the boy on the bicycle, with his protruding ears and big adult front teeth in his child's face, could you see his desperation.

5

Back in the double room, Underhill took off the black wide-brimmed hat and long black coat he must have picked up on Canal Street, and Poole called downstairs and ordered what looked like the best red wine on the Pforzheimer's list, a 1974 Chateau Talbot, and a Sprite for Underhill. They all wanted something to take the taste of their dinner from their mouths.

"You even put ketchup on your cabbage," Maggie said to Tim.

"I just asked myself, what would Conor Linklater do if he were here?"

"Who do we call first?" Michael asked. "Debbie, or one of the boys?"

"Would he have written to her?"

"Possible," Poole said, and dialed Debbie Tusa's number.

A teenage boy answered the phone and said, "You want my mom? Hey, Mom! Mom! A guy on the phone!"

"Who's this?" asked a tired voice a moment later. Poole could hear a television set bellowing in the background.

He introduced himself and briefly explained what he was doing.

"Who?"

"Vic Spitalny. I believe you used to go out with him when you both attended Rufus King High School."

She said nothing for a moment. "Oh, my God. Who are you again?"

Poole again recited his name and history.

"And where did you learn my name?"

"I've just been with Victor's parents."

"Vic's parents," she said. "George and Margaret. Well, well. I haven't thought about that poor guy in about ten years, I bet."

"So you haven't heard anything from him since he went into the service."

"Since long before that, Doctor. He dropped out of school in our senior year, and I had been going out with Nick, that's the guy I married, for a year already. Nick and I split up three years ago. How come you're interested in Vic Spitalny?"

"He kind of slipped out of sight. I'm interested in what happened to him. Why did you call him 'that poor guy' just now?"

"I guess that's pretty much what he was. I went out with him, after all, so I never thought he was as bad as the other kids did. In fact I thought he was kind of sweet, but . . . Vic wasn't what you'd call a real oddball, there was at least one guy who was worse off than what he was, it was just, nobody would give him a chance. He was kind of shy—he loved working on his car. But I hated going to his house."

"Why?"

"Old George's tongue used to drop out of his mouth the second I set foot on the sidewalk—he was always *touching* me. Ugh. I could see what he was doing to Vic—he just cut him down, all the time. I just couldn't take it anymore, eventually. Then Vic dropped out of school. He was flunking a lot of courses, anyway. And he got drafted."

"You never heard from him after that?"

"I just heard *about* him," she said. "It was in all the papers, when he deserted. Pictures and everything. Right before Nick and me got married. There was Vic on the front page of the *Sentinel.* Second section. All that stuff about his running away when that Dengler guy was killed—everything about that was *weird.* It was even on TV that night, but I still didn't believe it. Vic wouldn't do anything like that. It all seemed so mixed *up* to me. When the army guys came around after that—you know, investigating—I said, you guys made a mistake. You got it wrong."

"What do you think happened, then?"

"I don't know. I guess I think he's dead."

Room service arrived. Underhill let Maggie taste and approve the wine, tipped the waiter, and brought Michael a glass just as he finished his conversation with Debbie Tusa. The wine immediately dissolved the greasy taste of the sausage.

"Cheers," Maggie said.

"She doesn't even think he deserted."

"His mother doesn't either," Maggie said. Poole looked at her in surprise. She must have picked up this information on her Maggie-radar.

Bill Hopper, one of Spitalny's high school friends, said in the course of Michael's short conversation with him that he knew nothing about Victor Spitalny, had never liked him, and didn't want to know anything about him. Vic Spitalny was a disgrace to his parents and to Milwaukee. Bill Hopper was of the opinion that George Spitalny, with whom he worked at the Glax Corporation, was one hell of a good man who had deserved a better son than that. He went on for a time, then told Poole to get off his case, and hung up.

"Bill Hopper says our boy was a sicko, and nobody normal liked him."

"You didn't have to be normal to dislike Spitalny," Underhill said.

Poole sipped the wine. His body suddenly felt limp as a sack. "I wonder if there's any point in my calling this other guy. I already know what he's going to say."

"Aren't you going on the theory that Spitalny will eventually turn to someone for help?" Maggie asked innocently. "And here we are in Milwaukee."

Poole picked up the phone and dialed the last number.

"Simroe."

Poole began speaking. He felt as though he were reading lines.

"Oh, Vic Spitalny," Mack Simroe said. "No, I can't help you find him. I don't know anything about him. He just went away, didn't he? Got drafted. Well, you know that, right? You were there with him. Umm, how did you get my name?"

"From his parents. I had the impression they thought he was dead."

"They would," Simroe said. Poole could hear him smiling. "Look, I think it's nice you're looking for him—I mean, it's nice *somebody's* looking for him, but I never even got a postcard from the guy. Have you talked to Debbie Maczik? Debbie Tusa, she is now?"

Poole said that she had not heard from him either.

"Well, maybe that's not too surprising." Simroe's laugh sounded almost embarrassed. "Considering, I mean."

"You think he'd still be that guilty about his desertion?"

"Well, not only that. I mean, I don't think the whole story ever came out, do you?'

Poole agreed that it had not, and wondered where all this was going.

"Who's going to go check up on a thing like that? You'd have to go to Bangkok, wouldn't you?"

You would, and he had, Poole said.

"So was it just coincidence, or what? It sure seemed funny at the time. The only guy worse off than he was—the only guy who was as much of a loser as he was, actually more so."

"I'm not sure I'm following you," Poole said.

"Well, Dengler," Simroe said. "It sure looked funny. I guess I thought he must have killed him over there."

"Spitalny knew Dengler before they got to Vietnam?"

"Well, sure. Everybody knew Dengler. All the kids

did. You know how everybody knows the one kid who just can't get it together, whose clothes are all raggy—Dengler was a basket case."

"Not in Vietnam, he wasn't," Poole said.

"Well, naturally Spitalny hated Dengler. When you're down low, you hate whatever's beneath you, right?"

Poole felt as though he had just stuck his finger in a socket.

"So when I saw in the paper about Manny Dengler dying over there and Vic running away, I thought there must be more to it. So did most people, most people who knew Manny Dengler, anyhow. But nobody expected to get any postcards from him. I mean . . ."

When Poole hung up, Underhill was staring at him with eyes like lanterns.

"They knew each other," Poole said. "They went to school together. According to Mack Simroe, Dengler was the only kid who was even more out of it than Spitalny."

Underhill shook his head in wonder. "I never even saw them talk to each other, except that once."

"Spitalny arranged to meet Dengler in Bangkok. He set it up in advance. He was planning to kill him—they worked out a place to meet, just the way he did with the journalists fourteen years later."

"It was the first Koko murder."

"Without the card."

"Because it was supposed to look like mob violence," Underhill said.

"Goddamn," Poole said. He dialed Debbie Tusa's number again, and the same teenage boy yelled, "HEY, MOM! WHO IS THIS GUY?"

"I give up, who are you?' she said when she picked up.

Poole explained who he was and why he was calling again.

"Well, sure Vic knew Manny Dengler. Everybody did. Not to speak to, but to see. I think Vic used to tease him now and then—it was sort of cruel, and I didn't like it. I thought you knew all about it! That's why it seemed so mixed up to me. I couldn't figure out what they were doing together. Nicky, my husband, thought Vic stabbed Manny or something, but that has to be crazy. Because Vic wouldn't have done anything like that."

Poole arranged to meet her for lunch the next day.

"Spitalny came into our unit and found Dengler there,"

Underhill was saying to Maggie. "But everything has changed about Dengler—he's loved by everybody. Did he talk to him? Did he make fun of him? What did he do?"

"Dengler talked to *him*," Poole said. "He said, a lot of things have changed since high school. Let's just make like we never met until now. And in a way, they never had met—Spitalny had never met *our* Dengler before."

"When they came out of the cave," Underhill said, "didn't Dengler say something like 'Don't worry about it? Whatever it was, it was a long time ago.' I thought he meant—"

"I did too—whatever Beevers did in there. I thought he was telling Spitalny to cut himself loose from it."

"But he was saying it was a long time since Milwaukee," Underhill said.

"He meant both," Maggie said. "Backwards and forwards, remember? And he knew that Spitalny wouldn't be able to handle whatever happened to all of them in there. He knew who Koko was right from the start." Suddenly Maggie yawned, and closed her eyes like a cat. "Excuse me. Too much excitement. I think I'll go next door and go to bed."

"See you in the morning, Maggie," Underhill said.

Poole walked Maggie to the door, opened it for her, and said "Goodnight." On impulse he stepped out into the hallway after her.

Maggie raised her eyebrows. "Walking me home?"

"I guess I am."

Maggie moved down the hallway to her own door. The corridor was noticeably colder than the rooms.

"Tomorrow the Denglers," Maggie said, putting the key in the lock. She seemed very small, standing in the immense dim corridor. He nodded. The look she gave him deepened and changed in quality. Poole suddenly knew how it would feel to put his arms around Maggie Lah, how her body would fit into his. Then he felt like George Spitalny, drooling over Maggie.

"Tomorrow the Denglers," he said.

She looked up at him oddly: he could not tell if what he thought he had just seen, the increase in weight and gravity, had been real. It had been like being touched. Poole thought that he wanted Maggie to touch him so badly that he had probably invented everything.

"Want to come in?" she asked.

"I don't want to keep you up," Poole said.

She smiled and disappeared around her door.

6

Harry Beevers stood on Mott Street, looking around and thinking that he needed a killing box: someplace where he could watch Koko until it was time to either capture him or kill him. Spitalny would have to be led into a trap where Harry controlled the only way in or out. Harry considered that he was good at setting up killing boxes. Killing boxes were a proven skill. Like Koko, he had to pick his own battleground—draw his victim out into the territory he had chosen.

Some of Harry's flyers had been ripped off and thrown away, but most of them still called out from lampposts and shop windows. He began to walk south down Mott Street, sharing it on this cold day with only a few hurtling Chinese, heavily bundled and chalky with the cold. All he had to do was find a restaurant that looked quiet enough for his initial rendezvous with Spitalny—he would soothe him with food—and then work out where to take him afterwards. His apartment was out, though in some ways its seclusion was perfect. But he had to take Koko someplace which would in itself constitute an alibi. A dark alley behind a police station would be just about perfect.

Beevers could see himself slumping out of the alley like some heroic Rambo, heavy-shouldered, panting, spattered with his enemy's blood, gesturing a crowd of stupefied officers toward Spitalny's body—There's the man you're looking for. Jumped me while I was bringing him in.

He had to buy a good knife, that was one thing he had to do. And a pair of handcuffs. You could snap a pair of handcuffs on a man before he knew what was happening. Then you could do what you liked to him. And unlock the handcuffs before the body hit the floor.

On the corner of Bayard Street he hesitated, then turned east toward Confucius Plaza. He came to Elizabeth Street, turned in and walked back north a few steps before deciding it was all wrong—nothing but tenements and murky little Chinese businesses. Koko would see it for a trap right away—he'd know a killing box when he saw one. Harry went back to Bayard Street and continued on toward Bowery.

This was a lot more promising.

Across Bowery stood Confucius Plaza, an immense office and apartment complex. On one corner stood a bank shaped like a modernist pagoda in red lacquer, across the street a Chinese cinema. Cars swept unendingly around a long traffic island that extended from Bowery around the corner into Division Street. At the apex of the traffic island was a tall statue of Confucius.

This was too public for his meeting with Koko. He looked across the street to the Plaza. A lower building, of perhaps fifteen stories, fronted Bowery, blocking from view the lower half of the taller residential tower. The buildings had a slightly molded look that carried the eye along, and behind them, Harry thought, must be a terrace or a plaza—trees and benches.

And that gave it to him—at least half of it. Into his mind had come the image of the park bordered by Mulberry and Baxter streets near the western end of Chinatown. Now this park would be empty, but in the spring and summer the little park was crowded with lawyers, bailiffs, judges, and policemen taking a break from their duties. This was Columbus Park, and Harry knew it well from his early days as a litigator—he had never really connected it to Chinatown in his mind. Columbus Park was an adjunct to the row of government buildings lined up along Centre Street.

The Criminal Courts building stood between Centre and Baxter at the top end of Columbus Park; down at the bottom end was the smaller, more prisonlike structure of the Federal Courthouse; and further south, between Worth and Pearl streets, a block from the park, was the even more penitential structure, grim and dirty and oozing gloom at all seasons, of the New York County Courthouse.

Harry instantly discarded the notion of meeting Koko in a restaurant. He would ask him to meet in Columbus Park. If Koko had moved into Chinatown, he would know the park by now, and if he had not, the idea of meeting in a park would serve to make him feel secure. It was perfect. It would look good in the book too, and play beautifully in the movie, but it would be fiction. The meeting in Columbus Park would be part of the myth; it did not have to be real to be part of the myth. For Harry intended only to make Koko think that they would meet in the park. Harry would send him through somewhere else first, and that would be his killing box.

Harry stood freezing on the corner of Bayard Street and Bowery. A black stretch limousine pulled up to the curb before him and two short, pudgy Chinese men with glossy tiny feet got out of the backseat. They wore dark suits and sunglasses, and their hair was slicked back. They looked like twin dwarfs with zombie faces and stiff, self-important movements. One of them slammed the door of the limousine, and they strode across the sidewalk to push their way into one of the restaurants across from Confucius Plaza. One of them passed within a foot of Harry without in any way registering his presence. Harry thought that if he had been standing in his path, the little gangster would have knocked him over and walked across his body the way Elizabeth walked over Raleigh's cloak.

He moved across the sidewalk to the car. Harry felt even colder than before—in every car that sped down Bowery, in every apartment in Confucius Plaza, was a flat-faced chink who did not care if Harry Beevers lived or died. How had all the little bastards clawed their way up out of the laundries? He bent over the trunk of the limousine and looked down at sixteen layers of meticulously applied black lacquer. The skin of the car looked as deep as a lake. Harry gathered a good gob of phlegm and saliva in his mouth and spat it onto the trunk of the limousine. It began to slide a bit toward the fender.

Harry stepped back from the car and began to walk up the block. He was on the verge of thinking that now he was wasting his time here and that he should be checking out Bayard Street's western end when the smooth, unbroken row of Chinese restaurants ceased and he found himself staring into a cave. His feet stopped moving and his heart thumped like the kick of a rabbit's back legs. On both sides the tiles of the buildings folded in to form a wide passage. Of course it was not a cave. He was standing before an arcade.

Down in the distance he could see women's underwear in forlorn shades of pink and pale blue stretched across forms in a lighted window. Near it a pair of giant's eyeglasses stared out from an optician's window. Further back a restaurant sign floated in grey air. Harry walked into the arcade. One old Chinese woman shuffled toward him, in the dimness of the arcade no more than a wrinkled forehead and a pair of averted eyes.

Harry paused outside Chinatown Opticians and peered through the empty left orb of the giant's glasses. Behind the counter in the deserted shop a clerk with a punk crewcut and cheeks inflamed with acne stared into a Chinese-language edition of *Playboy*.

Tattered posters advertising a Chinese opera covered the walls of the arcade. Other posters concerned rock clubs. A few shops along, the gloom grew thicker and the arcade angled off toward what must be Elizabeth Street. The ripped posters led toward a shoebox-sized restaurant called Malay Coffee Shop, which showed a large white CLOSED sign on its door. A few feet farther, just before the angle in the arcade, a narrow tiled staircase led down to another level. A fat arrow had been painted on the side of the staircase, below it the words FORTUNE BARBER SHOP.

Harry went slowly down the steps, ducking his head to see how far the lower level extended. Two grey-haired barbers sat in their own chairs inside the Fortune Barber Shop while a third barber snipped at an old woman's hair. Two other shops, one with a poster in its window of a levitating Ninja with an outflung leg, filled out the short downstairs level. Harry stopped moving about halfway down the stairs. His eyes were at the level of the arcade's tiled floor. Nobody walking in would see him, but he would have a perfect view of them.

He moved a step up, and in the brighter outside air two short males moved past the arcade's entrance. The zombies. As soon as they had passed the entrance, they snapped back to reappear, looking into the arcade. Their sunglasses were like wide black holes in their faces. Harry moved quietly down a step and watched the two zombies glance at each other and take a step into the arcade. Their bodies blurred in the darkness. They came forward, stocky, almost stumping on their legs like sumo wrestlers. As they came nearer Harry saw that their hands were balled into fists. They stood three feet from him, their thick short arms swinging. One of them spoke softly in Chinese, and Harry understood the words as if they had been in English. *The bastard isn't here.* The second man grunted.

His life was not like other lives, other people thought the world was solid and were blind to the great tears and rents in the surface of existence. Harry's mind filled with the wingbeats of insects and the cries of children.

The surface of the world almost shredded and allowed his real life to take place.

The two men turned around in perfect unison, like dance partners, and went back outside the arcade. Harry waited on the steps a minute, two minutes, he did not know how long. The old woman from the barber shop came slowly up the steps, rapping on the tiles with a wooden cane. He moved aside to let her pass along the railing, and she wordlessly pulled herself up past him. He was invisible: no one had seen him. He wiped his wet palms on the flanks of his coat and went up to the main level of the arcade.

Empty: the world had closed up again.

Harry trotted downstairs to the Ninja shop and spent fifty-six dollars on a gravity knife and a pair of handcuffs. Then he mounted the stairs again.

At the entrance he bent forward and looked south down Bowery. The limousine was no longer parked in front of the restaurant. Harry smiled. Inside the chauffeur's once doubtless pristine white handkerchief was a fat yellow wad of Harry Beevers.

Someone was staring down from a window high up in Confucius Plaza; someone in a passing car turned his head to gaze at him. Someone was watching him, for his life was like a film and he was the hero of that film. "I found it," he said, knowing that someone heard him: or that someone watching him had read his lips.

Now all he had to do was wait for the telephone call. Harry began walking up toward Canal to start looking for a cab. Traffic moved past him in a seamless flow. He no longer felt cold. He stood on Canal Street and watched the trafflc sweep past him, tasting on his tongue the oil and bite of the icy vodka he had just earned. When the light changed, he crossed Canal to walk north on Bowery, rejoicing.

33

SECOND NIGHT AT THE PFORZHEIMER

1

Michael Poole came awake in cold darkness, the dream picture of a Chinese schoolgirl grinning at him from beneath the brim of a white straw skimmer vanishing from his mind. One of the large radiators clanked again, and Tim Underhill snored gently in the next bed. Poole picked up his watch and brought its face toward his until the hands became distinct. A minute to eight became eight o'clock as he watched. The first tendrils of warmth began to reach him.

Underhill groaned, stretched, wiped his hands over his face. He looked at Poole and said, "Morning." He sat up in bed—Underhill's hair stuck out on both sides of his head, and his white-blond beard was crunched and flattened on one side. He looked like a crazed professor in an old movie. "Listen to this," Underhill said, and Poole sat up in bed too.

"I've been thinking about this all night," Underhill said. "Here's where we are at the moment. We have Dengler spooking Spitalny, right? He comes up to him and points out that in a combat unit everybody has to protect everybody else. He takes him into Ozone Park, say, and he tells him that if he acts toward him in the old way he will mess with the lives of everybody in the platoon. Maybe he even says that he'll make sure that Spitalny will never come back from his first mission—whatever he says, Spitalny agrees to be silent about their old relationship. But this *is* Spitalny—he can't take it. He hates Dengler a little more every day. And eventually Spitalny follows Dengler to Bangkok and kills him. Now what I'm thinking is that Spitalny never was the original Koko. He just borrowed the name a decade and a half later, when he really slipped a cog."

"Who was, then?"

"There never really was an original Koko," Underhill said. "Not in the way I've been thinking of it." Excited by his thoughts, Underhill swung his legs over the side of the bed and stood up. He was wearing a long nightshirt, and his legs looked like pipe stems with knees. "You get it? It's like Agatha Christie. Probably everybody who wanted to support Dengler wrote Koko on a card at least once. Koko was everybody. I was Koko, you were Koko, Conor was Koko once. Everybody just imitated the first one."

"But then who was the first one?" Poole asked. "Spitalny? That doesn't seem very likely."

"I think it was Beevers," Underhill said, his eyes glowing. "It was right after the publicity began, remember? The courtmartials began to seem inevitable. Beevers was stressed out. He knew nobody would support him, but he also knew that he could claim to share whatever support Dengler had. So he mutilated a dead VC, and wore a word everybody associated with Dengler on a regimental card. And it worked."

Someone rapped at the door. "It's me," Maggie called. "Aren't you up yet?"

Underhill moved on scissoring legs toward the door, and Poole pulled on a bathrobe.

Maggie came in smiling, dressed in a black skirt and an oversized black sweater. "Have you looked outside yet? It snowed again last night. It looks like heaven out there."

Poole stood up and walked past smiling Maggie toward the window. Maggie seemed to be appraising him, which made him uncomfortable. Now Poole felt he could not trust any of his responses to the girl. Underhill began condensing their conversation for her, and Poole pulled the cord to open the curtains.

Cold bluish light slanted in the window and down on

the white street beneath him, pristine with the new snow and nearly unmarked. The snow looked like a good thick linen napkin. On the sidewalk a few deep footsteps showed where one person had mushed to work.

"So Harry Beevers is really Koko," Maggie said. "I wonder why I find that so easy to believe?"

Poole turned away from the window. "Does the word Koko mean anything to you?"

"Kaka," Maggie said. "Or *coo-coo*, meaning crazy. Who knows? *Cocoa*, as in the warm bedtime drink. But if Victor Spitalny knew that Harry Beevers had been the first to *use* it wouldn't he have an above-average interest in Harry?"

Poole looked at her wonderingly.

"Isn't it possible that he might want to eliminate Harry next, or before he retires or gives himself up or whatever he is going to do?"

"In fact," Maggie said, "Tina had probably been killed only because he had stayed at home. Tina was killed because he was there." She came to the window and stood beside Michael. "Koko even broke into 56 Grand Street, on the day Tina came uptown to fetch me back from where I stayed when I was not with him." A flicker of a glance toward Michael, who was frowning out at the dimpled snowscape of Maggie's heaven. And that, she said, was how Spitalny learned everything he wanted to learn.

"What was that?" Poole asked.

"Where everybody lived."

Poole still did not get it. Koko learned where everybody lived because Tina Pumo stayed at home?

"It was a night he still liked me," Maggie said—and then told him about Tina leaving the bed and finding that his address book had been stolen.

A night he still liked her?

"A few days later, it was all happening again," she said. "You knew Tina. He was never going to change. It was very sad. I came down to see just *if* he would talk to me. And that was how I nearly got killed."

"How did you escape?" Poole asked.

"By using a silly old trick." And would say no more about it. Saved by an old trick, like the heroine of a story.

"Koko knows how to find Conor, then," Tim said.

"Conor's staying with his lady love," Poole said. "So he'll be safe. But Beevers had better watch out for himself."

"Aren't you people ever going to get dressed," Maggie wanted to know, "all this middle-aged male beauty in disarray is making my stomach rumble. At least I think it's my stomach. What are we going to do today?"

2

What they did, once they had breakfasted in the Grill Room, was check out some of Victor Spitalny's old hangouts before rewarding themselves by visiting M.O. Dengler's childhood home and telling the Vietnam stories they had already told once, this time accurately. Stories and storytelling too had their gods, and it would be an act of homage to those gods to set the narrative record straight before Dengler's parents.

So they had begun with a round of the bars, or taverns, as these bars were known, in which Spitalny had spent his time waiting for his call-up—The Sports Lounge, The Polka Dot, Sam 'N' Aggie's, located within half a mile of one another, two of them a block apart on Mitchell Street and the other, The Polka Dot, five blocks further north, on the edge of the Valley. Poole had agreed to meet Mack Simroe there after work at five-thirty. Debbie Tusa had arranged to meet them for lunch at the Tick Tock restaurant, a block off Mitchell on Psalm Street. In Milwaukee bars opened early and were seldom without customers, but by noon Poole had become discouraged by the reception they had found in them. None of the people in either of the first two taverns had been interested in talking about an army deserter.

In 1969 army investigators had come to these same bars, looking for hints as to where Victor might be hiding himself, and Poole thought that the army's men had probably spoken to the same barflies and bartenders that he and Maggie and Tim had met. The taverns would not have changed at all since 1969 except for minor adjustments to the jukeboxes. Nestled in among the hundreds of Elvis Presley songs and hundreds more polkas—Joe Schott and the Hot Schotts?—had been a rare survivor of that era, Barry Sadler's "The Ballad of the Green Berets." In these taverns harsh light bounced off the Formica, the bartenders were pasty overweight men with tattoos and pre-modern crewcuts, and yellowbellies who deserted from the armed forces might as well go out and hang themselves from the oak tree in the backyard so as not to put someone else to the trouble. And you drank Pforzheimer's—you didn't mess around with lightweight stuff like Budweiser, Coors, Olympia, Stroh's, Rolling Rock, Pabst, Schlitz, or Hamm's. Taped to the mirror in The Sports Lounge were printed signs reading PFORZHEIMER'S—BREAKFAST OF CHAMPIONS and PFORZHEIMER'S—THE NATIONAL DRINK OF THE VALLEY.

"We don't export most of it," said Tattoo and Crewcut, getting yuk-yuk-yuk from his regulars. "We pretty much like to keep it to ourselves."

"Well, I can see why," Poole said, tasting the thin flat yellow stuff. Behind him E.P. groaned about chapels and momma and the difficulties of love.

"That Spitalny kid wasn't any kind of a man," Tattoo and Crewcut declared, "but I never thought he'd turn out as crummy as he did."

In Sam 'N' Aggie's the bartender, being Aggie, had neither crewcut nor tattoos, and instead of Elvis, Jim Reeves moaned about chapels and momma and the love that defied the grave, but the content of their visit was otherwise very similar. Pforzheimer's. Dark looks at Maggie Lah. You're asking about who is that? Oh, him. More dark looks. His dad's a regular guy, but the kid sure went wrong, didn't he? Another glowering glance toward Maggie. Around here, see, we're *real* Americans.

So the three of them marched in silence toward the Tick Tock, each with their own preoccupations.

When Poole pushed open the door and followed Maggie and Underhill into the small crowded restaurant half a dozen men had turned on the bar stools to gape at Maggie. "Yellow Peril strikes again," Maggie whispered.

A thin woman with frosted hair and deep lines in her face was giving the three newcomers a tentative wave from a booth at the side of the restaurant.

Debbie Tusa recommended the Salisbury steak; she chattered about the weather and how much she had enjoyed New York; she was having a little Seabreeze, that's vodka, grapefruit juice, and cranberry juice, would they want one? It was really a summer drink, she supposed, but you could drink it all year long. They made good drinks at the Tick Tock, everybody knew that, and was it true they were all from New York, or were some of them really from Washington?

"Are you nervous about something, Debbie?" Tim asked.

"Well, the last ones were from Washington."

The waitress came in her tight white uniform and checked apron, and everybody ordered Salisbury steak, except for Maggie, who asked for a club sandwich. Debbie drank from her Seabreeze and said to Maggie, "You could have a Cape Codder, that's vodka and clam juice?"

"Tonic water," Maggie said, and the waitress said, "Tonic *water*? Like tonic?"

"Like gin and tonic without the gin," Maggie said.

"A lot of people are talking about you, you know." Debbie inserted the tiny straw in her mouth and looked up at them as she sipped. "A lot of people think you people are from the government. And some aren't sure which government."

"We're private citizens," Poole said.

"Well, maybe Vic is doing something bad now, and you're trying to catch him, like he's a spy. I think George and Margaret are afraid Vic is gonna come back, and the news is gonna be just *terrible*, and George will lose his job before he gets his retirement—if Vic turns out to be a spy or anything."

"He's not a spy," Poole said. "And George's job would be safe anyway."

"That's what you think. My husband, Nick, he—well, that's not important. But you don't know what they do."

The waitress eventually set their food down before them, and Poole was immediately sorry that he had not ordered a sandwich.

"I know Salisbury steak's no big deal," Debbie said, "but it's better than it looks. And anyhow, you don't know what a treat it is to eat someone else's cooking. So even if you're all secret agents or whatever—thanks!"

The steak did taste slightly better than it looked.

"You didn't know that Vic and Manny Dengler were in the same class at Rufus King?"

"It was a surprise," Poole said. "There's a Dengler listed in the phone book on Muffin Street. Is that his parents?"

"I think his mom's still there. His mom was a real quiet lady, I think. She'll never go anywhere." A bite of steak, a swallow of the Seabreeze. "Never did. She didn't even go out when the old man was doing his preaching."

"Dengler's father was a preacher?" Underhill asked. "With a congregation and a church?"

" 'Course not," she said, with a glance toward Maggie—as if Maggie already knew all about it. "Dengler's dad was a butcher." Another glance at Maggie. "Was that sandwich any good?"

"Yum," Maggie said. "Mr. Dengler was a butcher-preacher?"

"He was one of those *crazy* preachers. He had little services in the butcher shop next to his house sometimes, but lots of times he'd just get out on the street and start yellin' away. Manny had to go out with him. Could be as cold as this, and they'd be out on the corner with the old man yellin' about sin and the devil and Manny singin' and passin' the hat."

"What was his church called?" Maggie asked.

"The Church of the Messiah." She smiled. "Didn't you ever hear Manny sing? He used to sing that—*The Messiah*. Well, not the whole thing, but his dad used to make him sing things from it."

" 'All we like sheep,' " Maggie said.

"Yep. See? Everybody thought he was goofy as batshit." Her eyes flew open. "*Excuse* me!"

"I heard him quote *The Messiah* once," Poole said. "Victor was there too, and Vic sort of mocked him as soon as he spoke."

"That sounds like Vic."

" 'A man of sorrow and acquainted with grief,' " Underhill said. "Then Spitalny said it twice, and said *" 'A man of sorrow and acquainted with dickheads.' "*

Debbie Tusa silently raised her glass.

"And Dengler said, *'Whatever it was, it was a long time ago.' "*

"But what was *it*?," Poole asked. *"A man of sorrow and acquainted with grief?"*

"Well, they had a lot of trouble," Debbie said. "The Denglers had a lot of trouble." She looked down at her plate. "I guess I'm done. You ever notice how you never feel like shopping for dinner after you eat a big lunch?"

"I never feel like shopping for dinner," Maggie said.

"Where do you suppose Vic is now? You guys don't think he's dead, do you?"

"Well, we were hoping to find out where he is from you," Poole said.

Debbie laughed. "I wish my ex-husband could see me right now. Screw you, Nicky, wherever you are. You deserved what you got when they sent your terrible old man to Waupun. Any of you guys want to change your mind about a drink?"

None of them did.

"You want to hear the worst? The worst thing? I said his butcher shop was next to the house on Muffin Street? You want to guess what the name of the butcher shop was?"

"The Blood of the Lamb Butcher Shop," Maggie said.

"Wow," Debbie said. "So close. Any other tries?"

"Lamb of God," Poole said. "The Lamb of God Butcher Shop."

"*Dengler's* Lamb of God Butcher Shop," Debbie said. "How did you know?"

"The Messiah," Poole said. " 'Behold the lamb of God, that taketh away the sins of the world.' "

" 'All we like sheep have gone astray,' " Maggie said.

"My husband sure did." She gave Poole a grim little smile. "I guess old Vic probably did too, didn't he?"

Poole asked for the check. Debbie Tusa took a compact out of her bag and inspected herself in its mirror.

"Did you ever hear Vic or anybody else sing something like *rip-a-rip-a-rip-a-lo* or *pompo, pompo, polo, polo . . .*?"

Debbie was staring at him over the top of her compact. "Is that the song of the pink elephants? Honestly. I gotta get back home. You guys feel like coming over to my place?"

Poole said that they had other appointments. Debbie struggled into her coat, hugged each of them, and told Maggie that she was so cute, it was no wonder she was lucky too. She waved good-bye from the door of the restaurant.

"If there's nothing to do now, I could go back to the hotel and work on some notes," Underhill said.

Maggie suggested that they try to call Dengler's mother.

3

"I said we just wanted to talk to her," Poole said, turning into Muffin Street. It was two shabby blocks long, the Old Log Cabin Tavern at one end, the Up 'N' Under at the other. Half of the buildings were small businesses; in half of these the windows had been boarded up and the signs had faded into blurs. A peeling frame building with a small front porch, like the Spitalny house, but listing to one side and so grimy it seemed almost to have been draped in cobwebs, number 53 leaned against a square smaller building with a sheet of plywood where it had once had a window. The Reverend Dengler had located the Lamb of God Butcher Shop two blocks away from the nearest shopping street, and like the TV repair shop two blocks away and Irma's Dress Shop it had quietly gone out of business.

"Nice," Maggie said as she got out of the car. "Very romantic."

They had to pick their way through the snow. Muffin Street had been plowed, but few of the sidewalks had been shoveled clean. The steps sagged and complained as they went up onto the porch. The front door opened before Poole could push the bell.

"Hello, Mrs. Dengler," Tim said.

A pale white-haired woman in a blue wool dress was looking out through the crack in the door, squinting because of the cold and the brightness of the fresh snow. Her hair was in tight tiny curls that had been dusted with powder.

"Mrs. Dengler?" Poole asked.

She nodded. Her face was square and private, white as a paper cup. The only color was in the almost transparent pale blue of her wide-set eyes, as odd in a human face as the eyes of a dog. They appeared slightly magnified behind a pair of round old-fashioned glasses. "I'm Helga Dengler," she said in a voice that struggled to be welcoming. For a second, Poole thought her voice was his wife's. "You'd better get in out of the cold." She moved no more than two or three inches out of the way and as Poole squeezed past her he saw the white flecks of powder in her hair sift down to the white scalp.

"You're the one who called? Dr. Poole?"

"Yes, and—"

"Who's that one? You didn't tell me about that one."

"Maggie Lah. She is a close friend of ours."

The odd pale dog's eyes inspected him. Poole had become aware of a close, dank, musty smell as soon as the door closed. Mrs. Dengler's nose was upturned and very broad, with three deep creases across its top just beneath the bridge of the old-fashioned glasses. She had virtually no lips, and her neck was very thick. Her shoulders too were thick, sturdy, and bent forward in a permanent stoop.

"I'm just an old woman who lives alone, that's all I am. Now, now. Yes. Come along." With little phrases she motioned them toward a coat rack and stood rubbing her hands over her wide upper arms. In the darkness of the hallway Mrs. Dengler's large square face seemed to shine, as if it drew all the light in the house to it.

Helga Dengler's pale eyes moved from Poole to Maggie to Underhill and back to Maggie. There was a sense of heavy shapelessness about her, as if she were far heavier than she looked. "So," she said. A staircase, in the darkness no more than an impression of a wooden handrail and newel posts, rose into the gloom at her back. The floor was slightly gritty underfoot. Dim light came through a half-open door down the hall.

"You're very kind to have invited us, Mrs. Dengler," Poole said, and Maggie and Tim Underhill said similar things that tangled together in the air and then broke off.

As if their words had reached her after a delay, for a moment she merely gleamed at them. Then: "Well, the Bible tells us to be kind, doesn't it? You men knew my son?"

"He was a wonderful person," Poole said.

"We loved your son," Underhill said at the same moment, and their sentences also tangled together.

"Well," she said. Poole thought that he could look all the way through her eyes and see nothing but the clear blue color of blue jeans washed a thousand times. Then he thought that their queer awkwardness was forced on them by her: that she had wished it upon them.

"Manny tried to be a good boy," she said. "He had to be trained to it, like all boys."

Again Poole had the sense of a missed beat, of a second that fell either into Helga Dengler or out of the world altogether.

"You'll want to sit down," she said. "I guess the living room is where you'll want to go. This way. I'm busy, you see. An old woman who lives alone has to keep herself busy."

"Have we interrupted something?" Poole asked. She smiled her hard twitch of a smile and motioned for them to follow her down the hall and through the door.

One low-wattage bulb burned beneath an ornate lampshade. The single bar of an electrical heater glowed red in the corner of the crowded room. Here the musty odor was not so noticeable. The furniture seemed to glow and ripple. Purple stained-glass tiger's eyes shone down from little shelves and from a table beside a couch of worn plush. "You can all sit there, it used to be my mother's." The rippling glow was reflected light streaking across stiff clear plastic covers which creaked when they sat down.

Poole looked sideways at the tiger's eyes on the round table and saw that they were marbles, cracked on the inside in such a way that they caught the yellow light. There were dozens of them fixed in an arrangement on a piece of black cloth.

"That's my work," the woman said. She was standing in the center of the room. On the wall behind her was a framed photograph of a uniformed man who in the general darkness resembled a Boy Scout leader. Other pictures, of puppies tumbled together and kittens entangled in yarn, had been placed in random positions on the walls.

"You can have your opinion, and I'll have mine," Mrs. Dengler said. She took a half-step forward, and her eyes seemed to swell behind the round lenses. "Everybody's entitled to their opinion, that's what we told them over and over again."

"Excuse me?" Michael said. Underhill was smiling either at Mrs. Dengler or at the pictures only half-visible behind her. "You said . . . your work?"

She visibly relaxed, and stepped backwards again. "My grape clusters. You were looking."

"Oh," Poole said. That was what they were. The purple marbles, he saw, had been glued to the black fabric in the shape of a cluster of grapes. "Very nice."

"Everybody always thought so. When my husband had his church, some of the congregation used to buy my grape clusters. Everybody always said they were beautiful. The way they catch the light."

"Beautiful," Poole said.

"How do you make them?" Maggie asked.

This time her smile seemed genuine, almost delicate, as if she knew she took an immodest amount of pride in her grape clusters. "You could do it yourself," she said, and finally sat down on a footstool. "It's in a pan. I always use Wesson oil. You use butter, it spatters. And it *burns*. My husband would use butter for everything, but he had the feeling for meat, you see. You use that Wesson oil, little girl, and you'll always get your marbles to crack in the right way. That's what nobody understands—especially in these times. You must do things right."

"So you fry the marbles," Maggie said.

"Well . . . yes. You use your pan and your Wesson oil. And you use low heat. That way they crack all the same way. That's the good part of it. They all turn out just right. Then you turn them out of the pan and run cold water over them for a second or two, that seems to *set* them somehow, and after they cool down you glue them to your form. A dot of glue, that's it. And then you've got your cluster, a beautiful thing for all eternity." She beamed at Maggie, all the light concentrated in the heavy, thick center of her face. "For . . . all . . . eternity. Like the Word of God. Each one takes twenty-four marbles. To come out exactly right and lifelike too. Well. Better than lifelike, in some ways."

"Being all alike," Maggie said.

"All just alike. That's the beauty part. With boys, you know, you can just try and try. You can do what you will, but they will resist." Her face closed up for a moment, and the center of her face seemed to dim. "Nothing in life comes out the way you expect, not even for Christians. You're a Christian, aren't you, little girl?"

Maggie blinked and said oh yes, of course.

"These men pretend, but they haven't fooled me. I can smell the beer on them. A Christian man doesn't drink beer. My Karl never touched a drop of liquor, and my Manny never did either. At least not until he got away, into the service." She glared at Poole as if she held him personally responsible for her son's lapses. "And never mixed with bad women, either. We beat that into him.

He was a good boy, as good as we could make him. And considering where and what he came from." Another sullen look at Poole, as if he knew all about *that.* "We got that boy to work, and work he did until the day the army took him. School is school, we said, but your work is your life. Butcher-work came from God, but man made schoolwork and reading any book but one."

"Was he happy as a child?" Poole asked.

"The Devil worries about happiness," she said, and the weird pale light went on in her face and eyes again. "Do you think Karl thought about such as that? Do you think I did? Those are the questions the other ones asked. Now you tell me something, Dr. Poole, and I'll rely on you to tell me the truth. Did that boy drink liquor in the service over there? And did he waste himself with women? Because in your answer I'll know what sort of man he was, and what sort you are too. The bad marbles crack all wrong, oh yes. The bad marble falls to pieces in the fire. The mother was one of those. Tell me—answer my question, or you can leave this house. I let you in, you're not a policeman or a judge. My opinions are as good as yours, in case they're not a lot better."

"Of course," Poole said. "No, I don't think I can remember your son ever taking a drink. And he remained . . . what you would call pure."

"Well. Yes. Yes, he did. This one thing I know. Manny stayed pure. What *I would call pure*," she added, with a blast of ice straight from her eyes into Poole's heart.

Poole wondered how she could have known that before he told her, and if she had known why she had asked. "We'd like to tell you some things about your son," he said, and his words sounded clumsy and ill-chosen.

"Go on," the woman said, and again used her peculiar psychic strength to alter both herself and the atmosphere in the room. She seemed to sigh inaudibly: both her thick body and the air grew heavier, as if filled up with dull unexpectant waiting. "You want to tell your story, so tell it."

"Did we interrupt your work, Mrs. Dengler?" Maggie asked.

A gleam of satisfaction. "I turned off my stove. It can wait. You people are here. You know what I think? We trained him more than most would, and some didn't care for what we did. You can't put your faith in what others say. Muffin Street is a world like many others. Muffin Street is real. You go ahead now."

"Mrs. Dengler," Tim said, "your son was a wonderful human being. He was a hero under fire, and more than that, he was compassionate and inventive—"

"You think backwards," she broke in. "Oh, my. *Backwards.* Inventive? You mean he made things up. Isn't that part of the original trouble? Would there have been a trial, if he hadn't made things up?"

"I would never defend his being court-martialed," Tim said, "but I don't think you can blame it on him, either."

"Imagination has to be stopped. You're talking about imagination. You have to put an end to that. That's one thing I know. And Karl knew it, up until the day he passed away." She turned almost in agitation to look at the rows of identical grape clusters, each grape with its identical flare of light within. "Well. Go on. You want to. You came all the way to do it."

Underhill talked about Dragon Valley, and the stories that had eased George Spitalny at first left her unmoved, then seemed to distress her. Pink crept into the whiteness of her face: her eyes zapped into Poole's, and he saw that it was not distress that made her flush, but anger.

So much for the gods of storytelling, he thought.

"Manny's behavior was fantastic, and he mocked his officer. Behavior should never be fantastic, and he should have respected the officer."

"The whole situation was a little fantastic," Underhill said.

"That is what people say when they try to excuse themselves. Wherever the boy was, he should have acted as if he were on Muffin Street. Pride is a sin. We would have punished him."

Poole could feel Tim's anger and sorrow even through Maggie Lah, who sat between them.

"Mrs. Dengler," Maggie said, "a moment ago you said that Manny was a good boy, considering where he came from."

The old woman lifted her head like an animal sniffing the wind. Unmistakable pleasure shone through her round eyeglasses. "Little girls can listen, can't they?"

"You didn't mean Muffin Street, did you?"

"Manny didn't come from Muffin Street. So."

Maggie waited for what was to come next, and Poole wondered what it would be. Mars? Russia? Heaven?

"Manny came from the gutter," Mrs. Dengler said. "We took that boy out of the gutter and we gave him a home. We gave him our name. We gave him our religion. We fed him and we clothed him. Does that sound like the work of bad people? Do you think bad people would have done that for an abandoned little boy?"

"You adopted him?"

Underhill was leaning backwards against the stiff plastic, staring intently at Helga Dengler.

"We adopted that poor abandoned child and we gave him new life. Do you think his mother could have had my coloring? Are you such fools? Karl was blond too, before he went grey. Karl was an angel of God, with his yellow hair and his flowing beard! Yes! I will show you."

She all but hopped to her feet, glowered down at them with her X-ray eyes, and left the room. It was like a grotesque parody of their evening with the Spitalnys.

"Did he ever say anything to you about being adopted?" Poole asked.

Underhill shook his head.

"Manuel Orosco Dengler," Maggie said. "You must have known something was going on."

"We never called him that," Poole said.

Mrs. Dengler opened the door, admitting a whiff of the odor of damp wood along with herself. She was clutching an old photograph album made of pressed cardboard treated to resemble leather. The corners and edges had frayed, showing the blunted grey edges of the layers of compressed paper. She came forward eagerly, open-mouthed, like a wronged defendant to the judge. "Now you see my Karl," she said, opening the album to an early page and turning it around to face them.

The photograph took up nearly the entire page. It might have been taken a hundred years earlier. A tall man with lank pale hair that hung past his ears and a pale unruly beard glared at the camera. He was thin but broad-shouldered and wore a dark suit that hung on him like a sack. He looked driven, haunted, intense. The nature of this man's religion rose off the photograph like steam. Where his wife's eyes looked through you to another world, dismissing everything between herself and it, his looked straight into hell and condemned you to it.

"Karl was a man of God," Helga said. "You can see that plainly. He was chosen. My Karl was not a lazy man. You can see that too. He was not *soft.* He never shirked his duty, not even when his duty was to stand on a street corner in below zero weather. The News would not wait for fine weather, and it needed a hard, dedicated man to tell it, and that was my Karl. So we needed help. Someday we would be old. *But we didn't know what was going to happen to us!"* She was panting, and her eyes bulged behind the round glasses. Again Poole felt that her body was gathering density, pulling into it all the air in the room and along with it all that ever was or ever would be right or moral, leaving them forever in the wrong.

"Who were his parents?" Poole heard Underhill ask, and knew that she would misunderstand.

"Fine people. Who would have had such a son? Strong people. Karl's father was also a butcher, he taught him the trade, and Karl taught Manny the trade so that Manny could work for us while we did the Lord's own work. We raised him from the gutter and gave him eternal life, so. He was to work for us and provide for our old age."

"I see," said Underhill, bending forward slightly to glance at Michael. "We'd also like to know something about your son's parents."

Mrs. Dengler folded the photograph album shut and laid it across her lap. Some of the musty smell had permeated the cardboard, and for a moment the odor eddied about them.

"He didn't have parents." She gleamed at them, self-satisfaction personified. "Not the way real people do, not like Karl and me. Manny was born out of wedlock. His mother, Rosita, sold her body. One of *those* women. She delivered the baby in Mount Sinai Hospital and abandoned him there, just walked out as fancy as you please, and the baby had a viral infection—he nearly died. Many did, but did he? My husband and I prayed for him, and he did *not* die. Rosita Orosco died a few weeks later. *Beaten* to death. Do you think the boy's father killed her? Manny was Spanish only on his mother's side, that's what Karl and I always thought. So you see what I mean. He had neither mother nor father."

"Was Manny's father one of his mother's customers?" Underhill asked.

"We did not think about it."

"But you said that you did not think the father was Spanish . . . Latin American."

"Well." Helga Dengler shifted on the stool, and her eyes changed weather. "He had a good side to balance the bad."

"How did you come to adopt him?"

"Karl heard about the poor baby."

"How did he hear? Had you gone to adoption agencies?"

"Of course not. I think the woman came to him. Rosita Orosco. My husband's church work brought many low, unhappy people to us, begging for their souls to be saved."

"Did you see Rosita Orosco at the church services?"

Now she planted both feet on the floor and stared at him. She seemed to be breathing through her skin. Nobody spoke for an excruciating time.

"I didn't mean to offend you, Mrs. Dengler," Underhill finally said.

"We had white people at our services," she said in a low, slow, even voice. "Sometimes we had Catholics. But they were always good people. Polishers. They can be as good as anyone else."

"I see," Underhill said. "You never saw Manny's mother at your services."

"Manny did not have a mother," she said in the same slow, evenly paced voice. "He had no mother, no father."

Underhill asked if the police had ever arrested the person who beat Rosita Orosco to death.

She shook her head very slowly, like a child vowing never to tell a secret. "Nobody cared who did that. That woman being what she was and all. Whosoever did it could come to the Lord. He is the eternal court of justice."

With hallucinatory clarity, Poole remembered the torture chamber in the Tiger Balm Gardens, the distorted half-human shapes kneeling before an imperious judge.

"And so they never found him."

"I don't recall that they did."

"Your husband had no interest in the matter?"

"Of course not," she said. "We had already done all we could."

She had closed her eyes, and Poole changed the direction of the questions. "When did your husband die, Mrs. Dengler?"

Her eyes opened and flashed at him. "My husband died in the year 1960."

"And you closed the butcher shop and the church in that year?"

The weird intimidating light had gone on in her face again. "A little bit before that. Manny was too young to be a butcher."

Couldn't you see him? Poole wanted to ask. *Couldn't you see what a gift he was to you, no matter where he came from?*

"Manny didn't have friends," she said, speaking almost as if she had heard Poole's thoughts. Some emotion swelling in her voice caught in Poole's inner ear, and it was not until her next sentence that he identified it as pride. "He had too much to do, he followed Karl that way. We kept the boy busy, you must keep your children at their tasks. Yes. *At their tasks.* For that is how they will learn. When Karl was a boy, he had no friends. I kept Manny away from other boys and raised him in the way we knew was right. And when he was bad we did what Scripture says to do." She raised her head and looked straight at Maggie. "We had to thrash his mother out of him. Well. Yes. We could have changed his name, you know. We could have given him a good German name. But he had to know he was half *Manuel Orosco*, even if the other half could become *Dengler.* And *Manuel Orosco* had to be tamed and put in chains. No matter what anybody said. You do this out of love and you do it because you have to. Let me show you how it worked. Look at this, now."

She flipped through pages of photographs, staring down at them with a rapt, abstracted face. Poole wished he could see all the photographs in that book. From where he sat, he thought he caught glimpses of bonfires and big flags, but he saw only blurred fragments of images.

"Yes," she said. "There. You see this, you know. A boy doing a man's job."

She held up a newspaper clipping preserved behind the transparent sheet the way her furniture was preserved beneath the plastic covers.

Milwaukee Journal, September 20, 1958 was written in ink at the top of the page. Beneath the photograph was the caption: BUTCHER'S BOY: *Little eight-year-old Manny Dengler helping out in Dad's Muffin Street shop. Dresses deer all by himself! This is believed to be a record.*

And there, in between, occupying half a page in the

old album, was the photograph of a small black-haired boy facing the camera in a bloody apron so much too big for him that it laps around him twice and encases him like a sausage skin. In his raised right hand, attached to his skinny angular eight-year-old's arm, is a massive cleaver. The photographer has told him to hold up the cleaver, for the instrument is too large for both his hand and the job spread out neatly before him. It is the headless body of a deer, stripped of its skin and cut neatly into sections, shoulders, the long graceful ribcage, the curved flanks, the wide wet haunches like a woman's. The little boy's face is Dengler's, and it wears a piercing expression which mingles sweetness and doubt.

"He could be good," his mother said. "Here is the proof. Youngest boy in the State of Wisconsin to dress a deer all by himself." Her face flickered for a moment, and Poole wondered if she were experiencing or even just remembering grief. He felt scorched: as if he had been swallowing fire.

"If they let him stay at home instead of taking him away to be with you and fight a war with—" A blast of ice at Maggie. "If not for that, he could be working in the shop right now, and I could have the old age I earned. Instead of *this*. This pauper's existence. The government stole him. Didn't they know why we got him in the first place?"

Now they were all included in her scorn. Her eyes snapped, and the color came up into her face and faded out again, like an optical illusion. "After what they said," she said, almost to herself. "That's the beauty part. After what they said, they were the ones who killed him."

"What did they say?" Poole asked.

She froze him now with a blast from her eyes.

Poole stood up and learned that his knees were shaking. The fire he had swallowed still burned all the way down his throat.

Before he could speak, Underhill asked if they could see the boy's room.

The old woman rose. "They stole him," she said, still glaring at Maggie. "Everyone lied about us."

"The army lied when Manny was drafted?" Poole asked.

Her gaze moved to him, filled with scorn and illumination. "It wasn't just the army," she said.

"Manny's room?" Underhill asked again into the strange cold frost the woman created about her.

"Of course," she said, actually smiling down. "You'll see. None of the others did. Come this way."

She turned around and stumped out of the room. Poole imagined spiders fleeing back up into the corners of their webs, rats scurrying into their holes, as her footsteps thumped toward them.

"We go upstairs, so," she said, and led them out into the hall and toward the staircase. The odor of must and wood rot was much stronger in the hallway. Every stair creaked, and brown irregular rust stains spread out from the heads of the nails that fastened the linoleum to the treads.

"He had his own room, he had everything the best," she said. "Down the hall from us. We could have put him in the basement, and we could have put him in the back of the butcher shop. But the child's place is near his parents. This is one thing I know: the child's place is near his parents. You see. The apple was near the tree. Karl could see the boy at any time. Every healthy child must be punished as well as praised."

The roofline narrowed the upper corridor to a walkway where Poole and Underhill had to bend their necks. At the end of the narrow corridor a single window, grey with dust and watermarks, gave a view of telephone lines capped with runners of snow. Mrs. Dengler opened the second of the two wooden doors. "This was Manny's," she said, and stood by the door like a museum guide as they entered.

It was like walking into a closet. The room was perhaps eight feet by ten feet, much darker than the rest of the house. Poole reached out for the switch and flipped it, but no light came on. Then he saw the cord and empty socket dangling from the ceiling. The window had been boarded up with two-by-fours, and looked like a rectangular wooden box. For a mad second Poole thought that Dengler's mother was going to slam the door and lock the three of them inside the windowless little chamber—then they would be truly inside Dengler's childhood. But Helga Dengler was standing beside the open door, looking down with pursed lips, indifferent to what they saw or what they thought.

The room could have changed only very little since

Dengler had left it. There was a narrow bed covered with an army surplus blanket. A child's desk stood against the wall, a child's bookshelf beside it with a few volumes leaning on its shelves. Poole bent over the books and grunted with surprise. Red-bound copies of *Babar* and *Babar the King*, identical to the ones in the trunk of his car, stood on the top shelf. Maggie came up to him and said "Oh!" when she saw the books.

"We didn't stop the boy from reading, don't think we did," said Mrs. Dengler.

The shelves provided a graph of his reading—from *Grimm's Fairy Tales* and *Babar* to Robert Heinlein and Isaac Asimov. *Tom Sawyer* and *Huckleberry Finn.* A toy car sat beside these books, two of its wheels gone and most of its paint worn off with handling. Books on fossils, birds, and snakes. A small number of religious tracts, and a pocket-sized Bible.

"He spent all day up here, when we let him," said the old woman. "Lazy, he was. Or would have been, if we had let him be that way."

The little room seemed unbearably claustrophobic to Poole. He wished he could put his arms around the little boy who had escaped into this windowless chamber and tell him that he was not bad, not lazy, not damned.

"My son loved Babar too," he said.

"No substitute for Scripture," she said. "As you can plainly tell by where these came from." In response to Poole's look, she said, "His mother. She bought those elephant books. Stole them, more likely. As if a baby could ever read such a big book. Had them right with her, right there in the hospital, and she left them behind with the baby when she took off. Throw them out, I said, they're garbage garbage garbage, just like where they came from, but Karl said no, let the boy have something of his natural mother—'*unnatural* mother,' I said, and the sour will soon spoil the sweet, but Karl wanted it and so it was. Books like those vanished from the church's rummage box, but they were different copies—Karl knew."

Poole wondered if she really took him in at all, or if she saw purple marbles ready to be cracked in the pan and glued into endless repetitions of the same pattern. Then he saw that she would not enter the room. She wanted to come in and pull them out, but her legs would not carry her inside, her feet would not move across the threshold.

". . . looked and looked at those books, the boy did. Won't find anything in there, I told him. That's foolishness. Elephants can't help you, I said, that's trash, and trash ends up in the gutter, I told him. And he knew what I was talking about. Yes. He knew."

"I think we could leave now," Underhill said. Maggie muttered something Poole did not catch—he realized that he had just been staring at Helga Dengler, who was facing him but looking at a scene visible only to her.

"He was just a little cuckoo we took in," she said. "We brought him into our nest, we were godly people, we gave the boy what we had, his own room, plenty of food, everything, and he laid it to waste." She stepped back to let the three of them come out of her son's room and then stood looking at them. "I was not surprised by what happened to Manny," she said at what seemed the last possible moment. "He died in the gutter too, didn't he, just like his mother? Karl was always too good."

They made their way down the stairs.

"You'll be going now," she said, and shuffled past them toward the door.

Frigid air rolled down the hallway as they buttoned up their coats. When she smiled, her white cheeks shifted like floured slabs. "I wish we could talk more, but I have to get back to my work. Take care now, get all buttoned up nice."

They stepped outside into the cold clean air.

"Bye-bye," she called softly from the door as they went down the porch steps. "Bye-bye now. Yes. Bye-bye."

When they got back into the car, Maggie said she felt sick, and wanted to go back to the Pforzheimer to lie down while the other two met Victor Spitalny's friend at The Polka Dot Lounge. "I need time to recover." Poole knew what she meant.

"So that was how Dengler grew up," Underhill said as they drove north on the frozen streets.

"His parents bought him," Maggie said. "He was supposed to be their slave. That poor little boy and his Babar books."

"What was all that stuff about 'them'? About lying? She never explained it."

"I have a feeling I'm going to regret this," Underhill

said, "but after we drop Maggie off at the hotel, I'd like you to take me to the main branch of the Milwaukee library. It's probably downtown somewhere, fairly close to our hotel. I want to look up some things in the Milwaukee papers. There were a lot of things that woman never explained."

Fifteen minutes early for his meeting, Poole pulled into the crowded parking lot beside The Polka Dot Lounge. It was a long, low gabled building that looked as if it should have been covered with ivy and placed in a German forest instead of on this steep gritty street leading down into the darkness of the Valley. Overhead, the long bridge the three of them had crossed on their way to the Spitalny house resounded with traffic. Oval lead-colored clouds that looked as solid as battleships hung motionless in the air further down, and bright red flames wavered at the tops of columns. Neon beer signs glowed in the tavern's small side windows.

Poole pushed open the door and entered a long, hazy barroom. Cigarette smoke and loud rock music eddied about him. Men in workshirts and caps already stood two deep at the bar. A blonde waitress in tight jeans and a down vest carried pitchers of beer and bowls of popcorn through the tables on a platter. Booths, most of them empty, stood along the walls. The floor was covered with sawdust, popcorn, peanut shells. The Polka Dot was a workingman's bar, not a puritanical neighborhood tavern with too many lights and lachrymose music. Most of the men at the bar Poole's age would have been in Vietnam —no college deferments here. Poole felt more at home in his first few minutes inside the Polka Dot than at any other time during his visit to the Midwest.

He managed to squeeze into an empty place at the far end of the bar. "Pforzheimer's," he said. "I'm supposed to meet Mack Simroe here. Has he come in yet?"

"Still a little early for Mack," the bartender said. "Take a booth, I'll tell him you're here."

Poole took a booth and sat facing the door. After fifteen minutes a huge bearded man in a ripped down jacket and a jungle hat came through the door. The man began to scan the booths, and Poole knew instantly that this was Mack Simroe. The giant's eyes found Poole, and the giant gave him a wide toothy smile from the center of his beard. Poole stood up. The big man striding toward him was congenial and puzzled and open for anything, all of which was visible in his face. Simroe engulfed his hand and said, "I guess you're Dr. Poole, Let's get a pitcher and make Jenny's life a little easier, what do you say, this stuff is better on draft anyway. . . ."

And then they were facing each other in the booth with a pitcher of beer and a bowl of popcorn between them. After being in the Dengler house, Michael felt peculiarly sensitive to odors, and from Mack Simroe came what must have been the undiluted breath of the Valley: a smell of machine oil and metal shavings. It would be the smell inside one of those leaden clouds of frozen smoke. Simroe was a fitter at the Dux Company, which manufactured ball bearings and engine parts, and he usually stopped in here at the end of his day.

"You knocked the pins out from under me," Simroe said, "asking about Vic Spitalny and all that. Sorta brought back a lot of stuff."

"I hope you don't mind talking a little bit more about it."

"Hey, I'd be here anyhow. Who else you been talking to?"

"His parents."

"They heard from him?"

Poole shook his head.

"George went off the rails when Vic got in all that trouble. Started drinking too much, and on the job too, way I heard it. Got in a lot of fights. Glax put him on leave for a month, I guess he discovered George Wallace in all his greatness around then. He started doing some work for Wallace and that got him back on the track. George still won't hear a word against Wallace. Who else you talk to? Debbie Maczik? What's her name now—Tusa?"

"I did."

"Nice kid. Always liked Debbie."

"Did you like Victor, too?" Poole asked.

Simroe leaned forward, and Poole was acutely aware of bulging forearms and his huge head. "You know, I can't help wondering what all this is about. I don't mind talking to you, buddy, not at all, but first I'd just kinda like to know the background. You were in the same unit as Vic?"

"All the way," Poole said.

"Dragon Valley? Ia Thuc?"

"Every step."

"And you're a civilian these days?"

"I'm a doctor. A baby doctor, outside New York City."

"A baby doctor." Simroe grinned. He liked that. "No cop, no FBI, no Intelligence or Military Police, no goddamned CIA—no nothing."

"No nothing."

Simroe was still grinning. "But there's something, isn't there? You think the man's alive. You want to find him."

"I do want to find him."

"He must owe you a hell of a lot of money, or you heard something about the guy—something bad. He's involved in something, and you want to stop him."

"That's about it," Poole admitted.

"So Vic is alive after all. I'll be damned."

"Most people who deserted are still alive. That's why they deserted."

"Okay," Simroe said. "Nobody who went into that war came back exactly the same way. You sort of think you know how far certain people will go—and maybe you don't. Maybe you never do." He downed a huge quantity of beer in one swallow. "Let me tell you how I got to know Vic. Back at Rufus King, I was kind of a half-assed hood. I had a big Harley, boots, evil tattoos—I still got those, but I hide 'em these days—and I tried to be a real badass. I didn't know what else to do. I was never a real hood, I just liked riding around on that big old bike. Anyhow, Vic started hanging around me. Vic thought the whole biker bit was cool as shit. I couldn't shake him off, and after a while I just gave up trying."

Poole thought of Spacemaker Ortega, Spitalny's only real friend in the service and the leader of the Devilfuckers—Spitalny had simply transferred his affection for Simroe to Ortega.

"And then I sort of got to like him. I got to thinking—here's this kid, kind of dumb, his old man's always breathing down his neck. I tried to give him advice. You gotta take care of yourself, you little asshole, I used to tell him. I even tried to get him to lay off Manny Dengler, 'cause there was a guy who had real problems, I mean who was in shit up to his neck all day every day. I mean, I used to *worry* about that little cat!"

"I saw his mother this afternoon."

Simroe shook his shaggy head. "I never met the lady. But the old man, Karl—man, he was something. Out there on those corners every morning, every night, yellin' into his little mike—little Manny singin' some stuff, hymns or shit, top of his lungs, and passin' the hat. And the old man would cuff him right there on the street. It was a show, man, a real show. Anyhow, right after I dropped out of school Vic dropped out too—I tried to argue him back in, but he just wouldn't go. I knew I wasn't goin' anywhere but the Valley, and I kind of wanted to get into uniform first, be a hero with an M-16, do my part. You know. And you were there—you know what happened. I saw good guys getting blown away for no reason at all. Fucked me up pretty good."

Simroe had been in Bravo Company, Fourth Battalion, 31st Infantry, the American Division, and he had spent a year fighting in 120-degree heat in the Hiep Duc Valley, wounded twice.

"Did you have any contact with Vic once you were both in country?"

"Just a couple letters—we were going to get together, but it never worked out."

"Did he write to you after he deserted?"

"I knew you were going to ask that. And I oughta dump this beer over your head, baby doctor, because I already told you I never heard from him. He just cut himself off from everybody, I guess."

"What do you think happened to him?"

Simroe pushed his glass through the puddles on the wet table. He looked up at Poole, testing his judgment, then back down at his glass. "I suppose I could ask you the same. But I'll tell you what I think, Doctor. I think he stayed alive about a month, tops. I think he ran out of money and tried to get into some action, and whoever he was with killed him. Because that's about what Vic Spitalny was good for. He was good for screwing up. I don't think he lasted six weeks, once he cut out on his own. At least I didn't think so until you showed up."

"Do you think he killed Dengler?"

"No way," said Simroe, looking up sharply. "Do you?"

"I'm afraid I do," Poole said.

Simroe hesitated and opened his mouth to say something, but then an uproar broke out at the bar and both men turned to see what had caused it. A group of young men in their twenties and early thirties had surrounded an older man with curly hair and the pudgy beatific face of a village fool. *"Cob,"* they were yelling, "Go, Cob!"

"Catch this," Simroe said.

The younger men milled around the one called Cob, punching his shoulder, whispering into his ear. Poole became aware of some bitter, familiar odor—cordite? napalm? Neither of those, but an odor from that world. *Cob,* they said, *come on, you fucker.*

The one called Cob grinned and ducked his head, pleased to be the object of so much attention. He looked like a janitor, a broom pusher for Glax or Dux or Fluegelhorn Brothers. His skin had an odd greyish tinge and in the curls of his hair were caught what looked like pencil shavings. *Come on, you dumb ass motherfucker. Cob! Do it!*

"There are guys in here," Simroe said, leaning across the table, "who claim they once saw Cob lift himself a foot and a half off the floor and just hang there for thirty-forty seconds."

Poole looked dubiously at Simroe, and heard a loud metallic noise like a series of backfires, or a burst from a machine gun, a *BRRRRAAAAPPPP!* that did not sound at all like a noise any human being could have produced. He looked sideways in time to see a torpedo-shaped sheet of flame four feet long shoot out toward the middle of the bar and disappear into itself. The cordite-and-napalm stench became much stronger, then disappeared.

"Clears the air, doesn't it?" Simroe said.

The younger men were banging Cob on the back, handing him bills. Cob staggered back a step, but caught himself before he fell. One of the men put a glass of beer in his hand, and he poured it down his throat as if dumping it into a well.

"That's Cob's trick," Simroe said. "He can do that two, maybe three times a night. Don't ask me how. Don't ask him either. He can't tell you. Can't talk—no tongue. You know what I think? I think the poor bastard fills his mouth up with lighter fluid before he comes in here, and stands around waiting for someone to ask for his trick."

"But did you ever see him light a match?"

"Never." Simroe winked at Michael, then poured another beer. "Another guy in here will eat his beer glass if he gets drunk enough." He swallowed beer. "You met Dengler's mother, you said? She tell you anything about old Karl's going off to jail?"

Poole's eyes widened.

"No, I don't suppose she did. Old Karl was arrested during our freshman year. A social worker came around to check on the kid and found him locked in the meat locker in the butcher shop, pretty well beat up. The old man got a little rougher with him than usual, and put him in the meat locker to get him out of the way until he calmed down. She called the cops, and the kid told them everything."

"What everything?"

And Mack Simroe told him. "How his old man, old Karl, used to—well, abuse him. A couple of times a week, starting from the time he was five or six. Used to tell him he'd cut his pecker off if he caught him messing with girls. Manny had to go to trial and testify against the old man. The judge sent him away for twenty years, but after he did a couple years he got killed in jail. I think he made a move on the wrong kid."

After what they said, Poole remembered. *Everyone lied about us.*

And: *We kept that boy busy.*

And: *He had to be put in chains. No matter what anybody said.*

And: *We closed the butcher shop a little bit before that.*

Michael saw Dengler's face glowing at him, uttering nonsense about the Valley of the Shadow of Death.

She said: *We didn't know what would happen to us.*

And: *Imagination has to be stopped. You have to put an end to that.*

He had ignored or misinterpreted all these things. At the bar, the man called Cob was smiling slackly upwards, his eyes unfocused and his skin some color between light purple and the grey of iron filings. *After what they said.* If a man could float up into the air and hang there for thirty minutes, that was what he would look like. Levitation took a toll. You had to pay a price. Not to mention what fire-breathing took out of you.

He made things up. Isn't that part of the original trouble?

It was the levitation that really did it to old Cob, Poole thought. One of the young men touched Cob's shoulders and revolved him so that he could see a number of shot glasses—Poole could not see how many, six, eight, ten—lined up on the bar in his honor. Cob began pouring the contents of the shot glasses into his mouth in a way that reminded Poole of a wild animal eating something it had killed.

"I guess that's news to you, isn't it?" Simroe said. "Manny Dengler stayed out of school for a year, and when he came back he had to repeat his freshman year. Of course he was treated even worse than before."

And Poole remembered: *Calm down, Vic. Whatever it was . . .*

"It was a long time ago," he said, finishing the phrase.

"Yep," said Simroe, "but I'll tell you what gets me. He was *adopted* by those people. Anybody could see Karl Dengler was crazy, but they still let them take him. And even after everything came out and Karl got sent to Waupun where some kid damn near took off his head with a homemade knife, Manny still lived in that house on Muffin Street. With that old lady."

"He started going back to school . . ." Poole said, his eyes still on Cob.

"Yep."

"And he went home every night."

"He closed the door behind him," Simroe said, "but who knows what went on behind that door? What did she talk about with him? I think he must have been damn happy when the army finally drafted him."

4

All this Tim Underhill had discovered in two hours at the library, going over microfilm of the two Milwaukee newspapers—he had read about Karl Dengler's trial and conviction, and about his murder in the state prison. "Sex Crime Minister," read the captions beneath photographs of wild-eyed Karl Dengler. "Sex Crime Minister and Wife Arrive for Tenth Day of Trial" beneath a photograph of Karl Dengler, grey felt hat on his head and staring straight into the middle distance while a younger, slimmer Helga Dengler, thick blond braids twisted around her head, blew the camera apart with one flat glare of her pale eyes. There had been a photograph of the house on Muffin Street, its porch empty and the shades down. Beside it Dengler's Lamb of God Butcher Shop already looked dispossessed. In the next few days, children would throw bricks through the shop's window. By the next day, as a *Sentinel* photograph showed, the city had boarded up the window.

SOCIAL WORKER PLEADS FOR FOSTER HOME, ran a subhead from the last day of the trial—forty-four-year-old Miss Phyllis Green, the woman who had discovered the child in the meat locker, severely bruised, half-conscious, and clutching his favorite book, had requested that the court find a new home for Manuel Orosco Dengler. A "spokesman" for Mrs. Dengler "vigorously opposed" the request, claiming that the Dengler family had already experienced enough pain. FOSTER CARE PLEA DENIED, announced the *Journal* a week after the verdict: in a separate hearing, a judge decided that the boy should be "returned to normal life as quickly as possible." The child was to be returned to his classes on the first day of the new term. The second judge advised that "this unfortunate history be put behind us," and that Helga and Manuel Dengler "get on with the business of living." It was "a time for healing." And the two of them left the courthouse, rode the bus to the South Side and Muffin Street, and closed the door behind them.

Everybody lied about us.

Timothy Underhill learned all this, and one thing more: Manuel Orosco Dengler's father was Manuel Orosco Dengler's father.

"Karl Dengler was his real father?" Poole asked.

He and Underhill were driving back to the Pforzheimer at seven-thirty that evening. On Wisconsin Avenue the lighted display windows of department stores slipped past like dioramas in a museum—lovers on a porch swing, men in loose, garish Perry Como sweaters and caps stiffly gathered on a golf course green.

"Who was his mother?" Poole asked, momentarily disoriented.

"Rosita Orosco, just the way Helga Dengler said. Rosita named him Manuel, and abandoned him in the hospital. But when she filled out the admission forms, she listed Karl Dengler as the baby's father. And he never challenged that, because his name is on Dengler's birth certificate."

"Are birth certificates on file in the library?" Poole asked.

"I went a couple of blocks to the Hall of Records. Something finally struck me—that the Denglers seemed to adopt this abandoned baby without going through any red tape. This Nicaraguan woman, a prostitute, comes into the labor ward off the street, has a child and disappears, and fifteen days later the Denglers have adopted the child. I think it was all arranged beforehand."

Underhill rubbed his hands together, his knees propped up before him in the little car. "I bet Rosita told Karl she was pregnant, and he reassured her that he would adopt the child, everything would be legal and above-board. Maybe he told her he'd marry her! We'll never know. Maybe Rosita wasn't even a prostitute. On the hospital form, she called herself a dressmaker. I've been thinking that maybe Rosita wandered into the Lamb of God church or temple or whatever Karl called it when it wasn't a butcher shop, and maybe Dengler came up to her as soon as he saw her and talked her into coming to private services. Because he didn't want his wife to see her."

Horns blared behind Poole, and he realized that the light had changed. He shot through the intersection before the arrow could fade and pulled up alongside the entrance of the hotel.

Poole and Underhill walked through the thick artificial light beneath the marquee toward the glass doors, which whooshed open before them. Out of the swarm of questions going through his mind, he asked only the most immediate. "Did Helga know that Karl was her son's father?"

"It was on the birth certificate." They moved into the lobby, and the desk clerk nodded at them. The lobby was almost opulently warm, and the big drooping ferns seemed to bulge with health, as if they could slide out of their pots and eat small animals.

"I think she didn't want to know," Underhill said. "And that made her even crazier. Dengler was the proof that her husband had been unfaithful to her, and with a woman who belonged to what she considered an inferior race."

They got into the elevator. "Where did they find Rosita's body?" Poole asked, pushing the button for the fifth floor.

"Beside the Milwaukee River, a block or two south of Wisconsin Avenue. It was the middle of winter—about now, in fact. She was naked, and her neck was broken. The police assumed that a customer had killed her."

"Two weeks after the birth of a baby?"

"I think they assumed she was desperate," Underhill said. The elevator stopped, and the doors clanked open. "I don't think they gave a damn about what happened to some Mexican hooker."

"Nicaraguan," Poole said.

5

Then they had to tell it all to Maggie, who said, "How do the Babar books come in?"

"It looks like Karl Dengler just took them from the rummage box, or whatever they called it, inside his shop and gave them to Rosita. She must have asked him for something to give the child, and he just picked up the first thing he saw."

The painted dogs stood guard over the bloody game, and the self-satisfied fat men looked out at them as if immensely pleased to be frozen in time.

"And he kept them until he was drafted."

"*Babar* is about a peaceful world," Poole said. "I suppose that was what he loved in it."

"Not that peaceful," Maggie said. "In the first pages of *Babar*, Babar's mother is shot and killed by a hunter. It's no wonder your friend Dengler kept the books."

"Is that right?" Underhill sat upright in surprise.

"Of course," Maggie said. "And here's something else. At the end of *Babar the King,* flying elephants labeled Courage, Patience, Learning, I don't know what else—Joy and Intelligence—drive away bad evil creatures labeled Stupidity and Anger and Fear, and a lot of other wicked things. Don't you suppose that meant a lot to him? Because from what I heard about Dengler, he was able to do that in his own life—to banish all the terrible things that had happened to him. And there's something else too, but I don't know what you'll think about this. When I was a child I loved a page in that book that depicted some of the citizens of the elephants' city. Dr. Capoulosse, and Tapitor the shoemaker, and a sculptor named Podular, Poutifour the farmer, Hatchimbombitar, a big strong street-sweeper . . . and a clown named Coco."

"Koko?" Underhill asked.

"Spelled differently. C-o-c-o."

Some realization almost moved into view between them.

Poole threw up his hands. "The only really important thing we learned here is that Spitalny knew Dengler back in high school. We're not any closer to finding him. I think we ought to go back to New York. It's about time we stopped humoring Harry Beevers and told that detective, Murphy, everything we know. The police can stop him. We can't."

He looked directly at Maggie. "It's time to do other things."

She nodded.

"Then let's go back to New York," he heard Underhill say. He either could not or did not want to take his eyes off Maggie Lah. "I miss Vinh. I miss working in the mornings and having him poke his head into that little room to ask me if I want another cup of tea."

Poole turned to smile at Tim, who was looking at him slyly, tapping his pencil against his front teeth. "Well, *somebody* has to take care of Vinh," he said. "The poor boy never stops working."

"So you're going to settle down and raise a family," Maggie said.

"Something like that."

"Lead a regular, moderate life."

"I have a book to write. I've been thinking of giving old Fenwick Throng a call, just to tell him I'm back from the dead. I hear Geoffrey Penmaiden isn't at Gladstone House anymore, so maybe I can even go back to my old publishers."

"Did you really mail him a turd in a box?" Poole asked. "Tina told me—"

"If you knew him, you'd understand. He was a lot like Harry Beevers."

"My hero," Poole said. He picked up the telephone and made reservations on the next flight to New York, which left at ten-thirty the following morning. Then he put down the telephone and looked at Maggie again.

"What are you thinking about?" she asked him.

"If I should call Harry now."

"Sure," she said.

He got Beevers' answering machine. "Harry, this is Michael," he said. "We're coming back tomorrow, arriving at LaGuardia around two o'clock on the Republic flight. No leads, but we found out a few things. I think it's time we went to the police with everything we know, Harry. I'll talk to you before I do anything, but Tim and I are going to see Murphy."

After that he called Conor at Ellen Woyzak's house and told him what time they would be arriving at the airport. Ellen came on the line and said that she and Conor would meet them at the airport.

They had a subdued meal in the hotel dining room. Maggie and Poole split a bottle of wine, and Underhill drank club soda. In the middle of the meal he announced that he had realized that it was a kind of anniversary—he had been sober for a little more than two years. They toasted him, but apart from that the meal was so subdued Michael feared that he had infected the others with his mood. Underhill spoke a little about the book he had begun in Bangkok after he had cleaned out his system and written "Blue Rose" and "The Juniper Tree"—something about a child made to live in a wooden hut at the back of his house, and the same child twenty years later—but Poole felt empty and alone, as cut off from life as an astronaut floating in deep space. He envied Tim Underhill his occupation. Underhill was itching to write: he had continued his work on the plane, in the mornings, and at night in their room. Poole had always imagined that writers needed isolation, but it seemed that all Underhill needed were legal pads and a supply of Blackwing pencils—and those, it turned out, had been Tina Pumo's. Tina had always been obsessive about his tools, and there was still nearly a gross of the Blackwings at the restaurant. Maggie had given four boxes to Underhill, who had promised to finish his book with them. They were *fast*, he said. With those pencils, you could *glide*. Underhill was already gliding, far away inside himself, soaring on a carpet of words he was impatient to set down.

When they went back upstairs in the elevator, Poole decided that as soon as he got back inside the room, he would let Underhill sail away on his imagination and his Blackwing pencils, and he would get into bed with *The Ambassadors*. Strether had just taken a short trip out of Paris for a day or two, and in the French countryside was enjoying what Henry James called "the general amiability of the day." At the moment he was eating lunch on a terrace overlooking a river. Everything seemed beautifully, luxuriantly suspended. Riding up five floors in a walnut-paneled elevator with Maggie Lah was about as close as Poole thought he would get to luxurious suspension —that, and reading his book.

The elevator stopped. They moved out into the wide cold corridor and turned toward their rooms. Underhill already had his key in his hand—he hardly knew they were there anymore.

Poole waited near Underhill's back as he opened the door, expecting Maggie to do no more than to smile or nod as she went into her own room. She walked past them, and then stopped moving as soon as Underhill had clicked the door open. "Would you join me for a little while, Michael?" she asked. Her voice was light and penetrating, the sort of voice that could pass through a concrete wall in spite of its softness. "Tim isn't going to pay any attention to you tonight."

Poole patted Tim's back, told him he would see him later, and followed Maggie. She was leaning out of her room on one leg, smiling at him with the same forced, powerfully focused smile she had turned on George Spitalny.

Her room was no more than a long box with one of the immense floor-to-ceiling windows at its far end. The walls were a dusty pinkish rose; there was a chair, a desk, a double bed. Poole saw the copy of *Kitty's Pretty Muff* on the folded coverlet.

Maggie made him laugh with a joke that was not really a joke but a sentence turned inside out—some piece of wit that flashed in the air like the swipe of a sword and made him think he ought to remember that way of putting things just before he forgot it. She whirled around and grinned at him with a face so wry and lovely that it, unlike her clever phrase, passed instantaneously into his permanent memory. She was still talking. She sat down on the bed, Poole said something—he scarcely knew what. He could smell a fresh, peppery odor that seemed to lift off her hair and arms.

"I wish you'd kiss me, Michael," she said.

And so he did.

Maggie's lips felt surpassingly cushiony, and the shock of being met with such welcoming softness went right through his body. Her round slim arms came up and pulled his whole leaning body toward her so that they fell back together on her bed. Her lips seemed enormous. Michael put his arms under her back, and together they hitched themselves further onto the bed.

At length, with real sweetness, she moved her head away from him and smiled. Her face was as enormous as a moon. He had never seen a face like it. Maggie's eyes were so quick and alive they looked defensive. "Good," she said. "You don't look so sad anymore. At dinner you looked wretched."

"I was just thinking about going back to the room and reading Henry James."

Maggie's face floated up toward him again, and her pointed pink tongue slid into his mouth.

Their clothes seemed to melt off their bodies, and they were clasped together like spoons in a drawer, like ordinary lovers in an ordinary bed. Maggie's skin was astonishingly smooth. It had no pores, it was all silken sheen. Her whole body seemed to expand and accept him. He kissed the palms of her hands, crisscrossed with a thousand tiny aimless lines. She tasted of salt and honey. He put his face deep into the smooth bend of her neck and inhaled her: whatever she had smelled of before, now she smelled of fresh bread.

"Oh, you beautiful man," she said.

He slid into a warm wet opening in her body that felt like home. He *was* home: Maggie almost instantly moved and trembled with an orgasm: and his entire body felt blessed. He was *home.*

Later Michael lay stunned, spent, and grateful, entwined in sleeping Maggie. It felt like travel: like a journey to a place that was not merely a country, but country-ness itself. Maggie Lah, the flag of her own nation, the treasure and the key to the treasure. Michael's happiness passed effortlessly into sleep.

34

THE END OF THE SEARCH

1

He could hardly sit still, he was *certain* that today everything was going down, that today would decide the whole rest of his life. He kept looking at the telephone, telling it to ring: *now*. He jumped up from the chair before the window and went to the telephone and touched the receiver with his fingertips, so that if the call came at that moment he could answer it almost before it rang.

Yesterday his telephone had rung, and when he had picked it up, not thinking, or stupidly thinking about something else the way you always do when the really important things happen to you, he had said hello and waited, his brain kind of on hold for a second while the person hesitated, and after a second or two he felt himself come into focus: all his nerves woke up because the person at the other end was still not speaking, and that person was Koko. Oh God, what a moment. He had felt Koko's hesitation, Koko's need to talk to him, and the fear that kept him from talking. It was like the moment when you feel a firm tug on your fishing line, and you know that something big and necessary is down there, making up its mind. "I want to talk to you," Harry had said, and felt the whole atmosphere charge with excitement and need. If there had been anything wrong with his heart, it would have blown itself out like an old tire right then. And Koko had gently, almost unwillingly, set down his telephone—Harry could hear the need and the regret, for at such times you hear *everything*, everything *speaks*, and had set down his own telephone with the knowledge that Koko would call again. Now Harry was like a drug he could not resist.

And the circumstances were perfect. Michael Poole and Tim Underhill, who in Harry's opinion had turned out to be a pure type of fifth wheel, were safely off in the Midwest, looking for Victor Spitalny's high school yearbook or something—and he was here at the center, ground zero.

Today he would lead Koko into the killing box.

He had showered and dressed in loose comfortable clothes—his only pair of jeans, a black turtleneck sweater, black Reeboks. The handcuffs went over his belt, hidden by the sweater. The gravity knife rested like a small cold sleeping animal in his side pocket.

Harry wandered over to his television set and switched on NBC. He jiggled his knee. Jane Pauley and Bryant Gumble were smiling at each other, sharing some joke—in a year, they would be pronouncing *his* name, smiling at *him*, looking at him with wonder and admiration. . . . They switched to the good-looking girl who read the local news. Dark eyebrows, wet full lips, that intense sexy look, *intellectually* sexy in that New York way. Harry put his hand on his groin and leaned toward the screen, imagining what the girl would say if she knew about him, what he was going to do. . . .

He walked to his window and looked down at the wage slaves leaving his building in groups of two and three. One girl slipped out of the building and turned toward Tenth Avenue in the cold wind. Ring, telephone. The girl moved toward Tenth Avenue, foreshortened by Harry's perspective but still walking on a good pair of legs, a good ass shifting back and forth under her coat—That Channel Four girl, Jane Hanson, a million guys daydreamed about meeting someone like that, but when all this was over, she would be talking about him. Before long, he would be in the studio, he would be sitting in Rockefeller Center—the trick was not in knowing where it was, the trick was in *getting yourself invited in.* Above the world of wage slaves was a world like a big party filled with famous people who knew each other. Once you were *invited in*, you were in the party. You finally had the family you deserved. Doors opened before you, opportunities came your way—you were where you belonged.

When he was twenty years old, his picture had been on the cover of *Time* and *Newsweek*!

Harry went into the bathroom and smoothed down his hair in front of the mirror.

He ate a cup of cherry yogurt and an old cheese danish he found in his refrigerator. Around ten-thirty, watching CNN now, he ate a Mounds bar and a chocolate chip cookie from the stash of goodies he kept in his desk drawer. He had this crazy yen to have a drink, but felt nothing but contempt for a man who would take a drink before an important mission.

Later he turned back to one of the regular networks, muted the sound, and turned his radio to a news station.

Around twelve-thirty Harry called a restaurant, Big Wok, right across Tenth Avenue, and asked for an order of sesame noodles and double-sautéed pork to be delivered to his apartment.

The programs ground on, one after the other, barely distinguishable. Harry barely tasted the Chinese food he put in his mouth.

At two-thirty he jumped up from his chair and switched on his answering machine.

The afternoon wore on. Nothing happened: a child drowned in the Harlem River, another child was severely beaten by his stepfather and then put into the oven and burned to death, thirty children in California claimed to have been sexually abused in nursery school—lying little bastards, Harry thought, next day there'd be another twenty kids yelling that their teacher had taken out their weenies or that he had taken out *his* weenie. Half of them probably wanted him to do it, they probably asked if they could play with it. Little California girls, already wearing makeup, earrings dangling from their pierced ears, tight little asses in their little-girl designer jeans. . . .

An earthquake, a fire, a train wreck, an avalanche . . . How many dead, altogether? A thousand? Two thousand?

At four-thirty he could stand it no longer, checked his machine to make sure it was still on, put on a coat and a hat, and went outside for a walk. It was a real end-of-February day, with that dampness in the air that found its way through your clothing and went right down into your bones. Still Harry felt liberated. Let the crazy bastard call back! What choice did he have?

Harry was moving very quickly up Ninth Avenue, walking much faster than anyone else on the street. Now and then he caught someone staring at him with alarm or worry on their innocent faces and realized that he had been talking out loud to himself. "It's about time we talked. We have a lot to say to each other. I want to help you. This is the whole meaning of both of our lives."

"We need each other," Harry said to a startled man putting a girl into a taxi at 28th Street. "You could even call it love."

On the corner of 30th Street he darted into a little deli and bought a Mars bar. In the artificial warmth of the shop he felt dizzy for a moment. Sweat streamed down his forehead. He needed to be outside, he needed to be moving! Harry thrust two quarters at the fat man behind the register and waited, sweat pouring from his scalp, for his change. The fat man frowned at him—the pouches under his eyes actually seemed to darken and swell, as if they might burst—and Harry remembered that he had given the man the exact amount, that candy bars no longer cost a dime, or fifteen cents, or whatever he had thought—and he had actually known this, for hadn't he given the creep the right amount? He whirled away back out into the cold, healthy air.

You came running out of the cave, Harry said to himself.

All his life fate had sparkled just over his shoulder, singling him out as one of the special ones who had been invited in. Why else had other people so envied and resented him, tried to hold him back?

You came running out of the cave to find us. You've been trying to get back ever since.

You wanted to be a part of it.

Harry felt his blood beating, his skin heating, his whole body steaming like a healthy young stallion's.

You saw, you heard, you felt it, and you knew you were at the center of your life.

You need me to get back there.

Harry stopped moving on the corner of Hudson and something, a car blared at him, and electricity coursed through his body. The long vertical sign of the White

Horse Tavern blazed in the darkness just across the street. *To get back there.*

Harry remembered the electricity pouring through his body as he stood with his weapon pointed at all those silent children the villagers from An Lat must have taken out later through the cave's back entrance. He remembered: in the phosphorous glare. Their big eyes, their hands held out to him. And him there, twice their size, an adult American male. Knowing what he knew. That he could do anything, really anything he wanted to, at this one golden godlike point in his life. The sexual thing blasting through him.

Let someone say it was bad—they had not been there. If your body spoke that loudly, how could it be bad?

Sometimes a man was blessed, that was what it came down to. Sometimes a man touched pure original *power* and felt it take over his whole body—sometimes, maybe once in your life, you knew whole worlds were coming out of your cock because at that moment *nothing you did could be wrong.*

His life was finally coming full circle. I almost laughed out loud, Harry thought, and then did laugh out loud. He and Koko were going to go back there again, to the hot center of their lives. When he came out of the cave this time, he was going to come out a hero.

Exultant, Harry turned back toward his apartment.

2

But by six Harry felt his energy finally begin to consume itself and turn into anger and doubt. Why was he sitting here, in the middle of this messy apartment, in these ridiculous Action Man clothes? Who was he trying to kid? He had finally lived long enough to be able to see what happened to his best, highest moments when their goals were suspended. The world turned black. Harry knew this had nothing to do with Post-Traumatic Stress Disorder or anything else undergone by weaker, shallower people than he. The blackness was simply him, part of what had always set him apart. At such times whatever it was that he wanted and needed and *knew he was going to get* faded away into a vaguer and vaguer future, and his whole character seemed no more than a façade of competence and stability over a spinning chaos. Once he had been on trial, accused of murdering civilians, and the world had come close to judging him a madman—what had been filled with blazing rightness was coldly evaluated as the act of a criminal. The demons had come in very close that time, he had heard them snicker and seen the red glitter of their eyes, felt the terror and emptiness they brought with them.

The demons had known his secret.

If Koko called him back, the world itself was in its proper shape: the center was the center, which was the secret, and the power of what Harry Beevers had felt and done radiated out through the rest of his life and took him where he had to be. Why else had Koko appeared?

Koko had appeared again in the world to give himself to Harry Beevers, he thought, writing this sentence in his mind as he half-heartedly watched a man turned dusty brown by makeup predict the weather for the next five days.

At ten o'clock he heard the radio repeating the same news—the earthquake, the flood, the dead children, disaster skimming over the planet like a great black bird that touched down with a claw here and toppled buildings with a wingbeat there, unseen, always moving.

Half an hour later one of its great wings seemed to flap directly over his head. He had given in and made a drink—his only one, to calm his nerves. Harry was pouring vodka into a glass when the telephone rang, and he sloshed some of the liquid onto the counter. He hurried into the living room just as Michael Poole identified himself.

Stay there another two days, Harry silently said, but heard Poole's voice telling him of arriving the next day on a certain flight at a certain hour. Then Poole spoke of going to the police. Poole's voice was earnest and concerned and kindly, and in its cadences Harry Beevers could hear the collapse of all his designs.

Later in the evening Harry got hungry, but could not stomach the thought of eating more Chinese food. Also nauseating was the idea of Michael Poole and Tim Underhill, both of whom had seemed to give up on sex, being with Maggie Lah—only he would really know what to do with a girl like that. This was so funny it hurt. He went to his refrigerator, thinking almost angrily about

Maggie Lah, and found within it a couple of apples, a few carrots, a wedge of cheese already beginning to go dry and hard.

Resentfully Harry dropped most of these things on a plate and carried it into the living room. If nothing happened—if his instincts had been so entirely wrong—he would have to go out to the airport and try to muzzle Poole. Maybe he could send him somewhere else for a day or two.

Late at night Harry sat in the dark with the telephone and answering machine before him, sipping his drink and watching the red message light on the machine. In the silver city light coming through the window, everything looked poised. Countless times Harry had waited like this in the jungle, not moving, the world suspended around him.

Then the telephone rang, and the message light began to blink. Harry extended his hand and waited for the caller to identify himself. The tape switched on, and a second of silence hissed through the speaker. Harry lifted the receiver and said, "I'm here."

It was not until then that he knew: he heard Koko waiting for him to say more.

"Talk to me," Harry said.

Tape hiss came through the little speaker in the answering machine.

"Backwards and forwards, isn't that right? You wrote that? I know what you mean. I know—you want to go back to the beginning."

He thought he heard a soft slow intake of breath.

"This is how we're going to do it. I want you to meet me in a certain place, a safe place. Called Columbus Park, right on the edge of Chinatown. From there we can cross the street and go into the Criminal Court building, where you will also be safe. I know people there. These people trust me. They will do whatever I say. I will take you into a private room. You'll be able to sit down. Everything will be over. Do you hear me?"

Hissing silence.

"But I want to be certain that I will be safe too. I want to see that you will do what I ask you to do. So I want you to take a certain route to Columbus Park, and I will be watching you all along this route. I want to see you follow my orders exactly. I want to see that you do exactly what I ask you to do."

When no words came from Koko, Harry said, "Tomorrow afternoon at ten minutes to three, I want you to start on Bowery, across from the north end of Confucius Plaza. Enter an arcade in the middle of the block between Canal and Bayard and walk through the arcade to Elizabeth Street. Turn left and go to Bayard Street. Walk west on Bayard until you come to Mulberry Street. Across the street is Columbus Park. Go across and enter the park. Go down the path and sit on the first bench. In exactly two minutes I will enter the park from the southern end and join you on the bench. Then it will all be over."

Harry took a deep breath. He could feel his whole upper body sweating into the turtleneck. He wanted to say something else—something like *we both need to do this*—but the other end of the line clicked down, and the dial tone began.

Harry sat for a long time in the dark. Then he switched on the desk lamp and called the Tenth Precinct. Without giving his name, he left a message for Lieutenant Murphy that Timothy Underhill would be arriving at La Guardia airport at two o'clock the next afternoon on a Republic flight from Milwaukee.

That night he lay awake in bed a long time, indifferent to sleep.

3

Crime and death surrounded the elephant, crime and death were the atmosphere through which he moved, the air he pulled into his lungs through his long grey trunk. And this is one thing Koko knew: though you move through the city the jungle stares at you, every step. There is no jungle but the jungle, and it grows beneath the sidewalks, behind the windows, on the other sides of the doors. Birds cry out in the midst of traffic.

If he could have gone up to the old lady on West End Avenue, she would have dressed him in fine clothes and tamed him by easing his heart. But Pilophage the Doorman had turned him away, and the mad beasts had growled and shown their teeth, and his heart had not been eased.

The door opened, and—

The door opened, and Blood the Butcher slid into the room. Here was the demon Misfortune, and with the demon came the wire-haired bat, Fear.

Koko sat alone in his room, his cell, his egg, his cave. The light burned, and the egg the cell the cave caged all the light and reflected it from wall to wall, let none escape for Koko needed it every bit.

Flames jumped from the floor of Koko's room but did not sear him. Dead children clustered round him, crying out, and the others cried out from the walls. Their mouths open, their elbows pressed close to their sides. The children exhaled the reeking breath of lions, for they lived in the cave as he lived in the cave, backwards and forwards.

The door opened, and—

A fire sprang up and a wind sprang up.

Spare my life, a child cried out in bat language.

Pilophage the General posed for his portrait before Justinen, the painter. The General looked grand and good, with his plumed hat beneath his arm. The Lieutenant stood in the dark cave, not good or grand, with his surfboard out before him. His shovel. And the girl in the alley off Phat Pong Road looked at him and knew.

Do you want to know what's dark?

The Devil's arsehole is dark. Koko went into the cave and into the Devil's arsehole and there met the Lieutenant, Harry Beevers, his surfboard his shovel his weapon out before him, being fingered, being fluted, being shot—shooting. You want a piece of this? The Lieutenant with his cock sticking out and his eyes glowing. Then the Devil closed his nose and closed his eyes and stuck his fingers in his ears and eternity came in a thunderclap, eternity happened all at once, backwards and forwards. The woman crawled up from Nicaragua and gave birth and died in a black cloud, naked and covered in frozen mud.

At the thought of Harry Beevers the children quailed and threw their arms around each other, and their stink doubled and redoubled.

Good afternoon, gentlemen, and welcome to the Devil's Arsehole. It is presently no time no date no year. You will presently take yourself to the Bowery Arcade, and there you will once again face the elephant.

4

And when Babar went to bed he could not sleep. Discord and misfortune had come to Celesteville. Outside Babar's window demons chattered. When Pilophage the General opened his massy mouth, snakes and bats flew out.

We have turned every one to his own way, every one to his own way.

Tapitor, Capoulosse, Barbacol. Podular. Pilophage. Justinen. Doulamor. Poutifor. Sturdy Hatchibombitar, whom the stunned child within Babar the King had loved best, with his red shirt and checked cap, his sturdy shoulders and broad back—the street sweeper, a man of no ambition but to keep the streets clean, a kind man, honest, sweeping and sweeping away the filth.

5

At the cusp of the night he heard outside his window the wingbeats not of birds, as at first it seemed, but of dark terrible creatures twice the size of bats. These creatures had come out of the earth in order to find him, and they would torment themselves at the window for a long time before wheeling away and returning to the earth. No other person would see or hear them, for no other person could. Harry himself had never seen them. The position of his bed in the little alcove beside the bathroom did not give him a view of the window. Harry lay in the dark for a long time, listening to the feathery, insistent sound of the wings. Eventually the din began to lessen. One by one the creatures flew back to their hole in the earth, where they huddled together squeaking and biting, dreamily licking the drops of blood from one another's bodies. Harry listened in the dark as their number shrank to a final two or three that actually thumped against the glass in their desperation. Eventually these too flapped off. Morning was only a few hours away.

He finally slept an hour or two, and when he woke up he faced the old problem of the reality of the creatures. In the light of morning it was too easy to dismiss them as imaginary. On the nights they came, four or five nights since he had been out of uniform, they were real. He would have seen them, he had known, if he had dared to look.

But they had failed again, and at nine he got out of bed feeling both tired and invigorated. He showered carefully and long, scrubbing and soaping and fondling, sliding his hand up and down the shaft of his penis, cupping his balls, rubbing and pulling.

He dressed in the same jeans and sweater he had worn the previous day, but beneath the sweater wore a fresh shirt, stiff with starch.

When he looked at himself in the mirror beside his bed, he thought he looked like a commando—like a Green Beret. He drank two cups of coffee and remembered how he had felt on certain mornings in Camp Crandall before going out on patrol. The bitter coffee, the weight of the automatic pistol on his hip. On some of those mornings his heart had felt as hard and tight as a walnut, his skin had tingled, it had seemed to him that he saw and heard like an eagle. The colors of the tents, the red dust in the roadway, the wire glinting on the perimeter. The slight hazy dullness of the air. Beneath all the other odors of men and machinery had been a live green scent, delicate and sharp as the edge of a razor. For Harry, this had been the basic smell of Vietnam. In Ia Thuc he had grabbed an old woman's shoulder and pulled her harshly toward him, shouting some question he could not recall, and beneath the coarse smell of wood smoke the green razor of this scent had sliced out toward him from her body.

If a woman smelled like that, Harry thought, she'd put a hook in you that you'd never get out.

He drank another cup of coffee on the fold-out couch and tried to visualize in sequence every action that would bring him together with Koko in the Bowery Arcade. At one forty-five he would take a cab to the northeast corner of Bowery and Canal. It would then be about two o'clock and Lieutenant Murphy and two or three uniformed policemen would just be meeting the Republic flight from Milwaukee at La Guardia. In Chinatown the day would be cold, grey, wintry, and few people would be on the street. Harry planned to walk across Bowery and station himself on the wide traffic island just north of Confucius Plaza for a fast look at the block containing the arcade. He visualized the long block, the tiled façades of the restaurants with their plate-glass windows. A few men and women moving quickly in heavy coats. If Spitalny had decided to conceal himself in a doorway or behind a restaurant window, Harry would see him, and immediately disappear into Confucius Plaza and wait for Spitalny to panic when he realized that something had gone wrong. When Spitalny came out of hiding, Harry could follow him and finish him off as soon as they were alone. If he did not see Spitalny waiting to ambush him—and he did not think he would—Harry planned to recross Bowery and make a quick pass through the arcade just to make sure that the staircase had not been closed or blocked. If anything unusual were going on in the arcade, he would have to follow Spitalny out onto Elizabeth Street and get up close behind him before he got to Bayard Street. Elizabeth Street was Harry's fallback—few restaurants, gloomy tenements. But if everything went as he imagined it would, Harry planned to go back across Bowery and conceal himself among the trees and benches at the base of Confucius Plaza. There he would wait until fifteen minutes before the time he had given Koko—until twenty-five to three—then he would cross Bowery one final time, make a final pass through the arcade to see that all was clear at the Elizabeth Street end, and then wait for Koko on the staircase.

Sitting on his couch and holding the warm mug of coffee, Harry envisioned the sweep of the tiled floor toward the wide entrance. Harry would see everyone who passed by illuminated by the natural light of the street—when they turned toward the entrance and faced him, it would be as if a spotlight had been turned on them. Victor Spitalny would be burned a little brown from years of living under the Singapore sun, there would be deep lines in his face, but his hair would still be black, and in his close-set brown eyes would still be the expression of baffled grievance he had worn throughout his tour of duty.

Harry saw himself moving silently up the stairs as soon as Spitalny had passed him, treading softly over the tiles to come up behind him. He would slip the gravity knife out of his pocket. Spitalny would hesitate before leaving the arcade, as he would hesitate before entering it. Stringy and ungainly inside his ugly clothes, inside his madness, he would stand exposed for a second: and Harry would clamp his left arm around his neck and drag him out of the light back into the arcade.

Harry brought his coffee to his lips and was startled to find that it had gone cold. Then he grinned—the terrible creatures had come for Victor Spitalny.

When he could no loger ignore his hunger, Harry went out to a deli on Ninth Avenue and bought a chicken salad sandwich and a can of Pepsi. Back in his apartment, he could only eat half the sandwich—his throat closed, and his body would not allow him another bite. Harry wrapped up the other half of the sandwich and put it in the refrigerator.

Everything he did seemed italicized, drenched in significance, like a series of scenes from a film.

When Harry came out of his kitchen, the framed magazine covers blared out at him like loud music. His face, his name. It took the breath right out of his body.

6

Before going downstairs for the cab, he poured himself a shot of Absolut. It was treacly from the freezer, and slid into his throat like a bullet made of mercury. The bullet froze whatever it touched, and evaporated into warmth and confidence as soon as it touched his stomach. Harry capped the bottle and returned it to the freezer.

Alone inside the elevator, Harry took out his pocket comb and ran it through his hair.

Outside on Ninth Avenue he raised his arm, and a cab swooped across two lanes and came to rest before him. The door locks floated up with an audible *pop!* Everything now was a sequence of smooth, powerful actions. Harry climbed into the back seat and gave the directions to the driver.

Down Ninth Avenue the taxi went, everything clear, everything seen in the frame of the moment. A tall window reflected a sky filled with heavy clouds. Above the roof of the cab Harry heard sudden wing beats, swift and loud.

He stepped out of the cab onto an empty sidewalk and looked south across busy Canal Street to the block that contained the arcade. A crowd of people carrying shopping bags and small children turned off Canal down Bowery. While Harry stood watching another small group composed of young Chinese men in suits and topcoats walked out of the Manhattan Savings Bank and also turned down Bowery. In a few seconds the second group had overtaken the first, and walked past the arcade without even glancing in. Suddenly all of Harry's plans and precautions seemed unnecessary—he was an hour early, all he had to do was go into the arcade and hide on the staircase.

He hunched his shoulders against this heresy as much as against the cold. Visualizing an action helped bring it into being. The preparations were themselves a stage in Koko's capture, an essential aspect of the flow of events.

Harry trotted through a break in the traffic and jumped up onto Stage Two of his preparations, the traffic island north of Confucius Plaza. He could see the entire block between Canal and Bayard, but he was exposed to anyone who would happen to look across the street. Harry backed away toward the far side of the island. The Chinese businessmen were waiting to cross Bayard, and the family with the babies and shopping bags was just straggling past the arcade. Nobody stood pretending to read the menus in the restaurant doorways, no faces were visible in the windows.

When the light changed Harry ran back across Bowery and ducked into the arcade for Stage Three.

It was even better than he remembered it—darker, so quiet it was hushed. One old lady dawdled between the shops. Today there were even fewer customers than he had seen two days before. The staircase to the lower level was nearly invisible, and when Harry glanced down it he saw joyfully that the bulb at the bottom of the staircase had burned out, and no one had replaced it. The lower level of the arcade was illuminated only by the weak light from the barbershop's windows.

He gave a quick check to the arcade's far end. A skinny Chinese in pajamas stared at him from the stoop of a tenement before retreating back inside.

Stage Four began at the base of Confucius Plaza. A few Chinese in padded coats came across the wide plaza and were admitted into the office building at Harry's back. They paid no attention to him. Half a dozen concrete benches sat among the trees and planters on the plaza. Harry chose one that gave him an uninterrupted view.

Now and then a truck stopped directly before him and blocked his view; once a delivery van parked directly in front of the arcade. Harry checked his watch as he waited for the van to pull away, and saw that it was two-twenty.

He felt for the knife in his coat pocket. The pocket seemed to be empty. Harry groped more industriously. The knife still eluded him. Sweat began to drip down into his eyebrows. He tore off his right glove and thrust his hand into the pocket—the knife was gone.

People passing in cars were pointing at him, laughing, leaving him behind as they swept by on their ways to parties, receptions, interviews. . . .

He poked his fingers to the bottom of the pocket and found a rip in the lining. Of *course* his pockets were ripped, the coat was eight years old, what did you expect? The knife lay inside the hem, useless as a toothbrush. Harry worked it up the lining, and gradually got it near enough to the rip so that he could thrust his fingers through and feel for it. A row of stitches popped, and the rip widened. He found the knife and drew it up and transferred it to his left pocket.

An eight-year-old coat! He had nearly lost everything because of an eight-year-old coat!

Harry sat down heavily on the bench and immediately put his left hand into the coat pocket and folded it around the knife. He had lost his focus. Harry wiped his forehead, put his glove back on, and folded his hands in his lap.

Trucks, cars, and taxicabs streamed past on Bowery. A large group of well-dressed Chinese men moved past the arcade. Watching them, Harry realized with a spurt of panic that anyone could have slipped inside from Elizabeth Street while he watched this end.

But Koko was a soldier, and he would follow orders.

The Chinese men reached Bayard Street and scattered with waves and smiles.

It came to Harry that he was sitting on a stone bench with a knife in his pocket, waiting not to capture someone but to kill him, and that he thought he could become famous for doing this. This idea seemed as cruelly barren as the rest of his life. For a moment Harry Beevers contemplated himself as just one man among a million men, a lonely figure on a bench. He could stand up, drop the knife into a planter, and go off and do—what?

He looked down at his body clad in loose dark uncharacteristic clothes, the clothing of an active man, and this simple proof of his uniqueness allowed him back into the heart of his fantasy. His rich destiny again embraced him.

At two-thirty Harry decided to alter his plan and wait out the time remaining on the staircase. It never hurt to be in position early, and being in position would mean that he would also see anyone who entered the arcade from the far end.

Harry stood up. His body was very straight, his head erect, his expression carefully neutral. Harry Beevers was *locked in.* The man was *wrapped tight.* He reached the curb, and his nerves reached out to every human being and every vehicle moving past. High heels clicked toward him, and a young Chinese woman joined him at the crosswalk. When she glanced at him—a pretty young woman, that silky Chinese hair, sunglasses even on a day like this—she was attracted to him, she found him interesting. The light changed, and they set off the curb together. In the middle of the street she gave him a rueful, questioning look. On the other side of the street the girl turned toward Bayard Street, stretching out the particular nerve that he fastened to her, drawing it out further and further like an unbreakable thread.

Harry moved quickly into the darkness of the arcade. From its far end came the sound of low voices and moving bodies, three bodies, and Harry casually moved nearer the wall and pretended to be interested in a large poster glued to the wall. X-RAY SPECS. THE BLASTERS. Three overweight teenage girls in duffel coats came slouching past the angle in the arcade. He recorded their brief acknowledgment of him, the way their eyes flicked sideways, and how they silently commented on him to each other. They carried knapsacks and wore scuffed brown loafers. The girls moved slowly down the length of the arcade and finally walked out into the lighter air, still pretending not to have noticed him.

Harry checked both ways—the arcade was empty, and the Bowery end gaped bright and grey—and crossed to the staircase. The burned-out bulb had of course not been replaced. He quickly went down half a dozen steps, checked back toward the Elizabeth Street entrance, and then went down the rest of the way. Harry unbuttoned his coat. He peeled off his gloves and shoved them into his pockets. The railing dug unpleasantly into his hip when he leaned against the side of the staircase.

At once an arm emerged out of the blackness behind him and clamped around his neck. Someone standing at his back pulled him off-balance and pushed a thick cloth into his mouth. Harry reached for the knife, but his hand tangled in a glove. Then he remembered it was the wrong pocket anyway, but in that second he was falling back and it was too late for the knife. He heard his handcuffs clatter onto the staircase.

35

THE KILLING BOX

1

Maggie saw the policemen first, and asked Michael what he thought had happened. They were halfway down the ramp to the terminal, and the two officers had appeared in the lighted square where the jetway ended. "I don't know," Michael said. "Probably—" He looked over his shoulder and saw Tim Underhill just emerging through the door of the plane, half a dozen people back. Maggie took his elbow and stopped moving. Michael looked ahead again and saw the big homicide detective, Lieutenant Murphy, staring at him with a set, furious face beside the two uniformed men. "Take it easy," Murphy said, and the policemen beside him braced themselves but did not draw their guns. "Keep on coming, people," Murphy said. The people ahead of Maggie and Poole had stopped short, and now the jetway was crowded with passengers. Murphy motioned the passengers in front toward him, and everyone began shuffling toward the terminal. Maggie was holding tightly onto Poole's hand.

"Everybody keep moving," Murphy said. "Keep moving and keep calm."

For a second there had been a shocked silence. Now a bubble of questioning, demanding voices filled the tunnel.

"Just proceed through the terminal normally," Murphy said. Poole glanced back at Underhill, who had gone pale but was moving forward with the other passengers behind them. A woman somewhere in their midst shrieked at the sight of the policemen.

Murphy was watching Underhill, and when Poole and Maggie finally reached the terminal he spoke without looking at them. "Take them aside."

One of the policemen took Michael by the arm Maggie was not holding, and pulled him off toward the window beside the gate. Another tried to separate Maggie, but she would not let go of Poole's arm, and so Poole, Maggie, and the two policemen moved crabwise to an empty space in front of the window. The gate had been roped off, and a wall of people stood at the rope looking in at them. Two uniformed policemen with rifles stood off to the side behind Murphy, out of sight of the passengers in the jetway.

When Tim Underhill came through, Murphy stepped forward, charged him with the murder of Anthony Pumo, and read him his rights from a white card he had taken from his pocket. The policeman who had taken Maggie aside patted Underhill's chest and sides, then patted down each leg. Underhill managed to smile.

"We were going to call you as soon as we got here," Michael said. Murphy ignored him.

The other passengers on the flight moved slowly toward the ropes. Most of them were walking backward, not to miss anything. The flight crew had clustered at the end of the ramp and were whispering to each other. Nearly all the passengers stopped moving once they reached the rope, set down their luggage, and stared.

Murphy's face flushed a dark red. He turned around and shouted, "Will you clear the area? Will you please get this area clear?" It was not clear if he was shouting at the policemen or the gaping passengers.

"Please move to the other side of the rope," said a young detective, a police dandy in a dark blue coat and soft wide-brimmed hat that made an umintentional contrast to Underhill's own big shabby coat and wide hat. Most of the passengers picked up their carry-on bags and moved toward the opening in the ropes. The entire terminal sounded like a cocktail party.

"Lieutenant," Poole said. Maggie glanced up at him, and he nodded.

"Keep your mouth shut, Dr. Poole," Murphy said.

"I'm arresting you and the girl too. There'll be plenty of time for you to say whatever you want to say."

"What do you think we were doing in Milwaukee? Could you tell me that?"

"I hate to think what you people were doing, anywhere."

"Do you think Maggie Lah would go anywhere or have anything to do with Tina Pumo's murderer? Does that seem reasonable to you?"

Murphy nodded to the dandy, who stepped behind Underhill and handcuffed him.

"Tim Underhill was still in Bangkok when Tina Pumo was killed—check the flight records."

Maggie was unable to stay quiet any longer. "I *saw* the man who killed Tina. He did not look anything like Timothy Underhill, Lieutenant. Somebody is making a fool of you. How did you learn that we were on this flight?"

"We had an anonymous tip." Murphy's face was still the same ugly purple it had turned just before his explosion.

"Harry Beevers," Poole said, looking down at Maggie.

"Look at my passport, Lieutenant," Underhill said in a quiet, reasonable voice. "I carry it with me. It's in my coat pocket."

"Get his passport," Murphy said to the dandy, who reached down into the nearest pocket of Underhill's long shapeless coat and found the small dark green booklet that was his passport.

"Open it up," Murphy said.

The young detective moved closer to Underhill. He opened the passport and riffled through the pages. There appeared to be a great many entries in Underhill's passport. The dandy found the last page of entries, examined it for a moment, then handed the passport to Murphy.

"I came back with Beevers and Dr. Poole," Tim said. "Mass murder was one of the mistakes I managed to avoid."

"Mass murder! Mass murder!" echoed through the crowd jammed against the rope.

Murphy's flush deepened as he stared at Underhill's passport. He leafed backwards from the last entry, looking for an earlier arrival in America. At length he dropped his hands, moved his feet, and turned to look at the scene in the terminal. People were pressing against the rope, and the police marksmen stood among the empty plastic chairs. Murphy said nothing for a long time. A flash went off as a tourist took a picture.

"You people have a lot of explaining to do," he finally said. He put the passport in his own coat pocket. "Cuff thc other two."

The two uniformed policemen snapped handcuffs on Poole and Maggie.

"Did this man Underhill come back from Bangkok on the same flight with you and Beevers and Linklater?"

Poole nodded.

"And you chose not to let me know that. You sat in my office and decided to let me chase after the wrong man."

"I regret that," Poole said.

"But still you people put up those posters all over Chinatown?"

"Koko had used Underhill's name."

"You wanted to find him yourself?" Murphy asked, seeming just now to have understood this point.

"Harry Beevers wanted to do something likc that. The rest of us wcnt along with him."

"You went along with him," Murphy said, shaking his head. "Where is Beevcrs now?"

"Mikey!" a voice called from behind the crowd at the ropes.

"Conor Linklater was going to meet us here."

Murphy turned to one of the uniformed policemen and said, "Bring that man here." The policeman trotted off toward the gap in the rope, and reached it at about the same time that Conor and Ellen Woyzak appeared at the front of the crowd.

"Bring them along," Murphy said, walking off toward the crowd, which began moving away from him.

"We were in Milwaukee to see if we could learn where Koko is," Poole called to him. "Instead we found out who he is. If you'll let me get some stuff out of the trunk of my car, I could show you what I mean."

Murphy turned around and glowered at Michael and Maggie, then, with even deeper distaste, at Tim Underhill.

"Hey, you can't arrest these people," Conor started to say. "You want a guy named Victor Spitalny—he's the one they were checking up on—"

"No," Poole said. "Conor, it's not Spitalny."

Conor stopped talking for a wide-eyed moment, and then stepped toward Murphy, holding his hands out. "Cuff me." Ellen Woyzak uttered a noise that combined a screech and a growl. "Put 'em on," Conor said. "I'm not gonna rest on my morals. I did everything these guys did—the buck passes here. Come on."

"Shut up, Conor," Ellen said.

Murphy looked as though he wanted to cover his face with his hands. All the policemen watched him as they would a dangerous animal.

Finally Murphy pointed at Maggie, Poole, and Underhill. "Put these three with me," he said, and charged toward the crowd like a bull in a bullring. More flashes of light exploded. As soon as he reached the gap in the rope, the crowd broke apart before him.

"Put them in the lieutenant's car," said the dandy. "I'll take Harry Truman with me."

Still red-faced but calmer than he had been in the terminal, Murphy had removed their handcuffs before they finally got into the backseat of his car. One of the young policemen was driving them across the Whitestone Bridge, and Murphy had twisted sideways to listen to them. Every few minutes his radio crackled, and cold air poured in through the imperfectly sealed windows. Another policeman was driving Michael's car, which they had taken from the airport parking lot and brought alongside Murphy's, back to the precinct house.

"On the plane?" Murphy asked. He was no longer as angry as he had been inside the terminal, but he was still suspicious.

"That's right," Poole said. "I suppose that right up until then Maggie and I had been thinking that we were still looking for Victor Spitalny. I guess I knew the truth, but I couldn't see it—I didn't want to see it. We had all the evidence we needed, all the pieces, but they just hadn't been put together."

"Until I mentioned Babar," Maggie said. "Then we both remembered."

Poole nodded. He was not about to tell the policeman about his dream of Robbie holding up a lantern beside a dark road.

"What did you remember?"

"The song," Maggie said. "Michael told me what the

man in Singapore and the stewardess said to him, and I—I knew what they had heard."

"The man in Singapore? The stewardess?"

Poole explained about Lisa Mayo and the owner of the bungalow where the Martinsons had been killed. "The man in Singapore had heard Koko singing something that sounded to him like *rip-a-rip-a-rip-a-lo*. Lisa Mayo heard the passenger sitting next to Clement Irwin singing something very similar. They both heard the same thing, but they both heard it wrong."

"And I knew what it was," Maggie said. "The song of the elephants. From *Babar the King*. Here—take a look at it."

Poole passed the book he had taken from the back of his car over the top of the seat.

"What the hell is this?" Murphy asked.

"It's how Koko got his name," Underhill said. "I think there were other meanings, but this is the first one. The most important one."

Murphy looked at the page to which the book had been opened. "This is how he got the name?"

"Read the words," Poole said, and pointed to the place on the page where the song was printed.

"Patali Di Rapata
Cromda Cromda Ripalo
Pata Pata
Ko Ko Ko"

Murphy read from the yellow songsheet printed on the page.

"And then we knew," Poole said. "It was Dengler. Probably we knew long before that. We might have known as soon as we went into his mother's house."

"There is a serious drawback to that theory," Murphy said. "Private First Class Manuel Orosco Dengler has been dead since 1969. The army positively identified his body. And after the army identified the body, it was shipped back home for burial. Do you think his parents would have accepted someone else's body?"

"His father was dead, and his mother was crazy enough to have accepted the body of a monkey, if that's what they sent her. But because of the extensive mutilation the body had undergone, the army would have strongly advised her to accept their identification," Poole said. "She never looked at the body."

"So whose body *was* it?" Murphy asked. "The goddamn Unknown Soldier?"

"Victor Spitalny," Underhill said. "Koko's first victim. I wrote the whole scenario in advance—I explained what to do and how to do it. It was a story I used to call 'The Running Grunt.' Dengler got Spitalny to join him in Bangkok, killed him, switched dogtags and papers, made sure he was so mutilated nobody could tell who he was, and then took off in the middle of the confusion."

"You mean, you put the idea in his head?" Murphy asked.

"He would have worked out something else if I hadn't told that story," Underhill said. "But I think that he used my name because he took the idea of killing Spitalny and deserting from me. He called himself by my name in various places after that, and he caused a lot of rumors that went around about me."

"But why did he do it?" Murphy asked. "Why do you think he killed this Spitalny character—in order to desert under another identity?"

Poole and Underhill glanced at each other. "Well, that's part of it," Underhill said.

"That's most of it, probably," Poole said. "We don't really know about the rest."

"What rest?"

"Something that happened in the war," Poole said. "Only three people were there—Dengler, Spitalny, and Harry Beevers."

"Tell me about the running grunt," Murphy said.

2

A man with deep broken wrinkles in his forehead and an air of aggrieved self-righteousness jumped up from a chair in the hallway outside the lieutenant's office as soon as Poole, Underhill, Maggie, and Murphy reached the top of the stairs. A cold cigar was screwed into the side of his mouth. He stared at them, plucked the cigar from his mouth, and stepped sideways to look behind them. The sound of the next group came up the stairs, and the man thrust his hands in his pockets and nodded at Murphy as he waited with visible impatience for the others to appear.

Ellen Woyzak, Conor Linklater, and the young detective in the blue coat and hat reached the top of the steps and turned toward Murphy's office. The man said, "Hey!" and bent over the railing to see if anyone else was coming. "Where is he?"

Murphy let the others into his office and motioned for the man to join them. "Mr. Partridge? Come in here, please?"

Poole had thought the man was another policeman, but saw now that he was not. The man looked angry, as if someone had picked his pocket.

"What's the point? You said he was gonna be here, but he ain't here."

Murphy stepped out and held open his door. Partridge shrugged and came slowly down the hall. When he walked into the office he scowled at Poole and the others as if he had found them in his own living room. His clothes were wrinkled and his unpleasant blue-green eyes bulged out of his loose, large-featured face. "So now what?" He shrugged again.

"Please sit down," Murphy said. The young detective took some folding chairs from behind a filing cabinet and began opening them up. When everyone was seated, Murphy perched on the edge of his desk and said, "This gentleman is Mr. Bill Partridge. He is one of the managers of a YMCA men's residence, and I asked him to join us here this afternoon."

"Yeah, and now I gotta leave," Partridge said. "You got nothing for me. I got work to do."

"One of the rooms under Mr. Partridge's management was rented to a gentleman calling himself Timothy Underhill," Murphy said, with more patience than he had displayed at the airport.

"Who skipped out," said Partridge. "*And* who ruined his room. I don't know who, but one of you people owes me back rent and a paint job."

"Mr. Partridge," Murphy said, "do you see the YMCA tenant who called himself Timothy Underhill anywhere in this room?"

"You know I don't."

"Thank you for coming in, Mr. Partridge," said Murphy. "I am sorry we took you away from your duties, but I'd like you to see our artist downstairs to work on a composite portrait. If you feel that the department owes you money, you can try submitting a bill to us."

"You're doin' a great job," Partridge said, and turned to leave the room.

Poole called out to him. "Mr. Partridge, what did the man do to his room?"

Partridge did a half-turn and frowned at Poole. "Let the cop tell you." He went through the door without closing it behind him.

The young detective moved to the door and closed it. He grinned at Maggie as he went back to his place beside the desk. He had a broad handsome face, and his teeth shone very white beneath his thick moustache. It occurred to Poole that both Murphy and the younger officer looked like Keith Hernandez, the Met's first baseman.

Murphy looked gloomily at Underhill, who sat in the folds of his big coat, holding his hat in his lap. "He was here to give us an identification, of course. Timothy Underhill checked into the YMCA on the Upper West Side on the evening of the day that Clement Irwin was killed at the airport. There is, by the way, no record of anyone named Timothy Underhill passing through Customs to get back into the country at any time during the month of January, so we know that he traveled under another name. We stopped examining the records before the three of you and Mr. Beevers came back, of course, because we knew our man was with us by then." He shook his head. "Partridge called us as soon as he looked inside Underhill's room. Once we got in there, we knew we had him. All we had to do was wait." He took a manila folder out of the middle drawer of the desk. "But after we waited all night, we thought he must have come back just after we showed up and saw our patrol cars. Which means that we missed him by no more than a couple of minutes. Take a look at the pictures of the room."

He took a handful of Polaroids from the envelope and passed them to the young detective. Grinning again, the man went straight to Maggie and handed the photographs to her.

Maggie smiled at him and passed the photographs to Michael without looking at them.

The walls of the room looked chaotic, with clippings

and photographs taped up above a wandering wavelike pattern that rose and fell through gouts of red paint. Another photograph showed a black and white picture of Tina, torn from a newspaper. In the third photograph, the undulating wave pattern finally came into focus. Poole swallowed. It was a crudely drawn mural of the heads and bodies of a lot of children. Chests had been exploded open, heads lolled on lifeless necks. Several of the children were naked, and the photograph clearly showed entry wounds in their trunks and stomachs.

Painted on another wall were the slogans A DROWSY STIFLED UNIMPASSIONED GRIEF and A MAN OF SORROW AND ACQUAINTED WITH GRIEF.

Poole passed the photographs to Underhill.

"I'll show you the other half of why I met you at the airport," Murphy said. He took a copy of a typewritten letter from the envelope and gave it to the young detective. "This time give it to Dr. Poole, Dalton."

Dalton smiled handsomely at Maggie and handed the sheet of paper to Michael.

"St. Louis police found it in his desk."

So this was how he had persuaded the journalists to come to him—Harry Beevers had been right. Poole read the letter very slowly:

> *Dear Mr. Martinson,*
> *I have decided that it is no longer possible for me to remain silent about the truth of the events which occurred in the I Corps village of Ia Thuc . . .*

He became aware that Murphy was saying something about Roberto Ortiz's apartment. The detective was holding up another typed sheet of paper. "It's identical to the one addressed to Mr. Martinson, except that the writer instructs Mr. Ortiz to reach him at an address on something called"—he glanced at the sheet—"called Plantation Road, in Singapore. Which is where his body was found."

"Only these two letters were found?"

Murphy nodded. "Some of the others must have done as he asked, and destroyed the letters. Anyhow, these letters and the room at the Y were the reason we were so interested in you, Mr. Underhill."

"Do you have any idea who placed the anonymous call?"

"Do you?" Murphy asked.

"Michael and Connor and I feel it must have been Harry Beevers."

"But if he got your friends to lie to me about your whereabouts, why would he send me out to arrest you?"

"You know why that asshole called the police," Conor said to Poole. "He was going to meet Koko, and he wanted you out of the way."

"So where is Mr. Beevers now? Trying to capture this man by himself?"

Nobody spoke.

"Get Beevers on the telephone," Murphy said, and with a final look at Maggie, Dalton hurried out of the room.

"If you people are hiding anything more from me, I promise you, you'll spend a lot of time wishing you hadn't."

They sat in silence until Dalton returned. "Beevers isn't answering his phone. I left a message for him to call you as soon as he got back, and I sent a car over to his place in case he's there."

"I think our business is over for the moment," Murphy said. "I really do hope that I am through with you people. All of you are lucky not to be in jail. Now I want you to get out of my way and let me do my job."

"Are you going down to Chinatown?" Michael asked.

"That is none of your business. You'll find your car out in front, Mr. Poole."

"Are there any caves in Chinatown?" Underhill asked. "Anything that might look like a cave?"

"New York is full of caves," Murphy said. "Get out of here. Go home and stay there. If you hear from this man Dengler, call me immediately."

"I don't know what's going on," Conor said. "Dengler? Will somebody sort of fill me in on what I missed?"

Underhill pulled Conor toward him and whispered something in his ear.

"I want to suggest something to you before you go," Murphy said. He stood up behind his desk, and his face mottled with the force of the anger he did not allow himself to show. "In the future, when you come across something important to this case, do not *mail* it to me. Now please let me do my work."

He walked out of the office, and Dalton trailed behind him. Conor said, "Mikey, what is this? Dengler?"

A uniformed policeman appeared in the door and politely told them to go away.

3

"I have to call Judy," Poole said when they got outside. "We have a lot of things to get straight."

Maggie suggested that he make the call from Saigon. Poole looked at his watch—four o'clock.

"Harry loved that bar," Conor told Ellen. "I think he spent most of his afternoons there."

"You're talking about him as though he was dead," Ellen said.

"I think we're all afraid of that," said Tim Underhill. "Michael told him our plane was getting in at two, and I bet he somehow managed to arrange a meeting with Koko around then. So it's been two hours—if Dengler called Harry in order to turn himself in and Harry tried anything tricky, which would be impossible for Harry *not* to do, probably nobody could save him now."

"Can you explain all this stuff about Dengler now?" Conor asked.

"That will require a drink," Tim said. "For you, not for me."

Poole opened his car, and Maggie stepped beside him. "There's someone uptown I want you to meet. My godfather." He looked at her curiously, but she merely smiled and said, "Can all of us really squeeze into your car?"

They all could.

As Michael drove off, Underhill began describing their visit to Milwaukee. Underhill had always been a good describer, and while Poole drove down Seventh Avenue he saw the Spitalnys' sad kitchen, and George Spitalny's attempt to seduce Maggie with an old photograph; he saw an enraged man pounding a tire iron against the back of a bus, and snowdrifts like little mountain ranges. *Kitty's Pretty Muff*, and the gas flares in the Valley. The smell of sizzling Wesson oil, Helga Dengler's dog's eyes. Little M. O. Dengler standing behind the body of a deer he had skinned and gutted.

"Michael!" Maggie screamed.

He twirled the wheel just in time to avoid ramming a taxicab. "Sorry. My mind was back there in that terrible house. And I hate the idea of giving up when there's some chance that Harry is still alive."

"And Dengler too," Underhill said. "Murphy said that New York is full of caves. Maggie, I don't suppose that you can think of anything in Chinatown that might even faintly resemble a cave?"

"No," Maggie said. "Well, not really. I used to go to this place with Pumo that was in an arcade. I suppose it was as close to a cave as you can get in Chinatown."

Poole asked where it was.

"Off Bowery, near Confucius Plaza."

"Let's go take a look at it," Underhill said.

"Do you want to?" Poole asked.

"Don't you?"

"Well," Poole said.

"You can't give up now, Poole," Maggie said. "You ate bad kielbasa in George Spitalny's kitchen. You waded through Salisbury steak at the Tick Tock Restaurant."

"I'm the explorer type," Poole said. "Conor? Ellen?"

"Do it, Michael," Ellen said. "We might as well try."

"You can tell she never met Harry Beevers," Conor said.

When Michael drove past Mulberry Street in the thick traffic on Canal Street, Underhill peered past the upturned collar of his huge coat and said, "Our friends are out in force. Take a look."

Poole glanced through the side window into Chinatown. Down on Mulberry Street, red lights spun on top of police cars drawn up to the curb; other red lights bounced off shop windows on Bayard Street. Poole glimpsed a group of policemen trotting diagonally across the street in a cluster, like a platoon.

"They'll find him," Conor said, sounding as if he wanted to make himself believe it. "Look at all those cops. And we don't know Beevers tried anything funny with Koko, not really."

Now they were passing the entrance to Mott Street. "I don't see anything down there," Poole said.

"It looks like two cops are going door to door," Underhill said. "But we really don't have any proof that

Harry is down here, do we, or that he tried to double-cross us and Dengler?"

"He wanted Murphy to stop us before we got any further than the airport," Poole said. He looked sideways into Elizabeth Street, which was emptier than the others. "That's proof of something. He wanted us out of the way."

Poole turned with the traffic toward the tall white towers of Confucius Plaza.

"There it is," Maggie said, gesturing to the far side of the street. Poole looked sideways and saw an opening in the row of shops and restaurants along Bowery. Light penetrated the opening for about five feet, then melted into shadow. Maggie was right. It did look like a cave.

Poole found a parking spot in front of a fish market on Division Street. When he got out of the car, he saw frozen fish guts and shiny puddles of ice on the sidewalk. "Let's just try to stay out of Murphy's way. After we check out the arcade we can go to Saigon, and I can begin figuring out where I'm going to live."

They began moving up Bowery in the stiff cold wind that came around the curved towers. A single policeman emerged from Bayard Street onto Bowery, and Michael realized that he did not at all want the policeman to walk into the arcade. Murphy and the rest of the policemen had Mulberry Street, Mott Street, Pell Street—all Poole wanted was the arcade.

The policeman swiveled toward them, and Poole recognized him—he was the fat-necked young officer who had led Michael upstairs to the meeting on the morning of the line-up. The man looked idly at Poole, then glanced down at Maggie's legs. He turned his back on them and walked down Bayard Street.

"Oink," Maggie whispered.

Poole watched the young policeman waddle down Bayard Street toward a patrol car beside which a band of uniformed men gazed into the windows of a grocery store while they stood around looking vaguely official.

Seconds later the five of them stood before the arcade. Maggie took the first step, and as they walked in they fanned out to cover both sides.

"I wish we were looking for something specific," Underhill said. He was moving forward slowly, trying to take in every inch of the floor.

"There's another level downstairs," said Conor, who was with Ellen on the arcade's right side. "Let's check that out when we're done up here."

"I don't understand why we're doing this," Ellen said. "Don't you think your friend would have arranged to meet Koko—this Dengler—in a park, or on a corner someplace? Or in an office?"

Poole nodded, looking at a dusty display of women's underwear. "If he just planned to meet him, that's what he would do. But this is Harry Beevers we're talking about." He moved past posters for a rock club, and looked back at Conor, who was leaning on the railing of the stairs with his arm around Ellen Woyzak's shoulders.

"And the Lost Boss wouldn't do anything simple," Conor said. "He'd cook up some plan. He'd tell him to meet him somewhere and plan to meet him somewhere else. He'd want to take him by surprise."

They went past the angle in the arcade and stood for a moment looking at cold grey Elizabeth Street.

"Let's say Koko finally answered his ads," Poole said. "It's not impossible."

"Tina always answered my ads."

"That's probably where he got the idea," Poole said.

"Okay, but why would he want to meet Koko in a cave?" Ellen asked. "That's why we're here, isn't it? Because this is the only place Maggie could think of in Chinatown that looks like a cave?" She looked at each of the three men, who did not answer her. "I mean, wouldn't it make more sense to get him to walk past a certain building and jump out at him? Or something like that?"

"Harry Beevers once had the time of his life in a cave," Underhill said. "He went inside it, and when he came out he was a famous person. His whole life had changed."

"Let's check out the stairs," Conor said. "Afterward we can go back to Saigon and wait for Murphy to tell us what happened."

Poole nodded. He had lost heart. Murphy would eventually come across Beevers' corpse in some tenement room. He would have a card in his mouth, and his face would be mutilated.

"Shouldn't there be another light down there?" Maggie asked.

They were at the top of the stairs, looking down into the darkness.

"Burned out," Conor said.

Weak light came out into the lower level of the arcade from the barber shop. Further back, the light from another shop cast a fan-shaped gleam out onto the tiles.

"No, it was taken out," Maggie said. "Look." She pointed at the empty socket set into the ceiling at the bottom of the stairs.

"Took it out because it was burned out," Conor said.

"Then what's that?" Maggie asked. In a corner of the bottom step, a nub of brass was just visible to them.

"Looks like the bottom of a light bulb to me," Ellen Woyzack said. "So somebody—"

"Not somebody. Harry," Poole said. "He unscrewed the bulb to conceal himself. Let's go down and have a look."

Strung out along the top step, they began to move down the stairs in unison. Harry Beevers had hidden on these steps, after having arranged a police reception for them at the airport. What had happened then?

"It's the whole bulb," Maggie said. She held it to her ear and shook it. "Nothing rattles in there."

"Well, looky here," Conor said.

Poole took his eyes from the light bulb and saw Conor holding out toward him a shiny pair of handcuffs.

"Now I believe all this," Ellen said. "Let's take the handcuffs to Murphy and get him to come back here with us." She wrapped her arms around herself and stepped closer to Conor.

"I think he'd toss us all in the slammer if he saw us down here," Conor said. "*Beevers* bought these, right?"

Poole and Underhill nodded.

"I want to see about something," Maggie said, and went down the rest of the way, still clutching the light bulb. Poole watched her go into the barber shop.

"I think Dengler took out the light bulb," Conor said. "I bet Dengler was waiting for him when he got here. And he took him somewhere, which means they aren't too far away."

Maggie came out of the barber shop looking very excited. "They *saw* him. The barbers noticed that the bulb was gone—burned out, they thought—early this afternoon. Later they saw a white man standing on the stairs. They thought he was a policeman."

"That's funny," Poole said. "Harry always wanted people to think he was a cop."

"It wasn't Harry," said Underhill. "They saw Dengler."

"Did they say anything else about him?"

"Not really. They said he stood there a long time, and then they forgot about him, and when they looked the next time, he was gone. They didn't see a struggle or anything."

"I don't suppose they would have," Poole said. "If you were going to take somebody quietly out of the arcade, which way would you go?"

"That way," Ellen said, pointing toward Elizabeth Street.

"Me too." Poole went up the steps ahead of the others.

"What are you going to do, Michael?" Ellen called after him.

"Take another look," Poole said. "If Dengler hustled Beevers out onto the street, maybe something else fell out of his pockets. Maybe Beevers was bleeding. Harry wouldn't have come unarmed, given what he intended to do. There has to be something out there."

It was almost hopeless, he knew. Koko could simply have shoved a knife into Beevers and dragged his body outside to a car. Anything Beevers would have dropped—a paper, a matchbook, a scarf—would have been blown away by the wind.

"What are we looking for?" Maggie asked as they walked out onto the Elizabeth Street sidewalk.

"Anything Beevers might have dropped." Poole began moving down the sidewalk, looking at the pavement and the curb. "Conor, will you take the middle of the street? Tim, maybe there's something on the other sidewalk."

"Conor," said Ellen.

Tim nodded, hunched himself against the wind in his big coat and hat, and crossed the street. He began making slow side-to-side sweeps up the opposite sidewalk. Maggie floated across the street to join him.

"Conor?" Ellen repeated.

Conor put his finger to his lips and walked out into the middle of the street. Poole moved slowly back and forth across the sidewalk, hoping to find anything at all that might tell him what had become of Beevers. Looking down for something he was not finding, he heard Maggie saying something to Underhill in her precise comedic voice, and then heard her giggle.

"Oh, hell," Ellen said, and went out into the middle of the street after him. "I suppose if we find any severed fingers or other body parts you won't object to my yelling my head off."

All Poole had seen on the sidewalk were two pennies, a punctured nitrous oxide capsule, and a tiny unstoppered vial which he failed to recognize as the former container of ten dollars' worth of crack. Ahead of him on the pavement were a discarded black rubber child's boot and something that looked like a damp ball of fluff but which Poole was certain would turn out to be a dead sparrow. More than two hours ago, Koko had caught Beevers in his own killing box. It was likely that Beevers was dead by now. What he was forcing the others to do was quixotic. Yet his body still felt a spurious excitement. They had been right about the arcade; they were standing on ground that M.O. Dengler and Beevers had crossed only an hour or two before. He had traveled thousands of miles to come this close to Koko. His whole body balked at the idea of yelling for Lieutenant Murphy and the fat-necked young policeman.

"Michael?" Maggie said softly from the other side of the street.

"I know, I know," Poole said. He wanted to throw himself down on the sidewalk and tear through the pavement with his fingernails, to rip through the concrete until he reached Koko and Harry Beevers.

If he did that, if he could do that, if he knew where to dig and had the strength and tenacity to do it, maybe he could save Harry Beevers' ridiculous life.

"Michael?" Ellen echoed Maggie.

He balled his hands into fists and held them before his face. He could barely see them. He turned around and through blurry eyes looked down Elizabeth Street and saw a stocky body dressed in a long blue coat swing into view like a wandering ox.

"Get back, hide, don't rush but get out of sight," he said.

"What—" Ellen began, but Conor grabbed her hand and began walking her up the street. Poole ducked his head and moved into the shelter of the arcade's entrance, trying to look like a preoccupied citizen on his way home.

He felt the policeman's eyes on him as he slipped into the arcade. He heard a wobbly, unearthly sound and realized that Conor was actually whistling. As soon as he got into the arcade Poole flattened out against the side and peeked out. The stocky young policeman was still looking in his direction. He seemed puzzled. Poole looked across the street, but Maggie and Underhill had disappeared into one of the tenements.

The policeman put his hands on his hips—something had disturbed him. Probably, Poole thought, he had just gotten around to recognizing Maggie and Conor and himself. He looked as if he was trying to work out what they could all be doing on Elizabeth Street. He looked back down Bayard Street at the other policemen, then took a step up toward the arcade. Poole stopped breathing and looked up toward the other end of the street. Conor and Ellen Woyzak were now doing a better imitation of a tourist couple who had wandered into unpromising territory. The young policeman looked behind him, then back toward the other officers. He stepped backwards and began motioning toward the policemen around the patrol car.

"Oh, shit," Poole said.

He heard a short, sharp whistle and thought that Conor had relapsed into his Gary Cooper imitation. Poole looked across the street and saw Tim Underhill, like a scarecrow in the voluminous coat and droopy-brimmed hat, just inside the arched entrance of one of the tenement buildings. Maggie Lah was standing slightly behind him, and behind her Poole saw a portion of a little courtyard. Maggie's eyes seemed very wide. Underhill was gesturing for Poole to join them, waving his arms like a traffic cop.

The young policeman stood down at the end of the street, waiting for someone—he was as impatient as Tim Underhill. Then the young policeman straightened up, and Dalton sauntered into view.

Poole glanced up the block: Conor and Ellen had disappeared around the corner. Dalton could see nothing but an empty street.

For a moment the young policeman spoke to Dalton. Dalton's only movement was to look once up Elizabeth Street.

Michael wished he could hear everything they said.

Are you sure you saw them? The same ones?

Sure I am. Dey were up dere.

Then did Dalton say *I'll be right back with Lieutenant Murphy,* or did he say *Keep an eye on things until we finish with Mulberry Street?*

Whichever it was, Dalton strolled back out of sight, either leaving Thick-Neck by himself or on his way to get Murphy. Thick-Neck turned his back to stare down at the crowds of Chinese on Bayard Street, and sighed so hugely Poole could almost hear it.

Poole looked back across the street. Underhill was practically exploding, and Maggie stared at him with wide eyes he could not read. The brooding young policeman did not shift his stance as Poole advanced out onto the street. Now Elizabeth Street seemed very wide. Poole moved as fast as he could, trusting that he would not hit a stone or make any noise. The wind seemed to roar around him. Finally he came up onto the opposite sidewalk. Underhill's whole face was blazing at him. Down at the end of the street, he thought he saw Thick-Neck's shoulders start to turn his way, a movement as slow and clumsy as that of a large machine, and he flew the final yards across the pavement and into the protection of the arch.

"He might have seen me," Poole gasped. "What is it?"

Underhill wordlessly moved through the arch into a narrow brick courtyard surrounded on all sides by the dingy high walls of the tenement. A smell of grease and sweat, odd and dislocating in the cold, hung in the air. "We saw it by accident, really," Underhill said. He was moving toward one of the entrances. Beside the rough peeling door to the ground floor and the staircase was a semi-circular well that allowed for at least one window in a room beneath ground level.

It was in that well, Poole knew. Tim Underhill had stationed himself beside the tenement door. He grimly looked down at whatever was in the well. Poole hoped that it was not Beevers' dead body. But that was what would be in the well. Koko had yanked Harry Beevers out of the arcade, dragged him through the arch, and then slit his throat. After he had performed the operations that were his usual signature, he had dumped Beevers' body into the window well. Then he had melted away.

For the first time, Poole really feared for his own life. He moved up to the well and looked down.

His certainty about what he had been going to see was so great that at first he saw nothing at all. The back wall descended seven or eight feet down to a dirty concrete floor before a window that had been painted black. Yellowed bits of paper and old beer cans lay on the dirty concrete. There was no body. He looked up at Underhill's face, then at Maggie's. Both of them were regarding him with a wild impatience. Finally Maggie pointed down at one of the corners where the curved brick wall met the tenement wall.

A shiny steel knife lay on top of a nest of old papers. A smear of bright blood lay across the blade.

Poole looked up and saw Conor and Ellen coming toward them through another arch set in the west wall of the tenement. They had circled around the block onto Mott Street and ducked into the first entrance they had seen.

"I think Lieutenant Murphy is probably right behind us," he said. "I want to go inside the building."

"Don't," Maggie said. "Michael—"

"I know Dengler. Murphy doesn't. Maybe Beevers is still alive."

"You might know Dengler," Maggie said, "but what about Koko?"

This was an excellent question, and the response that came immediately to Michael Poole's mind made so little rational sense that he stifled it before it was born. Koko's mine, was what he almost said—he belongs to me.

"He probably left hours ago, Maggie," Tim said in his low calm voice. "I'll come with you, Michael."

"If Murphy shows up before we come back, tell him where we went," Poole said, and pulled open the rough, sagging wooden door that was the tenement's entrance. Poole stepped inside and found himself before an iron staircase, painted dark green, which ascended up into the tenement; on its far side another section of the staircase went into the darkness beneath ground level. To his left was a door to one of the rooms. Poole rapped on the door, thinking that the tenant might have heard what had happened just outside his door. He rapped again, but no one came.

"Let's start taking a look through the building," he said to Underhill.

"I'm here too," Conor said from behind him.

Poole looked back and saw Conor pulling Ellen's fingers off his arm. "We'll be safer if we all go together."

Maggie put her arm around the taller woman.

Poole moved toward the staircase. For a moment he paused and looked up toward the six or seven flights through which the staircase turned; then he continued around the front of the staircase and took the downstairs steps.

As soon as his head passed beneath ground level, the staircase became as dark as a grave. The walls were cold and damp. Just behind him, Conor and Tim were moving so quietly he could still hear Maggie and Ellen Woyzak shuffling their feet on the floor above. Poole slowly groped down the steps. The air grew colder around him. Underhill had to be right: Koko, who had once loved Babar, had fled hours before, and somewhere down here in a cold shabby room, they would discover the dead body of Harry Beevers. Poole wanted to find it before the police did. He knew it would make no difference to Beevers, but he thought he owed him at least that much.

At last Poole saw yellow light outlining a door at the bottom of the stairs. He leaned over the railing and looked up. A milky nimbus of light hovered over the top of the stairs.

He came down onto the landing. Through the crack in the door he could see a fragment of wall painted the same green as the staircase. It was splashed with red and black.

Either Conor or Tim squeezed his shoulder again. Poole noticed a dark smear of blood on the section of landing before the door.

Poole gently pushed open the door. The chill inside the room, colder than the staircase, drifted out toward him. In the thick motionless light within the room, Harry Beevers sat strapped into a wooden chair facing the door. His body leaned against thick straps. Blood had run down the side of his face, over the white rags that gagged him, and down into his sweater. At first Poole saw that Beevers' left ear had been cut off, and he knew that Beevers was dead. Then Beevers' eyes snapped open, bright with pain and terror.

Spatters of blood lay on the floor around Harry Beevers. The walls were covered with waves and writing, and a slender man sat cross-legged on the floor with his back to them, gazing in rapt concentration at the painted walls. Directly before him was the crude representation of a small, black-haired Vietnamese girl, stepping forward with her hands outstretched, smiling or screaming.

Poole scarcely knew what he felt, or why—there was too much sadness in all this. Koko, who was M.O. Dengler, or was the person who had once been M.O. Dengler, seemed like a child himself. Poole did not know that he was going to speak, but he said, "Manny."

M.O. Dengler swiveled his head and looked at him.

4

Poole stepped forward into the cold green room. Until this moment, some part of him had resisted believing that Dengler really was Koko. Despite everything he had said to Maggie and Lieutenant Murphy, Poole felt as if the wind had been knocked out of him. He did not have even the beginning of an idea of what he was going to do now. It was still hard to accept the idea that Dengler could wish to do him harm. Harry Beevers uttered a keening sound through his bloody gag. Poole heard Conor and Tim pad in behind him and spread out on either side.

Dengler seemed not to have aged at all. He made Poole feel old and out of shape and almost corrupt with experience. He felt almost shamed before Dengler.

Over Dengler's alert nineteen-year-old face, Poole saw that what he had taken for a pattern of waves was a row of children's heads. Their bodies had only partially been painted in. Some held their hands upraised, others reached out with sticklike arms. Red paint wound through them like a skein. Dengler's young face tilted up toward Poole, his lips slightly parted as if he were going to say—*I was right about God.* Or—*Whatever it was, it was a long time ago.*

On the side wall had been painted, in large black letters, the same slogan Poole had seen in the police Polaroids: A DROWSY STIFLED UNIMPASSIONED GRIEF. And beneath that, in the same large letters: PAIN IS AN ILL-U-SHUN.

Poole took in all this in less time than it took to blink. He understood. He was in no-place, all right. He was back there. This was where Koko lived all the time, in that underground chamber he and Underhill had visited twice.

I'm here to help you, Poole wanted to say.

Dengler smiled up at him from the center of his uncannily preserved youth.

You been bad? Dengler seemed to ask him. *If you haven't . . .*

Harry Beevers squealed again, and his eyes rolled up into his head.

"I'm here to help—" Poole started to say, and the words seemed almost dragged out of him, as if he were in one of those dreams where every step requires immense effort.

"Come out with us, Dengler," Conor said, very simply. "It's what you want to do."

The smiling child with outstretched empty hands seemed to step out toward Poole as if from the back of a shadowy hootch, and for a second he thought he heard wingbeats in the cold air above his head.

"Stand up and come toward us," Conor said, taking a step forward with his own hand held out.

Beevers squealed in pain or outrage.

Then Poole heard the sound of men thudding down the iron staircase. He looked at Dengler's calm empty face in horror. "Stop!" he yelled. "We're all alive! Don't come any further!"

Almost before he stopped shouting at the policemen, Poole saw Dengler move up off the floor in a fluid, uncoiling motion. In his hand was a long knife.

"Dengler, put the knife down," Underhill said.

As Dengler stood and moved closer to the light bulb, the startling innocence and youthfulness of his face disappeared like a mirage. He smashed the bulb with the handle of his knife, and the room went dark as a mineshaft. Poole instinctively crouched.

"Are you okay in there?" called a voice from the stairs.

"Dengler, where are you?" Underhill whispered. "Let's all get out of this alive, all right?"

"I have work to do," came a voice that Michael did not immediately recognize. The voice seemed to come from everywhere in the room.

"Who's inside that room?" shouted Lieutenant Murphy. "I want to know who's in there, and I want to hear everybody's voice."

"Poole," called Poole.

"Underhill."

"Linklater. And Beevers is in here, but he's injured and gagged."

"Anybody else?" the lieutenant yelled.

"Oh, yes," came a quiet voice.

"Lieutenant," Poole called out, "if you come in here shooting, we'll all die. Go back up the steps and let us come out. We'll need an ambulance for Beevers."

"I want each man to come out alone. He will be met by an officer and escorted up the steps. I can offer the services of a hostage negotiator, if the man holding you will deal with one."

Poole steadied himself by putting his hand on the floor. That too was cold and wet, even sticky, and Michael realized that he was touching Harry Beevers' blood.

A high-pitched terrified squeal came to him from everywhere, bouncing from wall to wall.

"We're not hostages," Poole said. "We're just standing around in the dark."

"Poole, I'm sick of talking to *you,*" Murphy yelled. "I want to hear from this Koko. After we get you out of there, *Doctor* Poole, that's when I'm going to be interested in talking to you. Then I'll have a lot to say to *you.*" His voice grew louder as he bawled out the next words. "Mister Dengler! You are in no danger as long as you do exactly what I say. I want you to release the other men in the room one at a time. Then I want you to surrender yourself. Are you clear about that?"

Dengler repeated what he had said when he had put them in darkness. "I have work to do."

"That's fine," Murphy said. Then Poole heard Murphy say to some other policeman, "I have work to do. What the hell does that mean?"

A voice whispered into Poole's ear, so close and unexpected it made him jump. "Tell him to go all the way up the stairs."

"He says he wants you to go all the way up the stairs," Poole shouted.

"Who's that?"

"Poole."

"I should have known," Murphy said in a quieter

voice. "If we go back up the stairs, will he release all of you?"

"Yes," the voice whispered in Poole's other ear.

"Yes!" Poole shouted. He had not heard the faintest sound as Dengler moved around him. Now he could hear the sound of wingbeats again, which was really the sound of ceaseless movement, as of a large group of people moving all about him, whispering to one another. He could smell blood.

"Any other requests?" Murphy shouted, sounding sarcastic.

"All the police in the courtyard," the voice whispered directly into Michael's face.

"He wants all the police in the courtyard."

"While the hostages are being released," Murphy said. "He's got that."

"Conor, are you okay?" Poole asked.

There was no answer. The others were dead, and he was alone in the no-place with Koko. He was in a pool of his friends' blood and Koko was fluttering around him like a hundred birds, or bats.

"Conor!"

"Yo," came Conor's voice, quieting his dread.

"Tim?"

Again, no answer.

"Tim!"

"He's fine," came the whisper. "He's just not speaking at the moment."

"Tim, can you hear me?"

Something painful and red hot happened to Michael's right side. He clapped his hand over the pain. He felt no blood, but there was a long clean cut in the fabric of his coat.

"I went to Muffin Street," he said. "I talked to your mother. Helga Dengler."

"We call her Marbles," came a whisper from somewhere off to his right.

"I know about your father—I know what he did."

"We call him Blood," came the whisper from where he had last seen Conor.

Poole still held his hand to his side. Now he could feel the blood soaking through his coat. "Sing me the song of the elephants."

From different parts of the room Poole heard snatches

of unmelodic wordless song, the music of nothing on earth, the music of no-place. Sometimes it sounded as if children were speaking or crying out a great distance away. These were the dead children painted on the walls. Again Poole knew that no matter what he might hear in this room, he was alone with Koko, and the rest of the world was on the opposite side of a river no man could cross alive.

As Koko's song flew through the dark, Poole could also hear the sound of the policemen retreating up the iron steps. His side flamed and burned, and he could feel blood soaking into his clothes. The room had widened out to the size of the world, and he was alone in it with Koko and the dead children.

Finally Murphy's voice came crackling through a bullhorn. "We are in the courtyard. We will remain here until the three men with you have come out through the door. What do you want to do next?"

"We waste no part of the animal," came the hissing voice.

The dying children wailed and sobbed. No, the children were dead, Poole remembered: that was Harry Beevers.

"Do you want me to tell him you waste no part of the animal?" Poole asked. "He can't hear me anyhow."

"He can hear you fine," came the icy whisper.

Then Poole understood. "It was the motto of the butcher shop, wasn't it? Dengler's Lamb of God Butcher Shop. I bet it was painted right under the name. WE WASTE NO PART OF THE ANIMAL."

The voices all stopped, the nonsense song and the cries of the dead children. For an instant Poole felt violence gather in the cold dead air about him, and his heart nearly froze. He heard the rustle of heavy clothing—Underhill must have moved toward the door. Koko was going to stab him again, he knew, and this time Koko would kill him and tear his face from his skull, as he had done with Victor Spitalny.

"Do you think he killed your real mother?" Poole whispered. "Do you think he arranged to meet Rosita Orosco on the riverbank, and murdered her there? I do. I think that's what he did."

A low voice whispered a wordless exhalation from far off to Poole's left.

"Conor?"

"Yo."

"You knew it too, didn't you?" Poole said. He felt like crying now, but not from fear. "Nobody told you, but you always knew it." Poole felt his heart unfreeze. Before Koko killed all of them, or before the police ran in and shot them all, he had to say these things.

"Ten days after you were born, Karl Dengler met Rosita Orosco on the riverbank. It was the middle of winter. He stabbed her, and then he undressed her body and left her there. Did he rape her body, after he killed her? Or just before he killed her? Then he came into your bedroom, when you were a little boy, and did to you what he had done to her. Night after night."

"What's going on?" came Murphy's distorted, amplified voice.

"Night after night," Poole repeated. "Tim knew it all in some way—without really knowing anything about what had actually happened, he felt it, he felt everything. Your whole life was about the stuff that Underhill knew just by looking at you."

"Underhill goes out first," Koko whispered from behind Poole. A knife slid under Poole's ear, and the children wailed and begged for life. "First Underhill. Then you. Then Linklater. I'll come out last."

"I'm right, aren't I?" Poole said. His voice was shaking, and he knew that Koko would not answer him—because he did not have to answer. "Underhill is coming out first!" he yelled.

And a second later he heard Murphy's voice come crackling to him from the other side of the great rushing river. Murphy did not know about the river that surrounded the no-place and cut it off from every human place.

"Send him out," Murphy called.

Harry Beevers made a noise like a trapped animal, and creaked against his straps.

If Underhill were alive, Poole thought, Dengler was sending him out because he wanted Poole to go on with his excellent story. Maggie Lah was on the other side of the river, and he would never see her again, for on this side of the river was the bleak little island of the dead.

"Go, Underhill," Poole said. "Get up those stairs." His voice sounded stranger than ever.

The door opened a crack and an amazed Poole saw Tim Underhill's back slipping out onto the landing. The door slowly closed behind him. Slow footsteps went up the stairs.

"Hallelujah," Poole said. "Now who?"

He heard only the creaking and moaning that sounded like the cries of faraway dead children.

"It was whatever happened in the cave, wasn't it?" he said. "God help Harry Beevers."

"Send the next man," crackled Murphy's voice.

"Who's next?" Poole asked.

"It's different in here now," Conor whispered.

As soon as Conor spoke, Poole felt the truth of what he had said. The sense of prowling movement no longer surrounded him: the cold air seemed very empty. Poole stood in a lightless basement room—there were no faraway children and there was no river. "Let's go out together," he said.

"You first," Conor said. "Right, Dengler?"

Beevers protested with squeals and grunts.

"I'll be right behind you," Conor said. "Dengler, we're going."

Poole began moving toward the dim outline of the door. It was as if he had to unlock his arms and legs. Every step made the wound in his side screech. He could feel the blood sliding out of his body, and the floor seemed to be covered with blood.

Then Poole knew what had happened—Dengler had slit his own throat. That was why the voices had stopped. Dengler had killed himself, and his corpse was lying on the floor of his little cell in the dark.

"Someone will be down very soon to help you, Harry," he said. "I'm sorry I ever listened to anything you ever said."

Creaks and moans.

Poole attained the door. He pulled it toward him and a lesser degree of darkness enveloped him. He stepped out onto the landing. This had seemed like darkness when they had come down the stairs. He looked up toward the hazy nimbus at the top of the stairs and saw two uniformed policemen staring down at him. He thought of poor crazy Dengler, lying dead or dying back inside the room, and of Harry Beevers. He never wanted to see Harry Beevers again.

"We're coming," he said, but his voice was feeble, not his.

Michael pulled himself up the stairs. As soon as he was far enough up into the light to be able to see clearly, he looked at his side. He had to force himself to remain standing—an instant later he realized that there had been a deceptive amount of blood. Koko had meant to hurt him seriously, though not to kill him, but his heavy winter coat had lessened the degree of his injury. "Dengler killed himself," he said.

"Yep," Conor said behind him.

Poole looked over his shoulder and saw Conor coming up after him. Conor's eyes were the size of dinner plates. Michael turned back around and kept going up the stairs.

When he reached the top one of the officers asked him if he was all right.

"I'm not too bad, but I'll need that ambulance too."

Dalton poked his head into the entry and said, "Help that man out."

One of the officers put his arm around Poole's shoulders and assisted him out into the courtyard. It seemed warmer out in the air, and the gritty brick courtyard seemed very beautiful to him. Maggie cried out, and he turned toward the sound, barely taking in Tim's form slumped into his coat, his head bowed. Maggie and Ellen Woyzak stood in the far corner of the beautiful little courtyard, framed as formally as by a great photographer. Both women were beautiful too—overflowingly beautiful, in their different ways. Poole felt as though his death sentence had been commuted just as the blindfold had been tied around his head. Ellen's face ignited as Conor came through the door behind him.

"Get him to the ambulance," Murphy growled, lowering the bullhorn. "Beevers and Dengler are still down there?"

Poole nodded. With a little cry, Maggie jumped forward and threw her arms around his neck. She was speaking very quickly, and he could not make out the words—they seemed barely to be in English—but he did not have to know what she was saying to understand her. He kissed the side of her head.

"What happened?" Maggie asked. "Where's Dengler?"

"I think he killed himself, I think he's dead," he said.

"Get him in the ambulance," Murphy said. "Put him

in the hospital and stay there with him. Ryan, Peebles, get down there and see what's left of the other two."

"Harry?" Maggie asked.

Ellen Woyzak had put her arms around Conor, who stood as motionless as a statue.

"Still alive."

The thick-necked young officer moved up to Poole with an expression of great stupid satisfaction on his face, and began to urge him toward the arch that led out onto Elizabeth Street. Poole glanced at Underhill, who was still slouched against the wall beside the policeman who must have led him away from the tenement. Underhill did not look right, differently from the way Conor did not look right. His hat was pulled down over his forehead, his neck was bent, his collar was turned up.

"Tim?" Poole said.

Underhill moved an inch or two away from the policeman beside him but did not look up at Poole.

He was *small,* Poole finally saw. He was a little, a pocket-sized Underhill. Of course people did not shrink. A second before he realized what had happened, Poole saw the flash of teeth in an almost unearthly smile hidden in the folds of Underhill's turned-up collar.

His body froze. He wanted to yell, to scream. The wide black river cut him off, and the dead children wailed.

"Michael?" Maggie asked.

Michael pointed at the figure in Underhill's hat and coat. "Koko!" he could finally shout. "Right there! He's wearing—"

In the hand of the grinning man in Underhill's coat there had materialized a long knife, and while Poole shouted, the man sidled around the policeman beside him, clamped his hand on his arm, and shoved the knife deep into his back.

Poole stopped shouting.

Before anyone could move, the man had vanished through the arch out onto Elizabeth Street.

The policeman he had stabbed sat down heavily on the bricks, his face stunned and empty. Murphy exploded into motion, sending four uniformed policemen after Dengler, then getting the wounded officer carried into the ambulance. He took a last, infuriated look around the courtyard and then ran out through the arch.

"I can wait," Michael said when one of the policemen

tried to push him toward the arch and the ambulance bay. "I have to see Underhill."

The policeman looked at him in confusion.

"For God's sake, get him out of the basement," Poole said.

"Michael," Maggie pleaded, "you have to get to the hospital. I'll come with you."

"It's not as bad as it looks," Poole said. "I can't go until I see what happened to Tim."

Tim was dead, though. Koko had silently murdered him and taken his coat and hat and left the basement room in disguise.

"Oh, no," Maggie said. She made to run for the tenement door, but first Poole took her arm, and then Dalton restrained her.

Poole said, "Get down there, Dalton. Let go of my girlfriend and go downstairs and see if you can help Tim, or I'll pound the living shit out of you." His side flamed and pulsed. From out on the street came shouts and the sound of running footsteps.

Dalton turned slowly toward the arch, then changed his mind and moved toward the tenement's entrance. "Johnson, let's see what's taking them so long." One of the policemen trotted after him. Poole heard them clattering down the steps. "I mean that sincerely," he said. "I'll pound . . . the living shit . . ."

Ellen and Conor moved across the courtyard toward Poole and Maggie.

"He got away, Mikey," Conor said in a voice full of disbelief.

"They'll get him. He can't be that good."

"I'm sorry, Mikey."

"You were great, Conor. You were better than the rest of us."

Conor shook his head. "Tim didn't make any *noise*. I don't—I think—"

Poole nodded. He did not want to say it either.

"He cut you bad?"

"Not too bad," Poole said. "But I think I'll sit down." He put his back against the tenement wall and slid down onto the bricks, with Maggie holding one elbow and Conor the other. When he got down he felt very hot so he tried to take off his coat, but that made his side scream again. He heard himself make a noise.

Maggie knelt down beside him and took his hand.

"Just a twinge. A little mild shock too."

She squeezed his hand.

"I'm okay, Maggie. Just a little hot." He leaned forward, and she helped slide his coat off his shoulders. "Looks a lot worse than it is," Poole said. "That cop was hurt bad, though." He looked around for the policeman Koko had knifed. "Where is he?"

"They took him away a long time ago."

"Could he walk?"

"He was on a stretcher," Maggie said. "Do you want to go to the ambulance now? There's another one out there."

Then they both heard the heavy tramp of boots on the staircase.

A moment later two of the officers carried Harry Beevers out of the tenement. He had a big white cloth taped to the side of his head, and he looked like the victim of a savage street fight. Unable to stand by himself, Beevers wobbled between two policemen. "Where'd he go?" Beevers asked in a crushed, painful voice. 'Where is that asshole?"

Poole assumed that he meant Koko, and almost smiled—he had a right to ask that question.

But Beevers' intense unhappy eyes found Poole, and instantly filled with bitterness. *"Asshole,"* Beevers said. "You fucked everything up! What do you think you were trying to do down there? Get everybody killed?" Unbelievably, he tried to fight free of the policemen and come toward Poole. "What makes you think you can blame everything on me? You fucked up, Poole! You fucked up bad! I almost had him, and you let him get away!"

Poole stopped paying attention to Beevers' ranting. In the entrance to the tenement appeared Dalton and a tall, burly black policeman holding Tim Underhill between them. Tim's face was tinged with blue, and his teeth chattered. The side of his sweater had been cut open, and a large quantity of blood had stained his entire left side—like Michael, at first glance he looked as though someone had tried to cut him in half. "Well, Michael," Tim said while they carried him through the door.

"Well, Timothy," Poole said. "Why didn't you say something down there, when Dengler was pulling your clothes off?"

"Set me down next to Poole," Underhill said, and Dalton and the other policeman helped him across the courtyard and lowered him gently onto the bricks. Another policeman to whom Dalton had signaled came rushing in from the street with a blanket, which he wrapped around Underhill's shoulders.

"He tied something around my mouth," said Underhill. "I think it was Beevers' shirt. Was good old Harry wearing a shirt when he came out?"

"Couldn't say."

Lieutenant Murphy burst in through the Elizabeth Street arch, and both men looked up at him. His face was still purple, but as much with exertion as rage—it was just one of those Irish faces, Poole saw. By the time Murphy was sixty, his face would be that color all the time. When the detective saw Poole and Underhill leaning against the tenement wall with their legs out before them, he closed his eyes and his mouth became a taut, lipless line. He said, "Do you suppose you could manage to get another ambulance for these two idiots? This isn't a convalescent hospital."

"Dr. Poole wouldn't leave until Mr. Underhill came out," Dalton said, "and when Beevers got into the ambulance he threatened to sue everybody in sight unless they took him immediately. So—"

Murphy looked at him.

"Sir," Dalton said, and went out through the arch.

"Did you get him?" Poole asked.

Murphy ignored the question and walked across the courtyard to lean into the tenement as if he thought that someone else might be down there. Then he looked down into the window well. "Bag that knife," he said to one of the uniformed policemen.

"Did you?"

Murphy continued to ignore him.

A few seconds later they heard the wailing of an approaching ambulance draw closer and closer until it came up alongside the tenement and turned off its siren.

Dalton came back through the arch and asked them if they wanted stretchers.

"No," Poole said.

"Don't we?" Underhill asked. "Are stretchers effete these days?"

"What happened to the policeman Dengler stabbed?"

Poole asked. Dalton and the black officer were gently getting him up on his feet, and Maggie fussed around them, patting and touching.

"He died on the way to the hospital," Murphy said. "I just heard."

"I'm sorry," Poole said.

"Why? You didn't stab him, did you?" Murphy's face was blazing again, and he strode across the bricks to stand before Poole. "We missed your friend Dengler." His eyebrows nearly met at the boundary of a deep, angry-looking vertical crease in his forehead. "He dumped the hat and coat on the corner and took off down Mott Street like a rabbit. We think he ducked into a building somewhere. We'll get him, Poole. Don't worry about that. He's not going to get very far." Murphy turned away, clamping and unclamping his jaws. "I'll see you and your buddy in the hospital."

"I'm sorry that one of your men died, not because I had anything to do with it."

"Jesus Christ," Murphy said, turning away to precede them through the arch.

"Some people just don't understand sympathy," Underhill said to Poole as they were being taken toward the waiting ambulance.

5

Both Poole and Underhill were stitched up in an emergency room by a baby-faced young resident who pronounced their wounds identical but "all glamour," meaning that while they would leave good-sized scars, they represented no serious threat to life or health, facts that Poole had already ascertained for himself. After their wounds had been sutured, they were taken upstairs to a double room and told they would be spending the night by the officer who had ridden with them in the ambulance. This officer's name was LeDonne, and he had a neat moustache and kindly eyes.

"I'll be right outside the door," LeDonne added.

"There's no need for us to spend the night in the hospital," Poole said.

"The lieutenant would really prefer it this way," said LeDonne, which Michael took as the officer's polite way of telling them that they were under orders to spend at least one night in the hospital.

Maggie Lah appeared with Conor Linklater and Ellen Woyzak three hours after their installation in the room, and all three visitors described how they had spent the previous hours with Lieutenant Murphy. The lieutenant had heard the story of how they had come to the building on Elizabeth Street enough times to conclude that they were innocent of all crimes except foolhardiness and finally had charged them with none.

Maggie also told Michael and Tim Underhill, who had become slightly groggy from the effects of painkillers, that Koko had escaped the police in Chinatown, but that Murphy was certain he would be captured before nightfall.

Maggie stayed on after Conor and Ellen left to go to Grand Central for a Metro North train. Ellen kissed both men, and nearly had to pull Conor through the door. Poole thought that Conor almost wished he had been injured himself, so that he could stay with them.

"Where did they put Beevers?" he asked Maggie.

"He's three floors up. Do you want to see him?"

"I don't think I ever really want to see Harry Beevers," Poole said.

"He lost an ear," Maggie said.

"He has another one."

The light in the hospital room grew hazy, and Michael thought of the beautiful grey nimbus of light at the top of the stairs as he had emerged from Koko's cell.

A nurse came and gave him another shot although he said he did not want or need it. "I'm a doctor, you know," he said.

"Not now, you're not," she said, and slammed the needle into his left buttock.

After that he and Tim Underhill had a long conversation about Henry James. Later all that Poole could remember of this woozy conversation was that Tim had described a dream James had had as an old man—something about a terrifying figure trying to break into the writer's room, and the writer eventually attacking his own attacker and driving him away.

That day or the next, for Murphy had ordered them held over for at least another twenty-four hours, Judy Poole appeared on the threshold of the room just before the end of visiting hours. Michael could see Pat Caldwell standing behind his wife. He had always liked Pat Caldwell. Now he could not remember if he had always liked his wife.

"I'm not coming in unless that person comes out," Judy said. *That person* was Maggie Lah, who immediately began picking up her things.

Michael motioned her to stay. "In that case, you're not coming in," he said. "But I think it's a pity."

"Won't you see Harry?" Pat called to him. "He says he has a lot of things to talk about with the two of you."

"I'm not interested in talking to Harry right now," Poole said. "Are you, Tim?"

"Maybe later," Underhill said.

"Michael, aren't you going to get rid of that *girl?*" Judy asked.

"No, I don't think I am going to do that. Come in here so we can talk in normal voices, Judy."

Judy turned around and marched away down the hospital corridor.

"Lot of fun, being in a hospital," Michael said. "Your whole life appears before you."

Late the next evening, when Poole was lucid enough to feel the pain of the wound, Lieutenant Murphy came to the room. He was smiling and seemed calm and self-possessed, like the man Beevers had admired at Tina Pumo's funeral.

"Well, you're in no danger now, so I'm sending LeDonne home to get some rest. You'll be able to check out of here in the morning." He shifted on the balls of his feet, apparently uncertain of how to give them the next bit of information. In the end he decided on a mixture of optimism and aggression. "He's ours now. Thanks to you two people and Mr. Beevers, we didn't get him in Chinatown, but I told you we'd get him in the end, and we will."

"You know where Dengler is?" Tim asked.

Murphy nodded.

"Well, where is he?" Poole asked.

"You don't need to know that."

"But you can't apprehend him now?"

Murphy shook his head. "He's as good as apprehended. You don't have to worry about him."

"I'm not worried," Poole said. "Is he on an airplane?"

Murphy glowered at him, then nodded.

"Didn't you have people at the airport?"

Now Murphy began to seem irritated. "Of course we did. I had men at every subway station he might have used, we had people at the bus terminals, and at both Kennedy and La Guardia." He cleared his throat. "But he managed to get to New Orleans before we identified him. By the time we worked out what name he was using and where he was going, he had already boarded his connecting flight in New Orleans. But he's on that flight now. It's all over for him."

"Where is he going?"

At length Murphy decided to tell them. "Tegucigalpa."

"Honduras," Poole said. "Why Honduras? Oh. Roberto Ortiz. You checked the passenger lists and found the name. Dengler still has Roberto Ortiz's passport."

"I don't have to tell you anything, do I?" Murphy asked.

"Tell me you're going to get him this time."

"You can't walk out of an airplane. I don't think he's going to do a D.B. Cooper. And when the plane lands at the Tegucigalpa airport in four hours, we have a small army waiting for him. Those people down there, they want to be our friends. Those people, when we snap our fingers, they jump. He's going to be picked up so fast his feet won't even touch the ground." Murphy actually smiled. "We can't miss him. This guy might be the running grunt, according to you gentlemen, but this time he's running into a trap." Murphy nodded good-bye and went to the door; when he had gone out he had another thought, and leaned back in. "In the morning, I'll tell you how it went. By then your boy will be on the way back here." A grin. "In chains. And probably with a few bruises, and minus a couple of teeth."

After he left, Underhill said, "There goes Harry Beevers' idol."

A nurse came in and gave them another shot.

Poole fell asleep worrying about his car, which he had left parked at a meter on Division Street.

As soon as he woke up the next morning, Poole called the Tenth Precinct. On his bedside table was a vase of irises and calla lilies, and beside the vase was his copy of *The Ambassadors* and the two Babar books. During the night, Maggie had managed to rescue his car. Poole asked the officer who answered his call if Lieutenant Murphy was planning to visit St. Vincent's Hospital that morning.

"As far as I know he has no plans to do so," said the officer. "But I'm the wrong guy to ask."

"Is the lieutenant in now?"

"The lieutenant is in a meeting."

"Did the Hondurans arrest Dengler? Can you tell me that much?"

"I'm sorry, I cannot give you that information," the officer said. "You will have to speak to the lieutenant." He hung up.

A few minutes later a doctor came around to discharge them, and said that a young woman had come by that morning with a change of clothing for each of them. After the doctor left, a nurse brought in two brown shopping bags, each containing fresh underwear, socks, a shirt, a sweater, and jeans. Underhill's clothes were from those he had left at Saigon, but Poole's were new. Maggie had guessed at his sizes, and the shirt collar was a size too small and the waistband of the jeans was thirty-six instead of thirty-four, but he could wear it all. He found a note at the bottom of the bag: *I couldn't buy you coats because I ran out of money. The doctor says you'll be able to leave around nine-thirty. Will you come to Saigon before you go wherever it is you'll be going? Your car is in the garage across the street. Love, Maggie.* Clipped to the note was a tag from a garage.

"No coats," Poole said. "Mine was ruined, and yours is probably evidence. But don't worry—we can get something to wear. People are always leaving things in hospitals."

They signed form after form in the billing office. A young orderly, St. Vincent's own Wilson Manly, outfitted them, as Poole had foreseen, with overcoats that had been the property of two elderly gentlemen without family who had died during the week. "These are pretty shabby," the orderly said. "If you could wait a day or two, there'll probably be something better coming in."

Underhill resembled a middle-aged poacher in his long filthy coat; Poole's was an ancient Chesterfield with a threadbare velvet collar, and in it he looked like a run-down man about town.

When they had reclaimed the Audi, Poole sat behind

the wheel for a time before pulling out onto Seventh Avenue. His side hurt, and the Chesterfield smelled of wine and cigarette smoke. He realized that he had no idea of where he was going. Perhaps he was just going to drive forever. He stopped at the first light, and realized that he could go anywhere. For a moment he was not a doctor, not a husband, or anything at all to Maggie Lah: his greatest responsibility was to the car he sat in.

"Are you going to take me back to Saigon?" Underhill asked.

"I am," he said. "But first we're going to pay a call on our favorite policeman."

6

Lieutenant Murphy could not see them immediately. Lieutenant Murphy sent word that they could wait if they liked, but matters related to other cases were keeping him very busy; no, there was no information about the fate of the fugitive M.O. Dengler.

The young officer on the other side of the bulletproof Plexiglas refused to let them into the precinct house, and after a while avoided their eyes and kept his back turned while pretending to be occupied with something at a nearby desk.

"Did they get him when he left the plane?" Poole asked. "Is he coming back all wrapped up in chains and carrying a lot of fresh bruises?"

The officer said nothing.

"He didn't get clean away, did he?" Poole was speaking so loudly he was almost shouting.

"I think they might have had some trouble on the flight," the young officer said in a barely audible voice.

After they had waited half an hour, Detective Dalton finally took pity on them and allowed them into the station. He took them up the stairs and opened the door to room B. "I'll get him to come in here," he said, and grinned at Poole. "I like that coat."

"I'll swap you for yours," Poole said.

Dalton disappeared. Only a minute or two later, the door opened and Lieutenant Murphy came in. His skin had lost some of its angry healthy flush and his shoulders were slumped. Even the arrogant Keith Hernandez moustache looked tired. Murphy nodded at the two men, dropped a file on the table, and then dropped into the nearest chair.

"Okay," he said. "I don't want you to think I was avoiding you. I didn't want to call you until I had some definite word."

He spread out his hands as if he had said all there was to say.

"Hasn't the plane landed?" Poole asked. "What did he do, hijack it?"

Murphy sat slumped in the chair. "No, the plane landed. More than once, in fact. I suppose that's the problem."

"It made an unscheduled stop?"

"Not quite." Now Murphy was speaking very slowly and reluctantly, and his face had begun to show the first signs of spring. "Apparently the Tegucigalpa flights from this country always stop in Belize. We had men waiting there just in case Dengler tried something funny. Or so the forces in Belize tell us." Poole leaned forward to speak, and Murphy held up a hand like a stop sign. "It also regularly stops at a place called San Pedro de Sula, which is in Honduras, and where the Hondurans had people check everybody who left the plane. Now hold on, Doctor, I'm going to tell you what happened. What I *think* happened. Between San Pedro de Sula and Tegucigalpa there is only one more regularly scheduled stop." He tried to smile. "A place called Goloson Airport in a jerkwater town called La Cieba. The plane's only on the ground about ten minutes. Only domestic passengers ever get off there—they have different colored boarding passes from the international passengers, so everybody can see who they are. Domestic passengers don't have to pass through Customs, Immigration, any of that stuff. A couple Honduran soldiers were posted out at Goloson, but they didn't see anybody except domestic passengers."

"But he wasn't on the plane when it landed at Tegucigalpa," Poole said.

"That's right. At this distance, it's a little hard to tell, but it looks like he never landed there." He sniffed the air. "What's that smell?"

"The policeman at the desk downstairs said there was some trouble on the flight," Underhill said. "I can't help remembering what happened at Kennedy."

Murphy gave him a flat glare. "There was a little

trouble, you could call it that, I suppose. When the crew checked out the plane they found one passenger who hadn't left his seat. He was asleep with a magazine over his chest. Only when they picked up the magazine and shook him they found out that he was dead. Broken neck." He shook his head. "We're still waiting for identification."

"So he could be anywhere," Poole said. "That's what you're saying. He could have booked another flight as soon as he got off the plane."

"Well, now we have men at Goloson Airport," Murphy said. "I mean, they have men there." He pushed himself away from the table and stood up. "I think that's all I have to tell you, gentlemen. We'll be in touch." He began to move toward the door.

"But in other words, nobody's found him yet. We don't even know what name he's using."

Murphy made it to the door. "I'll call you when I have some positive word." He fled.

Dalton entered a second later, as if he had been waiting outside the door. "You have the story now? I'll take you back downstairs, you guys don't have any worries, you know, police all over Honduras are looking out for this guy. Hondurans will bend over backwards to do us favors, believe me, and our man will turn up in custody in a day or two. I'm glad your injuries weren't too serious. Say, Doctor, tell that good-looking girlfriend of yours if she ever gets sick of—"

They were out on the sidewalk in their dead men's coats.

"What's Honduras like?" Poole asked.

"Haven't you heard?" said Underhill. "They love us down there."

8
PART EIGHT
TIM UNDERHILL
8

And then what happened?

Nothing.

Nothing happened.

It has been two years since Michael Poole and I left the police station and drove back to Saigon, Tina Pumo's old restaurant, and nothing more has been heard of Koko, or M.O. Dengler, or whatever he is calling himself now. There are times—times when everything is going smoothly in my life—when I know that he is dead.

It is true that Koko must have yearned for death—I think he thought of himself as giving his victims the gift of freedom from the fearful eternity he perceived all about him. *"I am Esterhaz,"* he wrote in the note he left for Michael, and in part he meant that what happened on the frozen banks of the Milwaukee River never stopped happening for him, no matter how many times he killed in order to make it stop. *Backwards and forwards* describes an eternity which has become intolerable to the man caged within it.

Lieutenant Murphy finally sent Michael Poole copies of some photographs that had been taken from the room at the YMCA. These were photographs of convicted or accused serial murderers Dengler had clipped from newspapers and magazines. Ted Bundy, Juan Corona,

John Wayne Gacy, Wayne Williams, David Berkowitz—over each head Dengler had drawn a flat round golden ring: a halo. They were eternity's agents, and in my worst moments I think that Koko saw us, the members of Harry Beevers' platoon, in that way too, as dirty angels, agents of release from one kind of eternity into another. *I have work to do,* Koko said in the basement room on Elizabeth Street, and that we have not heard of him or from him does not mean that his work is done or that he has stopped doing it.

A year after Koko lost himself in Honduras, I finished the book I had been writing. My old publisher, Gladstone House, published it under the title *The Secret Fire;* the reviews were excellent, and the sales something less than that but at least good enough to make me self-sufficient long enough to write what I thought would be my next book, a "nonfiction novel" about M.O. Dengler and Koko. Now I know that I cannot write that book—I don't really know what a "nonfiction novel" is; you can't tie an eagle to a plough horse without making both of them suffer.

But as soon as I could afford to do it I took the same flight to Tegucigalpa from which Koko escaped while Michael Poole and I were being sewn up and sedated in St. Luke's Hospital. And with the novelist's provisional doubt I *saw,* as I *saw* the girl he had tried to murder in Bangkok, what happened on that flight. I saw how it could have happened, and then I saw it happen.

This is one version of how Koko came to Honduras.

The jet is small and so old it rattles, and few North Americans are on board. The Central American passengers have black hair and brick-colored skin, they are talkative and exotic, and I think Koko would have felt immediately at home among them. He too came out of the basement, he too left the children of Ia Thuc and the Patpong girl behind him in the basement, and now another language echoes about him. I think he closes his eyes and sees a wide plaza in a small sunstruck city, then sees the plaza littered with dead and dying bodies. On the steps of the Cathedral, bodies lie sprawled and twisted, their arms outflung, the fingers curled in toward the palms, the eyes still open, staring. The sun is very near, a large white hazy disc like a halo. Abundant flies. Koko is sweating—he imagines himself sweating, standing in the center of the plaza, his skin prickling with the heat.

When the little plane lands at Belize two people get off into a shredding dazzle of light that instantly devours them. At the back of the plane, visible to the passengers, two men in brown uniforms pitch a few suitcases out through an open bay. White cement, hard bouncing light.

In fifteen minutes they are back in that world above the world, above clouds and rainfall, where Koko feels himself freed from gravity and near to—what? God, immortality, eternity? Perhaps all of these. When he closes his eyes he sees a broad sidewalk lined with cafés. Rows of empty white chairs fan out from white tables with colorful sun umbrellas, and waiters in black waistcoats and black trousers stand in the open doorways of the cafés. Then the music of eternity swells in his mind, and he sees bloodied corpses sprawling in the chairs, the waiters slumped dead in the doorways, blood running into the gutters and moving slowly down the pitched street. . . .

He sees brown naked children, sturdy peasant children with stubby hands and broad backs, burned in a ditch.

Images, running without gravity or coherence, on a spool of film.

I have work to do.

When they land at San Pedro de Sula half a dozen suddenly impatient men and women thrust their way through the aircraft, carrying woven baskets and bottles of duty-free whiskey. The men's neckties are pulled off-center, and their faces are filmed with sweat. When they speak they growl like dogs, for they have evolved from dogs as some men have evolved from apes and others from rats and mice, still others from panthers and other feral cats, others from goats, snakes, some few from elephants and horses. Koko squints through the window at a dull white bureaucratic building, the terminal. A limp flag, half eaten by the light, droops over the building.

Not here.

After the pack has left the plane, a lone man carrying an orange boarding pass makes his way down the aisle to the last row of seats. He is a Honduran, a San Pedro de Sulan, in an ill-fitting tan sports jacket and a chocolate brown shirt, and his orange boarding pass means that he is a domestic passenger.

Just before the plane begins to move again, Koko stands up, nods at the stewardess (who has ignored him throughout the flight), and walks down the length of the plane to sit beside the new passenger.

"*Buen' dia,*" the man says, and Koko smiles and nods.

A moment later they taxi away from the white boxy bureaucratic terminal. Shaking and rattling, the plane rises up off the earth and again enters the world without time. There are twenty minutes before they will touch ground again, and sometime during that twenty minutes, perhaps at a moment when the stewardess disappears either into the toilet or the cockpit, Koko stands up and moves out into the aisle. His blood is zooming through his veins, and within himself he feels a sweet necessary urgency. Eternity is holding its breath. Koko smiles and points to the floor of the plane. He says, "Did you drop that money?" The man in the tan jacket glances up sideways at Koko, then bends forward to look down at the cabin floor. And Koko edges in beside him and puts his arms around the man's neck and gives the head a good firm twist. There is a *crack!* too quiet to be heard over the engine noise, and the man's body sags into his seat. Koko sits down beside the corpse. Now his feelings are impenetrable to me. There is that question the civilian world is forever asking combat veterans, silently or outright, *How does it feel to kill someone?,* but Koko's feelings at this moment are too personal, wedded to his terrible history, and that is a darkness I cannot penetrate.

Let us say: he hears the dead man's soul rushing out of the body beside him, and it is a confused, unhappy soul, startled by its release.

Or let us say: Koko looks straight through the roof of the airplane and sees his father seated in glory on a golden throne, nodding down at him with stern approval.

Or: he instantly feels the dead man's being, his essence, slip into his own body through his eyes or his mouth or the opening at the end of his penis and it is as if Koko has eaten the man, for thoughts and memories flare within Koko's mind, and Koko sees a family and recognizes his brother, his sister:

he sees a little whitewashed house on a dirt lane with a rusty car before it,

he smells tortillas frying on a blackened griddle. . . .

Enough.

Koko removes the orange boarding pass from the man's pocket and replaces it with his own. Then he reaches into the man's jacket and tweezes out his wallet. His fingers open the wallet, he is curious to know who he is now, who it is that he has eaten and now lives within him; he reads his new name. Finally he places over the dead man's face a magazine from the pouch before him and folds his hands in his lap. Now the dead man is sleeping, and the stewardess will not bother to shake him until everyone else is off the plane.

And then the plane begins to make its descent toward the tiny airport at La Cieba—

In a little while we will get to La Cieba.

Imagine that we are not in Central America, but in Vietnam. It is the rainy season, and inside the tents at Camp Crandall the green metal lockers shine with condensation. Sweet marijuana smoke hangs in the air, along with the music we are listening to. Spanky Burrage, now a drug rehabilitation counselor in California, is playing tapes on his big Sony reel-to-reel recorder, purchased in Saigon, the city not the restaurant, at a very good cost. In a large green holdall at the foot of Spanky's cot are thirty or forty reels of music recorded by friends of his in Little Rock, Arkansas. These are nearly all jazz tapes, and hand-lettered labels on the cardboard boxes identify who is on each tape: *Ellington, Basie, Parker, Rollins, Coltrane, Clifford Brown, Peterson, Tatum, Hodges, Webster . . .*

This is the brothers' tent, and in here music is always playing. M.O. Dengler and I are admitted here because we love jazz, but in truth Dengler, who is more or less loved by every soldier in camp, would be welcome here even if he thought that Lawrence Welk led a great jazz band.

The music sounds different here than it would back in the world: it has different things to say here, and so we must listen to it very carefully.

Spanky Burrage knows his tapes very well. He has the exact location of the beginning of virtually every song memorized, so that he can find any selection just by running the tape backwards or forwards. Therefore his memory allows him to play long sequences of the same song performed by different musicians. Spanky enjoys doing this. He will play an Art Tatum version of "The

Sunny Side of the Street," then one by Dizzy Gillespie and Sonny Rollins; "Indiana" by Stan Getz, then a version with the same chords but another melody by Charlie Parker called "Donna Lee"; "April in Paris" by Count Basie, then by Thelonious Monk; sometimes five versions of "Stardust" in a row, six of "How High the Moon," a dozen blues, everybody going to the same well but returning with different water.

Spanky always came back to Duke Ellington and Charlie Parker. And I sat in front of the speakers of the Sony beside M.O. Dengler maybe twenty times while Spanky followed Duke Ellington's "Koko" with the Charlie Parker song that had the same name. *Same name—*

"—but oh so different," Spanky says. And he whips the tape through the reels until the desired number comes up on the counter without his bothering to look at it, and drawing on a long cigarette rolled from Si Van Vo's finest, he pushes STOP and then PLAY.

In Vietnam, this is what we hear. The Ellington "Koko" first.

It is a music of threat, and it is world-music, meaning that a world is held within it. Long ominous notes on a baritone saxophone counterpoint blasts from trombones. A lurching, swaying, uneasy melody begins in the saxophone section. From the darkness two trombones whoop and shake, going *wa waaa wa waa* like human voices on the perimeter of speech. These are noises that jump right out of the speakers and come toward you like a crazy father in the middle of the night. The piano utters nightmarish chords which are half-submerged in the cacophony of the band, and at the end Jimmy Blanton's bass pads through the band like a burglar, like a sapper crawling toward our perimeter. It did not occur to us that there might be something deliberately theatrical, even comic, in all this menace.

"Okay," Spanky says, "the Bird." He snaps off the Ellington reel, snaps on the Parker. Spanky Burrage reveres the Bird, Charlie Parker. He threads the tape, advances to the correct number, but again he hardly has to look at the counter. Spanky knows when "Koko" has been reached. STOP. PLAY.

We are instantly in another world, one as threatening but far newer—a world that is still being mapped. This "Koko" was recorded in 1945, five years after the Ellington, and Modernism has finally come to jazz. The Parker "Koko" is based on the song "Cherokee," written by the English bandleader Ray Noble, though you would never know this unless you happen to recognize the harmonic pattern.

It begins with improvised passages of great complexity and urgency, and finally comes to a theme fragment, which is a brusque abstraction of "Cherokee," as unsentimental as a Picasso portrait of Dora Maar or a paragraph by Gertrude Stein. This is not the music of collective statement like the Ellington piece, but fiercely individual. After the abstraction of the theme is played, Parker begins. All through the first chorus has been a sense of impendingness, and it is for this that we have been prepared so efficiently.

For Charlie Parker begins *singing* at once, almost magically at one with his instrument, the harmonies of the song, and his imagination. He is overflowing, and he deliberately stutters at the beginning of a phrase, and the phrase says *I have work to do*. He immediately says it again, but more passionately, so that this time it is *I have WORK to do*. All through the long first section of his solo, he plays with absolute fluency over a tense and unrelenting rhythm.

Then an astonishing thing happens. When Parker reaches the bridge of the song, all that open-throated singing against threat is resolved in a dazzle of imaginative glory. Parker changes the beat around so that he actually seems to accelerate, and all the urgency is engulfed in the grace of his thoughts, which have become Mozartean and are filled with great calm and beauty.

What Charlie Parker does on the bridge of "Cherokee" reminds me of Henry James's dream—the one I told Michael about in the hospital. A figure battered at his bedroom door. Terrified, James held the door closed against the figure. Impendingness, threat. In his dream, James does an extraordinary thing. He turns on his attacker and forces open the door in a burst of daring. The figure has already fled, is only a diminishing spot in the distance. It is a dream of elation and triumph, of glory.

That was what we listened to in the dripping tent in the year 1968 in Vietnam, M.O. Dengler and Spanky Burrage and I. You could say . . . we heard fear dissolved by mastery.

You see, I remember the old M.O. Dengler. I rem

ber the man we loved. In the basement of the tenement on Elizabeth Street, if I had been faced with the choice of killing him or letting him go, unless killing him was the only way I could save my own life, I would have let him go. He wanted to give himself up. *He wanted to give himself up,* and if Harry Beevers had not betrayed him, he would have come in closer to our moral world. I believe this because I must believe it, and because I know that Koko could easily have killed all three of us down in his basement room. He chose not to. He had come close enough to our world to let us live. That is why Michael and I have matching scars that have turned us into brothers—the scars are the sign that Koko chose to let us live. He had work to do, *work* to do, and maybe that work was to—

I cannot say it yet.

Six months to the day after our release from the basement, Harry Beevers checked into a grand new hotel that had just opened in Times Square: one of those new hotels with an atrium lobby and a waterfall. He was given the suite he requested, rode up in the glass bubble of the elevator, tipped the bellman who had carried his suitcase with a ten-dollar bill, locked his door, opened the suitcase and drank from the quart of vodka that was one of the two objects inside it, undressed, lay down on his bed, masturbated, removed from the suitcase the .38 Police Special which was the other object he had carried from his apartment, put its barrel against his temple, and pulled the trigger. He died four hours later. A playing card was found on the sheet beside his head; I think the force of the bullet knocked the card out of his mouth. His life had become useless to him, and he threw it away.

Harry opened the door and stepped back to let the dark figure enter. He had no job, little money, and his imagination had failed him. His illusions were all the imagination he had—a ferocious poverty.

Perhaps in despair like Harry's, Koko once opened the door, stepped back, and let the figure enter.

Michael Poole commutes to the Bronx every day, where he practices what he calls "front-line medicine" in a storefront. Maggie is taking courses at NYU, but although she has the unmistakable air of a person with a goal, she will not speak about what she plans to do. Michael and Maggie seem very happy. Last year we built a new loft for them on the floor above Tina's old loft, where Vinh and Helen and I now live. I lead a regular, moderate life in the midst of these people, and sometimes at six o'clock I walk downstairs to have a single drink with Jimmy, Maggie's brother, who works behind Saigon's bar. Jimmy is a wicked character, and now that I know so few wicked characters and am no longer one myself, I rather cherish him.

I think Koko wanted to go to Honduras—I think Central America called to him, perhaps because of Rosita Orosco, perhaps because he imagined that there he could find his death. It would not be difficult to find a way to die in Honduras. And perhaps that is what happened, and for two years Koko has lain in a hurriedly dug grave, shot by the police or a gang of thieves or the militia or a drunken farmer or a frightened boy with a gun. He had work to do, and it is possible that the work was to find his own death. Maybe this time the mob caught him, pulled him to pieces, and scattered his body in a greasy field.

STOP.

PLAY.

I flew to New Orleans and went to the counter where the man calling himself Roberto Ortiz had bought a one-way ticket to Tegucigalpa. I bought a ticket to Tegucigalpa. Two hours later, I boarded the little plane and three hours after that we touched down in Belize. Heat rolled in through the hatch when the few passengers bound for Belize left the cabin. When the men in brown uniforms opened the back of the plane to take out a few pieces of luggage, hard flat light struck the white concrete and bounced straight into the cabin. The plane was sealed again, and we flew to San Pedro de Sula, where I saw the boxy white terminal with its dispirited flag. Hondurans with orange boarding passes joined the flight. We went up in the air again and almost as quickly came down again at La Cieba.

I pulled my overnight bag off the rack and moved forward in the cabin. The indifferent stewardess swung open the hatch, and I walked down a movable staircase into the world that Koko had chosen. Heat, dust, motionless light. Across the tarmac stood a low building, up on a platform like a loading dock, that could have been a bar or a failed inn, of unpainted grey boards. This was the terminal. Koko had walked across this tarmac toward the terminal, and I walked toward it and climbed the wooden steps to pass through the building.

The dark-haired girls in the blue airlines uniform sat on packing cases, their handsome legs thrust out before them. Koko too walked past these lounging girls. A uniformed boy soldier holding a rifle nearly as tall as himself barely glanced at him, his boredom too profound to be shaken by a white North American male. He did not even glance at my boarding pass. His contempt for *gringos* is unshakable, we are invisible to him. I wonder: does Koko turn around now, and what does he see? Angels, demons, elephants in hats? I think he sees a vast and promising emptiness in which he might again begin to heal. As soon as I walked past the boy soldier, I was in the rear section of the terminal, and after a few steps I came to a door, opened it, and was in the terminal proper.

We were in a long, hot, crowded space. Every seat was filled, fat brown mothers and fat brown babies everywhere. Latino men in broad-brimmed hats stood at the dusty bar, a few empty-eyed young soldiers yawned and stretched, a couple of pink North Americans looked up, looked away. We are not there anymore, we have disappeared.

Before me in both space and time, Koko passes through the entrance of Goloson Airport and returns to the strong direct sunlight. He blinks; he smiles. Sunglasses? No, not yet, his departure has been too hurried for sunglasses. I remove mine, which have round black lenses the size of quarters, from my shirt pocket and hook the ends of the wire temples around my ears. In darkened tones, I can see what Koko saw—the landscape that claimed him. He walks away from the terminal easily, loosely, not looking back. He does not know that at the distance of a year and then some I am watching his confident step take him down the narrow country road. Before us is a flat foreshortened landscape, a no-place, very green and very hot. A series of low, sparsely wooded hills rises up from the plain less than a mile distant. I think of Charlie Parker leaning as if into an embrace into the conditions that surrounded him; I think of the fat old Henry James throwing open the door and rushing forward; I wish I could flood my pages with the complicated joy of these images. The long, nearly leafless branches of the jacaranda trees droop in the punishing heat. It is the forest of no-place, of no significance in itself: simply the forest that grows on the low hills, and toward which the small lean figure is moving, a step now at a time.

***New York Times* Bestselling Author**

PETER STRAUB

Houses Without Doors 0-451-17082-2

This spectacular collection of thirteen dark, haunting tales by bestselling author Straub exposes the terrors that hide beneath the surface of the ordinary world, behind the walls of houses without doors.

"Straub at his spellbinding best."

—*Publishers Weekly*

Mystery 0-451-16869-0

Characters in a world of wealth, power, and pleasure fall prey to an evil that reaches out from the abyss of the past to haunt the present and claim the living.

"Mesmerizing." —*Chicago Sun-Times*

To order call: 1-800-788-6262

S411/Straub